OF MAN AND MANTA

The three battled the universe to return to their own world
and time. Veg struck out on his own, encountering a multi-
coloured blizzard, edible fog and giant, menacing plant life.
Cal and Aquilon, joined by the creature Ox, had found a way
to visit any world they had ever imagined – including the
dimension from which they had come.

But was there a chance for rescuing their lost friend Veg?
Could their frail human bodies withstand the strange forces
of Ox's vast powers? And most important, could this alien be
trusted to return them to the safety of their own universe and
time?

'A masterwork of imagination and a tribute to the creative
genius of Piers Anthony'
Things to Come, the magazine of the Science Fiction Book
Club

OF MAN AND MANTA

A Trilogy by
Piers Anthony

Omnivore
Orn
Ox

CORGI BOOKS

OF MAN AND MANTA

A CORGI BOOK 0 552 99214 3

First publication in Great Britain

PRINTING HISTORY
ORN
Corgi edition published 1977
OMNIVORE
Corgi edition published 1977
Corgi edition, comprising OMNIVORE, ORN and OX published
1986

This book is set in 10/11 point Sabon

Corgi Books are published by Transworld Publishers Ltd.,
61–63 Uxbridge Road, Ealing, London W5 5SA, in Australia
by Transworld Publishers (Aust.) Pty. Ltd., 26 Harley
Crescent, Condell Park, NSW 2200, and in New Zealand by
Transworld Publishers (N.Z.) Ltd, Cnr. Moselle and
Waipareira Avenues, Henderson, Auckland.

Made and printed in Great Britain by the
Guernsey Press Co. Ltd., Guernsey, Channel Islands.

CONTENTS

Part One

OMNIVORE

Chapter One

A LOAF OF BREAD

North of Appalachia an outcropping of wilderness survived. Subble aligned visible topography with known coordinates and guided his craft to a soft landing beside a thickly-spoked bull spruce. The distinctive gum smell of it surrounded him as he stepped out, and decades of rotting needles crunched underfoot.

The measured ring of steel striking hardwood led him past a grossly twisted yellow birch and into a subforest of tall beech trees. The forest was rather pleasant, in a disordered way; it occurred to him that few places on Earth remained so close to Nature's original.

The sound that had seemed so near was actually some distance away. Subble threaded his way through a thicket of young ash and maple and came at last to a forest trail: two slick brown ruts cut in the leafy floor. Clusters of toadstools sprouted periodically along it, and he spied one large bracket fungus embracing a decaying stump. Tiny gnats found him and hovered tirelessly before his eyes.

The trail debouched into an artificial clearing formed by a felled beech. A man stood facing away from him, one booted foot braced against the scarred trunk, his broad back flexing as he swung a heavy axe. The lumberman was powerful; it showed in the checkered bulge of sleeve and in the smoothness of the swing. Chips scattered with every second connection as the blade bit a growing triangular section from the base of a hefty branch.

The limb severed and crashed into a leafy jungle beyond the trunk. The man turned and saw Subble, balancing the axe in his left hand while wiping the sweat off his forehead with a meaty right forearm. 'Yeah?' he inquired, scowling.

This was the ticklish part. 'I'm an investigator,' Subble said, and kept his distance.

The man stiffened. Subble noted the slight elevation of the tendons along the back of the hand holding the axe, the sudden

11

creases in a normally amiable face, and the slight shifting of weight. 'Yeah?'

'All I want is information. If you are Vachel Smith, social code number 4409—'

'Cut it. I been Veg ten year and I ain't a number yet.'

Subble ignored the tone and the exaggerated accent. 'All right, Veg. I got a job, same as you, and I got to do it if I like it or not. Sooner we—'

Veg threw the axe at the beech stump, where it caught neatly, the handle vibrating. He closed his fists and took one step forward. 'Last time a damn city slicker talked down to me, I broke his collarbone. Speak your piece and get out.'

Subble smiled. 'Very well – I'll stick to my own language. But I must have your cooperation. There is information nobody else can provide.'

'Yeah? What?'

'I don't know. That's why I have to ask.'

'You don't know!' Veg seemed uncertain whether to laugh or swear, and his accent eased considerably. 'You come poking into my lot and you don't even know what you're looking for?'

It was best to keep him asking questions. 'That's right.'

But Veg did not keep asking. 'Mister, you're trying to make a fool out of me.' He moved in.

Subble blew his breath out audibly in a controlled show of exasperation. He was not as large as the lumberman nor as heavily muscled, but he did not back off. 'If you attempt to force me off your premises by physical means, I will have to employ certain defensive techniques at my command,' he said as Veg advanced.

'Yeah?' Veg leaped.

Subble stepped aside and put his right foot forward as Veg's right fist came at his head. He jammed his right toe against Veg's, bent his knees, grabbed the big man's shirt, spun around counter-clockwise and threw him over his shoulder.

Veg landed in the slippery moist earth of the trail, unharmed and undismayed. 'Yeah!' he said again, and launched himself a second time.

Subble ducked, caught Veg in the stomach with a shoulder block and followed it up with a quick and effective series of grips about the neck and shoulders.

Veg kept his feet, but his head lolled and both arms dangled. Subble let him catch his balance and recover the use of his extremities. 'I gave you fair warning.'

The lumberman shook himself and stretched his head from side to side. 'Yeah,' he said.

'Now I have to talk with you, because that's my job. I'll leave as soon as I have what I need. I'm willing to trade for what I get.'

'Mister, nobody ever bought me yet.'

'Nobody offered to. You take a break and I'll fill in for as long as it takes you to talk. That way you won't lose any time and I'll be out of your way in a hurry.'

Veg laughed, his good humour seemingly restored by his setback. 'You sure are a determined cuss. There aren't any fancy nerves you can pinch on a bolt of beech, mister. I don't know you and I won't tell you a thing.'

Subble was careful not to threaten the man. He looked around at the divergent timber, spotting a shy cinnamon-brown thrush with indistinct spots on its breast. 'Veery,' he said.

Veg followed his gaze. 'Yeah, I know him,' he said more softly. 'Comes around every two, three days. Got a hermit thrush, too – state bird, you should hear him sing! Never found the nest, though.' Then he remembered whom he was talking to and scowled again.

'I must have been pretty clumsy to set you against me so quickly.' It was a calculated overture.

'Mister, it's not you. Anyone who knows a veery when he sees one has some good in him. It's the government. We don't truck much with – you really don't know what you came for?'

'An agent's memory is washed blank before every assignment. I have been given three addresses and a caution signal. That was, literally, all I knew about you before I landed. Your name, where to find you, and a warning of danger.'

'That's crazy!'

'It prevents me from approaching the case with a bias. Everything must come from the case itself, nothing from my expectations or records which may be incomplete or distorted.'

'But if you don't even know what – I mean, I could lie to you and you'd never guess. I could tell you I'm a petty thief on the lam—'

'You aren't.'

'I thought you said you had no—'

Subble glanced at the tree again, but the bird was gone. So, oddly, were most of the other ubiquitous creatures of the forest. Something had subdued them. 'I was given no information, but my training enables me to obtain it very quickly. I know a good deal about you now.'

'Okay, Mister what's-your-name—'

'Subble.'

'Mister Government Agent. *How* do you know I'm not a thief?'

'I can give you a general idea. I'm equipped to pick up your respiration, heartbeat, muscle tension, the nuances of facial expression, vocal inflection, subvocal—'

'You saying you can tell when I'm lying just by watching me?'

'Yes. You are not a devious man.'

'I'm not a liar, either. But I'm not so sure about you.'

Subble took no offence. 'You are wise. I *am* a devious man. I am fully capable of lying when my mission requires it, and I am an expert at it.'

Veg touched his sore neck. 'More than that, I guess.'

'Yes – I could have maimed you or killed you. But that's my speciality, and I don't misuse my training any more than you would misuse your axe, or destroy that thrush's nest. You *could* cut down every sapling in the forest—'

'God, no! This's fourth generation timber now. I'm just cleaning out the weed trees and—' He paused. 'Yeah, I guess I see what you mean. You don't go 'round hurting people for the fun of it. But you still can't find out a thing if I don't talk to you.'

'I'm afraid I can, if there is no alternative.'

Veg studied him with genuine curiosity. 'How?'

'By making statements, asking questions, and reading your reactions.'

'Okay. I'm going to shut up now. You tell me what you learn.'

'You may not like this, Veg.'

The man picked up his axe and returned to the trunk he had been limbing.

'Are you a vegetarian?' Subble asked. 'Yes, you are,' he answered himself immediately.

'You already knew!' Veg shouted, shaken. 'You wouldn't even've *asked* that question if you didn't know!'

'I knew – but you were the one who told me. Your nickname, for one thing, and the smell of your breath, and your tension when I mentioned killing. You haven't touched meat for a decade.'

Veg's mouth was tight. 'Tell me something you couldn't've found in a government snoop-file,' he said. He didn't bother to chop any more.

'If you will put down your weapon—'

'Weapon? Oh.' He pitched the axe at the stump, missing this time.

'You see, you're upset now – and I would have to act precipitously if you were to attack me with *that*. Are you sure you—'

'Go ahead. Prove it.'

Subble's voice was low, but he watched Veg very carefully. 'Are you interested in baseball? ... No. Shakespeare? ... No. Any other playwright? ... Yes. Modern? ... Yes, but not *too* modern ... American? Foreign? ... Ah, English? Shaw, of course!'

Veg started to say something, but didn't. Stronger medicine was required before he would be convinced.

'How about women? ... Yes and no. Not just *any* woman. Are you in love? ... Yes, I see that you are, and not casually, but there is something wrong. Is she pretty? ... Yes, lovely. Have you slept with her, man to woman? ... No? But you aren't impotent ... No! Would she let you? ... She would, probably. Her name is Aquilon—'

Veg's lunge missed by several inches. 'Easy! The name happens to be the second on my list,' Subble explained. 'It was logical, in the circumstance, that she would be the one you – now don't charge me again.'

The big man halted. 'Yeah, you did warn me. Again.' He looked at Subble with a certain difficult respect. 'I guess I believe you.'

'I don't want to pry into your private affairs. All I want is the information I was sent for. My offer stands. If you want anything for your trouble—'

'Mister – Subble, you said? – you have more on the ball than I figured. But I already said: it's not you. It's the government. That's trouble every time. I have a notion what you came for, and I can't tell you. Not when some bureaucrat's going to—'

'I'm not an ordinary agent. What you tell me is held in confidence. I gather the information, assimilate it and make a single verbal report from which all irrelevancies are excluded. I may need to learn some personal matters in order to pursue my investigation and draw conclusions, but no one else need know.'

15

'You sound pretty sure of that.'

'I am sure. I'm sorry my word is worthless, since I could and would easily break it. I'll just have to assure you unofficially that I could be lying now, but am not. Your relationship with Aquilon has no relevance to – oh, oh.'

'Yeah. Just me and you, okay. But it isn't. It's my friends and the government, and I just don't have the right.'

Subble had expected something like this. The nature of the assignment was beginning to take shape, and he was now in a position to obtain a great deal from Veg – but his very training in prevarication, as with that in combat, made him exceedingly careful of the rights of others. An agent who gained his ends ruthlessly was apt to be unsuccessful in the end, since force inevitably inspired counterforce. And it was not wise to act in a manner that would increase the general distrust of agents as a whole. There was danger – extreme danger, he suspected now – and not from Veg himself. It was essential that no personal antagonism be added to it.

'Veg, I have all day, as far as I know, and tomorrow too. I'm not on a schedule, but I do have to get at the facts, whatever they may be. How about letting me stay with you for a few hours, so we can get to know each other, and you can tell me as much as you feel free to. I won't push you for any more than that, once you draw the line, and you'll have the confidence that you are not simply spouting off to a stranger.'

'What if I decide to tell you nothing?'

'Then you tell me nothing.'

Veg thought about it, scratching his sandy head. 'You going to talk to 'Quilon?'

'I have to. And Calvin. And anybody else who knows – whatever it is.'

'And you don't report till the end, just a summary?'

'That's right.'

'I guess I'd better, then. God, I sure don't like it, though.'

Subble smiled, but not inside. He could see that Veg had grave misgivings, and not on purely personal grounds. There *was* danger, and Veg knew it, and it was personal and immediate.

'I understand that you do not bear me any more than residual ill-will,' Subble observed. 'You respect physical ability, as many strong men do. But you are afraid that if I learn too much, I will be harmed

16

or killed, and that will make real trouble. I mention this only so that you will be aware that I know. And you are right: while I do not fear death, if I do die there will be a thorough and official investigation. You know what that means.'

'Yeah,' Veg said unhappily.

Subble dropped the subject. It was always difficult to obtain the trust of a normal person, but always necessary. He believed that frankness was best, and before long it would occur to Veg that he would be well advised to see that the agent got enough information at least to preserve his life. 'How can I help?'

'Well—' Veg looked about, searching for some pretext to accept the inevitable. 'Say – there *is* a little matter I've been saving up for a special occasion. This way.'

He trotted down the fresh logging track, intersecting another trail and following that. Subble saw the prints and ordure of horses, animals rarely seen today but still used in these protected tracts. Machines of all types were banned here; men harvested trees with hand tools and hauled out the logs with animal labour. Anyone who didn't care for the physical life was invited out in a hurry. There were too many people and too many machines in the world, and the fringe wilderness was a jealously guarded area.

Veg angled away from the trail, brushing by the round leaves of a young basswood and the serrated ones of the maples to jump over an ancient stone wall. Over a century ago men had built such walls by hand, using the great chunks of rock they cleared from their fields; such a wall had inspired the poet Robert Frost to discourse upon its mending, but no one cared to mend it now.

A sitting chipmunk dropped its acorn and scurried silently away. 'Sorry, pal – didn't see you,' Veg muttered as the handsome striped body disappeared. He pulled up under a huge blazed beech and put his hands to his mouth. 'Yo, Jones!' he yelled.

In a few minutes two dark men appeared and came to stand beyond the tree. 'What'sa matter – lonesome?' one inquired with blunt sarcasm. He was a husky individual, smaller than Veg but sure of himself. He wore the standard denims and checkered shirt, and a small neat mustache. His companion was similar, lacking the mustache.

'Naw,' Veg said. He put his hands on his hips aggressively. 'Remember that business about this boundary last month?'

17

'You mean when you tried to poach on our territory?'

'I mean when you hauled the marker-stone twenty feet out of line and claimed three of my best white ash and a rock maple.' He gestured, and Subble saw the stone some distance beyond.

'*Re*claimed, you mean.'

'And I said I'd take care of it when the time came.'

The two men nodded, smirking.

'Well, the time's come,' Veg said.

The mustached man approached. 'That your second?' he asked, glancing disparagingly at Subble. 'A city slick?'

'That's my second. Name's Subble.' He turned to Subble. 'This is Hank Jones. He and his brother work this lot next to mine – and some of mine, too.'

'City duds!' Jones said. 'Well, I reckon bound'ry jumpers can't be choosy.' He unlimbered a roundhouse left at Veg.

It was grandiose and clumsy by Subble's standards, but basic rules were evident. The two men moved out into the clearing beyond the tree, exchanging ferocious blows and taking almost no evasive action, but the object seemed to be to beat the opponent into submission without doing irreparable damage. Fists, feet and heads were freely employed, but never fingers or teeth, and eyes and crotches were left alone. Jones' brother called lewd encouragement and advice to his side, but did not interfere.

Veg took the first blow on the ear and shrugged it off. His own fist drove into Jones' belly, forcing the man away. Jones charged back headfirst, butting with such power that Veg fell to the ground. As he rolled to hands and knees, Jones put his boot up and shoved him down again, following this with a hard kick with the side of the boot to the shoulder. Toe-points also outlawed, Subble surmised, and heel-stomping.

Veg growled and leaped, fists alternating like pistons even before they met the target. He backed Jones against the beech and blasted mercilessly at his midsection until the man doubled over.

Jones' brother edged towards the pair, and Subble also moved in. Veg was an independent sort, and would not have accepted a 'second' unless he deemed it necessary.

The combatants bounced away from the tree, dirty and sweaty but with undiminished energies. Veg backed off to recover his balance, and Jones' brother surreptitiously poked a stick between

18

his feet. Veg tripped, and Jones was on him immediately.

Subble strode across the arena and stood before his opposite number. 'Friend, if you want to participate, pick your own fight,' he suggested.

The man scowled and swung. The attack was incredibly crude – but Subble accepted the blow on the shoulder and replied with a moderate jab to the gut. He had no need of his special skills here, and preferred not to display them. Obviously these encounters were family affairs, and all interested parties participated.

The single fight had become two – and privacy had dissipated. Only partially concerned with the mock-fight he was engaged in, Subble watched and listened to the other lumbermen as they emerged from the forest on all sides, until a great circle of cheerful faces surrounded them.

The sounds of extracurricular activity penetrated a long distance, it seemed, and the neighbors wasted no time dealing themselves in.

'Veg and Hank Jones are settling their account, as I make it,' one man explained to his companion. 'My guess is the stranger was standing in for Veg's second, and figured to keep Job Jones out of it. City man.'

'I'll second the stranger,' the other said. 'He's holding up his end okay, considering.'

'Yeah?' a third put in. 'I'm for Job.'

'Son, you picked a loser. Neither Jones can last long without his brother.'

The third raised his fist. '*I'm* his brother, far as you're concerned.'

And the third fight commenced. In like manner the two new antagonists were seconded, and soon a fourth battle was underway.

Subble laughed inwardly. He had been right: fighting was as much pleasure as business to these hardy folk, and any pretext would do. They could not stand idly by and let others war; they had to join in. But it was man to man, not group to group.

He ducked a swing from Job Jones and butted him in approved fashion. Job backed into another contestant, jarring the other man's aim as he cocked his fist. 'Sorry,' Job muttered. 'Forget it,' the other said, and proceeded with his own concern.

The ring was crowded now, resembling a ballroom filled with strenuous dancers. It was impossible to tell for which side any given man stood – yet each pair remained distinct and no one intentionally

19

struck anyone except his assigned antagonist. As in the dance, each couple created its discrete formations in the midst of babel. There even seemed to be music.

A hand fell upon his shoulder. 'Your turn's up,' Veg said jovially. 'Take a seat.'

Surprised, Subble broke. Job Jones quit immediately and went to the far side to join his brother, while Veg squatted down to view the melee. Hank Jones was playing a harmonica with some rude skill . . . so there *was* music now!

Before long the man who had seconded Subble joined them, his match lining up with the seated Joneses. New matches were still being formed from the uncommitted pool, distinguished by cleaner clothing and absence of bruises, and this in turn was constantly reinforced by arriving spectators. The men bore a common stamp of sturdy self-assurance and lusty living that contrasted with what Subble knew the city-norm to be.

'No room for everyone at once,' Veg explained.

Someone hauled out a guitar and began strumming more or less in time with the harmonica, and another man took a stick and began setting the beat on the scarred beech.

Subble was astonished at the scope of the battle. A dozen pairs were brawling in the clearing, and as many more men were scattered about the fringe. Someone had hauled in a wagon bearing a monstrous keg of beer, and wooden mugs of the frothing liquid were being circulated along with pails of forest berries and triangular beechnuts.

Subble accepted a warm beer and took a swallow. The activity had made him pleasantly thirsty – that, he realized, was part of the point of all this. It was technically a malt beverage – but home-brewed to about twenty proof. He smiled; he was sure the local soft-liquor taxmen had never met this keg.

Veg noticed his reaction. 'You didn't come for this?' he asked with sudden concern.

Subble drained his high-potency mug. 'You know it ain't!'

This time Veg did not take exception to the language.

The battle waned as the beer fumes drifted. The active partici-pants became ten, then eight, as each contest fissioned into thirsty individuals. The lines of the seated extended almost entirely around the circle, the men conversing contentedly and waving their mugs.

The show dwindled to two, and finally to a single encounter. The audience watched avidly now, rooting not so much for one man or the other as for the fight itself.

'Which one is ours?' Subble inquired, having lost track. 'Or does it matter anymore?'

'It matters,' Veg said. 'I hope it's Buff. He's a good man.'

Buff *was* a good man, and in due course he was conceded the victory. The last two grabbed mugs and gulped them pantingly as they plumped to the ground. the music finished with a flourish and an expectant silence came.

'Now the fun begins,' Veg muttered. Then, loudly: 'This meeting's to settle my boundary dispute with the Jones boys. Who did you second Buff, you lop-eared bastard?'

'Not you, turnip!' Buff called back. He finished his beer. 'I follow Zebra.'

'You with me, animal?' Hank Jones yelled next.

'Naw, brushface,' Zebra said. 'I'm with Kenson.'

And so it went, Veg and Jones taking turns challenging each ascending member of the victory chain, exchanging good-natured insults at every step while the keg gurgled to its steaming dregs and beechnut shells littered the ground. Long before the line finished Subble recognized its outcome, but refrained from comment.

'I follow this Fancy-Dan stranger here!' Subble's second proclaimed, and belched.

'And who the hell's *your* better man, you city refugee?' Veg shouted for the benefit of those who had joined the party too late to know.

'*You* are – in the daytime!' Subble cried. There was a burst of applause for the winner.

In moments a strong-backed crew had moved the boundary rock to the position Veg indicated, and an impromptu *a capella* group sang several verses of *The Frozen Logger*.

> I see that you are a logger,
> And not just a common bum—
> 'Cause nobody but a logger
> Stirs his coffee with his thumb!

Jones, it appeared, didn't feel like playing his instrument any more,

21

but he did come up to shake hands. 'I wasn't going to cut those trees,' he said.

The crowd dissipated, the men returning to their separate plots, happy for the break. The beermaster hitched his team and tilted down the track. Subble wondered who paid the cost of such refreshment, and decided that there were probably standing arrangements. Perhaps, instead of logging, he brewed – but received an allotment from the lumber mill anyway. Whatever it was, the system seemed to be functioning smoothly.

Subble mouthed the conventionalities, but abruptly his attention was elsewhere. At the fringe of it all something deadly watched, hardly more than a dark shadow lost behind the trees. He focused his trained perceptions and picked up a momentary flicker, a suggestion of motion, a subdued whistle. As a wolf might glare at the fires of early man, waiting for the embers to die, waiting for sleep . . .

'You did okay,' Veg said, and the shadow was gone. Subble sniffed, but picked up only the rotting leaves and pushing fungus of the forest floor. He had lost it.

They tramped back to the original work area, the forest as empty as before, though Subble knew that many men were still within a mile. Soon the distant sounds of their labours would resume.

Veg's tongue had been loosened by several mugs of brew. 'You catch on quick, and you fight fair once you get going. What do you make of our bunch?'

'It's a good bunch. I wish it were possible to—'

'Sub, don't start pulling that government-agent reserve on me again. We've been through a party together, and we won!' But it was Veg's own reserve that had dissipated.

A party: fists and drink and a symbol of friendship. Why was it that men so often could only respect each other after testing their respective mettles in combat? Here it was physical; but in the more sophisticated, less open gatherings, male and female, it also went on continually. Men and animals measured each other before giving of each other, establishing, if not a pecking order, at least a nuance order. Was this a fundamental characteristic of life?

Subble regretted that he was not free to explore this thesis thoroughly. Agents were doers rather than thinkers, however their inclinations might run. 'Well, there's little I can relate to,' he told Veg. 'My background is not like yours. I've never been to a – party –

like this before. I was raised more conventionally.'

Veg unpacked a collapsible saw from a cache in a tree. 'I'm not exactly bright, but I know your education was not conventional,' he said. He led the way to a pile of peeled spruce logs. 'Grab an end and we'll get to know each other.'

Subble accepted the proffered handle and fell into the rhythm of sawing. He knew that it was a matter of pull, not push, and that no weight should be applied; the saw's own weight would take it through the wood in its own fashion. The teeth were sharp and angled out alternately so that the cut was wider than the thickness of the saw; sharpening would be a tedious chore, but the saw worked well enough here.

What he hadn't known was the importance of a balanced, comfortable position that provided circulation for the legs and free play for arms and upper body. He was doing it incorrectly, and though he was not tired he knew that an ordinary man would wear out quickly this way.

Veg had marked off four foot lengths, and each time one bolt was severed he brought the next mark over the balancing point and began again. 'Now take me,' he said, pulling his end without noticeable exertion. 'Folks take me for an ordinary, no-count joker who won't eat meat, and that's okay. But I have things I—'

He paused, and Subble knew that he had almost let slip something about the menace that had cast its strange eye upon the party. He certainly knew about it, and the matter was definitely relevant to Subble's mission; the signals were strong. But Veg was not yet ready to speak of this.

They sawed for a while. Subble copied Veg's stance, and finally caught on to the swing of it. The motions were relaxing, vaguely similar to the steady beat of waves upon a lonely shore, leading the mind to introspection. Jets of sweet-smelling sawdust splattered across his foot and into the top of his sock, giving him another lesson in woodsman's clothing. The curlicues settled on his toe were twisted lengths, some like little worms, rather than the powder he had expected. The texture would depend upon the nature and hardness of the wood, he thought.

'Well, like why I don't eat meat,' Veg was saying instead of whatever he had intended. 'It's okay to talk about how the world's too crowded, not enough places to live, not enough food to go around, everybody going crazy because there's no room to holler in. So they tell me I get a neurosis from all that, and that's why I have to make it harder for myself. You believe that?'

'No,' Subble said, sensing the proper answer to the ambiguous question. Veg was trying to come to grips with the problems posed by the frustration of the territorial imperative, though he evidently was not familiar with the terms. Every creature sought out a territory of its own, distinct from that of other representatives of its species; birds sang, in part, to define by sound the limits of their domains, their foraging grounds, and men liked to talk of their homes as being their castles. The contest he had just participated in had been a rather tangible manifestation of that need; it was important for Veg to know exactly where his boundaries were, even though the land was his only to the extent of limited cutting rights. Successful defence of those boundaries gave him a fundamental satisfaction; he had fought for his territory and won. Neurotic? Hardly; it was a return to normalcy.

'You're damn right, no. Those headshrinkers never set their twinkletoes in the forest. They've never been off-world. That's why—'

Once more that pause. Veg kept approaching the key and shying away.

'You're a vegetarian – and this is part of what I may have been sent to investigate,' Subble said, helping him. 'But you don't feel free to tell me just what the connection is.'

'Yeah.' They sawed for another period in silence. An inchworm mounted Subble's shoe, struggling to navigate the unsteady sawdust strings and freezing when it thought it was observed. All creatures had their problems and their frights, he thought. An inchworm hid itself in stillness; a man in silence.

Veg tried again. 'Tell me if you ever heard anything like this. Maybe it makes sense to you. When I was a kid, my brother – well, he was a good guy. Everybody liked him. I liked him. We fought sometimes, but no real trouble – I mean, I had the muscle and he had the savvy, so we didn't feel crowded. We'd go around together all the time, but I knew he was the one going to make good. In the long run, you know, because of his brains. I didn't mind. He was right for it.

'Then he took sick. He was in the hospital, but he looked okay. I saw him there, and he said he felt fine, and that they told him he was

24

going to be back in school again soon and to keep up with his studies. I guess that's the only time I was jealous of him, a little, 'cause all he had to do was lie around all day, while I had all those dull classes.

'Then he died. A teacher just came up and told me one day, that he'd gone the way they always knew he would. From the first day, almost, they'd known. Only they never told him that, or his friends, or me. Cancer – and all those doctors lying about it, telling us he was getting better and all, when he was dying. Them and their hypocritic oath. I didn't believe it at first; I used to dream he was still there, only he'd broken his leg or something and they thought it was real bad, but it got better after all, you know? I guess it took me a couple of years to believe he was gone, all the way down in my mind.

'And it got to me. I mean, here was my brother, a good guy, nobody had anything against him, but he died. And it got in my head, if there'd been this god – I don't believe in God – this guy looking down, saying "One of these two boys has to go, there isn't room anymore for both," and he had to make the choice, see ... well, *I* was the one he should have taken, because I didn't have much to give the world anyway. You have to save the sheep and cast out the goat, or whatever, and he was the sheep.

'But this god took the wrong one. And there was this destiny, this good life, meant for my brother – and the wrong boy left to fill it. I was living *his* life, and it was all wrong, all wrong. But then I thought, now this mistake's been made, and it's too late to fix it, but it isn't all gone quite if I save as much as I can. What I have to do is, is – well, make something out of it the way he was supposed to make it, you know? Prove that maybe it wasn't a big mistake, just a small one, and not so much was changed after all.'

They sawed another bolt in silence. The inchworm had negotiated the shoe and disappeared into the crushed leafery beyond, and the sawdust was mounding tremendously – three or four inches high. A swift fly had settled upon it, savouring its freshness, perhaps. The scene darkened alarmingly, then brightened as an unseen cloud crossed the sun. It was amazing how absorbing the microcosm became with a little concentration.

'Any of that make sense to you?' Veg inquired after a bit.

'Too much,' Subble said, suffering a personal pang that surprised him.

25

'But it still hurt, knowing how he died,' Veg said, encouraged. How often people were afraid to express their true feelings, for fear of ridicule, and so presented artificial ones instead. Veg was concerned because he had let slip the mask and failed to be artificial, but now it was all right. 'I thought about it, and if there was one thing I was sure of, it was that death like that was wrong. I don't care what they say about statistics and survival – so many boys might've died, and him being the one that – but then I saw that those other boys were all somebody's brother too, you know, and probably if I knew them I'd know why they should live too. It wasn't all right to kill *anybody's* brother. And then I thought, what about the animals ...

'And when I stopped thinking, I wasn't killing anything that moved, or letting anybody else do it for me. It's as though that meat is *his* flesh.'

'But you will fight,' Subble observed.

'Yeah. I never did understand those pacifist types that preach nonviolence and demonstrate against war and then go home to a big juicy steak dinner. At least a man can fight *back*. Smack on the jaw doesn't hurt him, but—'

Subble moved so quickly that Veg, who was looking right at him, spoke the last several words and finished his stroke before realizing he was alone.

'Wha—?' But Subble was already coming back to resume sawing, disappointed. The menace at the fringe had moved faster yet, which deepened the mystery. Few animate things on Earth could elude an agent on the move.

'What kind of man *are* you?' Veg demanded somewhat belligerently. 'You were just a blur—'

'I was after that thing. It's been stalking us all afternoon. I'm pretty sure that's what I was sent for.'

'You *saw* it?' Veg made no pretence of ignorance, though this would have made little difference to Subble in any event.

'Only a flicker. Just enough to tell me it is animal and alien. You're fooling with strong medicine, Veg.'

'Yeah.' The big man seemed almost relieved to be committed. 'But it isn't what you think. I don't know *what* you think, but it isn't that.'

'I don't have an opinion. I was sent to gather information on a

26

matter relevent to Earth security. I make no judgement and no final decision. When I tell you that thing is dangerous, that's observation, not opinion. It reacted faster than I did.'

Veg's brow wrinkled. 'Just because it got the jump on you, it's a threat to the world?'

'I'm a very quick man, Veg. My powers *are* a threat to any normal community, unless completely under control.'

Veg was hostile again. 'So why should I trust you at all?'

'It's not a question of trust. You have to take me for what I am and make your decisions accordingly.'

'Okay – *tell* me what you are.'

'I'm a special breed of government agent. I'll have to give you some background—'

'Give.'

'This continent is lightly populated compared to some, but its economic and political organizations are still immensely complicated. Every facet contributes exponentially to the overall—' Subble saw that Veg wasn't following, so shifted his ground. 'Take crime. If a woodsman murders his neighbour to get his cutting rights, the other lumbermen will have a pretty good idea who did it, won't they?'

'Yeah. Not too many secrets hereabouts.'

'That's the "isolated community" approach. Everybody knows everybody, and trouble is easily handled by the group. But suppose *I* killed someone here, and went back home in my flyer before anything was done about it?'

'Guess we'd have to report it to the sheriff. But it'd be pretty hard for him to—'

'Precisely. Crime is no longer simple when there are many communities involved and interacting, and so many conflicting interests. Your sheriff's estimate of the situation would be valueless in running me down, because he wouldn't *know* me or my motives. I could walk into any body shop in Appalachia and have my facial features modified, hair restyled and recoloured, body profile altered by braces and injections – I could be quite unrecognizable to you in half an hour. Even if the sheriff had my exact identity – which he probably wouldn't – it could take enough time to run me down so that my lawyer could cover the evidence against me. And believe me, the changes a body shop could make in my physical appearance are

27

as nothing compared to what a lawyer can do to my *legal* appearance.'

'You telling me you can get away with murder?'

'Yes. In today's complex world, almost anybody can – if he knows how. All he has to do is avoid detection or capture for the few hours necessary to cover his traces – his legal ones – and the job of bringing him to justice becomes so complicated and expensive that it isn't worth making the attempt.'

Veg shook his head. 'I'm just a simple country boy. I'll take your word it's rough in the big city. What has that got to do with why you're here?'

'Obviously we can't let the murderers go free – or any other criminals. And that's only one section of the problem. What we need is a carefully trained and disciplined force of investigators, who can wrap up most cases so quickly that complications never develop. Men who can be assigned at a moment's notice and take hold immediately. Men who have the brains and muscle to act on their own, but the discipline to be inhumanly fair. Men whose reports will be so similar that a central computer can correlate them without having to make adjustments for individual ignorance or bias.'

Veg frowned again. 'You still aren't answering my question.'

Subble smiled in reply. 'I'm almost there. You wouldn't let Jones' brother arbitrate your dispute with Jones, would you?'

'Hell no! He'd—'

'So you understand what I mean by bias. The trouble is every person on this world is biased in some manner, even if he doesn't want to be. But when thousands of reports are being submitted by thousands of agents on thousands of unique situations every hour, bias is a luxury we can't afford. The computer has to be sure that the case is accurately presented, or the report is worthless. Yet it can't send out a bunch of identical robots—'

'You *are* a man?' Veg demanded.

'I am a man – but not an ordinary one. That is, not ordinary in the usual sense.'

'Cut the pussyfooting and *tell* me!'

'I'm a stripped-down human chassis rebuilt to computer-specifications – physical and mental.'

'An android!'

'No. I am a man, with a man's memories and feelings. I was born

28

and raised as you were, and I'm sure I had my problems and my successes – but the past I have *now* has been grafted on with the body.'

Veg struggled with the concept. 'You mean you aren't real? You can't—'

'I'm real – but not as I was born. Whatever I was was cut away, and the entire framework of the ideal agent substituted. My memories – all of them – are his memories, and my abilities are his abilities. There are thousands like me, male and female.'

'Just so your report will be like someone else's?'

'More or less. It's not merely a matter of standardization, but conformity to the highest qualifications. I can do things that my original personality could never have achieved.'

'Like moving in a blur,' Veg agreed. Then, after a moment: 'I guess I see why you understood about my filling in for my brother's life. That's what you're doing. You're another peavey made out of a cant hook – only you don't even *know* what you started out to be.'

Subble decided not to inquire what the difference was between a peavey and a cant hook.

They had finished the sawing. Veg stood up and stretched cramped legs. 'Sub, I guess I know everything about you I want to. I'll tell you as much as I can, but I can't tell you everything. I mean, I know more, but—'

'But there is Aquilon. I understand.'

'Yeah. 'Quilon and Cal and the rest of it. And when I stop, you don't ask any more questions, you just get out of here and I won't see you again, okay? And you don't poke around after what's in the forest, either.'

'Agreed,' Subble said. The discomfort normal people felt around the retread was a fact of his life, and did not disturb him. Perhaps some of the antipathy stemmed from the fact that agents only questioned people who had something to conceal. Veg had agreed to cooperate to a certain extent, and that was all that was required.

As Veg talked, Subble forgot the man's lingering homespun mannerisms and language and absorbed the episode as though it were his own. He imagined himself on a distant colony-planet, gazing at scenery unlike any on Earth, breathing through a filter in his nose and riding beside a lovely but unsmiling woman.

* * *
29

'Don't smile, 'Quilon,' the big man said, forearms flexing on the controls.

The girl beside him put both hands to her lips in a naturally graceful reaction, searching, as though afraid her features had betrayed her.

''Quilon,' Veg continued, 'you know you're a mir'cle of beauty in summer shorts. Be a shame to ruin it with a little smile, now.'

Aquilon leaned over, unsmiling, to rest her forehead against his muscular shoulder. 'Don't,' she pleaded quietly.

Veg stared ahead, realizing that he had hurt her but not understanding why. The truth was that he rather admired Aquilon's composure; it lent her features a classic splendor that few living women possessed. He had known many smiling females and respected none; they were always to be found hanging around the spaceport, eager for his money and his muscle and most of all for his notoriety: a spaceman. The mature ones were competent – and expensive – and not always trustworthy. The teeners were agog with puppylike willingness, anxious to question him on what simply *had* to be exciting, and too often taking the more prosaic truth for some veiled criticism of their feminine worth.

He was not a philosophic man, apart from one area that he kept to himself, and craved little more than physical pleasure and honest companionship; but circumstances had forced cynicism upon him. He was unsatisfied, and when driven to probe the reasons for this had realized that it was because he was in fact a non-person. The dedicated women of the spaceport were eager for news of space and for proximity to it – though not eager to undertake offworld voyages themselves. They had little interest in the personal needs or feelings of the man within the uniform. They paid off in sex and thought that was enough. It was true that he needed sex – but that was only the physical side of the coin. Sex was minutes; what about the hours remaining?

Aquilon was different. First, she had come to space herself, and that was a definite signal of determination, talent and courage. Second, she was young and astonishingly beautiful – an almost foolproof formula for serious trouble in space. She gave no shred of encouragement to any man – but she needed a man, if only to protect her boundaries from other males.

She had come to Cal.

If the choice seemed ludicrous, it was quickly apparent that it was not. Cal had no designs on her, and was knowledgeable about many things. She could talk to him without affectation or defensiveness, and touch him without being forcibly reminded that they were male and female. She could sleep in his cabin safely, for he forced himself on no person in any way. Indeed, she served him by bringing him books from the ship's library, by making up his bunk and cleaning his instruments and buttoning his uniform for him the few times uniforms were used in space. Cal was not always strong enough to do these things for himself.

But no one interfered. At first there had been a little restlessness, but Veg had talked to the men in question and it passed.

'As with Ferrovius and the Roman courtier,' Cal had remarked sagely. Veg had failed to comprehend, and so the little man explained. 'Ferrovius was a character in Shaw's play *Androcles and the Lion*. He was constructed somewhat like you, Veg, and I think there would be a fair comparison in temperament too. He was an early Christian, back in the days when such faith was unfashionable, and pledged to nonviolence. When the Roman struck him on the cheek, he dutifully turned the other cheek – but then he suggested that the Roman should try a similar exercise. "I sat up all night with that youth wrestling for his soul;" he tells us, "and in the morning not only was he a Christian, but his hair was as white as snow."'

After that Veg, who had little interest in literature, had taken the trouble to read the complete play, and had discovered that the Irish playwright himself was a vegetarian. Small cosmos.

At any rate, Veg had impressed upon the remaining complement of the ship that Cal was his friend. When Aquilon entered the picture, she became Cal's second friend. It was that simple. What upset her, upset Cal – and that in turn made Veg restless and brought about Ferrovian exercises of pacifism.

The relationship between Veg and Aquilon was somewhat cooler. It was absolutely polite, and there was even innocent banter, as there had been just now – but they did not quite understand each other, as the recent dialogue had just reminded him.

She touched his tense bicep. 'I'm sorry, Veg. My fault.'

'Naw,' he said, grinning. Suddenly his world was bright, though what he viewed was not. He swung the tractor around one of the giant fungi, wrinkling his nose at the fetid odor he fancied he smelled. He squinted through the front screen, trying to penetrate the haze that covered the planet of Nacre. The level plain ahead became lost in the gloom, its foreground broken only by the massive fungoid growths ballooning out of the fertile dust.

'Are we near the mountains?' Aquilon asked, slender fingers toying with a small but rather special art brush. Veg grunted.

The tractor accelerated, forging through the thick atmosphere. The wind whipped into the open cockpit, carrying Aquilon's hair out in short blonde streamers. She faced ahead, inhaling deeply through the concealed nostril filters. She did not smile.

Veg eased up as the mountain ridge appeared. Nacre had never been mapped, largely because there was no economical way to do it, but men were working on the problem now, and he enjoyed exploring. The outcroppings at the base of these hills of his were stark, while the tops projected into the encompassing mist and vanished. Aquilon's fingers moved in air, shaping the vision she saw, eager to express it on canvasite.

'Look at the vegetation!' she explained. 'The toadstools!'

Now that they were moving slowly, Veg could see what she meant. The plain had been largely featureless, a foggy desert, but the foot of the mountain at close view was covered with fungoid brilliance. What had seemed like bare stone was actually grey and blue fungus, its hugely spreading tops an umbrella over the lesser growths. What appeared to be sand was the salt and pepper of myriad tiny spokes emerging from a brown spongelike underpinning. Between were layered colours – red, yellow, blue and black, the individual plants shaped like funnels, horns, brackets, plates and, yes, toadstools. From a distance it was all a blur, largely the fault of the atmosphere; close, it was a wonderland of shape and colour. He pulled to a halt.

'Don't touch anything,' he warned her. 'Some of these mushrooms could be poisonous.' Then he felt foolish, remembering her training; she should be warning *him*. There was no danger of anyone taking a bite.

Aquilon unfolded a tripod from her pad and painted busily. She wore brown shorts and a white blouse and filled both so well Veg found it hard to look at her. He wondered again why she had deserted the popular life she could have had on Earth to venture into lonely space. But she offered no hint, as she twirled her brush and duplicated item after item in full colour.

He walked to the rear of the tractor and lifted the catch on the back equipment hold. There, suspended in a comprehensive padded harness, was a very small, thin, bespectacled man with sparse brown hair. His trousers and sleeves were full length, as though he did not want people to see his limbs, and his shirt came together in a snug collar about a small neck.

'How you doing, Cal?'

The little man smiled bravely. 'Well enough,' he said, but his face was pinched and white.

'We stopped to draw some pictures,' Veg explained. 'Maybe you want a few samples?'

The sunken eyes brightened. 'You found some distinctive varieties!' The emaciated hands came up to touch the fastenings of the harness, then dropped wearily. 'Perhaps you could select a few for me.'

'Sure,' Veg said, embarrassed. He could see that the ride had been hard on his friend. He kept forgetting that others did not always share his enthusiasm for speed. Cal had not adapted properly to the gravity of Nacre, though it was less than that of Earth, and the filters impeded his breathing. In space, under null-gravity conditions, he was all right, and he had a liquid suspension bath for conditions of acceleration. On land – he suffered. But Cal was Cal, and had insisted on coming on the exploratory excursion, rough as the journey might be. He was as excited as Aquilon about what might lie in the mountain range. It was not courage he lacked, but strength.

Veg donned protective gloves and marched toward the most luxuriant display. 'Not those!' Aquilon cried, startling him into drawing a breath through his mouth. Her voice was apt to do that to him. He expelled the air hastily, realizing that she wanted to preserve that particular group for a portrait, and moved over.

The atmosphere of Nacre had been exhaustively tested and pronounced safe – in moderation. A few breaths through the mouth would not cause serious discomfort, and all personnel were trained to breathe automatically through the filters, even in sleep. Veg knew this, but the unfiltered air seemed unclean and it upset him to inhale it.

The flora and fauna were another matter. Some of these were deadly in unexpected ways, and most had yet to be tested and

33

classified. The rule: Do not touch until the laboratory has taken apart and approved.

Aquilon glanced at him as he advanced upon the bend of the outcropping, but he did not interrupt her sketching. Veg stopped, spread out a collection sheet, and carefully reached out to grip the nearest offerings.

The fungi were even fancier than he had thought, and so thickly packed that there was no clear way to isolate them for individual harvest. Yellow goo flowed where his feet had crushed minute growths, and he regretted this accidental destruction. He reached for an Earth-sky-blue six-inch stink-horn, afraid the projecting tip would break off and crumble in his hand, but to his relief and surprise it was as solid as a stick of wood. He worked it free, sadly snipping off the wire-like root strands, and laid it on the cloth.

Farther along was a specimen about the size of a softball, with innumerable spaghetti-like threads twisting about. These moved as his hand approached, startling him. He jerked back, almost losing his balance, and glanced over the outcropping of mushroom-rock into the alcove beyond.

He stiffened. ''Quilon,' he called in a low tone.

She knew immediately that something important was there. She came swiftly and quietly and followed the direction of his gaze. 'I see it,' she said, as tense and quiet now as he.

It was a bay in the sea of dust, and squatting in front of a smaller inlet was a creature about the size of a small crouched man. From this vantage point the most distinctive feature was its enormous single eye.

'What is it?' she asked him. Veg did not reply. The creature stood unmoving, its eye, three inches across, focused unwaveringly upon them. The body was hunched into a globular mass balanced upon a single muscular foot.

They exchanged glances. Veg shook his head at the unspoken question. 'We're only supposed to note the lay of the land,' he said. 'We don't dare mess with the local life – not something as strange as this.'

'It doesn't look dangerous.'

'But eighteen men were killed before we arrived – by something . . .' He did not need to say more. They were conditioned to caution as members of a semiprivate trouble-shooting expedition investigating a promising but dangerous planet. Pay was to some extent contingent upon success in solving the problem, and qualified volunteers were scarce. Strange people enlisted and strange things happened – but individuals avoided risks not so much for personal safety as from consideration for the needs of the expedition. A foolishly brave man was a liability.

Veg had wondered from time to time why Cal was allowed to stick with the group, since he was most apt to get himself killed. Perhaps it was because he was also most apt to put his finger, feeble as it might be, directly upon the source of trouble, and thus save many other lives and much time.

At any rate, they were bound to watch this strange creature, but not to approach it, however much they might be tempted to.

Aquilon was already sketching, wasting no motions. Colour flowed from her brush, seemingly of its own volition. She flicked it, once, at Veg; a bright red dab flew to spatter against his cheek. Satisfied, she returned to her picture, the magic strokes quickly evoking a lifelike image of the animal ahead.

'Got a tail,' Veg said, wiping at his face with good humour, 'but no jaws. Not like the omnivore. How does it fight?'

She did not comment, rapidly filling new sheets of canvasite. All the animals they had observed on Nacre – and there were not many – were constructed on a roughly similar blueprint, as though radiating from a common ancestor. Just as the animals of Earth had settled on four limbs and two eyes, regardless of the vertebrate species, those of Nacre stayed with one foot and one eye. But, as on Earth, these animals diverged into large and small, bold and shy, predator and prey. The most savage of them all was the omnivore.

'Could have weapons that don't show,' Veg said, having nothing to do while Aquilon painted. 'That eye—'

Even from this distance the eye was impressive. It glittered from a convex surface like a lens, as deep and dark as a well. Inside, perhaps just beyond the visible spectrum, there seemed to be a flicker, almost a glow.

'... something about it,' Aquilon agreed, sketching an enlarged view of the organ.

Veg drew her back at last, his two hands on her slender shoulders while she continued to paint. 'We'd better get home and report this thing. Might be important.'

She acquiesced reluctantly. They backed away until the creature was hidden from view behind the projecting arm of the mountain; then Veg stood guard while Aquilon ran to the tractor to explain the situation to Cal. Veg kept his hand on his sidearm, hoping he would not have to draw it. For one thing, he never liked using a weapon, though he did when he had to; for another, he had no guarantee that the repellant fog it emitted would be effective, since this creature was quite different from any seen before.

After allowing Aquilon time, he backed the rest of the way to the tractor. He had been careless to harvest mushrooms without checking the area thoroughly first. The thing could have crept upon them silently ...

'That's all I got,' he said apologetically to Cal as he deposited the single fungus and closed up the compartment. The little man only nodded, and Veg knew he was wishing he had been able to see the new creature. A single glance would mean more to Cal than ten minutes to Veg. 'I'll glide by it as we go. You can watch through your periscope.'

'If only radio worked on this planet—' Aquilon complained as he joined her in the front. It was a familiar grumble; parties did not like being out of contact with the main base, but the dust seemed to blank out most electromagnetic radiation in the atmosphere. Later, alternative communication would be worked out; but now they had to desert a phenomenal discovery because they could not summon another party from the base. 'We may never see it again.'

He started the huge motors and ground slowly forward. The vehicle rounded the edge of the mountain and cut into the bay.

The animal remained, flickering inscrutably. Veg drew carefully opposite, then stopped and turned, hoping Cal was getting a satisfactory view. The man was fascinated by extraterrestrial life of all kinds, but especially by the larger animals. This would make his day.

The tractor spun to face its own retreating spoor. Aquilon, still curious, mounted the back of the seat to watch over the top of the vehicle as they departed. Veg glanced once at the several square inches of soft thigh exposed, then bit his lip and concentrated upon his driving. His expression was thoughtful.

The creature moved. Veg could see it in the rear vision screen. It made an awkward, high leap, twisting in the air to land on its foot a dozen feet nearer the tractor. The lambent alien eye still watched intently.

'I think it's as curious about us as we are about it,' Aquilon said brightly, still facing behind as they picked up speed. 'It's following us.'

Veg grinned, relieved now that the three were safely in the moving machine. 'Maybe it wants to race.' He accelerated to an even twenty miles per hour. 'Let me know when it gives up.'

'Not yet,' the girl said. She watched the creature leap and leap again, approaching the tractor, while Veg watched her watching. 'It's catching up to us.'

Veg grunted and played with the controls, letting out the mighty engine until the indicator registered thirty-five.

'It's still gaining,' Aquilon said, genuinely excited now and even more attractive in that condition. 'But – it isn't the same. I mean—' She faltered and glanced at him as though expecting a rebuke. 'It – I think it changed its shape. To hop faster.'

This was no overstatement, as he could see for himself. The body had flattened out and elongated, and the bounding effect was gone. The foot had become a pistonlike pushing member, touching the ground at intervals of twenty feet, sending the body forward in long shallow trajectories. The large eye was in the front of a head now tapered like a rocket, fading back into a neckless trunk, and the long tail streamed behind.

Veg tried to watch screen, girl and the view ahead, but had to alternate. 'We latched on to something here,' he muttered, rising to the challenge. 'But if it really wants to race—'

Once more the tractor accelerated. It had been built for high speed over rough terrain, and was as potent a machine as Earth produced. Veg switched on the headlights and maneuvred deftly around the rapidly looming fungi. Aquilon hung on to the hand rail behind the seat as the thick wind tore at her body. Her blouse inflated and hair shot over her face in a rigid bonnet. She faced back still, a look of solemn excitement on her comely features, lips parted but breathing through her nose, intent on the uniped behind. At sixty it began, slowly, to fall away.

Aquilon reluctantly lowered herself down into the seat, fighting the fierce currents and jolts. 'I never saw anything so fast—' She realized only then that her blouse had torn free of the elastic waistband and now hung loosely over the shoulders and arms.

Veg nodded appreciatively but made no comment. He wasn't going to get her mad at him again!

She tucked herself together and leaned over to view the screen before the driver. 'Look!'

Directly behind, the creature was gaining again.

Veg's mouth dropped open. 'But we're doing seventy-five!' he protested.

Aquilon watched closely, while Veg peered in frustration past her head. He did not really have the time to concentrate on the screen at this velocity. He was approaching the limit of forward visibility under Nacre conditions, and Cal would not be appreciating the roughness of the ride.

'It changed again,' she said, a little smugly, and described it to him. The thing no longer leaped or pushed at all; instead it stayed close to the ground, its foot moving so rapidly that it was invisible at contact. The body moved on an almost level course, flattened all the way into a thin disk ten feet in diameter. The vast front eye still stared ahead, hypnotic, glowing darkly.

'How could I have thought it awkward?' Aquilon whispered. 'It's the most beautiful thing, like a butterfly – no, like a swimming manta ray, back on Earth. Only it swims in the *air*, so swift—'

The tractor leaped forward, its motors roaring. 'This time,' Veg said with grim enthusiasm, 'this time I'm *really* going to show it dust!' He touched a button and an armoured canopy slid over the cockpit, killing the turbulence within. But heavy vibration jarred the occupants as the vehicle sped over the plain in a straight course, blasting apart the mists and shattering the fungi in its path. He was proud of the machine, with its engine composed of a motor for every wheel and its overwhelming impetus.

The thick dust stirred at last, obscuring the afterview, and once again the pursuer was lost to sight. But in a moment it reappeared, off to the side and still gaining over the tractor's speed of ninety-five.

'Is there any limit?' Aquilon breathed, staring raptly at it. 'Such a performance . . .'

As the tractor continued to accelerate, the flat thing outside slowly forfeited ground, and was finally lost again in the mists. This time it did not return.

Veg eased off slowly, somewhat intoxicated by the speed. He

seldom had a pretext to really push the tractor.

Aquilon was first to react, lifting her flaxen head like an alert doe. 'Burning,' she said. 'Something is burning!'

Veg laughed and pinched her bare knee with corded fingers. Then he smelled it. 'Oh-oh.'

The tractor slewed alarmingly. 'Wheel's froze up,' he grunted. 'Got to cut that motor. Damn dust must've—'

It lurched again, throwing them both to one side. Veg cursed and fought the controls; Aquilon unplastered her bosom from his shoulder and braced herself against the opposite corner. The dust ascended in surging clouds, hiding earth and sky.

The sturdy vehicle did not topple. They sat quietly while the pocket storm outside subsided, then choked jointly as the reek of well-charred insulation fumed in. Veg released the canopy and forced it back by hand. The incoming swirl of dust washed out the bitter air and gave their filters something tangible to work on.

'We're stranded,' Veg said bluntly. 'Own fault. This machine won't move for weeks.'

Aquilon worked it out for herself. 'In this mist and dust there won't be any tracks to follow by the time they realize we're lost . . . and we can't signal them. A full search pattern would take too long.'

There was a groan. Her eyes widened. 'We forgot Cal!'

Veg banged the door open and jumped to the ground. Aquilon slid over and dismounted more carefully. Together, they circled through the settling particles to the rear of the tractor.

Cal's glasses were broken and hooked over one ear, but there was no blood on his face. Veg unfastened the harness and lifted him down.

Aquilon flung both arms about the unconscious man and held him up while Veg checked his body quickly for injuries. 'He's okay,' he announced. 'Spinout must've made him light-headed.' He hoped he was right.

Aquilon set Cal on the ground and cradled his head upon her thighs. Before long his eyes opened. 'There appears to have been a – shake-up,' he murmured.

Veg relaxed, only now allowing himself to admit how worried he had been. The shock could have thrown his friend into a coma, and it there had been any internal injury – 'a shake-up! Friend, if *I* woke up in a lap like that, I'd be shook up, and I'd damn well think of something better to say than—!' He was compensating for his concern by showing mock gruffness.

Cal smiled but Aquilon did not. Veg turned away, irked yet again by his seeming ability to say the wrong thing. They all knew that his little jokes were just thinly veiled appeals for—

For what? For the same thing the spaceport professionals provided for pay or glamour? Was he that hard up already, that he had to chase after the friend of his friend? And if by some mischance he got her – would she then be no more to him than those contemptible others? Aquilon was a nice girl. What demon prompted him to dream of destroying her?

'Spores,' Cal said, sitting up with Aquilon's help.

'Spores?' For a moment Veg was afraid Cal's mind *had* been affected.

'This is a fungus world – insufficient light for chlorophyll plants, on the ground, at any rate. Much of this "dust" is in reality a surplus mass of spores, microscopically small, since that is the way most fungi reproduce. A palynologist will tell you that you could fit fifty sextillion of them in a level teaspoon. They float in the air and get into everything, and there are so many types that even on Earth they are constantly feeding on new materials. Probably some worked into the wheel bearings and sprouted in the oil, leading to—'

Cal was back to normal.

Veg moved over to stand before a locker in the side of the tractor. He stared silently into the interior, frowning.

'Supplies?' Aquilon inquired. Her head as she came to stand beside him, barely passed his shoulder.

'Steam rifle and a compass,' he said with disgust. 'We're in trouble Beautiful.'

She ducked under his arm and poked into the compartment. 'It's a complete survival pack' she said, pleased. 'Knives, matches, first aid, handbook ... We can hike back to the base, with this.'

Veg studied her.

'Why look' she continued innocently. 'The compass shows only twenty-four miles. That's not so far—' She broke off, noticing that Veg wasn't responding. 'What's the matter?'

'I never met a woman yet who could think straight. That score miles is straight cross-country; follow level ground, it's more like a hundred. We were a couple of hours out, in the tractor. You and I,'

'Quilon, might make it ...'

'Oh.' Her hand flew to her mouth. 'Cal ...'

'Yeah.' Veg got to work unloading the compartment and setting up the knapsack provided.

Already a thin film of the ubiquitous powder falling naturally had formed on the horizontal surfaces of the vehicle. Only the ghostly, dead, white fungus giants interrupted the obscurity of the shrouded plain. It was not cold, but Veg saw Aquilon shiver as he tightened the pack, picked up the rifle, and took his bearing from the compass.

'Couldn't you cut across by yourself and bring help?' she asked without particular hope. 'You could make it in a day and we'd be safe in the tractor.'

'If I knew the terrain, yes,' Veg said seriously. 'But there are some bad drop-offs around, worse because you don't see 'em. The camp sits right under a cliff. If something happened to me, or even if I were delayed only a little, you'd be finished. With only one real weapon, no food and precious little water, we can't split up.' He chucked her under the chin, trying to break the mood. 'Besides, I want you where I can keep an eye on you.' He pointed across the fog. 'That way – and pray it stays level after all. Help the lady, Cal.'

Aquilon caught the hint and took hold of the little man's elbow. They moved out, following Veg's lead. The pace was slow – hardly two miles an hour, but Cal stumbled almost immediately. He had discarded the useless glasses, but that was only part of the problem; he could see well enough at intermediate range, and wouldn't need to read on the journey. Sweat beaded his brow as he struggled to advance, but it was evident that even this slow pace was too much for his wasted body.

The woman, half a head taller than he and heavier, put her arm around his waist firmly and half-lifted him, helping him forward. Cal grimaced at the pressure of her arm but did not speak. Veg, rifle ready and eyes scanning the trek facing them, tried not to look back, but he slowed his pace until a balance was struck.

Two hours later they hove in sight of a group of animals. 'Herbivores,' Veg said. 'No danger.'

'Food,' Aquilon said. 'Why don't we wait here while you bring back a small one? We could use the break.' She meant that Cal could use it, principally.

Veg started to say something, then changed his mind. She had

41

forgotten; that was all. Still, he could bring back a live one for her . . .
He slung the pack to the ground and headed for the herd at a rapid
pace, still wearing the rifle.

Over twenty miles to go! He could make it so easily . . . and so
could Aquilon. But Cal—

The trouble was they could not do it at Cal's pace. That would
take three days at least, with the frequent rests, and while they might
last that long without food, the lack of water would bring them
down. He was thirsty already, and there was only a quart bottle of
sterile water, intended for first-aid use. They would drink that, of
course – but for how long?

Sooner or later it would occur to Cal that he was impeding their
chances. Then there would really be trouble. Veg had no intention of
deserting his friend. He would simply have to carry him; maybe that
way they could make good enough time. Aquilon could carry the
pack. He'd have to strip it down, throw out everything they weren't
sure they'd need . . .

He kicked at a football-sized fungus bulging out of a crevice in the
dust. It held its ground and absorbed his boot spongily, almost
tripping him. Veg cursed and recovered his balance, as angry at
himself for taking out his passion on an innocuous living thing as at
it for resisting the blow. There was transparent moisture dripping
from his toe; he had wounded it after all. He went on, nagged by
something but unable to place it, quite.

He approached the edge of the herd, not bothering to unstring the
rifle. The peaceful herbivores of Nacre were common, and no threat
to anyone. Their flesh *was* edible, but he did not propose to
slaughter one, not even for Aquilon. She would have to do that
herself – and he didn't think she would.

Like virtually all the animals here, these were one-legged. He
could see several hopping about, covering two or three feet with
each effort. Racers they were not; they did not travel much, and a
herd migrated only gradually in much the same manner as a dune of
sand: one particle at a time. There were about fifty members here,
and no more than half a dozen were moving, seeking fresher pasture
at the forward edge. The others were grazing, their long pink
breathing gills extending from the tops of their knoblike heads to
give individuals a faintly rabbit appearance. The group, inspected as
a whole, resembled a field of gently waving grain. He had heard that

those gills extracted water, among other things, from the atmosphere; too bad human beings couldn't do that!

The herbivores came in all colours of grey and all sizes of medium and grew, as nearly as had been determined, for life. A few were taller than himself and somewhat more massive. He stooped to pick up a medium-small representative that looked as though it weighed no more than fifty pounds. He had had contact with these creatures before, but had never quite overcome his amazement at the complete alienness of them.

He put his hands on this one's narrowest part, catching it just above the circular foot before it could realize what he was doing and hop away. He heaved. It came up easily, making no sound. The foot, splayed in a full circle to feed on the nutrient dust, flopped loosely as he lifted the creature into the air and held it before him.

The globular body rose in a hump like that of an octopus, and the single eye bulged placidly. The long breathing gill flowered at an angle now, an undulating mass of fine fibres.

The waving antenna brushed his face with a damp and gentle touch, and through it he saw Aquillon coming up to the herd. 'Your pet!' he shouted, knowing that the noise would not disturb these creatures; no animal so far discovered on Nacre made any vocal noise or possessed hearing apparatus. It was a silent planet – which, as Cal had pointed out, was strange, because the perpetual mist made sight a far less useful perception that it was elsewhere. The falling dust inhibited light and dampened out beams and signals of any—

The distance between himself, and Aquilon had halved, and she was waving her arms and shouting. 'Veg! Behind you!'

He whirled, still holding the herbivore. Something bounded out of the herd, rising far too high to be a normal member of its company. Sleek and black, its body contrasted sharply with the grey shades of its neighbours, too. A great eye shone from the thing, unnaturally malignant and totally unlike the empty mirrors of the herbivores. It landed at the edge of the group nearest Veg and moved towards him, flattening into a suddenly familiar shape.

'The manta!' Aquilon screamed.

Veg dropped his burden and slid the rifle into one hand with an experienced twitch of the shoulder. This was the last thing he had expected, and he felt naked in the presence of such a menace. A race in the tractor had been one thing; but to meet it in the open—

The heat chamber of his rifle flared as it built up pressure. His hands had been doing the right things automatically, as though they were more eager to kill than he was. It only took a few seconds for the steam to form – seconds that seemed very long, right now – but after that the rifle was good for service limited only by the aim of the marksman and the quantity of ammunition.

The manta came, shimmying towards the side, incredibly fast. Now he saw the whiplike tail, and with a sick insight he realized what that tail could do. He hadn't wanted to fire, but there was no longer a choice.

The steam hissed as he squeezed the trigger: once, twice. The manta came on, unhurt. Cursing, Veg ripped an explosive shell from the stock and clapped it into the auxiliary chamber. He held back another moment, however, despising the shell as, at best, unsporting.

The manta was little more than a thin line, head on, moving now at such a velocity that it was over Veg before he could aim properly the second time. It passed a foot above his head – but did not strike.

Now it landed between him and Aquilon, facing her. Veg saw her recoil in terror from its immense disk, she who had thought it so beautiful, with the trailing tail and the great eye that seemed to plummet through its entire length. It was after her!

Veg fired. This time the manta shook as the shell tore open its body. It spun, coalescing in mid-air, then fell heavily and moved no more.

He had killed it after all.

44

Chapter Two

A JUG OF WINE

The mountains gave way to the northern lakelands as Subble guided his flyer west, avoiding the crowded airspace above Appalachia. Then he cut south across the anti-pollutant smokestacks of the Midwest and angled on into the flat expanse of the intensive farmland beyond the Mississippi. Juggernauts trod along the endless plantations like mighty harvester ants, far too powerful to be challenged by barehanded man yet militant in the protection of the tenderest shoot of corn.

He drifted across the massed elevated pipelines of the rapidly depleting Oklahoma oilfields and landed at last upon one of the towering residentials just north of the Texas border. There was ample parking space on the broad asphalt roof of the address in his notes, and he taxied to the visitor's lot without event. A conveyor took him to the nearest elevator. The layout was standard, if unimaginative; so far everything was routine.

He stepped out on the twentieth floor down and navigated the cubistic maze until he found the proper apartment. The door opened promptly to his summons and warm air puffed out. A strikingly beautiful woman stood before him, the image of the girl of Nacre come stunningly to life in the long skirts and low bodice of a pseudo-gypsy siren. Her long fair hair was carelessly looped in a crude knot, as though tied in a preoccupied hurry, but this could not detract appreciably from the classic lines of her face. She was blue-eyed and barefooted and gently smiling.

'You are—'

...'Quilon,' she said immediately. 'Come in. I need you.'

Subble entered, picking up the spring essence of the simple perfume she wore. His perceptions told him that this woman was far more complicated and disturbed than Veg had seen her, but not dangerous in the physical sense. She was in many ways

45

complimentary to the bluff, powerful vegetarian, and it was not strange that they were in love.

'I am—'

'One of those agents,' she said. She handed him a folded stack of material. 'Put this on, please.'

Subble withdrew to her tiny bedroom and changed, setting his inconspicuous trousers and jacket carefully upon her bed. He did not worry about the things she might discover therein; only a trained weaponist would recognize the subtle modifications in cloth and leather, and in any event he would keep alert.

She had provided him with an archaic, outlandish space costume of the type reputed to have been employed during the earliest days of space exploration: cumbersome, heavy cloth and a bulbous transparent helmet. This *was* a costume, however, and hardly mistakable for anything else; the cloth was porous and the helmet fashioned of fibreglass mesh.

'Good,' she said as he emerged. 'Now stand before that backdrop and look tired. You're supposed to be the second man on the moon, back in the 1970's, lost in the shadow fringe with the sun coming up. You have to find shelter in six hours or less or Sol will fry you. That's good.'

She had set up an easel and was half-hidden behind a large canvasboard. Her right hand flirted with colour and image while her left guided him by signals into the exact posture she desired.

'Turn your handsome face away from me – down a little – bend your knees – more – good. Hold it there,' she said. 'Now you can talk or whatever it is you came to do, so long as you don't violate the pose.'

'You do commercial illustration,' Subble said, not moving.

'At the moment,' she agreed. 'But I paint all the time, whether I expect to be paid for it in money or not.'

'You receive payment other than money?' Though she had positioned him so that he could not watch her now, his ears and nostrils kept him informed of her exact position and mood. Her breathing was slightly irregular, her heartbeat accelerated, and the perfume could not conceal the odours of nervousness emanating from her. She was not nearly as sure of herself as she wanted him to believe.

'The best,' she said. 'Peace of mind.' But she was far from such reward at the moment. 'What do you want with me?'

'I'm not certain.'

She laughed. 'It is a strange man who says that to me! But that's right – they make you learn everything for yourself, don't they? To keep you on your ... toes. I should think that would be dangerous, though.'

'We are equipped for it.'

She was more at ease now, as though she had scored a point. 'I can see that. You hold that pose as though you're a statue. Not even a quiver. It takes a very special control to do that. But suppose someone simply refused to talk to you?'

'I can still learn much of what I need to. But I'd much prefer to have cooperation.'

She was nervous again. 'Change into this,' she said, bringing him another costume.

Subble returned to her room and switched outfits. He noted that she had none of her own paintings on display here, and nowhere were there any depicting Nacre.

The new costume was a conservative twentieth-century business suit, the sole incongruous note a bright campaign button pinned to the right lapel problaiming LET'S BACK JACK!

Aquilon had also changed, and stood in a head-to-toe scuba-diving rig that appeared to be genuine. The clinging rubberized suit displayed a figure that required no enhancement. She was one of the healthiest, loveliest women of the times, judged by his objective standards. It was unusual for such a creature to bury herself alone.

'This is for a period "confession" reprint,' she said. 'You just stand there full-face and look interested, as though about to fall desperately in love with a sweet girl. No, *not* lascivious. *Interested*. You see her as the ideal homemaker, wife and – No.' She tucked her brush behind her right ear and stepped from behind the canvas-board. 'Look at me. I am the future mother of your children, but you aren't in love with me yet. It's all potential. Raise your eyebrows a little, put one hand searchingly foward, fingers curved but relaxed, your weight on the balls of your feet but a trifle overbalanced as though you are about to take a step. Yes.' She took a breath which further defined her remarkable bosom. 'Now imagine me in a kitchen apron, ironing your shirts. This is 1960, you know; everything has to be ironed. It all has to show on your face, right down to the year and the season. Spring, of course. You know what they say: the desire of the man is for the woman, but the desire of the woman is for the desire of the man. But it has to be *clean* desire. This is a clean publication. You have to be the type of man whose desire the nice girl desires, if you see what I mean. There! Hold that expression.'

She painted industriously. 'Now show me how you're going to get information from an uncooperative client,' she said, her voice suddenly drained of animation. She, like Veg, demanded personal proof.

Subble watched her and discovered the trap. The board concealed the main portion of her torso, so that he could not directly observe the variations in her breathing and posture, and the opaque suit covered possible skin flushes and minute muscular reactions, as well as sealing in bodily odours. She lowered a tinted plastic face mask and breathed through a functioning oxygen system, so that there were no hints there either. He could still see her face – but it was as expressionless as a photograph.

Aquilon knew about special agents.

'Very nice,' he said. 'But the very fact you can turn off your facial animation gives me a starting point, and even if I had no other sources I could learn much by studying your apartment. If the need were urgent, I could strip you and so reestablish the physical signals. That would be interesting enough – they'd have to assign the competition handicaps if you entered a beauty contest. But I repeat: I want only what you will give me freely.'

She lifted the mask. 'Information, you mean.'

'Certainly.'

'I wonder. Is it true that you are wiped out after each mission?'

'It is true.'

'Isn't that like dying?'

'No. It's like freedom from dying.'

She shuddered expressively, no longer bothering to control her physical reactions. 'Why? I mean, what harm can a few memories do?'

'A great deal. The point is that we are virtually alike – every single agent – except for slight superficial variations in skin colour, weight, fingerprints, and so on. That's to avoid the appearance of duplication and lessen notoriety. We are almost identical where it counts, in

48

mind, physique and training. If an agent were permitted to retain individual experiences, he would shortly *become* an individual, and the objectivity of uniformity would be sacrificed.'

'But some memories might help you do the next job better.'

'Such memories are erased from the individuals, then implanted uniformly in the entire corps.'

She flushed. 'You mean if the computer thought you should remember me it would put me in thousands of minds? And every single agent in the world would know where I lived and ... everything?'

He smiled reassuringly. 'It could—'

'That's it! That's the expression.'

He held it while she completed her portrait, then went on. 'The computer *could* spread you across the globe, but it is unlikely that it would deem so unusual a woman as yourself to be suitable material for that. You can safely assume that our personal relationship is private.'

'I'll have to,' she muttered. 'Change again.'

This time it was a scant jungle-man costume, hardly more than a loin cloth. He had to dangle from a fixture set in the ceiling, by one hand, while holding aloft a papier-mâché 'club' with the other. Aquilon had also changed again, to an Asiatic toga.

'Try to look as though you're swinging on a vine,' she said. Then, as an afterthought: 'You do have nice musculature.'

'All part of the specifications, ma'am.'

She painted. 'Do they let you *live* between assignments? Or is it all work and no play?'

'We are given breaks after completing each mission,' Subble said. 'There are generally a number of agents of both sexes in the termination pool. But we *live*, as you put it, all the time. We encounter some fascinating people in the line of duty.' He was still hanging.

'But you can't *keep* it,' she said. 'They might as well line you up before a firing squad. And you *know* extinction is coming.'

'On the contrary. No need to italicize your words at *me*, miss. I told you before that we are free from dying. You look ahead to a tedious gradual ageing and loss of faculties and inevitable sickness and death. That is a lifelong dying. I look forward only to a completed mission and a paid vacation. I don't have to worry about age or disability, or even be concerned about the future. Death is not a spectre to me. I know that all of my conscious life I will be a virtual superman facing the world's most intriguing challenges. The best of any life is reserved for me.'

'Do you realize you've been hanging by one arm for six minutes?'

'Five minutes, thirty-five seconds at the mark,' he said. 'Mark.'

She looked at her watch. 'You *are* quite a man. You can let go now.'

Subble dropped noiselessly to the floor. 'Technically, I'm not a man, in that sense. I'm a number. I'm identified by a three-letter code, SUB, with a humanizing suffix. I differ from SUA or SUC or SUD no more than my code does.'

'I don't believe it,' she said, nettled. 'You must have feelings.'

'Not on duty. After this mission is over, I will have a few days to remember you and your friend Veg and appreciate your doubtless charming individual qualities. But at the moment—'

'Oh,' she said, rising to the challenge. 'So you have no normal human reactions right now. No pleasure, no anger, no . . . ?'

'I have them, but they are completely controlled.'

She was silent a few seconds. 'I have to do a series for a "Nature" magazine. The law doesn't allow it through the fax, but it still has a fair mechanical circulation. Just toss your Tazan suit over there.'

'You are asking me to pose naked?'

'Unless you have human scruples.' She poised her brush before a new canvas expectantly.

Subble removed the loincloth.

Aquilon stared at him for thirty seconds before speaking. 'This will illustrate the cover of an issue with a guaranteed circulation of four hundred and twenty thousand,' she said at last.

'Agents have appeared on covers before.'

'You go this far – just to obtain the answers to a few questions?'

'An agent will do anything within reason to maintain a harmonious relationship and uphold the integrity of the service. My body is public property, and you appear to have a valid use for it. Once you have confidence in me, perhaps you will no longer wish to withhold the information I need.'

'Put your arms forward as though about to dive into a pool,' she said. 'Give me a three-quarter view.' Then, as he posed, she began to talk about herself. 'It's a triangle. Veg and Cal and I – we're in love. I know that sounds funny. But I have to choose *one* of them, and I can't. I just can't make the decision. That's why we split up, mainly. It just wasn't possible, together, any more, in spite of – of what happened. I have to go to one of them – when I can.' She paused apprehensively. 'How much did Veg tell you?'

'That he loved you. That the three of you were marooned on Nacre. That he killed a "manta".'

'That was all? Just to the—'

'That was all. He felt that was his share, and that the rest belonged to you and Calvin.'

'Yes ...' She painted quietly for a while. 'Well, now I have to choose. I might make love with one, but then I'd have to do it with the other, too, to be fair. That would be promiscuity, and they'd both know it. I care too much for them both to hurt them like that. It's too intimate. I could sleep with someone I didn't care about, because that's only the body, public property, as you say. It's the emotion that counts. Who my heart sleeps with.'

She paused again, studying him frankly. 'I could sleep with you, the sexual part I mean, because I'm not involved with you. It would just be a physical release. An impersonal thing. Would you like that?'

'My preferences have no bearing on my duty.'

'So if I offered myself to you, physically right now, you'd decline?'

'Unless there were legitimate contrary reason, yes.'

'Legitimate reason!'

'Do you wish me to continue this pose?'

'No, but stay where you are. I want to know just how far this control of yours extends.' She touched her toga and it unwrapped languorously from her body. She wore nothing underneath. 'Now take a good look at me.'

Subble obliged. 'Is comment required?'

She sighed. 'You've proved your point, if that isn't an abysmal pun. You haven't been fooled at all, have you? You knew I meant to vamp you, to avoid telling you about Nacre.'

'Veg tried to use his fists.'

'With equivalent success, I'm sure. And Cal will use his mind. And you'll absorb it all unmoved and complete your assignment on schedule.'

'I have no schedule. I was impressed by Veg's nature, as I am by

51

yours. You should not mistake my physical control for disparagement.'

She marched to her collection of costumes and tossed him a man's bathrobe. 'Let's get drunk.'

Dressed in HIS and HERS robes, they started for her kitchenette. She put out a hand. 'Wait.'

He waited.

She made her decision and turned about. 'This way.'

He followed her out the door and down the hall to the elevator. She punched for the basement forty stories below. The other passengers stared straight ahead, not deigning to notice the intimate dishabille: loose hair, bare legs and feet, matching bathroom attire – but Subble could pick up the remarks of those who got off. He smiled. The basement *did* seem like a peculiar destination for such a couple . . .

The basement – actually, he was sure, the first of a number of unnumbered sublevels – was an austere compartment opening into several hallways. There was a directory billboard, but Aquilon ignored it. She led him down one of the central passages.

Pipes of tremendous girth crossed the low ceiling and, tunnellike offshoots led to pits with collections of valves and indicators. There was a light but pervasive aroma compounded of – he sniffed and isolated the principal components – mildew, animal dung, seed pellets, insecticide, ammonia, machine oil and offal. This would be the area's intensive livestock production unit; many residentials had their own, to avoid interstate controls, shipping charges and taxes.

One other smell: the same suggestion of alienness he had noted when searching for the vanishing trace of the thing in Veg's forest. The – creature had been here within a day. Was that why she had brought him here?

At the end of the hall a man sat at a desk poring over a chart. He looked up as they approached. He smiled. 'Good to see you, 'Quilon,' he said, rubbing his puffy eyes. Subble read the ingrained fatigue in him, the subdued desperation and misery. This man was unhappily married, sick of his job, bored and ridden with guilt. His pulse quickened as Aquilon came near him. He was not smitten with her, being too realistic for that, but he appreciated her physical qualities fiercely. He daydreamed, almost certainly, of an eventual liaison – but that was not the source of the guilt.

''Lo, Joe,' Aquilon replied, and smiled. The man's expression did not change, but Subble picked up the electric glow that shot through his physique and vitalized him; he was a sucker for the attentions of a lovely woman, particularly one so suggestively garbed. Aquilon, obviously, was using him; her smile was a cynical, calculated thing, as though the current were controlled by rheostat – yet she was prepared to arouse and oblige his passions in a certain not unlikely circumstance. She, like Veg, had come to terms with certain necessities – whatever these might be. It would be necessary to find out why she was cultivating Joe, Subble realized; probably it did involve the alien presence. The thing was hiding there, and a report by this man could betray it. 'I'd like to show my guest the farm, if it's all right.'

Joe looked at Subble. 'What's a government agent doing here?' he demanded suspiciously. 'We're inspected regularly. We're a top-classification unit.'

'Please,' Aquilon said gently, leaning over the desk. The man basked in her warmth, ready to yield her anything.

'But it's all in order,' he said in a final defensive reflex as he returned to his chart.

They entered the unit – and the smell magnified tremendously. 'He's really a computer programmer,' she said as she led the way down a narrow, straw-lined corridor. 'But they put him here because he was assigned to streamline the farm. He has to be thoroughly familiar with it before he can set up new flow charts. The distribution of feed, the percentage of calcium in the formula, the intensity of the light – the stock is sensitive to little things and the programme has to be modified for each unit or the profit ratio suffers.' Her tone showed that she had little sympathy with the suffering profit ratio. 'It's all automated, of course, so he's the only one on duty except for a mechanic, until he gets the job done. That makes him the veterinarian, now, even though he hasn't been trained for it. And he hates it.'

Subble nodded. Such things were common. Programmers too often wound up in *outré* situations, as did agents. Yet the popular imagination clothed them both in glamour and, oddly, a certain concurrent dislike.

'These are our bunnies,' she said.

They stood in a well-lighted room decked on either side with lined cages, the lowest set so close to the centre that there was less than a yard to walk in. The second layer was set back a foot, and the third another foot, so that there was a good deal of space at head height, just under the swishing air-ducts. The room was not air-conditioned; these appeared to be oxygenating units only, and it was hot. The odour was stifling.

'These are the growing hutches,' she explained 'See, they have no floors, just wire mesh so the droppings can fall through. The nesting boxes are more comfortable – they have solid plastic at the bottom and genuine bedding. How would you like to spend your life in one of these?'

Subble inspected the nearest cage at her direction. A conveyor-trough brought the nutrient pellets through and a drip-valve provided water. Another conveyor transported the descending dung away slowly. The cage was about four feet long and half as wide with clearance barely high enough for the occupants to assume a normal stance. Within it were a mother rabbit, pure white, and her litter of nine pink-eared babies.

'She has to raise twelve families in two years then she goes to the slaughter herself,' Aquilon said. 'Her pelt will find its way into some man's hat, and her delicate flesh will be packaged as quality broiler. She will never see honest daylight, and her only moment of pleasure, if that's what it is, is when the buck covers her. *He* doesn't get much leisure – he gets fed strictly according to the number of does he services, and if he falters, that's the end.'

She got ready to tell him something important, but balked and led him into another area. What was it that worried these people so? Veg, had not been frightened for himself, and neither was Aquilon, but both *were* frightened by something.

'Antibiotics are put in their food, but still a lot die in the cages. Flies get in somehow, and mold. Fungus pops up everywhere, and it seems to mutate so rapidly that they can't keep up with it.'

'As on Nacre?'

The question disturbed her. 'Sometimes I wish it were. This is the henhouse.'

Here the lights were low and red. Subble had no difficulty, but Aquilon had to wait a moment while her vision adjusted. 'It's so they won't flutter about and peck each other,' she said. 'Some are de-beaked anyway, or given blinders; but with only four to a cage there isn't too much trouble. It's all down to a science. The music helps, too.'

Sure enough: the speakers were playing Bach's 'Sheep May Safely Graze', as though sweet melodies could add to the freshness of the eggs.

'They aren't sheep, they can't graze, and they certainly aren't safe,' Aquilon remarked sourly.

The strains and harmonies were incongruous in the gloom and stink of the battery. The cages were similar to those for the rabbits except that their mesh floors were tilted to make the eggs roll into external troughs where they were borne gently away.

'What do you think of it?' she inquired as they proceeded to another room.

'Good, standard outfit,' he said. 'Seems as efficient as the state of the art can make it.'

She went on in silence.

The slaughtering section was more active, though also fully automated. The selected young chickens were funnelled into cul-de-sacs, urged on by moving brushes, where a machine looped cord about their feet, lifted them squawking and fluttering, and shackled them upside-down to an elevated conveyor-rod. At the end of the line another machine caught their struggling heads and slit their throats. The blood spouted into yet another trough.

'They aren't even stunned first,' Aquilon said, shuddering. 'Because their flapping helps the blood flow out more quickly, or something. I tried to have Joe write a stunner into the programme, and he wanted to, but he said he'd be fired if he tried to include anything that would increase the cost like that. He's trapped in the mess, just as we all are.'

Subble nodded agreement, though the realities of the situation did not strike him as a moral issue. A slaughter operation was not suitable for a man with scruples about pain – but the fate of a worker fired for inefficiency was not a sanguine one.

'If they don't die soon enough,' she continued tightly, 'the scalding tank takes care of that detail. Or the defeatherer, or the eviscerator. Most of the chickens, I'm sure, are dead by the time they are packaged, anyway.' She no longer tried to play down the irony. 'Still, their lot is better than that of the calves or pigs.'

Subble saw that she was quite upset about it. This was not what she had intended to show him originally, but the issue was a serious one with her. She must have looked for a place to hide the alien – and found this, then become concerned with the conditions she found in the farm.

'Let's get out of here,' she said. She had changed her mind again, still hesitating to reveal the secret overtly, though she must have realized that he would become aware of it. What held her back?

Back in the apartment she washed convulsively and in full view, as though her body had been soiled by flying blood. 'Do you understand, now?' she asked as she toweled arms and breasts and donned a new bathrobe.

He stripped and washed, knowing that she would find him contaminated if he did not. 'Why you have not eaten meat or eggs in several months? No,' he said, giving her a chance to explain it herself. She needed a case to argue before she could settle down.

'If we can do this to our animals today, what will we be doing to ourselves tomorrow?' she demanded. Her voice was bitter, her eyes becoming red. 'Don't you see how close we are already? This whole district – one mass of hutches for people, tier upon tier, each one fed by piped-in pellets called groceries and cleaned by communally flushing toilets. Every mind distracted by standard-formula canned entertainment that someone has programmed so there won't be too much fuss. They have to give tranquilizing drugs to the chickens so they won't turn to cannibalism when they get too crowded in their dark unnatural habitat – and we have drugs too, don't we, so we can stand it all a little longer.'

She walked jerkily to the kitchenette and brought out a quart bottle of gin. 'Come, deaden your mind with me,' she invited, pouring two four-ounce portions.

'It is no kinder in nature,' Subble pointed out. 'What man does in the effort to feed himself is only a more disciplined extension of—'

'I know,' she exclaimed. 'I know, I know! It's absolutely logical, this terrible cruelty. So we have to starve the little calves of iron so their meat will be white, and force naturally cleanly pigs to wallow in filth to save a few pennies. There's reason to it all – but where is the heart in it? Isn't there some better way than this?'

'Emotionalism doesn't help.'

'As chickens to the slaughter,' she declaimed, brandishing her empty glass, 'so mankind to the Bomb! I'm *ready*! Just water me and breed me and pluck me and—'

'If it is any consolation, I understand that intensive farming is on the decline,' Subble said, disturbed by her attitude. 'The need to rework the programmes is evidence of that. Synthetics are more efficient.'

'It doesn't matter,' she said, collapsing into despair. 'I still can't stand to be a member of a species that brutalizes this way. Veg is right. I'm an – an omnivore.'

'All of us must be what we are – and it is not entirely evil. There are redemptions, even glories. You know that.'

'My mind, not my heart,' she said, sipping at another glass. 'Ignorance is not bliss. I never knew what I was, until Nacre. Now I wish I could undo it all – a lifetime of thoughtless evil. I wish I were back there, the three of us back on Nacre, to stay forever and ever.' She changed the subject abruptly. 'You know, Veg called us "Beauty, Brains and Brawn",' she said, demure for the moment. 'I think of it as physical, emotional and intellectual – except I have the order mixed up – well, you know. But really it's – do you know Omar Khayyám?'

'The eleventh century astronomer-poet? Contemporary and friend of Hasan the Assassin, who—'

'Stop it!' she said with flash ferocity. 'I mean the *Rubaiyat* – the poetry. "A Book of Verses underneath the Bough, A Jug of Wine, a Loaf of Bread – and Thou."'

'"Beside me singing in the Wilderness – Oh, Wilderness were Paradise enow!" That would be Edward FitzGerald's rendition, third edition, I believe.'

She stared sombrely at him. 'You're getting even for all that posturing I made you do. All right, have your fun. What *is* the difference between editions?'

'According to the literal translation of Heron-Allen, the words are: "I desire a little ruby wine and book of verses/ Just enough to keep me alive, and half a loaf is needful;/ And then, that I and thou should sit in a desolate place/ Is better than the kingdom of a sultan." McCarthy had two prose variants. Whinfield an alternate, Graves another, and FitzGerald's own first and second editions differed somewhat. Do you wish them quoted?'

'Why didn't you become an English teacher? You certainly have the touch for ruining something beautiful!' But her desolate mood

57

had been broken.

'There may at some time be occasion to impersonate such a person. But more importantly, familiarity with literature, among other things, can lead to better comprehension of the key aspects of a complex situation. So we are educated rather carefully in this respect.'

'The way my knowledge of anatomy helps me as an artist?'

'Something like that.'

'Well, just don't try that stuff on Cal. He'll stand you on your literary head before you get the whole quotation out.'

'I'll remember,' he said, smiling.

She was on her third unadulterated glass. 'As soon as I saw your face,' she murmured into it, 'I knew what you were and what you wanted. But it isn't as simple as you think. No, I don't suppose you care whether it's simple or not. But this is – well, I just can't tell you what it is. Maybe if I drink enough I'll tell you. Maybe you'll have to make love to me after all to make me tell. You could force yourself, I'm sure. Maybe I'll just kill myself.'

'Are you willing to show me the paintings?'

She looked at him sharply. '*What* paintings?'

'The ones you don't have on your bedroom wall.'

'What's the use,' she said, plopping an ice sphere into her gin. 'He was bound to think of that. He's an agent.' She stood up unsteadily and went to a locked closet, rummaging in her purse for the key. 'I haven't shown these to anyone.'

She brought several large canvases to the table, propping them against its leg. She held up the first. 'That's the herbie herd,' she said. 'I repainted from my field notes.'

Subble studied it with interest. Aquilon had great talent, and her heart and soul had gone into this painting.

The landscape presented was dark: the misty world of Nacre, named for its brightness in space and not from the surface denied that light. The bloated fungi Veg had described loomed in the background. In the foreground was the herd: standing blobs like squid with their tentacles fused into fleshy columns. The pink gills were so finely drawn they seemed to wave.

But it was the technique that touched him more than the fidelity to an alien landscape. Somehow Aquilon had put emotion into this painting and made it live. It stirred him far more than her earlier nudity had, for this was genuine and without affectation. He glanced at her with a respect he had not felt before.

She brought up the second item: a smaller sheet glued to a board. 'This is the original,' she said. 'I did it on the mountain ledge after the first day's hike.'

Subble did not remind her that this had not been in the segment Veg had reported. 'You paint when you're tired?'

'I paint *because* I'm tired,' she said quietly. Her speech was becoming slow as the alcohol reached it. 'How else can I show my feelings?'

She reached for the bottle again, but Subble caught her hand. 'I'd rather you didn't,' he said. 'Alcohol has little effect on me because my subconscious is aligned with my conscious. There are no barriers to break down. But you—'

'What, *feelings* now? What do you care what I do?'

Subble did not reply immediately. He contemplated the picture, thinking of the circumstances of its creation. They must have been climbing, and Aquilon dead tired, for she had had to help Cal. Unable to relieve her feelings in normal expression, she had turned to her painting. Her eyes had focused on the phantom darkening grey of the sky while her brush formed a scene. The painting, though done on the spot, had to be from memory or imagination, for the haze, formed from the microscopic debris of the helioanimalcules high in the atmosphere – this much he understood about the planet – combined with the closing dusk to obscure everything more than a few feet from the open ledge. But it had taken shape steadily: an image of the trail those three had covered in the last hour, creeping around the corners of the mountain, fungus clinging like stylized puffs of cotton.

The trail over which they had travelled would have been tortuous and ugly, and Aquilon's rendition of it was striking. Her picture was a composite of all the features of the climb. The fatigue of the steep ascent was there, and the hardness of bare rock; the nausea of tired feet skidding on the slime of crushed fungus. There was a hint of the hopelessness of a man who lacked the strength or the will to live, and perhaps also that of a girl who would not, then, smile.

But the painting itself was magnificent.

And had she then set it aside, on that far world, and leaned back against the vertical stone wall rising from the inner ledge? The pale blue rock of the mountain she depicted would have contrasted gently with the dark haze of the sky beyond the drop-off, and here, ringed by the billowing white fungus, the lonely beauty of such a woman might have been at peace.

'When you tried to seduce me,' he said slowly, 'I was required to resist. That did not mean that I found you unattractive, or that I was indifferent to your welfare, as I tried to advise you. Now that you have shown me what is within you, I ask you not to demean it by – this.' He indicated the bottle, and discovered that he still held her hand.

This was an incidental intimacy more penetrating than all the dialogue and nakedness they had been practicing. She looked at him, realizing this, and gently disengaged herself. 'A jug of gin,' she said. 'I guess we got off on the wrong foot. I'm sorry.' She did not touch the bottle.

The third picture was quite different. Savagery dominated it. A monster glared from a single eye, and behind it rose the head of an incredible snake, all teeth and no eyes or nose. Subble had never seen a combination so menacing.

'The omnivore of Nacre,' Aquilon said.

The last painting showed the manta, immediately recognizable as the creature Veg had described. It was in full motion, probably as seen from the retreating tractor, and strangely beautiful.

'This is my mission,' he said, studying it.

'I know.' She laid her head on the table and cried.

Subble stood up and put the paintings away. He walked around the apartment and looked at the collected works, largely on mundane topics. Few of them had the magic of the four they had just looked at together. Aquilon had hinted that she disliked her present life, and her work proclaimed it. Her heart was on Nacre, with the two men she had known there and the creatures she remembered.

Behind him, she stirred, throwing away the bottle and going into the bathroom. He heard the water splashing wastefully, and knew she was trying to be sick.

He came across the pictures she had made of him: a spaceman staggering over a bleak moonscape, a handsome twentiety-century gentleman, an apeman swinging from a jungle tree, and a diver *au naturel*. Each likeness was accurate and detailed – and increasingly, from the first to the last, the special touch was there. The spaceman could have been anybody, but the diver was Subble. Not just an agent – Subble the individual. And, odd as it was to apply the thought to a picture of a naked man, Aquilon had put herself into it. She was astonishingly quick, for these were not mere sketches, and her skill was natural, not trained; her work really did reflect what was within her.

Subble was no artist, but interpretation of illustration was one of a number of things he was equipped to do with fair competence. He could learn a great deal about the character and mood of the artist by studying the technique.

He stood for some time contemplating the paintings.

His clothing still lay on the bed. He went to it.

Aquilon lay beside his suit, watching him. 'You're giving up?'

He picked up his clothing, intending to take it to the other room before changing 'Two men already love you.'

'And now you are modest,' she said. 'You don't want me to see your body again.'

He walked to the door.

'Come here,' she said.

He set his burden upon the chair beside the door and went to her.

Aquilon threw her arms about him and kissed him, drawing him down to lie beside her. 'You know we can't make love now,' she said.

'I know.'

They lay embraced, the bathrobes decorously closed. 'What happened to your invincibility?' she murmured in his ear.

'I saw what you are.'

She nestled her head against his shoulder. 'If only I knew what I am, I wouldn't be here.'

'You are a truly beautiful woman. Your body has nothing to do with it.'

His shoulder became damp from her tears. 'Will you help me?'

'I will try.'

'If only I were beautiful!' she exclaimed. 'But I'm ugly in a way nobody can cure. If only I could choose, one way or the other. Veg and Cal are clean, in their ways, but I'm dirty, and I just can't choose which one to – to inflict myself upon. And now I've come between them, because I can't decide. And I can't even—'

She tensed and bit the hard muscles of his shoulder. 'I can't tell

61

you that. It's up to Cal. All I can do is—'

She paused, then rolled onto her back, closed her eyes, took his hand and told him about the omnivore.

Cal was breathing in pitiful gasps, but he spoke as soon as Veg was gone. 'You shouldn't have done that, 'Quilon.'

Aquilon plumped down beside him and delved into the pack. 'He can handle that sort of thing much better alone,' she said. 'You and I would only be in the way.' She unfolded a survival cup and drew out the container of water. 'You'd better drink some of this.'

'I don't think you understand,' Cal said carefully, waving away the drink. 'How well do you know Veg?'

She looked up in surprise. 'Why, for three months of course. Ever since I joined the expedition. We've gotten along well enough. But I thought you two were old friends.'

'More than that,' he said morosely. 'We are a team: Brains and Brawn ... and now Beauty, of course.' Aquilon flushed gently. 'Didn't you realize—'

Her flush paled all the way. 'I forgot!' She scrambled lithely to her feet. 'I'll go after him. I never meant to—'

'Please.' Cal gestured her back tiredly. 'He would never kill a harmless creature. He will decide it was a joke. Perhaps he will actually bring back a herbivore for you to admire. Perhaps it is just as well.' He looked at the water she still held and turned away. 'We can hardly have come three miles. I can't make it.'

'Of course you can,' Aquilon said. 'I'll help you.' But she was tired already. Twenty-one miles?

Cal shook his head regretfully and tried to smile. 'It's not that, entirely. I could walk the distance, perhaps with your help. But you see, I can't eat, either.'

'You mean you're another—'

'No. It becomes ... complicated ... to explain. I can't eat off the land, as you might, and I have no supply of my own. I can't survive very long without it. The water might help, but I'll be dead long before we reach camp.'

Aquilon opened her mouth but was unable to speak.

'Don't feel that way,' Cal said softly. 'I brought it on myself when I insisted upon coming along. It was a calculated risk. I knew the moment the tractor failed that it was the end of me. The two of you will have a better chance if you don't wait for me to die.'

'Cal—' She faltered. 'I hardly know you as I thought I did, but—' She waved her hands in the air, characteristically trying to shape a concept that would not fit into words. 'I just can't leave you here, no matter what. The omnivore—'

The little man shrugged. 'I can only tell you that I have wanted to die for some time. Now fate has given me the opportunity. I'm not being sacrificial. For me, the end is clear – and I want to meet it alone.'

Aquilon stared at him, feeling the pupils of her eyes contracting to black pits in the pallor of her face. She tried to control her physical reactions, but she had been hit too suddenly by too much. Cal's gaze did not falter. He was not an old man, but the narrow lines about his eyes and mouth tokened appalling suffering. No, he was not being sacrificial.

She set down the cup, knowing that he had refused to drink so that he would die more rapidly. 'I'll go get Veg,' she said, unable to face him longer.

'Strange,' Cal said as he watched Aquilon work. 'If this creature is a true carnivore—'

Aquilon did not look up from the carcass. Veg had dragged it to their 'camp' and this surprising development had postponed discussion of Cal's fate for the time being. 'We really can't tell, can we?' she asked. 'We know the signals for Earth animals – the type of teeth, and so on – but this one doesn't have any teeth. I'm hoping that the lab experts will be able to tell from my pictures. But if it isn't like the herbivore or omnivore—'

'Call it a paleontologist's hunch,' Cal said with animation. 'This has the feel of a carnivore. The sleekness of it, the speed, the armament – look at the cutting edge of that tail! – this thing is organized to prey on the run. But what bothers me is, if it *is* our carnivore, why weren't the herbivores afraid of it? It must have been hiding right inside the herd.'

'You know, he's right,' Veg said, surprised. 'You saw it first 'Quilon. You say it came out of the bunch. But it just isn't natural for herbies not to be afraid of the hunter.'

Aquilon looked up this time. 'Herbies?'

'Well, what would you call them? You named the manta.'

63

'All right,' she said, 'Herbies.'

'Don't smile, now.'

Aquilon didn't smile.

'Unless they knew it was impossible to get away,' Cal mused. 'Its speed is fantastic.'

'But it only came out when we got there,' Aquilon pointed out. 'Why did it attack *us*, when the . . . herbies . . . were so much easier to catch?'

'It wanted to race again,' Veg said. 'Find out how it made out when we didn't have our machine along. Like a dog.' He became sober, for had he believed that, he would not have surmounted his aversion to taking its life. 'But we can't afford that kind of race, with it *or* the omnivore.'

There was silence for a time. Mention of the omnivore had a tempering effect.

'This eye,' Aquilon said. 'I've never seen anything like it. It's almost as massive as the brain – and that brain is heavily convoluted.'

'That, too, bothers me,' Cal admitted. 'I wish I could focus on the details, but without my glasses—'

Veg looked at the water container and put it aside regretfully. 'Just how well do you figure it sees?'

'The eye is almost nine inches long and three in diameter,' Aquilon said seriously. The sharp knife in her hand flashed as she aimed the spotlight at it and dexterously severed tissues. 'There are so many major nerve trunks connecting it to the brain that it's almost impossible to tell where one leaves off and the other begins. The eye itself is filled with some sort of refractive fluid. It's almost like an electronic tube. There's no guessing its properties – but my estimate is that the manta can see a great deal better than we can.'

'I agree,' Cal said. His whole attitude was different when he had a problem to wrestle with. 'This entire thing is an astonishing—'

'Barely an hour of daylight left, as I make it,' Veg interrupted. 'We have to move. We don't want to be caught in the open plain at night.'

Cal frowned. 'Veg, I want to tell you—'

''Quilon, you take the pack, if you can carry it; I'll handle Cal.' Veg picked up the smaller man and hoisted him over his shoulders with careful strength. 'We lost some time, here, but we can make it up if we move right along.'

Aquilon silently rolled up her anatomical sketches, plunged the dissection knife into the ground to clean it, and struggled into the straps. Veg set the pace, a good four miles an hour, burden and all. Cal didn't try to speak again.

There was a single half-hearted trail up the side of the mountain ridge, twisting narrowly among the rainbow fungi and over the ledges and slopes. At the foot the fungus was brilliant – horns, spires, skyscrapers of it, layer upon layer like a candy fairyland; but two miles up only tired white blobs clung to the ledges, unable to take firm hold on the outcroppings of rock and unwilling to surrender the slim beach-head that they had. Even the dust seemed sparse and dry.

It was a tortuous ascent – yet something had made the trail, and something must use it still. And it led, generally, in the direction they were going.

They sat propped against the mountain at dusk, recovering from the exertion. Veg had not complained, but Cal looked bad and Aquilon hurt all over from the chafing weight of the pack. The air was cooler now, but this only seemed to intensify her thirst; no one would touch the quart of water.

Veg lifted one of the football fungi from its precarious perch. 'You know, I kicked one of these, and my toe was wet.'

Cal lifted his head. 'Give me,' he said.

Veg passed it over and the little man squeezed it experimentally. A few drops of fluid fell to the ground. 'Let's look at this,' he said.

Aquilon passed him a cup and he squeezed some more, letting the juice collect. 'Here,' Veg said. He took the fungus and pressed with both hands.

Liquid spurted between his fingers, filling the cup and overflowing onto his legs. 'It's a water-sponge!' he exclaimed.

Cal held the brimming vessel and looked into its depths. The fluid was almost transparent. He sniffed it. He put the cup to his lips.

'Hey!' Veg and Aquilon cried together.

'Water,' Cal said complacently. 'We have to be practical. If I survive it, we have a usable source. You two share the jug. By the time you need more, either you'll have it or your load will be lighter.'

Aquilon looked at Veg and he looked at her. Cal was being practical, all right. He claimed to want to die, and without water he certainly would. He had nothing to lose from experimentation – and perhaps could gain a reprieve for them all.

They watched him drink down the cupful.

'I don't remember any mountain between us and the base,' Aquilon said doubtfully. 'Are you sure the compass—' She was fishing for a diversion from the morbid wait they were involved in.

'The compass is correct,' Cal said, stretching out comfortably. 'It works on the gyro-vector principle. This one was set at the base; as long as it runs, it has to be accurate.'

Veg looked at the forbidding trail ahead. 'I wish they'd made the distress signal on the gyro-victim principle, or whatever it is,' he muttered. 'Still almost twenty miles to go. Straight up and down, I figure.'

That brought the conversation to a halt. The dusk was intensifying slowly, but little time remained for them to find a suitable location for the night.

'No time for talk,' Veg said. 'If we can find a good level ledge or somewhere safe, we'll be okey. 'Quilon, leave that pack there; I'll come back for it. But we'd better ditch anything we can spare. You take the rifle and some ammo—' He browsed through the pack, searching for things to remove. Soon there was a meager pile beside the fog-pistol. 'No omnivores *here*,' he said, seeing her glance at it.

She started to protest, but realized that she lacked the strength to haul either the pack or the surplus items farther. 'You drink the water, then,' she said.

He nodded, to her surprise, and upended the quart. She was sure he wasn't being selfish, though her thirst abruptly multiplied; he had something else in mind. Possibly he intended to conserve his strength to carry *her*, if Cal—

Veg was already on the move. She dropped the strap and followed him meekly up the mountain.

They climbed. Veg, indefatigable, carried his companion without seeming to lessen the pace at all, and Aquilon, packless as she was, strained to keep up. Night tightened about them; the mist seemed to take on a more physical substance and close in until little beyond the immediate trail was visible. The dust stirred up by their feet coated her body with grime. The path went on, rising to its hidden climax.

'Luck,' Veg exclaimed. Aquilon, mistaking the word, caught up to him and looked ahead. They had come to an ideal ledge, hardly more than a widening of the path, but flat and almost level. The mountain sheered off so sharply above and below that it would be exceedingly difficult for any nocturnal prowler to approach them unaware.

Veg set Cal down. 'Got to pick up that pack,' he said to Aquilon, and disappeared into the night.

'Take the rifle!' she called after him. It was the one thing she had made certain not to leave behind, though even its slight weight had proved to be an enormous encumbrance at this pace. But he was gone, his quick heavy footsteps already muffled in the blank trail below.

Cal remained where he was, asleep or unconscious. Aquilon took off her blouse, afraid to think what his condition might mean, and rolled it up to place under his head so that he would not breathe the dust. She brought out her brush and sketching pad; these, too, she never forgot.

Cal opened his eyes a few minutes later to see her painting. 'My God – where do you find the energy to paint?'

'Your god?' she replied, puzzled, but thrilled to realize that he was better, not worse. Every moment that passed, now, was evidence that the sponge-fungus juice was safe to drink. 'You have such quaint expressions.'

He did not deign to reply, but watched her with a half-smile.

Aquilon faced the emptiness beyond the fungus-encrusted perimeter and stroked the brush across the surface of the canvasite. Color came once more in magical mechanism – but the mechanism stemmed from technology and the magic was her own. The brush was a compact, highly refined instrument, a sorcerer's wand in her practiced fingers. A touch on one of the concealed selection spots could produce and blend any combination of colours in the visible spectrum and feed it through the bristles in meagre or generous flow. Veg had marvelled that she could perform these shifts of hue and density so subtly, and she had told him that the brush was really an extension of her arm. That, said in jest, was close enough to the truth; she was no longer conscious of the control she exerted. She willed a shade of grey, it came; royal purple, it was there. The brush might as well have been programmed directly to her brain, or perhaps her soul, her creative being; the images she saw merged into a grand whole that reflected in the canvas.

People always asked her why she didn't use a camera. How could she explain to them the difference between a living brush and a dead machine? It was said that the artist distorted his image, while the camera was exact – but the truth was that the artist captured the living essence while the camera recorded one dead still-image, a mounted fragment of the animated series that was reality. In life there were no frozen scenes. If the lines of her brush were not as literal as those of the photograph, it was because the lines of *life* were less literal than those of death. By the time a living thing could be reduced to formula, it was no longer living.

But she had given up trying to explain this concept to people. Cal would comprehend it, and therefore he had never needed to ask. Veg had probably never thought about the matter; he accepted things as they were, and that too was good.

For the others – she murmured technical things, such as the fragility of good equipment and perishability of photographic emulsion; the distortion induced by alien radiation and wave-lengths, the awkwardness of carrying heavy supplies and setting them up in emergency situations. 'How could you make a color plate of an alien creature who appeared for only half a second unexpected-ly, and never again?' she demanded. 'But the brush is even slower!' the nameless arguer insisted. 'Not for me.' She meant that she could hold the image in her mind and paint it accurately before it faded, but they didn't understand.

No – the brush was compact and limitless, as the mind was limitless, and it would never be replaced by machine processing. Not on the frontier. Just as man would never be superseded by automation, where it counted. The machines and machine minds had tried to unravel Nacre – and the insidious molds and fungi had silenced them, while the explorer-colonists suffered and died.

'You match your painting,' Cal said sincerely.

Aquilon turned away from him, overcome by an emotion she did not understand.

'I'm sorry,' he said. 'I didn't mean to hurt you. You and your work are elegant. No man could look upon either and not respond.'

She put away her painting, but continued to look over the edge. There was nothing there to see; it was easy to believe that it was not a drop-off but a celestial curtain enclosing the ledge. There were no stars, of course. 'Do you love me?' she asked, surprising herself.

'I'm afraid I do.'

'That's really why you came – on the tractor.'

He did not deny it.

She faced him again, knowing that her face was now no more than a pale blur shadowed by her hair. The fungi around the fringe of their little camp were luminescent, and soft pastels glowed in silent levels, red, yellow, blue and green. She wished she had realized this before she put away her painting; but probably the effect did not materialize until darkness was complete. The colours seemed bright, but were not; Cal was visible only as a darkness cutting off the decorations.

'Cal,' she whispered, sounding like a frightened little girl. 'Cal – would you love me if I were not beautiful?'

'I would love you.'

She went to him, then, finding his hands in the dark and holding them in hers. 'When I was six,' she said, 'I was pretty. Then the virus came. I was only sick for a day – but after that . . . I didn't even know . . .'

'The sickness of our time,' Cal murmured. '"A terrible beauty is born."'

'I – I thought I was *smiling*,' she said. 'And they screamed. Every time I was happy, they beat me, and I didn't know why. I had to learn never to smile . . .' She caught her breath. 'And they – they named me after the Northwest wind . . . the cold north wind . . .'

He stroked her hair. 'That was cruelty.'

'They *knew*, while I was all confused . . .'

'"The best lack all conviction, while the worst are full of passionate intensity." Forgive me, 'Quilon, for retreating to literature, but I cannot improve upon William Butler Yeats. There is too much sorrow in our existence.'

'I don't *want* William Butler Yeats!' she flared. 'I want *you*!'

'Yet you would change me,' he reminded her gently.

She bowed her head so that the blonde hair obscured any of her face that might still be visible, still holding one of his hands. 'We're different, you and I and Veg. We look . . . normal . . . but we're not. We're torn and frightened and so very much alone . . .'

'That is a half-truth, 'Quilon. We—'

She laid her head on his shoulder, forgetful of his weakness. 'I never realized that before. That there were others. We need each other, Cal, because we're only half-people by ourselves. You don't have the right to die, not by yourself, no matter what happened to you—'

69

Suddenly, surprisingly, she was sobbing. Cal put his arms around her, leaned back against the rock and the resilient molds upon it, and continued to stroke her fine hair. His manner showed that he had been touched, but remained resigned.

'I wish I could smile again . . .' she said into his shoulder.

Aquilon woke when Veg's little spotlight played over them. Cal lolled against the rock; he had been too polite to ask her to move, and one of his hands still rested on her bare back. He too came awake, slowly.

'None of that now, friend,' Veg said, not unkindly. 'Put her down and come over here. We have a problem.'

Aquilon sat up, lifted Cal's head and rearranged the wadded shirt so that he could face Veg without moving; but he elected to get up anyway. She shrugged and remained to put on her blouse. There seemed to be no doubt now: the fungus water was a success.

Veg set the pack down and flashed the light on it. 'Do you see that?' he asked gravely.

'Somebody cut the straps!'

Veg laughed, a little hollowly. 'Some*thing*, more likely,' he corrected Cal. 'Genuine surplus alligator-hide leather straps. Never liked 'em much myself, but you know *I* didn't do that. I had a terrible time toting that bundle all the way up here, and holding the beam too, to see the trail. Had to hold everything in my arms.'

'But what could have—'

'Who else but Brother Manta?'

Aquilon considered, still on the far side of the shelf. 'Yes, the manta could have done it. That means there're more than one in this area. But I really don't see why . . . and why just the straps?'

'It's just as well those creatures aren't equipped to climb very well,' Cal said.

Veg took him by the shoulders and turned him around to face the trail below. Aquilon looked past them in the same direction.

There, less than twenty feet away, at the edge of the shelf, a single luminous eye was watching them.

Morning: the eye remained. They had slept, fitfully, under its awesome scrutiny. There was nothing else to do. Veg refused to fire at it, and they knew they could not escape it. This, she thought,

70

might be the attitude of the herbivores: why flee or fight such a creature? Neither attempt could help.

By daylight there was certainty. It was the eye of another manta, perhaps the third they had seen, hunched near the end of their little plateau. Its stationary form was not so frightening, but knowing what they did of its nature they were hardly able to ignore it, either.

Aquilon got up shaking off the inevitable film of dust and stretching her limbs in a natural but dazzling manner. 'I wish we'd saved the other one for food,' she said. 'I can mend the pack, but we still have to eat.'

'We can try some of the white fungus,' Veg said. 'If the water's good, maybe the rest of it is too. That'll take care of us, at least until we get to the base.'

'But even Earth mushrooms can kill you, and many of these are worse,' Aquilon protested. 'How can we take the chance?' She was hungry enough to do it, however.

'I tried some last night,' Veg said, a little sheepishly. 'Tasted terrible, but didn't hurt me. Better than the dust.'

So he had followed Cal's example that quickly! 'The dust?' she asked, shocked. 'You tried eating—'

'The dust is organic,' Cal said. 'The sun never touches the surface of Nacre. That's why you don't see anything green, except as an occasional fungus decoration. But the living cells drift down steadily. Highly nutritious sediment, if you can stomach it, and the herbivores evidently have no trouble.'

'Oh, I see,' she said. 'And the omnivores eat the herbivores . . . and so must our manta.'

'The ecological pyramid,' Cal agreed. 'It has to exist. Of course, the omnivores eat dust too, and fungus, or they'd be misnamed.'

Veg carved a chunk from one of the more succulent footballs. 'Whatever the manta is, it sure is fast on its foot. Probably has to be, to keep clear of the omnivore.' He glanced at the animal, which sat unmoving at the edge. 'Try this, 'Quilon, if you're hungry.' He held out a chunk of white substance.

She reached to take it.

The manta bounded into the air, its body assuming something like the dread racing shape. It hurtled between them.

Aquilon fell back with a cry. Veg stood frozen as the creature came to rest beside him, near the fungus. They stared at it.

71

'Are you *sure* it's tame?' Aquilon asked facetiously.

Veg watched it baffled. 'I thought I was done for, last night,' he admitted. 'When I saw that eye coming after me, and me without the rifle. But all it did was follow – that's when I began to be sorry about blasting that other. Maybe it *wasn't* attacking.'

Cal spoke up from the far side. 'I don't think it was attacking just now. It seemed to be trying to keep the two of you apart.'

'Hands off the damsel?' Veg asked thoughtfully. 'But last night the two of you were pretty close—'

Aquilon flushed. 'Maybe it thought we were—'

'Now wait a minute,' Veg exclaimed in mock anger. 'A moralistic manta I can do without – at least, if it figures *me* as the extra man.'

'Perhaps we should marry?' she murmured sweetly.

'I could never marry a—' Veg stopped, but it was there between them, a joke that hurt. She had mistaken his gallantry for genuine interest and he had set her straight. They were man and woman, but there was a fundamental difference in practice. She had thought his vegetarianism was only a personal preference, but now she saw that it affected his whole outlook on life.

By mutual consent they turned away from that subject, too.

'The fungus!' Aquilon said excitedly. 'Maybe it *is* poisonous. Maybe it was trying to stop us from eating it!'

Veg still held the white mass. Slowly he brought it to his mouth, eyeing the creature beside him. The manta looked back, motionless. Veg took a bite.

Nothing happened.

'You try it,' he said, tossing the remainder to Aquilon.

She caught it deftly and repeated the process as the manta swivelled smoothly to watch her. The faint putrescence of it made her gag. It was like eating rotten potato, but she forced her teeth to close on it. The manta did not respond. She looked at Cal, offering the morsel, but he shook his head negatively.

Veg shrugged. 'I'll prepare a full, er, repast,' he said, taking up the knife.

Aquilon went over to Cal. She knew he was hungry, and that for him a few hours of undernourishment were like starvation for a normal man. He simply did not have the physical resources to stand up under it. 'What are you going to do?' she asked, looking into his eyes. 'You told me you couldn't eat—'

72

'I don't suppose it would do any good just to tell you to leave me here and get on back to the main camp.'

She shook her head no. 'If you'll just tell us how we can help you—'

'You can't help me. I will die in a few hours, no matter what you do. If I could only convince you of the truth—'.

Veg, slicing into more fungus, had been listening intently. 'Maybe it's time you did tell us, Cal. I've known you for three years, and you never let out a word. You never come to the mess hall. What's the matter with you? Why are you always so weak you can hardly walk? Why can't you eat any of our food?'

Cal closed his eyes as if in pain. 'You wouldn't understand.'

Aquilon took his hands, as she had the night before. 'We aren't going to let you die, Cal,' she said. 'We'll all stay here together.'

Veg chewed on fungus, not disagreeing.

'Death is my destiny,' Cal said, the words, from him, quite unmelodramatic. 'Anything else I might tell you would be a lie.'

'Then tell us the lie,' Veg said around his mouthful.

Aquilon started, surprised by the simplicity of it. She kept forgetting that the big man's unsubtle mannerisms did not denote any obtusity of mind or feeling; he would not have been permitted in space were that the case. At one stroke he had nullified Cal's elaborate defensive structure.

Cal watched them both for some sign of relentment, but found none; Veg consumed his fungus entrée and Aquilon imitated him, more to keep up appearances than from present appetite. The stuff was foul.

'A story, then,' Cal said at last. 'Then you go on – the two of you.'

There was no response.

'I was only a paleozoologist searching for fossils,' Cal said, closing his eyes. 'You can't generally locate a given specimen just by digging a hole in the ground. My speciality was Eocene insectivores and I was running down a rumor that a primitive primate shinbone had been spotted in a sedimentary outcrop. It happened to be in a restive corner of the world, and I hadn't paid sufficient attention to local politics. I didn't even speak the language.'

'I don't believe a word,' Veg said equably.

'I was arrested as a spy – that was one word I picked up in a hurry! – and was unable to convey the true nature of my mission to them.

My captors didn't understand paleontology; I think their religion renounced any nonbeatific derivation of man. They were convinced I was concealing information, and they had devious methods of coercion. They were not backward in the *modern* biological sciences. Odd how retrogression and advancement sometimes co-exist . . .' He trailed off.

'What did they do to you, Cal?' Veg inquired. 'According to your story, I mean.'

Cal went on with a visible effort. Aquilon was shocked to see the fatigue and misery of years so deeply etched upon his face. 'It doesn't matter now, except for one thing. My diet became . . . restricted. They fixed it so that I can't live on anything but—' He stopped.

'We have to know,' Aquilon said softly.

'. . . blood.'

There was silence for several minutes.

Veg walked over to the pack at last and withdrew a cup. He squatted down. 'Can you take it straight,' he asked abandoning pretence, 'or does it have to be by transfusion?'

Cal's self-control dissolved, embarrassing Aquilon acutely. What had happened to the intellectual power she had so admired in Cal? This was a moaning baby of a man. Would it have been kinder to let him die?

'They made me into a vampire,' Cal whispered. 'I've been living on plasma . . . have to go to the doctor for my meals. He's the only one on the ship that knows. The grouping – RH factor – doesn't matter; I take it orally. How I've wanted to die!'

Aquilon whirled as the meaning of Veg's question sank in. 'You can't—' she cried.

Veg was carefully sterilizing his knife in the flame of one of the matches. 'Keep out of this,' he said gruffly.

He must have known. He had taken the last of the water so that he would have . . . blood. 'But you can't even kill a herbivore,' she said, distracted. 'How can you—'

Veg wiped off his arm and readied the knife. Aquilon made as if to throw herself upon him, then subdued herself.

She had thought she understood the motivations of these men, and thought they understood each other – but her knowledge of anatomy, human and animal, and her associated studies left her convinced that Cal's story *was* a lie. No drug or surgical technique

74

she knew of could possibly do to a man what Cal claimed; the nearest approach would be regression to an infantile dependence on milk, which was in fact very similar to blood. But if it *could* be limited specifically to blood, yet not so narrowly as to restrict the condition of that blood or the animals from which it came, a chemically similar substitute could certainly be prepared in the laboratory in quantity. The oral dosage was the give-away – a transfusion was a precise business, but the digestive tract of man was equipped to handle a variety of things.

Cal had indeed made up a story, as he had threatened – and Veg must have recognized it for what it was. Why, then, was Veg accepting the fiction as fact – *and acting upon it*? How could he donate, literally, his own blood, for the perpetuation of a charade?

And then she understood.

'I don't think I ever knew what real friendship ... was,' she said quietly. 'But you have to save your strength to carry him. Otherwise we won't get back at all, any of us.'

Veg hesitated. 'He's got to eat.'

She held out her own arm. 'I don't have to carry anything,' she said.

Veg studied her and nodded. 'You're pretty much of a woman,' he said, and there was a double meaning there, as there had to be. It erased his prior reaction to the bantering suggestion of marriage, and the motive behind it.

He lurched to his feet and charged past her.

Turning, she saw the reason. Cal had almost made it to the edge. There could be no doubt about his intent. Veg caught the little man and carried him back to the inner side.

'You don't know what you're doing,' Cal gasped weakly. 'I *need* to die—'

'You don't have a choice,' Veg said. 'Unless you want to spill *her* blood into the dust,' He returned to Aquilon, carrying the knife.

Once again the manta moved, flashing between them with alarming speed.

'What the—' Veg grunted, angry now. 'You can touch Cal, I can touch Cal. But it won't let me touch you. What's the matter with the critter?'

'Throw me the knife,' Aquilon said.

Gritting her teeth against the pain and shock, she made a neat

75

surgical slice across the fleshy part of her forearm and let the rich blood drip into the cup.

The four moved on up the slope. Veg led the way, carrying Cal on his shoulders; Aquilon followed, bearing the rifle and her sketch-pad; last came the manta, hopping erratically. It evidently wasn't accustomed to slow travel. Aquilon remained nervously aware of it, almost feeling the slash of the tail down her exposed back, but it never came too close.

The sheer side of the mountain began to level out, as they neared what had to be the top of a convex slope. The spherical fungi became larger and more numerous, lining the trail like fat snowmen, and the candyland smaller growths re-appeared.

The ground shuddered. Loud crashing and pounding approached from the obscurity above. Something was charging down the trail! Veg lowered Cal to the side and whirled. 'Only one thing makes a noise like that,' he said grimly.

Aquilon gripped the rifle and pressed the ignition stud, feeling the warmth of the chamber in her hands. It occurred to her now, as she saw the jet of water vaporize inside the translucent barrel, that they could have distilled the fungus-water, cooking out the bacteria and eliminating the poisons that might have been in the solution.

The rifle was hot and ready to fire. Veg strode towards her, reaching for the weapon. The manta leaped and flared ominously. He backed away. 'Throw it here!'

Too late. A great mottled shape came hurtling out of the mist ahead. It would weigh, Aquilon knew, in the neighbourhood of a thousand pounds. Its spiny, discoloured skin hung in huge folds, making the creature resemble an enormous horned toad. A single tiny eye was embedded in the flesh of its forepart, glaring balefully out. This was animosity incarnate. This was the omnivore.

Cal, nearest to it, huddled on the ground. The savage beast leaped, too anxious for its prey, and the great blotched shape passed over him, the sharp teeth of its striking tail clashing together just inches from his head.

Aquilon was before the monster now, the rifle hissing in her hands. The omnivore turned on her, raising its stout tail overhead. The vicious jaws in it gaped as that tail wove from side to side like a deadly serpent, doubly dangerous because it was a most specialized

76

weapon of offence. There was no connecting alimentary tract, no soft tissue, no weak spot. Those jaws could crunch a human arm in half, and the tail could hurl a human body into the air and dash it against a rock or under the slavering underside.

Her bullets only strung it, and she had no time to put a shell in the other chamber. The massive propulsive muscles of the omnivore's single foot bunched, ready for the next leap.

Veg stepped in from the side, shouting, trying to distract the omnivore's attention, though he was armed only with the puny knife. The monster swivelled, aware of him in spite of the foolish cries; it could not, of course, hear him, but its perceptions were more diversified than those of other Nacre creatures, and it could smell him and feel the warmth of his body. The jaws of its tail clashed together loudly as it turned on this new adversary.

The manta, temporarily quiescent, came back to life. It rose into the air, once more assuming the shape that had earned it its name. The eye seemed to flash as the creature banked around both humans and landed before the omnivore.

Facing the monster, the manta was tiny. Four feet tall when stationary, it could not have weighed more than eighty or ninety pounds, Earth-gravity. Yet the bulking omnivore recoiled; it leaped back, turning in the air. Its toothed tail came back as a kind of rear guard, intersecting the second jump of the manta.

The disk of the manta spread out, suddenly huge. Aquilon could feel the wash of air as it took off. It passed over the omnivore. There was a sharp Crack! as of the snap of a whip – and the gruesome jaws at the tip of the monster's tail were flying through the air directly at Veg. He jerked back – and toppled over the edge of the path.

With a cry, Aquilon rushed to the brink, light-headed from the exertion and the loss of the blood she had donated. Veg was rolling helplessly down the side, puffball fungi shattering and squirting under him but cushioning his descent. He careened into one of the giants, bounced off as though it were a rubber boulder, and fetched up with his head buried in a smaller growth.

Aquilon scrambled down to help him, glad that the slope was less ferocious here than it had been lower on the mountain. As she got there, panting and dizzy, Veg straightened and spat white chunks out of his mouth.

'Are you all right?' she asked foolishly.

77

'Gimme a little – phew! – kiss and we'll find out,' he replied, smiling. It was more fungus he was clearing out, not an insult to her.

Overcome by relief, she returned the smile.

She saw him blink, then tighten his jaw muscles in a spastic effort at facial control. Horror showed in the narrowing of his eyes.

Behind him the shape of the manta appeared, sailing down the steep slope. Its eye centred on Aquilon. Suddenly the body folded and swerved in a tangible double-take.

Too late she realized what she had done. Veg had seen. She had appalled him with her smile, that shameful thing she had tried never to show again. Now anything that might have built between them was gone. She knew what it was to wish for immediate death. Death . . .

'Cal!' she cried, remembering. 'He's still up there with the—'

Veg launched himself up the slope, followed lopingly by the manta. Aquilon started after them, but her head began to spin again almost immediately. She had exerted herself too much already, and there had been the shock of the . . . smile. But life went on, and there were other things to worry about. She eased her pace and picked her way up carefully.

She reached the trail, afraid for what she might see. There had been no sound from Veg – or anything else. It was too quiet.

The omnivore lay dead, its body slashed into tattered sections as though a cosmic knife had dropped upon it. Pale blood dripped from the carcass, forming rivulets across the flesh and soaking into the dust beneath, as thick and slow as that of a man. Cal was trying to gather some of it in his cup.

It was a horrible sight, ludicrous and pitiful at once. Somehow the notion that Cal should try to drink the blood of the omnivore disturbed Aquilon even more than had the donation of her own. Yet it was the obvious solution, if they were to survive at all as a group; her present disorientation proved that her resources in this respect were severely limited. The wrenching of it suppressed the shock of the other thing, the smile, for the moment.

It was right. It was a stroke of fortune. The omnivore could feed them, and the risk the consumption of its flesh and blood entailed was no greater than the one they had already taken eating the loathsome fungus or drinking its juice. If it worked, it spelled life for all of them, instead of a cruel death.

It was still sickening.

Something nudged her foot, making her jump and look down. The jaws of the omnivore's tail were lying there, like the head of a mutilated dog, snapping reflexively with a lingering life of their own. Muscle fibres trailed from the stub, tangling with the dust in clotted strings.

Aquilon leaned over the edge and gave way to silent nausea.

Chapter Three

A BOOK OF VERSES

Cal's house fronted the flexing water of the Gulf of Mexico. Subble had looked in vain for a private landing spot in the intensely developed suncoast of Florida, and had finally had to settle on the water, to the distress of the water-skiers ranging there. He anchored his flyer to the shallow bottom-land, allowed for the change of tide, and swam to shore.

Cal was working in the sun just beyond the seawall. He was small, standing a little over five feet, and not well-fleshed, but his skin was tanned and his movements sure. He gave no sign of any unusual weakness.

Before him, or rather around him, was an electronic device comprised of massed wires, a television chassis, ham radio equipment and laboratory mechanisms ranging from a pencil-soldering iron to a sophisticated pocket oscilloscope.

'Good,' Cal remarked as Subble swam to the wall and heaved himself onto the pavement. 'I need extra hands at this point.'

'Aquilon called you,' Subble said, shaking off the salt water.

'And Veg. Those two try to look out for my welfare, as I think you know. I owe them a great deal.'

Subble nodded, remembering the bloodletting episode Aquilon had described. He also understood by the man's entire attitude and immediate reactions that Cal was by far the most formidable of the persons on his list, physical evidence to the contrary. The man was extremely intelligent, and evidently approached the interview with a clinical rather than defensive manner. There was no bluster in him and no overconfidence; Subble was a situation to be explored and a hypothesis to be verified.' Cal would ascertain the facts and let the consensus be his guide. Yet he was concealing something important, just as the others had done.

'I think we understand the situation,' Cal said. 'And this

equipment should be no mystery to you.'

'A jury-rigged closed-circuit television transceiver adapted to the signal emitted by the manta's eye,' Subble said.

'Yes. We were slow to comprehend the nature of the creature. We assumed that it saw in much the way we do, though 'Quilon's dissection refuted that. But of course ordinary optics would be ineffective on a hazy world like Nacre. Just as the fish of the sublevels of the ocean become luminous—'

Subble was studying the schematics. 'This is highly adaptable.'

'Highly imprecise, you mean. I am not an electrical engineer, and until this is tested in the field it must be generalized. And testing is a problem.'

'I saw the manta in the forest with Veg, and I smelled another in Aquilon's basement,' Subble said quietly. 'I presume the first fed on wildlife and the second on rats. At least two other mantas have been at this spot within the past two days, and your equipment has been in operation. Why is testing a problem?'

Cal was not alarmed. 'Importation of unregistered aliens is illegal, for one thing. We called them pets, but that was a misnomer, and your presence here indicates that the government is getting suspicious. These creatures are dangerous, for another thing. Even you, with all your strength and skill, would be virtually helpless against a single manta.'

Subble did not comment. He explored a large fibrous container, noting the pockets and fastenings inside. It was designed to hold the assembled transceiver, and to float on water. He glanced out over the gulf.

'Yes, they can "walk" on water,' Cal said. 'At high speed the water presents a surface as solid as the dust nature trained them for. But the air here is thin, for them.'

'When will I meet them?'

Cal shook his head. 'I know you have no fear of death – but a premature encounter would be disastrous, for you and perhaps for Earth.'

'Not for the manta?'

Cal tried to lift an energizer pack into the basket, but his strength was insufficient. Subble took it from him and fastened it in the proper place. Obviously the little man had not intended to take this equipment out to sea by himself.

'We live in a charged environment,' Cal observed. 'So many billions of sentient individuals, such intense war hysteria, cultural unrest, pressure to succeed. Most of the people of this planet are desperate to get away from it all – but there is nowhere to go. Only a few qualify for space. And so they grasp at anything in reach, and pull it down in the belief they are climbing—'

Subble remembered the misery of the programmer in charge of the cellar farm, and Aquilon's own distraught emotionalism. He quoted:

> The Sensual and the Dark rebel in vain
> Slaves by their own compulsion. In mad game
> They burst their manacles and wear the name
> Of Freedom, graven on a heavier chain!

'Coleridge,' Cal agreed. 'He referred to the French Revolution, of course, two hundred years ago, but he spoke for humanity as well, as the great poets do. "When France in wrath her giant limbs upreared" – how easy it would be to transpose that for today!'

Subble smiled. 'When Man in wrath his nuclear arms upreared, And with that oath which smote air, earth and sea, Fired his great jets and swore he would be free— Bear witness how I hoped and feared!'

'Except that some of us no longer hope. Man is an omnivore, figuratively as well as literally. He consumes everything—'

'An omnivore,' Subble murmured remembering Aquilon's remarks.

'You begin to see the problem. Man is the true omnivore, far more savage than the creature we designated by that term on Nacre. I'm afraid it hit 'Quilon pretty hard when she realized—'

'It did. She won't touch meat now.'

'I know exactly how she feels. Nacre was a pretty drastic lesson. But none of us realized the really fundamental difference between man's nature and that of the creatures of Nacre. As it was, we were casting about blindly.'

'So am I,' Subble hinted. 'What is this "fundamental" difference, if it is not the ecological adjustment or the methods of perception?'

'I can't make that clear unless I tell you first about the third kingdom.'

82

'I don't follow you.' This sounded like a fairy tale, but the man had something concrete in mind.

Cal nodded. 'Probably you overlook it just as we did on Nacre. I certainly had little excuse. All the learning in the world can't make a man grasp the obvious, when that learning contributes to a prescribed mode of thinking. This, more than the sensory differences, makes it difficult to establish full contact with the manta.'

Subble studied him, but found no evidence of equivocation. The man had a concept that was not easy to accept or discuss, particularly for him, and the odds were good that it had direct bearing on what Veg and Aquilon had not felt free to tell him. There was a major section of the puzzle missing. 'What must I do to acquire this information?'

'It is not information per se; it is a way of thinking. I haven't mastered it myself, and may never do so, though I like to think I am gaining ground. But it is a difficult route, especially for someone like yourself. You have too much contemporary power.'

'Too *much*?'

'That can be a liability. There are realms only the impoverished can achieve.'

Subble smiled again. 'And again I say unto you, it is easier for a camel to go through the eye of a needle, than for a rich man to enter the kingdom of God.'

'I'm afraid that's what I mean. You have chosen one of the most popular misquotes of the language, and are probably not even aware of it.'

'I assure you the quote is exact. King James Version, Matthew XIX:24.'

'Precisely. You have been indoctrinated with a standard education, and a remarkably comprehensive one. You therefore have not reaped the benefits of genuine scholarship. You are limited by the standard restrictions and errors. I daresay you can quote the entire Bible—'

'I can.'

'Yet you have never thought to question the version or translation. Otherwise you would have suspected that Jesus of Nazareth, in whatever capacity He existed, probably never spoke of a camel attempting anything so ludicrous as climbing through the eye of a needle. I believe the original term was "rope", or "camel-hair", miscopied and never corrected.'

Subble was silent. It was true: he had no means to verify or refute this statement, but it had the ring of authenticity. It made no difference whether the little man was right or wrong; he had the advantage because his knowledge was more pertinent than Subble's own. Cal had pinpointed the weakness of a man who had his entire education grafted on, and Cal was in control.

For the time being. Well, Aquilon had warned him.

'The information doesn't matter,' Cal said. 'It is the *attitude* that counts. You were sure of yourself because you knew you had your quotation straight. You were right, yet wrong. That's why your rich man has so much difficulty – he can't bring himself to part with his wealth, even when it becomes an impediment to the achievement of his basic desires. The poor man has no moral advantage; he simply has less to lose. So he can travel where the rich man can't.'

'You are telling me that I must give up my knowledge if I am to complete my mission?'

'Essentially, yes. At least you must set aside your confidence in it. Your certainty will betray you, here.'

'Can you provide me some more tangible reason for doing so?'

'That sounds like my cue to condemn you as a materialist who will never achieve the kingdom of heaven! But I don't require blind faith in anything, including faith itself. I can give you reason: you must learn to communicate with the manta, and the manta is alien. Much more alien than its actions or appearance indicate. Perhaps in time normal man will hold meaningful dialogue with normal manta – but not for many years, I suspect. You need to do it *now* – and that means you must go to the manta. You have to meet it on its own territory, in its own framework. No human conventions will help you; they'll only interfere. You may never get a second chance, if you blunder early.'

Again Subble remembered Aquilon's episode, and knew that what Cal said was true. The manta's appearance was strange and its actions stranger – and the reactions of the three who had dealt with it on its home world were stranger yet. If he were to learn the whole truth, he would have to finish with the mysterious manta – and it obviously was alien. He could not trust the second-handed impressions of others.

But if he set aside his formidable training, he would be vulnerable

– as perhaps the starfaring trio had been. Assuming that he *could* set it aside. 'Do you realize what kind of conditioning I have undergone?' Subble inquired. 'No casuistry can shake my logic; no torture can break me; no brainwashing can overcome my loyalty to my mission without first killing me. How do you propose that I accomplish what my entire existence was conceived and shaped to prevent?'

'I'm not sure, but I believe you can approach the third kingdom – and with that and my equipment you have a chance. The trick is to lead you there without destroying your mind. Trust me and let me guide you as far as I can and – we'll see.'

'Why should I trust you?'

It was Cal's turn to smile. 'Because I am completely sincere. You can read my emotion easily, and I know it and you know I know. You must believe me – or renounce faith in your own abilities, which is the same thing. So you have no choice.'

Mousetrapped again, this time by paradox. His abilities *did* inform him that he had to question them. 'This statement is false,' he said, musing at it. Taken alone, those four words negated themselves, and forced a new framework which excluded them. An intellectual toy – but it had come to life. 'All right. Lay on, Macduff. Lead the way to the third kingdom. I follow.'

'And damn'd be he that first cries "Hold, enough!"' Cal said. He went inside and returned with an ornate copper vessel resembling an antique teakettle, but slung lower. He set it on the pavement and touched a lighter to its spout. After several attempts he got it going with a tiny greenish flame perched just beyond the projecting tip.

'A lamp,' Subble observed. 'Aladdin's lamp?'

'Something like it. It generally takes a little while for Myco to appear, however. We'll talk; you tell me when you see him.'

'Myco – a combining form applying to fungus. An unflattering designation.'

'Not necessarily.' Cal indicated a spot beside the lamp and they took their places crosslegged on the tile.

Subtle perfume wafted from the flame; cedar and more obscure aromas blended in a harmony new to him. He ticked the ingredients off in his mind, classifying each automatically, but there was a residue that escaped him. An unusual incense, certainly, but harmless. Evidently Cal was trying to create a mood for whatever he was leading up to.

'You have met Veg and 'Quilon already,' Cal said, 'and you know something of the situation we found ourselves in on Nacre. You know about the omnivore?'

'Yes.'

'I suppose it seems a striking coincidence that our particular trio happened to possess the very qualities necessary for survival there.'

'Yes. My boss views such coincidences with distrust. There is generally more to them than what is visible on the surface – or in the official reports.' Subble stared at the flame, waiting for the trap to spring. He detected no aliens nearby, but Cal was expecting something momentarily.

'Actually, there was no coincidence at all,' Cal said. 'Our unusual qualities were at best incidental to the problem, and contributed to some confusion. We just happened to be the group that became isolated on Nacre at the time contact was scheduled to be made. Anyone could have done it.'

That was not precisely true. Cal had hold of information which frightened him thoroughly, and his bodily processes reflected it on every level. Veg and Aquilon had suspected, but Cal *knew* – whatever it was.

'Chance threw us together, but it meant nothing,' Cal said. 'I wish it would throw us together again.'

'Triangle and all?'

'Triangle and all. 'Quilon has this thing about choosing, when really it isn't necessary. Love is not exclusive.'

'She said she felt "unclean".'

Cal sighed. 'The sensual and the dark rebel in vain,' he said. His form was hazy through the gathering smoke of the lamp. 'Slaves by their own compulsion. Earth has become a population of neurotics, turning inward what they can no longer dissipate outward. Acquaint yourself with virtually any person living today and you will discover it. Suppressed madness. That much certainly is not coincidence. No unique qualities remain – only unique ways to express the horror of continued existence. Some call it creativity, others psychoneurosis – but it remains the madness of a people who have lost their last rational frontier.'

'Veg—'

'Convinced himself that death was the evil he had to fight.

86

Fortunately, he was satisfied to restrict it to the refusal to kill unnecessarily, or to consume the flesh of any creature with a tangible instinct of self-preservation. He was never deeply touched, and remains one of the best adjusted members of our society. He's happy – while his forest lasts.'

Subble had his doubts about that, but was trying to follow Cal, not debate with him. 'Aquilon—'

'Was hit by it in childhood. She was a pretty girl, envied for her appearance. Some chance occurrence suggested to her that she should punish herself by sacrificing her smile. That way the others would not resent her. She took the injunction too literally, and the retribution was far more savage than the offence. Oh, yes, she was beaten – but that was the ignorance of her family, who took the symptom for wilful meanness, though she was actually a rather wonderful person underneath.'

'Yes,' Subble said, remembering. 'But she smiles now.'

'And she's worse off than before. She's caught in a more devious complex. When she believed that the destruction of her smile exonerated her, she was free of other phobias and compulsions. Now she searches for them. She's trying to follow Veg's path, as though death were the ultimate evil – and of course it isn't. *Life* is our world's problem. Too much human life on Earth, crowding in so tightly that territory and freedom are largely concepts of the past. Death is the greatest privilege granted to man; death is responsible for his very evolution. Death is not our enemy – it is our salvation.'

'That's an unusual view in itself.' The perfumed smoke was exhilarating.

'It is the paleontologist's view. Anyone who studies the history of life on Earth must come to respect death as a vital force. Without death there would be no natural selection; without selection, mammal and man would never have arisen. The weak, the deviant, the outmoded – these must all make room for progress. Species radiation and selection: constant variations, some good, most bad, but on the whole the good ones survive and propagate. When you interfere with the selective process, you destroy man.'

'And we have interfered,' Subble said, seeing the reasoning but not the point of it. Cal was still working up to it. 'We have preserved *every* human life, strong and weak, and nature cannot act.'

'Oh, nature can act – but not in what we consider to be normal fashion,' Cal corrected him. 'I think our genie is on his way. Do you see him?'

Subble peered at the flame. He had been about to inquire about the nature of Cal's own malady, but had missed his chance. Or perhaps he had been outmaneuvred again. 'Myco of the third kingdom? I'm afraid not.'

'There above the lamp – like a little whirlwind, growing. Grey, at first, becoming lighter as it expands. Stop trying to be reasonable and *look*.'

'If you insist.' Subble concentrated – and saw it. The green flame flickered, changing colour, gold, purple and bright red, and from the spout emerged a fine column of smoke, grey and whirling swiftly. As he watched it increased, a dust-devil, miniature tornado, a burgeoning dervish, suddenly exploding into a giant dusky man garbed in streamers of thick smoke. 'I see it,' he said.

The genie placed clublike hands on hips and stared at him.

'Good,' Cal said. 'Myco will guide us to the third kingdom.'

Subble jumped up, realizing that he'd been had again. 'Psychedelic drug! Lysergic acid diethylamide—'

The genie laughed, and the sound echoed. The back of his head resembled a coloured toadstool and his teeth were tusks.

'LSD? No,' Cal said. 'This is a hallucinatory agent, though both are derived originally from mushrooms. Their properties differ in ways that wouldn't be important to you.'

'This is the basis of your new philosophy?' Subble inquired, disappointed. He reached to snuff out the lamp.

'No. It is merely a vehicle, a channel – that may or may not lead to the contact we seek. Give it a fair trial before you turn away.'

'There is nothing in my mind not already available to me,' Subble said, but he let the flame be. 'No mysteries can be unveiled where none exist. But the distortion induced by the drug can prejudice my effectiveness.'

'Your mind is still closed. Look at yourself: are you elated? Depressed? Do you feel as though you are floating? Have your horizons become limitless? Are you nearer to God? Sexually precocious? Just what effect has the drug had upon your system? How has it incapacitated you?'

Subble ran through a quick series of physical and intellectual exercises. 'It has affected my system very slightly,' he admitted. 'Not

88

enough to interfere with my performance significantly.'

'In what way has it changed you, then?

Subble looked at the standing genie, who stared contemptuously back at him. 'It has provoked a sustained hallucination.'

The genie bellowed. 'O fool of a mortal – and I breathed upon thee one tiny breath, thou would fly into the sea and drown most foully, nor could thou do aught contrary!'

'Don't provoke Myco,' Cal warned. 'In the physical world, you may be supreme – but this is not your world. It does not follow your rules.'

'Yeah,' Myco said with satisfaction.

'Whose rules does it follow?' Subble inquired, interested.

'Mine,' the little man said. 'This drug produces hallucinations without inhibiting the conscious mind or affecting the thinking processes, except to the extent the hallucinations themselves affect them. You are in complete control of your mind and body – but *I* control the habitat.'

'A shared dream?'

'Call it that for convenience. Actually, your view is built up from discreet hints I provide – key words and the use of the lamp which you could not fail to associate with Aladdin's escapade – but what you see naturally differs somewhat from what I see, as our knowledge and tastes vary. When it comes down to it, this is a fact of life anyway; one person can never be certain, for example, that the colour he sees as red is not blue to his neighbour: the blue his neighbour calls red. In this respect the change is not great, and perhaps the drug really produces a closer accord, since any honest difference can quickly be reconciled, when challenged, with the dominant view. The weaker will conforms to the stronger will.'

'How can you be certain that your will is stronger than mine?'

'Do you want tangible proof or a reasoned explanation?'

'Both.'

'Is Myco wearing a turban?'

'No – his head is blatantly bare.'

'Look again.'

'He is wearing a turban.'

'You are mistaken.'

The genie was bareheaded again. Subble concentrated, trying to visualize the turban that had appeared for a moment, but nothing changed. Myco grinned at him, enjoying it. 'It appears the genie obeys his master,' Subble admitted.

'Yes. First, he is *my* image, a figment of *my* selection, well rehearsed by me, while you are meeting him for the first time. I probably know much more about Arabic mythology than you do, and that gives me power, just as my attitude towards the Bible translation gave me the advantage there. Now the situation is clearer, thanks to the literal nature of the drug's imagery. You could not control Myco unless you knew more about him.'

'Yeah,' Myco repeated.

'Second, I have been here many times before under the drug, I mean – and I have developed tolerance and control. I am under less deeply than you are, though we have taken the same dose, and that gives me a firmer grip on objectivity as we both know it. Experience is the best teacher, particularly here.'

Subble studied the genie, intrigued by the creature's evident reality despite agreement that he was a product of the imagination. Realization that a fear was groundless was supposed to banish it – but he knew it often did not. Knowledge that an illness was psychosomatic did not always ease the pain, either. Suddenly he sympathized with a host of problems he would ordinarily have observed dispassionately – the problems of desperate individuals on a crowded world. He *knew* the genie did not exist – but this didn't change a thing. There it stood, as the unfounded fears and problems stood before others.

'I can read thy mind, too,' Myco said. 'Not that it pleasureth me.'

'Finally, your own preference betrays you,' Cal said. 'You do not *want* to take control, because that would abort your mission. You don't need supremacy, you need information – and you know that I can only give it to you this way.'

'I do not remember past experiences, of course,' Subble said, 'but I suspect that you and Veg and Aquilon represent the damnedest trio I have encountered. I'd certainly like to see the interplay between you when you three are together.'

Cal smiled a little sadly. 'It is a quartet now: physique, emotion, intellect – and spirit. Perhaps, soon, we *shall* be together again. We cannot endure apart.'

Subble perceived that the little man was not thinking of the romantic aspects. There was something else, just as there had been for the others. Cal had been correct: every person on Earth was pressured into an odd configuration, but these three had a peculiar interaction that gave them something special.

'But we have other business,' Cal said briskly. 'Myco, show the vault.'

'I hear and obey!' the genie boomed. He stooped and touched the floor. A great silver ring appeared, arabesqued inside and out, and screwed vertically into the centre tile. Myco hauled on this and the slab came up to reveal a staircase going down.

'Down there?' Subble inquired, no longer bothering to distinguish between types of reality. 'Not the black hole of Calcutta?'

'Another fallacy,' Cal said. 'That episode is entirely fictional. It was a rumour which even historians took as fact, since it seemed to justify British policy in India.'

'I see. But in *this* edition your genie could shut us in securely and take over the hallucination.'

'An interesting thought,' Cal said. 'But a chance we'll have to take. You have to experience the marvels of the third kingdom, to appreciate them properly. This is important.'

'As you say,' Subble agreed. His remark had not been serious, but now he wondered.

Myco shrank somewhat in size, manifested a torch, touched it to the flame of the lamp and held it there until it caught. He led the way into the ground.

The stairs descended into a vaulted corridor lined with heavy closed doors. 'The third kingdom is rich in all the needs and comforts of man,' Cal said. 'Here is the chamber of food. Observe it well.' The genie opened the door with a flourish and stood beside it at attention as the two men entered.

It was a gourmet's delight. An enormous banquet table had been set up, groaning with exotic delicacies. An entire stuffed pig squatted in a platter at the head place, garnished with fragrant herbs and spices and relishes. Beyond it was a monstrous roast turkey nestling in matted parsley, and beyond that a line of salmon steaks decorated with stewed raisins and sliced lemon.

They walked down the interminable length of it, past creole shrimp, meat loaf and lamb shish kebab. There were towering salads – chicken, tuna, potato, gelatin and fruit, with dressings too numerous and exotic to number. There were steaming tureens of soup and aromatic breadstuffs and pastries. There was chocolate cake and strawberry pie. Fresh corn on the cob steamed beside golden carrots and thick pods of okra ... jelly omelette ... potato pancakes. Table wines of every description stood adjacent to their traditional dishes, and after them were boiling coffee and frosty ice cream.

Agents sometimes found themselves in odd situations, in the line of duty.

They completed the gustful circuit and returned to the hall. 'Impressive?' Cal inquired, and again there was a subtle extra meaning there.

'Impressive. Can any of it be eaten?'

'Oh, yes, and most enjoyably. But you would be hungry again the moment the vision ended. That's the trouble with magic – no residual effect.'

'Suppose there were actually more commonplace food available?'

'You could feast on it delightfully, and afterwards you would have a full stomach and a pleasant memory.'

Subble appreciated how easily a craze could form.

Myco had not bothered to accompany them inside. He stood at the door holding his nose.

'Our next display is within the chamber of health,' Cal said, gesturing. The door opened.

The room was large – so large it seemed they were emerging into a valley. Just ahead was an open plain bounded by vigorous trees: beech, ash, maple and a solitary bull spruce. Bronzed Greek athletes were taking exercise: one throwing the javelin, another heaving the discus, four indulging in a foot race and two wrestling strenuously. Down the valley two vibrant young women in shorts were playing tennis. The men looked like Veg, the women like Aquilon. A man resembling Subble himself was practicing elaborate dives into a rippling pool, naked.

The air was bracing, with a crisp occasional breeze. The grass underfoot sprang up luxuriantly, and nothing showed, animal or vegetable, that was not in the prime of life.

'And wealth,' Cal said, leading the way to the third chamber. Myco had disappeared.

It was a palace comprising many chambers in itself. The first was filled with gold and silver coins of rare and handsome design, some round, some hexagonal, some holed in the centre, overflowing from great jars and piled haphazardly upon the floor. Subble estimated the weight of metal and calculated its net value in modern terms: over eleven million dollars for what was visible in this room alone, discounting the antique or archaeological enhancement of the strange old coins.

The second room was more impressive: jewels of every colour and description – blue diamonds, green emeralds, red rubies, star sapphires and assorted lesser gems, some splendidly faceted, others gleaming in natural crystalline formations. There were strings of pearls and intricate rings and bracelets.

The third room held priceless paintings and statuary: Subble recognized the handiwork of Michelangelo, Da Vinci, Van Gogh, Picasso and many other masters, all represented by originals. A number he did not recognize, except by type: Chinese Ming, Maya Jaina, Egyptian Middle Dynasty, Mandingo leatherwork, a Gupta Buddha – artifacts which could not be valued because of their immense social and historical significance, as well as their artistic merit. And at the far end, the Nacre landscape Aquilon had painted, at last in the appropriate company.

The fourth room was a library of first editions, the finest volumes produced by man. Every author, every researcher he valued was there, every book in perfect condition though some like the Caxton *Le Morte d'Arthur* were centuries old.

'And finally the chamber of Life and Death,' Cal said as they returned through gallery and treasure-rooms to the hall. He opened the last door.

Armies were arrayed on either side: on the left a Roman phalanx, on the right the mounted horde of Ghenghis Khan. Subble had wondered idly, just as he was sure all agents wondered, what would be the outcome of such an encounter. The Romans had been supreme in their day, owing this largely to their discipline and training, but the Mongols of later centuries were a horde in name only: they were actually among the most methodical fighters and slaughterers of all time. Numbers being equivalent, the nomad riders were probably superior to any military force prior to the advent of firearms, and had they *had* rifles . . .

Still, nothing was certain until the armies actually met. Generalship was a vital matter, and morale, and circumstance.

As the two visitors emerged from the hall, the horsemen charged, screaming and firing arrows from horseback while the Romans advanced stolidly, shields overlapping, long spears thrust forward.

Cal was looking at him questioningly, and then he remembered: the phalanx was not Roman, but Greek and Macedonian! He was guilty of another carelessness, and now this anomaly was engaging the enemy. Exactly how *was* the Roman legion armed and organized? The short sword, flexibility—

'This is visual, auditory and olfactory only,' Cal said, mistaking his concern. 'The images will pass through us without effect, or vice versa.'

It was good to know. The armies met, and Subble found himself in the midst of a savage engagement. The horses reared up against the massed shields, striking them with their hooves and beating them back with the weight of their bodies. One hoof struck at Subble, passed through him, and churned up turf and sand. The brown-skinned rider swung his curved blade at a break in the phalanx and the Roman fell, his ear cut off. A spear lashed out, lodging in the belly of the horse, and the rider came down as gore spurted.

Then it was an indecipherable melee, suffused with the stench of blood and iron and sweat and urine and crushed vegetation, the screams of animal and man, the sight of carnage and agony. Subble was acclimatized to violence, but the brutality of this encounter disgusted him. And he *still* wasn't certain whether the Romans had ever employed the true phalanx, or whether the Mongols ever stayed put for a pitched battle. The violation of history, after allowing for the basic anachronism of the situation, was probably worse than that of the slaughtered men.

Cal drew him back into the hall and closed the door. The bloodletting was cut off abruptly. 'Come and relax for a while,' he murmured. 'I have some questions.'

The end of the hall opened into a twentieth-century living room, air-conditioned and with the FM playing soft music. Subble realized with a start that it was the same piece he had heard at the intensive farming unit he had toured with Aquilon. The animals were pacified by music – and drugs – while they girded their corpulence for the butcher-machine.

'Please describe to me what you experienced,' Cal requested.

'You weren't watching?'

94

'I wish to make a point.'

Subble described in detail what he had seen in each chamber, a little embarrassed about the last. He was sure Cal would have some pointed corrections to make.

'Your verses differ from mine,' Cal said. 'You are still clinging to your own expectations. This is what I warned you against, and one reason I brought you here. It would be disastrous if you strayed this far during a meeting with the manta. Clear your mind of everything and follow me, and this time I will show you the true nature of the third kingdom.' The little man was becoming more and more didactic, but Subble accepted the rebuke and accompanied him back to the fourth chamber.

It was empty. 'Look at the ground,' Cal said.

Ground appeared then: rich, dark earth. 'See that mushroom?' Cal suggested, pointing.

A single mushroom sprouted, bursting from the soil in accelerated motion and opening its soft umbrella, white and delicate. 'This is a saprophyte,' Cal said.

'A saprophyte – an organism that feeds on dead organic matter,' Subble agreed. 'This is a characteristic of the mushroom and related fungi, while others are parasitic.'

'Think about it.'

Then Subble made the connection. Fungus – a thing that took its life from death, locked behind the door of Life and Death. This was a much neater definition than his vision of battle had been. And he had worried about military detail! Fungus – and Nacre was a world of fungus forms, to the exclusion of chlorophyll plants. Death – and Cal was obsessed with it, personally and philosophically. The genie Myco, whose name meant fungus; the hallucinogen, derived from another variety of fungus.

And the mysterious third kingdom itself—

Animal – Plant – and Fungus! Animals were animate, possessing, among other things, the powers of motion and conscious reaction. Plants performed photosynthesis, drawing nourishment from in-organic substances. But fungi neither moved nor drew energy from light – yet they lived and thrived. They had found an alternate route, and some experts – mycologists – considered them to represent a kingdom of their own, distinct from plants.

A kingdom that had ousted plants, to become dominant on Nacre.

'Forget about Nacre, for now,' Cal said. 'I want to show you what the third kingdom means to Earth. Mushrooms, fungi, mould, mildew, yeasts, bacteria – a little more heat and humidity and this kingdom would dominate right here. Fungi can live off almost anything organic: meat, vegetables, milk, leather, wood, coal, plastics, bones. The strains adapt rapidly. Develop a new jet fuel, and before long you will find a fungus feeding on it. The spores are tougher than we are; cold will not kill them, heat must be extreme to damage them all, dehydration – they can be dried and saved for years and grow again when conditions change. Fungi can grow at phenomenal speeds. Some are, as you know, parasites – their food doesn't *have* to be dead. Some change back and forth. One fungus can release hundreds of millions of spores in a few days – and those spores are everywhere, floating invisibly in the air we breathe and settling upon every mouthful of food we eat, no matter how "clean" we think it is.'

'In other words, they are pervasive,' Subble said. 'But at least they are under control, here.' But he remembered the infestation of the cellar-farm, and wondered.

'That is a matter of opinion. Man cannot exist without them, while the fungi can certainly exist without us – in fact, without the entire animal kingdom.'

'Evidently my programming isn't up to date on this subject,' Subble said. 'How is a parasite or saprophyte to exist without animals, live or still, to feed upon? And in what way am I personally dependent upon that little mushroom or its brethren? I can eat it, if it isn't poisonous, but I certainly don't have to, and I wouldn't miss it much if it vanished forever.'

'To answer your first question: parasites and saprophytes cannot exist in isolation, naturally, but the plant kingdom is sufficient for their dietary needs, so animals are unnecessary. The answer to the second is more devious – but also more important, because *both* plants and animals are now dependent upon the fungus kingdom. Are you familiar with the oxygen–carbon dioxide breathing cycle?'

'Of course. Animals take in oxygen and release carbon dioxide. Plants require carbon dioxide for photosynthesis, and give off oxygen. It's a rather neat balance.'

'No. It is not neat at all. Animal respiration provides only a quarter of what is needed by the plants.'

96

'A quarter? That doesn't add up.'

'The rest is a by-product of decomposition.'

'And decomposition—'

'Is the service performed by bacteria and fungi. Without these, dead organisms would remain as they died, sterile. Their elements would never be returned to the earth or atmosphere. Three quarters of the carbon dioxide, among other things, would be permanently trapped, the percentage growing, and the plants would be on a one-way track leading to extinction. And with the end of the plant kingdom—'

'The end of the animal kingdom. I follow you now.'

'And without decomposition, no higher creature could have evolved on Earth. There would be no regenerative cycle; the first micro-organisms that ever formed would be with us today, two or three billion years dead but as durable as stone. Natural selection would never have had a chance. No room, no food, no air. As a matter of fact, to the best of our present knowledge, the presence of fungi of some type is essential to the development of *any* higher forms of life anywhere.'

Subble looked at the mushroom with new respect. 'I congratulate you, little saprophyte.'

Cal led the way to the third door, that had previously opened on money, gems, works of art and a library. Again the room was blank until he spoke.

'You saw wealth in conventional terms. Most people do. But in reality, wealth is not money, art or literature; it is the improved standard of living these things represent. A man can starve, locked in a roomful of gold, or in a library. The gold must be traded for functional products, the books interpreted to apply to tangible things. What you saw were the convenient *symbols* for wealth, material and intellectual – handy for tabulations and comparisons and storage, but not directly contributory to personal well-being.'

'No argument there,' Subble said. This certainly *was* a lesson in how far afield a mind could go when not corrected.

'Instead, let's look at the things we can *use*. Observe the healthy expanse of growing barley, wheat, rye and oats – the breadbasket of a nation, a world.'

Subble saw the patchwork of fields as from an airplane, stirred like standing water by vagrant breezes. 'And peas, tomatoes, onions,

97

potatoes.' The plane swooped low to bring these into view. 'Cattle, sheep, horses.' Livestock ranges appeared – the old kind, before the animals were herded into darkened buildings for confinement and forced feeding.

'But these are ordinary plants and animals,' Subble pointed out.

'But they are dying. See, the leaves are wilting, the animals are feeble.' And they were; a massive blight swept over the fertile scene, destroying flora and fauna alike.

'They have been attacked by tiny eelworms, nematodes,' Cal explained. 'We are shrinking now, rapidly, down to rat size, mouse size, insect size – but the destroyer is neither rodent nor insect.'

The airplane vanished and the fields zoomed closer, as though they were falling, and expanded voluminously. Then the two men stood on the ground and watched the world explode around them. 'We are an inch tall, a tenth of an inch, a hundredth.'

The world was an animated microscope slide. 'We are in a chamber in the soil, the humus just below the surface. This is the most active biologic zone of the world, the vital key to the entire ecological cycle. This is the fiercest battleground of the three kingdoms – they fight ruthlessly, you know – and there are monsters here more astonishing than any we know in the macrocosm.' He gestured. 'Before us is one such: the nematode, the most successful wormlike organism on Earth.'

Subble looked at it: an eyeless python twenty-five feet long, according to present perspective. The semi-transparent body behind the bare oral openings was a foot in diameter. 'It eats anything, but especially root hairs,' Cal continued, 'and it can lay its own weight in eggs in a week. It is one of the most savage destroyers we know of, and the plants we cultivate have little effective defence against it, since we corral them in so tightly. A cultivated field is like an open supermarket, for the worm.'

The nematode slid towards them, its body slimy and rank. Subble stepped back. 'Do other animals handle it satisfactorily?'

'It would dominate the world, if not stopped – and neither plant nor animal seems capable of controlling it. It parasitizes larger creatures, too. It can expand its length a thousandfold, in time, in the intestine of a mammal. No sizeable crops would survive its ravages, and—'

'I understand the gravity of the situation,' Subble said, retreating another step as the blind orifice quested after him. 'Just what *does* stop it?'

Cal pointed to the side. 'Now here is a handsome clump of saprophytic fungus. Perfectly harmless – we can pass among the threads – the mycelium – without danger.'

'Third kingdom to the rescue!' Subble said, climbing through the spongy brush he pictured. At least it offered some tacit resistance to progress of the hungry worm. But the nematode remained intent on their trail, and forced its way through the mycelium close behind.

'But you see, the nemin coating the creature's body has a peculiar effect on the fungus. As soon as a nematode approaches, short branches sprout with loops at the ends.' The loops appeared, each about a foot in diameter. The worm ignored them, thrashing after the retreating men with almost mindless determination. Subble still did not feel at all comfortable so close to its eagerly sucking mouth.

But the loops became so profuse that they were unavoidable. The men pushed them aside, but the nematode didn't care; it poked its front end into one and came on, sliding through it easily. But the thicker central part of its body jammed; the loop was just too small to permit free passage. The creature struggled, attempting to withdraw or squirm on through the construction – but the loop inflated like a rubber tyre and pinned the worm securely about the middle.

Now there was furious thrashing. The monster whipped its head and tail back and forth with frightening violence, but the booby-trapped ring only bound it more tightly. The nematode was far larger and heavier than the fungus, but it was not anchored and its leverage was poor in this position. It was unable to break the narrow band.

Gradually its struggles diminished, and it expired.

'Some species of fungi touch sticky knobs to the worm, holding it down, then grow strands into its body to consume its innards. Others deposit spores that germinate and parasitize it,' Cal said, watching the dying worm dispassionately. 'In any event, it is indeed the third kingdom that saves our crops, in this important instance, and so is the protector of our wealth, much more significantly than your hoard of gold. It kills animal parasites, and in many cases sets up symbiotic relationships without which even mighty trees could not flourish. We have just seen an omnivore fall prey to something it didn't even notice was dangerous, but that is only one aspect of the story.'

That was significant. An omnivore brought down by a seemingly innocent fungus. Even through the layers of hallucination, he perceived the stress Cal placed upon the concept. Man's appetite was very like the worm's, 'Evidently you have been researching the matter.'

'I reviewed it, at any rate. After Nacre, I had to. The representatives of the third kingdom are primitive, here, perhaps because there is always food for them and further evolution is not essential to survival – but they remain the best key to the advanced species there. I haven't begun to cover the economic importance this kingdom has for Earth. We use moulds in industry to synthesize the acids employed in the manufacture of plastics, new paints, photographic developer, bleach, ceramics, monosodium glutamate ... fungus to break down petroleum and detergent ... electric batteries powered by yeast action. And the wealth of knowledge provided in the laboratory: molds and bacteria are the most primitive organisms containing DNA, the basic molecule of life.'

'Wealth indeed,' Subble said, impressed. The DBA/RNA researches were leading to tremendous breakthroughs in the life sciences already. 'But I'm not certain how this will help me to complete my mission.'

'It is not my place to tell you that,' Cal said soberly. 'But my hope is that somewhere in this demonstration you will discover the clue I couldn't. We should be better able to understand the advanced fungi once we study the primitive ones. I'm afraid we made a bad mistake on Nacre, but I can't bring myself to define it and have no idea how to undo it. That is what you have to learn – and I think only the manta can complete the picture for you. You must learn to communicate on its terms, as you are now learning to do so on mine.'

'So I understand.' And that would be the reason for the drug. Cal could have presented the material directly, but not the experience of the hallucinogen, the training in personal submersion in order to respond to another person's slightest concept. With an alien, there might be no standard communication, and the nuance response would become all important. He was mastering the technique now – but he certainly would not have wanted to practice while facing the

100

manta.

'Let's check the other rooms,' he said.

They expanded to normal size. 'Was it not a mushroom Alice ate in Wonderland, to change her size?' Subble inquired, requiring no answer. The third kingdom was pervasive, now that he had become aware of it as such.

'Health,' Cal said at the next door. 'Most people are aware of mycotic infection – ringworm, athlete's foot, histoplasmosis – but don't realize how much more they owe to fungal antibiotics and drugs. You saw an array of healthy people – but how many would have stayed that way without penicillin and the other fungoid derivatives?' He opened the door.

A foul odour wafted out. The chamber was filled with a monstrous bubbling vat, churned constantly by a mighty paddle wielded by the grinning genie. 'Surprise!' Myco cried. 'This is where I live.'

It was pencillin mould, stimulated to grow in aerated nutrient fluid.

Cal closed the door, cutting off the smell. 'Not to mention the work still being done with yeasts in connection with radiation sickness and cancer and memory restoration.'

'Or with mental health, via the mind-opening drug therapy,' Subble added. 'That's a little fungoid trick I will not forget in a hurry.'

There was a clap of laughter from the health chamber; Myco, it seemed, appreciated the feed-back.

'Or mental control,' Cal murmured. 'Knowledge does have its dangers.'

They stood before the door of the chamber of food. 'Let me guess,' Subble said. 'Edible mushrooms of splendiferous variety: morel, puffball, shaggymane, polypore, truffle ... and breads leavened, liquor fermented, cheese ripened, all by virtue of yeasts and fungi cultures.'

'Only partly,' Cal said, smiling. 'I could add the biblical manna from heaven to your list, since that was another fungus product that people have eaten directly in time of need, but I was thinking along another line. Actually, it is not necessary to give up your original banquet. I can double or triple it via the third kingdom.'

'By feeding mushrooms to livestock?'

101

'By feeding garbage to yeast.'

'Don't open that door!' Subble exclaimed. 'The penicillin was bad enough. Let me remember my banquet as it was. Just tell me about it.'

This time Cal laughed. 'The processing is rather interesting, but I admit there are uncomfortable elements. Even our sewers have become marvellous fonts of nourishment.' But he dropped his hand from the knob.

'Today there are six billion human beings on Earth, and not more than ten percent are actually hungry. We're feeding our population better than ever in spite of its appalling growth rate. You can't do that on steak, no matter how brutally you intensify your farming. A steer yields less than a pound and a half of dried beef for every hundred pounds of feed provided it, and it takes many months to do it, and copious rangeland if you insist on a really healthy product. Much of what those impacted livestock batteries turn out is technically unfit for human consumption: tasteless, non-nutritive meat contaminated with residual insecticides and deleterious hormones.' This seemed to disturb him more than the idea of food from sewage.

'A pig yields six pounds of pork for the same bag of feed, and does it in less time and much less space,' Cal went on. 'But still there isn't room or food for the porcine billions that would be required to feed us if that were the major dietary staple. Other animals are no better. Plants are more efficient as food converters – barring nematode infestations! – but there is only so much arable land. We use artificially illuminated interior farms, multi-levelled, certainly, and we also farm the sea and to a limited extent the atmosphere – but our biggest single source of protein today is torula yeast.'

'*Yeast?* Straight?'

'Not exactly the variety that makes bread rise,' Cal said. 'But the principle is the same. Torula feeds on almost anything organic – refuse from sawmills, molasses, rotten fruit – even petroleum and coal tar.'

'Another omnivore!'

'You could call it that, yes. It produces sixty-five pounds of edible solids for every hundred of feed, which is ten times as good as any animal, and what it consumes is foodstuff that would otherwise be largely wasted. And it does it on no more land area than that required to support the vats, multiplying its original weight many times in a single day. It can be mixed with other foods, indistinguishable by taste and rich in nourishment. Half of what we eat today is in fact processed from varieties of torula – and the average man doesn't realize it. Your turkey, your stuffed pig – if those were standard brands, much of their weight was textured and sculptured torula protein. A lot of artistry goes into blending it.'

'It must,' Subble agreed, 'if the banquet in my own imagination is made from fungus I didn't know about!'

'You're in good company. Our spacemen are fed their own waste products, broken down by the yeast. Anyway, *this* is the true breadbasket of the world – and man can no longer survive at his present level without the generous assistance of the third kingdom.'

They mounted the steps and emerged upon the terrace. 'That's it,' Cal said. 'That's what the third kingdom means to Earth. Remember that Nacre is an advanced fungus world; it is billions of years ahead of us in that respect. Somewhere in all this information is the key to disaster, perhaps, for all of us.' He stooped beside the lamp, still quietly burning, and snuffed out the little flame.

Almost immediately the nether staircase faded. 'No residual effect?' Subble inquired, indicating the lamp.

'Not with this dosage. You would not want to overdo it, however. None of the hallucinogens are mere amusements.' He considered for a moment. 'I'm not sure what would happen if a person ever became entirely subservient to this drug. It isn't addictive, theoretically, but it's potent stuff. We sat about a yard from it, which diluted it sufficiently, but if you inhaled directly over the flame—'

'My antibrainwash syndrome could trigger self-destruction,' Subble finished.

'Yes. It would in effect give you a psychoneurotic disorder, and you haven't been conditioned to it as we have.'

'You showed me all this for a reason – not just background or practice. What reason?'

Cal would not meet his gaze. 'I lack the courage to tell you. I hope most urgently that I am wrong – but you must discover that for yourself, then do what you must. Perhaps you will find, incidentally, some solution for our more personal problems.'

Subble nodded. 'I promised to help Aquilon, too. That's really the price for your cooperation. I'll do what I can. But first I'll have to take your lamp and your communication device and go to meet the manta directly. That is where it will end.'

'I don't know whether to wish you success or failure.'

'One other thing,' Subble said. 'I want your segment of the Nacre adventure. I only have part of the story so far.'

'Yes – there is that,' Cal agreed wearily. 'I had forgotten. We'll have some torula pancakes and . . .'

Hours later, away from the stench and gore, they camped on another thin ledge and spread out on the ground. Veg and Aquilon were tired, and quiet for their own reasons; the manta was as inscrutable as ever. It had fed upon the omnivore's carcass, absorbing the juices through its digestive underside, and now seemed content to relax. Aquilon had looked at the remains and decided to continue eating fungus after all. Only Cal was possessed of new strength.

'Do you know,' he said, 'that manta must be the most formidable fighting machine on the planet! Did you see the way it cut apart the omnivore? Our rifle didn't faze the monster, but the knife-edged tail of the manta slashed it to pieces. And the omnivore knew it; it was afraid.'

'We – didn't see all of it,' Aquilon said. 'But why doesn't the manta attack *us*?' Her motive seemed to be more to encourage him than genuine curiosity. 'Why does it keep Veg away from me, and not from you?'

'I've been thinking about that,' Cal said. He was buoyed by some nameless excitement, as though the horrible encounter had released him from a coma. He would have to explore the reason. Could it be some invigorating chemical in the omnivore blood he had eaten – or had the revelation of his vice brought relief instead of shame? No, there was something else, something highly significant, that he could not pinpoint yet. 'I've also been wondering why the herbivores weren't afraid of the manta. And I think I have the answer.'

Veg stared morosely into the ground, facing away from Aquilon. Something had passed between them, something Cal didn't know about, that left both pensive. But what? There had been no time for any private dialogue, and the battle with the omnivore should not have prejudiced their interpersonal relationship.

The entire complexion of their little group had somehow been changed. Veg had been dominant at the beginning of the adventure, running the tractor and determining their route back towards the camp. Then, with the slaughter of the first manta, Veg had given way subtly to Aquilon, the artist and anatomist. Now the immediate problems of survival for the three of them had been surmounted, and their eventual return to the base seemed probable – if they could grasp the special nature of their contact with the manta. Obviously it could kill them all, and might do that, if they gave it incentive. Now was the time for intellectual exercise, for problem solving on other than a physical basis. Now it was Cal's turn to be dominant. But that was not the source of his exhilaration.

Aquilon was curious. 'You can explain the manta's actions?'

'I think so. But it's not simple, and the implications may not be pleasant.'

'I think we'd better know,' Aquilon said. 'If it affects our safety . . . and it isn't as though there hasn't been unpleasantness already.'

Cal looked at her, concerned for the effect his words might have upon her. She was a very sensitive girl. He glanced at Veg, but knew the big man would shrug off the implications. 'It does affect our safety – and our pride,' he said. 'On Nacre, the ecological chain seems spare: one species of herbivore, one of omnivore, and also, apparently, one of true carnivore. But that's only a very small part of the story. It is impossible for animal and fungoid life to exist to the exclusion of the photosynthesizing plants. Those are the ones that manufacture food from light and inorganic substances, using chlorophyll, the green pigment. Everything else feeds on these, directly or indirectly.'

Veg began to take an interest. 'None of those here.'

'They *are* here, though. They have to be. They're in the atmosphere, microscopically small, circulating in the higher reaches where sufficient sunlight penetrates. As a matter of fact, the evidence is that the major ecological chains are completed in the atmosphere, and that the ground is merely a wasteland for the debris. Thus the plant life remains primitive, since it can't establish a ground base, send out roots, form a woody structure, flower and so on. It is like plankton in Earth's sea, floating and growing where conditions are favourable, and falling to the bottom when it grows too large to remain suspended. That's our dust – the perpetually sinking plankton. The plants really seem to occupy a subordinate niche here, perpetually retarded, just as many fungi are on Earth. That's an

105

oversimplification, of course—'

He saw their restlessness and realized he was lecturing. 'At any rate, the ground habitat is restricted enough so that three major species of animal have been able to dominate, at least in the section we have seen. The so-called herbivores feed on the dust, and are easy prey, but without them the other species would perish. It would be easy for the omnivore to wipe them out, seemingly—'

'But what about the manta?' Aquilon asked. 'It should be even more—'

'Let him talk,' Veg growled. Nettled, Aquilon shut up.

'The manta, the true carnivore, would maintain the balance by preying on the omnivore, which in turn eats anything available, from dust to men. But the manta shouldn't require the herbivore for food at all—'

'That's it!' Veg exclaimed. Aquilon gave him a look. 'The manta doesn't eat herbies. It protects them!'

'Let him talk,' Aquilon said.

'If I'm right,' Cal continued quickly, 'these creatures would instinctively define everything in terms of their own system. There would be just three animal classifications: herbivore, omnivore and carnivore, preying, respectively, upon no creature, upon all creatures, and upon just one: the middle. So the herbivore would have to fear only the omnivore, and might even be protected by the manta. They would distinguish each other by type, not physical appearance, since their shapes are somewhat flexible – and may even be able to distinguish similar divisions in unrelated species. As fate would have it, the three of us represent—'

The other two came to life. 'Herby!'

'Omnivore!'

'And carnivore,' Cal finished. 'In that light, the manta's motives are clear. To it, Veg is a helpless creature in need of protection. Every time a manta has seen him, it has followed, probably in response to that impulse. Naturally it has to safeguard him from the menace so close at hand.'

'It was protecting *him* from *me*,' Aquilon said, not entirely pleased.

'That time in the herby herd,' Veg said, running it down. 'The manta sailed right over me. It could have sliced me in half with that tail, but it was headed for her. And when that omnivore attacked,

106

our manta didn't budge until I got in the way. It must've figured Cal could take care of himself, and it didn't care about 'Quilon . . .' He paused. 'And I killed the first one. It was trying to help me, and I shot it down—'

'It might have killed 'Quilon, otherwise,' Cal reminded him.

'But why,' Aquilon said, beginning to comprehend her personal danger, 'why didn't this one attack me right away, instead of watching?'

'It must have realized that all three of us were alien,' Cal said, finding the need to offer something though this question bothered him considerably. 'It may not know quite how to deal with us, and is holding off until it can make up its mind.'

'Still no call to cut the alligator pack-straps,' Veg muttered.

'Don't you know the difference between alligator and granulated pig leather?' Aquilon demanded. 'Those straps are omnivore hide.'

Veg looked embarrassed.

'After a rude surprise like that, no wonder it wanted to keep an eye on us,' she continued.

'A large eye,' Veg said, staring at it.

'But when it finally comes to a decision—'

'I suggest that we get back to the base before it comes to that,' Cal said.

Aquilon looked at the manta's well of an eye and shuddered. Death stared back at her.

They climbed with new incentive. The manta followed, declining to take action – yet.

The trail ended in midafternoon. One moment they were toiling past coral cones and hanging yellow strings crowding the path in increasing proliferation; the next, they faced a vast level plain extending into the haze. To either side the fungus coloured the brink, setting it off, but most species did not venture far onto the plateau.

Veg studied the compass. 'Six miles. But we can't make it today.'

'So close?' Aquilon asked him. 'But why not?'

'We could make the level distance, all right. It's the up-down that bothers me. We must be a mile in the air. Got to be a drop-off somewhere . . .'

'Oh.'

'One more night on the road won't hurt us,' Cal said. 'Manta

107

permitting. I'd certainly like to know just how smart this creature *is*.'

'Smart as a man, you figure?' Veg asked.

'I didn't say that. We know that it has a complex brain, or something analogous, and its actions certainly show something more than blind impulse. But with its superb fighting equipment, it doesn't really need intelligence as we think of it. There isn't enough challenge. It *could* have genius, but—'

Aquilon's brush and canvas appeared. She seemed to have shaken off her apprehension about the manta. Once again the vitality of her personality showed in two dimensions as the brush created its extemporaneous colour. Sitting before the manta, trying to conceal any nervousness she might have felt, she painted its portrait: the midnight hump of a body, the flickering depth of the mighty eye that transfixed her with unblinking candour, the cruel whip-length of the tail, now curled on the ground in a circle about its foot.

The manta sat through this, quite still.

'Try one of the omnivore,' Cal said, understanding her purpose. Aquilon obliged, producing from memory an effective rendition of the charging monster. She represented it to the manta, but met with no response.

She tried a herbivore, a fungus, an enlarged manta eye, all to no avail. It would not be possible to establish communication unless she could find some point of reaction. At Cal's further suggestion she drew an omnivore charging at a group of herbivores. Still nothing. She went on to portray lifelike caricatures of the three human beings. Finally she drew a picture which she concealed from the men, showing it only to the manta. When that also brought no response, she hesitated, flushed gently, and signalled to Veg, who was getting ready to backtrack for the pack down the trail.

'Something I can do for you, Beautiful?' he inquired. Cal noted this with interest; apparently whatever had soured them earlier was fading, and the subdued flirtations were recommencing. Thus encouraged, Aquilon beckoned again.

Veg came – and the manta moved. Dust swirled as its flat body angled between them. Aquilon cried out and dropped the sketch, while Veg jumped back.

'Still forbidden,' he commented sadly. 'That thing sure watches out for what it thinks are my interests. Otherwise you know what I'd—'

His eye fell on the picture, lying face up on the ground. 'Yeah, I guess you do.'

Cal looked at it. It was a picture of Veg embracing Aquilon.

The following day opened with uneasy turbulence. On Nacre, the shrouded planet that sparkled in space like a pearl, the wind was seldom more than a wash of mist, and the day-to-night extremes of temperature fluctuated within ten degrees. There appeared to be no rain other than the constant fall of dust – yet on this morning something was developing, something very like a storm.

They moved on, traversing the last few miles towards the base. Veg's estimate was verified within two hours: there was a sheer drop at the other side of the plateau. The human base was so close that they could hear the distant clank of machinery, but it remained invisible in the mist.

The cliff was authoritative, here; there was no feasible way for them to scale it. A few puttylike fungi leaned over the edge, but did not brave farther. Veg shouted into the gulf, but without effect. There would have to be a detour.

As suddenly as it had come, the manta left. It sailed off the edge, spiralling down to disappear in the dust.

Veg peered after it, astonished. 'It can fly,' he said. Then his mind reverted to first principles. 'Chaperone's gone!' He caught hold of Aquilon's slim waist and drew her close. He kissed her.

'Not bad,' he said after a moment. 'For an omnivore ... maybe we *should* marry.'

She kicked him and moved out of reach. Cal still wondered what had caused the rift, now evidently healed and more than healed, but did not care to inquire. He felt no jealousy; it was enough that dissension had been removed.

With something less than enthusiasm they turned to the right and proceeded down a slight incline parallel to the cleft. Two miles to go and they had had to turn aside.

An hour later they had to halt again. Across the sloping plain a thin line of discs appeared, emerging from the obscurity with astonishing rapidity.

'Mantas,' Veg said. 'Dozens of them.'

'I'm afraid Ragnarok is at hand,' Cal said. 'Our guardian has returned with his company. If only we had been able to make some

109

kind of contact.' But he was not seriously worried; had immediate death been the verdict, the original manta would have handled it alone. This was something else, and therefore promising.

In moments the line of sailing creatures closed the distance and circled the human group. It was strange to see so many at once, after the three contacts with individuals. A single ring of them settled down, a manta every five or six feet, eyes facing into the centre where the human trio stood. Most were sleek and black, though they were of differing sizes and variable posture. There was no way to distinguish one from another with certainty, since the shape of each body was not fixed, except by size. Cal could not even be sure that their erstwhile companion was among them.

'They found the one I shot!' Veg exclaimed. 'They're here for revenge.'

'I doubt it,' Cal said. 'How would they know which one of us fired the weapon?' But that suggested a manta investigation, a trial ... 'Probably they are merely curious how this weird collection of aliens manages to associate in harmony.'

He hardly believed this now, and was sure neither other person was fooled. There was too much they did not know about these creatures. The mantas must have surrounded them for some purpose. Did they have a leader? A decision maker?

He spied a huge grizzled individual, two hundred pounds at least and almost five feet tall. It's eye bore upon him. Menacingly? Intelligently? Could size be an indication of status, since presumably the largest was the oldest?

Outside the immediate ring the smaller mantas moved about, leaping and cruising in widening spirals, their paths crossing and recrossing. It seemed to be an aimless pattern, antlike; and like ants, each member hesitated as it met another, exchanging glances and dodging by.

Cal observed all this with growing excitement, 'That eye – why didn't I think of it before! It is constructed like an electronic tube, a cathode. It must generate a communication signal!'

'But why didn't my pictures—'

'I see it all now,' Cal rushed on, hardly hearing her. 'Why, more straight perception must be massed in that one optic than in all our multiple senses. It would be a highly effective natural radar device, emitting a controlled beam and coordinating the data returned. The

110

dust would prevent confusion by limiting the range. I wouldn't be surprised if it detected depth by analyzing the time-delay of the returning signal.'

'But if it could see that well—' Aquilon began.

'That's the reason! We see by our own "visible" spectrum, but the manta wouldn't necessarily operate on that level at all. Even if it could make out the colours, it would hardly interpret them as a representation of a three-dimensional object. Its vision wouldn't utilize the same illusions of perspective as our own. You may have been showing it a flat, blank sheet.'

Veg had been walking around the circle. 'So it sees too well for us?' he asked.

'Partly that, but—' Cal drifted off, working it out. 'We know from that dissection that virtually all of the manta's brain is tied directly to the eye. If it emits a modulated signal – why, its whole intellect is keyed in. Think of the communication possible, when two of them lock their gaze. The full power of each brain channelled through the transceiver . . . pictures, feelings, all of it in an instant . . .'

'They must be pretty smart,' Veg said.

'No, probably the opposite. They—'

Both stared at him curiously. He tried again. 'Don't you see – so much of man's vaunted intelligence is required simply to transmit and receive information. Each of us has a wall of isolation, of ignorance, to transcend. We have no direct communication, and so we have to master complex verbal codes and symbolic interpretations, merely to get our thoughts and needs across. With such second-hand contact, no wonder a powerful cerebral backstop is necessary. But the manta must have virtual telepathy: one glance, and communication is complete. It needs no real intelligence.'

'Yeah. Sure,' Veg said dubiously.

The grizzled leader (presumed) swivelled to meet the glance of a travelling manta as a strangely hot gust of air washed over the assemblage. Then it was moving, and so were the others.

'There's something else going on,' Aquilon said nervously. 'I don't think they care about us. Not to talk with, anyway.'

'It only we had the proper equipment here – a television transducer, perhaps – we might be able to establish direct contact,' Cal said, disappointed. 'We could photograph their signal and analyze it. But right now we have no way to know their motives.' But he knew that she had a good point. It was a strange day in a strange area, and the strange actions of the mantas were more likely than not to be connected. Had the human party overrated its importance?

Across the plateau the grey mists parted. A brilliant light appeared, widening rapidly. The mantas scattered across the plain reacted with bursts of energy that tore up the ground.

'Look at them move!' Veg exclaimed admiringly.

The light expanded, sweeping towards them in a burning arc. 'What is it?' Aquilon demanded, clutching Veg's arm. 'That light – like a furnace. Where is it coming from?'

She realized what she was doing and jerked her hand away, but the sweeping shapes paid no attention. The mantas seemed possessed, darting about in a crazed firefly pattern.

More flares appeared, as far as he could see across the plain. It was a phenomenon that extended for miles, if what he observed were typical. Volcanic eruption? Then where was the noise, the earth-shuddering? This was silent light, flaring intermittently as though a curtain flapped before a projector.

Then he understood. 'The sun – the storm has let in the sun!'

The advancing light struck one of the billowing fungi spotting the plain in this neighborhood. Almost immediately the structure began to twist and shrivel; then, as the radiation and heat penetrated its rind, the dormant gases inside expanded. The skin of the fungus distended in gross blisters; then the entire growth shattered.

'I never thought of that,' Aquilon said, fascinated. 'Nacre hardly ever sees the direct light of the sun. The native life isn't conditioned to it.'

'Like a forest fire,' Veg agreed. 'Wipes out everything it touches, and nobody knows how to get away.'

It occurred to Cal that this could explain the barrenness of the upper plain. The higher elevation might predispose it to such breakthroughs, letting the sun blast away all life periodically. Had the mantas come to warn them? Convection currents at the edges could keep enough new dust stirred up so that the fungus there was protected.

The sky opened near at hand and the terrible brilliance flamed down almost where they stood. Cal visualized the weight of the suspended plants becoming too great for atmospheric conditions, forcing an occasional massive inversion, just as sometimes happened

112

in Earth storms. The overturning could become so violent, here where the lay of the land forced air currents up, as to create a rent from top to bottom and lay the ground open to the sun. But it could hardly last long; more ordered dust would soon fill in from the sides.

The mantas must have known it was coming. They had acted in foolhardy fashion, coming here for any reason at this time, unless the storm held some particular fascination for them. Now they leaped in masses over the edge of the fault, fleeing the blazing path of light.

'Look!' Aquilon cried, pointing. One manta had been trapped within the sunlit area. It cast about violently, unable to find shelter.

She started forward. 'The sun is killing it. It can't see to get away!'

'There is nothing we can do,' Cal cautioned her. 'We can't interfere—'

'We can't let it die!' she cried. Veg caught her arm, but she knocked his hand away without even looking. He reached for her again, trying to restrain her, but she was away, running fleetly across the plain. She plunged into the sunshine without hesitation, straight toward the blinded manta.

In moments she reached it. The thing was writhing on the ground, and Cal could see the dangerous tail snapping without direction. It was trying to get its eye into shadow, but there was none.

Aquilon stopped briefly, looking at it. Cal knew the reason for her hesitation: she had never actually touched a live manta with her hands. Then she ripped off her light blouse and threw it over the creature's tortured eye. It would offer scant protection, but the idea was good. She circled both arms around its globular, contracted body and picked it up. Burdened with its weight, she ran heavily out of the light. The tail dragged on the ground behind.

Veg ran forward to help her, but she was already out of the danger area, putting down the manta. It was of medium size, or about fifty pounds.

The sun storm was over, as though it saw no point in continuing now that its victim was gone. Singly and in groups the mantas returned. Aquilon stopped to unwind the blouse from her manta's head. 'I never knew they were cold-blooded,' she said, as though that were the most significant thing of all.

The circle reformed. The largest manta came forward, and Aquilon stepped out of its way. It contemplated the quivering creature on the ground; then without warning it was airborne. The body of the blinded one shook as the tremendous disk passed over and cut it to pieces with invisible slashes. Soon there was nothing but a pile of tattered flesh.

'No, no!' Aquilon cried. She strained, but this time Veg's grasp was firm. She struck at him ineffectively, then fell sobbing into his arms. 'I only tried to save it ... did they think my touch contaminated—'

'Look out!' Veg shouted, throwing her to one side and lunging to the other. The great manta was coming, its fierce eye glittering. The disk seemed to expand enormously. Veg spread his arms as though to intercept and halt the creature by the mass of his own body, but it pleated in mid-air and funnelled by him.

Aquilon looked up – and screamed as the manta struck. Four times the tail knifed into her face before she could protect it with her hands. Then the vengeful shape was gone and she fell, knuckles to her cheeks, blood welling between the fingers.

Veg knelt at her side immediately, gripping both her wrists in his large hands and pulling her hands away by main force. Cal peered over Veg's shoulder, sick at heart. As Aquilon raised her face he saw her flowing tears mixed with the smeared blood. Cheek and jaw on both sides had been deeply slashed, but the blood was running, not gouting. Her eyes had not been touched, and no artery had been hit.

His gaze fell on her bare shoulders and back. The skin was red and beginning to blister from the brief exposure to the rays of Nacre's sun, the damage extending down to her bra strap.

Cal removed his own shirt, the need for cloth overcoming his extreme disinclination to expose his skeletal body. He handed it to Veg, who accepted it unceremoniously and wiped Aquilon's face as clean as he could. The cuts were sharp and well defined, not ragged, and the flow of blood diminished quickly.

'Need a clean one,' Veg snapped; then, realizing what it was: 'Hey!' He looked at Cal, embarrassed, then gripped the short sleeve of his own shirt and wrenched. Muscles bulged as the tearproof fabric tore. He moistened it with his tongue and carefully wiped away the remaining smears.

'I can do that,' Cal offered.

'Maybe you'd better,' Veg said grimly, remembering something. 'I have business with Brother Manta.' Rising, he strode to the rifle and picked it up, activating the flare-chamber immediately.

'No, stop!' Cal called, seeing his intent. 'You can't judge the manta by our standards. We have no way to know its motives. It could have thought 'Quilon was responsible for torturing and blinding that young one. They must have no real conception of the sun . . . perhaps they even worship it as the embodiment of evil. They might even believe that we *brought* the light . . .'

Veg paid no attention. He was stalking the large manta.

'They could even be right,' Cal went on desperately. 'Our ships go up and down, disrupting the atmosphere as we ferry supplies. Remember – man *is* an omnivore . . .'

Veg stood still, holding the rifle ready, chamber hot. Cal knew the weapon could do a lot of damage as its steam fired a rapid stream of projectiles at the standing mantas. Its chief advantages were silent operation, except for the hiss of the escaping gouts of steam, and safe ammunition, since the motive power came from the rifle and not from explosive bullets. But it would be disastrous to fire it now; the mantas would very quickly realize its purpose and wipe out the attacker. A good weapon in the hands of an angry man . . .

'If *I* can live with the omnivore,' Veg said, 'so can the manta. She saved one from the sun– and that big bastard killed it and went after her. It tried to blind her. You saw.'

'But she *didn't* save it from the sun!'

Aquilon looked up, startled.

'That manta had been blinded by the light,' Cal said, hoping he could hold Veg's attention until he cooled off enough to remember he didn't believe in killing. 'Remember, their eyes must be far more sensitive than ours, and the sun may be deadly to them. The first few seconds may have destroyed its vision utterly, as surely as though a glowing poker had been rammed into its eye. There would be no possibility of salvage, with such a delicate mechanism.'

'But it lived,' Veg said. 'She saved its life.'

Cal sat back and looked at him. 'Life,' he said. 'You worship life. You think everything is all right so long as you do not kill – except maybe for revenge. You are a fool.'

'I th-thought I was helping it,' Aquilon said, putting her hand to her face to feel the wounds. She had not been seriously hurt; that was now obvious to all of them. The manta's attack had not been to kill – or, perhaps, to blind, either.

115

Cal shook his head, meeting her gaze. 'You mean so well, 'Quilon – but you are thinking with your emotions, not your mind. Don't you understand – the manta *has* no other perception besides its sight. A man has eyes and ears and so many other senses that the loss of one doesn't really hurt him; he can function perfectly well with one or two impaired. You dissected the manta's brain two days ago; you know the eye is the only perceptory connection to speak of. Our own eyes are such feeble candles, ranged against that. But when it is destroyed—'

He took another breath. 'When it is destroyed, the manta's *total contact* with its environment is severed. In such a case, it is only mercy to terminate its life quickly. Believe me, I know.'

'Okay,' Veg said, softening. 'Now tell me why it went for 'Quilon. If it had so much mercy—'

'I'm afraid it *is* an animal,' Cal said sadly. 'Not capable of understanding that an omnivore is not necessarily an enemy. And yet – it could so easily have killed her. Those little cuts won't even mutilate her face permanently. They're neat and precise, almost like surgery. A token punishment—'

'I don't think so,' Aquilon said, speaking with difficulty. Her words were blurred as though she had trouble controlling her facial muscles. The cuts began to bleed again, and he hastily dabbed some more.

'Look!' Veg cried, still facing the main group. 'Little mantas!'

The mass of moving bodies parted. It was true. There, herded by a grown one, were eight tiny mantas, the first babies they had seen. Their miniature leaps were uncertain, their landings awkward, and they had not yet learned to flatten their bodies properly for control in the air, but mantas they certainly were. They could not have been more than a few days old.

'They *did* understand,' Cal said.

By expert snaps of her whiplike tail the adult drove them in a course that led directly to Aquilon. Cal got up and moved away. As they came to rest in front of her, the adult left. Mantas and humans waited, intent upon that scene.

Astonished, Aquilon looked down, at the tiny group. From a six-inch elevation, eight sober little lenses looked back, flickering tentatively. Touched, she leaned over and spread out her arms, and the babies hopped into their circle trustingly.

116

'They are for me,' she said in wonder.

'Too young to be afraid of the omnivore,' Cal murmured. 'Could a human mother ever show such trust? These eight will come to understand our ways. We'll be able to colonize, now. And—' here he broke into a smile that set the years of agony aside – 'we shall come to understand *them*.'

'For me,' Aquilon repeated, holding the little bodies.

'Don't smile, 'Quilon,' Veg cautioned, then bit his lip. Cal saw the motion and began to see what had happened to make that joke unacceptable.

But Aquilon did smile. Gradually, in the reflex suppressed for so many years, the corners of her delicate lips upturned. Her face lighted, casting an emotional radiance that touched man and manta alike, reflecting from the watchfull extent of the manta's gift – the physical pretext and the psychological reality – she showed the beauty that was in her heart unfolding like a brilliant flower; warm and clean and fine, so full of rapture that the onlookers were stunned.

Chapter Four

WILDERNESS

But the loveliness of a blooming flower may be a fleeting thing, Subble thought as he stroked through the water. Nacre had not solved any problems, it had only graven their names on heavier chains. So long as home was a ruinously impacted Earth, the horrors would remain in one form or another.

He towed a basket by a cord looped around his waist. A mile ahead rose the offshore key – a semi-tropic island preserved as a wilderness park, inhabited only by birds, rodents, arthropods and elements of the second and third kingdoms. It was dusk, the island was outlined against the sunset, black palm against red cloud. A few gulls wheeled, and there were sundry movements in the shadowed tide beneath him. That was all.

He swam, enjoying the feel of the cool gulf water, the slap of salty spume against his shoulders and face. There was discovery and danger ahead, perhaps death – but death was an impersonal thing to him. He had a mission, and its completion was at hand – whatever that might mean.

The story of Nacre ran through his mind. What an adventure it had been, for the diverse trio! A vegetarian, a normal omnivore and a technical carnivore, solving the riddle of a world whose fauna mirrored their own habits. Yet the solution had not been complete, for now the deadly canivores were on Earth, and there was danger no one quite comprehended yet all suspected. Not the human problems of the male-female triangle; that would be resolved quietly in its own fashion once the principals got together again. Not the risk of an alien scourge on Earth, for the mantas were highly ethical creatures; they *could* attack man, but would not. They had come to comprehend, he was sure, not to conquer.

What, then? There *was* danger, terrible peril. His trained perception was suffused with it. Veg, Aquilon, Cal – all carried the

118

aura of fear, tied in with the manta. There was a potent mystery to the presence of the creature on Earth, and it was not a matter of diet or savagery or even intent. The future of Earth itself might hang upon the success of his mission – and he still could not grasp *how*.

Early night, and the isle loomed close before him. Subble turned on his back and looked up at the still trees, and beyond them to the cold stars. He had never been away from the planet himself, he was sure; agents had to be specially conditioned for extraterrestrial duty, and there would be no point in utilizing an Earth-trained unit for it. He understood that the average man felt a nameless emotion when viewing the stars, a kind of compulsive awe, a yearning to reach them and also a deep loneliness. Subble felt nothing except a mild intellectual curiosity. Probably he had been conditioned to cleave to Earth, and could not leave it without suffering from the same kind of emotional malady the normals suffered just existing upon it. Or perhaps it was because he needed no sense of continuity, of timelessness, since he had no past and no future. There was only the mission, and the stars were elsewhere.

There had been other missions before, but no trace of them remained with him. He might have had severe adventures in prior assignments, and could be fated for worse ones to come – but such speculations were hardly worth the effort it took to dwell upon them now. Death did not frighten him, and neither did the termination of his mission. Failure was the only spectre, and he was not a man to fail easily.

No, there was one realistic fear for him. Sometimes, he knew, an agent became stranded. For some reason it might be impossible to complete the assignment and check in promptly, and an agent caught in that situation was obliged to continue indefinitely, gradually growing old and losing the edge of his powers, missing the automatic updating provided by the reconditioning. It could be due to a continuing relationship – marriage in the line of duty, for example – in which a substitution would be inexpedient. Of course, if a female agent happened to be involved ...

Occasionally there was an accident; the agent was reported lost in action and his file discontinued prematurely while actually he survived to strive futilely for termination. It could happen to him! The unit SUB could be incapacitated upon this island, unable to return or report, yet alive. It could be months or even years before a follow-up located him, during which period he would be without a mission.

The thought was horrible. His body was nothing, his life irrelevant; pain and pleasure were only commodities of existence. But the mission – that was paramount, and without it he was wasted. Waste was the only intolerable. Better a clean death in the line of duty; better by far.

His feet found the sand beneath the shallows, and he drew his basket to the beach. A score of tiny brownish fiddler crabs scuttled sideways away from him as he emerged. They disappeared into their peppered holes in the damp sand. He waited while one big-clawed giant, well over an inch long, tried vainly to get into two of the pencil-sized holes and finally squeezed into the third. He wondered whether the burrows were linked underneath, like Aquilon's residential section. Did they have air-conditioning and colour television? Well, running salt water, perhaps.

The isle was quiet; no frogs or crickets chirrupped, and the birds held their peace. They were present, though; as he concentrated his faculties he perceived them all about, hearing their surreptitious motions and smelling their furtive animation behind the drifting odours of seaweed and rot. The animals would return to normal activities when assured he was not a menace. Already the fiddlers were peeking out.

It was a normal beach. The packed, even sand gave way to a line of tumbled larger shells just beyond the high-tide line: clam halves ranging from several inches across down to half-inch coquinas, broken red and white conches with the inner spirals exposed, bleached sand-dollars decorated with five-leaf clover designs. Farther back the weeds and creepers sprouted between occasional driftwood and dessicated palm fronds. Whitish morning-glory type flowers nestled upon beach-running vines, and towards the forest line the jointed, head-high sea-oats waved beside the great round sea-grape leaves.

He set up the electronic equipment and tested it. Cal's notion had been good: duplicate the frequency and quality of the manta's eye-beam and emulate the patterns of communication with the guidance of the oscilloscope. Cal had had limited success; he thought he had the proper channel, as it were, but had trouble gaining the cooperation of the mantas. Subble believed that the groundwork was good; now it was up to the faster responses of a trained man: himself. He would try it first without the hallucinogen; he was not convinced that this aspect of Cal's regimen was either appropriate or safe. There was no guarantee that the fungus drug would bring him closer to the representatives of the fungus world. It was as likely to give him the illusion of liaison, which was hardly his mission, and if, like an addict, he lost his perspective and inhaled an overdose—

It was dark when he finished, but this was no disadvantage. Subble, as a fully equipped agent, was at home in the night. He knew the mantas were largely nocturnal on Earth; they, unlike man, were severely handicapped by bright daylight, and only in the gloom of the forest or closed buildings could they function well. An overcast day might allow them to go abroad, however. It was not so much the sensitivity of the single eye as of the body: sunlight would burn away the delicate skin and interfere with the pressure responses essential to precision control of movement. This would be a fact of life for any creature with the properties of the manta; specialization inevitably brought special liabilities.

He was ready. Cal had said that the mantas would find him, once he made himself available – if they wanted to. They were half-grown now and knew their way about, preying on fish and rodents. They would come. After that—

Subble resigned himself to a long wait. If they did not seek him out tonight, he would look for them by day. It was pleasant enough here upon the spongy sand, contemplating the mosslike growths and ribbonlike weed – but the mission could not wait upon alien capriciousness.

There was no wait. They came over the beach, flying saucers kicking up gouts of wet sand, twenty feet apart. No evasion, no maneuvring; they came to rest in a wide circle around him, six one-eyed humps, now absolutely still, tails curled around their feet. The party was on.

He assessed each in turn, turning slowly in their cynosure. He had not seen any this close before, and had had only the descriptions of the three spacefarers to guide him, apart from the evanescent flash in Veg's woods and Aquilon's portrait. These were young individuals, smaller than the ones the trio had encountered; he judged their weight at forty-four pounds, plus or minus three percent. He was not yet certain of the specific gravity of manta flesh. The colour was

121

nongloss black. The six together would outmass him only moderately, and in this thin – for them – air their flight would suffer somewhat, requiring a greater spread for a given speed. Their eyes would suffer from increased signal-loss, too, since there was not so much atmospheric opacity to bounce it back. It seemed unlikely that they represented the physical threat to him that Cal had suggested, though he had come without his most formidable armament. Their concerted attack could be severe, however.

Subble had not come to fight. He was trained to assess the physical potential of any man or animal or machine he met, and this was an automatic process that signified no aggressive imperative. It was intellectual contact he required, on whatever level available. He turned on the communicator.

One manta hopped forward. A single bound, a single yard, and the tableau was as before, the circle broken only at that spot. Subble aimed the projector at the proffered eye and adjusted the settings.

Was all this paraphernalia necessary, he wondered? Surely the creature could read the nuances of human countenance by now with a facility impossible to any man or Earth machine. Selected frequencies probably penetrated the subject in the manner of an X-ray to read internal configurations, perhaps the convolutions of the brain itself. The manta might not have olfactory apparatus, but could actually *see* the minute particles arising from all objects, that men interpreted as smell. Sight could replace several of the conventional senses. This was sight quintessential, more potent than man's diversified hearing, smell, touch, balance, tension and fragmented other bodily perceptions. Sight, bringing almost total information, geared directly to the brain and thus the most efficient communicatory instrument ever devised or evolved.

But as Cal had theorized, this did not guarantee intelligence as man defined it. For man, communication was an effort; but the manta could convey its entire world-view in the blink of an eye. Not literally: the eye did not blink. The external lens seemed to be crystalline, requiring no lubrication; he wondered what mechanism kept it clean. At any rate, it could represent a barrier to increasing intelligence by its very effectiveness. Ants and termites had evolved complex societies without intelligence; instinct was more than sufficient. Mantas could easily have done the same, using neither intelligence nor instinct, but simply their version of complete communication.

Cal had hoped that he had discovered an alien civilization, but now, after further study, he was not certain at all. Cal wanted complete understanding, but had become resigned to the fact that he could not achieve it on his own, for reasons that eluded him. He had helped Subble as much as he could, though desperately afraid of the consequence.

Cal was not a man to be frightened by phantoms.

'Say something, Brother,' Subble urged the manta.

The screen came to life. Meaningless patterns played across its surface, whorls and lines shifting in kaleidoscopic confusion. Meaningless to *him*, Subble reminded himself; the signals might be direct and plain if he could interpret them properly. Cal had succeeded in aligning the equipment to manta impulses, but the fine tuning still had to be done. This first step was equivalent to establishing radio contact while remaining ignorant of the language.

'Let's revert to sign language,' he said. He brought out the light-pencil and played it over the separate photoelectric screen. Scribbled lines appeared in its wake, as though he had run chalk over a blackboard randomly.

He hooked the screen into the main circuit and began to draw. He had, in effect, a two-way contact: his probe could initiate designs that were transmitted to the manta frequency, albeit crudely, and the screen would reflect impulses originated from the other end as well. Their minds could meet via this circumscribed channel – if the manta desired it.

'Observe.' Subble drew a line of light and waited. The screen could only be activated by a steady, controlled impulse, and this had been demonstrated to be within the capability of the manta – when it chose to employ the technique. The transitory flickerings of the screen faded, indicating that the creature was following him, but there was nothing more.

He drew a second line beside the first. 'Come on, whip-tail – make like an artist,' he suggested. Still no response – yet the manta would not remain before the equipment unless it understood its purpose.

He added a third and a fourth line, and finally it happened: a fifth appeared.

'Now we're in business!' The manta was participating at last.

Subble erased the screen and drew a circle – and suddenly it was

123

filled with duplicate circles and wiped clean again, with no action on his part. It was as tangible an expression of impatience as he could imagine. There was at least minimal comprehension, and phenomenal manipulative ability. 'So you can make symbols,' the manta had remarked, in effect. 'So what? Stop wasting my time.'

Could it simply have been tedium that had interfered with Cal's efforts? The little man was a deliberate thinker, checking and rechecking before taking any new step. Quite possibly the volatile manta had given up in disgust while Cal deliberated.

'I doubt it,' he said aloud, finding it easy to maintain the one-sided verbal conversation while working out new lines of play on the board. That smacked of the same simplicity as the 'revenge' motif when one of the mantas of Nacre had struck Aquilon in the face. The truth appeared to be immensely more complicated. The simple answer's main asset was its convenience for simple minds. There had to be more to the present problem than impatience – and already he had had far more specific success than Cal had described, despite his lack of experience with the manta.

'So you just didn't *want* to talk to Cal,' he said, as his electronic pencil moved as swiftly as his heightened ability could control it. 'Why not? Why do you speak to the stranger and not to your friend? Isn't that a little fickle?'

He drew a man, simplified and stylized but recognizable, he hoped. The manta produced an identical figure, seemingly instantaneously. Subble drew a flying manta and this too was reproduced.

Was he achieving anything? Mere imitation proved only that the line was open. He needed intelligent application, and he hadn't found it yet.

He drew a slightly larger man, and opposite it a Nacre herbivore. 'You know Veg, right? And this is Aquilon, who brought you here, but didn't want to keep you all cooped up in her apartment. She's an omnivore – like this Nacre specimen, make of that what you will. And this smaller male-symbol is Cal, who is—' He left the opposite space blank, and waited. If Aquilon's technique had been soundly conceived—

The manta figure appeared in the appropriate space. Success! It understood the parallel.

A dotted X appeared, superimposed over the entire screen, but the picture remained. Then, rapidly, a standard man-symbol appeared beside the female, and the herbivore and the carnivore sets vanished. The manta was telling him that it knew that most men were omnivores; the screen quickly filled with human figures, the straight men and the bosomed women. But why the X?

Was the manta saying 'I understand your point, but it isn't valid'?

Then the slate wiped clean again, to be renewed by a group of Nacre omnivores. Subble's estimate of manta intellect jumped abruptly as he watched what followed.

For the figures were animate, no longer stationary symbols. The omnivores quivered and pounced, horribly real, and now they took on colour and a fungus background of the Nacre habitat. Their size expanded until the screen was a picture of a single living creature, leaping heavily and carelessly crushing the smaller mushrooms beneath its muscular foot.

A placid herbivore came into view, as though a television camera were centring on it – and the omnivore leaped upon it, tore away great juicy hunks of soft flesh with the toothed tail, and settled upon the spread remains to feed. Subble could even see the digestive acids flowing over the carcass, breaking the flesh down externally so that the predator's underside could absorb the jellied essence.

Then a single manta appeared, much smaller than the omnivore, but also much swifter. They fought, and the manta won and began feeding on omnivore meat.

The scene shifted to Earth: a recognizable tropical jungle. Subble now appreciated one of the reasons Cal had chosen to make his fungus commentary the way he had – in scenes. He must have suspected that the manta would employ this camera-mode.

A striped tiger prowled fretfully, the play of the great muscles beautifully pictured. A man appeared dressed as a hunter, with a heavy rifle in his hands. So accurate was the detail that Subble was able to identify the make of the weapon: one of the vintage gunpowder models. The tiger sprang; the man wheeled, brought up his rifle, and fired. The tiger fell and rolled on the ground, snapping and dying.

'Right,' Subble said. 'On Earth the omnivore prevails over the carnivore – and all other creatures. So long as he has his trusty technology at hand.'

Now the picture split: the victorious manta on one side, the man on the other. The backgrounds metamorphosed into sand and palm trees: the island upon which they stood. The line between them faded. Man and manta stepped towards each other.

And the screen went blank.

The manta hopped out of the circle, past its companions, and found a place in the centre of the beach. It waited. None of the others moved to utilize the electronic setup.

'Oho!' Subble exclaimed. 'So that's the way the jet fires. You don't care to talk to me either.'

He turned off the set. There was no use running down the battery until they settled this matter. The manta had proved beyond question that it *could* communicate – when it chose. It had gone as far as it intended to, and the next gesture was up to him.

Why? Because it did not respect the omnivore? Subble could understand this. He would be unlikely to treat a pig with respect unless the creature first demonstrated qualities deserving such attention. Unless, in fact, it were in a position to *command* respect – by superior intellect or physical prowess. Swine in a muddy pen were one thing; a great boar hog in the wilderness another. Wild tusks were more effective arguments than tame pork.

What did man have to distinguish himself? A technology that was superfluous to the framework of the manta, and rather crude where intelligible. Man's weapons were little more than an extension of the innate savagery of the species. Not an impressive total.

But Aquilon's act of faith and courage on Nacre had brought a limited response. That had been the first solid example of omnivore compassion the manta had observed and understood, and it had replied in kind. The seed had been planted.

Perhaps if the hunter saw the wild boar spare a human child, he would be constrained to hold his fire – but not necessarily to adopt that pig into his family. Respect had to be earned step by step; it could not be given as a gift.

The manta, it would seem, had returned Aquilon's favour and gone one step farther. It had sent its representatives to Earth. Now it was up to a designate of Earth to prove himself – step by step.

And the foundation had to be laid in the field of arms. The root of respect was almost always physical, no matter how tempting it might be to consider it otherwise. Man and manta had won their respective places by becoming the most deadly fighters of their worlds. The order of precedence had to be established before higher negotiations could begin. This was the essence of natural selection; not pretty, but necessary.

'So you wouldn't fight handicapped men,' he said. 'You insisted on a really capable specimen, so that there could be no excuses.' That was why Cal had had no success.

The manta was waiting.

Subble looked at it. 'Well, you've got one.' Was he to pit his devastating physical attributes against a half-grown animal? Immediately he caught himself. He had just had formidable evidence that the creature was alert and sapient, yet he still thought of it as an animal. Acceptance was a two-way business!

Still it bothered him. Inherent in ritual combat was the concept of fair play, and this was evidently highly developed in the manta. They had not simply attacked him; they had explained first, and now awaited his acquiescence. Fine – but he was probably a match for several of the creatures facing him, while only one made the offer.

Subble's reflexes were keyed to speeds far beyond those of ordinary men, and his weapons were the finest Earth technology could provide. He was a superman; no creature on the planet could match his strength, speed, endurance and general command of combat technique – except another agent. These mantas, on the other hand, were adapted to another planet, used to a thicker atmosphere and a steadier clime. They should hesitate to commit their forces in unfavourable terrain, just as an agent like himself would consider it bad tactics to engage, barehanded, a killer whale in the water.

Perhaps they had not completely understood the situation. He would clarify it.

'If you will direct your attentions to the inland vegetation ...' he said, gesturing, but none changed position. One was already facing that way, however.

Subble's hands touched the band of his trunks. Two lances of fire appeared and disappeared. Two fronds on separate palm trees dropped to the ground, their blasted stems smoking.

Not a manta moved.

But distance weapons were not part of the manta's framework, though they evidently knew something about them. Subble stepped out of the armoured trunks and dropped them beside the equipment.

He removed his rather special watch, a potent ring, and certain portions of his bridgework. A naked man against a naked manta – that was closer to it.

'But it still isn't entirely sporting, Brother,' he said. 'You weigh in at forty-four pounds, no hands.'

Subble moved: five steps, turnabout and somersault, in the time it would have taken an ordinary man to focus his eyes – and he had swept up a sturdy length of driftwood and shattered it with one blow of one hand.

The single manta waited.

'You offer me no apparent choice,' he said regretfully. 'I'll have to kill you before the others will believe.' He knew there could be no mercy in such a confrontation, for mercy in elementary battle was weakness.

He was prepared to do what had to be done, efficiently and supposedly without regrets – but he regretted this. His mission required the exchange of information with the mantas, to complete the picture, and a subsequent report. That was all – but they refused to cooperate until mastered. It was such a waste, to destroy an intelligent creature so casually – but necessary.

He strode to the centre of the beach, fifty feet from the selected manta. As he did so the others bounded outward, taking up positions several hundred feet distant at either end of the long strip: two and two, with the fifth beneath the blasted palm on the inland side.

Subble paused, assessing the slope of the beach and testing the footing offered by the sand. He would do best to stay clear of the dry area, since that would be powdery and contain prickly sandspurs; he needed good leverage more than the manta did. Then he marched towards his opponent.

He was uncertain how to kill it cleanly. He could not expect to strangle it, since it did not breathe in an Earthly fashion, and the tail would be dangerous in close work. He could not expect to stun it with nerve blows because he did not know enough about its nervous system, which could be simplified and well protected. As a matter of fact, he realized belatedly, he knew much less about it than it knew about him. Perhaps the match was not so uneven after all.

The best choice, in the face of his ignorance, was a quick series of blows, crushing the head section. The eye was the obvious vulnerability, and he did not wish to torture it by a slow death or dismemberment. The slaughter had a bad taste, but at least suffering could be minimized.

The manta did not move as he walked up. At twenty feet it looked pitifully small, an innocuous black hump with a single eye, something like a negative shmoo. Had he made an error? Had he misread its intent, and seen combat to the death where some gentler dialogue had been proposed? What a terrible mistake, if—

The manta was airborne, leaping away from him. He would have to catch it first – and one thing he could *not* do was outrun it. Even handicapped by Earth conditions, and under-age, it was probably capable of forty miles per hour over the sand. He would have to wear it down, or outmaneuvre it, or mousetrap it as it assailed him. He was glad; it was too noble a creature to die ignominiously.

'The recipe for rabbit stew ...' he reminded himself. *Could* he catch it, if it stayed clear?

It angled into the air, a disk a dozen feet in diameter. The foot disappeared into the body in this attitude, streamlining it, and he could see the flux of the surface responding to air resistance. The thing was both kite and glider, as much at home in the air as on land, though technically it could not fly. Beautiful control.

The manta swooped at the ground – and suddenly it was coming directly at him at double its prior velocity. Subble threw himself prone, clapping one hand over the back of his neck and the other over his spine while his face dug into the sand. It passed over him, the tail striking down as he squirmed to the side.

He was on his feet again immediately, facing it, but the manta settled a hundred feet up the beach. He glanced at his hand, the one that had protected his neck, and saw a long shallow slash beginning just below the wrist and running eight inches down the forearm.

Then he knew what he was up against. The wound was not dangerous, and in moments his physical control had sealed it off almost bloodlessly. But it was at the wrong angle. The manta's tail, moving forward in line with its body, should have cut crosswise over his wrist. Instead it had sliced at right angles to the creature's flight.

The manta had not only had time to select its target carefully, but had had the control to make a rather awkwardly positioned cut.

There was a similar incision along his other arm.

It had returned Subble's warning demonstration: this pass had been to alert him to its capability, not to incapacitate him. Now they both knew where they stood.

It was probably the first time he had ever seriously underestimated his opposition, for he would not have been available for this mission otherwise. He had allowed for exaggeration in the Nacre episode, for the observers had had other concerns to distract them from really objective views, and he had allowed for his own surprise when the manta moved in Veg's forest. Now he knew that these reasonable allowances for human error were faulty. He was in a battle for his life, and it was not possible to anticipate the outcome.

The tail was too fast for him. After appreciating what it could do in a controlled run, he knew that it could crack the sonic barrier when snapped with force, just as a whip could. He had no defence but interference and avoidance. He had to keep the manta out of range while in striking position or it would blind him or slit his throat or lay open some other part of his body on the next pass.

The manta lifted, flattening as it gained speed, coming at him. Subble dived for the water's edge and scooped up a handful of pebbles. He whirled and began firing them as the disk approached, his throws rapid and accurate.

It dodged easily, rippling to let the stones pass harmlessly, but it slowed; Subble was aiming for the great eye and knew that should the manta grow careless and allow a hit it would be in serious trouble. He began feeding his shots in pairs, forcing double dodging, and abruptly the creature gave up and swerved aside.

The manta touched the sand and catapulted ferociously at him again. But this time Subble was not to be surprised; he leaped – high into the air, directly at the manta.

Its velocity was too great to allow it to swerve in time, and his body was far too big for it to dodge like a pebble. A collision would favour him, because he massed over four times as much as it did, and his body was comparatively bony. He reached to enclose it, knowing that its delicate extensions would be highly vulnerable to the grasp of his hands. The striking tail would be ineffective in the face of such direct bodily contact.

The manta flexed and passed under him, going out to sea, and Subble landed on hands and feet, his nose not far from a pretty two-inch corkscrew shell lying just beyond the water. He jumped sideways and whirled, rearmed with stones, but the creature had not turned. It sailed over the rounded waves, the beat of its pumping foot casting up thin sprays of water.

Subble watched, startled, though he should not have been. Cal had remarked on this, and it was obvious that at the speed the foot struck, water was as good a medium for leverage as any. It was possible for a man to water-ski upon his two bare feet, if towed at sufficient speed, and the manta's foot-area at contact was far wider than man's. That was why they had chosen an island: the sea was a private highway.

But only at speed, surely. Were a manta actually to fall into the ocean, it would not be able to get up sufficient velocity to become airborne again, and its pusher would be virtually useless for swimming. That was worth remembering.

It was coming in again, flat and deadly as a flying knife. He could not hope to avoid it indefinitely; the manta was too fast, its tail too accurate. He could not run it down in his own time, either, since it could 'walk' on water. If it became fatigued, it could cross to another island and recover at leisure; if he tried to swim after it, he would be subject to immediate attack in the water, where the disparity in their maneuvreability would be greatest.

The manta gave him no time to think. It rose to an altitude of nine feet above sea level and sailed over the choppy waves of the incoming tide, too high for him to block effectively but just right for its own striking range.

Subble lurched to the side, and the manta shifted angles to head him off. But the mid-air maneuvre cost it velocity that it could not regain without coming down. He ran along the beach, seeking the hard-packed wet sand at the very edge of the water and moving at thirty miles per hour: a feat impossible for any normal athlete.

The manta altered its course to follow him, touching the ground. It gained momentum. Subble heard it approaching, closing the distance between them rapidly. He could maintain this pace for only a few seconds, yet it was easily outrunning him. In a moment it would draw abreast, and the tail would flick across to touch the throat, the eye, perhaps the hamstring tendon above the heel, and he would be pinned for the kill.

It drew within ten feet. It was silent, except for the staccato beat of the great foot and a faint whistling of air. He positioned it by sound: two feet above the sand, six feet behind. It would have to get close, beside him or over him, to utilize the tail, unless it could whiplash over its own head ...

Four feet, three – and Subble stopped. He braked with all of his force, driving his feet into the sand and throwing back his body. His arms went up over his head, as stiff as ramrods, fists clenched.

But the manta too had profited from experience. At forty miles per hour it could not stop within a yard; its foot was structured for forward drive, not braking. As old Ettore Bugatti had protested when cautioned on safety: 'I make my cars to go, not to stop!' Again Subble was using his less specialized physique to good effect; he could do more things than the manta could, even if he could not compete in its specialities.

It could not swerve aside in time, nor could it rise the six feet necessary to avoid him without totally disrupting its aerodynamics and looping out of control. It was made to go – but it had come prepared.

It accepted the collision.

The soft ball of it smacked into Subble's back – and bounced. He twisted around, grabbing for it again, but already it was bounding high into the air, ten feet, and opening into its travelling form, unhurt. One more trait had been revealed: the manta could protect its eye temporarily by englobing it in its own flesh, and its bonelessness prevented internal rupturing.

Why had it not done so in the Nacre sun storm? Probably because the light burned its skin and never let up; there it could not rebound and recover.

Subble scrambled beneath the spreading mantle, knowing that it lacked the proper leverage for a tail-strike when almost stationary. It was not the manta's own small mass that anchored it, but the resistance of the air to its spread body. That same resistance provided the real forward impetus, too – the foot pushed primarily *up*, but the sail tacked against the stable air and sent the body shooting forward much faster than otherwise. The manta was a creature of motion, and could not even achieve its full umbrella without sufficient velocity. Now it was almost still, and had to descend for at least one push before getting away. To this extent it had miscalculated.

And Subble was under it. 'Come to Papa,' he said as his hands reached up, enclosing the vainly fluttering shape. But he kept his face

132

averted; it could blind him yet, as his grip on its body provided some of the vital leverage. He would have to fall upon it, crushing it into the sand, encumbering the tail—

A sledgehammer struck his head.

Subble fell, stunned by the blow. The shallow water came up to meet his face, and the bright shells under the surface, though the night was black. The manta had driven its foot at his head, perhaps instinctively, and almost broken his neck! His brain had been severely jarred; unless he brought his bodily reactions under control immediately, he would lose consciousness – and life.

And mission. The phosphorescent surface smacked against his face. It was sheer luck; the external shock stimulated adrenalin and gave him momentary control. He brought his knees up under him and pushed for deeper water.

Or was it Enrico Ferrari who made his cars to go?

The manta was coming again, ready this time for the kill. Its black shape passed a few feet to the side, visible only as a moving shadow. Subble placed it principally by ear, discovering that he had temporarily lost his infrared vision, more sensitive to damage than normal sight because it was artificially implanted. He was, in this situation, virtually blind.

A searing blade slashed across his shoulders, laying the flesh open. Painful, but not crucial – but the end was near if he could not get away in seconds.

Subble dived. The ocean was only four feet deep here, but it was enough. The dread tail could not strike at him through very much water. He was safe – so long as he could hold his breath.

He could hear the foot pounding against the surface as the manta circled above, frustrated for the moment. It would slice away the top of his skull as soon as it appeared above the water – but he would drown if he did not come up within another minute. He had good resources here too, and could ordinarily stay under a long time, but he had entered the water disadvantageously. Unless he could deceive the manta in some way, gaining time for a breath—

The shape passed directly over him as he continued to stroke out to sea. Subble lunged for the surface and gulped air before it could turn. The manta's liability here was that it could not remain stationary on the water; it had to keep moving, and that allowed a few seconds between passes. By the time it could return, he was below again.

But how long could he hold out? At best this represented a standoff, and at worst defeat for him, if the manta learned to time his rise for air and lash out then. He could not overcome his opponent by hiding from it. If he lasted this way until daylight – still many hours away – the creature would probably retreat to shade on another island. Then night would come again . . .

The beat of the foot stopped. Subble listened, interpreting the cessation of the loud clear sounds conveyed by the water, and the strange substitution. The manta was coming at him – *under the surface!*

But almost immediately it was out of the water again, resuming flight. Now he realized what had happened: the manta had cut below the waterline much as a flying fish cuts above it; a shallow, temporary incursion dependent upon initial velocity. This was a dangerous maneuvre. One second too long, and it would be trapped, lacking the speed to angle successfully back into the air.

Why had it taken such a chance? Unless it could not locate him from the surface—

He worked it out. The manta was dependent upon one perception: sight. It was a phenomenal perception, but still subject to the limitations of the medium. It was necessarily narrow-beam; an eye which provided its own radiation had to limit its energy output stringently or essential resources would be drained from the system. Even a simple flashlight soon exhausted its batteries. Human beings, who utilized external sources of illumination, used as much as twenty-five percent of their bodily energies in connection with their eyes alone. The ratio would be worse for the auto-illuminants of Nacre, unless they were considerably more efficient.

But a narrow beam was virtually useless for locating a specific object in space. Even the wide-beam perception of Earthly eyes required special synapses to call motion to the attention, which solved most problems. A warty toad was lost amid the dry leaves of the forest floor, though in plain view – until it moved. Peripheral vision and sensitivity to motion: these were vital to a moving creature. the manta seemed to have neither; it played its fine beam over all objects and knew by its biologic radar what they were and how they moved.

What would the refraction of water do to this power? For man, the apparent displacement of objects beneath liquid, and the reflective properties of the surface were merely oddities and occasional nuisances. Man had other ways to plumb the depths. For manta – it could be a complex problem indeed. It had no verifying senses except the touch of foot and tail and skin, and these were almost useless here. Yet it was experienced enough to realize that the medium *did affect* the impulse, as a man might see a mirage and hear a ringing in his ears while knowing that these things did not reflect the true situation. Indeed, as a man might perceive a complete framework of stimuli, and know them all to be false ... as he had done himself under the influence of the hallucinogen.

As it was, that dialogue had disturbed him. Now he was uncertain about little things, such as exactly what a given racing-car pioneer had said. It *must* have been Bugatti!

So the manta could not trust what he saw beneath the shifting waves. Still, it could wait for the telltale appearance of his head above water – except that its narrow-beam vision made this largely a matter of chance. How likely was a man with a small beam to spot a figure in a dark ocean – a head that appeared only a second or two every three minutes or less?

The odds were with him after all! He could swim underwater and come up near the manta at any time – and duck when spotted. He could find a pole and jab it, spearlike, at the passing enemy, without emerging at all. No wonder the creature was desperate to locate him!

Subble broke surface and looked about. He was in deep water now, and had the whole gulf to hide within. It was still dark to his gaze: apparently his infrared was done for the duration. He could compensate to a considerable extent, since that seemed to be the worst of his injury, apart from the slash across his back and a headache he was able to suppress. He could see the white beach and the tall stars; only the black on black of the manta evaded him visually. But he could hear it well enough, ranging at a distance, and smell its distinctive, funguslike aroma.

He had lost some blood and his neck was stiff; he had gained a major tactical advantage. He was, all in all, in good shape.

'Over here, Brother!' he called.

And the manta looped about and came towards him. It had heard! Subble submerged hastily and sought a new location. How could a creature without auditory apparatus respond to sound waves? Cal had shown him a copy of Aquilon's dissection pictures: the manta had no ears and its skin was not attuned to sonic vibrations. It had only the eye.

Unless it could actually *see* sound waves . . .

He could not chance it. Obviously it *could* locate him when he made a noise, and if it missed the tiny splashes of his lifting head in distant water, it would not overlook those noises near at hand, or the vapours of his breath. Impasse again.

He came up, spotting it near his last emergence. But as he did, it changed course and zeroed in on him. Once again it had profited from experience, recognizing the noises characteristic of him and watching for the expanding atmospheric waves that were his sounds. He had thrown away his major advantage.

Again, his choices were continuing retreat – or death. This ocean episode had given him a limited reprieve and educated him somewhat, but it had not forwarded his mission particularly. Better to meet the foe on land, where, if defeat were more likely, so was victory. If only he understood the manta better!

And suddenly he did. The thing that Cal had hinted at and had not been able to say; the thing that made the manta incredibly dangerous to civilized Earth; the obvious rendered obscure by a mind trained to expertness at conventionalities – the pieces of the puzzle began to fall into place at last, and hinted at the devastating consequences of ignorance.

He took a breath and stroked powerfully for the cache of equipment. He stayed under as far as the diminishing depth permitted, then emerged silently, holding his breath. The tide was at its height, the surges almost touching his basket, but it was undisturbed.

Beside it sat a dark hump. The manta had anticipated him!

But it did not attack. He realized with relief that this was one of the watchers, a noncombatant. It would leave him alone – he hoped.

Carefully he knelt at the basket and drew out the lamp. He found a match – still the surest route to fire! – and thumbed it to life. As it flared the distant manta veered, aware of the sound or the radiation of heat or light or some other ambient characteristic of fire. He touched it to the spout of the lamp, willing it to catch quickly. It did, and he moved to the centre of the beach, nostrils close to the flame.

The manta left the water and shot across the narrow beach, its eye bearing upon him with the typical flicker; he could see that much directly now. Subble readied a fistful of shells and pebbles, but it sheered away from the steady green flame. Did the hallucinogen affect it too? Or did it suspect some more suble trap?

Subble inhaled, knowing he was taking too much but urgent for the drug to take effect, while the manta circled warily. Cal had been right; this was the only reasonable avenue for comprehension, in the circumstances. And he had to understand the creature before he dared to kill it.

The old one was dying. Laboriously it made its way to the place of decease, climbing the narrow trail though hardly able to spread its brittle aerofoil. Periodically it rested, its massive body sagging with fatigue, the eye staring lethargically. The younger, vigorous ones passed it in salute and went on, sparing it further exhibition of its incompetency. The last trip had to be alone.

The old one came at last to the highest plateau and collapsed ignominiously upon the level dust. It was the end – but life remained behind the glazed eye, flickering into the final configuration. Blind, the old one rose on its flaccid foot, the globe of its body swelling tremendously. The extinguished eye bulged and exploded; the body split asunder. A cloud of smokelike particles puffed into the air, spreading slowly through the staid atmosphere.

The body collapsed, an empty husk devoid at last of animation, awaiting only the periodic annihilation of the fire from the sky. No omnivore would defile the remains after that cremation. Life had not been destroyed; it had passed on, into myriad microscopic free-floating spores. The old one had contributed its genes to the world.

The spores ascended, diffusing as they drifted over the face of the cliff and caught the circulating breezes there. They travelled, half an octillion strong: five times ten raised to the twenty-sixth power, or a numeral followed by twenty-six zeroes. Their motions were random, within reasonable meaning of the term; they were governed by trace eddies and currents, and by the gentle static repulsion contributed by their common charge. They were male and female – that is, complementary half-chromosome arrangements – in even numbers, but the static prevented them from mating with each other. And so they spread and merged with the inanimate dust and wandered wherever fate decreed, almost indistinguishable from their environment.

Time passed. Quintessentially decimated, the spores continued, settling on cliff and plain, on animate and vegetative, rising into the sky and sinking into the water. Fungi fed upon them, and grazing herbivores. Some died and rotted, while others achieved the pinnacle and were destroyed by the fierce radiation of the upper sunlight. Some were buried, encysted, and lay dormant interminably, waiting for the destiny that did not come. Quintillions remained, distributed across the planet. Then quadrillions and finally only trillions.

Other spores from other ancient mixed with these: plants, molds, animates in countless species. The old one's spawn was long lost in the proliferation. Now there was no way to estimate their diminishing number, and seldom did any approach a sibling close enough to react to the repulsion. But some few did encounter similar spores released by other members of the species, and where sexually compatible they merged. Union had been completed, and the two spores became a single embryo.

Perhaps no more than a million of the old one's seed achieved such matings in the course of the fertile years, and for almost all it meant destruction. Merged, they had to grow – and there was little opportunity for it. Where they landed they sprouted hyphae and formed cords of mycelium, seeking nourishment – but there was seldom anything they could use, since their diet was precise. Some seemingly similar embryos flourished in organic dust, and thousands competed for it vigorously, but the old one's minions perished there. Others fell upon carrion and reveled in the inert meat – but not these.

Time ran out. The mated spores grew without intake and bled their energies into extinction. Some were preyed upon by omnivorous animalcules. Some found suitable lodging, but could not grow, inhibited by inherent defects or harmful radiation or rough treatment or environmental incompatibility. Some grew too slowly, and were eliminated by rivals for the food, and some were unsuccessful mutants.

One endured all hazards and became established: a parasite upon the body of a tremendous beast. This one developed the characteristic symbol that would identify it as an individual for the rest of its lifetime: an intricate network representing a compromise between the symbols of its unknown parents. Cruder intellects would fashion

138

it a geometric diamond with unimportant structural deviations.

Diam had achieved incipient sentience.

The host-beast charged and fought, and the unfelt parasites upon its skin were crushed and bruised and brushed away. Only Diam survived long enough, and at such time as to develop mobility before the host terminated its own violent existence in battle with another of its kind.

Diam tore free and fled, a leaping midget the size of an insect, before the body of the omnivore dissolved beneath the digestive secretions of its conqueror. Hitherto only chance had dictated his survival; now he had control, and would live or die depending upon his fitness. He lived. He preyed upon the baby omnivores feeding on dust and corpses, and he grew.

In time he encountered an adult of his kind: a full-grown carnivore. The manta took Diam in charge and helped him find proper sustenance. Others were similarly salvaged, until there was a flock of diversely parented hoppers: Diam and Circe and Star and Pent and Hex and Lin and sibling symbols. Secure, for a time, they grew fat and clumsy as they learned to communicate with each other and to recognize individual patterns.

Increasing size brought problems, for the aerodynamics of a creature weighing less than an ounce changed when it came to weigh more than a pound in a comparatively short segment of its life. Gravity became a significant and objectionable factor; a clumsy landing hurt. The tremendous growth rate kept Diam and his foster siblings continually off-balance, and the magnifying complexities of communication also strained their as yet diminutive faculties. So much was demanded!

Then, just as they were coming in sight of mastery, they were given onerous instructions, taken to the place of decease, and there put into the charge of a blind alien omnivore. It was the beginnings of an exile that they knew meant a lifelong separation from their kind for most of them, and dishonourable death.

The two-footed pseudo-omnivore stood over Pent's crushed body, its slick round-pebble orbs shifting whitely. The five-faceted symbol would speak no more; eye and brain had been crushed beneath the savage and abruptly knowledgeable force of the stranger.

It was good: the omnivore had proven itself. It had risen above the terrible limitations of its physique to meet a civilized creature on even terms. Now at last it was permissible to converse with it without restraint, while Pent dissolved into smoky spore vapours. The other omnivores had been innocuous pets, unable ever to comprehend the code of the warrior, unworthy to share the information of the elite. This one – this one was contemporary.

Diam took his stance before the clumsy artificial eye the omnivore had brought. It was uncomfortable, communicating via such a mechanism, but no more so than the concept of a sapient omnivore, or a world in which green plants retained their life to anchor on the ground and magnify grotesquely. If the stranger learned quickly, the machinery might soon be dispensed with.

The ball-eyed one gestured crudely with its forelimb. A pictorial representation took shape, so abbreviated that it was hard to follow. Surely there was some better way to do the job! Complete understanding would be extremely tedious if all communication had to be filtered through this obstruction.

The omnivore seemed to realize this. It sucked in more of the primitive fumes emerging from the burning container and returned to try again.

Then it began to learn. Ratios clarified, symbols danced through permutations, and the creature became more and more responsive to suggestion. A truly powerful intellect was beginning to emerge. But – an increasingly ill one.

'Like the slime mold!' it projected, showing in summary the life history of the local example. A slimy, jellylike plasmodium crept under the moist vegetable leaves fallen on the floor of the monster-plant forest, surrounding the organic matter it discovered and digesting it comfortably. Then, emerging into the light, the yellow creature shifted into inanimate status and fruited: brownish balls ascended slim orange stems and opened to release the floating spores; these, falling on water, germinated and put out tiny flagella to enable them to swim. Two came together and mated, found land and grew into the original slime formation.

'You actually evolved from the third kingdom – from fungi!' the omnivore stated, as though this were not obvious and reasonable. The parallel to the primitive slime mold was imperfect, but certainly such a creature could have been ancestral to all the sentients of Nacre. The astonishing thing was that it had not happened similarly on Earth. Here the fungal forms had failed to advance properly, while the plants overran the planet, and the animals – who neither created food from light and mineral nor broke down residues to complete the cycle – somehow had become dominant over it all. The notion of a life-form that served no useful purpose appearing and achieving sapience was appalling – but nevertheless a fact that had to be recognized.

These things maintained two discrete sexes throughout life, and generated their spores long before death. They omitted the atmospheric floating stage entirely, preferring to confine their embryos within their living flesh.

What other monstrosities were to be found in the universe?

Circe, symbol of the circle, was to claim this episode, though Diam read it first:

'The mantas saw *us* as pets?' Aquilon demanded, amazed. 'After we raised them and brought them all the way to Earth?'

'Not exactly. But it was hard for them to refrain from killing you as a matter of habit or instinct, without some innocuous designation.' Subble watched her move about the apartment, her body lovely under the translucent shift. 'They saw all three of you as omnivores from the start. They were soon aware of your diets – I mean, the mantas on Nacre were aware – not from any mysterious aura, but from simple observation. Veg had no flesh adhering to his teeth, and his breath reflected this, for example. They could see the microscopic particles in the air that we discern as smell. But the species Homo sapiens *is* omnivorous, and the attempted deviation of individual members is an oddity, apart from the oddity of the entire form of life. They could not imagine a *Nacre* omnivore settling down to graze peacefully among the herbivores. They marvelled at this for a long time, wondering whether the inconsistency was a characteristic of the kingdom.'

She came and sat in his lap and ran her hand over his cheek. 'Then why did that one manta stop Veg and me from getting together? If it *knew* we were all of the same kind—'

Subble found the trigger-thread and pulled. Her shift fell open. 'Because it did not fully understand the rules of your game. Your nature was omnivorous, but your practice deviated, not just dietetically but in your evident concern for each other. True omnivores never cooperate. It wanted to study the three of you, and for all it knew, Veg might be along solely to serve your hunger when the time came. Apart from its natural aversion to cannibalism – another omnivore trait – it wanted to fathom you as a group, and had to play safe until it was sure.'

'Before we make love,' she murmured, 'there is something you should know.'

'I know you are beautiful,' he said.

She smiled – and with that expression her lovely features became flaccid, grotesquely homely. The vibrant body seemed to cave in on itself, becoming a mushy mannequin; the shape was there, but not the glory. It was the death of rapture.

Subble shoved her away. 'That ties it. You were cured of that. I saw you smile, before.'

He stood up and marched towards the lamp he now spotted on the floor. 'I'm still under the hallucinogen. Damn overdose!' He reached to snuff it out, though it flared violently.

Circe erased the rest.

The mangled bodies had long since been eaten, the alien structures that were bones scattered, but the old stockade still seemed to reflect the night of ravage that had wiped out the off-world colony. Fungus grew richly out of the crevices of the tumbled buildings; dust and debris covered the inert machinery. Measured plots of Earth plants remained only in outline; they rotted where they had died when the mechanics who ran the sunlamps vanished.

Star moved on. Never before had his people slaughtered an entire population, and even traversing the scene in the eidetic memory provided by the elder who had been there was objectionable to him. He did not regret the action, for anything the group decided upon was proper, but he disliked the waste. These had been dangerous omnivores, yes, that insisted upon killing indiscriminately as was their nature, and so had set the precedent – but their flesh had proved to be of an entirely different order of construction and quite difficult to digest. Disposal of all eighteen bodies had been a terrible struggle – but the manta was bound to eat all it killed.

The aliens had seemed monstrous, with their inability to communicate, but subsequent developments had thrown into question their need to be put entirely out of their misery. Perhaps it would have been better to study them more carefully.

Then another party had descended from the blazing sky, and set up a more powerful base, preventing contact until a trio became isolated. The opportunity had come – if the individuals could be protected from the dangers of the world and their own quixotic nature. The first to spot them had lost them again as they fled in their machine; the second had died as they misunderstood his purpose. The third had made contact at night, and shepherded them to the place of dying, where the group could assemble. They were partly tame by then.

Then the ugliest omnivore had become less frightening. Star had it all in the transferred images, and it helped them comprehend the astonishing and descending mind of the present omnivore. These creatures were not entirely savage.

Diam:
　'Report!'
Subble stood before the pickup of the Director's dais and spoke to the man or men who controlled him – men he had never seen. 'I interviewed the three names on the list and determined that the problem involved them only indirectly. Each person provided a segment of their joint experience on the planet Nacre, but the whole remained incomplete. The key actually lay with the representatives of the dominant species of the planet, imported by the trio as theoretic pets and approved by quarantine as sterile and distributed among the three at the ratio of one, one and six when they resettled on Earth. The humans feared for the eventual security of these alien carnivores, so hid them diversely; and there were personal problems encouraging a temporary separation. These circumstances—'
　'We are aware of the circumstances. Proceed.'
Subble did not show surprise at this evidence of a parallel investigation. 'Full contact was not feasible until one of our own species earned the respect of the manta by meeting it in honourable battle. With them, as with us, physical appreciation must precede intellectual appreciation. I met their representative on an isolated beach and—'
　'We know the details. Proceed.'
　This time he hesitated visibly. 'It was an impasse. I finally took the hallucinogenic drug again in order to establish a close enough

143

rapport with my opponent so that—'

'Naturally! Proceed.'

'After I killed it, I realized that their fungoid nature was an appalling danger to—'

'Proceed!'

'Because Earth itself is now largely dependent upon—'

'Proceed!'

'The moment one dies—'

'Proceed!'

Subble leaped upon the dais and knocked aside the screen. A single manta stood there, glaring into the translating mechanism.

Subble grabbed the lamp and flung it against the wall. The oils poured out; the green flame expanded hungrily.

Diam faded from view. So did the dais and the rest of the set. There was only the heaving, animate fire.

'Next verse!' Subble cried.

Five mantas:

Subble stood on the sand watching Pent move. He had taken the drug before he killed the manta – which meant that everything since the moment of inhalation was suspect, even the killing itself. He could trust none of it – and he could not risk igniting the lamp again.

Pent circled but did not charge. Why hadn't the creature killed him while he stood bemused by wish-fulfillments? What held it back now?

Was it afraid of mycotic hallucinogen? Did the drug that induced spurious images in the mind of a man have a similar effect on the manta? Or was the result more severe, for it?

His hand hovered over the lamp, hesitating to snuff it out.

Then he realized: he had tried to kill that flame twice – and had not succeeded. He had merely stepped into a new sequence. What guarantee did he have that this was not yet another nightmare, and the lamp an illusion?

How could he put it out – if the act of quenching it was itself a dream?

Subble smiled. The manta hadn't attacked because it did not understand his ploy. Why should he stand on land, after establishing that his tactical posture was deficient there? Why – unless he had come up with something special?

144

And perhaps he had. He was not the same man who had begun the contest. The things he saw were entirely different now. He appreciated Pent in a new and marvellous perspective, and would not react as he had before. The information had been delivered hallucinogenically, as though he had been listening to the manta's quarter of the story, immersing himself in it as he had during the human quarters – but that did not mean that it was invalid.

On the contrary. He must have killed Pent and earned contact, learning to interpret the peripheral signals, to operate without dependency upon the transceiver. The drug made his mind responsibe to suggestion, even alien suggestion. When he had taken it in the presence of the manta he had recreated the world-view of the manta, and had seen to some extent what the manta saw, modified somewhat by his humanity. Somewhat . . .

Yet Pent circled still, alive. He could as easily have invented the entire thing, including the fungal origins of the manta. Was he victor or vanquished?

Twice the vision had become dominated by his own ambitions – and twice he had realized this and cut it off. Agents were not supposed to be subject to ambition. Such visions indicated personality breakdown, making him unsuitable as an agent. He had been moved by beautiful Aquilon's body, so he had recreated her in a willing situation, much as he might have done subconsciously had he possessed a differentiated subconscious. Balked, he had jumped ahead, then, to the completion of his mission – and perceived the distortion more readily, that time.

The drug affected his perception, making real any transitory thought that had sufficient force. He had taken an overdose, but it did not impair his reasoning facilities – *faculties*! – or his memory. He had entered a world of hallusions – but he could control them.

At this moment he was matching hal – *ill*usion to reality. He could now snuff out the flame successfully – and did not need to. Assuming that his reasoning were valid. Otherwise he was trapped anyway.

He tested. The genie Myco appeared, grinning. 'Put on your turban!' Subble said. The slave obeyed.

'Kill Pent.'

'Master, Pent is dead already.' The language was wrong; Myco should not be speaking modern.

'Well, kill him again!'

'Gladly!' Myco swelled up, launched enormous jewelled hands at Subble's throat.

The five watched him die, unable to protect the omnivore from himself. Contact had been a failure after all.

Cal woke with a start, the dream fading. Strange, the way it had become an obsession: the simple fact of drinking the blood of the Nacre omnivore. He knew now that he had suffered from the same compulsion syndrome that Veg and Aquilon had – except that they had not possessed the intellectual determination to carry it to such a macabre extreme. The simple refusal to eat meat, or to smile – but *he* had made of his entire life a nightmare, like the man who believed he must commit a crime every day or die. Cal had taken unto himself the action he considered most reprehensible: the parasitic consumption of the blood of other animals.

Though the origin was psychasthenic, the effects were real. He had wanted to die, and for years had driven himself to it, fighting the internal censors of self-preservation ... only to be balked at the climax by the blind faith of friends. A man who gave of his strength, a woman who bled herself – to show their faith in *him*.

He opened his eyes and saw Star standing at the window. Was someone coming?

That had been the breaking point, he thought, resuming the chain. They had beaten him, for he could not bring himself to sacrifice either the man or the woman he loved to his own morbidity. Veg would have driven himself, like a faithful horse, to a running collapse, travelling two miles loaded for every mile while others went unburdened. Aquilon would have bled herself dry – to save the feeble creature they called friend. The two had overcome his death-wish by tripling the cost of success. Better that he should live, than they die.

And so he had been given the impetus for change, and had searched for a pretext. He had taken the blood of the omnivore and thrived upon it – knowing, beneath a new suppression, that it was a nutrient fluid unrelated to human or Earthly blood except in general function. How could it be blood – drawn from the corpse of an animate fungus? And from that first exhilarating step, that concession to the needs of life and health, he had progressed steadily towards a more normal diet, and gained back much of the strength the years had dissipated.

Yet, like Aquilon, he had replaced his chains with stronger ones. He had accepted life for himself – at the possible expense of that of his species. Thus his new nightmare stemmed from that cup of blood – Aquilon's or Nacre's, he was not sure – and climaxed in rivers of the blood of man drenching the earth of Earth.

'Wake and dress immediately,' the voice said, and for a moment it seemed the manta had spoken. 'I will carry you.'

That was what had disturbed Star. A man *had* been approaching. 'Subble!' he said. 'Did you—?'

'No. I am Sueve, assigned to complete this aspect of the mission. Subble is otherwise occupied.'

Cal dressed hurriedly. Now he heard the movements of trucks outside, of human activity. 'What's going on?'

'Evacuation.' Sueve picked him up and strode to the door.

'But my books, my notes—'

'Sorry. Nothing but yourself. Your clothing will be destroyed when you enter decontamination.'

'What's *happening*?' But Sueve did not reply. He was running now, down the street that covered the length of the beach establishments, avoiding the slowly maneuvring army trucks and confused, milling people, while Star kept up easily. The wind whistled by Cal's ear; the agent was astonishingly strong and swift.

It was early dawn, still too dark for the birds to sing. The greens and whites and browns of the plaster and wood houses were only shades of grey. 'Truth is a shade of grey,' he thought, and wondered who had said it first. Now and then the gulf was visible, its water dark and still. Palmettoes and pines leaned over the winding street, and large century plants spoked beside it. The bright signs of the all-night stores, the motels and restaurants catering to restless tourists, these shone eerily in the absence of their proprietors and clientele. The evacuation was almost complete already, proceeding with a swiftness he had not thought possible as the sealed trucks moved out. The drivers wore bacterial masks. But there were no sirens, no shrill radio exhortations or loudspeaker warnings. All was accomplished silently. Why?

Sueve was cutting across the barbered golf links. In the centre of the convoluted greens stood a ship. A booster rocket, grossly misplaced here. Then they were inside. Sueve – so much like Subble!

147

– set the controls and tied Cal into a deep acceleration couch, while Star braced against what was coming.

'What happens to all the other people? Why them, too?'

'They are being interned for the duration.' The panel was clicking off the countdown.

Yet he was sure there had been no declaration of war, no reports of oncoming hurricane or other natural calamity. This was a sudden, complete and secret evacuation of the beaches – and he could think of only one reason. The one he had dreamed about so guiltily.

'What about the ones who refuse to go? Who demand reasons? Who hide, who are missed?'

'They remain.' The rocket ignited and acceleration crushed him back into sleep.

The line of men in fire suits combed through the forest, driving everything before them by spraying a toxic chemical. Where they passed, the green foliage wilted and dead insects and small animals littered the leafy floor.

'Hey!' Hank Jones exclaimed. 'This is *my* land! Get outta here!'

Then, seeing that they paid him no attention, he took up his axe. 'Go get Veg!' he yelled to Job. 'He'll help. Tell 'im it's an invasion – they're laying down mustard gas!'

Job bolted as the second line of invaders, masked and armed, conducted Hank away. Job leaped over the wall and pounded down the trail to the neighbouring work area.

But Veg was the major object of the advance. He had problems of his own, that early morning, as the troops converged.

Hex, knowing the meaning of the weapons and the spray and the hovering ring of helicopters, permitted himself to be herded in with Veg. The omnivore had little sense of individual ethics. The only defence here was no defence.

Behind them, as the flyer lifted, the reluctant smoke of burning greenwood pushed up from the dying forest.

Joe looked up from his computer flow chart, but there was nothing in the hall. The noise came from the air circulation vents: not a hiss, not the usual knocking of incipient breakdown, but a suble change in rhythm, as though the texture of the air had changed. A fine haze emerged.

He reached for his phone. He had authorized no addition of chemicals, and certainly not so unselectively as via the air. What was good for the rabbits was not necessarily good for the hens, and—

He slumped over his chart, letting the receiver fall. In their cages the animals also slumped. In minutes all were dead.

Incendiary gas now descended from the vents, filling the chambers. A spark, and it burned fiercely but not explosively, charring everything in almost complete silence. The farm had become a thorough oven by the time someone realized that there had been a small error: the man was supposed to have been evacuated first.

Circe alone escaped. She well knew the nature of the omnivore, and had been alert for the telltale sonic waves of the first faint preparations. She sped for the elevator before closure was complete. Its mechanism was powered by the same trunk line as the air circulators, and by the time the omnivores realized their oversight, Circe was out of the death zone.

But Aquilon's apartment too was a trap. Woman and manta were caught and sealed in a pressurized capsule: air and water but not freedom. The capsule was taken from the building secretly as the suited demolition crew razed the apartment, burning the furnishings and paintings and melting down all other fixtures.

The faceless units of the incendiary crews moved relentlessly, guiding their tanks delicately down the length of the beaches spraying gasoline and igniting it with bursts from the flame throwers. Men ran screaming from the fired houses: the ones who had avoided relocation by intent or mistake, fearing the quarantine stations, the loss of their expensive properties and household possessions, or just plain ornery about their rights. The omnivore cared nothing for their rights. They ran, touched by jets from the tanks, their clothing and then their skin dropping from their bodies in bright embers, and after them their women and children, crying skinlessly. Some tried to attack the massive tanks that crushed their homes – and were themselves crushed beneath the unswerving metal treads. Some dived into the ocean, swimming beneath the hovering white-breasted gulls, and the burning oils pursued them across the water, converting the grey-green depths to orange and black.

It was swift, it was merciless. Lin, symbol of the line, paced the length of it, observing the omnivore in action. What the tanks did

149

not destroy, the napalm bombers did. By the time the sun appeared in the sky, the beaches for a hundred miles had been levelled. If anything survived there, it regretted it.

Lin left, urged by time and the increasing light. Beyond the beaches the nets extended, reaching far into the sea and penning all surface marine creatures behind them. Ships patrolled this perimeter – robot vessels, armoured, no man upon them, diffusing deadly fluids to plumb the lowest regions. Automatic weapons shot down everything that approached from either side – flights of birds, a straying pilot, even large insects. Here, too, the closure was complete.

Lin joined the others at the robot shuttle that bore them rapidly away, but he knew what happened behind. A single missile arched over land and water, homing in on an isolated island. A hundred feet above the tiny beach where Subble lay it disappeared.

The island became a ball of incandescence as land and water vaporized.

Where it had been, a monstrous mushroom sprouted.

'You mean – *everything's* gone?' Aquilon asked, shocked. 'Veg's forest, the whole cellar farm, all the gulf beaches?'

'They had to go,' Cal said. They were crowded with the seven mantas into an orbiting chamber awaiting decontamination: a thoroughly unpleasant process. 'There is no other way to be *sure* – and even the two hours they allowed for evacuation before ... liquidation were a calculated risk.'

'I don't get it,' Veg said. 'Why did they leave us alone so long – no quarantine, no trouble – then suddenly, pow!'

'Because it took the bureaucracy some time to become aware of the danger. They suspected that the mantas might revert to a dangerous wild state, or something minor like that, I think. When Subble figured it out and made his report, they had to act immediately. We're extremely fortunate they decided to save our lives; that surprises me, as a matter of fact.'

'*What* danger? The mantas have no diseases, and they know they aren't supposed to attack people.'

Cal sighed. 'It is complicated, but I'll try. Briefly, the danger is inherent in the nature of the mantas and the other creatures of Nacre. They are of a fungus world, where animals of our type never

150

evolved at all. The mantas are the most advanced representatives of the third kingdom. They are in fact evolved from parasitic fungi resembling our slime molds, while the ones we call herbivores are similarly advanced saprophytes. Naturally they couldn't be true herbivores, with no living vegetation on the planet's surface, and they certainly aren't plants themselves.'

'I never thought of that!' Veg exclaimed. 'No trees, no grass, no flowers—'

'Then – they aren't really animals, even?' Aquilon wanted to know.

'Not as we think of them. Parallel evolution has brought the Nacre animates to a state surprisingly similar to the higher Earth animals, which is why we made the mistake we did. But their life cycle remains mycotic – that is, they reproduce by spores, and at some period they are unable to move independently.'

'But so do Earth fungi,' Aquilon said.

'Precisely. And Earth fungi are exceedingly important to Earth's economy, as I explained to Subble. So important that no interference with their development and exploitation can be tolerated. If we lost our food-yeasts alone, billions of people would starve before alternatives were developed. And if the carbon-dioxide cycle were broken—'

Veg was shaking his head dubiously, and Aquilon seemed uncertain also. He kept forgetting that although they had been on Nacre, the chemistries of ecology meant little to them. But there were other facets.

'Can you imagine what havoc would be wreaked in our civilization if an octillion super-advanced fungus spores were released in our atmosphere to mix with these here? There could be millions of mantas overruning the planet, looking for omnivores – *men*, that is – to feed upon; and the next generation would see more mantas than men in the world.'

They looked at him, trying to visualize it.

'Or the spores might succeed in merging with local spores to produce Earth-Nacre half-breeds that might very well displace all other life on Earth. The mantas by themselves, you see are self-limiting; they feed only on omnivores, whether animal or fungus, and have the intelligence and conscience to preserve some equitable balance. Man can live with them, though perhaps not as master. But

151

the halfbreeds could be—'

'Omnivores,' Aquilon breathed. 'Beasts with *no* controls . . .'

'Worse. They could operate on the molecular level, and start our common molds and yeasts changing, leapfrogging freakishly along the path of a billion years of evolution. That's what would hit our food supply. We are able to work so effectively with our fungi because they are primitive. But we know now that their evolution can lead to forms in many ways superior to us. Since most mutations are not beneficial, all life as we understand it today could be imperiled while savage semi-primitive strains competed for dominance. Our yeasts could begin feeding on *us*.'

'But I thought different species could not mate unless they were closely related,' Aquilon said. 'The Nacre spores should be quite different from ours.'

'Perhaps. Perhaps not. We know so little about the third kingdom that we just can't be certain. There is no such thing as complete convergence in the animal kingdom – but spores are about as hardy and versatile an instrument of reproduction as exists. Some may grow to maturity without mating, but ingest other spores they encounter. Alien enzymes in a local predator could result in modification. There are so many billions of spores in our atmosphere that some kind of mutation becomes a probability rather than a possibility. The danger is theoretical – but so great that every vestige of alien life must be expunged from the planet. Our existence may depend upon it.'

Veg thought about it, obviously following only part of the technical discussion. 'We've been back on Earth several months and I haven't seen any new things appearing. Why all the hurry now? All the – burning.'

'And why *did* they capture us and the mantas alive?' Aquilon added.

'I think they did it because they had to get the mantas alive, or completely sealed in at death, and that would have been almost impossible without us. We're the only ones who actually associate with mantas; they'll come with us, while they might never be captured alive in a hunt.'

'Yeah, but—'

'You see, the creatures of Nacre don't spore until death. In the natural course, as I make it, they dissolve into spores at the end of an active life. But if they anticipate death, they can prime themselves for emergency reproduction. They're sexless in the active stage, actually; the spores are the ones that mate. So an individual manta can release a complete collection of spores, and ours are primed for it, even though they are not full grown. If any die now, their bodies will quickly fall apart into billions of spores – and the siege is on. Each is a hopping bomb, on Earth.'

Aquilon looked at the mantas. 'I see,' she said soberly. 'They don't *want* to die, but if they do, the species goes on.'

'Yes. The only safe procedure is live capture and deportation – and sterilization of the territory they occupied, no matter what the cost. Any person, any animal, any gust of wind could carry devastating spores. Everything that leaves the zones of exposure has to be decontaminated, and those who refuse to leave—'

'What about *us*?'

'We're isolated now. I suppose we'll be exiled to Nacre. Perhaps they'll let us return once the mantas are landed there.'

'To Earth?' Veg remarked sourly. 'After they burned my lot? I'd rather stay on Nacre.'

'I would, too,' Aquilon agreed. 'I didn't know how – close – Earth felt until I came back. I—' She looked at the mantas. 'One of them is missing! What happened to it?'

'I'm afraid Subble killed it. That would have been what precipitated – this. They only burned the forest and cleaned out your room, but the mantas' island—'

They looked out the vision screen and watched the enormous cloud below. The station was orbiting at such a distance that they remained above the general area of the gulf, but even so the effect could be discerned.

'The spores were already in the air—' Áquilon murmured.

'Why would he do a thing like that?' Veg demanded. 'He seemed like a pretty straight guy to me, considering.'

'And me,' Aquilon whispered.

'We may never know. He went to meet the six mantas on the island last night; that's all I know.'

'And he didn't return . . .' she said, staring down.

Diam, reading the compressions and rarefactions of the ambient gases by which these omnivores communicated, understood, just as he had finally grasped the terminal signals of the stronger omnivore

153

on the island. The Subble-creature had achieved dominant status by meeting Pent honourably and crushing him, but even as full communication was attained he was reeling from severe distortion of perception. Subble's intellect, once unmasked, had been monstrously powerful; had the ritual conflict been mental instead of physical, he could have mastered them all in concert. They had had to change off to assimilate it all, even though his mind had wandered erratically and finally lost contact entirely as he died. They had drawn from him all the information they could, and tried to give him what he had come for, but by the time they understood the situation it was too late for him.

Their presence on Earth was already forfeit. Pent's spores would not produce new mantas; the conditions were wrong, and there were no matching spores from others of their kind. But the risk of mutation did exist.

They had come to comprehend, not to destroy. Destruction was a characteristic of the omnivore, not the manta. This was a wilderness world without true order: the life forms were far more vigorous and tenacious than those they had known. But Subble had approached sentience, and his kind deserved its chance.

The omnivore was savage, but with certain redemptions. Diam had known what would happen when he activated Subble's equipment and made the coded report Subble would have made, had his overdrugged mind not destroyed itself. Diam had modified the report only to protect his brothers and the three original contactees, seeing that desire in the man's mind at the end. The omnivore had done his best, and it was proper that his victory and his sacrifice be honoured.

The three lesser omnivores – whose minds, Diam now realized, were also far more powerful than his own, but almost entirely nullified by their physical and sensory limitations – these three had problems he could not comprehend. But it was better to give them the chance to work them out together, than to leave them at the mercy of the corporate omnivore. None of them would have survived that.

Yet his major thought was with Subble, who had expired the way he wanted to: with his mission. Now Subble's incandescence blended with that of the periwinkles and sand dollars and fiddler crabs and Pent's incipient spores, and it was fitting.

Part Two
ORN

Chapter One

ORN

Orn woke exhausted. His body was cold and somewhat sticky, and his muscles were uncertain. He could not remember how he had come here, but he knew it was not safe to yield to his confusion now.

Something was wrong. He lifted his head and forced open eyes that had been sealed shut by goo. At first the brightness hurt him; then it settled to a wan glow as his sensitive eyes protected themselves. He was in a cave, and it was half-light: the start or end of a day. That much he grasped, remembering the inanimate cycle.

He was sprawled awkwardly across cold stone. He wedged four sticky, clumsy limbs under his body ungracefully, then rose to stand with greater confidence on two.

Yes – in the gradually brightening light he made out the flat floor and naturally corrugated ceiling, both descending into darkness beyond him. Nearby was a voluminous tumble of dehydrated stalks: a nest, containing a single monstrous, elongated egg, and sticky fragments of another.

Orn brushed gingerly against the whole egg. Cold – nothing would hatch from this. Beyond it and the nest were rocks and bones and other debris of indeterminate origin. All dead.

He walked unsteadily towards the light, avoiding the scattered joints and droppings and teeth and dehydrated leaves and sticks that lined the track. The exertion warmed his body, and he began to feel better. But with this physical improvement his mind seemed to backslide, to lose coherence. Strange visions passed through his awareness, incredible peripheral memories that could not be his own, that faded as he became aware of them.

He relaxed, not attempting to scrutinize the twitchings of his brain, and then the pictures perversely took on a sharp focus.

Memory. It began far, far back in the half-light, wetter and warmer than since. He floated in a nutrient ocean and absorbed

157

what he required through his spongy skin. He reached for the light, a hundred million years later, needing it ... but recoiled, burned, finding it too fierce to approach. He had to wait, to adapt, and this did not come easily. He held his position and ate what he could and expanded his mass slowly, very slowly, a billion years slowly. But somehow the larger he grew, the greater became his hunger. He could not get enough nourishment. Never enough, never enough ...

The odd memory dissipated as he turned the corner and stood in the stronger light at the cave's mouth. Green shrubbery showed beyond, and the intense grey-white of the sky. This was morning: not the steamy dawn of twenty million years ago, but a chilly and empty rising of the sun.

The corpse of a mighty bird lay on the ground, astride the opening of the cave. In life it might have stood so tall as to brush the very ceiling, and it had a thick, slightly curved beak, stubby wings, and cruel, forward-reaching talons. Under the disarray of grey feathers the long strong muscles of the thighs still bunched, as though it had been running – or fighting – when it died. The powerful neck was twisted so that the head stared stiffly to the side, and dried blood fouled the upper plumes. One eye peered into the sun, the orb already shrunken with the dehydration of its tissues. Once-handsome tail feathers were broken off in the dirt.

There had been a desperate battle, and the bird had lost, but the victor had not paused to consume the flesh. This too was strange.

Looking at her – for he recognized the corpse as female as readily as he was coming to identify all the things he saw – Orn felt a vague alarm. He did not conjecture the meaning of his own awakening beside the abandoned nest of this creature, nor did he wonder what had vanquished her. Instead he searched his troubled memory – and found the bird within.

Sixty to eighty million years ago the hot-bodied aves had completed their divergence from their rep ancestry, conserving the produce of their internal furnaces by means of scales lengthening into fluffy down. They lived in tall pines and rocky gullies, where it grew cold at night, and needed continuous warmth in order to stay alert and alive in those windy heights. They spread all four legs with strengthened coverts to add buoyancy, and leaped and glided to safety at the slightest provocation. For some of the predator reps could climb, and all were hungry. The tree-leaper who fell to the ground was dead, and not from the fall.

But soon one line of aves had grown too large to escape through the air, and while its light-boned, light-brained cousins ascended ever higher into the sky and pumped their expanding front wings and let the hind wings shrivel into claws, this nether line planted its hind limbs firmly in the dread earth and discarded flight. Here only the fleet of foot survived at all, and the strong of beak, and the firm of memory. They had to run at times, and fight at times, and to know without hesitation when each was appropriate in the stronghold of the reps.

They succeeded. They were able to forage in colder areas than the reps, and to travel at night. Other land-bound lines diverged.

All this Orn knew, his memory triggered by the need, by the sight of this ultimate bird. She was not a creature of terror to him, but of history, who had come fifty million years along her line to die so brutally before this cave. Orn did not sorrow for her; such was the nature of existence. The weak, the careless, the unlucky – these died and were replaced by others.

He stepped around the body and stood in the sun. A towering pine ascended from the nearby turf, as ancient and grand in its fashion as the bird. The ground was covered with tall ferns, and cycads shook their fronds in the light breeze. Similar plants had dominated the landscape for a very long time, Orn knew. Only recently had others come to contest the land, and those others had not been very successful here.

He scratched the ground experimentally while the rising sun took the chill off the land. His digits were feeble and tender compared to the thick horned toes of the dead bird, but a few tentative scrapes exposed the underlying structure. Beneath the surface leaves and twigs and needles lay a spongy humus teeming with its own awakening life. He put one eye down and concentrated, bringing the miniature landscape into focus.

Here were cricks and roaches and black-shelled beets busily scavenging microscopic debris. Tiny springs, those wingless arths who jumped by flipping forked tails against the ground – these too scrambled for cover, disliking the sun.

Orn knew them. The arths had diverged very long ago, so far back that he had no memory of their early evolution. Somewhere – sometime in that hot sea as he struggled between the freezing darkness and the burning light and satisfied his compelling hunger by growing into an absorptive cup, a cylinder, a blob with an internal gut, as he extruded fins and nascent flukes and swam erratically after game, and formed eyes to harness the light at last and gills to breathe the water and the lateral line system to navigate by – somewhere during that complex billion-year development that preceded his rise to land the little arths had taken their own mysterious but highly successful course. Now they crawled and flew and fashioned webs and hives and cocoons and burrows and lived their hasty lives in many-legged, many-winged, virtually mindless certainty ...

Orn moved on, observing everything but questioning nothing. Timorous hairy mams scooted from his path, afraid of him; these represented innocuous lines. He travelled a shallow valley that led gradually downward towards a body of water. Soft, flat vegetation of the new type crowded the edge of the water and floated on the surface, an increasing amount of it bearing flowers. Small fish, piscs, flashed where a streamlet flowed over naked stone and coursed between round mossy rocks; they were an ancient and multiple line, and now and then one came to kiss the surface of the lake.

Once more Orn remembered: the flowing water was a different medium from the passive depths of the sea, as different in its fashion as air from land. The flaccid flesh of the calm ocean depths had had to develop a stiffened but flexible rod of gristle along its length, lest it be tumbled into danger by the new phenomenon of current. To this gristle the expanding muscle tissue was anchored; progress was no longer random but forward, against the flow. Before his line diverged from that of the piscs, they had invaded the less-habited regions up the current, and changed in the process. The spinal rod protected increasingly important nerves, for coordination had become essential; then the gristle hardened into cartilage and then into bone. The skeleton was the gift of flowing fresh water, and so the land had already affected life in the sea.

But the rivers of the past were fast and shallow, and they flowed from the bleak inhospitable mass of substance that formed the continent, and from time to time the ambitious swimmer was stranded in some stagnant pool. He had to gulp life from the surface, even as these fish in the lake did now, and hold the bubble in his mouth in an effort to absorb from it the breath that had left the

160

water. But his mouth was now encumbered with jaws and teeth and tongue, all needed for feeding. Thus he was forced to develop a special cavity in the throat, a bag, a chamber – a lung. When the water of his isolated pool finally sank to nothing, his fins had to strengthen into four stout limbs to support the body against the gut-wrenching land gravity, and the new lungs sustained life entirely. It was a brief but awful trek, that first journey over the cruel land, and almost every fish who tried it perished; but that fraction who were not only determined and strong but fortunate as well – Orn's own line – won reprieve in a deeper, fresher pool.

Orn remembered the orignal home: the water. He remembered the gradually lengthening adventures over a land inhabited only by pulpy vegetation and rapidly scrambling arths, until most of his life was spent upon it and he was no longer a true fish. He remembered the hardening of the rind around the soft eggs, until they withstood to some extent the ravages of sun and air. A small step, but significant, for it meant that the sea had let slip its last lingering hold. A complete life cycle could occur without the intervention of the ocean.

By the shore of the lake he found the body of the male bird. This one, too, had perished violently – but unlike his mate, he had taken his enemy with him. A long, powerful rep lay belly-up on the sand, its tail in water, its eyes two bloody sockets, its gut an open cavity. Gore on the beak and talons of the bird betrayed the savagery of its attack, here at the fringe of the rep's demesne; but the scattered feathers and blood on its breast showed that the teeth of the croc had not fastened on empty air.

Had the rep reached water before the bird attacked, the rep would have won the battle easily. But it had not, perhaps because of wounds inflicted by the female bird. Now all three combatants were food for the clustered flies.

The croc: as Orn gazed at it he comprehended the course it had taken since its ancestors branched away from his own, more recently than the fishes. His line had stayed on land in the trees before returning to the ground, climbing and leaping from branch to branch, becoming warm of body, omnivorous of diet, and highly specialized of brain. But the croc had returned part way to the water, hiding behind horny skin, preying on anything that fell in or strayed too near.

This time the croc had ventured too far from its region of strength, perhaps seeking to raid the enormous eggs in the cave nest while one bird was absent, thinking the remaining bird would not fight . . .

Orn did not attempt to work out the details further in his mind. He was weak and tired and alone, and now ravenously hungry. His heritage of memory finally closed the gap between his evolution and himself, and he undertood that there would be no outside help for his distress. He was a member of the most advanced species yet to tread the earth of this world – but he had nothing more to sustain him at the moment than his generalized body and the knowledge within him of the genesis of living things.

He did not pause to consider what would have happened had the croc reached the two eggs before the parent birds returned, or the happenstance that the elder egg had been on the verge of hatching the instant the fatal encounter took place. The mother's warmth had been taken away at the critical moment, forcing activity or death for the chick. He did not ponder the coincidence of destiny; he did not contemplate revenge. His mind was designed for far-reaching, comprehensive racial memory rather than true thought. Racial memory was his instrument of survival – a device like none ever employed by another species.

Orn shook out his stubby, still-featherless wings and advanced on the piled meat before him. Flies swarmed up as his beak chopped down. He was hungry, and there was no one to feed him.

Chapter Two

AQUILON

For two days they orbited: three humans and seven mantas. The shell was tiny for ten occupants, the sanitary facilities embarrassingly unsophisticated and, the food monotonous. But the mantas were siblings who could range leagues or freeze in place for hours without suffering, and the human beings were two men and a woman said to be beautiful. Because the mantas were of fungoid metabolism (though this description was about as precise as 'heated protoplasm' might be for the humans), their body processes complemented those of the humans, freshening the air to a certain extent. It was a tidy circumstance, though machine revitalization was still essential for oxygen.

Nevertheless, it was crowded.

By the time the shuttle came to grapple the capsule and haul it in entire for decontamination, the trio had talked out almost everything inconsequential.

The mantas faced each other in a ring, or perhaps a seven-pointed star, or yet again a hemisphere, depending on how one viewed the topology of the shell's interior. Each gazed for a period of seconds into the eye of his opposite, three pairs engaged at all times, one individual sitting out. Then the pattern would shift for new combinations. What philosophies they contemplated so raptly Aquilon could not guess, but certainly something was being discussed at length. She cursed her female curiosity, but did not attempt to query a manta.

There was a jolt as the capsule was caught by the shuttle and braked. The spin that had provided a kind of gravity stopped, and they all had to cling to handholds to keep from somersaulting in free-fall. The mantas had no hands, but each had a mass approaching fifty pounds in normal gravity; they bounced against the wall and each other like so many huge rubber balls. She almost laughed.

163

'Prepare for decontamination,' the speaker said.

Veg braced himself before the exit port, automatically assuming the lead for what promised to be an unpleasant procedure. Aquilon had been through it before, of course, as had the two men – but familiarity did not bring composure. Decontamination covered a good deal more than the external physique.

Watching Veg, Aquilon smiled, though not with her lips. She was tall for a woman, but Veg dwarfed her. He was as powerful a man as she had ever met, with one exception she preferred not to think about. She peered at his broad back through the mesh of blonde hair waving across her face in the free-fall. Who would normally suspect this two-fisted roughneck of compulsive passion for the well-being of all living creatures? Yet it was so. Only against men did Veg use his muscle, and then by way of demonstration, rather than coercion, except in rare instances.

She removed her gaze, and it fell naturally on the other man. Cal was superficially the opposite of Veg. He was tiny – hardly up to her own shoulder, and thin and weak. But his mind was frighteningly sharp, capable of appalling concepts, and he had the courage of his strange convictions. Cal seemed to fear death not at all; indeed, he seemed almost to worship it.

Aquilon loved both men. The physical side of her leaned towards Veg, the intellectual towards Cal. Yet it was Veg's intellectual example she followed now, for she had stopped eating meat, fish, and fowl. She needed something tangible that she had not been able to find or assess, except that it related to them. And both men believed they needed *her* – but the truth, it seemed to her, was that they needed each other, and she was only in the way. They had been good companions before she met them – better than they were now, though neither man spoke of the subtle, insidious change occurring. Could she abscond with Veg's body and Cal's mind? Was she selfish enough to interpose her femininity (more bluntly, her female-ness) between them, drawing to herself the life-preserving dialogue they had for each other?

It would be better if she stepped out of their lives entirely. If only she had the ability to devise a clean exit, and the emotional stamina to follow through . . .

Now, she thought sadly. Now, during the decontamination. They segregated the sexes for that, thank God, and she could simply request a transfer to some other planet, and she would never see them again, even for a fond farewell. It would break her heart, but she had to do it.

'Cancel,' said the speaker, and she jumped guiltily. The port remained sealed. 'Your unit is to be transshipped entire. There will be no processing.'

Veg looked about, perplexed. 'This isn't SOP,' he said.

Cal frowned. 'That business below may have put us in a special category. One of their agents died—'

'Subble,' she said tersely. 'Subble died.' She had only known the man, really, for four hours, and known him as an enemy. But it was as though a lover was gone.

'And the problem the manta represents is critical. They may have decided not to expose any of the station personnel to—'

'But what about the *Earth* germs?' Aquilon demanded. 'Decon is both ways. We don't want to infect Nacre with—'

The communications screen glowed. A face appeared, supported by the lapels and insignia of the Space Police. 'Your attention please. Your attention please.'

'Does he mean us? Does he mean us?' Aquilon inquired mockingly in the same tone. She resented being treated impersonally.

'If they had television, why did they use the speaker all this time?' Veg wanted to know.

Cal smiled. 'That's still the speaker. The picture has merely been added. It means we've switched from voice to film.'

'About time, after two days,' Veg said, missing the irony.

The face on the screen frowned. 'This is a live transmission. I am addressing you three in the capsule. I can hear you.'

Veg closed his mouth, embarrassed at having been overheard. Aquilon had to suppress her smile. She also envied him his essential simplicity.

'Please respond as I call your names,' the man said. 'Vachel E. Smith.'

There was a silence. Aquilon noted Cal struggling similarly to void a smile. Veg did not like his proper name, and seldom answered to it. After the tedious confinement here, he was even less likely than usual to be tractable in the face of authority.

'Vachel E. Smith!' the official repeated impatiently.

'What's *your* name, noodlebrain?' Veg demanded. This time Aquilon did let out a noisy breath, attracting a momentary glance from the interrogator. She felt giddy, as though she were a schoolgirl testing the grouchy teacher. Confinement and near-free-fall could do that, particularly after the horror they had so recently experienced on Earth. They were all acting like gradeschoolers – but she felt like enjoying it while she could. It took her mind off what she would have to do.

The man in the screen brought up a clipboard and made a checkmark. 'Deborah D. Hunt?'

Suddenly Aquilon appreciated Veg's ire. She had fallen out of the habit of using her own name since meeting Veg and Cal, and the derogatory nickname imposed on her during a childhood illness had become her badge of honour. She even signed her paintings with it. Now her real name sounded strange and obnoxious, an epithet rather than an identification.

The officer made another check. 'Calvin B. Potter?'

'Present,' Cal said, not acceding to foolish gestures. 'All present. What is your business with us?'

'Wait a minute,' Aquilon cried mischievously. 'You haven't checked off the others.'

'Others?' The officer peered at her.

'The mantas. They're individuals too. As long as you're calling off names by remote control—'

Veg broke into a grin. 'Yeah. Everyone gets on the roll. Call 'em off.'

'The animals hardly qualify for—'

'I should advise you,' Cal said to the screen, 'that the mantas do comprehend human speech to a certain extent, even though they may not choose to acknowledge it. Actually, they are somewhat more civilized than we are, but their definitions differ from ours.'

'That's *why* they're more civilized,' Aquilon said.

The officer maintained his composure, obviously comprehending the ridicule. 'I do not have names for the fungoids.'

'It's very simple,' Aquilon said, hoping her twinkle didn't show. 'Each manta is represented by a characteristic symbol rather like a snowflake, no two alike. If you have an oscilloscope handy, they might feed in the patterns—' She hesitated, not wanting to confess how recently the trio had acquired this information. Cal had suspected it for some time, but it had taken Subble to break through and achieve complete communication – by whatever means would be forever a mystery. Now Subble and one manta were dead, but the other mantas demonstrated by their reactions that they understood a good deal of man's vocabulary and custom. The period in the capsule had brought out the eight names and a system for limited dialogue.

'If you will provide the names, I will add them to my roster,' the officer said.

'Well, first there's the symbol of the line,' she said brightly. 'Of course it isn't exactly a line, but to our crude human perception that's the closest—'

'The name, please.'

'Lin. Lin for Line.'

One of the mantas bounced from one side of the capsule to the other, and ricocheted to the communication screen. Its single foot struck the oblong of light squarely.

The officer flinched. 'Lin,' he said, marking it down.

There was now a faint line across the screen, cut into the plastic by an unseen slash of the manta's whiplike tail. If Aquilon had had any doubt before about the ability of these creatures to understand human dialogue, this dispelled it. Intrigued, she strung out the game.

'Next we have the symbol of the circle, Circe. She's the one who stayed with me, and fed off the rats in the cellar-farm. Of course the mantas are all neuter, technically; only their spores have sex. But since she stayed with me, and *I'm* female—'

'Circe,' the officer said, not rising to that particular bait. 'The sorceress.'

A second manta caromed off the screen. Behind it was left a neat circle. The juxtaposition of symbols made a bisected loop. '*Not* the sorceress,' Aquilon said. 'The circle, as you see it there.' But she wondered whether the man's observation didn't have merit.

'And the triangle, Tri,' she continued. The third manta added a triangle, its three points neatly touching the perimeter.

The officer allowed his mouth to fall open momentarily. This was impressive sleight of hand. He was not ready to believe that the mantas themselves were responsible for the geometric markings so accurately inscribed. 'Tri,' he said.

167

'And the diamond, Diam,' The parallelogram was added to the figure.

Aquilon became serious. 'Unfortunately the pentagram, Pent, is not with us. He – died. We don't know exactly how or why, but we think it has something to do with your agent Subble, who is also dead. You dropped a missile on the island and killed some citizens—'

Yes, she thought. The spores of the dead manta were in the atmosphere, threatening to contaminate all Earth and perhaps mutate its tame molds and fungi, harming its food-protein industry. So a Florida resort area had been bombed in the attempt to eradicate those spores. It had not been pretty.

After that she didn't feel like playing the game any more, so Veg took over. 'Hex,' he said. 'He was *my* manta, in the forest. The forest you burned to the ground—'

'I neither originate nor execute landside policy,' the officer said primly. 'Nor am I informed about it. I'm sure there was good reason for whatever action was taken.'

'*Omnivore* reason,' Aquilon muttered. The omnivore she meant was man, the most brutal killer known, and the only one who rationalized the misdeeds of his brother by pretending not to be responsible.

'And Star,' Veg continued. 'One of the six who stayed with Cal. And Oct, the last one.'

The screen was now thickly crossed with lines, all geometric figures inscribed within the circle as though constructed by compass and straight edge. The officers image came through as though he stood behind transparent stained glass.

'I believe I have all the names now,' he said. 'It is my duty to inform you ten that computer headquarters has recommended that you be assigned to a new mission. You will not be returning to Nacre.'

Aquilon exchanged glances with the two men, and the mantas looked at each other. The harried officer was having the last laugh after all!

'In fact, you will not be visiting any of the listed planets, and it is unlikely that you will ever return to Earth. This is not to be considered an exile so much as—'

The voice continued, but Aquilon tuned it out internally,

168

horrified. Banishment, not only from Earth but from all known colonies! So that was their punishment for the trouble the mantas had caused by their presence on Earth. She should have known that the powers that governed the planet would not destroy several billion dollars worth of development and landscape and wipe out a number of innocent lives, and then merely reprimand those who were to be the scapegoats. The trio had broken the law by importing unauthorized alien creatures to Earth, as many travellers did. They had not intended any harm – but this time great harm had come.

No, she could not protest lifetime exile. Worse things were possible. She had wanted desperately to leave Earth again, yet now that her wish was being granted, she felt perversely nostalgic. She did not *like* Earth or feel at ease upon it – but it still was harsh to be denied it for life.

However, that did not really affect her decision to separate from the two men. That had made it impossible for her to go to Nacre anyway.

'... first habitable alternate, as determined by soil, sea, and air samples,' the officer was saying. She had missed something important! 'But there are several problems. First, our connection is tenuous. We can ferry any amount of material over, but only when the phase is proper – and that's infrequent. Second, we can not alter the point of contact without risking complete severance, and it could take us a century to re-establish contact if we lost it now.'

That didn't sound like ordinary space travel. But he had used the word 'alternate'. Could this mean—?

'And, unfortunately, this contact occurs under the ground. We have sent in borers to open passages to the surface, but another complication—'

She tried to pay attention, but her mind refused. An alternate world! This was exploration of an entirely different order. But if it were another Earth, why was it the 'first habitable'? That implied that there were others unfit for human occupation. What true 'Earth' could be unfit, except a devastated one? And even for another Earth, there should be decontamination processing; a virus virulent on one world should thrive on the other, if introduced.

No, she did not like the sound of this.

Cal's silent touch on her thigh jogged her to attention. He was not looking at her, and she would have supposed the contact to be accidental had she not known that nothing Cal ever did was accidental. Particularly not a goose with the thumb. She followed his gaze.

There was a map on the screen – a globe marked off with meridians of longitude and latitude, as though it were the Earth proper. But the continents and great islands were strange; it was obviously a different world.

Cal touched her again. Then she understood. She unobtrusively brought out her pad and brush and quickly sketched the outlines of the map. As she worked, the geography was replaced by the face of the officer, but she held the prior image in her mind and continued to work on the picture, employing the trained short-term eidetic memory that helped make her the artist she was. Cal would have good reason for this subtle directive – reason he did not want the officer to know.

She put the finishing touches on the map as the dialogue continued, then quietly put the pad away. What secrets had Cal read in this seemingly routine illustration? She was now alive with female curiosity. But how would she learn, if she were to part from the two men now? For that matter, how would she deliver the map to Cal? She could not pass it over now without giving away the show.

'Your assignment is to enter this alternate and make casual survey of its flora, fauna, and, as far as practicable, its mineral resources. You'll be supplied from Earth, but there may be danger. You'll be expected to report—'

'Yeah, we know the route,' Veg said. 'We did it on Nacre, remember?'

The officer bore with this insolence. 'Radio relay to the transfer point, where the recording will be brought back at such time as this phase permits, probably within two months. Analogous but not identical to your prior—' He paused. 'I have just been informed that an excellent contact has developed in the past few minutes. Perfect phase, but it won't last long. We may have to wait a month for another, so we'll act immediately.' He paused again, verifying instructions from an offscreen source. 'The port will open. Move at once to the transmission chamber. Good luck.'

Once more they exchanged glances. This was too sudden, too

convenient; even Veg realized that. They were not being told something. Ordinarily the wheels of Earthly bureaucracy preferred a month to a minute for even a minor decision. Why should—

The port opened.

Before the humans could move, the mantas did. Three of them angled around Veg and launched through the hole, flaring into the flying shape as they emerged into the pressured connecting tube. There were no other spacelocks here; the passage entered the main station directly. The three were out of sight in a moment.

'What?' Veg exclaimed.

Then he piled out after them, determined to find out what they were doing. Cal and Aquilon followed. The four remaining mantas stayed in the shell, motionless.

Shouts and noises sounded ahead. Aquilon pulled herself along by the deep corrugations of the tube, floating after the men. She was surprised the mantas had been able to move so well in free-fall – though she realized, now that she thought about it, that it was air resistance that stabilized them, not gravity. They were like powered kites, perpetually tacking against the wind, except that they were doing the moving, not the air. One pushing foot, one sail —

There was gravity inside the station proper. A guard was rolling on the floor, clutching his hand. Aquilon stopped automatically to help him – and recognized the clean wound of a manta attack. The manta's tail was a deadly weapon, capable of indenting a television screen – or of severing the human hand from its wrist. In this instance the hand had only been cut. She saw the anesthetic gun on the floor and realized that the manta had merely disarmed the man. Few people could fire before a charging manta struck.

But why? Why had those three mantas bolted?

'They were going to ambush us,' Veg said angrily, watching the guard. 'Kill us out of hand—'

'Ridiculous,' Cal snapped. Somewhere down the hall there was a continued commotion, and cries of anguish. 'There are innumerable ways they could have dispatched us and the mantas without ever releasing us from the capsule, had they wanted to. Those three mantas provoked this.'

'Then why did that bastard have his gun drawn?' Veg demanded. 'He never could have reached it if he waited until he saw them.'

He was right. The guard had to be waiting with the weapon ready,

171

or he would have been struck down with it still in his holster. Or, more likely, not struck at all, since the manta would not have *had* to disarm him. But Cal was right too, for it was a sleep-gun, not a kill-gun.

Then she remembered: no deadly weapons were permitted in a normal orbiting station. The risk to personnel was too great, but that answered only the smallest part of it. The guard could have been instructed to stand by with weapon at the ready, just in case; that did not necessarily constitute aggressive intent. He would have tried to use it when he saw the horror shape of the manta coming at him, however.

She helped the guard to his feet. 'Better get over to sick bay, mister. Your hand's laid open to the bone, and that's arterial bleeding. Next time remember: never point a weapon at a manta. They know what guns are, and their reflexes are faster than yours.'

Dazed, the man departed. She wondered how it would have turned out had the guard been an agent. Agents' reflexes were super fast, and with the gun already drawn – but the mantas had obviously been ready for trouble. Could there have been such an encounter between Subble and Pent on the defunct island? Had Subble won, then been killed by the others? She really would have to inquire about that.

'I think we'd better get back to the capsule and wait,' Cal said. 'We weren't ambushed – but we weren't told the truth, either. I'm sure the mantas had reason for moving out like that. Notice how neatly executed it was – three took off, four sat tight.'

They returned with alacrity. The four mantas remained, immobile as the fungi they were kin to. Somewhere in the bowels of the station a commotion continued, showing that the three were still on the rampage. The screen in the shell was still lighted, but now no face showed.

Cal faced the mantas. 'All right, comrades – what is your purpose? Are we in immediate danger?'

One of the four flexed its tail twice, making a double snap: the signal for 'no'.

'Maybe they went beserk!' Veg cried. 'Being cooped up for so long—'

Three snaps: question mark.

172

'Berserk,' Cal explained, first to recognize the problem. 'Going wild, acting unreasonably, making unnecessary trouble. A form of insanity.'

Again the tail: no.

'Find out whom we're talking to,' Aquilon suggested, wondering how long they would be allowed before station personnel closed in. 'And who's left.' She was not in the line of sight of the answering manta, but it made no difference. They had no ears, yet picked up human speech and other sounds quite nicely by seeing the compressions and rarefactions of the atmosphere that comprised sound. In effect, they could hear with their eyes – and very well, too.

Four snaps, answering her implied query. 'Diam,' she said recognizing the code. The four-sided symbol, the diamond.

Another manta moved: two snaps. 'Circe,' she said. 'The two-sided symbol – inside and outside. I'm glad you're still here.' It was a foolish sentiment, but it did seem to her that she could tell her erstwhile companion from the others, and that Circe had more personality, more feminine attributes.

A third snapped: six. 'Hex,' Veg said. 'My pal. I knew it was you. You have more savvy than those others.'

Personification, she thought.

And at last: seven. 'Star.'

'That means Lin, Tri, and Oct are gone,' Cal said. 'But we still don't know why. We weren't in physical danger – none that we weren't in all along, at least. They must have had a reason, just as the station personnel had one for rushing us. I think we'd better discover what that reason is. I wish we'd taught them Morse code.'

'The mantas only learn what they choose to learn,' Aquilon said. 'We're lucky they communicate at all. They never did before.'

'Your attention, please.' It was the officer on the screen again. 'There has been a disturbance.'

'Now he tells us,' Veg muttered.

'Your beasts attacked station personnel. We had understood they were tame.'

'That's why you had guns on 'em,' Veg said sarcastically. 'Real brave.'

'How can civilized individuals be "tame"?' Aquilon demanded in her turn. 'Do you have tame men, tame computers?' But she wondered. She *had* thought there had been an understanding with

173

the mantas, and this breach of manners didn't jibe. Why had they done it?

'What happened to the three?' Cal asked, more practical.

'One is dead. The men cornered it with bayonets and stabbed it through the eye. The others—'

Aquilon flinched, knowing how terrible a wound of that type was to a manta. The eye constituted the substantial majority of its apperceptive mass; a blind manta was virtually a dead manta, except for the suffering.

'How many men dead?' Cal inquired softly.

'No fatalities. Our men are trained for trouble. Several lesser casualties, however – mostly cuts on the hands.'

Thank God, she thought. The mantas weren't on a killing spree. They were merely trying to avoid capture. But again: why?

'We're in a hurry,' the officer said. 'Ordinarily there would be severe repercussions – but the phase is beginning to slip. Can you keep your remaining animals under control?'

'Yes,' Cal said before anyone else could comment. Aquilon understood, then. The station personnel still thought the mantas were merely pets – dangerous when out of control, but basically subject to man's will. The demonstration of the manta's geometric ability had been deemed a stunt, no more. If these people realized the truth, after what had just happened—

And she had been trying to blab it out! She could have cost the lives of all the mantas!

That made one more reason to separate from this group, to go her own lonely way. They would survive better without her.

But Veg was hustling her along, and this time the mantas followed docilely behind. They had made their move, whatever it was. She was unable to make hers.

She felt a terrible relief.

Chapter Three

ORN

It was an island he dwelt on. Orn's explorations had long since verified that no exit from it existed for him, since he could not fly and did not care to swim. But his memory informed him that this bit of land, which he could cross many times in the course of a single day without fatigue, was not the total of the world. He was able to appreciate its recent history to a certain extent because there were evidences of many prior nestings of his species, and his memory suggested that land had been here several million years ago. Spot details, such as the cave he had hatched within, were too transitory to register; but the body of rock itself was stable enough to be familiar.

Orn's ancestors had ranged the entire continent, mapping its shifting configurations in the memory of fifty million years. Orn saw portions of the whole whenever he contemplated the local landscape. He was aware that this island was a tiny fringe of the great land mass, a part of it really, despite the gulf of sea cutting between them. The island rode the continent's western perimeter. He was aware too that the continent itself was moving, and had already travelled many times the breadth of the island, though slowly. Ponderous upheavals had split the original continent apart, fragmenting it. Though changing bridges of rock connected the new subcontinents, the last of these had severed hardly ten million years ago, isolating an entire ecological population. The influx of new species of animal from far regions had halted, ranging grounds had become comparatively restricted, and the increasing violence of the geography had led to the decline of certain established creatures and the sudden rise of others. The great reps had largely vacated the cool northern regions and the mountainous terrain, though they still predominated in the southern marshes. The tiny mams had overrun those deserted areas and, more importantly the orders of aves had

175

flourished. A new balance of nature had occurred.

Orn's memory faded out for the most recent period. It required many generations for the racial record to become firmly established, so that he was clearest on the situation of five to twenty million years before. Prior to that period his memory became more general, being specific only in relation to his own line. Even much of that had faded as he grew farther away from the egg; he no longer remembered the impressions of swimming or conquering the land.

Some recent images were clear but uncertain, others foggy, and some so transient as to be meaningless. Had his parents lived, they would have educated him to the specifics of contemporary existence; memory was less important than example for day-to-day life. Lower creatures like the arths made do entirely on memory – but this would not do for himself. His own experiences would be added to that mass of memory already inscribed within his genes, strengthening some images infinitesimally and weakening others that were no longer applicable. His descendants would benefit accordingly.

The western section of this travelling subcontinent had buckled as it moved, tripping over the sea floor it overrode in its geologically precipitous traverse. An expansive shallow interior sea arm had drained away as the land wrinkled into a tremendous mountain range instead. Thus one natural barrier had been replaced by another, and the range was still rising as Orn's memory faded out. The flora had changed rapidly here; flowering plants had spread explosively over the highlands, leaving the old varieties to the warmer lowland coastlines.

Orn knew the geologic history of his present island mainly by extrapolation from precedent. This was a volcanic framework. It had risen out of the sea as the residue of frequent emissions of liquid stone and airborne ash. From a single cone it had grown to three, all feeding on that same restlessness inspired by the larger motion of the continent much as thunderstorms fed on the motions of large air masses. Though two cones had subsided, the third and smallest still erupted periodically over the centuries. Orn had seen the traces of its erstwhile furies, recognizing the typical configurations though the vegetation now covered them richly. It was from its subterranean furnace that the heat had come to make the island pleasant; Orn's memory implied that the surrounding geography grew distressingly cold in winter – too cold for his kind to nest.

It was summer now, better than a year after his rude awakening here. Orn had grown to better than half the mass of the avian parents he had never known in life, whose rotting flesh had sustained him those first difficult days after hatching. They had done that for him, at least: given him food when he was too small to hunt effectively himself. Now his feathers had filled out comfortably, white around the neck and handsome grey on the breast, and his wings and tail were sturdy. He could twist his neck to reach any part of his body, and his beak was a respectable weapon. His thighs were well muscled for running, and his flesh well toned. He had grown up strong and fleet and smart; had it been otherwise, he would not have grown up at all, even in this protected locale.

He was aware that most birds of his type had parental care in the chick state, and were sheltered from the savagery of climate and predators. He had suffered, at first. But he was also aware that his particular parents had chosen their nesting site well; few really dangerous animals lived here. The croc that brought tragedy had come wandering from another isle, a loner, and with its demise the area had been rendered safe again. Occasionally Orn had seen another such croc swim by, but had hidden and it had not noticed him. Yes – his parents, by their sacrifice, had made it possible for him to survive even without their immediate care. They had been resourceful birds.

Once, he knew by the traces, many couples had nested here, and many eggs had hatched. Now he was alone; somehow his species had declined over the millennia along with the reps. Oh, there were birds on the island – more lines than ever before – but none of his own species. He did not wonder why the same circumstance that encouraged a general avian radiation simultaneously discouraged his particular line; he merely knew it was so. He did feel a general loss, a loneliness, and was from time to time disturbed by it.

Now, as he grew into his second year, he became aware of a more immediate problem. The island underpinning was building up to one of its periodic eruptions. He could feel the ground shuddering and swelling, and he could see and smell the increasing gases emerging from the active cone. He read the multiple signals: danger.

The other creatures were aware of it too, but largely helpless. Fish floated belly-up in ponds grown hot; tiny, warmbodied multis

177

scrambled by day in the open, driven from their caved-in burrows. Birds hovered in the sky, afraid to perch for long on uncannily vibrating branches.

The aves at least could fly; Orn could not. Had he thought in those terms, he might have envied his distant cousins their ability to depart so readily. But he knew that physical escape was only part of it; their home was being destroyed as much as his own was. He paced the shore facing the mainland, peering at the mountainous vista so near by air, so far by water. He was not an efficient swimmer, and the sea had its own threats.

Yet even the mainland was restive. Dark clouds drifted above the mountains as other great cones vented their fury. There were tremours not of the island alone, but of the area, and the tide was off schedule.

He had to remove himself from this locale. He would not have chosen to travel in a half-grown state, but survival required it. He had to get across the water and away from the shore, and soon. But how?

Any decision he might have made became irrelevant. The crisis was on him even as he balked at the water.

A tremendous quake shook the island, making the ocean dance and the trees splinter and tumble. The ground lifted, dropped, and lifted again, throwing him violently on the side. As he scrambled back from the beach large cracks opened in the ground, grinding against each other noisily and spewing up gravel and mud. The sea pulled back momentarily, as though afraid; then it rushed at the beach in mighty waves, smashing into the rocks and foliage there and foaming well beyond the normal high-tide limit. The water was brown, and where it passed a coating of mud and debris remained.

Then it was very quiet, but Orn knew that the island was doomed. His ancestors had tended to nest in similar places, and had met this situation before, and the warnings in his memory were lucid. He had to flee it, for there was no memory of those who had not done so; none of those had become his ancestor.

That memory also guided his course of action. He ran to the single river that wound down from the oldest and largest mountain and gathered token tributaries to itself. There should be trees in it now – floating trunks toppled by the quake and wrestled about by the current. He might board one there, where he could reach it, and ride

178

it into the sea. With that extra mass and buoyancy he might achieve the crossing he could not hope to accomplish alone.

His trip was wasted. The river had been dammed by a mass of rock, and was already backing up into what would develop into a small lake. There were floating logs – but on the wrong side of that barrier.

Again the ground shook, less violently but more persistently than the last time. Before the vibration subsided there was a subterranean *snap*! followed by a different and, to Orn, more ominous type of rumbling.

Alarmed, he looked up at the tremendous elder mountain. His fear was justified: yellowish gas was rising from its weathered cone. The fire mountains never really died.

Even as he looked, a vent opened in the side of the cone and a monstrous belch of vapour emerged. It formed a bulging cloud, completely opaque, that gathered, swelled, and *rolled* down the incline towards the river. Behind it was conflagration: a swath of blistered rock, shorn of its former veneer of life.

The cloud was large – he could see the top of it even as it dipped into the gully of the river several miles upstream. He heard the hiss of boiling water, and in a moment saw the cloud expand enormously as water vapour distended it.

The mountain trembled again, roused into action by the initial quake and now finished with the preliminaries. From the vent in its side poured a golden syrup, splashing down the smoking channel left by the cloud. Where it spread to touch the fringe of vegetation, flames erupted and smoke gouted up. The lava, like the gas, obliterated everything in its path except the ground itself.

Orn knew about this also. Perhaps the searching molten rock would solidify and stop before reaching the sea, but probably more would come, overriding the first mass as it cooled, until the entire island lay buried beneath it and all life was gone.

Fire now raged through the forest, charging the air with its odours. Minor tremours continued. Tiny animals fled the forest and milled on the beach, doomed.

Orn waded into the water, knowing he could not afford to wait longer. There was a chance that the ocean predators would be frightened or confused by the shocks, or even stunned, so that he could swim across with no more than the water to contend with. A chance – but he entertained no unrealistic hopes.

The water appeared calm from a distance, but this was illusory. The surface had been churned into ugly foam. Hidden objects banged into his feet and chafed his legs, and the violent currents beneath the froth tugged strenuously at his balance, He flapped his wings, fouling them in the dirty spray, and held his beak high – but for nothing. He was soon swept off his feet and dunked in the grainy liquid.

He swam, using his legs as ballast and rudder, while paddling messily with his wings. Aquatic birds had webbed feet, but his own were clawed and virtually useless for propulsion in the water. Everything was wrong for him; he was poorly structured for swimming and had to hold his head low lest he capsize. That interfered with visibility. His nictitating membranes protected his eyes from the salt spume, but the constant dousing inhibited his breathing. He was not enjoying himself.

Storm clouds gathered overhead and wind whipped savagely across the surface. Orn rode the growing swells, up and down, up and down, fighting for equilibrium and orientation. The gusts of air were warm, not cool, and carried the stifling fumes of the volcano. Substance descended from the storm above – not rain but particles of rock-ash that chipped away at his feathers and smeared his plumage dark. Only his acute sense of direction kept him facing the invisible mainland.

Then his feet banged into something solid. For a moment he thought he had made it across, but his vector sense reminded him that this was impossible. But he was also far from the island. A sand bar must have developed since the crossings of his ancestors, for there was no hint of shallow water here in his memory. Full grown, the prior crossers had been more powerful swimmers and had made competent surveys of the local geography; there was a firm image of deep water here. The contours of the land and island had changed, fuzzing their images, but the depth of the water had been stable.

He stood, and the ocean fell away around him while the windborne fragments pelted down. A ridge of land ascended from the waves, mottled with fragments of seaweed.

No – this was no sand bar, though the bottom was not as deep as it had been at one time. Instead, the water was receding, laying bare the ocean floor.

He could walk to the other side, but he realized that the chances for his survival had just dropped again. To the earthquakes and volcanos had been added a third threat.

He trod upon an old-time coral reef, the shells now largely broken and compacted. Great sponges branched out of the crevices, and jellyfish lay sprawled helplessly. Most of the true fish had escaped with the water, but a few were wedged fatally in barnacle-encrusted declivities. Crabs scrambled frantically, their claws suddenly dead weights, and a starfish that had folded about a clam now found itself prey to circumstance.

This was a world less familiar to Orn, and despite the danger – or perhaps because he had given up hope of living when he realized what the dropping of the sea meant – he contemplated it avidly. There were many marine plants he had seldom tasted, even in memory, so many exotic forms of life. Many of them had changed little since his ancestral line left the water; others were quite new. He had so little time to live; he wanted to learn as much as he could before he lost the opportunity forever.

He had been picking his way along, and had made incidental progress towards the shore while he observed all this. Now he began to give way to his reflexes, despite the uselessness of this. Behind him it was coming, as he had known it would: a massive swell of water travelling better than ten times his own maximum running speed. Around his feet the level was rising, seeping in quietly. But the major wave was another matter.

The wave would crush him; there was no way he could get out of its range in time, nor had there been since the water dropped. But the blind instinct for survival swept through his body at that sight, and he had to yield to it. He flapped his wings and stretched his neck forward, putting all his strength into the sprint, running over the ragged coral without regard for his feet. He could hear it now, as the giant wave tripped over the shallow island shelf, looming higher and higher. It had exchanged forward momentum for elevation, but still closed the gap rapidly.

That slowing of pace as it gained height had not been clear in his memory. He had more time than he had supposed, though still not enough. He kept running.

Suddenly the mainland beach was there, and he was scrambling across it. He charged into the brush, leaping over what he could and tunnelling through the rest, heedless of the plumage torn out in the process. It was growing dark; the shadow of the wave was enveloping him. The breeze was suddenly chill – and it moved *toward* the water.

Still he ran, over rocks, around trees, up and away from the shore. He had expected the leaning wall of water to fall on him before this, ending everything, but that doom hovered, hovered.

And fell. It struck so abruptly that he wasn't aware of it until he found himself caught up and hurled forward, completely inundated and helpless. It was as though he were drowning in a fierce ocean current – but as he was whirled about, he saw a landscape in the sky, falling sideways.

Then he was sinking through increasingly tenuous foam, losing support yet not really falling. He flapped his wings and felt froth splashing against them. His rump landed hard, and he clutched at foliage with his beak, afraid of being sucked back out to sea though the alternative was to be dashed against the ground and crushed.

But he had already landed, and was no longer moving. Somehow he had survived the blast, through no doing of his own.

The water continued to subside, leaving him on a green island. He was dizzy but whole – and on the mainland! He looked about.

He was perched on the stout upper foliage of a broken-topped fir, six times his own height above the ground.

Chapter Four

VEG

They were in a cavern – not a natural one. Solid rock had been melted to form an irregular chamber, in whose wall was set the receiving focus. Below that entrance were scattered boxes of supplies, as though they had simply been dumped without supervision.

Just the way the seven of them had been, Veg thought. It was a pretty unimpressive way to begin a mission.

'No receiver, since this is what might be termed a probability shift,' Cal observed. He seemed to have worked it all out already. He always knew the score before the game got started. 'The effect would resemble that of a spurting firehose: it can affect the volume in front of the nozzle, but not very much behind it. They must have fired a heat-beam through and melted out a cylindrical cavity. Then supplies, never risking any men . . .'

The mantas were already spreading out. One had found a drill hole projecting straight up, and was shining its eye into it; another poked into the dark horizontal recess.

'But where did all the stone go?' Aquilon asked. 'Solid or melted, it can't just disappear.'

'Not if they reverse the flow and suck it out through the aperture – or rather, let its own gaseous pressure drive it through. A ticklish operation, but feasible, it would seem.'

Veg followed the manta – Hex, he was sure – beyond the tumble of supplies, his flash beam flicking about. A yard-high tube curved away into darkness. 'No sense sitting around until our air runs out,' he called back.

Aquilon joined him, seeming to agree. They were committed; it was pointless to procrastinate. A new adventure beckoned.

'That would be the corkscrew leading to the surface,' Cal said. 'The small vertical shaft would have been intended to provide air, but of course that failed. I imagine they used it to fire up the observation rocket instead, then let it seal over again. There's a fair amount of work ahead before we leave this region.'

Veg moved along, knowing Cal was probably right, but disinclined to dawdle while the tunnel lay unexplored. He did not suffer from claustrophobia, but did prefer open range when available. He slung the flash around his neck and proceeded on hands and knees. He could hear Aquilon following, and wished he had a pretext to glance back at her in that position. She was a well-structured woman.

The passage curved steadily to the left. He soon lost his orientation, retaining only the nebulous impression that he had navigated at least one complete circle. His knees were chafed; there was not room to go on hands and feet. But with Aquilon behind (and not complaining about *her* knees), he could not hesitate. Hex had long since disappeared ahead, managing to travel nicely in the confined tube.

The loops were interminable. The officer, noodlebrain, had said something about using a borer to cut through the rock, but he hadn't hinted at the distance! Veg was beginning to feel constrained.

At last he came up to the manta Hex, who was humped before a metal barrier. This was a plug that filled the tunnel almost completely, rimmed by a rubberlike flashing that squeezed tight against the circular wall. In the centre of the plug was a dial and knob resembling the face of a combination lock. That was all.

'What's the matter, slowpoke?' Aquilon inquired. It meant nothing negative and nothing positive, but he felt a certain happy tension whenever she addressed him, especially with a friendly teasing comment like this.

'Can't get around Hex,' he said, straightening so that there was room for her to squirm up beside him. She did, moving lithely – but the process still entailed a certain amount of contortion and physical abrasion. As if anything as rounded and resilient as Aquilon's torso could abrade in any but an esthetic sense. Esthetic? Least of all that!

'That's not Hex,' she said. 'That's Circe.'

What a woman she was! Since he had met her, Veg had lost interest in the fleshy shells that masqueraded as human femininity. He had not realized how deeply Aquilon affected him until they had parted, after Nacre. On Nacre, home planet of the mantas, he had bantered with her in the midst of mystery and danger, thinking it no more than a passing fancy; but back on Earth when the trio split up in order to protect the growing mantas—

'Wake up, vegetable,' she said, snapping her fingers under his nose. Even those were slender and shapely. 'I said you had the wrong manta.'

'You're crazy,' he mumbled, embarrassed at the chain of thought her nearness had started. Yet what other thoughts were possible when she was this close?

'And you claimed you knew your own manta!' She dismissed the matter as though it were settled (as probably it was; he hadn't identified the manta that surely) and peered ahead. 'Must be an air-lock.' Her lovely face with its tangled blonde hair was so close to his that her breath caressed his cheek. The skin stretched over the delicate curve of her chin, close enough to kiss. She lay on her left side, he on his right.

Dolt that he was, he hadn't realized how strongly he felt about her until that government agent, Subble, had tricked him into the admission, after beating him in a fair fight . . .

'There must be some way to open it,' she continued, oblivious to his turbulent yearnings. 'Is that a combination lock?'

'Maybe.' There had been no element of flirtation in her contact. She was unaware of the electrifying effect of a perfect breast as it touched a man, even sheathed as hers was by layers of clothing. Once it had seemed that she returned his developing interest, but obviously that had passed. She did not need to say a thing; her indifference to his maleness was manifest in so many little ways. He was a friend, not a man friend.

'Let me try it.' She brought her right arm up, threading it between them and reached for the dial. As she twisted, Veg was treated to a scenic view of her right breast flexing under the coverall in response to the motion of her arm.

A woman with a mind, yes. But not one of the pinched genius types. He had regarded the gender with a certain veiled contempt in earlier years, to be appreciated in purely physical fashion – until he discovered in Aquilon what a woman could be. A *complete* woman. She had said she did not eat meat any more . . .'

Yet of course he had little to offer a real woman. He appreciated intellect without being intellectual himself, much as a working man appreciated wealth without possessing it. And no windfall income could rectify *that*.

There was a click, and Circe moved aside somewhat. 'I've got it,' Aquilon exclaimed. 'It's not really a combination, just a kind of safety catch. I'll have it open in a moment.'

Her eyes, as she peered up, were grey-blue; her lips, as she talked, compelling. 'Moment,' she had said – that word like two kisses strung together.

'Careful.' It was Cal, behind them, startling them both. 'Remember, we're under water.'

Aquilon's hand froze on the knob. 'Water!' she exclaimed, as though she hadn't known.

'That's right, I forgot!' Veg said, taken aback. He imagined a torrent of salty liquid smashing in, washing them down the tube as though it were a drainpipe, swirling them in among the boxes of supplies like so many drowned rats. What would they do without Cal's innate caution?

'That would be the borer,' Cal said, shining his own light between them. Grotesque shadows blotted out most of the beam. 'Probably it is watertight, and of course we'll use it as an exit-lock, once we have our diving suits on. But it would be wise to verify—'

'The borer?' Aquilon asked.

'My dear, I fear you were not paying proper attention to that attendant's lecture,' Cal said reprovingly, and her fair skin coloured slightly in the angled beam. Veg saw it then: if she had real interest in either man, it was Cal. Cal, with his brain, was the trouble. A woman without a mind looked for a strong man or a handsome one; a woman *with* a mind looked for an intelligent man. The kind of woman Veg could appreciate was also the kind who would naturally prefer Cal. Cal was only small and weak when you looked at him, never when you listened to him.

The borer, as Cal explained for Aquilon's benefit (and for Veg's too – he had not paid proper attention to Noodlebrain's lecture either), was a tractorlike device with a diamond-surfaced bit that ground into rock and pulverized it. The dust and chunks were blown back down through the tube for disposal. In this instance the borer had been stopped the moment its nose projected into the water, so as not to flood the passage. It could be entered by reopening the sealed exhaust section, and also by the service gate set into its side. The dial in its rear would indicate internal pressure and the proper setting would activate the water pump and evacuate the interior as required.

In the end Veg had to back away so Cal could pass him and Aquilon and Circe had come up to manipulate the control. Veg felt as though he had been demoted – but it was good that *someone* here knew what he was doing! The thought of all that sea water pouring in—

'Clear,' Cal announced. He clicked the dial. 'Should come open now—'

It didn't. Cal manipulated the knob again, puzzled, but still nothing happened.

'Must be jammed,' Veg said. 'Want me to—?'

'There's no handhold,' Aquilon pointed out. 'No way to yank. Unless the dial can be—'

She was right. He remembered the featureless wall of metal. And obviously it would be unwise to tug too hard at the knob. He pictured delicate wiring tearing, tumblers jamming, so that the group was sealed in permanently behind a ruined mechanism. A fine report to take back to Earth: 'Sorry – the door was stuck!'

But if the connection to Earth was out of phase, or whatever that problem was, they could stay cooped up in the worm-bore for weeks or months. How much canned air did they have?

'I'm afraid Veg is right,' Cal said after another fruitless minute. 'It is jammed. It should open but it doesn't.'

'We could try it again in a few hours,' Aquilon said without enthusiasm.

'And let it rust even worse?' Veg demanded. He put one large hand on Aquilon's slim ankle and tugged gently. 'Back off, both of you. And Circe too. I'll get it open!'

The others allowed themselves to be bullied away from the barrier, and Veg came up. Circe retreated a little, so that he had an entire segment of the tunnel to himself. He braced, brought back his arm, and slammed his fist sidewise into the panel beside the dial.

It was that simple. The metal gave. Opposite the dial a semicircular section swung out, spraying flecks of dirt into his face, and cold water gushed forth.

'Oops!' Aquilon exclaimed as she got soaked.

But it was only the token backlash of inanimate perversity. Veg

187

had won the round and the way was open. He blinked his eyes clear and caught the panel. It rotated around a vertical column, the dial set in its centre, leaving a vent about a foot wide on either side. Wires trailed from the backside into the body of the borer.

'I must admit you have your uses,' Cal said, coming up. 'Now this should slide out—'

The borer chamber was about eight feet long, with a bank of dials on the far wall. Beyond it, Cal explained was the motor, and beyond that the drill itself – now projecting harmlessly into the water. Along the sides of the compartment were indentations for the caterpillar housings, making the available space quite narrow.

'We'll have to haul our supplies to this point, then ferry them through the lock,' Cal said. 'The outside man will have to wear a diving suit. According to soundings and the record of the photographic rocket, we're only two hundred feet below the surface of the water, so it shouldn't be too difficult. Still, it might be wise to climb to the top and take a sighting, before we commit outselves too far.'

'Climb?' Aquilon inquired from behind the manta. 'Don't you mean *swim* to the top?'

'Swimming would be risky until we know more about the local currents,' Cal explained. 'And the suits are weighted. We'll send up a balloon and climb the ladder that anchors it to the borer. If we spot land, we'll *walk* to it – across the bottom.'

Aquilon was silent, and Veg appreciated the reason. On Nacre, Cal had been near death, and the other two had assumed the leadership and organized the trek from the wreck of their vehicle back to the camp. Now Cal was healthy, and it was evident that he was the natural leader of this trio. It simply took some getting used to.

There was a winch in the borer, powered electrically with cartridge capacitors. They removed it and got organized on an assembly-line basis. Cal connected the line to objects in the proper sequence, Aquilon ran the winch from a location just below the borer, and Veg was outside man. The line was actually doubled, passing through a pulley at the base of the tunnel so that it was not necessary to reset it by hand after each haul. But because of the narrowness and curvature of the passage, they had decided to run only one load at a time; a break or jam would be awkward to fix otherwise.

The diving suit was rather like a space suit, but built to resist pressure at key points rather than to contain it. It was quite heavy. He got it on, then had to squeeze himself into an uncomfortable knot inside the borer and push closed the panel. It sealed into place as Aquilon worked the knot control. Then water began to flow in through a vent in the floor. It entered with some force, splashing against him and collecting in a puddle beneath, as though he were lying in a filling bathtub. As the water rose up around his faceplate he began to feel that claustrophobia he thought he didn't suffer from. He knew he couldn't drown in the sealed suit, but the suggestion was powerful. He couldn't move, he couldn't escape; he had to lie here and let the liquid claim him! One leak . . .

Once the chamber was full the effect vanished. It was the sight of the advancing water line that did it, he decided. Now he was floating and felt comfortable.

He tried the side port. At first it wouldn't open, and he realized that the pressure hadn't equalized yet. He tried again after a short wait, and it yielded readily. It swung out, a blister of metal, and he peered into the darkness beyond.

He activated the suit's helmet light and looked again. The beam struck through cloudy water and faded in the distance. Like foggy Nacre, he thought; and this must be what the manta's vision was like: just a tunnel of light in the opacity. A manta could not see anything that wasn't directly in front of its eye. But it certainly saw everything that *was* in front. Even sound waves . . .

He pried himself out of the borer, feeling like old-time toothpaste inching from the tube. The borer manufacturer had not had a man of his dimensions in mind!

At last he stood beside the borer. The suit seemed light now, and he was glad for the weights that kept him gently anchored. He knew that without that ballast he would be borne helplessly to the surface by the buoyancy of the air encasing him in the suit. And without that shield of air he would be pretty cold in this water, not to mention squashed and suffocated. He had to admit that things had been pretty well planned.

He looked about. Cal had been right about the position of the borer: its gleaming blades projected into the water, reflecting the beam of his helmet in a spray of light. How much diamond had gone to coat that massive screw?

Beyond the borer was the floor of the ocean. He was surprised to discover that it was not level here, but hilly; somehow he had visualized the depths as similar to the surface – flat with small waves. The borer projected from a steeply slanting face of rock. Had the slant been the other way, the machine would have had to grind a long way farther before emerging. He saw some small fish, but could not identify their type; certainly they were not like the ones he knew. All in all, the unfamiliar detail made him uneasy; he expected oddities on some far planet, but here in the water he had no proper emotional framework.

He was startled by a knocking from within the borer. Three taps: their joint human-manta code for question. Aquilon wanted to know how he was doing.

He tapped back once, affirmatively, and pushed closed the port. He heard the click as it locked in place. The evacuation pump started up, and he saw the seaweedlike growths wave as the water was spouted out of the bottom aperture.

In a few minutes bubbles emerged, the current stopped, and assorted rumblings emanated from the interior of the unit. Then there came a banging, not a signal; Aquilon was pounding on the panel, trying to open it.

In a sudden mental illumination he understood the problem: the air forced into the chamber to evacuate the sea water had to be under high pressure. Once the water was out, that pressure remained; it had nowhere to go. And the bulkhead to the tunnel was designed to open only when the pressures were equalized, in and out, to prevent leakage.

There should be a valve to release the surplus pressure within the chamber, once the water was out. Probably it had gotten plugged. He had pounded open the panel by sheer force, but Aquilon did not have his strength.

Here he was with both the muscle and the insight – where neither could be applied to the problem. How were they going to get the supplies through?

A large, sleek fish nosed up to him. Veg cast about for some weapon, but had none. Anyway, he had no idea whether this creature was dangerous. It must weigh more than he did – or *would* weigh more, out of the water. What would he do if it attacked?

It did not attack. It merely continued to snuff him and the borer as though curious. He wished he could identify it, in case it were a shark. But he didn't want to be on the defensive if it turned out to be some entirely innocuous or even friendly prowler.

There was a deeper *thunk*! and under his hand the metal shook. The fist jerked back, alarmed. What had happened? He tried to pry open the port, but it was tight, as of course it would be. Whatever had happened inside – had happened. There was nothing he could do.

'What's your opinion, Sam?' he asked the fish. He doubted that any sound left his helmet, however.

Then bubbles shot up from the top pipe, and he knew that it was all right. The water cycle was starting over.

This was too much for Sam, however. The big fish coursed away into the obscurity of the surrounding ocean.

Before long the bubbles stopped. He tried the port again, and it opened. He aimed his light within. There was a cylinder, a roll of nylon-cord ladder, and a balled balloon. He took them out, wondering how Aquilon had gotten around the pressure problem.

He tied one end of the cord to the borer, looping it around just below the bubble chimney. He threaded the other end through a gross needle eye in the base of the balloon and knotted it tight. Finally, he hooked the nozzle of the tank into the balloon and fastened it in place. He turned the tank's cock.

Helium gas whistled coldly into the balloon. The ball unrolled as though it were a Halloween toy and inflated into a yard-long tongue, then became a long gourd, then a water-melon. It began to lift the tank, hauling up on the nozzle.

Hastily Veg flung another loop of the ladder around the borer and clung to it. The balloon dragged the tank up to the limit of its play, twelve feet above the borer, and held it there.

Stupid! He had forgotten that the thing would rise as soon as it was inflated, and he had made no preparations. As though a ball of helium, light enough to lift a dirigible in air, would sit still under water . . .

Expansion levelled off when the balloon was about a yard in diameter. Veg climbed up the ladder, now taut, and tied off the sphere, letting the tank drift down. He watched the flow of bubbles from the borer's chimney go by within a foot of him. Then he descended to the floor and wrestled with the segment of ladder he had tied to the borer. It was too rigid to move.

Meanwhile the next cycle had been completed. He gave up on the ladder and opened the port.

A head poked out, followed by a body that was feminine even through the crude folds of the suit. Aquilon had joined him.

She glanced around, shining her headlight, entranced as he had been by the scene. Then she saw the tangled ladder.

She could have spoken to him by touching her helmet to his – or maybe even directly through the water, since this was *not* a vacuum between them – but did not, to his relief. His stupidity was obvious. He'd had no idea the pull would be so strong with such a small balloon.

Together they worked the ladder over the body of the borer, seeking to pass it off the end. Suddenly Aquilon stopped, pointing to the diamond-edged drill. Of course! Friction against that could sever the rope, or at least damage it and make it unsafe.

Aquilon tried another ploy. She picked up the slack length of the ladder between the first and second loops and began pushing it under the borer. Veg saw what she was doing and assisted. The idea was to carry the slack around the borer, so that the second loop would in effect be brought adjacent to the first, allowing all the intervening ladder to ascend to the surface. The cord was very fine, and there appeared to be well over two hundred feet of it – more than enough.

They bunched it up and shoved – and abruptly the whole length of it was rasping through, and the balloon was rising out of sight. They stood back and watched it. Veg appreciated how narrowly they had missed making another mistake: had a hand been caught when the rope let go—

The motion stopped, and there was slack at last in the main line. Quickly they re-anchored it so that the ladder was vertical and firm; then Veg began to climb. Belatedly he realized that he could have had a free ride up, had he clung to a rising rung. Now he had the easy but tedious job of mounting it step by step.

By step. He lost count of the rungs somewhere between sixty and eighty, not certain whether he had skipped seventy or repeated it. The water around him was featureless; even Sam the fish would have been welcome company. Was he really ascending, or just working a treadmill through nothing?

At last he reached the top. The balloon floated amid a choppy sea, and white clouds decorated the blue sky spreading overhead.

He looked out over the waves, standing with his feet hooked into the top rung of the ladder and his arm about the bobbing balloon. He saw – more waves.

He craned his head about.

Behind him, perhaps within a mile, perhaps much less, was a mountain.

Veg smiled, let go the balloon, and drifted down towards the floor of the ocean, mission accomplished.

Chapter Five

ORN

It was a strange world he ranged. The familiar palms and cycads were rare, their places taken by burgeoning flat-leaved, flowering trees and bushes. He knew these newer plants, but here they thrived in unprecedented profusion, dominating the landscape rather than occupying their occasional nooks, and that was hard to accept readily. His reflexes were wrong for this, his expectations constantly in error, and that upset him. The mighty firs still stood in thick forests – but these forests were smaller than they had been. Ferns were still common, but stunted; if their form was little changed from those of his twenty-million-year memory, this was small comfort.

Orn did not speculate on the meaning of these changes. He was concerned with what had been and what existed now, not with what it might portend. Every object he saw evoked its peculiar history, clear with the vision of countless generations of his observant forebears. Change was in fact uncomfortable for him – but he had been forced by his orphan status and the pressure of invincible events to adapt more readily than had his ancestors. Perhaps his very isolation had facilitated his survival, for had he been trained in the usual fashion by careful parents he might not have had the initiative to escape the island when that became necessary.

He was familiar with the mainland as it had existed many millions of years before, and was hungry for fresh information. But this normally would have meant slight changes in geography, flora and fauna, instead of the catastrophic alterations in all three he actually discovered. These flowering plants – never had anything leaped into prominence so explosively before.

Orn was hungry physically, too. His appetite was unspecialized, omnivorous. Leaves, fruits, mams, arths, occasional gulps of water, pebbles to aid digestion – whatever had food value could be his meal, provided it was not poisonous. But he lacked the imagination to

194

search actively for specific meals. He ate whatever was available.

He scratched away the dried, mottled leaves beneath his feet. His two front toes had long sharp claws, while the rear toes that bore much of his weight were stubby and solid, the claws more like hoofs.

Yes – the little arths were there, just as they had been on the island. The land had changed; the soil had not. Some flying aves fed exclusively on the tasty arths, and so could he if he could only find enough. But these vanished even as he uncovered them. He required more substantial food for his travels. And he had to travel, for he knew that the lull in the volcanic activity was temporary.

Orn's beak was not adapted to snare the fast scrambling creatures, but he scratched again and ran out the sticky tip of his tongue to spear several before they found cover. They were delicious as they passed into his crop – but such a meagre repast only intensified his hunger.

He straightened up, casting about for prey that would satisfy him for many hours. Hunting was difficult in this unfamiliar territory. He listened.

From far above came the cry of one of his primitive cousins, a flying bird. Orn looked up and saw it swoop over the trees, searching out the flying arths. He flapped his wings experimentally, momentarily wishing he could do likewise. Many hundreds of lines rode the air now, more than ever before. But this had been impossible for his own line for so long that he had only the dimmest specific memories of flying. His wings were mainly for display and defence now; the weight of his large head, with its burden of memories, prevented him from even jumping high, let alone flying.

Another, gentler sound came to him. It was the trickle of water over naked stone. A stream!

Orn found it immediately. He stood at its brink and studied the narrow channels as the bright liquid coursed between the rocks, then plunged his beak into it and drank. Unlike his cousins, he was able to suck in water without lifting his head to swallow. But he did not need the voluminous quantities that poured through the little systems of the mams. *They* survived by tanking up sufficient liquid to last them for a reasonable period in spite of copious urination; *he* survived by being efficient. That was one reason his line was superior to theirs, apart from the factor of memory.

Small fish flashed by, reminding him fleetingly of the swimming stage of his ancestral line. The notion of feeding on creatures like those he had derived from did not disturb him; in fact, he rather cherished the connection. He stalked upstream in quest of a pool that might contain fish large enough to be worthwhile.

Something moved nearby. Orn swivelled his neck to fix one eye on it, and spied the disappearing tail of a good-sized snake. This line of reps had recently dispensed with legs and become slithering creatures. He had eaten a few on the island, but this one was fatter and longer. He pounced on it, pinning its head with one foot while his beak cut through the neck.

The raw segments of it were cool and juicy and delightful as they collected inside him, assuaging his hunger.

Highlands existed where he remembered swamps, and the drainage of the landscape had changed. The nights inland were cool, the days hot. Orn, in the days of travel away from the treacherous volcanoes, was finally able to set aside his expectations and accept what he found, and his emotional distress diminished.

Birds were everywhere, none intelligent but in other respects more advanced than those of his memory. They swooped cleverly through the air and swam in the small, cold ponds. The families of arths were fabulously abundant. And the little warm hairy juicy mams had emerged from their tunnels and hideaways to tread boldly in the open, overrunning forests and glade.

Orn found a number of the mams easy prey. The largest were hardly a danger to him, and most were so small he could swallow them in a few bites, wasting only a few hot drops of their substance. It was not that they were not cautious, but that the larger ones did not seem to expect trouble from a bird. This allowed him to get quite close before they took proper alarm, and a quick neat pounce usually brought him a pleasant meal. The mams learned quickly, however, and he found them to be much more wary of him after one or two of their number had been taken from any particular assemblage. But since he was travelling, this hardly interfered. He had never eaten better.

He continued to feel a vague disturbance, however. Something was missing – but he could not identify it until such time as he actually saw it. He knew that life was too easy for him here; that there should be more danger. But again – he had to experience that danger to identify it. His memory was very long, but also very selective.

Gradually he overcame his initial difficulty in appreciating the new forms of animal. Had his ancestors watched these creatures evolve for a thousand thousand generations, the picture would have been strong. A million consecutive lives, each life a single, momentary picture: the whole making a composite creature. But this single flash was too brief for him to assimilate properly, even though it occurred in the present and consisted of many hours and days. His ancestors had been confined beyond the rising mountains recently, making too few forays through the changing passes and over the moving continent to form the necessary pictures of the fast-changing animals.

But some few lines were clear. The cautious marsups were little changed. The plant-feeding multis were more difficult, for they were larger and more diverse now, making a jump in the memory pattern. Some he had come to know on the island, and that helped him make the adjustment. But the arth-eaters had diverged prodigiously, feeding on the vast numbers the flowering plants supported. Now there were many major lines, few of which retained their original nature – and these creatures with small pasts were largely invisible to him.

This was dangerous, as he realized almost too late.

The thing was coming at him before he comprehended its menace – much as he had come at careless small prey. This was a mam, but almost as massive as himself, and far more ferocious than he had come to expect. Vaguely he fathomed its ancestry: one of the lines of tiny tree-dwelling insectivores that expanded their scope to feed as well on nuts and carrion, quivering as the tread of giant reps shook the ground. Somehow these unprepossessing midgets had descended to take over the reps' terrain, and now were becoming large and bold themselves.

For a moment Orn seemed to grasp what had bothered him most about this land, but he was allowed no time to fix on it. The adjustment to the present creature was too rapid. He did not have its entirety in mind, and so did not know how to handle it. Rapid thinking was not his forte; he depended on the reflexes engendered by millions of years of experience. Given time, he could adapt to this situation, though with difficulty – but the animal was attacking *now*.

Its tiny claws of Orn's memory had become talons worthy of an ave; its teeth, though small, were thick and sharp. It moved with a sinuous grace almost like that of a snake, yet it carried its bulk on four muscular legs, and was capable of alarming speed.

A killer mam.

He countered as it pounced. He spread his wings, squawked, and jumped to the side, stabbing forward with his beak. His pattern was clumsy because of the oddity of the creature; had it been a rep of similar size he would have scored upon an eye socket. But his action caused it to veer off, and he had a momentary respite while it slowed, turned, and came back.

Classify it as a new creature, Orn decided. Once it had been an insectivore, but now it was a carnivore, a creo. Its legs were springy, its snout blunt, and it used its feet for fighting as well as its teeth. It was as alert and swift as Orn himself – not astonishing in a warm-bodied mam, but horrifying considering its grotesque size.

If only he could *see* it! But his ancestral images simply did not match the immediacy; his memories were too far out of phase to be meaningful at once. He had to guess at much of the creo's nature, and he was not good at such extrapolation.

Had the mam been familiar, he should have been able to defeat it in combat. He was, after all, Orn. But as it was, he would be its meal.

It sprang. Inspired in an uncharacteristic fashion, Orn visualized it as a running rep of similar mass, and reacted accordingly. He brought up one foot, spread his wings for balance, and struck for the tender nostril.

His blow missed, since this creo was faster than a rep and had a shorter snout. But his talon caught it in the neck and raked a bloody furrow across its hairy hide – something the scales of the rep would have prevented. He followed up with another beak stab at its eye, and scored on its pointed, flabby ear.

The creo howled and snapped sidewise, but Orn was out of its reach already. He brought his foot up again, and this time caught it in the muscular jaw with the downstroke. Flesh tore from its cheek as his claw carried through; blood and hot saliva sprayed out. Again it snapped sidewise, towards the injury – and because that was exactly what a rep would have done, Orn was prepared once more. His beak speared its eyeball and penetrated its brain, killing it abruptly.

Again Orn struck, reacting to the greater life tenacity of the rep, and had its belly torn open before he realized that it wasn't fighting any more.

He stood back then and gazed at it, knowing that he had been fortunate to survive. Had he not summoned an image that enabled him to fight *something* efficiently, creo would now be looking down at his own corpse.

But he did not waste undue time in contemplation. He finished the work of dissection, studying each soft organ as he consumed it, and when his crop was full he had some better understanding of this mam. Should he have to fight another, he would be better prepared. But he would not battle another voluntarily – not this agile, clawed, toothed monster! Better to avoid creo and all large mams.

But it did make an excellent meal.

Chapter Six

CAL

Cal lay in the bore hole, his light off, just below the winch. Circe stood above it. He doubted that the mantas had anything resembling human sentiments, and certainly they were sexless. But it did seem that Circe was female, and that she looked out for Aquilon's interests. The other mantas remained below, taking no part in the human activity, sitting beside the supplies like so many toadstools. Circe had stayed with Aquilon throughout, the only one never to leave her, and there was now a certain flavour of Aquilon about this manta. Perhaps some manta lottery had decided which one would associate with which human – but Cal suspected something more than that.

It was too easy to personify all the mantas. Actually they were alien; indeed, in some ways man was more closely related to the birds, snakes, or spiders than to these third-kingdom sentients of Nacre. On that far planet a germ plasm of something akin to slime mould had evolved into complex, motile forms, superseding the entire animal kingdom. The internal chemistry of the Nacre creatures remained largely a matter of conjecture, since their bodily energies came from breaking down organic substances, not building them up. The mantas were the pinnacle of fungoid evolution in much the way man was the end result of animal evolution on Earth – so far. The astonishing thing was how closely the two species resembled each other in areas that counted. Man had two eyes; the manta had one. Man had a powerful brain; the manta had a lesser brain, but was able to communicate more effectively. Man was omnivorous, the manta carnivorous, in relation to its framework. Strictly speaking, all the creatures of Nacre had been herbivorous until man arrived there, since there had been no animal kingdom to prey on.

Yet these were picayune distinctions. Converging evolution had brought the two species to the point where they had more in common with each other than with a number of the variants of their own lines. It was as though nature had intended them to meet and coexist.

But why had those three mantas made their suicidal dash for freedom? They must have understood a good part of the official's presentation, and so been aware that no harm would come to them, even though they were not to be returned to Nacre.

Not to be returned to Nacre.

He lay there, chagrined at his own obtuseness. Of course the manta would rebel at such a sentence of exile! Even the human trio had not been happy on Earth, crowded and sick as mankind was; how could they have supposed the mantas would like it any better? Sparsely settled Nacre was the best place for the mantas. They must have eagerly awaited the chance to go home, after learning the ways of man and establishing a line of communication. To have had that expectation, that dream, so rudely cancelled ...

But only three had bolted.

'Circe,' he said.

The manta made a tail-snap noise: It seemed strange to speak in the darkness and have her respond, when he knew she heard with her eye. But the darkness was to his eyes only; the mantas generated their own illumination in the ultra-violet range, so were independent of outside sources. Circe could see his speech.

'Did you seven agree that three of your number would make the break?'

Three snaps: question.

He had phrased it in too complicated a fashion. He tried again: 'Lin, Tri, Oct – you knew?'

One snap: yes.

So it had been planned. The mantas had had ample opportunity to work out a detailed plan of attack, since the full power of each mind was channelled through the single eye. A man might require a full hour to convey a single nuance of feeling, and even then not succeed; but the mantas could project it all in a fraction of a second. They were not more intelligent than man, merely more efficient.

'You – sent them?' He had to keep it simple. Perhaps the manta vocabulary was still small. Perhaps they did not ordinarily think in word forms. He suspected that the manta's capability in theoretical matters was considerably smaller than man's. The same efficiency that promoted communication also militated against high intelligence. Man's brain had not evolved appreciably since he achieved competent verbal communication because there had no longer been a competitive advantage in higher intelligence. He had risen above the hurdle that isolated him socially, and so achieved the stability of water flowing over a dam. Barriers were necessary to progress; neither water nor brain capacity rose without compulsion. That was the way of nature, a mere permutation of physics. The ant had remained virtually unchanged for millions of years, once it achieved a satisfactory social organization; it did not need size or intelligence, so had not achieved them. Man did not need *more* size or intelligence than he had. Why should the manta differ in this respect?

Circe had answered with another snap. Yes, three had been selected to make the attempt, while four played it safe.

It did make sense, tactically. 'Who died?'

Three snaps, followed by eight. So *two* had died: Tri and Oct. Cal wondered how Circe knew. Had the spores of the descendents already circulated through the station before the others left?

That was another thing about the mantas. They reproduced by spores, and the spores were released only at death. Microscopic in size, those spores could be filtered out of the air only with difficulty. Now two sets of them suffused the station. That meant that individual male and female spores could mate with their opposite numbers, to develop with luck into new mantas. Provided they found omnivores to ride on . . .

There was going to be real trouble aboard that station! Cal could not evoke much regret; his sympathy was with the mantas. But it would not be wise to count on much assistance from the station soon. The personnel would be very busy at first, very angry later.

'Lin escaped?'

Yes.

So Lin would, circumstance permitting, go free. Perhaps he would actually manage to hitchhike back to Nacre and report to the manta society there. That would probably mean even more serious trouble for Earth. After all, the visiting mantas had seen the planet in all its squalor and savagery, and mantas had died. But he couldn't help hoping that Lin made it. In many respects the manta society was admirable compared to that of Earth.

There was a *thunk*! from outside, transmitted through the layers of metal. That would be the outer port closing. Aquilon was coming back.

He turned on the light and watched the panel, though he knew it would be a few minutes before the evacuation cycle finished. Aquilon affected him that way, making him yearn to catch the earliest possible glimpse of her. She was such a lovely creature, the first woman who had ever treated him as a man, and he loved her. While not brilliant, she possessed more than the average sensitivity. This showed in her artwork. Perhaps it was her painting that he loved, rather than herself. Certainly she was not for him physically – he knew that, whether she was aware of it or not. The physical, the sexual part – he lacked the capacity and the desire, largely. Oh, there were times . . . but it was the intellectual side that intrigued him, and he was attracted less to Aquilon's comely physique than to her female mystique.

Still, he liked to look at her.

The dial showed the completion of the cycle. 'Go to it, Circe,' he said.

The manta leaped and bounced off the panel. The impact of the single foot jarred it open. Air exploded into the tunnel, creating a kind of shock wave but not hurting anything. They would have to do something about that inoperative pressure-equalization valve; this was a cumbersome way to open the chamber.

Aquilon crawled in, unfastening her helmet as she came towards him. 'There's land!' she said, her beautiful face alight. 'Veg climbed up and saw it. An island, we think – but within a mile.'

'Good,' he said, feeling enormous relief. He had not realized until this moment how important that was to him. Land, even an island, meant that they could be independent, at least to some extent, of the tunnel and its supplies. Independent of Earth. They could not suddenly be recalled by angry station personnel, or wiped out by a heat-beam fired through the aperture. And the mantas would be safe.

The map he had had Aquilon sketch had not been detailed enough to show the configuration of land and water within a hundred miles of the aperture, so the issue had been in doubt. If the significance of that map dawned too soon upon the military organizers of this expedition, there would also be trouble. It tied in, in fact, with the ramifications of the mantas' violence at the station. He and Veg and Aquilon and the four mantas particularly were in dire peril – until they got far away from here.

Aquilon completed the removal of her suit, folding it carefully and placing the bulky, weighted wad beside the winch. Her coverall clung to her economically; she was sleek and strong. 'We might as well move out what we'll need, for now,' she said. 'I'd like to spend the day on land.'

Yes – she understood, at least intuitively, the need for a prompt exodus. Wordlessly he crawled down the wormbore, so that he could hook the next box.

It was an island, swept by steady west winds. A small beach well laden with shells gave way to an interior spread of massed palmetto. A number of off-brown birds nested in that tangle, feeding on the surrounding insects and sea life of the beach. Cal watched them, but was unable to identify their specific species. They had beaks and feathers and birdlike ways, but matched no genus of his experience. most were not really good flyers; they were too heavy for their size, and had to rest often. He wondered how they had reached this island. Storm-blown, perhaps – and then could not escape it.

The insects and arachnids, on the other hand, were familiar. Flies buzzed about the foliage and inspected the human visitors hungrily. Some were mosquito like, some wasp like. A drab butterfly skirted his display and moved on. A black-armoured beetle mounted a spire of driftwood. In the trees he had spotted the trailing lines of spiders, too. Liquid repellent discouraged most of the biters, however.

Crabs and snails occupied the salty perimeter, and schools of small fish traversed the shallows. Both air and sea were warm and clean. Cal was invigorated by the surf as he waded in and bent to pick up an assortment of shells. There was something about the smell of the sea ...

In due course he had a basketful of hardware. He brought it to the beach, cleared off a section of sand, and arranged the shells in neat columns by type. Some were flat, some spiral; some were drab, others ornate. He turned each over, contemplating it, and bit by bit an incredulous excitement grew in him. First the hint of the map, now this confirmation ...

He thought for a moment, his heart beating with unaccustomed vigour. Then he proceeded to the supply depot they had set up near the brush and picked up his voice-typer. He selected a shell and began dictating.

Cal laid out his last shell and spoke into his typer: 'phylum *Mollusca*, class *Pelecypoda*, order *Taxodonta*, suborder *Arcacea*, family – forget it, I'll have to look it up. Call it an Arca, two-inch diameter, mint condition.' He smiled privately and paused to review his display affectionately: a score of clam shells. Taxodonts, with their small numerous hinge teeth; a number of Dysodonta, like assorted scallops; burrowing Desmodonta; a single weird Pachyodont; several unclassified. These shells offered only a rough guide to this world, since the pelecypods as a class had diversified early and evolved thereafter quite conservatively. In four hundred million years of Earth's history there had been only nominal modifications of most orders.

He moved a few paces to the gastropod display. Here there was much greater variety, for the shells were coiled, ridged, and spired diversely, and several were very pretty. But these too were not definitive for his purpose.

It was, in fact, mainly what was missing that fascinated him. There were very few cephalopods. He had searched diligently and come up with only two shells, both belemnites. That was highly significant, for the cephalopods had dominated the seas of Earth for three hundred million years before suffering certain selective but drastic extinctions. The belemnites had given way to their squidlike cousins – but the geological period in which belemnites had existed in the *absence* of ammonites was restricted.

The picture described by his carefully ordered collection of shells was remarkable. He was not properly versed, without his reference texts, in every detail of invertebrate fossilography; but he was certain that coincidence did not stretch this far. The fauna of the shallows here matched those of Earth, order for order, and probably species for species. Not contemporary Earth, no. Not truly ancient Earth, either. But definitely Earth.

In fact, the evidence of the sea shells reinforced that of Aquilon's map in exactly the way he had incredulously anticipated. He had recognized its configuration without daring to believe it, and suppressed his burgeoning excitement. The Earth authorities, unused to paleogeographical perspective, had apparently missed its significance. Now he looked at shells that suggested either a preposterous coincidence of convergent evolution, or—

Or they stood upon an island in the oceans of an Earth of sixty-five million years past. No – not *an* Earth—

The Earth.

Aquilon walked up the beach, resplendent in a one-piece bathing suit. It covered more of her flesh than certain contemporary fashions would have, on or off the beach; but she was perfect in it. Her hair in the sun was almost white, in contrast with the black of the suit, while her skin already showed an enhancing tan.

'Have to come in before I burn,' she said, joining him in the shade of the display tent. 'And I'd better catch up on illustration, too.' She brought out her brush – somehow she was never without it – and began sketching the shells of the display.

Should he tell her what he had discovered? No – not right away. It would only disturb her unnecessarily. Time travel, after all . . .

'This is Earth, isn't it,' she said calmly as she sketched.

'Yes.' So much for feminine histrionics. Would he ever fully understand this woman? 'How did you know?'

'Your silence, mostly. You should have been exclaiming over divergencies, and parallels, since this is by any reckoning a sharply Earthlike world. If it were a true parallel, it would be contemporary, and even *I* can tell it isn't. And you knew something when you had me sketch the map – yet you never spoke of it again. When I thought about it, I realized that there was a certain familiarity about that map, as though it were a gross distortion of the geography we have today. Earth might once have looked like that, millions of years ago – and you would be the first to spot it. But you shut up – and you're wound up like one of these shells.'

Had he shown his tension so obviously? 'You've been apprenticed to an agent, I suspect.'

She did not reply. Low blow, he realized then. The agent Subble had made an impression on her, how much of one he was only gradually coming to appreciate. Best to move off that topic. 'Does Veg know?' he inquired.

'Maybe. It doesn't matter much to him, though. When is this – the

Permian?'

'Off by two hundred million years, 'Quilon. It's the Paleocene.'

'The Paleocene,' she mused, placing it. 'Dawn of the age of mammals, if my girlhood schooling does not betray my aging memory. Vice versa, I mean. I think we should have been safer in the Permian, though.'

'Oh, there are few dangerous landbound forms in this epoch. With the reptiles decimated—'

'Safer from paradox, I meant.'

There was that. Could their actions here affect the evolution of man. It seemed incredible, yet—

'What are these?' she inquired, her brush moving and rendering as of its own volition. Shape, shade, and colour were artistically duplicated, the pigments flowing from the brush in response to subtle signals from her fingers, without dipping, without rinsing.

It was an abrupt change of subject, but he accepted the shift with relief. 'Phylum *Mollusca* – or as Veg would say, shellfish.'

'You underestimate him, difficult as that is to do at times. He calls them clams and conks.'

'He's right. The hinged shells are pelecypods, commonly known as clams. Most of the others are gastropods – Greek *gaster*, meaning stomach, and *pous*, foot. This army really does march on its stomach—'

'Like the manta,' she said.

Cal paused, surprised. 'Yes indeed. Strange that that similarity hadn't occurred to me.'

'But the mantas don't carry their houses on their backs.' She turned over a gastropod shell in order to get a new view for sketching. 'I studied tetrapodal anatomy, but I'm beginning to wish I'd learned more about sea life. These shells are beautiful.'

'Anything you paint is beautiful.'

She ignored that. 'What do the live animals look like?'

'Like snails. That's what they are. As they grow larger, they add on to their domiciles, forming the spirals you see. Because the result is really a horn – an expanding tube – it is possible to sound a note on the empty shell, when it is properly prepared. Thus Veg's conch, or "conk". He'd have trouble sounding a blast on an ammonite, though.'

'Which of these are ammonites?'

'None. They're extinct. That's one reason I know this is the Paleocene and not the Cretaceous period.'

'How can you be sure? Maybe you just didn't happen to scoop up any ammonities.' She was teasing him, anticipating his reply.

He made it anyway, enjoying her smile. *Any* dialogue with Aquilon was pleasant. 'My dear, you are asking for a tedious narration of marine paleontology—'

'Oops – not that!' She continued painting.

'The major distinction between the shells of the gastropods and those of the cephalopods is compartmentalization. The snail shells are hollow throughout, forming a single valve; but those of the cephalopods—'

'You forgot to tell me what cephalopods are,' she said. 'What do *they* look like, in life?'

'Squids in shells. Your snails and clams are sluggish in the mature state, but the cephalopods are active. They have keen eyesight and are strong swimmers, despite their hardware. They have a number of tentacles around the mouth. The cephalopods as a class have been abundant and important in the seas for well over three hundred million years, and are the only invertebrates able to compete actively with the ocean vertebrates. The giant squid—'

'But you were talking about shellfish, not squids!'

'*Mollusca*. Some wear their shells outside, some inside. The squid's shell is vestigial and internal, so you're not aware of it. The ammonite shell is external and, as I was *about* to explain, chambered. Segments of the interior are walled off as the creature grows, and these are filled with gas to make the dead weight more manageable. A sophisticated, highly successful format – and the ammonites were virtual rulers of the sea for a length of time that makes the tenure of the great reptiles on land seem brief. Yet the ammonites suffered a series of calamitous decimations, marking off the Triassic, Jurassic, and Cretaceous periods, and finally became extinct just before this Paleocene epoch. Their passing is, to my mind, a more subtle and significant mystery than that of the complex of reptilian orders that claims popular attention. In fact, the ammonites passed at about the same time as the dinosaurs.'

'The same time,' Aquilon repeated, seeming to appreciate the significance of that. 'But some reptiles did survive, and some molluscs.' She had finished her painting.

'A few reptiles like the lizards, snakes, and crocodiles. And turtles. But none of the ammonites, only the related but more primitive Nautiloids. They have the septa in the shell – simple, saucer-shaped partitions – but with comparatively unimaginative convolution. The ammonites in their time developed extraordinary elaborate fluting, and with much greater variety.'

'We shouldn't stay here,' she said, evidently tired of paleontology at last, 'on the island.'

'I've hardly begun to catalogue—'

'Circe says something is happening.'

He studied her, realizing that she was seriously concerned, and had only listened to him in order to have time to settle her own thoughts. Circe was her manta, just as Hex was Veg's, and news from that source had to be taken seriously.

'Can you be more specific?'

'We don't have the terms, the words. But it's something big. She doesn't know whether its dangerous, but it might be. Something about the water.'

'Storm?'

'I don't think so. And we'd know about that ourselves, wouldn't we?'

'We should. We have a fair selection of meteorological instruments. The barometer doesn't indicate trouble, and we'd have some advance warning if a hurricane were coming. Enough to retreat to the undersea tube, I'd think. Could the water be polluted in some way?'

'We'd know about that too, wouldn't we? What would pollute it, here?'

He shrugged. 'What indeed, without man's machine age. Perhaps I should question Circe directly.'

He could tell by her attitude that this was exactly what she'd had in mind. Aquilon put two fingers to her mouth and delivered a piercing whistle, astonishing him. In a moment the disk shape of a travelling manta rounded the curve of the island, moving at a good thirty miles per hour over the water. Circe.

'What's this I hear about the water?' Cal inquired as the creature came to rest before him.

Circe did not move or snap her tail, but Aquilon responded. 'She doesn't know what you mean, Cal.'

'There is something wrong with the water,' he said, making it a statement.

Now Circe snapped her tail twice: no.

'Something *will be* wrong.'

Three snaps: question.

'The water will change.'

Yes.

'Warmer.'

No.

'Colder.'

No.

'Higher.'

Yes.

Suddenly it clicked. 'A wave!'

Yes.

'Tsunami!'

Question.

'A big wave caused by movements of the land. Very big.'

Yes.

'How soon? One day?'

No.

'Sooner?'

Yes.

'Twelve hours?'

No.

'How many hours?'

Six snaps of the tail.

Cal stood up. 'Get Veg. We have to get off this island in a hurry. We have just about time to batten down before it hits.'

Circe was up and away, though he had been addressing Aquilon. That was just as well; the manta could spread the news more efficiently.

But Veg, when notified, threw an unexpected block. 'No. I'd rather ride it out right here. I don't want to go back in the can.'

'It would only be for a day or so,' Cal explained, but privately he shared the big man's reluctance. They joked about Veg's obtuseness, but he generally knew what was going on. And by this time the spore problem at the orbiting station would be in full swing, and the personnel could be in a very bad mood. 'Until the danger is over.

210

Then we can resume work here.'

'Well, I've been thinking,' Veg said. 'Out here in the sun and spray, no problems, no people crowding together, not even rationed cutting rights. I like it. It's the way a man is meant to live. Down there – we'd be walking back into the tin can, squeezed tight. That's what the trouble is back on Earth. Crowded. Here it's good; there it's bad. I don't want to go back. At all. Not even for a day.'

Oh-oh. When Veg 'thought something out' he could be obstinate, and the irony was that Cal agreed almost entirely. It was possible that they would be in greater danger in the tunnel than on the island, though from a different source. But at least they could remain near the borer exit. 'Let me explain what a tsunami is,' he said carefully. This was for Aquilon's benefit too, to be certain everyone knew what the choices were. 'An Earthquake or erupting volcano can do enormous damage on land, but if it is in or near the sea it acts in a different way. It makes a wave – a shift in the level of the water, a number of inches or feet. This wave travels at a rate governed by the amount of the disturbance and the depth of the water; it is a top-to-bottom matter, not just a surface ripple like those the wind makes. In deep water its forward velocity can exceed six hundred miles per hour. Because the vertical displacement is proportionately small, ships at sea may not even be aware of the tsunami's passage – but once it strikes the shallows, its full impact is felt. Forward momentum is converted to vertical displacement. The water can rise up in a wall a hundred feet high, and demolish shore installations with its impact.

'Now we don't know how bad this one is – but this is a small island without any really high land. A large wave could inundate it completely. Back on Earth such waves used to kill thousands and carry ships miles inland. Here—'

'Only three people, and four mantas,' Aquilon said. 'Hardly worth its while.'

Veg retained that determined expression. 'You said ships could ride it out.'

'Ships in deep water, yes. Not those too near the shore.'

'How about a raft?'

'A raft!' Aquilon repeated, becoming interested.

'The matter is academic,' Cal pointed out. 'We don't have a raft – unless you're thinking of the emergency balloon-type craft. I

211

wouldn't care to risk it. One puncture—'

'How about a log raft? Good solid timbers, rudder, cabin, sail—'

So that was what Veg had been doing! Trust an outdoorsman to put his talent to work. 'All right, Veg. Let's see it.'

The raft floated in a cove on the far side of the island, about twelve feet wide and twenty feet long, fashioned of stout, round palm logs bound together by nylon cord set into notches. In the centre was a cabin six feet square, and from the centre of that rose a ten-foot mast of sturdy bamboo.

'Haven't made the sail yet,' Veg admitted. 'But she has a six-foot keel and the cabin's tight. I call her the *Nacre*.'

'And you hope to ride out a tsunami in this?' Cal shook his head, though he was impressed with his friend's accomplishment.

'Why not? You said ships wouldn't even notice the wave. *Nacre*'s unsinkable. And we have to look about this world sometime.'

'It seems reasonable to me,' Aquilon said.

Cal tried to marshal his objections, but saw that he had already been outvoted. Or was he compensating for his own unreasonable desire to get far away from the works of Earth-contemporary? Or could he actually *want* to reach some area of this world where their actions might prejudice the development of the primates, and therefore abolish man from the globe entirely? No, the paradox inherent made that notion ridiculous. 'I hope there is a survivor to tell the tale,' he said morosely.

It required four hours of strenuous group labour to load their supplies and tie everything down. Cal had to agree that it would not have been feasible to convey everything to the undersea tunnel in that period. They would have had to sustain a serious loss of supplies, unless the wave were minor. But Circe could probably not have detected the advance tremours of a minor one. Perhaps this raft, fragile as it seemed, *was* the best alternative. But with only two hours to reach deep water, and no sail—

They boarded and pushed off without ceremony. Veg poled the craft out from the island while Cal and Aquilon paddled as well as they were able with splayed palm-flower pods, and the four mantas circled on the water. Cal was glad he had recovered enough of his strength to make a decent show of it. Six months ago he would not have been able to lift the crude oar, let alone use it effectively. He owed his resurgence to Nacre – the planet, not the raft – that had been inhospitable to man's physique but excellent for his spirit.

No – the planet had been no more than the locale. The benefit had been due to the friendship of two people – *these* two people – that had faced him back towards life.

He continued to row. His arms were tired, but the thought of that approaching wave kept him working. How *had* the mantas known of the tsunami? They could not have detected a shock wave in the water, because the wave *was* the shock. Yet he was sure they were correct, for they did not make mistakes of that nature. Something important would happen with the water, and if not a wave it was because he had misinterpreted Circe's message. There must have been a vibration that their peculiar eyesight had picked up, or a radiation typical of large land movements. Something that not only signalled trouble, but allowed the mantas to judge its time of arrival.

There was still much to learn about these fungus companions. And much to learn about tsunamis.

All loose equipment was in the cabin, and that tiny enclosure was tied together and sealed as well as limited time and resource permitted; but Cal retained grave doubts about the outcome of this jaunt. He was not afraid of death – actually, he rather approved of it as a natural institution – but disliked contemplating the premature termination of the young lives of those who had befriended him. And there was the group's mission to be considered: the charting of life on this Paleocene planet. Better to die after the mysteries of this world had been fathomed and the report made; then the effort would not have been wasted.

Veg took over Cal's oar as soon as they were out of poling depth, and Cal moved gratefully to the rudder. This was little more than a paddle tied between two projecting logs, and in view of the *Nacre*'s overall clumsiness seemed almost useless. But they did make steady if tedious progress towards the open sea.

They had hardly gotten far enough before their time was up. Cal had carefully directed them away from the direction Circe indicated for the oncoming tsunami, so that the island stood between them and it. He hoped they would thereby escape the worst of it even though the water was still too shallow for safety. The swell should bear them *away* from land, rather than into the turbulence of the shallows.

The time came – and nothing happened. 'False alarm,' Aquilon announced, sounding uncertain whether to be annoyed or relieved.

'Not necessarily so,' Cal cautioned her. 'The first signs of the typical tsunami are inconspicuous. A very small rise in the water level, followed by a deeper trough. But the second or third real wave shows its full mischief. Keep paddling.'

Aquilon looked dubiously at the serene island behind them. 'I somehow thought a tidal wave was a tall wall of water striking without warning,' she said.

'That may be true enough, for those on land who aren't alert for the signals. Of course "tidal wave" is a misnomer. The phenomenon has nothing to do with the tides.'

Veg kept paddling.

Fifteen minutes passed placidly. They nudged farther into the ocean.

'Are you *sure*—?' Aquilon inquired.

'Of course I'm not sure,' he told her. 'It is possible that we misunderstood what Circe was trying to tell us. It is also true that most tsunamis are not serious affairs; that depends on the severity of the incitation and its distance from the observer's position.'

'Now he tells us,' Veg muttered.

'However, Circe was alarmed, and I suspect she had good reason,' Cal said. 'Because of the masses of water involved, the waves may be over a hundred miles apart. I wouldn't count the danger as over until a couple more hours pass.'

Veg shrugged and kept working on his oar. 'Quitest calamity I ever survived.'

The four mantas had been ranging out, then returning to the raft to rest. They seemed to require frequent quiescence. Cal had never had the opportunity to watch them in action for days at a time like this, and it was instructive. On Earth he had found them a secluded island to camp out on, and had seen them only occasionally thereafter. There had never been a laboratory analysis of their metabolism, but he suspected that it was not conducive to sustained energy output of the level of Earthly animals. They were cold-blooded, for one thing. Not that their body fluid resembled blood in any chemical way, or that it was actually cool – but it did suggest a basic conservation of energy. Cold temperature inhibited them; that was probably the main reason the majority had elected to stay with him in the subtropics, on Earth. They were saprophytes, feeding on the breakdown of organic matter; to what extent did temperature affect their chemistry? Or were they inhibited now because they were primed to spore upon death – a state that must be equivalent to pregnancy in a mammal? The mantas he had seen die on Nacre had not spored, since their deaths had been unexpected and they had not been primed.

Now they were resting. Fatigue, boredom – or in preparation for some unusual stress ahead? It pained him to be so ignorant.

Forty minutes after the scheduled arrival of the tsunami, Veg saw something. He stopped rowing and watched. The others, noting his reaction, did the same.

It was as though a weathered mountain were rising on the horizon behind the island. The water humped up grotesquely, its main height concealed by the island foliage. Even so, the swell was not really striking; the highest point could not be much more than thirty feet above sea norm.

'We could have weathered that,' Veg remarked.

Cal kept his peace. He knew what was coming, and his mind's eye augmented the visible traces. The wave was rising on the shallows leading up to the island, the same submarine slant they had walked up from the tunnel. From the look of it, there was a fairly extensive submerged reef angling across the path of the tsunami shock wave.

Near the island the rolling swell became a peaked wave at last, showing a tumbling white crest and emitting an increasing roar. The water formed into a vertical wall – he heard Aquilon's intake of breath – and crashed over the green landscape. A cloud of spume went up, as though a tremendous explosion had sundered the island. A rainbow appeared in the sky, tribute to the water sprayed high into the atmosphere.

'We could have weathered that!' Aquilon said, mimicking Veg's remark without malicious intent.

Then the misty wake was upon them. White foam surged by the raft, lifting it precariously and causing the logs to shift against each other, and bits of island debris bobbed about.

The swell subsided and they viewed the island again. From this distance it seemed unchanged, but Cal knew that terrible havoc had been wreaked there. The mantas' warning had been valid.

Reminded, he turned to check on their otherworld associates. Circe, Diam, Hex, and Star stood on the roof of the cabin looking

215

miserable. They would have had difficulty running over this wave; its changing configuration and bubbly surface could easily have inundated them. Though a manta could 'walk' on water, it could not swim within it, except for very brief scoops at speed. A manta had to keep moving swiftly or stop entirely, when the surface was liquid. These four needed the raft more than the humans did in this instance.

Yet they could have avoided the problem nicely by travelling over deep water, where the swell of the tsunami was mild. Did they feel an emotional loyalty to the human party? It always came back to what he did not know about them. Right now, however, his job was this planet, not manta.

In due course the second wave crashed over the isle. Others followed at about twenty-minute intervals, but the worst was over. the raft had saved the party.

'I believe it is safe to return now,' Cal said at last.

'Why?' Veg asked.

Cal looked at him, so tousled and sweaty and strong. 'Are you implying that the raft is better than a land base?' The notion was foolish; there was not room to spread his shells or keep them secure, let alone acquire more.

'I'm implying we can't travel far on an island.'

'Travel! These winds are obviously seasonal. Once we drift from this vicinity, we'll be unable to return for months.'

Veg nodded.

So it was coming into the open already: the decision to mutiny, to break contact with the Earth authorities. Not completely, for the radio equipment could keep them in touch. But since they would be unable to return if so directed . . .

Veg wanted simply to isolate himself from a hateful influence, and Cal understood this entirely too well. Yet he could not so casually justify the abrogation of the mission. They were not here on any vacation, and too obvious a balk could trigger the trouble already building for them.

In addition, if this were Paleocene Earth, the consequence of activity on the mainland could ramify appallingly. What *about* the paradoxes of time travel? They had not yet done anything significant, for their traces on the island would have been wiped out by the tsunami – but such good fortune could not be perpetual. What would happen when some action of theirs threatened to change the nature of their own reality? Such paradox was patently impossible – but the situation could be extremely delicate.

'It seems to me we would have to move about a bit to gather information,' Aquilon said. 'For a proper report, I mean. We should at least map the continents—'

'Map the continents!' Cal knew she meant the floral and faunal features, since they already had the map, but still it was an excuse. 'That would take a full-fledged survey party several years with a cartographic satellite. And we already know what they would find.'

'That reminds me,' she said. 'That map. How do you know—'

'I'd have to go into paleogeography to explain that. It—'

'Summarize it,' Veg said, irritated. He was holding his paddle and seemed anxious to use it, rather than talking. But Aquilon must have brought up this matter now in order to make sure Veg knew about it.

Summarize the concept of drifting continents? Cal sighed inwardly. It had to be done, though, and now did seem to be the time. Now – before they committed themselves to the mainland. 'Well . . . the crust of the Earth may seem solid and permanent to us today, but in fact it is boiling and moving steadily. Like the surface of a pot of cooking oatmeal (he saw they didn't comprehend the allusion, but let it stand), it bubbles up in some regions and cools and solidifies and sinks down in creases elsewhere. Segments of the more solid, lighter material float, collecting above the creases until large masses are built up by the action. These are the continents – or rather, the single continent, that formed billions of years ago, then broke up as the convection patterns changed, drifted, reformed. Two hundred and fifty million years ago there were two great continents, two halves separated by narrow seas: Laurasia in the north, Gondwanaland in the south. These broke up into the present continents, and changes are still occurring. In time the Americas may complete their journey across the oceans and rejoin the main land mass from the other side—'

'Watch it,' Veg said. 'You're theorizing.'

'Now I remember!' Aquilon said. 'They verified the continental drift by checking the magnetism of the ocean floor. The metal in the rocks that bubbled up was aligned with the magnetic poles as the material cooled and hardened, so there was a record, and they could tell where it had been when.'

217

'Something like that,' Cal agreed, surprised that she had made the connection. 'There were other ways to corroborate the phenomenon, too. Computer analysis showed how certain continents, such as Australia and Antarctica, made a precise fit despite being separated by two thousand miles of water. The underlying strata also matched. All over the world, the changing continental geography could be interpolated to show the configuration for any particular period. The map I had you sketch strongly suggested the Paleocene epoch, since the major continents as we know them had only recently severed from the main masses and remained relatively close together.'

'So where are we now – on Earth?' Veg asked.

'Our island here is some distance off the coast of what will be known as California. In our time western America has overridden one of the Pacific rifts and so developed the San Andreas Fault, a source of regular earthquakes. This has been an active area of the world for some time, and no doubt this tsunami stems from—'

'We can't just sit here talking,' Veg grumbled. 'There might be another wave.'

'And we really should take a look at California,' Aquilon said. 'The westerlies should take us right there, and I could paint some of the animal life for your report.'

Cal perceived that she had an ulterior motive. She didn't truly comprehend something until she painted it, and she was intrigued by the notion of treading the soils of the past. She was not concerned about paradox.

'We aren't operating as an isolated party,' he said. 'There could be consequences—'

'Maybe we should take a vote,' Veg suggested.

Cal already knew the outcome of that. Trust the group to revert to elementary democracy in this wilderness world. The others were not trained to appreciate the enormous fund of information available on the single island, or to anticipate the vagaries of seemingly steady wind. It would be far safer to remain here, and more efficient. Though there *was* that matter of the spores in the station ... and he could not outvote the two of them.

'Four out of seven?' Cal inquired.

Veg and Aquilon exchanged glances. They had not thought of this. If the precedent of voting on key decisions were established, the precendent of including the mantas as franchised individuals would also be in force.

'Manta suffrage,' Aquilon murmured.

In the course of a difficult discussion the nature of the voting concept and practice was conveyed to the mantas: each entity to cast his ballot, the minority amenable to the will of the majority. Cal wondered whether the fungoid creatures really understood. They could easily cast a bloc vote. Should they have been considered as a single entity, one vote for the group of them? Too late now.

Cal called off the names in alphabetical order. Each voter would advance to the bow if he wished to travel on the raft, and to the stern if he wished to remain based on the island.

''Quilon.' She stepped to the bow, and the tally stood one to nothing, raft.

'Cal.' After he spoke his own name, he moved to the rear. The truth was that he did want to explore, and to get away from Earth's influence – but he did not want to alarm the others by giving his reasons, or to have it on record that he approved the jaunt. There were sometimes distinct advantages to a split decision, particularly when the results would be recorded and evaluated by unfriendly officials.

'Circe.' Here was the test: which way would the manta jump?

Circe hopped to join Aquilon. Two to one.

'Diam.' This could decide it, for Veg surely wanted to explore, and that would make a majority.

Diam bounded into the air, shaking the raft by the force of his takeoff, flared, and came down beside Cal. Two to two – and they were *not* bloc voting!

'Hex.' That was Veg's companion. But if Circe had joined Aquilon from personal sentiment, Hex could not do the same, for Veg had not yet formally committed himself.

Hex joined the bow party, and it was three to two. The outcome was no longer in doubt, but the vote had to be officially completed.

'Star.' Star had stayed with Cal throughout, as had Diam. Would he choose accordingly, as a matter of academic curiosity?

Star did. Three to three.

'Veg.' And of course Veg went forward. The issue had been decided, and – what was far more significant – the mantas had voted as individuals.

The party of seven was about to travel, and Cal was glad.

219

Chapter Seven

ORN

Time was long, yet it was nothing, for he only wandered and grew. He crossed inland mountains – the kind that developed from shifts and buckles of the ground, rather than from ash and lava – and plains and swamps, bearing east. Though he ran his limit each day. stopping only to feed himself, the summer was waning before he reached the new ocean formed from the widening chasm between land fragments. He had verified his general map: this land was now far away from its origin, and was still moving.

Increasing cold nudged him south. Many things had changed, and much of the landscape differed substantially from that of his memory, but that was the way of the Earth. It always changed, as the waves on the seas changed, and so had to be resurveyed periodically for posterity.

The mams were everywhere. Small primes twittered in the occasional grassy areas, burrowing for grubs and tubers, and some peered at him from trees with great round eyes. They were generally fragile and shy, yet numerous; he fed on them frequently. Every so often he brought down a dino, horned, but clumsy and not very bright. This creature tended to become absorbed in his browsing and not be alert for danger.

There were also a number of snakes, and many liz and small amphibs, all feeding on the plentiful arths. And Orn did too, tearing open anthills with relish and picking up the scurrying morsels with his gluey tongue. Never in his memory had there been such regular feasting!

Aves filled the trees, benefiting even more from the arth supply. The birds had become more diverse than ever, and were now excellent fliers. Several lines swam in the ponds and rivers, and others ran along the ground as he did, though none of these were closely allied to him. His line had been land-bound longer, and during more dangerous times; thus he was larger and swifter than these newcomers. Many of the others would never have been able to survive attack by a running rep.

Winter promised to be far more severe than his prior one on the island. Orn continued driving south, making good progress; yet the cold stalked him. There was nowhere he could set up a regular abode. He could withstand freezing temperatures for short periods, but this sapped his strength. His plumage was not thick enough to protect him against a prolonged siege, even though many smaller birds endured winter well enough. He was becoming tired of perpetual travel; he was almost full-grown now, and beginning to respond to developing urges for other things.

He did not recognize in himself the nesting impulse, for only the sight of a nubile female of his species would clarify that. But he carried on with increasing and undefined hunger, hurrying somewhere while wanting to stay where he was. It was not only the onrushing season that disturbed him.

At last his southward progress was blocked by mountains. They were volcanic, and therefore to be treated with respect and fear. He trotted west, seeking a way around them, but was met after a day by a great ocean. He had crossed the continent again, intersecting the coastline here where the land mass narrowed. He had either to give up or to proceed on through this region; the nights of the inland area had become far too cold now for his comfort.

The range extended into the sea, the individual summits diminishing to islands and finally reefs. These isles would be warm, he knew – but Orn did not care to set up residence in such a precarious locale again. He could abide a quiescent volcano, or an island, but not the combination. That was too much of a trap.

So it had to be the land route. He had no memory of the territory ahead; the configurations of this landscape had shifted too rapidly and drastically in the last few million years. The wall of volcanoes was new, certainly – and if any prospective ancestor had penetrated it, that bird had never emerged to sire his line thereafter. Sometimes what Orn could not remember spoke as eloquently as what he could.

He found a promising avenue a few mountains from the coast and moved in. It was a pass of a sort – a fissure between two of the lesser peaks, overgrown with bracken and a tough new strain of grass. Some water trickled along it, but not enough; he risked thirst here.

But better that than the other flow – of liquid stone.

The mountains were dead. He could read their histories as he passed, observing the remnants of ancient lava fields and mounded ash. The sides of the gully were weathered and overgrown with brush. He made a foray up one slope and brought down a young, slow-footed ambly who had strayed into this inhospitable region. He severed its jugular with a single contraction of his beak muscles, and fed quickly on the warm carcass. There was far more meat than he could consume at one time, but he had to tolerate the waste this time because of the need to save his strength for the climb ahead. An arduous, tedious search for small prey at this time would have worn him down, though ordinarily he killed no larger than his hunger, however vulnerable the prey.

The air was cold as he fed, and the warmth of the flesh he swallowed was fleeting. Almost, he desired a little more activity in the old fire cones. Almost.

In the morning he outran the cleft and crossed the steep side of the smaller mountain, stiffening his feathers against the chill wind that struck at this height. Then he was over the pass, and it was warmer on the other side. Too much so: he smelled the fumes of an active volcano.

There was no way to avoid it. The cold of the heights forced him to seek the lowest valleys, and from the great basin ahead rose the live cone. Fires danced upon its rim, reflected from the hanging clouds above it, and as Orn approached the ground quivered omniously.

It took him a full day to skirt it, and he watched its every malignant gesture. This was not a lava mountain; this one was the more deadly gas and ash type. No plants grew near it. Yet he found arths amid the tumbled rocks of its perimeter, and one semi-stagnant pond, so his hunger and thirst were partially abated.

On the southern slope the volcano caught him. Monstrous gases swirled out of its cruel orifice, forming a burgeoning cloud that glowed of its own accord. As night came this cloud drifted south – following Orn. As it gained on him, slow-moving as it seemed, the thing began to rain: a downpour of incandescent droplets that accumulated voluminously on the ground.

Orn fled before it, knowing that the smallest touch of that fiery storm meant annihilation. He did escape – but his retreat had been

222

sealed off. He could not know what lay ahead, but death lay behind.

Exhausted, he perched at last upon a jagged boulder and slept nervously amid the drifting fringe gases of the storm. In all that murky region there was nothing alive but him.

Next day he came across a spring of boiling water. Where it overflowed into a basin and cooled sufficiently, he washed the cutting grime from his feathers and felt clean again. Once more there were arths; he scratched for grubs and had a partial meal.

After that there was more even ground, and he made good time though the unusually rough turf abraded his feet. The rocks were warm, and not entirely from the sun, with many heated ponds. He washed cautiously and drank the richly flavoured water dubiously, but found no fish. He avoided the boiling mud and steaming fumaroles, and particularly the active cones.

It was an awful landscape, jagged in the distance, bare and dead up close. He longed for the end of it, but feared that there was no end. He felt too vulnerable without his memory to guide him.

Gradually the land levelled into a desert, and though Orn made excellent time here, he had to go without food and water for two days. Because of his rapid metabolism a third day would finish him. Not at once, but by crippling him and thus preventing any possible escape. Yet he also lacked the resources to retreat. He pushed on. There was nothing else to do.

Though the evening brought relief from the ambient heat, this was scant consolation. The cold was severe, and he had to roost on the ground and half bury himself in dust as a hedge against it. Now he had no way to cleanse his feathers properly or to slake his terrible thirst. He almost felt like a mam, the way this territory wrung the moisture from his body; but no mam could have travelled this far.

On the second morning he lay stiffly for a time, waiting for the sun to restore what energy it might to his body. His flesh, under the battered and poorly insulating feathers was dehydrated – yet he knew that the day would soon dry it out farther. Would it be more comfortable to rouse himself for the terminal effort, or to lie here and let death visit him peacefully?

Across the brightening desert he saw the sunlight stab at a rising wisp of mist, giving it momentary brilliance as the beam refracted. This was the single instant of the day that these barrens had beauty, however slight.

Then his memory informed him what mist meant. Orn lurched to his feet, flapping his stubby wings in his eagerness, and staggered forward. He was weak, his feet were bruised, his muscles hurting, and he doubted that he could crack open a hard nut with his beak – but he covered the ground.

There was a gully where the mist had been. Within this depression was a cleft similar to the one he had followed into these badlands. And at the bottom of this crevice was a tiny flow of water.

Orn dug a pit in the sand with his broken talons and set his head in it. He lay there and the water trickled over his tongue.

He remained there all day, and by night he was not thirsty any more.

He followed the riven gully down, too hungry now to sleep. A quarter day's trek below his point of interception the first stunted vegetation appeared. He dug it out in the dark and swallowed it, hoping to find nutritious grubs within. He had not recovered enough to be able to tell by smell. Then he relaxed.

The following day was better. The cleft, at first only a few wingspans across, broadened out into a winding canyon, and creeping foliage covered its shadowed sides. It was hot, but not nearly as bad as the burning desert. The minuscule water had been reinforced from offshoot crevices and gathered into a running brook. Orn travelled slowly and recovered his strength.

At last there was enough water pooled for a proper washing, and he bathed with delight. Once more he could fluff out his feathers and protect himself better from cold.

But on the second day he climbed the canyon wall and poked his head over the rim and spied – a steaming mountain. He was not out of the volcano belt yet; the desert and cleft had been only a hiatus.

The canyon widened out and finally the water in it levelled and became salty. He was back at the sea.

But with a difference. He had passed the first major belt of mountains and reached a warmer area. He might be able to make a winter nest in a burrow by the water, within the protected canyon, and feed on fish.

Then he discovered the underground river.

It opened into the canyon wall: a squat tunnel from which warm water poured. He braced himself against its gentle current and entered the cavern. Light spilled from natural vents in the ceiling,

224

and he saw stone columns he recognized as typical of such places. His ancestors had often stayed in caves. This was better, much better; he could winter here in comfort, going outside only for forage.

Unless other animals – predators – had the same notion.

Orn sniffed the slowly moving air. The worst came to him then, hidden before by the lingering insensitivity left over from his desert thirst: the rank odour of a large rep.

He sought out the source, alert for rapid retreat. Not all reps were inimical, and this smell was borderline.

He found it lying half-submerged. It was a Para, five times Orn's own length and many times as massive. Its four feet were webbed for efficient swimming, and its tail was long and powerful. There was no armour on its body. Its head was equipped with a large scooplike bill that Orn remembered was used to delve into the soft muck of shallow ponds. It had a monstrous bony crest that projected back so far that it effectively doubled the length of the head. Through this process the nasal passages ran, and to it the hot blood of the active animal was pumped for cooling in the heat of the day. Too much heat was deadly to reps, and the large ones had trouble dissipating it; thus this evaporative cooling system gave the Para an advantage over his cousins. Neither exertion nor noon sunlight was likely to harm him.

Nevertheless, the Para was dead, its flesh rotting.

This was a creature of the old type. Orn had not seen such a rep in anything but memory before, except for the crocs, but it was familiar in a way the tiny mams were not. Paras were among those reps who had dominated the world for much of his memory, and who until this moment had seemed to be absent from it.

Yet something had killed it. Not an animal enemy, for the creature was unmarked except for those bruises typical of inanimate encounters, and post-mortem infestation. Not thirst or hunger, for it was sleek and in potable water.

If this superbly equipped animal had succumbed within this cavern, far more its natural habitat than Orn's, how could Orn expect to survive?

Better to brave the dangers he knew, than to subject himself to the sordid and fatal mystery of this place. He would have to continue his journey.

225

Chapter Eight

AQUILON

They sailed due east. The *Nacre*'s yardwork was crude – a wedge of rubberoid sheeting buttressed by palm fronds suspended on half a dozen transverse bamboo poles, vaguely in the manner of a Chinese junk. Nothing better had been available. It would have taken them weeks to form a suitable sail from natural materials, and they might not have held the wind any better than this cut-and-stretched balloon material.

When Veg wanted to slow progress, he let out a supportive rope and the sail collapsed in a mess of sticks; when he wanted full power, he hauled it back up, using all his brute strength.

It functioned, anyway. When the breeze was stiff, Aquilon judged that they made as much as five knots. Ordinarily the rate was more like two. Thus they traversed from fifty to a hundred miles per day, for the *Nacre* never rested. Respectable progress!

The sea air was balmy, the day clear. But the perpetually rolling waves lifted the raft, tilted it, dropped it, and lifted it again interminably, and very soon Aquilon was feeling more than queasy. She was sure the men had a similar complaint. She felt sorry for Cal, hanging bravely to a rope knotted around a log. Not only did he seem to be in continual peril of being washed overboard – that was why he had the rope – but he looked quite sick. Veg didn't complain, but he hadn't eaten all day. Aquilon herself had simply puked into the water and felt better for a while – until being blessed with the dry heaves. She wondered whether the mantas, perched in the cabin shade, had equivalent difficulties.

She tried to distract herself by watching the sights. The heaving seascape was no help at all, but she found she could see a good deal by donning her diving mask, immersing her head, and peering down through the water. Once she learned the trick of compensating for the flexing façade of the surface.

The sea, at first glance so desolate, was actually full of life. Aquilon had some familiarity with fish, having painted them many times and she had also done a number of dissections for anatomical illustrations. The species here were not identical to those she knew, but they fell into similar patterns, and some were so close she was sure only an ichthyologist would be able to differentiate the types. A school of herring drifted directly under the raft, flanked by a shark she couldn't quite see. Then a four-foot tuna cut across, and suddenly several flying fish broke surface and skated over the water, their fins spread like the wings of insects. Half an hour later she spied several cod, then some jacks, and finally a great lone swordfish fully eight feet long.

She lifted her head at last and doffed the mask, deciding that her seasickness was coming under control. It was late afternoon. The two men seemed listless, perhaps dulled by the monotony of the waves. Veg was spume-flecked; Cal now leaned against the cabin. The four mantas remained where they had been. They would not venture forth in direct sunlight, of course; that was too rough on their eyes.

'Tennis, anyone?' she inquired with mock cheer. 'Or maybe supper?'

But no one replied, and she wasn't hungry herself. There were supplies on board for several days, so foraging from the sea was not necessary. Yet.

She pondered this, since she was already feeling dismal. Suppose the map were wrong, and California was not within three or four hundred miles? Suppose they had to remain on the raft for two weeks? By then the stored food would run out, and the canned water. If they were to survive, they would have to fish, consuming the flesh and grinding out fish-body fluids to drink. It was feasible; they all knew the techniques, and the necessary equipment was part of the lift-raft package. But Veg would not touch fish, himself, and might refuse to bring in any for the others. She could do it herself – but she now shared Veg's viewpoint to a considerable extent, though her rationale was different, and wasn't sure she cared to go back to an omnivorous diet. It would make her feel unclean. Would she eat fish if she got hungry enough, and drink fish juice? Would she kill another living, feeling creature in order to slake her own needs? She didn't know – but the feeling that she *might* made her feel again.

227

What value was a moral standard, if it disappeared the moment it became inconvenient or uncomfortable?

They took turns sleeping, one at a time – not from any urge for privacy but to insure that two were always alert to the vagaries of the sea. Their collective motion sickness was responsible for the pessimistic outlook for the voyage, she was sure, but meanwhile caution was their only resource.

She lay alone in the cabin, listening to the slap of the waves against the logs and trying to ignore the swells of brine that inundated the nethermost centimeter of her torso at irregular intervals. In time, she knew, she would acquire the reflex to hold her breath even in her sleep for those essential seconds, and would not even notice the involuntary baths. Human beings were adaptable; that was why they survived.

Survival. It seemed to have less to recommend it recently. How blithely she had cast her ballot in favour of this stomach-wringing journey! Cal, at least, had forseen what it entailed. One overruled his judgement at one's peril. Now it was far too late to change course; the force of air driving them along would not permit it. With this clumsy vehicle they could not hope to tack into the wind effectively – and even if they could, it would take twice as long (at best!) to return to their island as the outward trip had taken. There was no way to escape at least another day of oceanic violence.

Yet she was dead tired, and sleep had to come. The mantas seemed to be comfortable enough on the cabin roof, so why couldn't she be likewise here? Gradually she acclimatized and passed into a fitful dream state interspersed with ten-second cold shocks as the pseudo-tide touched her again and again.

She found herself – no, not back in her cosy Earth apartment, for that physical comfort was empty in the face of the intellectual horror on which it rested. She did not like Earth; she had no fond memories to bind her to it. Space meant more to her, Nacre meant more, and the easy, sexless companionship of these two men. Her dream was of current matters, her nearest approach to joy: the day and night just passed on the island.

She stood conversing with Cal, and he was taller and stronger than in life, and simultaneously she painted the shells of his collection. They were ammonite fossils, extinct just yesterday, geologically speaking – extinct, that is, barely ten million years ago. And her picture grew as she filled in the colour; it swelled and became real, and then she was walking into it, or rather swimming, for it was a living ocean habitat. All around her floated the cephalopods, their shells coiled, straight, or indecisive. Most were small, but some were large – fist-sized, even head-sized, their tentacles spread out hungrily, fifty or a hundred for each individual, plus the two larger feeder tentacles.

She was stroking lithely, but these clumsy-seeming molluscs were more agile. Their bodies matched the specific gravity of the water so that they neither lifted nor sank involuntarily, and they moved rapidly backward as they jetted water from their hyponomes. She could not catch any in her hands, try as she might. Soon she gave up the attempt, and then they drifted confidently closer to her, shells sparkling iridescently.

It was a wonderland of bright living coral and sponge and jellyfish and crabs and forestlike seaweed, with the abundant 'bony' fish circulating everywhere. But the cephalopods dominated the scene – small squids shooting past in shoals, almost indistinguishable from fish at that velocity. There were also the relatives of the cephalopods: the belemnites, and the nautiloids and ammonites. The molluscs did not swim in the manner of vertebrates, however; they all moved by that same jet propulsion, using their finlike members only for guidance. The belemnites were cigar-shaped shells completely surrounded by flesh, almost like little manta rays with backbones fused.

They were feeding now, culling animalcules and tiny fishes from the water with their myriad tentacles and bearing them in to the mouth parts. Their big round eyes stared at her as she went along. The individuals were getting larger; some were more than a foot in diameter across the coiled shell, and their short tentacles were six inches.

Their shells were varied, but nowhere did the markings of the septa show. She remembered that Cal had explained about that: the sutures were the internal joining places of the septa, analogous to the dark rings inside a poorly washed coffee cup. They did not ordinarily show externally. Where the septum, or disc blocking off a segment of the interior was flat, the suture merely ringed the inside of the shell. But the more advanced ammonities had fluted sutures, reflecting a convoluted septum. She visualized the situation, using a straight shell for convenience rather than a normal coiled one:

LIVE   FLAT   FLUTED

The sutures became more and more complex as the ammonoids developed, until in the middle Cretaceous they were phenomenal. Loops formed within loops, resembling the profile of elaborate branching coral.

Aquilon contemplated an ammonite fully eighteen inches in diameter, tentacles as long as her hand reaching out from it. The creature was impressive in much the manner of a monstrous spider. She waved her hand at it, and it snapped back into its shell, closing its hood over its head. She laughed, making bubbles in the water (where did she find air to breathe? she wondered fleetingly, but this was immaterial) and waited for the cephalopod to lift its anterior portcullis and peep out again. So much like a hermit crab, she thought – only this was a hermit octopus, who constructed its own shell.

'Take me to your leader,' she said as its eyes reappeared.

The ammonite nodded with its entire body and jetted away, its tentacles streaming behind. She followed, not really surprised.

Through bays and inlets of coral they swam, by algae-covered rocks and sea moss like green waving hair, and now and then a stray brown kelp anchored to the bottom with its top held near the surface by small bladders of gas. Purple, green, orange, solid or tenuous, the shallow-water plants decorated the reef. Starfish crowded near vaselike sponges, and beautiful but dangerous sea anemones perched on stones or the backs of crabs. Green spiked sea urchins and dark sand dollars dotted the bottom sand (where sand occurred), and green lobsters gestured with their terrible pincers. She had to swerve to avoid a giant ancient horseshoe crab. And the bivalves – they were everywhere!

She longed to stop and begin painting – but then she would lose the guide, for that fast-jetting mollusc gave her no time to lag. Tragedy!

Then, abruptly, she faced it; a coiled ammonite shell over six feet in diameter. Her guide was gone, perhaps afraid for its own safety, and she was on her own.

The tremendous hood hoisted up, a gateway almost as tall as she was in that position. Yellow tentacles snaked out, writhing towards her. She was frightened now, but she stood her ground as well as her buoyancy permitted. An eye the size of a small saucer fixed on her.

'Yes?' the king of the ammonites said. No bubbles rose, for it was not an air breather.

She didn't want to admit that its speech surprised her, so she asked it an inane question. 'Are your sutures fluted?'

A hundred tentacles formed a frown. 'Are they fluted, *what*?'

She blushed. 'Are they fluted, *Your Majesty*?'

The frown writhed into neutrality. 'Honeyshell,' King Ammon said, 'my sutures are royally fluted and convoluted, each in the shape of a finely crafted crown. Would you care to examine them from the inside?' Its purple tentacles were extending towards her, each a yard long, and its mouth pried itself open.

'No,' she said, quickly, backpedalling.

'One does not,' Ammon remarked slowly, 'say no to the king.' Several of its red tentacles were coiling around projections in the coral reef, as though ready to pull the entire shell forward suddenly.

'I meant—' She cast about for the proper phraseology. 'Your Majesty, I meant that I could never think of doubting the statement of the king so it would be insulting to suggest any closer inspection, Your Majesty.'

The tentacles relaxed while Ammon considered. 'There is that.' Somehow she had the impression the king was disappointed. Now he was green.

'What I came to ask,' she said humbly, 'was why? Why do you need such a complex pattern, when no one can admire it ... from outside?'

'*I* can admire it very well from the inside – and my opinion is the only one that matters. And I am hungry.'

'Hungry?' She didn't make the connection, unless this were a hint

231

that she should get farther out of range. But the king surely could move through the water faster than she, and he had so many appendages! Brown, at the moment.

'I perceive you do not comprehend the way of the ammonite,' Ammon remarked. 'You vertebrates are powerful but clumsy. You have only four or five extremities, one or two colours, and your shell is obscure.'

'We do our best to live with our handicaps,' she said.

'Actually, you're decent enough, for a lower species,' Ammon admitted graciously. 'It behooves me to educate you. Pay attention: our primitive ancestors, the Nautiloids, had simplistic septums, hardly more than dismal discs, and so their sutures were aconvolute. They scrounged and scavenged after a fashion, gobbling down anything they could catch, and doubtless made a living of sorts. But we ammonites learned the secret of specialization: by varying the size of the space between the torso and the outermost septum, the early ammonite was able to change its specific gravity. Larger air pocket (actually a unique gas – but you would not comprehend the secret formula), and he floated; smaller, and he sank. Do you understand?'

'Oh, yes,' she said. 'That would be a big advantage in swimming, since you could maintain any level without effort.'

'Hm.' King Ammon did not seem to be entirely pleased. 'Just so. Now with a flat septum there is not much purchase, since the body is anchored only at the rim and the siphuncle. You know what the siphuncle is, of course?'

'No, sir,' she said.

'Hm.' The mollusc was pleased this time. 'That is the cord of flesh that passes through the septa and chambers of the shell, right back to the very end. Have to keep in touch, you know. I suppose your tail is a clumsy effort in that direction. At any rate, a convoluted septum, matching the configuration of the body surface, is a more effective base for adjustment of the volume of that gaseous partition. So we ammonities have superior depth control. That enables us to feed more effectively, among other things.'

'How clever!' Aquilon exclaimed. 'I can see how you grew so large. But what do you eat?'

'Zilch, naturally. What else would a sapient species bother to consume?'

'I don't think we vertebrates are that advanced. I don't even know what zilch is.'

Ammon's tentacles writhed and went rainbow at this astonishing confession of ignorance, but he courteously refrained from remarking on it. 'Call it a type of marine fungus. There are quite a number of varieties, and naturally each ammonite species specializes on one. I imbibe nothing less than Royal Zilch, for example. No other creature can feed thereon!'

'By kingly decree?' She had not realized that ammonites were so finicky.

'By no means, though it is an interesting thought. No lesser creature has the physical capability to capture a Royal Zilch, let alone to assimilate it. It is necessary to lock on to its depth and duplicate its evasive course precisely, or all is lost. One mistake, and the zilch eats *you*.'

Oh. 'That's why your convolutions are so important. Your hunting is dangerous.'

'Yes. I can, among other feats, navigate to an accuracy of two millimetres, plus or minus 15 percent, while interpenetrating the zilch with seventy-three tentacles.' Grey members waved proudly. 'And I've seldom been slashed.'

This was beginning to sound like doubletalk to Aquilon. But she remained entirely too close to the king to risk contradicting him directly. He might yet develop an appetite for bipedal vertebrate à la blonde. 'I'm amazed you can coordinate so well.'

'Your amazement is entirely proper, my dear. You, with your mere five or six appendages, can hardly appreciate the magnitude of the task. And every unit has to be under specific control. The nervous system this entails – you know what a brain is?'

'I think so.'

'Hm. Well, I have a sizable brain. As a matter of fact, the convolutions of my septa merely reflect the configuration of the surface lobes of my brain, which are naturally housed deep within my shell for proper protection. It is my advanced brain that sets me off from all other species; nothing like it exists elsewhere, nothing ever has, nothing ever will. That is why I am king.'

Aquilon searched for some suitable comment.

Suddenly Ammon turned orange and lifted grandly in the water. She had supposed him bottom-bound because of his size, but he

233

moved with exactly the control he had claimed, smoothly and powerfully. 'There's one!'

She peered about anxiously. 'One what?'

'One Royal Zilch. My meal!' And the king jetted off.

Now she saw his prey, a flat grey shape. 'No!' she cried with sudden horror. 'That's Circe!'

But the chase was already on, the monster cephalopod shooting backwards in pursuit of the fleeing manta. She knew how helpless the mantas were in water, and foresaw only one outcome of this chase. 'No!' she cried again, desperately, but the bubbles merely rose upwards from her mouth, carrying her protest snared within them.

She woke with a mouthful of sea water, her body soaking and shivering, and she still felt sick. She clambered out into the chill breeze. It was 4.00 a.m., or close enough and time for her shift on watch to begin.

Veg had the four-to-eight sleep, and she didn't envy him his attempt in the watery cabin. The mantas wisely remained on the roof, seemingly oblivious of the continual spray. A gentle phosphorescence showed the outlines of the rolling waves, and the wind continued unabated. Now that she was fully awake and erect, she found the chill night breeze refreshing.

There was not much to do. Veg had lashed the rudder and cut the sail to a quarter spread, and the *Nacre* was stable. They had merely to remain alert and act quickly if anything untoward happened. She did not expect to see more than routine waves, however.

'Cal,' she ventured.

'Yes, 'Quilon,' he said immediately. He did not sound tired, though he could not have had any better rest than she had had, during his turn in the cabin. This was a rough vigil for him. The fact that he was able to bear up at all meant that he had gained strength considerably since Nacre. That was reassuring.

'The ammonites – could they have been intelligent?'

She was afraid as she said it that he would laugh; but he was silent for a time, considering it. She waited for him, feeling the damp air in her hair, the vibrations of the shifting logs underfoot. No, Cal was not the one to laugh at a foolish question; he always took in the larger framework, the reason behind the statement.

'Highly unlikely, If you mean in any advanced manner. They had neither the size nor the metabolism to support extensive brain tissue, and water is a poor environment for intellectual activity. It—'

'I mean – the big ones. As big as us.'

'Most ammonites were quite small, by human standards. But yes, in the late Mesozoic some did achieve considerable size. I believe the largest had a shell six and a half feet in diameter. However—'

'That's the one!'

He glanced towards her in the dark; she could tell this by the changing sound of his voice. 'Actually, we know very little about their biology or life habits. The soft parts are not ordinarily preserved in fossils, and even if they were, there would be doubt about such things as colour and temperament. But still, there are considerable objections to your thesis.'

'In short, no,' she said, smiling. She liked to smile, even when no one could see; it was a talent she had not always had. 'Try this: could they have eaten a kind of swimming fungus exclusively, and become extinct when it disappeared?'

'One would then have to explain the abrupt extinction of the fungus,' he pointed out.

'Maybe it emigrated to Nacre ...' But this was another dead end. It had been quite convincing in her dream, but it lacked that conviction here. The mystery remained, nagging her: why had so highly successful a subclass as the *Ammonoidea*, virtually rulers of the sea during the Cretaceous period, become abruptly extinct? Survived only by its far more primitive relative, the pearly nautilus ...

'What, if I may inquire into such a personal matter, brought the status of the cephalopods to mind? I had understood these were not of paramount interest to you.'

'You showed me those shells and explained, and I – had a dream,' she said. 'A foolish, waterlogged vision ... if you care to listen.'

'Oh, I have enormous respect for dreams,' he said, surprising her. 'Their primary purpose is to sort, assess, and file the accumulated experience of the preceding few hours. Without them we would soon all be thoroughly psychotic, particularly on so-called contemporary Earth. Adapting to this Paleocene framework is difficult, but have you noticed how much less wearing it is intellectually than was merely *existing* on Earth? So it is not surprising that your dreams reflect the change. They are reaching out into the unbounded, as your mind responds to this release.'

The odd thing was that he was right. She had longed to return to Nacre, because of the relief it offered from the tensions of home – but this world served the purpose just as well. She would rather be battered, seasick, and in fear of her life *here*, than safe and comfortable *there*.

But it was not entirely the freedom from Earth that was responsible, she knew. Cal, Veg, the mantas – she loved them all, and they all loved her, and Earth had nothing to match that.

She told Cal in detail about colourful King Ammon, and both laughed and it was good, and her seasickness dissipated.

At eight, daylight over the water, Veg came up to relieve Cal. 'Do snails have false teeth?' he inquired groggily. 'I had this dream—'

Direct sunlight hustled the mantas back inside the cabin, the solar radiation too hard on them. There had been tree shade on the island, and irregular cloud cover; apart from that they tended towards the night. It was not that they were naturally nocturnal; but high noon on the planet Nacre was solid fog, and the beam of the sun never touched their skins. These four were more resistant to hard light than were their kin on Nacre, for they had been raised on Earth – but environment could modify their heredity only so much. They could survive sunlight here, but not comfortably and not long.

The day swept on, the wind abating only momentarily. Her heart pounded pusillanimously during such hesitations, anticipating the consequence of a prolonged delay in mid-ocean. What use would land within a hundred miles be, if they had to *row* the clumsy craft there? And should the wind shift . . .

At dusk, windchapped and tired, they watched the mantas come out and glide over the water, their pumping feet invisible as they moved at speed. How clearly this illustrated the fact that mantas did not perambulate or fly or swim! They jumped, and their flat bodies braced against the air in the manner of a kite or airplane wing, providing control. They either sat still and lumplike, or travelled at from thirty to a hundred miles per hour; they could not 'walk'. They were beautiful.

And they were hungry. Circling near the raft, they lashed at surfacing fish. She heard the whip-snap of their tails striking water, and saw the spreading blood. Cal brought out a long-handled hook

Aquilon hadn't known was aboard and hauled the carcasses in. She spread them on the deck, and one by one the mantas came in to feed. Circe first – and Aquilon watched her chip the fish up into small chunks with her deadly tail, then settle on top of the mess for assimilation. Cal had placed a section of sail over the logs so that the fluids of this process would not be lost.

Veg did not watch, and neither, after a moment, did Aquilon. They all understood the necessity of feeding the mantas, and knew that the creatures could not digest anything but raw meat, and would not touch any but the flesh of omnivorous creatures – but this proximity was appalling. Circe had fed on rats in the theoretically aseptic far-cellar of Aquilon's Earth apartment building, and this had been accomplished privately. No doubt Hex had similarly isolated himself from Veg in the forest at feeding time. Now it was hard to accept physically what they had known intellectually. Only Cal seemed unaffected – and of course he had foreseen this problem too.

Aquilon called herself a hypocrite, but still did not watch. Perhaps it was because she knew herself to be a member of an omnivorous species – evolved to eat anything, and to kill wantonly. Whatever brutality was involved in the manta's existence was redoubled for man's. What could she accomplish, deciding to stop eating flesh after indulging for a lifetime, and spawned from millions of years ancestry of flesh eaters? Years would be required to expel the tainted protoplasm from her body, and the memory would never be expunged. Yet how could she kill, now that she comprehended the inherent evil of the action?

She felt sick again. Damn her subjectivity!

In five days they spotted land.

'There she blows!' Veg sang out happily.

'That's land ho!' Aquilon corrected him. 'Fine lookout *you'd* make.'

But she was immensely relieved, and knew the others were too. Diminished appetites had extended their stores of food, but the men were looking lean and the limit had been coming distressingly near. Their camaraderie had never been tested by real hunger. Certainly it would have been ugly – a compulsive meat-eater, a vegetarian, and a woman wavering unprettily between, and nothing but fish . . .

But she was relieved because of the change in scenery, too. The sea, after the first day, had become monotonous; it had seemed as though they were sailing nowhere, accomplishing nothing.

The *Nacre* tacked clumsily along the shoreline, seeking an appropriate landing. Aquilon could not be certain whether it was mainland or merely a large island, but it was obviously suitable for foraging and camping. No smog.

'No really formidable land animals on Earth during the Paleocene epoch,' Cal remarked, as though to reassure them.

'Good for Paleo,' Veg said.

'Paleo?'

'Here. You want to call this world Epoch instead?'

Cal did not argue. Veg tended to identify things simply, and the names stuck. Henceforth this planet would be Paleo.

Soon a calm inlet opened, and Veg guided the craft so neatly into the cove that she knew it was blind luck. She watched for a suitable beach, wondering whether this was San Francisco Bay. Probably not; everything could have changed. Palms were in view, and conifers, and populous deciduous trees. Birds flitted through the branches, uttering harsh notes. Insects swarmed. Flowers of many types waved in the breeze.

'Look – fungus!' she exclaimed, spying a giant puffball. For a moment she thought of Nacre again, the planet of fungi. But Paleo, really, was better, for here the sun could shine. In fact, she was coming to realize that Nacre itself had represented little more than an escape from Earth for her; there was nothing inherently appealing about it otherwise, except for the mantas. And it was not the *planet* Earth that soured her, but the human culture that infested it. Yes, yes – Paleo was better.

The raft drifted close. The bottom of the bay was clear now, small fish hovering placidly. The smell of woods and earth came to her as the wind subsided, cut off by the land. The soil-loam-humus *cleanness* of it filled her with longing.

Veg touched her arm, and she looked up with a start.

Near the shore stood two hairy animals. They were four-footed, thickset and toothy, with long tails and blunt multiple-hoofed feet. Small tusks projected from their mouths, and their eyes were tiny. The overall aspect was like that of a hippopotamus – except that they were far too small. The highest point of the back was no more than a yard off the ground.

'Amblypods,' Cal remarked without surprise. '*Coryphodon*, probably. Typical Paleocene fauna.'

'Yeah, typical,' Veg muttered. 'You never saw it before, but you know all about it.'

Cal smiled. 'Merely a matter of a decent paleontological grounding. I don't really know very much, but I'm familiar with the general lines. The amblypods are distinctive. One of the later forms, *Uintatherium*, had the bulk of an elephant, with three pairs of horns on his—'

'You figure any of those are around here?'

'Of course not. *Uintatherium* was Eocene. He could no more show up in a Paleocene landscape than could a dinosaur.'

Veg's eyes ranged over the forest. 'I sure would laugh if a dinosaur poked his head over the hill while you were saying that. You're so sure of yourself.'

Cal smiled again, complacently. 'When that happens, you'll certainly be entitled to your mirth. The shellfish I studied on the island were decisive.'

Veg shook his head and guided the raft to shore. Aquilon noticed irrelevantly that his face was filling out with blond beard. The amblypods, startled by the intrusion, trotted off, soon to be lost in the forest.

Smoothly the *Nacre* glided in, cutting the gap to land to twenty feet, fifteen, ten—

And jarred to a halt, dumping Veg and Aquilon into the water. 'Oops, struck bottom,' Veg said sheepisly. 'Wasn't thinking.'

'Wasn't *thinking*,' she exclaimed, cupping a splash of water at him violently. But she was so glad to touch solid land that she didn't care. the sea was hip-deep on her here, and she waded ashore gleefully, pulling strings of seaweed from her torso.

Veg, meanwhile, went back to fetch a rope and haul the craft about by hand. Cal, never careless about his footing, had held his place, and helped unwind the coil. Soon they had the raft hitched loosely to a mangrove trunk.

Aquilon wandered inland, content for the moment merely to absorb the sights and smells of this richly primitive world. Ferns grew thickly on the ground, and she recognized several species of bush and tree: sycamore, holly, persimmon, willow, poplar,

239

magnolia. Mosses sprouted profusely, and mushrooms were common; but she saw no grass, to her surprise. Still, there had been bamboo on the island, and that was a form of grass.

Something launched itself from a shrub ahead, and she jumped in alarm. It was a brown streak that sailed through the air, away from her. She caught a glimpse of extended limbs, a web of skin, an oblong shape. Then it was gone; she heard the rustle of its ascent in other foliage. It was not a bird.

'*Planetetherium*,' Cal said behind her. 'Primitive insectivore, one of the prime mammalian stocks. A glider.'

'Yes ...' she said, seeming to remember it from her studies. She really had no excuse to be ignorant of mammalian lines, but time and other considerations had let her knowledge fade. Cal, with his appalling intellect, seemed never to forget a thing.

'Perhaps you should change,' Cal suggested, 'before you become uncomfortable.'

She looked down at herself. Her clothing was plastered against her body, and she knew the salt would chafe as the moisture evaporated. Cal was right, as always.

Yet the air was pleasant, and despite the shade of the trees there was no chill. She wished she could simply remove her clothes and glide nymphlike through glade and fern, free of all encumbrance.

'Why not?' she said rhetorically. She began to strip, handing her wet garments to Cal stage by stage. He made no comment, and did not avert his gaze.

So she ran, nymphlike, through glade and fern. It was every bit as glorious as she had imagined, except for a thorn that got in her foot. She had shed the restraints of civilization with her clothing, and was whole again.

Veg's mouth dropped open appreciatively as she burst upon him, but he said no more than Cal had.

The *Nacre* was tight against the shore: Veg's muscle had come into play. Her dry apparel was aboard, but she hesitated to seek it. Wouldn't it be better if they *all* were to—

No. Sexual tensions existed among them already at a barely submerged level. It would be criminally foolish to do anything to heighten them needlessly. Subdued, she boarded the raft and dressed.

* * *

They spent the night on the raft, anchored just offshore. There might be no dangerous species, but they preferred a little more time for acclimation.

In the morning the insects and birds were clustered thickly on the shore. The first were familiar, the second strange. Several large grey sea fowl swam around the raft, diving for fish. Aquilon stood on the deck and painted them, intrigued by their fearlessness. Were there no significant predators on the water? Or was the raft so unusual as to be taken for an artifact of nature? Or did they know instinctively who was a threat and who was not?

Veg brought the *Nacre* to shore again and tied up. This time there was no premature jolt. She wondered whether he had scouted the bottom to locate a suitable channel for the keel, or whether he had excavated one himself.

They ventured inland several miles, as a party. Here were oaks, beeches, walnuts, and squirrellike creatures sporting in them. Occasional tufts of grass sprouted in the hilly country, where the thickly growing trees permitted. So it *was* present, but not well established. Ratlike creatures skittered away as the human party approached.

'Were there true rodents in the Paleocene?' Aquilon inquired.

'Not to speak of,' Cal said. 'These are probably ancestral primates.'

'Primates!' She was shocked.

'Before the true rodents developed, the primitive primates occupied that niche. They descended from trees, like most mammals, and took to the opening fields. But there wasn't enough grass, as you can see; it occupies a minor ecological niche until the Miocene epoch, when widespread dry plains developed. And the primates weren't completely committed. So the true rodents eventually drove them back into the trees, this time to stay. The primates never were very successful.'

'Except for man ...'

'A minor exception, paleontologically. Man happened to wobble back and forth between field and forest just enough to remain more generalized than most of his contemporaries. If he hadn't been lucky and clever, he would not have survived.'

'I see.' She wasn't certain how serious he was.

'Quite often it is the less specialized creature that pulls through,' he continued blithely. 'Conditions change, and the species fully adapted to a particular environment may have to change in a hurry or perish. Often it can't adapt. But the generalized species can jump either way. So although it seldom dominates, it may outlast those who do. Probably that explains the marginal success of the primitive nautilus, while the specialized and dominant ammonite vanished.'

She had never thought of it quite that way. Man – as an unspecialized, lucky, but clever species, thrown into prominence by accident of circumstance ...

A large running bird with yellow tail feathers appeared and scooped up a careless mammal that resembled a kangaroo rat. The bird, a good two feet tall, passed quite close to them before passing out of sight. Aquilon wondered whether the rat could have been an ancestor of hers, then chided herself: dead, it could not have sired much. At any rate, it would be foolish to interfere. Suicidally foolish, possibly, for *any* change in the life patterns here might affect those of her own time.

'The birds showed considerably more promise, initially,' Cal said. 'Actually, throughout the Cenozoic until the present, they have dominated Earth, reckoned in the normal manner.'

'By number of species,' she said. 'So I understand. But diversity isn't everything, fortunately.'

'Fortunately?'

'You don't approve of man winning out?'

'I believe the world would have endured more amicably without him. It is not good to have a single species run amuck.'

She saw that he meant it. She thought of contemporary Earth, and understood his point. Paleo was clean, unspoiled. Better that it remain that way, paradox aside.

The next few days they ranged more widely. They encountered more amblypods and both doglike and catlike carnivores. The pursuers, Cal explained, had long snouts for reaching out on the run; the hide-and-pouncers had sharp claws for holding and slashing, and short snouts. The ambushers buried their dung, to mute the giveaway odour; the chasers did not bother. The physical properties of what were later to be canines and felines and ursines were not random. Another line was the fairly substantial *Dinocerata*, ancestors to the monster *Uintatherium* of the later epoch. But all these mammals were stupid, compared to those that were to evolve; none would have survived readily on Earth of fifty million years later. She painted them all, and Cal made many notes on his voicetyper. She learned to ignore the monotonous murmur of his descriptions as he made his entries.

This was a warm paradise – but she became restless. There was nothing, really, to *do*. It had been nice to dream of a life without responsibility or danger or discomfort, but the actuality palled rapidly. It was late summer, and a number of the trees bore small fruit, and there were berries and edible tubers. Food was not a serious problem. She talked with Veg and Cal, but knew them both too well already, and she did not care to get too personal lest it came down abruptly to the male-female problem. She had not decided between them, yet; that was what restrained her, she decided.

'Going to get cold,' Veg observed. 'Fall's coming.'

Of course he was right. They didn't know their exact location, and it probably could not be matched precisely to a modern-Earth geography anyway, but the number of deciduous trees said things about the seasons. There might be no actual snow here in winter, or there might be several feet of it – but it would be cold enough to make leaves turn and drop. They would have to prepare for the worst, or – 'Let's go south!' she cried. 'To the tropics, where it is warm all year round. Explore. Travel. Survey.'

'You sound as though we're staying here indefinitely,' Cal remarked, but there was something funny about the way he said it. *He's afraid of something*, she thought, and that made her uneasy. Was it that a long-term residence would force them to revert farther towards the natural state, mating and homemaking? Or that doing so would upset the existing balance of nature and imperil the status quo on Earth, because of the paradox effect? Her inclination was to ignore that; somehow she doubted that what they did *here* could affect Earth *there*, whatever the theory might be. And if it did – well, so be it.

'Actually, there appears to be more than enough data on hand to render a report on Paleo,' Cal continued.

She felt the skin along her forearms tightening – a nervous reaction once more common than now. She *had* forgotten, or tried to forget, their assigned mission. The truth was that she viewed the prospective return to Earth, or whatever other mission awaited next, with misgiving bordering on alarm. She liked Paleo, bored though she had been with it a moment ago. She liked its wildness – 'In wildness is the preservation of the world,' she remembered from somewhere – and she would far rather tackle its problems than those of Earth society.

But they had little excuse to tarry longer. The onset of winter could be of little concern to them if they were to return to the station and report. Their radio equipment was in good order, and they could find the way by homing in on the master unit remaining in the tunnel.

But she was sure, now, that Cal did not want to go back, though she also knew it would be useless to challenge him on that. He comprehended something she did not, something that worried him deeply, but that he chose to keep to himself. He might allow himself to be persuaded to travel south – or somewhere, anywhere but back – if she could provide a strong enough pretext.

Yet she did not care to admit her true feelings yet. How did Veg stand?

'Can't sail back against the wind,' Veg said. 'More likely sink, tacking the whole way, and it'd take us a month in clear weather. Going to get hungry on the way.'

Bless him! She felt a surge of special affection for the big, simple man, so naïve in manner but practical in action. They *couldn't* go back without enormous preparation.

'Of course,' Cal said, unperturbed. 'I was thinking of a radio report. We can not make a physical return until the wind shifts with the season – though that may occur any day now.'

That did not reassure her particularly, though she wasn't sure why. Cal seemed to be agreeing to some procrastination, and a radio report would keep them officially on duty.

'I thought your report came at the end,' Veg said.

'Not necessarily. We were to determine the status of the planet, then put the report on record for the next in-phase connection to Earth. It was presumed that these various delays would make the report wait a month or two, perhaps longer. But we've done the job. This is definitely Paleocene. All the fauna and flora check. We have exceeded coincidence by a millionfold; this can not be a foreign planet.'

'How about the geography?'

244

'I explained about that. Their map seems accurate, and it *is*—'

'We could follow the coast a little and find out, maybe,' Veg said. 'Make sure there isn't some out-of-place continent, or something.'

Clumsy, clumsy, she thought. That tack would never work.

Cal smiled ruefully. 'In other words, you're voting with 'Quilon again.'

Was he *asking* to be outvoted? What was on his mind?

Veg shrugged, missing the implication. 'There's time to kill, and maybe we'll learn something new for your report. Better than sitting around here waiting for the wind.'

'That's a transparent appeal to the researcher in me,' Cal said. 'You know I don't like to make a premature statement, and so long as the possibility exists of discovering something significant—' He sighed. 'All right. I know how the mantas feel. They all want to remain here indefinitely. So a full vote would change nothing. We'll leave one of the two radios here under cover and mark the place. That way, if anything happens to the raft, I'll still be able to make my report.'

Aquilon smiled uneasily. Cal had yielded almost too readily.

They sailed by day, tacking along the shore and covering about twenty miles before searching out a harbour for the night. It was good to be moving again, even though there was now no tangible destination.

A month passed like the breath of the breeze, and it was good. Gradually the curve of the continent brought them around so that they were sailing south-southeast and largely before the shifting wind. They had come perhaps eight hundred miles, and only verified that the Paleocene landscape was remarkably uniform, though she realized that this could be because their progress south roughly matched that of the coming fall season.

The mantas rode the raft the first few days, then took to travelling on land. They would disappear in the morning and reappear at the new camp in the evening. Sometimes only one or two would show up, the others ranging elsewhere for days at a time. Yes, they liked Paleo!

It was Circe who broke the lull, bringing news to Aquilon just before dusk. 'Mountains? Tall ones?' Aquilon inquired, reading the manta's responses so readily now that it was almost the same as human dialogue. 'Unusual? Snow-capped? And—'

She spoke to the others, excitedly. 'It seems there are extremely large mountains about two hundred miles south of us. Twenty thousand feet, or more. They form a virtually solid wall, and a number are actively volcanic. The mantas can't get past, on land, because of the cold, and they don't trust the water route either.'

'How can an active volcano have snow on it?' Veg demanded. 'It's hot, isn't it – or else the snow would put it out.'

'Silly! Volcanoes aren't on fire,' she reproved him. 'One could shoot off in a snowstorm – or underwater, as many do.' But she was thrilled. They were finally coming up to something atypical, something not suggested by the map or Cal's knowledge of Paleocene geography. Massive, active volcanoes, shoulder to shoulder, in America.

The mantas had been ranging far ahead, scouting the territory, yet had been baulked by these, both on land and water. A mighty barrier indeed, for the manta's travelling range was good.

'If that's the region the tsunami originated from,' Cal said, 'we had better approach it with exceeding caution.'

Aquilon nodded soberly, but she was singing inside. This promised to be an unforgettable experience – and that, despite all the undertones, was a thing she ardently craved.

Chapter Nine

ORN

The mountains were high, and chill winds swept through the pass. The range was new; Orn's memory of the landscape of this tropical section of the subcontinent indicated a flat plain sometimes submerged by an inlet of the ocean. Natural forces had come into play in unusual fashion to bring this orogeny where none had occurred before. Yet it was possible that his mental map was inaccurate, for this was at the fringe of it. None of his ancestors had gone far beyond this place, having been stopped by the sea. The range, and whatever land might lie beyond it, must have risen complete out of that ocean in the past few million years.

Orn would have turned back and sought another route, but it had been a long, difficult climb, game was scarce, and he was hungry. Prey might be near ahead; it certainly was not near behind. He ran on, generating new warmth to replace what the wind tore from him. If the lie of this pass were typical, the descent would begin soon.

It did. As Orn passed the ridge, the weather changed. The cold dry air became cold damp air that steadily warmed as he went lower. The stinging snow became ice mist, then rain.

He adjusted his wings to shed as much water as possible in their oil-starved state and went on. He wanted to reach the lowlands by nightfall, and fill his crop. The vegetation was increasing, but the ferns and palmetto bore no fruit.

It was getting warm. Orn recognized the type of soil underfoot. Volcanic in origin. This alerted him; he knew firsthand, and many times over, how dangerous volcanism was. Instead of getting out of it, he was going deeper in.

There seemed to be more regions of such activity than ever in the past, and had his mind worked that way Orn would have wondered what the world was coming to. Great changes were taking place all over the land mass, apart from the visions of plant and animal life. It continued to be unsettling.

He came across a streamlet, and followed it down rapidly. Dusk was coming. Just as it became almost too dark to forage by sight, he found a shallow pool stocked with fat lazy fish, teleos. He jumped in with both feet and scooped two out before they took alarm.

He fed well and spent the night in a dense mag tree. The hazard of the mountain range had been overcome.

In the clear morning Orn looked out over the landscape. The stream fell away in a series of rapids and finally disappeared in a tangled mass of vegetation at the foot of the slope. A short distance beyond that lay the shore of a wide shallow lake. Many thickly overgrown islands spotted it, and portions were little more than liquid swamp. Far in the distance across that water rose another ridge of mountains.

The valley was hot. Jets of steam plumed from the bay nearest the live volcanoes and thick mists hung over much of the lake.

The valley was flat. Nothing stood taller than the height of the trees, and the majority of it was open water. It was, on the whole, familiar: this was the landscape of twenty million years ago, sharpest in his memory, though in greatly reduced scale.

He followed the stream down. Rushes and horsetails grew at the edges of its shallows, and leafed plants bordered it everywhere. Tufts of grass were present high on the mountainside, but disappeared in the lowland, unable to compete there. Orn did not miss it; grass was tough and tasteless stuff and its seeds were too small for his appetite.

As the land levelled out, Orn lost sight of the overall valley. He discovered that it was not as flat as it had seemed from above; mist had filled in irregularities, concealing banks and gulleys and gorges. The stream plunged into a mass of tall trees. A few were of the seasonal leaf-dropping variety that had taken over the continent of the north, but most were the memory-familiar ginks and firs. Here full-sized fern trees prospered, and many treelike varieties of cycad.

Game was especially plentiful. The little primes peeked out from the branches of the larger leafed trees and liz were abundant on the turf. Flying arths hummed everywhere.

He cut away from the river that was degenerating into swamp, and shortly came out on a bushy plateau punctuated by short barrel-bodied cycads and shrublike angios. Moss covered the occasional rocks. He trotted after a particularly large four-winged drag, not with any real hope of catching it but content to explore this wonderful, unexpected reincarnation of familiarity. Any pretext would do.

A huge, low shape rose before him. Orn was almost upon it before he was aware, having allowed pursuit of the winger to take up more of his attention than was wise. He had become careless, in this season of innocuous animals. He had smelled no large mam, so had relaxed. Foolishly.

It was a rep – a big one. It was not as tall as Orn, but that was because this creature's whole body was spread out against the ground. Its head was low and armoured with bony scales, and four toothlike horns projected sidewise. Similar scales extended the length of the body, making the back a broad impervious trunk. Stout spikes lined each side, some as long as Orn's beak and as wickedly curved. The tail was a blunt, solid mass of bone.

Orn remembered immediately. This was an Anky, one of the lines of great reps. It was four times his own length and disproportionately heavy and powerful, but no aggressive threat to him. Its massive armour was defensive, and it was a herbivore.

This was the second giant land rep he had seen here. The first had been in the cavern, mysteriously dead, but this one was healthy. Orn did not concern himself with the complex ramifications of his discovery, but did understand that where there was one live monster there were likely to be more. His relaxing reflexes were brought once more to full functioning, and he looked around alertly and somewhat furtively.

The Anky, slow-witted, became aware of him, and flexed its tail. Orn leaped back. A single sweep of that bludgeon could destroy him, were he so careless as to step within its range. The Anky was harmless – but normal precautions had to be taken. It could kill without meaning to.

The Anky took a slow step forward, the muscles in its short thick legs making the scales bulge outward. It was curious about him, in its dull way. He could easily outrun it, but preferred not to. Guided by a memory functioning for the first time the way it should, Orn stood still. The Anky hesitated, then lost interest and took another mouthful of leaves from the nearest shrub. What did not move and did not smell threatening did not exist as a danger to it. Anky had forgotten him.

Orn moved on, alarming the rep again. This time he was not concerned; he had verified the reliability of his memory, and would trust it within this valley. The sun was high now; the mists had cleared and the brush ahead thinned out into a field of low ferns.

A herd of large animals came into view, grazing peacefully. Orn recognized these too: Tricers. Larger than the ones his ancestors had known, more horny – but also harmless, for him, when undisturbed.

He approached them cautiously, but they took no notice of him. Nearest was a large bull as long as the Anky, but taller than Orn, with a monstrous shield projecting from the back of the head. Three heavy-duty horns curved slightly downward from the region of eyes and nose, and mighty muscles flexed as it swung its head about. This was an animal no sensible creature tampered with.

Orn skirted the herd of fifty or more individuals and travelled on towards the main lake. The turf became spongy and the horsetails tall. And, significantly, the small birds became silent.

A head appeared above the mixed foliage. Orn jumped, spreading his wings in a reflex, that had nothing to do with flying. He recognized this rep, too – and now he was in for trouble. This was a Struth.

The Struth was about Orn's own height, and rather similar in physique at first glance. It stood on long slender hind legs, and its small head topped a sinuous neck. It was omnivorous, but did not attack large prey. Its diet consisted of arths, aves, mams, and anything else that offered, such as eggs and fruit. It was fleet.

The resemblance to Orn ended about there, for the Struth had small forelimbs in lieu of wings, and a strong fleshy tail in place of Orn's tuft of feathers, and a mottled smooth skin and a much uglier beak. Its body, like that of any rep, varied in temperature with the heat of the day.

But its similarities to Orn were enough to constitute a problem, for the two shared, to a considerable extent, an ecological niche. They were direct competitors.

Orn had never physically encountered a Struth before, but his memory covered all of this. The rep, possessing some faint hint of the species recollection so highly developed in Orn, knew the competitor instinctively. They were not enemies in the sense of

250

predator/prey, but the one could not tolerate the other in his foraging ground. The rival for food had to be driven off.

The Struth, despite the similarity in size, outmassed Orn considerably, for it had fat and muscle where he had down and quill. It was fresh, while he was lean from the difficult trek over wasteland and mountain. In the chill of night or height, Orn would have contested with it nevertheless, for his warm body did not become lethargic as the temperature dropped. His reactions there would be faster, his blows surer, his perceptions more accurate.

But this was the heat of the day, and of the lowland, and the rep was at its best in its home territory. Orn, in these circumstances, would be foolish to fight it now.

The Struth was aware of its advantage. It charged.

Neither bravery nor cowardice were concepts in Orn's lexicon. He battled when it behooved him to, and avoided trouble at other times. He fled.

The Struth had routed its rival – but was not bright enough to realize it yet. The chase, once commenced, had to continue until it terminated forcefully in some fashion.

Orn was a swift runner, as he had to be as a landbound bird. But the terrain was new to him in detail, and the somewhat marshy ground was poor footing for his claws. He started with a fair lead, but the rep was gaining. This pursuit might be pointless for *it* – but it could also be fatal for *him*.

Orn dodged to the side, seeking to avoid the Tricer herd. The Struth cut across the angle, narrowing the gap between them rapidly. Only five body-lengths separated them now.

It would be useless to seek out the water and wade into it; the rep would merely follow, making better progress because of its solidity. Orn could swim on the surface, as the Struth could not – but deep water was dangerous for other reasons. He would need time to scout it out thoroughly before trusting himself to it, regardless of the chase.

The ground became mucky, inhibiting him more. The wet sand and clinging mud encumbered his feet, slowing him down critically and tiring him rapidly. It interfered with the Struth too, but not as much. The gap was down to three body-lengths.

Orn ran on, not exhausted but straining to his utmost. Soon he would have to stand and fight – and unless he were unrealistically fortunate, the outcome would be the same as that of the chase. He could hurt the rep, perhaps cripple it – but could not expect to overcome it.

A single bull Tricer grazed in the cycads at the edge of an inlet of marsh. Orn saw that in his haste he had trapped himself: ahead and to one side was a bubbling swamp that he dared not enter unprepared, even granted the time to do so, and to the other side was the massive horned herbivore. He had nowhere to go.

Except—

He did it, hearing the Struth one length behind. He lunged towards the bull as though to impale himself on the ferocious horns.

The Tricer looked up, huge and stupid. A green strand dangled from its beak. Its tiny eyes were obscured by the two vicious horns overshadowing them, and the semicircular flange of head armour stood higher than Orn himself. Yes, a most dangerous creature – but slow to initiate business. Its eyesight was not good, so it judged a potential enemy primarily by size and smell – and did not fear birds, Provided that it recognized them in time.

Orn ran up to it, fluttering his wings and squawking so that his avian affinity was quite clear – to almost any creature. He passed within a wingspan of the Tricer's head . . . and the bull merely stood there, attempting to make up its mind.

The Struth, however, did not dare try such a stunt. It was a hunter, and therefore not completely dense. Though too small to be a threat to the bull, it was too large to be tolerated by the herd. Orn saw the juvenile Tricers sporting near their dams. Actually, few reps guarded their eggs or protected their own young, but those infants who stayed with the herd tended to survive more readily than those who wandered free, so the effect was much the same. No – no predator was welcome here.

But the Struth, intent on the chase, did not sheer off in time. It approached the bull moments after Orn passed: just time enough for the monster to make up his mind. The Tricer sniffed, snorted, and whipped his terrible shield about, making ready to charge.

Already the Struth realized what was happening. The delay had been in implementation rather than cognizance. Now it halted and pulled back, the bull following. Finally the Struth ran back the way it had come, its original mission forgotten. The Tricer pursued it a few paces, then stopped and resumed grazing. The episode was over, and Orn was safe.

Just as well. He had had no real quarrel with the Struth, and was happy to honour its territorial integrity. His only concern had been to protect himself.

He walked through the herd unmolested. This was good, because it gave him respite, but he could not remain here indefinitely. A Tricer cow might absent-mindedly step on him. And if anything should happen to alarm the herd, to send it milling or stampeding, he could be crushed between the bruising bodies.

Yet where was he to go? This was a pleasant and memory-familiar valley in type if not in detail, and he could reside here comfortably for some time. But it did not have that something which had increasingly urged him on.

He left the herd and struck for the mountain range that defined the valley. There at least he could find arths and fish to satisfy his returning hunger, and probably that elevation was free of large predators. With this return of the old world had come the old dangers. He had allowed himself to become used to sleeping safely, and until he recovered his proper nocturnal reflexes he did not dare to sleep amid the reps. Though he could not visualize these until he saw them, he was aware that far more dangerous creatures prowled this valley than the ones he had encountered so far.

This, at least, was the gist of the diffuse array of thoughts Orn had as he climbed the slope.

He returned to the descending river and the volcanic soil, because these were now familiar. Familiarity was life to him. There was danger from the heated earth and the rumbling mountain, but this known hazard militated against *unknown* hazards. The volcanic threat applied to *all* creatures, particularly the reps, and the environment was in fact more hostile to them than to him. He would utilize it until a larger area had been properly scouted.

He encountered no more of the large reps, though his sensitive eyes and nose picked up their profuse traces. There were numbers of them, mostly young, but these hid from him. The valley was not really more crowded than the surrounding areas beyond the badlands; it merely seemed that way because its denizens tended to be larger and more familiar. There were small mams in far greater abundance in the north country, while the huge reps were comparatively sparse. A few crocs, a few snakes. What had happened, there?

He dined on fish again, and splashed the clear water over his feathers, refreshing them. Time had passed, and now it was afternoon. He began to search for an appropriate lodging for the night. He preferred not to roost directly on the ground, but an ascent into a tree was impractical, here where the trees were stunted and scarce. Possibly a good thicket of thorns—

This was a serious matter, and Orn undertook his search carefully. He was looking for a permanent roost – one he could depend on during the entire period of his stay within this valley. Later he might develop other roosts, so that he could canvass more distant sections of the valley without having to make a long trek back; but this first refuge was essential.

The sun dipped towards the far side, making the range there thrust up in silhouette, and the clouds became pink. But still he had not found a suitable spot.

The ground was becoming warm again, signal of another subterranean furnace ahead, or at least a vent from the depths. It was as though the entire range were riddled with hot conduits. Orn became nervous, reminded again of what could happen in such terrain. He did not think of it at other times; the immediacy, as always, conjured the painful image. Yet he felt there was a certain security in water. Though the river channel might shift, it was protection against actual fire.

Accordingly, he followed an offshoot of the stream up towards its snowy source. He could, if necessary, spend this night in the coldest heights. The reps certainly would not be there. But this would not be comfortable, and it was too far away from the valley proper to be convenient as a regular thing.

He came across a waterfall, as the sun touched the far mountains. The brook passed over an outcropping of hard rock, forming a pool above and another below, and splayed in a shallow falling sheet between the two. The drop was somewhat more than Orn's standing height, but the force of the water was not great.

He recognized the construction. Behind such a sheet of water would be a concavity, where the less durable substrata melted away in the course of millennia. This was the way, in the life cycle of rivers. Sometimes there was space enough underneath for a large bird to roost.

Orn braced himself and poked his beak into the waterfall. The

cold water split, and his head went on through. There was space –
but no adequate footing. In an emergency he might grasp one
slanting ridge of rock with one foot, and hang on to the carved
backwall with his beak, but certainly not by preference. This was
not his roost.

Then something activated every perception and conjured a
barrage of images, one tumbling over the other in unique confusion.
Orn snapped back his head and stood rocking in the spuming water,
sorting it out while his wings fluttered spasmodically.

The thing he had been unknowingly searching for – the nameless
mission – the object of his quest—

Excitement! For he had seen the traces of a prior occupant of that
emergency roost. The scrape of claw, the mark of beak—

The unmistakable spoor of another bird of his species. Another
'Orn' – his own age, and female.

Chapter Ten

VEG

It was a truly awesome range: scarred volcanic cones set almost adjacent to each other to form a wall, seemingly solid, extending right into the sea. The ambient fumes suggested that the volcanic activity continued beneath the water, too, and there were very few fish.

'I don't understand this,' Cal lamented. 'This should be about where Baja California terminates, or will terminate, on our globe. This formation, to put it euphemistically, is atypical.'

Veg manoeuvred the *Nacre* into deep water, unconcerned with that aspect. He could see why the mantas hadn't fooled with this section; it was a real wasteland.

The mountains were followed by much more active cones. An almost impenetrable fog of gas and floating ash obscured portions of the shore. After that came desert, rent by jagged rifts. They drew the raft in only enough to view the desolation under strange foul clouds, and did not touch land.

At one point the wind reversed, pushing the *Nacre* far out to sea before he could angle it back. The smell was appalling. They had to tie shirts over their heads to keep the stinging particles out of eyes and lungs. The four mantas huddled inside the cabin, no more comfortable, though of course they did not need to breathe.

After days and nights of this another range appeared, even more massive and imposing than the first. Its oceanic barriers extended far out, becoming mighty reefs with jigsaw-puzzle elevations poking through the surface. It was as though grotesque statues stood upon the water, mocking Jesus Christ.

Twice the *Nacre* was snagged, forcing them to disembark and struggle waist-deep in the gritty fluid to free it. But there were some few fish here, and corals, and crabs, and barnacles. To their dismay, they had to wear shoes in the water, for the fish had teeth and the crabs pincers, and the coral was sharp.

'But where there's life, there's hope,' Aquilon said. Veg didn't think it was funny, but agreed that some sea life was better than none, for things must be about to ease up.

At last they spied deep water – but had virtually to portage across a final band of shallows. The solid raft, even without their weight or that of the mantas, projected too far down to make navigation easy, and it was crushingly heavy to haul about by hand. The palm wood had become waterlogged, making it worse. Veg had to dive under and remove the keel, and even so the raft caught on every conceivable piece of reef. He braced his feet against the rocklike coral foundation and hauled on the front rope, while Cal and Aquilon pried with poles.

Busy as he was, he couldn't help noticing Aquilon's anatomy as she strained at the raft. Her shapely legs were bare from the water level up to her brief shorts, and her midriff was open too. Her bosom flexed as her arms moved, each breast a live thing straining at the halter. Her blonde hair was tied back, but several major strands had pulled away and now whipped across her face erratically.

Ah, she was lovely now – far more so than when she had affected nudity that one time just after they landed. Clothes made the woman, not the man, for they supported and concealed and enhanced and made mysteries where mysteries belonged. Not that she was unattractive, nude; oh no! But now – now he felt like charging through the water, sweeping her up entire, and—

And nothing. With Aquilon it had to be voluntary – even in his fancy. The mere touch of her fingers on his arm meant more than the definitive embrace of any woman he had known before. Her smile gave him a shortness of breath, though he had loved her long before he had seen her smile. Even that time on planet Nacre, when she had made that shocking expression, as though the muscles of her face were connected up the wrong way – even then, his horror had been because he *cared*. In fact, it hardly seemed that there could have been a time when—

The raft broke away from whatever submarine object had held it, and Veg stumbled forward into deep water. He let go the rope and clamped his mouth and eyes shut as he hit. The warm bath tugged at his clothing, and trapped air hauled him immediately back to the surface before bursting out of his shirt in an embarrassing bubble.

257

For an instant his eyes opened under water. It was clear, here.

A gigantic fish was coming at him. It resembled a swordfish, but it had a fin on its back like that of a shark and its eyes were each as big as a human head. The creature was well over twenty feet long, sleek, swift, and strong.

Veg propelled himself out of the depths and onto the reef in a manner he could never afterwards recall. He stood at the brink, dumbly pointing.

The fish broke surface and leaped partially into the air, its tremendous nose-spine opening to reveal many small teeth. Vapour spouted from a blowhole over the eyes.

'That's no porpoise!' Aquilon exclaimed, amazed.

Cal stood open-mouthed. Veg had never seen the little man so surprised.

The creature departed as rapidly as it had come, never bothering to attack. Veg's knees felt weak. That dinnerplate eye! 'Never saw a fish like that before,' he said shakily.

'Fish?' Cal was coming out of his daze.

'Didn't you see it? With the beak and the—'

'That was *Ichthyosaurus*!' Cal said, as though it were marvellously significant.

Now Aquilon began to react. 'The reptile?'

'The reptile.'

Veg decided there was something he was missing, but he waited until the *Nacre* had been reloaded and they were on their way again before challenging it.

The treacherous reefs enclosed a moderately shallow ocean basin about thirty miles across. Into this projected two large islands separated from each other by a one-mile channel. They were mountainous; ugly black cones rammed into the sky from each, and yellow-brown vapour trailed from one.

'Scylla and Charybdis,' Aquilon murmured. 'Let's go around.'

Veg obligingly angled north so as to pass Scylla on the western shore, heading in towards land. His keel, replaced, was not properly firm, but the weather in this cove was gentle and he had no trouble. About three miles separated the island from land, and on both sides were small white beaches backed by tangled jungle. Nearest to the water were tall tree-ferns, but inland, up the mountain slopes, he could make out the solid green of stands of pine and fir. There was a light haze, and every so often he sneezed.

'Heavy pollen in the air,' Cal explained.

'Now that we're on the subject,' Veg said, 'what's wrong with that fish being a reptile?'

Aquilon looked at Cal. 'He just won that bet about the dinosaurs, though he doesn't know it!'

'I did?' Veg asked. 'All I saw was a big-eyed fish, dark grey with a light-grey belly and a snout that almost rammed me. And you—'

Cal looked serious. 'Nevertheless, its presence forces us into a considerable reappraisal.'

'Funniest looking dino *I* ever saw! How long did you say they've been dead?'

Aquilon reached up to ruffle his matted hair. She, at least, was at ease. 'Extinct is the word, not dead. And it's been about seventy million years, on Earth. The dinosaurs died out at the end of the Cretaceous.'

'So they've been gone five million years, here – and we haven't seen one yet, and maybe we won't unless we go back into the Bodacious.'

'Cretaceous,' Cal said, missing the outlandish joke – another sign that the man had been badly shaken up. 'The name comes from the Latin word *Creta*, meaning chalk. So it's the chalk age. Chalky limestones such as the White Cliffs of Dover—'

'So the dinosaurs were full of chalk,' Veg said, wondering how far to take this game. 'Used it in their big bones, I guess.'

'I'm afraid that's not quite it. The chalk came from the compacted skeletons of billions of single-celled animals, the *Foraminifera*, who lived in the shallow seas. But such animal chalk deposits are hardly more than an episode in the seventy-million-year period of the Cretaceous.'

Veg remained solemn. 'On Earth, maybe. But this isn't Earth.'

'But it *is*,' Aquilon murmured. 'Paleocene Earth. Dawn of the age of mammals.'

'I *know* what mammals are,' he said, looking at her bosom.

'Mammaries,' she said, correcting him without embarrassment. 'Typical of the mammals.'

'Whose distinguishing trait is – hair,' Cal added, suppressing a smile.

Veg let that pass, seeing that Cal had gotten over his disturbance.

259

'So if there are dinosaurs, this would be Creta instead of Paleo. Now how about this famous fish?'

'Cal just explained,' Aquilon said. 'It's *not* a fish. It's *Ichthyosaurus* – a swimming reptile. Its ancestors walked on land, and it breathes air.'

'Same as a crocodile. What does that prove?'

Cal took over. '*Ichthyosaurus* is a member of class *Reptilia*, order *Ichthyosauria* – the swimming reptiles. It is not considered to be a dinosaur. The dinosaurs are actually a popular composite of two reptilian orders, the *Saurischia* and the *Ornithischia*, respectively "lizard-hips" and "bird-hips". They were primarily land or swamp dwellers.'

'Somewhere in there I think you brushed near my question. Icky is not a dinosaur, just as I thought. Good. So now tell me why you figure it's so significant, this fish-reptile. What's it got to do with dinosaurs?'

'He's got you there,' Aquilon said to Cal.

'They were contemporaneous phenomena. The Cretaceous was the zenith of the reptilian radiation. Almost all the lines flourished then – and almost all died out before the Paleocene. The *Ichthyosaurus* passed before a number of the land-dwelling forms, so—'

'So if Ichy's still here, so are the dinos,' Veg said. '*Now* I make the connection. It *is* like a dinosaur poking his snout over the hill.'

'Of course that doesn't necessarily follow—'

'Oh, no, I'm happy to have it follow. Serves you right.'

'But you see, this *is* the Paleocene,' Cal said. 'The ocean fauna, and everything we have observed on land – the evolution of the other species is cumulatively definitive. Dinosaurs have no place here, no place at all, unless—'

'Unless?' Veg and Aquilon were both curious.

'Unless there is an enclave. An isolated carryover of the Cretaceous fauna – doomed to extinction, but surviving the demise of its age by a few million years. Those sea reptiles that fed on fish or belemnites might endure, such as the particular ichthyosaur we encountered, but not those specializing in ammonites. Though why there should be no fossil record—'

'It *could* have happened on Earth,' Aquilon said. 'We might yet discover a submerged bed of fossils that proved—'

'Down!' Veg whispered ferociously.

They obeyed immediately, cutting off the conversation. In silence they followed his gaze.

They had been rounding the green bend of the island Scylla, Veg now poling the craft along. Standing, he had the best view, and so had seen it first – but it made them all flinch. In the silence one of the mantas poked around the shady side of the cabin: Hex, getting his own eyeful.

It was a tremendous serpentine neck, seeming at first to be truncated just short of the head. The column projected fifteen feet from the water and was barely a hundred feet from the raft. It was smooth and round and gently tapering – and as Veg examined it more closely, he found that it terminated in a head hardly larger than the neck's smallest diameter. An eye was half hidden under a kind of fleshy crest, and beyond that was a rounded, wrinkled snout. Despite the small appearance of the head, he judged that the jaw was a good two feet long. That creature could, Veg reflected, finish a man in just about three bites lengthwise.

Plumes of vapour formed above the crest, signifying the location of nostrils, and now Veg could hear its heavy-bellows breathing. There had to be a lot more body out of sight beneath the water, for he could make out no expansion and contraction of the visible portion as the air rushed in and out.

As they watched, the minuscule head dipped in towards the land, to take a swipe at floating foliage there. The teeth were pegs that clamped rather than cut or chewed. The creature either hadn't noticed them, or it considered them to be beneath notice.

Veg poled the *Nacre* quietly backwards. Slowly they rounded the turn of Scylla, passing out of sight of the monster as it lifted its head high to swallow.

'That is the biggest snake I ever heard of,' Veg announced when they had achieved the limited safety of distance.

'No snake could lift its head like that, that far,' Aquilon said, obviously shaken. 'Not unless it were over two hundred feet long – and that's unlikely. I think that's some other swimming reptile. There was one with a long neck, wasn't there, Cal?'

Cal smiled with some obscure satisfaction. 'Yes there was, 'Quilon. Some types of plesiosaurus. But such a creature could hardly stand still in the water like that, and would not feed on watercress. This is a reptile of quite a different nature – a true dinosaur, in fact. We saw only a tiny portion of it.'

Aquilon stood up straight. 'Of course! The thunder lizard – *Brontosaurus!*'

'No. Not quite. The head does not conform. The brontosaur's nostrils were at the apex, and I doubt that many survived much beyond the Jurassic. This would be its later cousin, the largest of them all: *Brachiosaurus*.'

'Brach,' Veg said, pinning down the name. 'Sounds like some fantasy hero.'

Aquilon merely shook her head, not recognizing the designation.

'*Brachiosaurus* – meaning "arm-leg", because its arms are longer than its legs, in a manner of speaking. *Brontosaurus* was the other way round, its hips being higher than its shoulders.'

'I always thought Bronto was the largest dinosaur,' Aquilon said.

'Bronto weighed as much as thirty-five tons. Brach may have gone up to fifty tons.'

'Oh.'

'Quite innocuous, except through accident. The sauropods are herbivorous, and would not become violent unless hard pressed. But their size—'

'Vegetarians,' Veg said. 'Good guys. Let's get acquainted, then.'

'With fifty tons of nearly mindless reptile?' But Aquilon shrugged. She, like Veg, seemed to have become inured to a certain extent to personal danger – and Paleo, so far, was as safe as Nacre had been.

They advanced again, cautiously. The head and neck remained, feeding as before, resembling a crane as it hoisted up and down, with visible bulges from the down-travelling boluses of greenery.

'Harmless, you said,' Veg murmured, losing his bravado as he was forcefully reminded of the scope of this creature.

'Bear in mind that the sauropods are not very bright, as 'Quilon mentioned,' Cal said. 'And as *you* mentioned, big vegetarians—'

'Are good guys – but sometimes squish nasty little carnivores by accident,' Veg said, smiling.

'The carnivores were not necessarily small, in the age of reptiles. But as I was explaining, this creature may run eighty feet in total length, and it takes time for the neural impulses to travel along its—'

'Yeah, I know about that.' They were whispering now, subdued by the presence of the giant. 'So if Brach thinks we're food, some kind of new turnip maybe, and wants to take a bite, it'll be a while before he gets around to doing something about it.'

Aquilon was now busily painting the portrait of the fleshy column. 'By the same token, if it changes its mind and decides *not* to take a bite, we may be halfway down its gullet before it desists.'

Cal smiled. 'Actually, it could probably desist from *biting* quickly enough, since its brain is adjacent to its eyes and jaws. But larger motions—'

They were now quite close to the feeding head, lulled by its pacifistic and plodding manner. Down – bite – up – swallow, and repeat. Veg glanced into the cabin to see how the mantas were taking it, and discovered that only two remained. The others had evidently left during the excitement, perhaps taking advantage of the temporary overcast that now existed. But he couldn't spare the time to investigate; Brach was too important.

Closer yet, and an impressive view. The skin of the neck, rather than being smooth, was covered with wartlike tubercles, and on the head wrinkles overlay creases on bulges, the topology changing with every slow shift of the jaw. The mouth swept up leaves, stems, water, and mud from the bank, straining some of it back out in the haphazard process of mastication. Brach was either very old or very ugly. But the muddy water still concealed the rest of the reptile's body.

'I heard once that if a dinosaur were walking along,' Aquilon remarked, 'and discovered that it was about to step over a cliff, by the time it could make its legs halt it would have gone over. So its very size led to its extinction.'

'Like much hearsay, not true,' Cal said. 'I suppose that if a creature the size of *Branchiosaurus* were proceeding on land at a full gallop, its mass could carry it over the cliff in such a situation. Fifty tons do not stop on a dollar. But Brach would never find himself in such a predicament.'

'Why not?' Veg's own query, though he was hardly interested. This dialogue was merely a way of rationalizing the incredible and postponing healthy fear. They were talking too much. Yet the monster went on feeding.

'Because Brach would not be found innocently trotting along like that. Full-grown, he's far too heavy to walk on land with any comfort. He must stick to water, or at least swamp, so that his body is buoyed up.'

'So I see,' Aquilon said.

'Brach, much more than Bront, is adapted for deeper water,' Cal continued. 'Note the placement of the nostrils and the angle of the head. But his range is sharply limited to the coastal shallows. His presence here, rather than Bront's, is an indication that the flat swamps are less extensive than they were. And of course we've seen that directly. Evolution is never random.'

'Perhaps we should get moving again, if we're going to,' Aquilon said gently.

'But all we've seen is his head!' Veg protested facetiously. Fifty tons was too large, even if all he could actually see were two or three tons; it alarmed him.

'That's all anyone usually observes,' Cal said. 'Assuming that anyone before us has had the opportunity. Better be satisfied.'

Veg was willing to be convinced. He poled the craft into deeper water, and he and Aquilon took up the paddles. They passed about forty feet behind the busy head. He judged that Brach was standing in about twenty feet of water – and that implied much about its size.

His paddle struck something. 'Obstruction!' he said. 'Log, maybe, under the surface. Sheer off before we—'

Too late. The raft collided with the object, jarring them all. Veg felt the rending of the keel as it tore off. There would have to be substantial repairs.

'Reef?' Aquilon inquired, brushing back hair that had fallen across her face.

Veg probed with the pole. 'Water's deep here. I can't find bottom,' He angled the pole forwards, searching for the obstruction.

Cal had been shaken harder by the bump, partly because he was less robust physically, and partly because he had not been anchored by a paddle. He must also, Veg thought, have been preoccupied. Veg himself was able to accept something like a dinosaur on Paleo, but the concept evidently came harder to Cal. The little man was sitting very still now, recovering his wind while the others assessed the situation.

'Move out – fast!' Cal snapped.

Again they responded to the need of the most urgent member. First it had been Veg, spotting Brach; now it was Cal, not as winded as he had appeared. They had worked together long enough on Nacre, and now on Paleo, to know almost intuitively when life depended on instant cooperation.

As the raft began to move, thanks to the strenuous efforts with the paddles, Cal explained: 'That was no log or reef. That was the tail.'

Aquilon looked at the troubled water behind. 'The tail – of the dinosaur?'

But again events provided confirmation. From the water came the tip of a massive fleshy extremity, stirring up waves.

Veg peered across at the head. 'It's still feeding. This can't be the same—'

Then the head stopped chewing and sifting. It lifted and rotated to face them, while the tail struck the water furiously.

'. . . that slow reaction time,' Aquilon murmured.

'Keep moving,' Cal said urgently. 'It's aware of us now, and that blow to the tail must have hurt. If it decides we're an enemy—'

'Harmless, you said,' Veg repeated, with some irony.

'Oh, I'm fairly certain it won't attack. It's natural inclination would be to flee from danger. But—'

'We *did* bruise its tail,' Aquilon said.

They could all see it now, as the tail lifted clear of the waves again. Diluted blood streamed off it. Their keel had cut a gash in the spongy flesh – not a serious injury to an animal of that size, but enough to colour the surrounding water.

'Smarts, I'll bet,' Veg agreed with some sympathy. A wound of that magnitude in a lesser creature would have been fatal. It was several feet long and inches deep.

Then the water churned in earnest. Brach had made its decision.

'Move!' Cal cried. 'He's running!'

The two mantas remaining in the cabin popped out, though there was still direct sunlight. They sailed over the surface. Veg knew they couldn't keep it up long; the sun would burn them terribly and injure the eyes.

But the dinosaur was coming *toward* the *Nacre*! The tiny yet ponderous head looped about, gliding low over the water, and the neck threw up a white wake. The tail retreated, its tip skipping over the waves smartly. Between the two – a distance of about fifty feet – something like a whirlpool formed, and from it several tiny indentations spun off.

'Divert the head!' Cal called. 'Don't attack! Herd it!' He was addressing the two mantas, who now circled the raft uncertainly.

'Bluff it! Move it aside!'

Hex and Circe (Veg was sure he recognized them) seemed to understand. In turn they swooped at the head, banking with kitelike flares of their bodies. The head reacted fairly quickly, flinging away from them, but still approaching the raft. As Cal had explained, it took time to change the course of such a mountain.

Brachiosaurus came at the trio – but the head missed by twenty feet, the eyes not even focusing on them. Water surged aside, rocking the raft as though a huge mass trailed that worm-like forepart. In a momentary eddy they saw the speckled flank, and the muscular rhythm of it.

The body missed them by only ten feet, and that because the raft moved with the current of water thrust aside.

Then the main torso was beyond, and they balanced precariously on the swell, relieved. In that unguarded moment the tail struck. It was not the cutting whip of the manta, but its blind ponderosity was fully as devastating.

The tail rose from the water under the rear edge of the *Nacre* and flipped it over.

Aquilon dived away sidewise, hitting the water before the raft toppled. Veg hooked his right arm around Cal's mid-section, lifted him as the *Nacre* came up, and shoved off to the left. The raft bobbled endwise, sinking into the water; then it rebounded and seemed to fling itself on over. Veg kicked his feet, keeping his arms wrapped around Cal, driving away from the splash.

The waves subsided. The dinosaur was gone, the raft inverted but steady, and already the two mantas perched on it. Aquilon waved, showing that she was all right. And, blessedly, a cloud dimmed the sun, giving the mantas relief.

Veg lifted up Cal, hoping the man had not taken in much water, but his concern was needless. Cal blew out the breath he had held during the upset, smiling. Veg kept forgetting that his friend had recovered considerably since Nacre. Cal remained small and light, but by no means infirm.

Veg let go, and together they swam back to the raft. Aquilon joined them there. They peered at one another over the shattered keel, and at the two mantas.

'Does this seem familiar to you?' Aquilon inquired with simulated brightness. Her hair was dark and lank, now that it was wet, and her eyes more grey than blue.

He knew what she meant. Back on Nacre, at once like yesterday and a decade past, they had begun the adventure that was to meld them into the trio. Beginning at the corpse of a tractor, and knowing that their journey back to the human camp would be a terrible one. Blood had been shared, literally.

He clung to the edge of the raft and looked about at the debris. A can of kerosene floated nearby, but there was no sign of the lantern it serviced. Beyond it was a wicker basket, empty of the food it had carried. Aquilon had found ways to occupy her nimble fingers during the long southward voyage, fashioning things from natural materials; it hurt him to see her handiwork adrift. Most of their equipment remained lashed to the raft, for the bindings were tight. It would be a tedious job getting it loose safely, but could be done.

Their radio set, so carefully conserved if used, had ripped away from its mooring, and now surely lay in the bottom of the channel. Their theoretical contact with civilization was gone.

Yes, it was like old times – and he wasn't sorry. They could stay lost forever here, and he'd be satisfied. A friend like Cal, a woman like Aquilon ... and of course the mantas.

At least the paddles remained. One was broken, but could be mended or replaced: palm fronds were plentiful. The stout bamboo pole was undamaged.

It would be pointless to try to right the raft here. They would have to haul it onto land, then see what they could salvage. Most of their supplies could survive such a dunking.

Hex and Circe took off and pounded over the water. At once they circled back. 'Oh-oh,' Veg said. 'Trouble?'

Two snaps, almost in unison: each manta agreeing. They seldom spoke at once like this.

'Predators!' Cal cried. 'I should have thought! The wound—'

He meant the blood that still discoloured the water around them. Veg knew that Cal still did not like to say that word – blood. Of course the flavour would attract the vicious creatures of the sea. Brach must have bled gallons, kegs, barrels ...

'Sharks!' Aquilon exclaimed.

And the three human beings were out of the water and aboard the inverted raft. Veg was sure that neither of the others was aware of scrambling up, any more than he was. When one thought of sharks

267

or crocodiles while swimming, one left the water in a hurry, that was all.

It was no mistake. There were sharks, invulnerable to the lash of the mantas' tails because they swam below the surface. Veg splashed with the good paddle – how had he brought that up with him? – and they retreated, but not far.

Cal's face was pinched. 'The sharks won't come up after us,' he said. 'But the reptiles – if *Kronosaurus* ranges these waters—'

'Who?' Aquilon had the broken paddle, and was fishing with it for the floating pole. Veg let her fish; if he moved over to her side, the raft would tilt, and stability was suddenly very important.

'*Kronosaurus* – a short-necked plesiosaur. Fifty feet long, jaws twelve feet long, the size of a small whale—'

'I get the message,' Veg interrupted. Prodded by this vision, he thought to pry his own paddle against his side of the raft, pushing forcefully outwards so that the *Nacre* nudged towards the pole Aquilon wanted. She hooked it in, then went after the kerosene.

They conferred hurriedly and decided on the obvious: landfall at the nearest point. That way the *Nacre*'s beach-head could mark the spot where the lost radio lay on the ocean floor. Assuming recovery of it would do any good at this stage, since it hadn't been sealed against such total and prolonged immersion. He and Aquilon started paddling.

'Harmless, you said,' Veg muttered, his spirits rising as they passed out of the pink water, spotting nothing but frustrated sharks. 'Would run from danger, you said.' But he was smiling.

'It *did* run, if you mean Brach,' Cal replied. 'But it ran to deeper water. Most of its enemies are land dwellers.'

And they had been between the dinosaur and deeper water, and Brach was not very bright. It figured.

He still had not seen the creature. Only its head and tail, and a portion of its shoulder.

The sharks, apparently satisfied that no advantage remained in following the raft, disappeared. But no one offered to swim.

Laboriously they brought the raft to poling depth, and then shoved the ungainly monster up against the shore.

Fern trees leaned over the water, giant cousins of the plants Veg once had picked by hand near his cutting acreage on earth. A strange conifer rose above them, its needles bunched peculiarly. He saw no grass, no flowers. Half-floating water plants massed at the tideline.

'Cretaceous landscape,' Cal murmured. 'Astonishing.' But he sounded awed rather than surprised.

There were, fortunately, no shore-dwelling predators in sight. Calf-deep in muck, Veg and Aquilon hefted the loaded raft up. But it was far too heavy to be righted this way. They would have to hold it while Cal braced it with sticks; in this marshy terrain there were no rocks to set under it, and no really solid footing. But first they had to slide it up beyond the level of high tide, so that it would not be carried away in the night. ''Quilon, you steady it while I heave,' Veg said.

They tried, but the *Nacre* lifted only inches while his feet skidded away in brown slime. 'No use,' he grunted. 'We'll just have to take it apart and rebuild it right side up. Might as well make camp.'

He was not unhappy at the prospect. Sailing, he decided, was not his forte; hiking and camping were better. It reminded him of their other hike together, on planet Nacre. Something had begun then between him and Aquilon. Something intriguing. More and more, his mind was coming to dwell on that.

His gaze met hers, over the raft. She realized it too. Their return to Earth had cut off what had been developing; she had wanted it that way for some reason. But now – now there could be a middle and an end to that beginning.

No, he did not mind being stranded for a few days or weeks or longer. He did not mind danger or hardship. To be here in the ancient forestland with Aquilon, here for the second session . . .

'Probably Brach wouldn't have been feeding here if it weren't fairly safe,' Cal remarked. 'A large land carnivore might bite off Brach's head, and that would be, eventually, fatal. Reptiles die very slowly. So while I couldn't call our encounter with the monster exactly fortunate, it does have its redeeming aspect. We can't tell what we might have met, farther in.'

'Still, let's not try to camp right here,' Aquilon said, looking down distastefully at the bubbling goo covering her feet. 'Sleeping in a flooding cabin was bad enough, but this—'

There was something hilarious about it, and Veg laughed. Aquilon tried to glare at him, but looked at her mired ankles again and joined in.

Yes, it was good to be back. Earth was like a pressure cooker with the temperature rising and the escape valve blocked. They were better off here.

The two remaining mantas, Diam and Star, had rejoined them at some point, perhaps while he was preoccupied with the problem of landing the raft. Veg was sure they agreed. They hadn't been scouting this territory just for the fun of it.

Night found them camped under a large tree whose stout branches and small twigs gave it the aspect of a stiff-armed octopus. Each twig had a cleft, fan-shaped leaf, unlike the branching greenery of conventional trees. This was a ginkgo, and Cal seemed to feel it was something special, though he claimed they existed on contemporary Earth.

They were in a lean-to improvised from cycad barrels, palm fronds and fern leaf, on a rise overlooking the beachhead. Cal had designed it, showing more practical ability than Veg had expected. Veg had done the brute work, collecting the peculiar wood. Aquilon had plaited fibres to make the roof tight. Yes, they were a functioning team, a good one.

The finishing was a more tedious task than the designing or building, and Veg had time to loosen the nylon bindings of the *Nacre*, get the logs enough apart to free the supplies within the crushed cabin, and begin ferrying supplies to the camp. Cal and Aquilon remained cross-legged by the lean-to, weaving fern stems in and out.

Veg kept a sharp lookout for life, hostile or otherwise, though Hex was with him and made an effective bodyguard. He did not know much about dinosaurs except that they were big and dangerous – even the herbivorous ones, as the wrecked raft testified. Brach would not be wandering on land, however, if what Cal said was true – and of course it was. But other creatures might be found anywhere. Brach would not have been so ready to flee to deep water unless there were things on land it feared.

A creature that could frighten a fifty-ton dinosaur could hardly be ignored by a one-tenth-ton man.

Unfamiliar birds twittered in the tree-ferns, scouting for bugs. Small things scuttled in the brush. Fish swam in the water. There was plenty of life, but nothing to fear, yet.

He lifted the last of the cases they had decided to move, brought it to his shoulder, and tromped through the sludge. Yes, they all had to be alert here, on guard against unknown menaces. But the air was wet and warm, the biting insects had not yet discovered him, and he felt marvellously free. Perhaps he would die tomorrow in the jaws of some monster whose name he could not pronounce – but he would die a man, not a sardine.

Hex ranged ahead as they came out of the swamp and recovered firm footing. It was dusk, growing too dim for him to see clearly, but he liked the challenge. The manta drifted to one side and stopped beside a tree – a maidenhair, Aquilon called it, but it looked exactly like the ginkgo – and stood as a black blob. By tricks of vision – looking slantwise at specific objects, narrowing his eyes – Veg could still make out good detail. What was Hex looking at?

He came up and peered. Was that a—?

It was.

Veg squatted down beside the manta, holding up the teetering carton with one hand while he cleared away obstructing foliage with the other.

It was the print, in hardening mud, of either a bipedal dinosaur or a very large bird. Three sturdy clawmarks, the points digging down and forward, no rear toe showing. Whether toothed or beaked, a land walker armed with effective talons that could gut a man in a hurry.

The creature was somewhere within range of their camp. Veg was glad the mantas would be mounting guard this night.

Chapter Eleven

ORN

The spoor was not fresh; only its protected location had preserved it. It could have been made a season ago, since the merest suggestion of odour remained. But it was sure, for his memory was strongest of all on such identification: a female of his species had roosted here.

Did she remain in the valley? Was she still alive? Could he locate her? These questions were vague and peripheral and largely beside the point. His mind grasped the fact that she existed, and his glands responded and ruled. The mating urge was upon him, no longer to be denied.

Orn spent the night under the waterfall. It was uncomfortable and tiring, on top of his preceding labours, but the discovery of a trace of his own kind prevented him from leaving. He had to begin here and follow the trail until it became fresh. Convenience was unimportant. If there were another male – but there was not; the trace was that of an unbred bird. Such things were specific, in his line.

In the morning he explored the neighbouring terrain. She had been here; there had to be signs of her avenue of departure. He would discover them, however faint or fleeting.

It was not easy, but he was geared for this. He would not be able to perceive so old a trail at all, were it of any other creature. But his pumping glands sharpened his senses, and all his memories focused on this one task. His search pattern identified another trace, downstream, and a third, and he was on his way.

In two days he located fresher spoor, and in another day the roost she had used for a time. It was in the raised hollow of a rotting flat-leaf tree. Nose and eye and memory informed him that she had departed when a predatory rep had scouted the region. She had lost some feathers, but not her life.

She had fled into the mountain, perhaps as recently as Orn's meeting with the expanding sea on the other side of the continent.

This season, certainly. Here the trail became exceedingly difficult, for she had passed over shuddering, heated rock in her effort to shake the pursuit. But Orn widened his search pattern and persevered, as he had to, and in time picked up the spoor again where she had descended to the valley.

Her prints and smell became mixed with those of many animals, as though she had frequented the haunts of a herd of Tricers. Again he had to cast a wider net, seeking a line of emergence, and again he succeeded, as he had to. Days old now, her trail stimulated him exquisitely. She was alone and nubile, and not very much older than he; she wanted a mate, but had found none. All this he read in her spoor, knowing the signals from millennia past, and his desire for her became savage.

But he did not find her. She found him.

She had come upon his own trail, in her roundabout rovings, and recognized it immediately. In less than a day she had caught up.

Orn looked up from the newly hatched brach he was feeding on, suddenly aware of her presence. Across the open space of the deserted Tricer stamping ground they peered at one another. His beak was smeared with the blood of the fleet young rep, his nose suffused with the fresh odours of its open carcass, and in this delicious and romantic moment he viewed the bird who was to be his mate.

Ornette: she was shorter than he by the width of one dry tail feather. Her beak was slender, a delicate brown matching the scales of her muscular thighs. Her eyes were large and round, half shuttered by the grey nictitating membranes. The white neck feathers were sleek and bright, merging gracefully into the grey breast area. Her body plumage fluffed out slightly, lighter on the underside, for she had been moving through high brush. Her wings were well kept and handsome, looking larger than they were because of the unusual, almost regressive length of their primaries. Her tail, too, had sizable retrices, and the coverts displayed the grandeur of the nuptial plumage. Even the claws of her feet glistened with natural oil. From her drifted the perfume of the distaff, at once exciting and maddening to the male. She was beautiful and wholly desirable.

Then she was away, whirling her shapely sternum about and running from him; and he was running after her with all his strength,

273

his meal forgotten. She disappeared into high palmetto brush, outdistancing him; but it was a chase he was certain to win, for his thews were heavier, his masculine endurance greater. This was the way it was meant to be, and had been, throughout the existence of the species.

She fled towards the swamp, passing into the territory of the Struth, that zealous rep so like Orn himself. That surely meant trouble, but there was nothing Orn could do about it. If he tried to circle to head her off, he would only lose distance, for she was for the moment as fleet as he.

She dodged around a giant fir, sending green sprigs flying, and sheered away before encountering the Struth. She knew! She bore north, much to his relief, though that was territory he had not scouted. Her pace slowed as the ground became marshy – but so did his own. It would be a long time before he caught her, this way. This, too, was as nature had decreed.

She ran north for a time, then veered west, towards the mountains. Soon they were ascending, leaving the steamy valley below. Flying aves scattered from their path and grazing young reps scooted away. A wounded adult Tricer, come this far to die, looked up startled. Through increasingly leafy trees they went, where mams twittered in the branches, and on into the grassy elevation where arths swarmed in sunlight, but Ornette did not slacken her pace, running up until the air became cool; on until the snows began. But Orn did not feel the cold. Slowly he gained on her.

She changed course at last, running north along the fringe of white while the sun dropped towards the mountain crest. Then down again, into the valley, into the thickest greenery, spreading her wings to aid control in the precipitous descent. She gained on him again, utilizing those longer feathers, but on the level bottom where the reps roamed he got it back. And up again, almost to the snow, and still Orn gained on her, though he had never run so long without resting.

The second time they came down at the northern apex of the great valley, beyond the swamp. Here there was a higher plain, too dry and cold for the comfort of most reps though the little mams were plentiful. And here, abruptly, the light of the sun was cut off by the mountain range. It was early dusk.

Ornette stopped, panting. Orn, hardly two wingspans behind,

stopped also. The chase had to halt when the sun dropped, to resume in place when it rose again. The night was for feeding and resting and ... courtship. Thousands of generations before them had determined this, and the pattern was not to be broken now.

The swamp spread out below from a comparatively tiny tributary stream here, and there were fish in it and mams in burrows adjacent and arths available for the scratching. They hunted separately, and fed separately. Then, as full darkness overtook them, they began the dance.

Ornette crossed the plain, away from him, until she was a female silence in the distance. Orn stood, beak elevated, waiting. There was a period of stillness.

Then Orn stepped forward, spreading his wings and holding them there to catch the gentle evening breeze. He gave one piercing, lust-charged call. She answered, demurely; then silence.

Orn moved towards her, and she towards him, each watching, listening, sniffing for the other. Slowly they came together, until he saw the white of her spread wings. The remiges, the rowing feathers, were slightly phosphorescent when exposed in this fashion, slick with the oils of courtship exercise; and so she was a winged outline, lovely. He, too, to her.

In the sight of each other, they strutted, he with the male gait, she the female. They approached, circled, retreated, their feet striking the ground in unison, wings always spread. Then Orn faced her and closed his wings, becoming invisible, and she performed her solo dance.

Wings open; wings closed. On and off she flashed, a diffuse firefly, her feet beating the intricate courtship meter, now steady, now irregular, always compelling. Far back into her ancestry the females had done this series for waiting males, taunting them with the nuptial ritual.

Then her dance halted, and the plain was quiet again. Orn's turn. He spread, commenced the beat, closed, whirled, jumped, spread, and instinct carried him on irreversibly. Tap-tap-tap against the turf, the flapping of wings measured by that cadence but not matching it. A faster, fiercer dance than hers, domineering, forceful, signifying what male expression in any species signified, but artistically, and not without gentle undertones. Forward, back, around; one wing flashing, then the other, as though he were

275

jumping back and forth. But silent, except for the feet; a pulsing ghost. Finally an accelerated beat, wings and feet together, climbing as though into takeoff – and silence.

The dance was done. Orn rested, alone in the dark, letting his heart subside. It had been a good effort, following a good chase – but better things awaited the morning. He made his way to the roost he had selected while foraging. Ornette, out of his sight as the ritual dictated, did the same.

A quick meal at daybreak. Then, as the sun struggled over the eastern pass, the chase resumed. She was fresh again, recovering better than he, and she was familiar with this terrain, and he lost ground. Up the face of the northern range, across a low, hidden pass leading into another rich valley – but she turned back into their own, south. Even to the verge of the swamp she ran, passing briars, moss, and fungus that wrenched feathers from him or powdered him with spores as he charged carelessly through. At one point she intersected the spoor of a giant rep predator, and reversed her field hurriedly. It would not do to have trouble of that nature on this romantic occasion!

Up to the snows again, across a hot stream that melted its own channel through ice, down ... and before noon Orn was gaining on her again. She was tired; her feathers no longer glistened sleekly, her beak was no longer held high. She made to ascend once more, but he shortened the distance between them so rapidly that she desisted, staying on the contour. They were near the southeast corner of the valley now, separated from his original entry by swamp and bay.

Orn approached within a wingspan, no longer straining. She was so worn he could keep the pace easily; his season's travel had conditioned him for this, and he had recovered his strength during his days in the valley. And – he was male. But the time to catch her was not quite yet, and he dallied.

Aware of her defeat, Ornette stumbled and hardly caught herself in time. In desperation she waded out into the shallow water of the bay, towards a nearby island, but she was so gaunt and tired that this was even worse, and she had to turn back.

Orn was waiting for her, victorious. As she climbed slowly to the bank he pounced on her and buried his beak amid the tender down feathers of her neck, but did not bite. She hardly resisted; she had been conquered. She dropped to the ground and lay there at his mercy.

Orn shook her once, not hard, and let her go. He trotted to a nearby bed of moss. He gathered a succulent beakful and brought it to her as a counteroffering. She sniffed it weakly, looked at him through the nictitating lid, and accepted.

With these first tokens of submission and of the nest they were to build and share, their courtship was done. They had found each other fitting; soon they would mate and settle, uniting their memories in their offspring.

Another morning – the first of their new life. They scouted the vicinity and decided to cross to the island Ornette had not been able to reach before. This was thickly wooded with firs, and seemed to represent a suitable haven from most carnivores. The big land walkers would have difficulty crossing to it, while the sea dwellers would be unlikely to venture among trees of such size, even if they were able to leave the water.

The two waded in and paddled with their abbreviated wings, entering the water while the chill remained in the air. The sea itself was warm, and they would be vulnerable to submerged predators. But the reps of the surface or shore would still be torpid, and so less dangerous than usual. Morning was the best time to forage when such creatures were near.

Not a ripple disturbed the sea, apart from those of their own motions. They crossed quickly and safely – but this was not a risk they would take again soon.

The island ground was spongy but not soggy; the matted fir droppings made an excellent fundament. Though the island was small, it was not flat. The trees ascended a mound in the centre. Orn perceived it for what it was: the tip of a submerged mountain. Once it might have stood as tall and cold as the peaks of the ranges enclosing this warm valley, but its understratum had given way and allowed the bay to encroach. Its original formation had been volcanically inspired. None of that animation remained to it now, or Orn would not have stayed.

Near the water were thick stands of club moss, the tops of the plants as high as his head. Once this species had been a giant many times that height, but somehow it had diminished to this innocuous status, and was still shrinking elsewhere on the continent. Horsetail

277

rushes were also abundant, though similarly restricted in size.

At the fringe of a twisting inlet they discovered the ideal nesting site: a mossy peninsula sheltered within a northern baylet. It was protected from the harsher waves of the ocean, and from the openness of the main island. The bridge to the site was narrow, so that a single bird could defend it, and the bay itself was deep enough to discourage wading. Yet the mouth of the inlet was toothed by jagged rocks, preventing access by most large sea creatures. A stand of several pines served as a breaker against offshore wind, and the main body of the island guarded against the sea wind. The soil was rich with grubs, and small fish teemed in the inlet, and clams in the gravel below it.

Ornette was pleased, already casting about for the specific spot for the nest. But Orn was more cautious. The experience of his ancestry told him that seemingly ideal locations generally appealed to more than one individual or species. Sometimes a flawed site was actually superior, because of this competitive factor. And he was directly aware of the fate of his parents, who had nested on another apparently ideal island. Orn did not want his own chicks to be orphaned as they hatched.

The smell of rep was strong here, and there were many droppings. Something used this peninsula regularly but he was unable to identify the particular creature before actually seeing it.

Ornette, female, had few such compunctions. Defence of the nest was not her primary responsibility; filling it was. She scratched the earth in several areas and fluttered for his attention. This spot? This? Or nearer the water?

Unable to subdue her enthusiasm without unreasonable gruffness, Orn approved a site beside the inlet. This was atop a large elevated stone, concave above, that he deemed secure from both flood tide and the intrusion of egg-sucking reps and landbound arths. A wingspan across and half that high, it was large enough for a proper nest yet had a sharply defined perimeter. The eggs would be as safe there as anywhere in the open, and of course they would never be left unattended.

If only he knew what manner of rep frequented this locale. It might be innocuous.

All afternoon they worked on the nest, foraging amid the pines for needles and cones, and fetching moss for spongy lining. Ornette

278

wove the long stems of shore plants into a great circular pattern and calked the interstices with the clay Orn scooped up from beneath the water. The nest would have to bake for a day in the sun before the padding was installed, and if it rained they would have to repeat the calking and wait again. Orn hoped that such delay would not happen. The nest had to be complete before mating occurred.

As the sun touched the bright crest of the mountain wall, shapes appeared in the sky. They were the huge gliding forms of the ptera, largest of the flying reps. Orn recognized the creature now, as the visual trigger activated his memory. The trees, the droppings, the odour – this was a nesting site for the enormous gliders.

The shapes came in, drifting on the rising currents in the atmosphere but steadily approaching the island. Orn stood in the centre of the peninsula beside the stoutest tree and made ready for the confrontation that had to come. Ptera generally did not get along well with true birds.

Three spiralled towards him. Their wings were monstrous: four times Orn's own span. Their heads were large, with long toothless beaks and crests of bone that extended back as a counter-balance. A flap of skin stretched from the crest back above the body, serving as a rudder that oriented each creature into the wind. Their bodies had neither hair nor feathers, but scales as fragile as natal down and hardly more protective.

Orn continued to watch, remembering more. The ptera, like the other larger flyers among the reps, had tiny legs to which the rear of the wings attached. The tail was so small as to be useless. The forelimbs that braced the wings were many times the size of the hind limbs, and the fourth phalange extended half the length of each wing. Ptera, able to glide all day without respite, could not walk on land. There was nothing to fear from this particular species; any individual who tried to attack him in the air would be at a severe disadvantage because Orn could knock it down and kill it while it flopped helplessly on the ground. A ptera could not fly from ground level.

Orn dropped his fighting stance, though he kept close watch on the visitors. One could never be certain what a rep would do, though the ptera were not notably foolish.

The three circled overhead, then evidently decided that he was not a threat and swooped at one of the pines leaning over the water.

Each passed over a horizontal branch high on the trunk, let down its little legs, caught hold with marvellous accuracy and spun around.

Then the wings folded and they hung inverted, three suddenly smaller bodies wrapped in folded leather, the downy scales outwards. They were well beyond Orn's reach and he, effectively, was beyond theirs. Friends the two species were not, but coexistence was feasible.

The mystery of the rep inhabitant had been alleviated. The three ptera combined would mass no more than Orn alone, for they were insubstantial things despite their monstrous wingspan. And if they nighted safely here, so could he.

Ornette was unconcernedly scooping small fish from the water. She had known it all along.

They fed together and slept that night beside the half-constructed nest, the head of each tucked under the wing of the other, sharing warmth and love. It rained, forcing them to scramble to shelter the nest with their spread wings; but it was a good night.

The ptera were not early risers. Long after the birds had foraged for their morning meal, the three reps hung from their branches tightly cloaked. Only when the sun itself touched their bodies did they move, and then stiffly. The scant chill of this valley night was enough to incapacitate these creatures who lacked internal control of their body temperatures. Even the hairy mams were better off than that.

The nest was baking. For the present, the birds had nothing constructive to do, so they explored the peninsula thoroughly, searching out the best fishing area and the richest infestations of edible arths – and watched the reps.

The three began to stir more actively as the sunlight heated them. Their heads rotated and the small claws at the break of their wings flexed. They began to flutter gently, opening their membranes to the warmth. Those tremendous wings could trap a large expanse of sunlight, heating the entire system.

Then, one by one, the reps dropped. The first fell almost to the water before levelling out, then swooped perilously close to the surface. Its wings stretched out so thinly that the sunlight made them translucent, the veins showing dark like the web-work of deciduous leaves. The ptera flapped clumsily, its very bones bending in the desperate effort to gain altitude, and Orn felt a surge of longing.

Once his own line had flown, and take-off had resembled this. He knew the rep had to reach an updraft quickly, for its reserve of energy was small and a descent into the cool water would be fatal.

It found a favourable air current and fought its way to a safe height. The second ptera dropped, following a similar course. But the third, the largest, did not. The wind had shifted, and that particular corridor to the sky was closed. Anxiously it manoeuvred from side to side, but remained too low. The tip of one wing as it banked touched a wave, jerking the creature about. It righted itself, but now was too low even to flap without disaster.

The drama was not over. Carefully the ptera circled, coasting closer and closer to destruction but never quite touching the sea. It came in towards the island, towards Orn's nest.

Alarmed, Orn ran to protect their property. But the ptera was only trying to reach land before falling that last bit. It did not succeed. With a sick splash it struck the water, so close to the nest that Orn spread his wings quickly to intercept the flying droplets before they wet the clay and forced the postponement of his nuptial.

The ptera had reached the shallows, however, swimming ineffectively but determinedly, and was able to struggle the small remaining distance to the shore. Dripping and bedraggled, it climbed to land and lay there for a moment, watching Orn.

The creature was exhausted, cold and helpless now; it would be easy to kill. It had very nearly killed itself, bouncing over the rocky barrier to the inlet. But Orn, imbued with the romance of his newly completed courtship and sympathetic to a certain extent to the rep's plight, did not attack. Anyway, there was very little good meat on it, and he was not hungry at the moment. Had such a creature fallen near him as he struggled through the desert, it would have been a different matter.

After a while the ptera pulled itself away from the bank, scraping along on bedraggled, wet, folded wings and weak legs. It was unable to stand or walk, but it could crawl. It seemed surprised that no attack had come, but was not remaining to contemplate the matter. Indeed, Orn was not certain he had done the right thing; it went against his nature.

The ptera scrambled awkwardly to its tree, then hooked its wing claws into the bark. Laboriously it climbed, clinging to the trunk with its wings draped down from the bend, a dripping cape. Only when it reached its branch did it rest again, flopped halfway over the wood with its long heavy head hanging in fatigue.

At last it assumed the sleeping position, but did not sleep. It walked out from the trunk, sidestepping upside down, until it had good clearance. It spread its wings so that the sun caught them and warmed them and made it entirely dry. Then it dropped again.

This time it completed the manoeuvre successfully, and disappeared proudly into the sky.

That day they watched the pteras feeding by swooping low over the waves and scooping small fish into their long bills. Because they did this at high speed and always facing the wind, they were able to touch the water and recover elevation without being immersed and trapped, and the massive rearward bones of their heads balanced the weight of the solid morsels they lifted. It was a graceful operation.

Orn hardly cared about the life and fate of any given rep, yet in some fashion his act of mercy enhanced his relationship with Ornette. Together they gathered the last of the supplies they required. All day the sun shone without remittance – unusual, for this valley – and by late afternoon they decided the clay was firm enough. They packed in the lining layers and made the nest smooth and comfortable.

That night they occupied their nest for the first time, snuggled pleasantly together within its bowl. And Ornette presented, and they mated at last, while the three ptera hung silent.

Chapter Twelve

AQUILON

She had slept in close proximity to these two men before, both on the planet Nacre and the raft *Nacre*. She knew them well and loved them both. But now she felt an increasing discomfort, a sense of impropriety. She had almost decided to leave them rather than continue to come between them, back when they had orbited Earth in the quarantine capsule. Events had prevented that, but did not really dispel the mood that had precipitated the decision. For surely she *would* come between them, and be the cause of sorrow and misfortune, if she remained a member of the party. She felt the female urges within her, compelling her to—

She peered at the roof of the lean-to, invisible in the darkness but present in her mind's eye, for she had spent hours plaiting it. Yes, she felt compelled – but to *what*?

To choose.

Aquilon was a woman. She had breasts and they were not simply for appearances; she had thighs and not entirely for walking. She was long past adolescence. But she had not felt the need of the physical male until – that agent Subble had aroused her, somehow, back in her tight Earth apartment, and turned her down. She had never realized before that a man could do that to her, and it had been a shock. When she had had no smile to show the world, she had bypassed social life, of course; but that new smile had seemed to open all the world to her, to lay waste all prior mysteries. Subble had routed that euphoria.

She had not loved him, those few hours they conversed, but she had felt his controlled masculinity tangibly. He had made her realize that the love she professed for Veg and Cal was an intellectual thing possessing no physical substance; a sympathetic resonance of the love they professed for her. She had never actually imagined herself undertaking a sexual relation with either.

283

Subble had been an agent, in more senses than one. He could move with seemingly irresistible speed and force and accuracy, yet hold a difficult pose indefinitely without sagging. He could talk philosophy and he could kill without compunction. He was handsome, yet ruthless even in his kindnesses. He was a body like Veg's, a mind like Cal's. He had understood her.

Subble had died, making any consummation with him, however theoretical, a waste of emotional effort. Of course there were hundreds, perhaps thousands, of agents virtually identical to him, and, designed to be exactly that, computerized. But it had not been the assembly-line physique and mind that made the connection between him and her; it had been their mutual experience. *The* Subble was gone forever; the close resemblance of other agents was irrelevant.

That threw her back into the trio – with a difference. It had taken her this long to realize it.

But what to do about it?

She fell asleep without an answer. Her dreams, however, were not of love; they were of *Brachiosaurus*.

The explorations of the next week banished any doubt they might have entertained about the nature of this region. They had struck paleontologic gold. This was a thorough Cretaceous enclave in the Paleocene world. The full spectrum of the golden age of reptiles was present – a vast pyramid of ecology, with inordinately plentiful small forms, largely mammalian, and lesser numbers of larger, dominant reptiles. Here, in fact, there were dinosaurs.

Ten miles up the shore, northwest from their camp ('There's nothing so permanent as a temporary camp,' Cal remarked, and smiled for some obscure reason), the ocean inlet became the delta of a southbound river. It was evident that the towering mountain chain had once enclosed a salt-water bay some forty miles across and sixty miles long, but almost all of it had been filled in by the rich silt and debris of the river to form a tremendous warm swamp. Its centre was a freshwater lake, swollen daily by ungentle rain, overgrown by soft vegetation, while its fringe rose up into the foothills of the giants. All of it was tropically warm, near sea level, the nights dropping down to a temperature of about 65° F, the days rising to – 85° F, with the predominating level towards the higher end of that scale.

In the direct sun it was much hotter, of course. At midday hardly a reptile moved. They were all hiding in whatever shade was available, predator and prey together. Aquilon had forgotten how much reptiles liked to rest.

The corner of the delta nearest them was the sporting place of several families of duckbill dinosaurs. Cal insisted on using the proper classification terms – the 'family' being ranked below 'order' and above 'genus' – and of course the reptiles did not have families in the social sense. But they did associate in small or large groups, except for the carnivores, and Aquilon preferred to anthropomorphize to that extent.

In the liquid portion of the swamp a lone *Brachiosaurus* browsed, perhaps the same one they had encountered so awkwardly upon their arrival. It consumed anything soft that grew within range of its neck, and once she saw it scoop up a fair-sized rock. Cal had abated her astonishment: it developed that such reptiles normally swallowed rocks to aid in their digestion of sturdier morsels. Long periods of stasis were required while the voluminous and tough material being processed was crushed and gradually assimilated; this was one reason, he explained, why mammals and birds were far more mobile than reptiles on a twenty-four-hour basis. Superior digestion eliminated that torpor. She decided that she'd feel torpid too if she had to let rocks roll around in her stomach.

Sometimes the sauropod disappeared entirely, and she presumed it was taking a nap under the surface. It was an air breather, but probably it could hold its breath for a long time without particular discomfort, much as a whale did – or would do, tens of millions of years hence.

Across the bay near the eastern mountains were more duckbills, these ones grotesquely crested; she meant to have a closer look at them in due course. And in the plainlike reaches between slush and mountain, where fern trees and cycads were particularly lush, were herds of *Triceratops*, plus scattered *Ankylosauruses*, both armoured reptiles of considerable mass. Truly, it was a paradise of paleontology.

And Cal, the paleontologist, was becoming more and more depressed. She found this hard to understand. Cal had a pessimistic view of life, but there was always sound reason behind his attitudes. If only he would explain what was bothering him!

Meanwhile, she drew a map and filled in all the details observed and conjectured to date. She put in the volcanic mountains, and Scylla and Charybdis, and their camping place. She marked a dotted line to show their route of entry. Perhaps this could serve as an adjunct to Cal's eventual report.

They found a better location about twenty-five miles north and made a second, more permanent camp beside a streamlet coursing down from the western range. She updated her map accordingly. There was a pleasant waterfall nearby, and hilly ground that seemed to be secure from the plains-dwelling armoured dinosaurs, and the air was cooler here. She liked it very well. Veg, exploring indefatigably, said there was a snowy pass through the range at the head of the stream, and some hot areas of ground: even the silent volcanoes were far from defunct.

There was danger here, certainly; there were savage predators larger than any existing on Earth before or after, though she had seen only their tracks so far. But danger was not objectionable per se, so long as one did not push one's luck. This was a visit in history, in historical geology, an experience like none possible to any home-bound person. So very like Earth...

Like Earth? It *was* Earth, according to Cal, though he hadn't spoken on that topic in the past month. She kept forgetting that. Perhaps it was because she thought of Paleo as a world in its own right; or maybe she simply could not assimilate the notion that something she might do here could change her own world, perhaps even eliminate the human species and extinguish her too. Then she could *not* come here, because she didn't exist, so no change would be made after all...

No, it made no sense, and this was Paleo, and she refused to be ruled by fears of paradox.

But there were mundane problems. The insects were fierce, after they had zeroed in on the new arrivals, and all three of the humans, and for all she knew the mantas too, had welts from nocturnal bites. Someone had to keep watch part of the night, because they had agreed that it wasn't fair to make the mantas assume the whole task. That meant that one of the three was generally short of sleep and temper. It was surprising how quickly a nagging itch and insufficient rest could flare into personal unpleasantness. And the food—

Her hands were raw and her nails cracked from scraping in the dirt for edible tubers. Veg ate no meat at all, and she had stopped doing it the past few months, but now the thought of roasted fish was tempting indeed. Coconut was fine, and so were the few small berries growing on the mountainside, and she had pounded nutlike fruits down into powder for something vaguely like bread, baking it laboriously over the kerosene burner. But the lush greenery of the waterside was tough and stringy and internally gritty even when thoroughly cooked, and tasted of creosote. It made her appreciate why Brach needed rocks in his belly to grind it up; he couldn't stand to keep it in his mouth long enough to chew it! The Tricers didn't bother; she had seen them biting off entire fern trees, and chewing up the trunks, their beaks and phenomenal back teeth like saw-mills. Cal had explained that too: the Tricers had multiple rows of teeth set one on top of the other, the worn ones being replaced automatically with new. And the upper jaw did not meet the lower directly; the teeth slid past each other in a sheering action controlled by jaw muscles a yard long. To think that some researchers had theorized that the dinosaurs died out because they could not chew the flowering plants!

For the supposedly superior dentition of the human beings, the softer tubers were better – but some made her sick, and she could not be sure, yet, which. The effect seemed to be delayed and inconsistent. Cal did eat fish, and also cooked fat lizards without compunction, and had no trouble. By unspoken agreement he did it alone; none of them were sure to what extent their dietary differences were ideological or physical, but no one criticized another in this one area, even when tempers were shortest.

She saw it coming: in time she would change over again. On Earth she had been appalled at the way animals were raised in cruel captitivy for slaughter, but here the animals were wild and free and able to look out for themselves, and it was the natural order that the weak or slow or stupid became food for the strong and swift and clever.

But mainly she was hungry, and her tastes were falling into line. What held her back was the fear that the moment she reneged on vegetarianism, Veg would turn from her, and thus she would have made her choice of men involuntarily. Perhaps Cal, with his brilliant mind and strength of will, would be the one anyway – but she wanted to make the decision freely, not via her intestines.

Meanwhile, too, there was considerable drudgery in paradise.

She broke from her task – picking over a basket of objects resembling beechnuts Veg had gathered from somewhere, to eliminate the green or rotten or wormy ones (about half the total!) – and picked up her sketch pad. At least she still had that: her painting. She headed downriver, in the direction of chopping noises.

Veg was hacking down selected hardwood saplings, comparatively rare in this valley, and skinning them. He had a row lying nude in the sun, each about six feet long and one to two inches in diameter, depending on the end. He was using his hefty scout knife, rather than attempting to harvest the slender trees by axe, and his large arm muscles bunched handsomely as he worked.

Yes, she thought, he was a powerful man, if not really a handsome one. Hardly the kind she would have taken for a vegetarian, a hater of killing. A strong, strange man, for all his simplicity.

'What are you making?' she inquired at last.

'Quarterstaffs,' he grunted.

'Quarterstaff? Isn't that a weapon?'

'Yeah. We lost our steam rifle in the turnover, and there are animals here even that wouldn't faze. Got to have something. Staffs are defensive, but effective.'

'But a weapon—'

'Defensive, I said!' Last night had been his turn on watch, the human half, and he had whistled cheerfully. But now he was feeling it. She knew what four hours of sleep felt like, but still didn't appreciate his tone.

She kept her voice level. 'You mean against a dinosaur?'

'I figure you could jam it down his throat, or maybe stop his jaws from closing on you, or just bop him on the nose. Lot better'n bare hands.'

She eyed the slender poles dubiously. 'I wouldn't care to try it on *Triceratops*. He'd bite it right—'

'Nobody's making you!' he snapped.

Affronted, she walked away. She was disgusted with herself for reacting emotionally, but she was angry at him too. He didn't have to yell.

She found Cal farther downhill, north of camp, observing a small tame dinosaur. She had seen quite a number of these innocuous, almost friendly little reptiles about, for they usually grazed in herds of a dozen or more. This one was about five feet tall with a head of considerable volume compared to the average species of reptile. Brightly coloured tissue surrounded its face, red and green and yellow; it circled all the way around its head and rose above in a spongy dome. Aquilon had no idea what such a display did for its possessor, but remembered that evolution always had realistic purpose.

The creature was nibbling bracken, and though it looked up as she approached, it returned to its meal when she halted. Harmless, certainly; had it been a predator, it would have attacked or retreated immediately. Aside from that she could tell by its tooth structure that it was herbivorous.

She came to stand behind Cal, knowing the sound of her voice would spook the beast. She opened her sketch pad and painted the dinosaur's portrait, not one to miss the opportunity. Her paper, fortunately, had been salvaged from the raft wreck, though each page was discoloured around the rim. Perhaps it was not as valuable materially as the radio equipment, but she was much happier to have it.

She was intrigued by this reptile. It looked defenceless, and its head was so large and tall! Did it have a brain capacity rivalling that of man? Could it be intelligent, in human terms? Its actions suggested nothing of the kind, but—

When she finished, Cal handed her a sheet of his notes. Usually he employed the voicetyper, but this time he had been doing it by hand, to preserve silence. She looked at the crude writing: 'TRŌŌDON, "bonehead" ornithischian. Solid bone skull, small brain.'

Solid *bone*? That skull she had thought to contain a massive brain ... What a waste of space!

There was more, but she looked up to see one of the mantas approaching. The little dinosaur took alarm and bounded away like a huge rabbit, keeping its head erect.

'Why all bone?' she demanded, free to speak now. 'Doesn't it just slow it up, when there is danger?'

'That has bothered paleontologists for some time,' Cal admitted. 'I'd very much like to see Trōōdon in a situation of hazard, and make notes. At present I can only conjecture. A large carnosaur would ordinarily bite the head off one that size, as the best way to kill the creature rapidly. The body would still cast about a bit, but the predator would be able to hold it down and feed on the carcass at leisure. But if it sank its teeth into Tròòdon's soft-seeming skull . . .'

Aquilon laughed. 'No teeth! It wouldn't try *that* again!'

'Not exactly. There are several inches of fleshy padding around the bone, that would cushion the impact. And the carnosaur would soon learn to take in the entire head, not part of it, and so succeed. But this would still be a respectable mouthful, perhaps quite tasty – yet unchewable. I think that by the time the meat were off the bone, the others in the herd would long since have taken advantage of the carnivore's preoccupation to get away. So it would be an indirect measure, protecting the herd more than the individual.'

'That's a grisly mechanism!'

'Yet it would seem to limit herd liability, and perhaps discourage careless predators entirely. We do observe a thriving population of these species, at any rate.'

The manta had arrived and settled into its lumplike posture. 'What is it, Circe?' she inquired, knowing that there would be valid reason for such an interruption. More and more, the mantas were keeping to themselves, associating only loosely with the human party. One always showed up for watch at night, and they certainly were not hiding; but they seemed to prefer their own company. Communications were adequate; she could understand Circe quite well now.

STRANGE – IMPORTANT, the manta signalled with that combination of gesture and tail snaps they had gradually worked out as their code.

'Dangerous?' She remembered how well Circe's warning had served the first time, when the tsunami came.

NO. But the denial lacked full force, showing probability rather than certainty. THIS. And Circe snapped her tail in the dirt four times, leaving a mark like a footprint.

'The bird!' Cal exclaimed. 'The bird that made those tremendous prints we saw at Camp One!'

YES. TWO, Circe indicated.

'What's so distinctive about a large bird, here in the land of giants?' Aquilon asked Cal.

'It may be our substantial evidence that this is a discrete world.'

'Discreet? Oh, you mean "e-t-e" – discrete, *separate*?'

'*Alternate*. A world parallel to our own in virtually every detail, but distinct. The concept is certainly more sensible than that of temporal displacement.'

'Temporal—? Time travel? Changing the past? Paradox?' As though she hadn't worried about it too!

'Something like that. The resemblance of Paleo to Earth is far too close to be coincidental. The size of it, the gravity, atmosphere, every matching species – but we've discussed this before. I've been assigning Earthly nomenclature because it fits, but I simply can not credit time travel. There has to be another explanation, and the alternate-worlds framework can be made to fit.'

'Back where we started from,' she murmured. 'But Earth didn't have dinosaurs during the Paleocene.'

'We can't be sure of that, 'Quilon. This is an enclave, isolated rather stringently from the rest of the continent. It could have happened on Earth, and have been entirely destroyed, so that no fossils remained as evidence – or merely be buried so deeply that we haven't discovered them yet. This location, particularly, would be subject to such an upheaval. I'll certainly check that out when . . .' He paused, and she knew he was remembering their banishment. They could not return to Earth soon, if ever, even if they wanted to. 'It *could* have happened, and I rather think it did. The San Andreas Fault of our time is the landward extension of a Pacific ocean rift. The continent has overridden it, burying enormous amounts of undersea landscape. This valley could be part of that vanished structure, the mountains a reaction to the extreme turbulence of the area. There is nothing here inherently incompatible with what we know of our own world.'

'I'm not sure I follow all that,' she said, wondering which of them he was straining to convince, and why the point was suddenly so important. 'But I gather that Paleo either is or is not Earth.'

He smiled momentarily. 'That would seem to cover it. This *could* be Earth – except for that pair of birds Circe reports. Everything else fits, except the chronology of some of the reptiles, such as the pteranodons. They should have become extinct before—'

'But a big bird *doesn't* fit? I'd think that two birds would be easier to explain than a whole enclave of anachronistic dinosaurs.'

'Not so. The enclave is merely a remaining pocket, a brief, geologically speaking, carryover. The bird – one of this nature, this early – would have had to evolve over the course of millions of years, and it would have ranged widely. There would have been fossils, other evidences of its presence.'

'Cal, that sounds thin to me. There are so many giant gaps in the fossil record—'

''Quilon, we are faced with drastic alternatives. If this *is* Earth, we are faced with paradox. Paradox can't exist in practice; nature will resolve it somehow, and we might not like the manner of that resolution. Not at all. Principle of the monkey's paw.'

'The what?'

He didn't seem to hear her. 'But if this is *not* Earth, the implications are equivalently awkward. It is necessary to know.'

'But it's ridiculous to claim that one bird – I mean *two* birds – that we haven't even seen—' She stopped. She had just left an argument with Veg, and now was provoking one with Cal. Whatever the geological, ecological, paleontological, philosophical implications, their discussion would not affect the truth, and it was silly to let it prejudice their personal relations. Cal obviously had something more than a mere bird on his mind; that was a pretext to cover what he refused to discuss. Otherwise he would surely have seen his own illogic.

It was her place to smooth things over, not to aggravate them. 'Let's go see!' she said.

Cal nodded.

They rejoined Veg, who seemed to be in better spirit now that his self-appointed task was done. Aquilon didn't mention their prior exchange.

'How far?' was all Veg asked.

Circe explained: twenty miles across the water.

They used the raft, rather than make the dangerous trip around and through the unexplored swamp. They backtracked to Camp One, rebound the *Nacre*, and poled as far as the remaining day permitted.

It was good to be afloat again, Aquilon thought, as she lay wedged between the two men in the cabin. Somehow, aboard the raft at anchor, decisions were not so urgent, and she appreciated the fact that the security of their position allowed all three to sleep at once. It would otherwise have been her night to stand guard . . .

They had merely to pull together as a team of three, while the mantas relaxed, wherever it was that the four were spending this

292

night. Let the theoretical questions settle themselves. Here it was nice.

'Oh!' She jumped as a cold wash of water slid over the cabin floor, soaking her derrière. She had forgotten about that hazard. Tomorrow she would set about recalking the *Nacre* ...

Next day they beached the *Nacre* on the south shore of the small island Circe indicated and proceeded forward overland. They were quiet and cautious, so as not to frighten the anticipated birds. Each carried one of Veg's new quarterstaffs, just in case.

There was no excitement. The island was nothing more than the long-eroded peak of an ancient volcano, covered with firs and pines and surrounded by deep water. No large reptiles were in evidence, though there were some duckbill footprints. The human party crossed without event to the north side and discovered a tiny peninsula-and-inlet complex.

A bird five feet tall stood guard at the neck of the peninsula. Veg marched at it, poking with the end of his quarterstaff. 'Shoo!' he said.

The bird did not squawk and flutter away in the manner Veg evidently expected. It spread its wings, which were quite small for its size, and struck at the pole with its great curved beak. As Veg drew back, surprised, the bird raised one powerful leg high in the air.

'Careful, Veg,' Cal called in a low tone. 'That's the one we're looking for, and it's dangerous. It's a predator – a killer. Look at that beak, those talons, those muscles. It could disembowel a man with one stroke of that foot.'

Veg had come to the same conclusion. He brought the quarterstaff around sharply, striking the bird midway down its long neck. The bird fell back a pace, hurt.

'Oh,' Aquilon exclaimed, putting her hand to her own neck. She didn't want the bird to be injured, particularly if it were as rare and significant as Cal intimated. It wasn't, of course; it could not be. But it was a remarkable specimen in its own right.

She looked beyond it and spied the second bird, perched on a rock near the water. Worse and worse – that would be the standing one's mate, sitting on her nest. She would have moved by this time, either to come to the aid of the male or to join him in flight, if she were free to do so. The fact that she stayed put meant that she had eggs to protect and warm.

The humans were intruders on a nesting site, troublemakers.

But Veg had now seen this too. Embarrassed, he retreated. 'Sorry, pal,' he said. 'Didn't know it was your home. Thought you were just getting in the way. Sorry.'

The bird watched him, standing unsteadily, neck crooked where it had been struck. The second bird watched also, from the nest.

Veg, backing away, had forgotten where he was. He stepped off the narrow bank and toppled beautifully as his foot came down on water. The quarterstaff flew up as he went over, flailing. There was a tremendous splash.

Aquilon couldn't help laughing. The change from crisis to ignominy had been so sudden. Then, to cover up, she trotted to the bank to see what help she could offer.

Circe stood a few yards away, watching but not participating. What had passed through the manta's mind as she watched this farce?

The male bird peered at the scene but did not move either. As Veg staggered out, dripping, and Aquilon assisted him, it unkinked its neck and reached down to peck exploratively at the forgotten quarterstaff.

The human contingent withdrew. The manta observer disappeared. The bird remained at the neck of the peninsula until contact was broken. Aquilon held back just long enough to sketch its proud portrait.

They camped on the (calked) raft again, anchored south of the island. They consumed their respective suppers without conversation, and lay down together in the cabin when it became dark.

'That bird is intelligent,' Cal said. 'I suspected as much from its foraging habits. Did you observe the way it reacted? None of the blind animal instincts. It was studying us as carefully as we were studying it.'

'I wish you'd told me that was the bird we were looking for,' Veg complained. 'Here I was, trying to scare it away – I thought you wanted some giant!'

Aquilon stifled her laugh. The unforeseen problems of communication! Veg must have imagined a bird proportioned on the scale of *Brachiosaurus*! The fabled roc . . .

Then she thought of something else. 'How did you know how it foraged?' she demanded of Cal.

'I followed its tracks, naturally.' She heard Veg stifling his own laugh, at her expense. She had overlooked the obvious, much as he had.

'I lost the trail in the marsh,' Cal continued, 'but I learned enough to convince me that the originator resembled class *Aves* about as much as man resembles class *Mammalia*. That was significant. So I asked the mantas to watch for it.'

'Now he tells me,' Aquilon muttered chagrined. Of course a really intelligent bird would be a different matter. She, like Veg, had been thinking only in terms of size, and probably it hadn't occurred to Cal that either had misunderstood him.

'Now that I have seen it directly, I'm almost certain,' Cal said enthusiastically. 'No such creature walked our Earth in Mesozoic or even Cenozoic eras. This is Earth – but a parallel Earth, not our own. Very similar, but with certain definitive differences developing. And there is a displacement in time, so that this world runs about seventy million years behind our own, geologically. Perhaps there are an infinite number of alternates, each displaced by an instant of time instead of by physical distance. Our connection happened to be to this particular alternate, Paleo – a purely random selection. We could as easily have landed on a world removed by a single year, or by five billion years.'

'Or one ahead of ours, instead of behind,' Aquilon murmured. Cal had not been joking about the implications being as severe as time travel. What Pandora's box was opening up for mankind with this discovery?

'It may be possible to trace the entire history of our own Earth, simply by observing the progressive alternates, once the key to their controlled discovery is perfected. But in the interim we are free to manipulate this specific world to our advantage, knowing paradox is not involved.'

There was something about that phrasing Aquilon didn't like.

'I don't know what you mean, friend, but it doesn't sound good,' Veg said. 'What do you want to do with Paleo?'

'Why, open it for human colonization, of course. It is ideal for Earth's population overflow. Same gravity, good climate, superior atmosphere, untapped natural resources, few enemies – apart from certain reptiles of this one enclave, and perhaps scattered others. This could be preserved as a zoo; it will be invaluable for research.'

'Colonize?' Aquilon didn't like the sound of this any better than Veg did. 'This is an independent world. Who are we to take it over for our convenience?'

'We are men, generically. We must consider the needs of men. To do otherwise would be unrealistic.'

'Now let me get this straight,' Veg said in his play-dumb fashion. She could feel the tenseness of his body as he lay beside her. 'You say we should turn in a report saying that *Paleo* is A-O.K. for people to come in and settle, and make it just like Earth. And if a few birds or lizards get in the way it's their tough luck?'

'Well, provision should be made for the fauna. I would not condone genocide, particularly in so fine a paleontological laboratory as this. But apart from that your summary is essentially correct. This is a wilderness area, and Earth needs it desperately; it would be a crime against our species to let it lie fallow.'

'But the bird,' Aquilon protested, her heart beating too strongly. 'You said it's intelligent. That means Paleo is technically inhabited—'

'Intelligent for *Aves*: birds. That can't approach human capability. But yes, it is most important that this – this *Ornisapiens* be preserved and studied. It—'

'Orn,' Veg said, simplifying again. 'In a zoo.'

'No!' Aquilon cried. 'That isn't what I meant. That would kill it. We should be *helping* it, not—'

'Or at least leaving it alone,' Veg said. 'It's a decent bird; it didn't jump me when it had the chance, and after I'd hit it with the staff, too. We don't need to lock it up *or* help it, just let it be. Let them all be. That's the way.'

'We appear,' Cal remarked, 'to have a multiple difference of opinion. Veg feels that man can not sit in judgement over the species of Paleo, either to assist or to exterminate.'

'That's what I feel,' Veg agreed.

''Quilon feels that the bird, Orn, deserves assistance, because of its apparently unique development as a creature distinct from Earthly genera. Obviously Orn is not common here, and may be in danger of extinction.'

'Mmmm,' Aquilon agreed. Cal was that most dangerous of

opponents: the one who took pains to comprehend the position of his adversary.

'While *I* feel that the needs of our own species must take precedence. It is nature's decree that the fittest survive in competition, and if Man *can* control this world operating from a tiny beachhead in the Pacific, he deserves to and is required to. The fact that the animals here resemble those of our own past is irrelevant; our species must have room to expand.'

'*Lebensraum*,' Aquilon whispered tersely.

'Adolf Hitler's term,' Cal said, picking up the allusion immediately, as she had known he would. 'But he used it as a poor pretext for conquest.'

'Aren't *we*?'

Cal shrugged in the dark.

She felt herself getting flushed. 'Suppose some other species – maybe an advanced version of Orn – had felt that way about our own Earth?' she demanded. 'Suppose they had come when we were apelike primates, and used advanced technology to push us out?'

'We'd have deserved it. We're *still* apelike primates.'

'Maybe we should vote,' Veg said.

'No problem,' Cal said. 'Are you ready, mantas?'

From the roof came a tap – the contact of a manta's tail on the wood. Aquilon was startled, though she should not have been. They had probably come after dark and viewed the leaking sound waves, thus picking up the entire conversation. Cal had certainly been aware of the audience, and he seemed to have confidence in the outcome. Why?

Veg was silent also, probably wrestling with similar concerns. How, she wondered hurriedly, would the manta mind view this crisis? They saw things in terms of their own Nacre framework, manta framework – carnivore, omnivore, and herbivore – with rights and wrongs being interpreted through this. Veg's vegetarianism had been the original key to contact with these creatures, since they had seen him as theoretically in need of protection from the omnivore of the party: her. It wasn't as simple as that, Cal had maintained; but as an analogy it would do. Of course she had shifted from omnivore type to herbivore type, while Cal had gone from carnivore to omnivore; apparently the mantas were now wise enough to the ways of man to accept these changes. All human

297

beings were true omnivores, regardless of their diets of the moment; man's brutal nature defined him.

'What do birds eat?' Veg inquired.

It was a stupid question and no one replied. Veg knew what birds ate; he was a veteran birdwatcher. Funny, she realized now, that he had treated the Orn so brusquely. Perhaps he only identified with small birds, the seed-eating, fly-chasing kind. As a species, of course, birds were omnivorous.

Omnivorous.

The question had not been stupid at all. Suddenly she knew which way the manta vote would go. 'No,' she said, trying to control the tremor in her breast. 'Don't vote.'

'Why not?' Cal asked her. He knew his advantage, and was pressing it ruthlessly despite the mild words. In body he was small, in mind a giant – and that went for discipline as well as intelligence.

'It's too important,' she said, dissembling, knowing she could not prevail against him, and that Veg would be even less effective than she. Cal had the brain and the votes. 'Before, it was only where we wanted to go as a group, not a really critical decision. This time it's the fate of an entire world. *Our* world, or one very like it. This isn't the manta's business.'

She saw the teeth of the trap and scrambled to avoid them. 'Colonization would destroy Paleo as it is, you know that. They'd decide the dinosaurs were a menace to tourists or navigation or something, and wipe them out. So we can't decide a question like this by ourselves.'

'I was hardly suggesting that we should,' Cal replied calmly. 'We have merely to make an honest report to the authorities on Earth, and let *them* decide.'

'But they're omnivores!' she cried, knowing this implied that she endorsed a dishonest report. Omnivore – she meant it as a description of character, not diet. The omnivores of the planet Nacre were utterly savage, with virtually no redeeming qualities, in her terms. This was in contrast with the innocuous herbivores and deadly but disciplined carnivores. The term 'omnivore' had come, for her, to represent all that was despicable in life. Man *was* an omnivore, and had already demonstrated his affinity to the Nacre breed. That ruthless action on Earth itself to eradicate potentially dangerous fungus spores—

'So is Orn,' Cal said.

'That isn't what I meant!' she exclaimed, defensively angry.

'You're being emotional rather than rational.'

'I'm a woman!'

There was a freighted silence.

Cal was right, but she knew he was wrong, ethically. Cal had decided against Paleo the moment he was assured that it was safe to do so. The mantas wouldn't care. The Earth authorities would be concerned only with exploitation of natural resources and the temporary relief of population pressure. They would much prefer to devastate another world, rather than to abate the mismanagement of the first. There was no one she could appeal to.

'I can't participate in this,' she said at last. She got to hands and knees and crawled out of the cabin, leaving the men lying there separated by a woman-sized gap. She was dressed; the niceties of contemporary convention were ludicrous here.

She stood aboard the raft in the gentle night wind, looking across the moonlit water towards the island. Large flying insects hovered about her head and tried to settle on her. She jerked her hood up and fastened the mesh over her face, batting it against the sides of her head to clear it of trapped arthropodic life. Then she drew on her gloves, so that no portion of her skin was exposed. The night was warm, and this confinement made her hot, but it was better than submitting to the appetites of the winged ones.

It was stupid, it was cruel – but it would be worse to go along with this genocidal majority. She had witnessed the ways of man on Earth, and could not bear the thought of the rape of Paleo that was surely in the making. So – she had to go her own way, whatever that might mean.

She looked over the black water. She would have to swim. At least that would cool her off! The chances were that no large marine predators were near. The reptiles didn't seem to be active at night, generally, and their size kept their numbers down. Still, she hesitated, sadly confused inside. She tried to tell herself it was because she knew *Ichthyosaurus was* a night hunter, because of those pumpkin-sized eyes ... but it was the separation from those she had thought lifetime friends that really dismayed her. How could she return, once she made this break?

There was the scuffle of another person breaking through the cabin net, and Veg stood up beside her. 'Better your way than his,' he said.

She experienced a choking surge of gratitude towards him. She had made her decision on her own, not presuming his. The ties between the two men were strong, however different their temperaments and physiques might be. She had not even thought what she might do, by herself, or how she would live. Now she was immensely relieved to know that she would not be alone.

'We'll have to swim,' he said, echoing her own thought. 'You were headed for the birds, weren't you?'

She hadn't planned that far ahead, but it seemed to fit. The schism had started with the birds, really.

She touched his arm, not wanting to speak within the hearing of Cal, or even to gesture, knowing the mantas were watching. Cal was the weakest member of the group (physically!) and the raft required muscle to operate. Muscle the mantas could not supply. By leaving him, they were marooning him.

'I'll check back in the morning,' Veg said. 'We'll work it out.' He dived into the water, making a phosphorescent splash.

Relieved, she followed him.

Chapter Thirteen

ORN

Well after dusk Orn lifted his head, disturbed. Beyond the normal noises of the night he perceived a differing manifestation, and in a moment placed it: the awkward progress of the monstrous mams.

The confrontation of the day still distressed him. The really strange or inexplicable or completely unremembered bothered him because he did not know how to deal with it, and this recent encounter had been all of that. Mams themselves were familiar enough; they were everywhere, more plentiful by far than the reps even here in the heart of this enclave. Elsewhere on the continent they were larger and bolder and farther developed than were the primitive samples here. But nowhere did they approach the size of either Orn himself or any of the larger reps, except perhaps for their largest and stupidest herbivores. He had adapted to the changed situation in the world and learned to cope with the new creatures, before settling into this more familiar valley. But to be so abruptly confronted by bipedal mams larger than himself!

That shock had very nearly cost him his life. He had stood bemused by the appalling gap in his memory, trying to fathom the life history of the species so that he might know how to deal with it. Size was only one feature of many; these mams were *different*. Their myriad peculiarities had rendered them nearly invisible to him at first. Only his prior practice in visualizing unfamiliar creatures in terms of familiar ones had enabled him to grasp their nature at all.

Meanwhile, one of the creatures had approached and made contact. Orn, mindful of Ornette and their two precious eggs, had had to react to repel the intrusion.

The mam had struck him with an inanimate object, another astonishment. Orn had never realized that such a thing was possible. Inanimate things could be used for roosting or nest-building, or even riding across rough water, but never for the work of claw or beak.

301

Hitherto. What could it mean?

And the final fluke: the mam, having by its alchemism rendered him vulnerable, had failed to kill him. The creature had instead plunged into the water and retreated, and the others with it. If they had come to fight and feed, this was nonsensical.

He remembered the way he had spared the ptera, that first day of their nesting. It was possible to abstain from easy victory, in the absence of hunger. Yet that offered no comprehensible clue to the behaviour of the big mams.

Orn ruffled his wings restlessly. He was not equipped to think things out; his memory ordinarily made such effort unnecessary. But now that huge mam was coming again, in the night. Orn had to react, and to protect himself and their nest more effectively than he had before. No ancestor had faced this particular problem.

At least this night attack was in character. The mams, like the aves, were able to move about as readily by night as by day, and a number preferred the cover of dark for their foraging. Indeed, many would not survive long in this homeland of the reps otherwise, for there were many empty bellies and sharp teeth on patrol by day, and mams were tasty morsels. Only by occupying regions too cold for the reps and by feeding at night had the mams prospered.

But these were so clumsy! If the creatures – only two were coming this time – were hunting, they would never overtake their game so loudly. If they thought they were hiding, they were disastrously inept. Was it that they were so large for their type that they were stupid, like the brach swamp dweller whose plentiful young were such ready prey? But even the mam amblys were more careful of their own well-being than that!

Yes, they were coming here. Orn raised himself from the nest and Ornette moved over to cover the eggs fully. One of them had to warm and guard the eggs at all times, and Ornette, gravid with the third, did not forage at all now. Three times they had made connection, and two of the eggs were incubating. The final one was due tonight, and a disturbance would be harmful. He had to guard the nest from every threat.

He strode to the isthmus and waited for the two lumbering mams. Male and female, both grotesque in their inept giantism. What their mission was he could not know, for they lacked the furtive manner of egg stealers. But he would turn them back. There was a bruise under the feathers of his neck, from the previous encounter, and the muscles there were sore, but it had been an important lessen. He would not let such an object strike him again, not stand dazed. He would kill the first mam immediately and be ready for the second.

They arrived. Orn waited, standing just behind the narrowest section of the isthmus so that they would have to approach singly. Perhaps they were egg stealers after all, depending on brute strength rather than stealth. He twitched the claws of one foot in the turf, ready to lift and slash ferociously. The eggs must not be imperilled!

'He's there.' It was the male, making some kind of hissing growl that still did not quite resemble a challenge to battle.

'Veg, he thinks you're after the eggs. Don't go near him.' That was the female, her growl more sustained and variegated. It was as though she were cautioning her mate about the coming encounter.

The male halted in bright moonlight about four wingspans from Orn. He held a length of tree in his paws – the same object that had surprised Orn before. It was in fact a substitute beak or claw, for the mam had no effective armament of its own. Orn visualized it as the latter, for it attached to the limbs. He would have to strike around it, diving for the open throat or gut.

But the mam did not make an overture for combat. He stood for an interminable period, while the female stroked a twig against a flat object. Orn comprehended neither the action of the female nor the inaction of the male.

'I've painted his portrait. We'd better leave him alone.' Noises from the female again, as she concealed her twig and tucked the flat thing under one forelimb.

As though that senseless series of female squawks were a signal, the male dropped his length of barkless tree and took a step forward.

'Veg!'

There was no mistaking that cry of alarm. She understood, at least, that the male was on the verge of an encounter likely to end in disembowelment. Orn would not permit it near the nest.

Still the creature approached, taking great slow steps, pausing between each. Now it had its fleshy forelimbs behind it, exposing his entire torso. It was only two wingspans distant, entirely unarmed and vulnerable; Orn could leap across that space and stab the large mam heart he sensed, then retreat to the superior position on the isthmus. But he held back, leery of attacking when he did not

303

comprehend the meaning of the mam's actions and could not interpret them in terms of any similar creature. It could easily be a death trap for himself.

Another step, and now he was aware of the tension in the mam. It was afraid yet determined, not in a kill fury. Did it want to die? Certainly it did not want to fight! It had made itself entirely vulnerable to Orn's beak or talon, while its mate whimpered behind.

Then everything fell into place. These huge, awkward, bumbling things – they didn't know *how* to fight. They could strike out with pieces of tree, but were unable to follow up any advantage gained. Both would soon become prey to a predator rep unless they found sanctuary somewhere. So they had come to this isolated island, and, still afraid, had sought Orn's protection.

He would ordinarily have killed it anyway, or at least wounded it sufficiently to drive it off, this alien male. He was not hungry for the meat. But the very nest that made him stand his ground against an unremembered antagonist also made him disinclined to kill unnecessarily. His being was suffused with the juices of cohabitation and protectiveness; he had his own mate to comfort and eggs to warm, and bloodshed made a poor nesting mood.

The mam kept coming. Orn had either to kill him or let him pass, thereby extending his protection to the strange pair.

He heard Ornette pant with the first laying pangs.

Orn stood aside.

The female crossed then, and the two mams joined appendages and skirted the opposite shore of the peninsula. Orn stepped backward towards the nest, anxious to be with Ornette in her time of pain, but compelled to watch the mams lest they make some hostile move. He was profoundly uncertain, more so than he had been when he spared the ptera, but at least he had avoided battle and killing.

He came at last to the nest, and stood beside it for some time, listening to the mams while one wing touched Ornette's back. The creatures were behind the clustered pines, scraping the ground with their soft digits and uttering their ugly, drawn-out cries, but never coming towards him. They seemed to know that they lived on sufferance, and that the vicinity of the nest was forbidden. He would have to kill them if they came near Ornette or the eggs, particularly tonight.

Finally they settled down, and only their vocal noises persisted. That was their oddest trait: the perpetual and irrelevant sounds they made in their throats and mouths.

'I wish there were some other solution.' The female making tones of disturbance. 'I hate to leave him alone like that.'

'He's got a lot of know-how.' Now the male was replying with assurance. Their moods were not so different from those Orn shared with Ornette; only their vocalizing differed substantially. They employed drawn-out, modulated chains of sound in lieu of simple pitched honks. Apart from the clumsiness of the mode, it served. Everything about these ungainly mams was like that, however. Even their fur was matted and creased as though it had been baked in mud until it hung in chafing sheets. Nets of hair had fallen over their heads as well, obscuring their vision and smell perceptions and surely interfering with feeding.

'He'll know better than to try to go anywhere.' The female was uttering modulations of self-reassurance now. 'The mantas will protect him.'

'Yeah.'

One thing about their continuing utterances: it enabled Orn to keep track of them without leaving the nest or straining his perceptions. He settled down beside Ornette, who was relaxing for the moment, and listened.

'I wish we could get dry.' Female. 'I know it isn't really cold, but with this soaking and the sea breeze – I'm shivering.'

'I brought a tarp in my pack,' Male. 'Make a passable blanket, if that helps. It's watertight.'

'You're thoughtful, Veg. But the wet clothing is right next to my skin, and the tarpaulin would prevent it from evaporating. I'll have to take my things off.'

'I'll set up shop in the next gully.'

'But you're cold too, Veg. You're just as wet as I am, and there's only one tarpaulin.'

'I've roughed it before, 'Quilon. Don't worry about me.'

They were doing something. Orn heard the rustle of something he could not identify. Not leaves, not bark, not tangled fur. Concerned, he stood up quietly and moved to where he could oversee the mam camp.

The male was drawing flexible material from a rock-shaped

object. It was as though a giant clamshell contained matted ferns. He spread it out, a single sheet, so that it settled over the female.

It was all right. They were merely spreading bedding.

'Veg—'

''s okay. The tarp's dry. I had it sealed in. Got a dry T-shirt for you, too. Wrap it tight to keep the bugs out though.'

'Veg, you're not very bright sometimes.'

'I know. I should've thought of dry clothing before diving in. In the morning I'll go back and pick up some. Now you fix yourself up, and I'll go down a ways and—'

'Veg, if we sleep apart we'll *both* be cold.'

'I know, but no sense getting everything wet again with my sopping rags. You're better off by yourself.'

Orn realized that they were disagreeing with each other in some awkward mam way. The female wanted something but the male didn't understand.

'Veg, remember when I spoke about making a choice?'

'Yeah, 'Quilon. Back when we broke it up on Earth. I never forget things like that.'

'I made it.'

The mams were silent for a moment, but Orn, watching and listening and sniffing, was aware of a continuing tension between them. Some kind of understanding was incipient. He flexed his claws, ready to move if the creatures attempted to make a night raid on the nest.

'Yeah, I'm not very bright.' Male sound again: comprehension and triumph.

Then the male put his soft mam digits to his own fur and ripped it apart. It fell from his body in wet lumps, leaving him plucked. The female stood up and did the same. Orn was amazed; he could never have removed his own feathers like that, or have endured the pain.

The mams got down together and wrapped the big sheet around them, as though they were two hairless worms in a single cocoon.

Orn listened for a while longer. Then he realized the significance of their actions. *They were nesting!* What had passed before was their odd mam courtship, and now they were ready to copulate.

Relieved, he returned to his own nest. At last he understood the complete motive of this pair of intruders. They had sought a safe place to reside during their mating and confinement, and so had chosen to make common cause with his own family.

The big mams were not as stupid as he had supposed, merely strange.

That night, while the mams embraced cumbersomely and made sounds reflecting labours of universal significance, and while the three ptera hung in cold silence from their branches, Ornette gave birth to the final egg.

Peace and joy were upon the peninsula.

The mams woke in the morning but remained in their bundle for a time, waiting for the sun to strike away the chill. As the ptera began to stir, the mams unwound, attended to their special toilettes, and climbed back into their ugly fur. They ate from a cake of scorched, impacted plant stuff and drank copious quantities of water from a strange container. Like all mams, they imbibed and ejected an appalling amount of liquid.

'Look at the pteranodons!' The female was making her excited noises again. Orn, initially irritated by this constant and useless chatter, was becoming used to it. He accepted every creature for what it was, and it seemed the giant mams were noisemakers.

Then a trach crossed the water from the mainland and sported about the peninsula, browsing for shore herbage. This rep fed mainly on pine needles and cones, grinding them up with its flat bill full of little teeth. Though it was large, standing four times Orn's height and possessing a flat, sleek muscular tail, it was harmless unless provoked. It needed its full height to reach the succulent (to it) needles growing from the lower branches of the tall trees. It was related to the para Orn had first seen dead beyond the mountain range, but lacked the elaborate bonework on the head. A para could thus outrun a trach, because it ran cooler; but the trach was of sturdier construction.

Orn stood by the nest and let the rep graze as it would, leaving its webbed prints in the muck. That was why the island location was so good: most large reps that were able to reach it and climb on land were those that ate neither flesh nor eggs, and so were reasonably safe. Like this good-natured trach.

The mams also watched, but with greater caution. Their exclamations suggested that they were not accustomed to such proximity to the trach. Soon they relaxed, however, watching the rep's easy motions.

'I better check on Cal.' And with that utterance the male was off, charging through the brush like a small tricer. The female remained to watch the trach play and feed.

Ornette rose from the nest, and Orn covered the three living eggs while she exercised her legs and wings and cleaned herself off at the edge of the water. She had had a hard night, and was not entirely easy about the presence of the mams or the trach, but deferred to his judgement.

Orn watched the female mam speculatively. Most mams did not lay eggs, of course; they gave live birth, like the ichthy rep of the sea. After the authority of the mating ritual of the night just passed, this process was surely commencing within this female. Would the two mams remain on the island for the denouement? Perhaps the mam litter would grow up with Orn's own in compatible proximity. This would be a curious phenomenon, but not objectionable, so long as there was no strife between them concerning tasty grubs and such. His ancestors had nested upon occasion in harmony beside tròòs and even ankys, though the parent reps never went near their eggs once they had been deposited. Rep nests were far more transient than those of aves, so it didn't matter. But his species had never shared territory with struths or tyranns or crocs of any age; indeed, Orn would smash and consume any eggs he found of these creatures. It depended on the type of rep.

It depended on the type of mam, too. He would just have to be alert.

It was during this contemplative interlude that the first tremor struck.

Chapter Fourteen

CAL

It hurt Cal, this schism; he could not deny it. The group had come upon it almost incidentally, yet he had known it was brewing, and it had bothered him increasingly. They had been fortunate that it had not occurred on Nacre. Veg believed in life, however naïvely; Cal believed in death. Aquilon fell between, vacillating, but tended towards life. This was not so simple a concept as good and evil; both qualities were represented on either side of this issue. It was primarily a question of what was necessary.

The four mantas understood that much, as they had demonstrated by their action at the orbiting station. Their view of man's endeavours was dispassionate, as was their view of the entire animal kingdom, since they were not of it. They remained with him because they knew that his approach to the problem of Paleo was realistic rather than emotional. Had it been otherwise—

He sighed. Had it been otherwise, he would have relegated all Earth to limbo, for the mere love of Aquilon. He acted as he had to, but this did not alter his love for her. Nor did her figurative elopement with Veg affect this; he was aware that the simmering chemistry of heterosexual existence had to boil over at some point. They loved life, and this was the essence of life; the fact that Cal had increasing yearnings of his own of that nature could not change his overall orientation. They were his friends, and he had more pressing responsibilities; he could not begrudge them their joy.

Meanwhile, he had a job to do. Paleo was suitable for colonization by Earth, and no report he could make could conceal that. In fact, it was vital that he make the matter entirely clear, though this would sacrifice this beautiful world, for there were larger concerns. If the rape of Paleo diverted mankind long enough to allow information to circulate to those who could and would be stimulated to ensure proper protection for the other worlds of the alternate framework – the positive backlash – the end did in this case justify the means. Whatever Aquilon might think. This would necessarily entail the retirement of certain native fauna, and was certainly regrettable; but nature's way, properly guided, was best. No species could prevail by holding back. That was the way of self-extinction. The philosophy that saw virtue in the preservation of species and systems unfit to survive competitively – that philosophy was quaint but futile. Nature had no such sentiments.

Cal studied the raft in the morning light. He would have to arrange to sail it back across the bay by himself, then make the trek overland to Camp Two for supplies. Then a longer sea voyage back to their Paleocene camp, where the one remaining functional radio was located. After that it would be merely a matter of waiting. Earth would decide.

It was not an easy journey he contemplated. Veg could have done it, but Cal was a far cry from that! Still, his philosophy accounted for this. He would make the attempt. If he failed, the report would not be made, and perhaps Veg and Aquilon would have their way. If he failed, he deserved to fail.

His strength was not great, but it was more than it had been. He could rig the sail, tie it in place, and handle the rudder provided the winds were moderate and favourable. He would have to be alert for large reptiles and stormy weather, assuming that either could be avoided. How he would navigate the barrier reefs he did not know; possibly he could map a channel through them at low tide, then follow that course at high tide. He judged that the odds were against his completing the trip, but with proper application and caution he hoped to make a worthy run for it.

'Ahoy!'

It was Veg hailing him from the island. Cal waved.

'How're you doing?' Veg called. Then, not waiting for an answer, the big man dived into the water and stroked for the raft.

'I'm going back to the Paleocene camp,' Cal said as Veg clambered aboard. 'The radio is there, and I believe the winds are shifting enough to make it feasible.'

'Feasible, hell. You can't make it by yourself. Why don't you talk to 'Quilon again? We shouldn't split like this.'

'Three, as the saying goes, is a crowd.'

Veg covered up his embarrassment by going to the tied mound of

310

supplies. Most of their equipment remained at Camp Two, but they had come prepared for several days. 'She needs some dry clothing, okay?'

'She is welcome. Take some bread, too. She made it, after all. I'll be moving the *Nacre* out soon.' There had not been any official division of spoils, but it was tacit: Veg had the woman, Cal the raft. And the mantas.

'You'll kill yourself.'

Cal shrugged. 'Death is no spectre to me.'

'Here.' Veg busied himself with the sail, hauling it into position and tying it securely. 'If you get in trouble, send a manta.'

They shook hands awkwardly and parted. Already the *Nacre* was tugging at the anchor.

The wind was fair and gentle, the sky overcast, and progress was satisfactory. The mantas sailed out over the water, stunning fish with their tails. Cal scooped them in with the net and piled them aboard the raft so that the mantas could feed at leisure.

It was interesting that the sea there was completely Paleocene. No ammonites, no rudists. Would Aquilon have dreamed about the rudist bivalve if he had described it to her as another typically Cretaceous sea creature? Only the reptiles had retained their hold on the sea, as part of the enclave. What did this signify about the relation of land and sea forms? There had to be some continuing link between the reptiles of land, sea, and air, so that they became extinct almost together . . .

The island was a mile astern when the tremor came. The water danced as though rain were hitting the surface, but there was no rain. The mantas, disgruntled, closed hastily on the raft and boarded. Debris sifted down from the trees visible along the shore, and dust came up in peripheral sections of the valley.

A tremor – no more than fifteen seconds in duration, not really severe. Cal did not react with unreasoning dread. Perhaps this little shake signified nothing – but it could be the prelude to a far more violent siege.

Veg and Aquilon were on the island, stranded there until they could construct a second raft. Certainly they would not attempt to swim to the mainland during the heat of the day; the carnivores of water and shore forbade it. But of course there was no security from an earthquake. They were as safe on the island as anywhere. Perhaps safer, when the great land predators, surely roused into anger by the shake, were taken into account.

He could return, but it would not resolve their interpersonal dilemma. The arguments had been made, the positions clarified. Best to continue as he had planned.

In the distance, in the strait between the islands Aquilon had dubbed Scylla and Charybdis, he made out animate activity. The water dwellers had indeed been shaken up by the tremor, and were casting about, trying to flee or attack but finding no way to isolate the cause. Cal decided to steer well clear of them. Most were far smaller than *Brachiosaurus*, but many were more predacious, and even a herbivorous dinosaur was dangerous when alarmed, as the battered craft testified.

Tremendous pteranodons sailed in the sky, the only creatures unaffected. No – as he watched, the winged reptiles changed course en masse. The wind had shifted, as though blunted by the tremor.

That meant trouble for him too. He had travelled under fair auspices so far, but any change in the wind would be the worse for him.

He untied the sail and began to haul it down. Now his lack of strength was critical, for what Veg made seem easy was a tremendous strain on his own resources. The sail, under tension, resisted his efforts.

Then the wind shift caught up. The sail fluttered violently as it was struck almost at right angles, and the raft began turning. Cal knew how to adjust the sail and use the rudder so as to tack into the wind, but he also knew that he had neither the agility nor the strength to perform the coordinated tasks required. Sailing a clumsy raft was at best a two-man job, and tacking took muscle.

He did the next best thing. He steered the *Nacre* around forty-five degrees, heading northwest instead of west. This would bring him to land too soon, but seemed to be his safest course.

The mantas perched on the cabin roof, unable either to assist or to offer advice.

All too rapidly the *Nacre* came at the shore. This was the swampy region where certain tribes of duckbills foraged, but none were in evidence at the moment. Just as well. They were not inimical to man, but would have reacted unpredictably to a charging raft.

Now was the time to drop the sail, but the line was still jammed.

312

The *Nacre* was driving relentlessly for the bank of land, carving a ragged course through the water plants.

The mantas dived for the sides. So did Cal.

He hit a cushion of soft plants and took in a mouthful of warm, slimy, but not salty, water before finding the mucky bottom with feet and hands. The depth here was about a yard.

The *Nacre* ploughed on, slowed by the thickening growths. Then the keel scraped into something more solid than the bottom mud, and the whole thing crunched to a halt, upright and listing only momentarily. The jammed rope let go, and the sail dropped resoundingly to the deck, releasing the raft from the urging of the wind.

Cal had taken his plunge for nothing.

He waded up and sought the crude anchor. This might not hold against a determined offshore wind, but again there was nothing better he could do. He would have to leave the *Nacre* and hope it remained secure for a day or two, until he could return. He was, at least, on the right side of the river.

He donned a small pack, taking only enough baked fish to last him a day, since he hoped to pick up supplies at Camp Two. He would be foolish to wear himself out prematurely, on this easiest leg of his journey.

As an afterthought, he took his quarterstaff too.

It was now early afternoon, and he knew he could not make the twenty miles the compass indicated before dark. He would have to husband his strength and do the job in stages. Time was as critical as survival.

He trekked through the slough all afternoon, resting more frequently than he needed to. His strength was for the moment his most precious commodity, and he guarded it jealously. The mantas stayed with him though they would have been happier on their own; they were evidently concerned for his safety. By dusk he had achieved higher ground. He threw himself down, eyes closed, not bothering at first with any formal bedding.

Veg could have made this distance in an hour, he knew. But to Cal it was a victory, for a year ago he could not have made a tenth of it. He was tougher than he had been in a decade, and he took an unobjective pride in it.

But he still assessed his chances of success at less than even.

313

He ate a salted fish for breakfast and moved out. His legs were stiff, but he felt stronger than ever. This was the first time in many years he had travelled by himself, and he was pleased to discover how well it was going. He was making much better time on this firm terrain.

There were more deciduous, broad-leafed trees than he had supposed at first. Counting them idly, he found that fully a third of the substantial growth were familiar hardwoods – beech, birch, maple, ash, elm, and so on. Though the typically Cretaceous flora predominated, the balance was even now shifting to these newer types. The land, like the ocean, was advancing relentlessly into the Cenozoic Era. Only the reptiles lingered.

By noon he was within five miles of the camp. The intricate distance-gauging compass assured him of that, since it had been keyed to Camp Two. He stopped to eat the last fish and sup water up from a small rain-formed pond, and the mantas ranged out to bring down their meals too. He was not worried about nourishment; the mantas would gladly kill for him if that became necessary, and show him the way to fresh water. He would spend the night in the lean-to, then attempt to make the return trip in one more day. There would have to be many such journeys, of course, for he could not carry much at a time – but the exercise over a familiar trail should toughen him up for the major journey ahead. Perhaps he could fashion a harness-drag, and transport a greater weight at one time. He felt better able to cope than ever before.

Hex came in, tail snapping. Trouble!

A predator dinosaur had come across his trail and was pursuing him. The mantas had tried to distract it harmlessly, but it was intent on one scent. This was what they had been alert against. A big one, Hex clarified: *Tyrannosaurus Rex*, king of the carnosaurs.

The creature could be stopped, of course. The mantas could harass it and probably blind it. *Tyrannosaurus* was far larger than the omnivore of Nacre, but no more dangerous to the swift manta. Four against one—

'Do not attack it,' Cal said.

Hex didn't understand.

'This creature's world is on trial. If I get to the radio and send my report, my people will come and exterminate the biological system that now obtains. Not all at once, but over the years, the centuries,

314

until the only dinosaurs remaining are caged in zoos, and the same for most of the primitive Paleocene fauna. Modern mammals will be introduced that will compete aggressively with the less sophisticated natives, and the trees will be cut for timber and pulp and the rocks mined for precious minerals. So *Tyrannosaurus* is fighting for his world, though he doesn't see it that way. If the reptile brings me down, the report will not be made, and man will not come here – at least, not quite so soon. If I escape the reptile, I will have vindicated my right, according to the implacable laws of nature, to supersede it on *Paleo*. It is a contest between us, and the prize is this world.'

He had issued a statement whose entirety they could hardly be expected to grasp, but it seemed better not to confuse things by attempting to simplify a difficult concept. The mantas should understand that he did not want them to intercede on his behalf, and that he had reasons that were sufficient for his own mind. That should be enough.

The other mantas came up, and an eye-to-eye dialogue followed. Would they acquiesce?

'Let me meet Tyrann alone,' he repeated. 'You watch, but do not interfere. Mammal against reptile, the chosen champions, one to one.'

Hex snapped once. Yes, they accepted it. The mantas understood the rite of personal combat.

The four spread out to the sides and disappeared amid the cycads. Cal was on his own.

But not for long. A mile back, the giant was coming, crashing through the brush horrendously.

It had been easy to commit himself, for that was necessary by his definitions. It would not be as easy to survive the consequence of that decision. He was hardly the best representative of his species or class for such an encounter. But that was the way circumstance had offered, and he was ready to abide by nature's verdict. He had never been one to avoid confrontation with death.

Cal waited where he was. He wanted to face his opponent. It would be no good for him to sneak away, even if that should fool the reptile. He had to stand up to Tyrann, let the thing know he was challenging it. Then he could make his escape, if it was in him to accomplish it.

The ground shuddered, and not from any geologic tremor.

Tyrannosaurus was closing in, unsubtly. Every step rocked the land, and the crashing of saplings became loud. This was the pinnacle of reptilian predatory development; no more massive carnivore had ever walked the earth.

The slender fern trees swayed aside, as though reaching to the ginkgo for comfort. A terrified bird flew up. Through the palm fronds poked a gaping set of jaws – fifteen feet above the ground. Then the whole of it came into view: seemingly all teeth and legs, so tall that a man could pass upright under its thighs and tail without stooping. A roar like none ever to emanate from a mammalian throat shook the air, and the tiny cruel eyes peered down.

Tyrann had arrived.

Chapter Fifteen

AQUILON

'He's sailing the *Nacre*,' Veg said as he reappeared. 'Going back to the radio and sending the message.' He threw down the pack of supplies he had brought from the raft.

Aquilon was appalled. 'He can't possibly do it by himself!'

He shrugged. 'Can't stop him from trying.' But his jaw was tight.

He knew the mantas represented a formidable bodyguard, but there were things they could not protect Cal from. Drowning, physical injury, heatstroke—

Still, Veg was right. If Cal insisted on attempting a suicidal journey, that was his concern. At least, so long as the break between them continued.

If only it were something other than the future of a world at stake! She would gladly have gone along with Cal for the sake of unity on any lesser matter. But his report to Earth would damn Paleo by its praise, and she could not go along with that. It would violate all her most cherished, if uncertain, principles. The wolf should not be loosed at the lamb, not this way.

She felt guilt for either outcome: Cal's success or his failure. She knew he would not change his mind. If he lived, Paleo would die.

Now, too, she felt uneasy about her night of love with Veg. She had made her choice – but she had done it because of the convenience of the moment, and that was not far clear of prostitution, in retrospect. And she suspected from Veg's silence on that score that he felt the same. They had wronged Cal, whatever the merit of their respective positions.

The Orn birds went about their business, first one sitting on the nest, then the other, but usually the female. There were eggs, naturally; she had not glimpsed them, for the birds were sensitive about any human approach to the nest. But nothing else would account for such care.

The first day passed in beauty. She watched the *Trachydon*, the large duckbilled dinosaur, feeding among the pine trees. It was sleek in the water, with webbed feet and a tail flattened like that of a crocodile. When it stood on land it was fifteen feet tall, resembling an outsize kangaroo, and the hind feet were revealed as possessing tripartite hoofs. Duck*billed* – but not duck*like*!

Trachydon spent most of its time chewing, as though its digestion not only began in the mouth but ended there. Its hide was pebbled, without scales or other armour, and the play of the creature's musculature was quite clear underneath the skin. Its underside was whitish, reminding her of a snake. Its sheer size fazed her at first, but Trach was really quite likeable when familiar. It also seemed to pose for her, remaining impossibly still except for its jaws, and she painted many portraits. She was sorry to see Trach go, once its belly was full of pine.

At night the pteranodons returned to their bough to sleep, and that was another impressive spectacle. She had somehow imagined all dinosaurs to be ravening monsters or dim-witted behemoths, before coming to Paleo; this day on the island, watching *Trachydon* and pteranodon in life, banished that prejudice forever. These reptiles had individual personalities and problems, and were bright enough about the latter.

She also saw, that first day, the raft sailing before the wind, angling in toward the mainland, and finally anchoring there. She knew why: the wind had shifted after the tremor, and Cal had been unable to sail directly back to Camp One. At least he had made it safely to shore.

The second night she and Veg slept under the tarpaulin but did not make love.

Two nights and a day on an isle very like paradise – but the tension was cruel. What was Cal doing? He was so small, so weak; he could be lying exhausted in the swamp ...

No. The mantas would come back and report. He must be all right.

Still—

'One's coming!' Veg called, looking up from the new raft he was building.

She ran to his side to see. A lone manta was speeding across the water toward the island. Circe!

The story did not take long: a tyrannosaur was after Cal. He had forbidden the mantas to help. Circe departed.

'The crazy fool!' Veg cried. 'He's suiciding again!'

But it was not that simple. Cal *wanted* to fight the dinosaur, according to Circe. Ritual combat.

'I know how he thinks!' Veg said. 'He wants to prove he can do it by himself. And he can't.'

'You mean, prove he's better physically than a dinosaur? That doesn't sound like the kind of thing—'

'That he can get through and send his message, no matter what. Our leaving him didn't stop him, Tyrann won't stop him. That makes it right, he figures.'

Suddenly she saw it. The mammals against the reptiles, each represented by its most advanced stage, one individual meeting the other on the field of honour. The decisive combat. The carnosaur had size and power; the man had brain. It *was* a fair compromise, a way to settle an otherwise insoluble dilemma. If Cal won, he would send his message and be justified in the spoils; if he lost – well, it was an answer, and he had chosen the way to come by it.

'I'm going over there,' Veg said.

'Veg—'

'I'll have to swim to the mainland and run along the shore. Cross the river up where it's narrower, nearer Camp Two. Hope I can pick up his trail, or maybe a manta'll show me. Fastest way. Might make it in time to haul him out of there alive.' He was fastening his clothing for swimming as he spoke.

'Veg, I think we should let him do it his way. On his own. That's the way he wants it.'

'He'll get killed!'

She hesitated. 'Maybe – that's best.'

Veg stiffened. Then, so suddenly that she did not realize what had happened at first, he hit her. His arm came back in a hard swing that caught her across the side of the head and sent her reeling to the ground.

By the time she righted herself, he was in the water, well on his way. She must have blacked out momentarily, for she had not seen him go.

Her hand lifted to touch the stinging, swelling side of her face gingerly. His wrist had struck against her cheekbone; there was no blood. Veg had not even paused to see whether she was hurt. Thus eloquently had she been advised of his first loyalty.

Had she worried about coming between these men? She should have known there was no danger of that!

Yet it still seemed to her that Cal was not only courageous, but right. She could abide by the decision, made that way. Veg, long as he had known Cal, loyal as he was, did not understand. Nothing would be settled if he got there 'in time'.

She turned to find Orn – yes, that was the name that fit – standing behind her. He was close and quite formidable, suddenly, with myriad tiny scars showing on his legs and beak, and some feathers not completely grown out to replace lost ones. He could have struck her down easily while she stood bemused, but she sensed no hostility in him.

Hesitantly she reached toward him, experiencing an overwhelming need for companionship of any type. She was alone now, on a strange world, without any genuine hope of seeing either man again. Cal's mission was suicidal – but so was Veg's. It might be that the only company she would know henceforth would be that of the big birds.

Orn opened his mighty beak and caught her hand within it – and did not bite. She felt the knife edges of his jaw and knew that her fingers could be severed cleanly by its vicelike compression. But the touch was token.

Then Orn dropped her hand and returned to his nest. It was as though he had touched her in comfort, but not remained to make an issue of it. She was deeply grateful for the gesture.

She roused herself after a time and foraged for edible roots on the main body of the island, since her supplies would not last indefinitely. Her heart was not in it, but she did have to eat. She found a lone banana plant, but the fruit was not ripe. It was afternoon, and she knew nothing of the progress of the two men. She might have expected Circe to stay with her, but the manta was away on some other business. The rapport she had thought she had with the creature of Nacre was fading ...

A second tremor came – a stronger one. The ground did not shudder, it rocked. It was as though the soil had turned liquid, and she was riding the waves. She kept her feet with difficulty.

She had a sudden and ugly premonition of what such a quake

would do to a nest built on a rock, and to the fragile eggs within that nest. She ran swiftly back to the peninsula as the motion of the ground subsided.

The site of the nest was chaotic. Both birds were standing beside the rock, fluttering their vestigial wings. The worst had happened.

They did not challenge her as she approached, too upset, she realized, to maintain their guard. The nest was damaged but largely intact. The eggs—

Fragments of thick shell projected up, and white and yellow jelly filled the base of the main cavity. The eggs had been shattered by the quake. The birds seemed stunned by the calamity. She visualized the mutilated corpses of human babies in place of the smashed eggs, and thought she understood how the Orns felt.

But one shell appeared to be intact. Aquilon touched it hesitantly with a finger and found it warm and firm. It was eight or nine inches long and slender in proportion, the surface rough. She reached both hands around it and lifted the object out, careful not to let it slip in the slick fluid around it.

Both birds were still, watching her helplessly. 'This one's all right,' she said.

From somewhere in their throats came an incredulous, hope-dawning cooing.

She carried the egg to a dry hollow and set it down. 'Keep it warm,' she said. 'You can make another nest.' She backed away.

After a moment the female – Aquilon thought of her as Ornette – came over and studied it. Then, in a kind of nervous collapse, she sat on it.

But one crisis had passed only to lead to another. The odour of the broken eggs had attracted a predator. Sleek and very long in the water it came – a giant crocodilian reptile, not closely related to the modern crocodiles of Earth but similar externally and every bit as dangerous. Twenty feet from snout to tail, it hauled itself out of the water at the rocky mouth of the inlet and scrambled overland towards the nest.

Orn charged it, squawking loudly and beating the air with his wings, but the armoured reptile only snapped sidelong at him and continued without pause. Nothing Orn's size could hurt it seriously; that was obvious.

Would it stop with the nest? Aquilon knew it would not. It must

321

have swum over from the main swamp, for she had seen nothing like this near the island before. The duckbill would hardly have been so casual, either, had it sniffed this predator. Perhaps the quake had jolted it from its accustomed beat. It was hardly in a mood to be reasonable by any mammalian or avian definition. Now that it was here, it would pursue all food available – and that meant the third egg, and the bird protecting it, and probably the stranded bipedal mammal, herself, as well.

Aquilon fetched her quarterstaff. She held it by one end and ran at the crocodilian as though she carried a lance. The forward end struck the creature's leather-tough neck and bounced off, denting it only slightly but delivering a severe jar to her.

The long head swung about, jaws gaping. Aquilon braced herself and swung the pole like a club, striking that snout resoundingly. Unhurt but annoyed, the reptile charged her, its horrendous teeth leading.

Fighting instinctively, she drove the quarterstaff lengthwise into its mouth. To her horror, the entire pole disappeared into that orifice, and the snapping jaws barely missed her hands. She scrambled back.

But it was enough. The crocodilian coughed and shook its head, pained by the object in its throat. Unable for the moment either to swallow it or spit it out, the monster abruptly plunged into the water. It swam to the rocky inlet mouth, jammed itself between the stones so violently that it left scrapings of flesh, and departed. As it passed from view, she heard its teeth clashing together as it sought vainly to bite down on the obstruction anchored neatly between the dental rows.

Aquilon sat down hard, discovering herself panting desperately. She had expended more energy than she realized during the excitement, and was nearly exhausted. But she had won! Her omnivore heritage had come to her rescue and she had driven off the predator.

At the cost of the only weapon she had. Well, she could make another.

Was this the type of creature she was striving to protect from Earth's ravages? A twenty-foot, merciless egg-eating carnivore?

With this in the water, and others like it – had Veg even made it to the shore?

322

Dusk was coming – where had the day vanished! – and with it the pteranodons. Aquilon got up, still too tense to eat, and began to walk to the tarpaulin on the other side of the peninsula.

Orn blocked her way. She stared at him blankly, then tried to step around. He blocked her again, herding her back by spreading his wings. They were larger than she had thought; their total span, tip to tip, was about five feet. Far too small to enable him ever to fly, but handsome in their own right. The under surfaces seemed almost to glow. Some of the feathers had been freshly broken off, courtesy of the crocodilian. But Orn's manner was not threatening.

She turned and walked toward the makeshift nest, now buttressed by bits of moss Ornette had found within reach. Orn followed. She got to her hands and knees beside Ornette, then curled up and lay beside the huge bird. Orn settled down at her exposed side, spreading one wing to partially cover her body. It was like a thick, warm blanket – and yes, it made her feel immeasurably safer.

No – *this* was what she was fighting to save! This unique, intelligent family, related to her only in spirit.

Comfortable and secure between the two great warm bodies, she slept.

Chapter Sixteen

CAL

It was mind against matter. The mind of man against the matter of reptile. One would prove itself superior in this contest, and to that one would go this world. That was the way it had to be. Except for one small factor—

Tyrannosaurus rex – the tyrant lizard king – charged down on him, banishing that speculation. Yet in this moment of confrontation he had an aberrant vision of Aquilon, so lovely she blinded even his mind's eye. She would have understood this, had she known of it, and perhaps she would also have approved. Had he known this opportunity would arise, he could have arranged to avoid the schism in the human party.

But Veg would not have gone along. The big man tended to overlook the nuances of interspecies morality, and so relied on conformance to a simplistic code. Thou Shalt Not Kill – except when threatened. And who could say what constituted a legitimate threat? The corollary was taken as Thou Shalt Not Eat the Flesh of Any Member of the Animal Kingdom – forgetting that man was a natural predator, owing much of his progress to his diet. So how could such a code solve or even ameliorate the myriad problems of the species? No matter; conform.

All this, in fragments, while Tyrann crashed towards him, head swaying from side to side for balance, eyes fixed on target. The reptile was now within a hundred feet: twice its own body length, five times its height. It was moving forward in a roughly straight line at some twenty miles per hour, ten tons of malevolence. Perhaps it was disappointed in the size of its quarry, hardly worth the effort – but this did not slow it.

No, Veg would not have understood. So it had to be this way: a battle without witnesses, except for the alien mantas. If he lost, his friends would assume he had been suicidally foolish. If he won, lucky. But *he* knew, and that was what counted.

Time to stop reminiscing and start competing.

Cal waited until Tyrann was within a single body length, calculating the time factor. Fifty feet at twenty miles an hour would be about a second and a half until contact — too brief for fine adjustments on its part. The maneuverative advantage did not lie with size. At that critical point – fifty feet – Cal dodged to the side.

His velocity from a standing start was slower than that continuing motion of the dinosaur, but he had a smaller distance to go. He covered only fifteen feet before the six-inch teeth clashed where he had been, and another ten by the time the tremendous thigh and foot rocked the ground behind him. But the margin had been sufficient.

Tyrann, discommoded by the miss, drove his nose into the dirt and came to a roaring halt. He lifted his mottled head, dewlap stretching, small eyes peering balefully about while leaves and twigs tumbled wetly from his jaws. It took him a moment to realize what had happened, but not a long moment. He was a predator, and few of that ilk were stupid or slow when hungry. He had been fooled once by a seemingly petrified morsel, but now he knew it for one of the quick-footed mammals, and he would not underestimate its agility again.

Cal, meanwhile, had made it to the nearest large palm tree, holding his quarterstaff aloft. He had won the first pass by utilizing his advantage of mobility. His shorter neural chains permitted faster responses; the distance from his brain to his feet was a fraction of the corresponding connection in the dinosaur. But the overall advantage remained with Tyrann, who could outrun him on the straightaway and catch him when the dodging slowed.

Of course even that was not clear-cut. Tyrann had a great deal more mass to sling about, and a sprint would wear him out rapidly and overheat his tissues. Cal could probably outrun him in the long run, if he survived the short run.

The reptile sniffed the air and oriented on Cal's tree. There, too, was a weapon: the predator's well-developed nose. There was room in that huge head for capacious nasal chambers, and though the gleaming teeth were superficially impressive, they were dependent on the functioning of that nose. The eyes and ears were less important, since Tyrann was not a sneaker. He required one sure way to locate his prey, and the nose was it.

Fortunately for Cal, the sense of smell was ineffective as a guide to the whereabouts of a fast-maneuvering creature. Cal could not hope to hide long or steal away any great distance, but right now he could force the carnosaur to use his less effective senses. That was the function of his brain: to divert the contest to his opponent's weaknesses, his own strengths, and thus prevail.

Maybe.

Tyrann charged the tree. It seemed ludicrous to imagine weakness in connection with twenty thousand pounds of predator, or of strength in his own hundred pounds. But – that was the thesis he intended to prove.

Tyrann knew about trees. He did not bite the palm or crash into it. His forelimbs, smaller than his own great toes, were useless; they were hardly more than toothpicks projecting from the neck. Literally: Tyrann cleaned his teeth with those vestigial, two-clawed arms, though even that made him contort his neck to make the connection. So it seemed that he could not get at Cal, so long as the man kept the broad trunk between them.

Not at all. The dinosaur turned and swept his massive tail against the trunk. The tree vibrated; loose fronds dropped, forcing Cal to cower. A spearlike dry seedpod plunged into the ground next to his head: the thing was a yard long and well pointed. He jumped away from the tree, realizing how hazardous its cover was – but stopped, realizing that that was what Tyrann intended.

The tail itself whipped around, a scarred column of flesh, and caught him smartly on the hip as he was trying to get back to the palm. Its force had been broken by the trunk, and its vertebrae did not permit much flexibility, but the residual nudge was enough to send him lurching away from his cover again. His quarterstaff was jolted wide, and he had no chance to recover it. Now he lacked even token armament.

And of course Tyrann was ready. He pounced.

Cal ducked under the dinosaur, avoiding the gaping jaws again by the surprise of his motion. Tyrann had anticipated flight *away* from him, and had compensated accordingly. Cal bounced off the hanging skin of the reptile's neck, scraping his arm against the horny creases, and jumped for the tree again, panting.

He was thankful he hadn't tried to escape by climbing the palm. He would have been an easy target for that tail. Tyrann could not use it to reach or clutch or coil, but that brute banging against the base of the tree would have shaken almost anything loose.

Tyrann swung around again, watching Cal with one eye. The tail lifted, swung.

Cal didn't wait for it this time, he sprinted away from the trunk, eyes open. As the tail struck and whipped over, he threw himself down flat and let the tip pass over him. Immediately he was up again and running for the next tree, legs and lungs straining.

Tyrann let forth a bellow that sounded like gravel being dumped on a metal roof. He followed. Cal didn't stop at the tree; he passed it and angled for a small forest of firs he saw a few hundred feet ahead. His breath rasped in his throat, saliva streamed back across his cheek, and a pain in his side blossomed into a square foot of agony, but he could not stop.

The dinosaur was impeded by the trees, since he had to circle them with wider clearance, but still was making better speed. His two feet came down like pile drivers, shaking the earth with an oddly measured beat.

Cal's heart was pumping harshly, and now his entire chest was aflame. He saw that he could not make it to the pines, the spruce. Tyrann should be getting winded himself by this time – but it seemed that the dinosaur's strides were so long that this pace represented walking, not running, and so was not tiring. Cal dived behind a leaning oak and propped himself against it, too fatigued to do more than watch Tyrann.

But here he had a fortunate break. The small-brained reptile had forgotten his quarry's predilection for changing direction, and charged on by the tree. Then, realizing the error, Tyrann cast about, but could not immediately recover contact. The smell of the mammal was stronger behind then ahead, and that did not make immediate sense to the reptile.

Cal slid around the tree, aware that the accidental respite had probably saved his life. But he knew very well that the war was not over; this was only an intermission, and a momentary one.

Tyrann got his bearings and approached the tree. This time he waited to see which way Cal would bolt, not aware that the man had scant energy left to move at all. Yes, the dinosaur learned by experience – but not quickly enough, in this case. He lunged ahead when caution was best, and practiced caution when the direct approach would nab the prize. But that was his handicap: he was bright enough for a reptile, but hardly in the intellectual league with a man.

The truth was that Tyrann would be better off giving up on Cal and looking for some careless upland-dwelling baby *Brachiosaurus*; those young did not reside in the water until their developing mass required it, and by then their numbers had been thinned to the verge of extinction. The adult female Brachs made annual pilgrimages upland to lay their eggs, and they too would be easy harvest for Tyrann. But this dinosaur had determination; he had settled on Cal as prey for the day, and would not give up. Cal respected that; this was a worthy opponent, over whom a victory would be meaningful.

By the time Tyrann decided that the prey was not going to move, Cal had recovered the better part of his wind, and the pain in his bowels had abated. Oddly, he felt stronger than ever, as though tempered, as though his exertions had been pouring energy into him rather than drawing it out. This was possible: his weakness had been a sympton of an Earth-nurtured psychological syndrome, rather than anything initially physical. At Nacre he had tasted his first hint of freedom from it, aboard that sparsely populated world and with staunch companions. On Paleo he had his second experience – and though there were elements of disharmony, the overall effect was beneficial. And by this very chase he was resolving the last of that internal conflict. The long agony of indecision was over; he would prove himself – and his species, and his genus, family, order, and class – or die. He did not need to cripple himself any longer.

So now, perhaps, the bodily resources that had been so long suppressed were reappearing, and he was ready for the dinosaur. It was a good feeling.

Tyrann lunged at the tree, but this time did not swing about to threaten with his tail. He put his head beyond the slanted trunk and stopped.

Cal scooted a quarter of the way around, but halted when he saw that his opponent was there too. One giant leg came down beside the tree, while the nightmarish head descended from the opposite side. Tyrann *could* close the circle, when he happened across the right technique!

But with difficulty. This was an unusual maneuvre, and the dinosaur's reflexes were geared more for crashing through than for

328

curling around. The closure occurred slowly, and the tail could not make it at all. The highly flexible neck was the principal instrument, coming to meet the tremendous thigh – Cal between.

Saliva dripped from the grinning mouth, spilling over the double-edged teeth. The stench of reptile was oppressive. Cal peered into the near eye, just a yard away and huge from this vantage. The lower jaw widened just below it, making anchorage for bulging facial muscles. The skin was rough, covered irregularly with tubercles, puckered in the region of the ear hole, and hung below the chin in a kind of extended wattle: the dewlap. Oh for the lost quarterstaff now! He could have used it to poke out that eye!

He glanced down, seeking some weapon, but there was only loam and acorns. A handful of coarse gravel hurled into that eye might start the job; but *acorns*?

Slowly the jaws parted, the lipless skin peeling back from every dagger-jagged tooth, and sliding across the muscle-filled fenestrae, the windows in the skull. The alien reptilian breath blasted out, hot, not cold. It was a misnomer to describe reptiles as cold-blooded; their body temperatures were variable, determined by external conditions and exertion. In this warm valley, the reptile ran about as hot as the mammal and functioned about as well.

The stunted forelimbs turned out to be as large as Cal's own arms, their claws long and sharp. Useful for holding the slowly dying meat firmly against the mouth, certainly: much as a busy executive might hold the telephone receiver against his ear by hunching his shoulder, aided by a little harness. Hardly essential, but useful upon occasion.

One tooth was broken, leaving a gap, and the gum there was black. Tyrann's temper could hardly have been improved by that recent accident! But already the replacement tooth was pushing up.

This was a strange situation: he was about to be bitten in half, in slow motion! If he ran for it, Tyrann would catch him; he could see the tension on the ponderous leg muscles, ready for that forward thrust around the tree. But if he remained—

Closer. Tyrann's nostril, inconspicuous from a distance, now seemed large enough for Cal to put his fist into. But the eye, though within reach, was guarded by a heavy overhanging ridge of bone and skin; he was sure that if he struck at it the eye would blink shut, and he would smash his hand against that protection painfully. The ear indentation did not even penetrate the head; skin covered the canal just inside the depression. Yes, the dinosaur was well protected.

Still, Tyrann could hear well enough. Cal leaned towards the head until only inches separated his face from the skin of the monster. The rank odour made him want to gag, and he could see body parasites in the folds.

'Boo!' he yelled.

The dinosaur jumped.

Cal was off and away, springing again for the copse of assorted firs. Tyrann recovered in a moment, merely startled by the unexpected noise, but too late. A jump reaction, in a creature of that size, was a matter of seconds from start to finish. The prey had won another round.

The firs were not large, but were close together and thickly spoked. The proximity of the trees served to break off useless lower limbs – but many of the stubs were jammed into neighbouring trunks, forming rungs. Cal scraped himself getting through them, but was grateful for their protection. Tyrann had to crash through headlong, and that was noisy, painful and time-consuming. Cal was able to catch his breath again as he slowed to a walk and scramble, threading past the worst of the maze.

But it was another brief respite. Tyrann could knock aside those slender trees and bulldoze them down, and was doing so. The stand was not as extensive as Cal had hoped; a few minutes would see little besides cordwood here. And the dinosaur, stung by repeated jabs of fir spokes, was beginning to grow perturbed.

Beyond this was palm-dotted prairie. That was sure victory for Tyrann.

Except – there was a herd of *Triceratops* in sight, lazing in the shadow of the trees and browsing on the fronds. If he were able to play one species off against the other—

Cal ran out towards the herd. A bull winded him and looked up, a morsel of palm stalk projecting from his tremendous beak. Then the Tricer spotted the carnosaur behind. Why the herd hadn't noticed the intrusion before, Cal could not say. Perhaps they had been aware of Tyrann right along, but had known he was after other prey and therefore no immediate threat to the herd. That, combined with the discomfort of having to walk through the sun to find other shade, must have kept them where they were. It was a complacency that armoured brutes of this magnitude could afford – but no lesser creatures!

By running at the herd, however, Cal was luring Tyrann too close. The bull gave out an oddly regressive hiss, and suddenly there was motion elsewhere. The adult Tricers bullied their young into a confined area adjacent to the trunk of the largest palm, then turned about and formed a ring outside, just at the fringe of the shade, armoured heads pointing out. It was a formidable phalanx, executed with military dispatch.

Cal was daunted himself. These were tremendous animals, and dangerous. Those beaks, intended for slicing through palm wood, could as readily amputate his limbs; and as for the horns . . . ! But he had no choice. Tyrann was closing the gap again, and there was no other cover. He ran at the defensive circle of behemoths.

The nearest bull didn't like it. He hissed his challenge again and charged out of the pack. Sunlight glinted from his polished horns. The adjacent bulls rocked over to fill the gap, keeping the circle tight.

Cal, perforce, brought up short. No living animal ever resembled a tank more than *Triceratops*. Then he used the trick applied earlier to Tyrann, and jumped to the side.

Almost eight tons of armoured flesh thudded by. The Tricer was not as large as Tyrann, but was more solidly built. It body, exclusive of the tail, was twenty feet long, the head taking up about a third of it. Two devastating horns jutted above the eyes and a third, shorter but thicker, perched on the broad beak. Behind the head was a tremendous bony shield large enough for a man to ride on. The astonishing jaw muscles anchored to this, making even Tyrann's face seem flabby in comparison. There was more bone and muscle on Tricer's head than in the entire body of most other creatures. The skin of the rest of the torso, though technically unarmoured, was ribbed like the hide of a crocodile, and Cal was sure it was just as tough.

Now Tricer confronted Tyrann – a situation neither had sought. Tyrann tried to skirt around the bull to get at Cal, but Tricer would not permit an approach near the herd. To it, the small mammal was an annoyance – but the carnosaur was a threat.

And so they came to unwilling battle, these two giants of the age of reptiles. The one would not relinquish his chase; the other would not permit passage.

Tyrann, goaded to fury by the unreasonable interference of the bull, roared and gestured: an impressive spectacle. Tricer merely waited, the three fierce horns focused on the enemy. Tyrann skittered to the side, seeking a vulnerable point beyond horn and shield. Tricer whirled with surprising finesse, the neck muscles flexing hugely, and gored him in the thigh.

Tyrann screamed and bit at the briefly exposed rump. The teeth sank in, but Tricer whirled again, the three horns swinging about like the machine-gun turret of the tank he resembled, and the hold was broken. Cal observed that the broad bony shield did double duty: the neck musculature also anchored to it. Just as a flying bird needed a strong keelbone to brace the flying muscles, so Tricer needed that shield to whip his massive head about. What an engine of defence!

Blood speckled each combatant, but inhibited neither. Tyrann did not take lightly to being balked, but Tricer would not give way.

Then a second bull came out, and Tyrann backed off hastily. *Two* trios of horns could destroy him. But this one was after Cal, and the man had to flee even more precipitously. Apparently the herbivores had decided that he was too much trouble to entertain. Or they had realized that Tyrann would not leave until the mammal did.

The two bulls were between Cal and Tyrann, each herding its object before it. Cal was amenable; this allowed him to increase his distance from the carnosaur. He spied an inlet of water and headed for it, congratulating himself for a winning tactic.

Tyrann finally freed himself from the harassment of the bulls and charged in Cal's direction. Cal threw himself down a short steep bank and into the bay.

It was shallow. He had succeeded in covering himself with muck, but knew that two feet of water would hardly balk Tyrann for long. the carnosaur probably chased after water reptiles to depths of ten feet or so. He had made a tactical error.

Tyrann splashed down, sending muck flying. And sank in to *his* tall knees. Instead of firm bottom, it was ooze bottom, and the dinosaur's much greater weight put him as deep, proportionately, as the much smaller man. They were even. Cal chided himself for not realizing that beforehand. So far, he had prevailed more by chance than by application of brain, and that was not as it should be, if he were to prove anything.

332

Again in grotesque slow motion, man and reptile staggered through the swamp. But again the pursuer was gaining. Cal had supposed that Tyrann was basically a hide-and-pounce hunter, or a take-from-other-hunter bully: neither occupation requiring much stamina. But this chase had passed beyond that stage.

Cal looked for deeper water, hoping to lure Tyrann out beyond his safe depth. He was sure the dinosaur could not swim. Both of them would risk attack by swimming predators, but Tyrann would be the prime target there.

This, however, turned out to be a slender ribbon of swamp, extending like a tongue into higher ground. Deep water was too far away. He would have to slough along for a mile or more, and that was out of the question.

He heard Tyrann panting behind him. At least this was taking as much out of the carnosaur as the man. The creature had a lot more mass to haul around, and his energy requirements right now must be phenomenal.

Cal angled to the far bank and scrambled up. He gained distance as he hit the firmer footing. With another belated inspiration he ran along the bank instead of away from the water, tempting the dinosaur to chase directly after him. Tyrann did not understand about vectors; to him the direct route was the fastest and surest, whatever the terrain. So he waded after Cal rather than cutting to the bank and gaining high ground first. Cal's lead increased dramatically.

Tyrann was almost out of sight behind when the terrain shifted to favour him again. Nature played no favourites! Cal had been running downhill, towards the main swamp, and the land was becoming generally lower and flatter. Soon he would have no firm footing remaining, and would have to wade or swim again. That might get him away from Tyrann – but without that close pursuit, there would be nothing to distract the attention of the water predators from him. They were as dangerous in their medium as Tyrann was on his – and Cal's contest was with *this* reptile, not some aquatic monster. If he had to be eaten, it was only proper that Tyrann be allowed the honours. He had already earned this meal!

Cal reversed his field and ran headlong the way he had come, ducking down to avoid Tyrann's sight. It worked; the dinosaur continued sloshing downstream. By the time Tyrann realized what had happened, Cal had a lead of half a mile.

He needed it, in order to cross the plain and achieve new cover. Tyrann came into sight again, making excellent time, probably spurred by increasing appetite. Nothing like a walk before dinner! But the reptile's persistence was amazing. The chase had lasted a couple of hours now, and was far from over.

Yet this, of course, was the way Tyrann obtained his meals. He was not a swift runner compared to *Struthiomimus*, the 'ostrich dinosaur', or an agile hunter compared to even primitive mammalian carnivores. He was limited largely to land, which meant that he seldom dined on *Brachiosaurus* in quantity. The young Brachs were of course available – but swift and small, and the fleet amphibious duckbills were similarly elusive. Stealth was not, as it turned out, Tyrann's way, nor was he particularly clever. Probably he dined on carrion as often as not, sniffing out the rotting carcases of creatures who had perished by other means, then driving off other predators. But this would be an uncertain living at best, and live meat was a treat worth striving for.

No – *Tyrannosaurus* succeeded largely by determination. Once he fixed on his prey, living or dead, he never relented. Other things might intersperse themselves, such as the fir grove, a *Triceratops* herd, and swamp channel, but Tyrann would keep after his original objective until he ran it down. That way his meal was certain, eventually. And his meager intellect was not strained, and his energies not wastefully dissipated in fruitless asides. Even the fleetest prey must succumb in time.

It had become a contest of endurance. Though the carnosaur was wounded – Cal could see the blood along the thigh where the bull had gored – he still had substantial physical resources. But the prey, in this case, had equivalent *mental* resources. Which would prevail – muscle or mind?

Cal headed uphill. Right now he'd be happy to trade a few points I.Q. for a few pounds of striated tissue in the legs and torso. The vagaries of the chase had caused him to bypass Camp Two, and he was ascending the mountain face beyond it. The climate was changing rapidly, both because of the waning of the day and increasing elevation. This had to shift the balance somewhat in his favour, because he was a controlled-temperature creature while Tyrann was not. He could function efficiently regardless of the external temperature, theoretically. A reptile in the cold was a reptile helpless.

Yet Tyrann continued to close the gap, and once more was within a hundred feet. Now Cal had to dodge around trees and rocks, lest he be overrun. Damn that giant stride of the dinosaur! This should have been superior terrain for the mammal, with its myriad crevices, but none were secure for any extended stay. He had to keep moving.

He was tired. He was in excellent condition, considering his past history, but a pressing chase of several hours was more than his body had been geared for. Tyrann, on the other hand, seemed to have most of his original vigour about him. Endurance: yes. Or merely pacing.

Cal fell. At first he thought that fatigue had brought him low; then he realized that the mountain had thrown him down. The earth was rocking violently, and Tyrann was screaming with cantankerous surprise. It was an earthquake – far more severe than the tremor he had observed while on the raft yesterday.

Cal was small, light, and lucky. Tyrann was none of these. The dinosaur was upended and rolled several hundred feet downhill to crash into the brush. Nature had played favourites this time.

Cal needed the reprieve, but he resented it. He wanted to win by his own abilities, nothing else. He sat down after the earth was still and waited for Tyrann to resume the chase.

The dinosaur was slow in doing so. A roughing of that nature was hard on him, because of his size. A mouse might fall a hundred feet straight down and survive nicely; an elephant might fall its own height and be killed on the spot, because of the problems its magnified mass brought. Tyrann had merely rolled – but that probably represented the most brutal punishment he had ever had. Internal organs could have been ruptured, bones splintered . . .

But no. Tyrann got up and resumed his ascent – but with only a fraction of his previous vigour. Now Cal could stay ahead without panting.

So it continued, slower. The air became cool and more than cool as dusk and height came together. Even through his exertions, Cal felt it; his clothing had dried on his body and was fairly good insulation, but still he was not dressed for freezing weather. Yet Tyrann continued, bruised and scarred and shaken in more than the thigh, but seemingly unaffected by the temperature.

Of course! The dinosaur had considerable mass, and so was slow to cool. And his giant muscles would generate a large amount of heat, keeping him going longer. Tyrann could probably keep up the chase as long as Cal could, even into the snows of the upper mountain.

Unless Cal could trick him into remaining stationary for a few hours ...

Meanwhile, he would have to drop down into the warmer region. He was quite tired now, and the buoyancy of the chase was giving out. If he rested in hiding, the cold would get him. And he couldn't hide anyway, even in the dark, because Tyrann would locate him by smell.

Yes, it was brains against brawn – but in what manner could brains mitigate the cold? If only he had warm clothing! Then he could ascend into the very snows, while the dinosaur slowly capitulated to nature. The mammalian form *was* superior; a hairy animal could have lost Tyrann easily here, or even turned and challenged him. A woolly elephant—

Cal stumbled, pushing himself up with difficulty. Why dream? It was his own body he had to make do with, and his own brain he meant to apply. Tyrann was still hardly more than fifty feet behind, but Cal had become used to that distance. They both knew that the chase had come down to its essential: the first to give way to exposure and exhaustion would forfeit the game. The sudden charges and matching dodges were over, as were the peek-a-boo games around trees. The rules were set, and the mammal could afford to stumble so long as he got up promptly.

Still he hesitated – and Tyrann hesitated also, as though waiting for him to proceed. They had become accustomed to each other, the tiny man and the giant reptile. They had been over much territory together, shared many experiences – even an earthquake. There was a camaraderie of a sort in experience and fatigue.

But he knew the dinosaur would gobble him up when that phase ended. Camaraderie did not presume amity. It was merely a kind of appreciation in adversity. He hesitated not from any sense of safety, but because something was trying to impress itself on his cold-dulled sensitivities. Something – warm.

Warm. The ground was wet and the wetness was soaking through his footwear and in that moisture was heat, as though he had stepped in the drain chute of an outdoor bathtub. But the temperature of the air was near the freezing point of water. What was this – a hallucination brought about by his deteriorating condition? Was he about to imagine himself falling into a lush warm paradise, a tropical garden near the snowline where rapture abounded ... while in reality his feet froze and the jaws of the carnosaur crushed out his life?

Tyrann approached at last, and Cal moved – uphill. His feet sloshed in the drainage and absorbed heat. The dinosaur's feet also sloshed, and he paused to sniff the ground suspiciously. No hallucination.

A quarter mile higher it was warmer than ever, the air and earth as well as the trickling water. They were in a high valley, a kind of cleft in the mountain; not far away Cal could make out light snow, still bright in the fading day. But within this deepening hollow it was beginning to be comfortable. Ferns spread richly at the bottom, and toadstools and moss, and tiny salamanders scuttled out of his way.

Cal recovered energy as his surroundings became conducive, but Tyrann remained slow. One advantage of smaller mass was a faster response to changed circumstances. Conditions were improving; he knew it, but Tyrann did not yet. But in this narrow chasm he would hardly be able to close his pursuer, and there were no hiding places. It was risky comfort, this winding summer crevice.

Unbidden, the explanation came to him. Volcanism! This was an overflow of a hot spring, the water emerging from conduits passing near the perpetual furnace of the volcanic mountain. The gully owed its warmth to the same force that heated this entire Cretaceous valley. No mystery at all, but something he should have anticipated. And that very realization, even so late, gave him the clue to victory!

The vegetation diminished as the temperature continued to rise, and he knew he was approaching the outlet of the flowing water. If it were a bubbling spring, he was in trouble; but if—

He came into the presence of the upper end of the cleft abruptly. This *was* a drainage ditch, formed by erosion, and above the emergence of the water the normal contours of the mountain resumed. The outlet pipe was a cavern, as he had hoped.

Sweating now, Cal plunged in. The river here was too hot to touch for any length of time – perhaps 130° F. – but there was clearance at

337

the brim. The opening was large: large enough for Tyrann. But still it meant mammalian victory.

He moved ahead, unable to see anything inside. Tyrann's outline showed against the faint light of the entrance, but Cal knew the dinosaur would not follow.

The key was this: while cold was inconvenient for the great reptiles, and slowly fatal in the regions of its intensity, heat was more critical. A reptile's peak efficiency was at a body temperature of from $95°$ to $100°$ F. – about the same as for mammals and birds. But above that, the reptile would succumb more quickly than a mammal, because it lacked any internal heat-control mechanisms other than inaction. Cal could survive for a reasonable period in an environment of $115°$ F. or more; a reptile in the same situation would cook, literally.

If Tyrann were to enter this cave and remain for any length of time, he would die. Dinosaurs could not sweat.

On the other hand, Tyrann would soon grow hungry waiting outside. Indeed, he must be ravenous already. There was no food nearby. Cal would suffer too, of course – but he could rest in warm comfort, and drink water to ease the pangs.

He heard a funny lapping sound and peeked out. Tyrann was hunched before the cave licking his wounds. There was blood on his body in many places besides the Tricer's gore wound. That earthquake had really battered him! No wonder he had settled for a relaxed pace at the end. The wounds that didn't show, the internal ones, must be even worse.

Cal found himself a comfortable ledge, sprawled out, and fell into a perspiring stupor. It occurred to him that one of the duckbilled dinosaurs, such as *Parasaurolophus*, might have entered this cave safely. That creature's nasal passages traversed the entire length of its enormous crest. This would make for super-efficient smelling ability – but probably also provided efficient cooling of the blood by evaporation from those passages. Perhaps more than one duckbill had escaped Tyrann by entering such a cave. However, hunger and the rising heat inside the mountain would have killed any creature venturing too deep, too long. Perhaps there were mysteriously defunct bodies washed out in the lower subterranean rivers every so often . . .

He slept.

338

Chapter Seventeen

ORN

'*Tyrannosaurus rex* was galloping after Cal, those awful double-edged half-foot teeth snapping inches short of his frail palpitating body, the feet coming down on him like twin avalanches. Snap! and the rag-doll form was flung high into the air, striped grisly red, and that colour reflected in the malignant eyes of the carnivore. One giant claw toe came at that torn form where it landed, crushing it into the ground; the jaws closed, ripped off an arm. Cal's tiny head lolled back from a broken neck, the dead eyes staring at me not with accusation but with understanding, and I screamed and woke.'

Orn saw that the mam female was troubled. She had slept restlessly and awakened noisily, and now was in a continuing state of agitation.

'How close to reality was that dream? How great is my guilt? Cal wouldn't have gotten into that thing, if I hadn't forced the issue. If he's dead – I'm afraid to think of it – it's my fault.'

Orn stood up and stretched his wings. There did not seem to be anything he could do for her. Her mate had deserted her.

'And Veg – I dreamed of him too. It wasn't love, it was sex, and ugly. I tried to split their friendship, and now they're both – gone. I should never have come with them to Paleo.'

Ornette still slept, fluffed out over the single egg. It was the youngest and fairest of the three, and now it was everything. Orn had picked the site for the nest, and he had erred; now two of his three chicks were gone. He could not mourn specifically, but he felt keenly that he should not have come to this island.

'But it wouldn't make sense for me to chase after them. I couldn't do anything, even if it weren't already way too late. All I can do now is hope. Hope that the two men I love are still alive, and that this strange but beautiful world can live as well.'

Orn intended to guard that last egg more carefully. The mating

339

cycle was over. There would be no new eggs until next season. This egg had been shaken by the earth one day, and almost smashed the next; another siege could occur at any time. Could he protect the egg against that? He felt the need, but could not formulate a resolution.

'I know what's bothering you, Orn. That egg's in a precarious spot. I'll move it for you, if we can find a better place. I might as well help *someone*. Maybe the worst is over . . .'

The sun was lifting, a bubble of light behind flashing mountain silhouettes. Soon it would touch the hanging pteras and animate them. Daybreak was such a struggle for that type!

The mam got up and crossed to the main island. Orn knew she had to attend to her eliminations and did not wish to soil the nest area. Not all mams were that considerate.

He looked about. Several of the pines had been overturned in the quake, and the configuration of the peninsula had changed. Now a second bridge of land joined it to the island. That was not good; it would be harder to safeguard now. Another shaking like the last and there might be no peninsula at all! He had seen what the ground could do on the island of his own hatching.

The mam returned and began to forage for edible roots. She had what smelled like food in her nestlike container, but appeared to be storing that. She found nuts from two varieties of flat-leaved trees and seemed to have enough to sustain her, though Orn could tell she was not fully satisfied. He, meanwhile, had hooked some fat fish out of the inlet and gutted them with beak and talon, offering the delectible innards to Ornette first. He wasn't certain whether this mam ate fish also. He offered her one but received an indefinable response.

'I think the main island is better for the eggs.' She had started with her noises again. 'It's less likely to sink under the wave.' She was trying to convey something to him, and he had an idea what. He could feel the continuing tension in the rocks, the distant motions increasing local stress. The earth would twitch its tail again, soon. His memory informed him that changes normally requiring millions of years could occur in an instant, when the ground got restless.

'I'll scout for the best place, Orn.' For a moment something like the innocent levity of a hatchling chick lifted her. 'And you can call me 'Quilon, since we're on a first-name basis now. Short for Aquilon, the northwest wind. 'Quilon.'

She tapped her own body as she repeated a certain sound, as though identifying her species. Of course such sounds were meaningless, but he would now think of her as the quilon giant mam.

She departed again, questing for something. He watched her thoughtfully as she retreated. Yesterday he had extended his tolerance to this quilon whose mate had deserted her (no bird would do that!). Then the earth had moved and slaughtered two of his chicks and put the third in peril, and the quilon had helped him save the last. But for that, the problems of his own hatching might have been repeated here: one egg surviving, both parents dead fighting a crock. Now his egg would have a better chance, for there were three to guard it, counting the quilon. Perhaps it was her blunted nesting instinct: she guarded his egg because she had none of her own.

Mams were not notably trustworthy around eggs, but the circumstance was special. This was a strange, huge, clumsy, yet brave and loyal mam, with surprising comprehension despite her annoying noisemaking. It was almost as though she had her own type of memory, so readily did she grasp things. And she had saved the egg. She deserved his companionship.

The egg had to be moved. It was not safe here; a single tilt of the land could roll it into the sea, where the penetrating chill of the water would quickly extinguish it. But he could not move it; only the quilon could do that. Fortunately she was warm; that was the trait the mams had acquired even earlier than the aves. She could touch the egg without hurting it, and her digits, because they were soft, could lift it. He had no memory of any creature with this ability to turn seemingly useless appendages to such direct purpose. Limbs were generally adapted to running or foraging or fighting, while these unspecialized mam limbs turned out to be adapted for carrying a single egg!

But all this thinking and reasoning was hard. His brain had not been evolved for this, and only his solitary life and the radical change of the world had prompted this quality in him. Ornette depended on her memories far more than he did. It was as though his mind had mutated into something else in a jump like that of the strained earth – something unique and unnatural.

Then he felt it: the earth was beginning to break. He ran towards Ornette and the egg, but there was nothing he could do except settle down next to them and try to shield it with his body. If the ground jumped again, even this would not save it from cracking, for there was no proper padding beneath the egg.

The quilon ran after him. She scooped up the egg as Ornette jumped nervously aside, and held it cushioned in those almost hairless fleshy forelimbs.

Then the land broke apart. Orn was hurled into the water, to scramble back dripping; Ornette fell in the opposite direction, flapping her wings. Only the quilon remained upright, flexing her tremendous legs and leaning over the egg, protecting it.

The motion changed. Orn felt it: somewhere deep below a support had snapped. The land on which they huddled was sliding down, away from the island, becoming an island of its own. The water surged around it. The shudders continued, rocking the diminishing perch farther. The pines were standing in water now, and falling as the land slowly tilted.

There was nothing in his memory to account for this particular sequence, and he could tell that Ornette was as mystified as he. The quilon just stood with the egg, looking about. There was nothing any of them could do.

It occurred to him that the reason he had no memory of such an event – a fragmenting, slowly sinking island – was that no potential ancestor had survived the experience.

The last of the pines crashed down, tumbling over its fallen neighbours and splashing into the water. Orn thought of using it to float to safety, but realized that the quilon could not do this while carrying the egg. Without that egg, and within it the nascent memory and experience of all his ancestry and Ornette's, there was no point in escape.

At last the motion stopped. Their new island was separated from the larger one by the length of a full-grown brach rep, and it was only slightly greater than the length of yesterday's croc in its diameter. They stood on its highest point: a terrace near the original site of the next bounded by an escarpment leading into the water where the isthmus had been before; the land had actually risen slightly here. But on the opposite side the surface tilted down more gradually. Had the trees remained standing they would have been at an angle.

Where would the ptera sleep now? They would perish in the night unless they found new roosting.

The quilon settled down, supporting the egg on her thighs. She leaned over it, keeping it warm with her body and forelimbs. Ornette looked, but did not challenge; it was safest where it was, and this entire sequence had left her confused. It was hard to accept, this control of the egg by the mam, but it seemed to be necessary.

How were they going to get away from here? This was no longer a suitable nesting site, yet even the short distance to the larger section of the island was dangerous for the egg. Unless the new bay were shallow ...

'We might build another raft. Maybe the one Veg started is around, or pieces of it.' The quilon was beginning to make sounds again, which meant she was returning to normal.

Orn stepped into the water, testing the depth. The footing was treacherous; he slipped and took a dunking. It *was* too deep, and far too chancy for the awkward mam. They would have to remain here at least until the chick hatched. They could forage on the island, swimming across individually. It would be an uncomfortable existence, but was feasible.

He sniffed. Rep, gross. Trouble!

As he scrambled back on land, he saw it: the towering head of an elas, the great shallow-water paddler. The quilon uttered a cry: 'A plesiosaur!'

Orn had few direct memories of this creature, because its sphere of operations seldom overlapped that of his own species. He was aware of its gradual evolution from minor landbound forms struggling to come even with the large amphibs, finally returning entirely to the sea – and then a memory gap broken only by glimpses of the larger sizes, some with lengthening necks and others with shortening necks, until this line attained its present configuration: eight full wingspans from snout to tail, the neck making up half of that. It was primarily a fish-eater, but it would consume carrion or land life if available. Orn would not care to swim while an Elas was near, but had no particular awe of it while he stood on land.

The rep came closer, its tiny head carried high. It smelled them, and it was hungry.

'The quake shook it up. It's crazed, It's coming after us!'

Orn would have preferred that the quilon not choose this moment to make her meaningless noises. Now the Elas was certain there was a meal here. The length of its neck was more than half the breadth of

343

the island fragment. There was no section it could not reach from one side or the other, if it were determined. It could not leave the water, for that would destroy the mobility it required for balance – but they were vulnerable despite being on land.

They would have to fight it off, if that were possible. The ground and sea motion must have crazed the rep, so that it was not aware that it was fishing on land instead of in water. It was not particularly bright, but *was* dangerous.

The head hovered above the island, twice Orn's height. The neck curved back from it, then forward, in the manner of a wind-twisted rush. The alert rep eye fixed on Orn.

He leaped aside as the Elas struck. Like a plunging coconut the head came down, jaws gaping. The flat-flippered body lunged out of the water with the force of that thrust, and the jaws snapped within a beak-length of Orn's tail feathers.

This much his memory had warned him of: the Elas fed by paddling behind a fish and flinging its head forward suddenly, to grasp the prey before it could escape. Had Orn not jumped when the motion began, he would have been lost. Too quick a jump would also have been fatal, for the Elas could crook its neck about in a double spiral, and small corrections were routine for it.

But now the rep was in trouble. Used to dunking its head under the surface in the process of catching fish, it had not considered that land was different. It had bashed its snout hard against the ground. The jaws had actually snapped at the level of Orn's body, but reflex and follow-through had carried head and neck on down. Now its neck was spread full-length on the dirt and its mouth was bleeding where its teeth had crushed against stone and earth. Yes, it was crazed; it would ordinarily have been more cautious this near land.

Orn whirled and struck at the exposed neck near its joining with the torso. The creature was vulnerable now but would be deadly in its rage once it got reoriented. He dug his talons into the glistening, smooth-skinned column and probed with his beak for some vital or crippling spot. But the mass of flesh was too great and strange; he did not know where the key tendons were, and claws and beak were lost amidst its layer of blubber.

Elas emitted a high-pitched squeal and hauled its neck up in a magnificent undulation. The head looped back to come at Orn from the side, and he was unable to break loose immediately because his

344

members were mired. He was lifted helplessly into the air, dangling by both feet.

Ornette leaped to help him. She aimed her beak at the rep's eye, but the Elas turned on her quickly and met her with wide-open mouth. She squawked once, pitifully, as the pointed teeth closed on her wing and breast; then she was carried upwards.

Orn fought loose and fell into the water a wingspan from the rep's front flipper. He tried to attack again, but the Elas was already paddling away, Ornette dangling.

Pursuit was useless. Orn could neither catch the Elas nor harm it, and Ornette was already dead.

Orn climbed back on the island, blood-tainted and disconsolate. It was not exactly grief he felt, but a terrible regret. Ornette had died defending him, as he would have died defending her, and both defending their lone egg. Now her companionship had been severed and he was alone again.

Except for the egg! The most important part had been salvaged.

The quilon still warmed it. She had not moved during the struggle, and this was right. Ornette would not have attacked the Elas had the egg not been secure without her protection. Nothing took precedence over that egg.

Again the oddness came to him: stranded on an exposed island, he without his mate, the mam without hers, the two of them guarding the egg neither had laid.

What was there to do but go on?

Chapter Eighteen

VEG

Veg recovered consciousness painfully. He was lying on a hard beach, his face against a wet rock, his feet in water, and he was hot. He did not know where he was or how he had come there. His head was aching, his innards soggy, and the rest of him was hardly robust.

He sat up carefully and waited for the resultant dizziness to pass. The beach was scant, hardly more than a hesitancy between land and sea, and the land itself was brief. In fact, it was no more than a pylon of rock jutting up from the waves, with a single ledge he perched upon. Similar to the jigsaw reefs separating this section from the main ocean, really – not that that improved his position.

He had lost his quarterstaff, but retained his knife. The quarterstaff idea hadn't turned out very well; nobody had gotten any good use from the weapons. Well, next time he wouldn't bother. His clothing was torn, and his neck was welted with insect bites where it had been exposed. He wished he could puke up some of the muddy water he must have swallowed – but then he would probably feel hungry.

Strength seeped back unwillingly, and with it some spongy memories. He had fought a government agent – no, that was back on Earth, too long ago, and the man had turned out pretty decent in the end. Veg had been arrested and put into orbit with Cal and 'Quilon and the eight, no seven, mantas. Then – here to Paleo, with four mantas and a trip on the ocean. And a bash with Brach, the arm-leg lizard ten times life size. And a bird, and—

He had made love to Aquilon! 'Quilon!

After that it became fuzzy. Her soft thighs, and Cal in trouble, and guilt and a swim and a run through the swamp and—

And here he was, tossed on a rock by himself. No friend, no manta, no woman, no bird. Time had passed; now he had a memory

346

of shivering in the night and fading out again.

Why had he done it? After all this time, on three worlds – why had he taken her? It had not been a physical thing between them, only a promise. Now that promise was gone.

Then he remembered the rest of it. Cal – they had broken with Cal! The tyrant lizard was after his friend, while Veg had been mucking about with Aquilon. Too late he had remembered his loyalty and tried to get there. On the way there had been another quake that threw him into the water, and he had swum blindly, trying to get out of it.

He had been lucky he had not drowned. The waves had been bad enough, and any of the great sea animals could have gobbled him en route. Unless those swimmers were as shaken by it all as he.

He peered over the level water. They would not be shaken now – and the tide was rising. He had perhaps another hour before his island disappeared entirely.

Well, better get on with it. Maybe Cal was dead, and Aquilon too. But maybe they were just waiting for him to find them. He'd save his regrets for the facts.

He faced towards land and dived in, the splash a mark of defiance. The impact of the water against his skin invigorated him, and he stroked strongly for the shore. There were scratches on his back, and the salt sting did its part to spur him along.

Salt? He had thought this area was fresh water, from the stream and swamp. But maybe that was only when the tide was out, or in the river channel itself.

Something moved in the ocean. A snout broke the surface – a mighty beak. Veg saw it coming towards him.

A swimming Tricer?

It was a huge sea turtle, attracted by the splashing. Veg had little concern for turtles ordinarily, but this was hardly the kind he was accustomed to. It was twice as long as he was, with a heavy leathery skin instead of a true shell, and its beak was horrendous. Its two front flippers were roundly muscled paddles, propelling it rapidly forward. This was the beast that Cal had termed *Archelon*, when they had observed it from the raft. The only reason Veg remembered the name was its resemblance to Aquilon. Arky, he had dubbed it, and forgotten the matter; but it didn't seem quaint or funny now. The head alone must weigh as much as Veg did!

347

He treaded water, uncertain how to react. He didn't *think* turtles ate people . . .

Arky glided up, sleek and swift in its element. Veg realized that he had been foolish to judge its capability by those of its cousins he had observed on land. This was a mighty creature, capable of wiping him out casually. He gripped his tiny-seeming knife. Would it even pierce that skin?

The turtle sniffed him. Veg wasn't sure that was possible with its head under water, but it remained the best description. Then it decided he was not edible, and nudged away, its ballroom carapace brushing his legs. He felt giddy with relief – a sensation rather strange to him. Obviously he wasn't as much recovered as he had thought. The cuts on his back smarted again.

Arky lifted its head above the water. Veg followed its seeming glance – and spied a ripple coming in from the open sea. It was another creature.

And – he saw the disk of a manta, also coming towards him. That was immensely reassuring. Hex, probably, on the lookout for the lost party. Now he could get in touch again, and find the others.

Provided they still lived. That quake had been rough.

Hex arrived before the sea creature, but not by much. The turtle floated just under the surface, twenty feet away, facing the swimming newcomer. Veg, now assured of his safety, stroked once more for shore.

He heard the thing come up behind him, splashing softly, and had to look. It was a mosasaur – the most vicious reptile of the sea. Thirty feet long, the torso highly flexible, the tail splayed vertically and quite powerful enough, and four paddle-shaped limbs. The head was narrow, the nose pointed, but the jaws were lined with ample sharp recurved teeth. A kind of crest or ridge commenced at the neck and trailed all the way back into the tail, and this waved ominously just above the water as the creature swam. It was as though the worst features of crocodile, turtle, and shark had been combined and magnified – and Veg was frankly terrified.

Suddenly Hex's protection seemed scarcely sufficient. Mosa was too big, too ugly – and most of its body was shielded by water. It could come at him from below, and the manta would be unable to strike.

Mosa circled both him and the turtle, as though considering which one to attack first. Arky, fully alert to the danger, rotated in

348

place, always facing the predator lizard. Evidently the turtle did not trust its armour to withstand Mosa's teeth, though possibly it was only the turtle flippers, which could not be withdrawn into the body, that it was concerned about. If *Arky* were worried, how should *Veg* feel?

The shore was far too far away; he could never make it now. The diminishing rock he had nighted on was still fairly close, thanks to his dawdling – but he couldn't get there either while Mosa was watching.

Hex paced above the water, making a tight circle inside that of the mosasaur. The reptile was aware of the manta, but not particularly concerned. Probably it thought Hex was a pteradactyl, waiting for the remnants.

Veg was pretty sure Mosa would decide on the warm, unarmoured appetizer: himself. Then, invigorated by the morsel, it could tackle the tougher turtle at leisure. No particular genius was required to select the easy prey.

Mosa decided. It angled smoothly in towards Veg.

Hex struck out the exposed eye.

The reptile didn't seem to realize what had happened, immediately. It continued its charge, drifting in the direction favoured by the remaining eye, its teeth snapping.

Veg started to swim for the rock. Mosa spotted the motion and came at him again, jaws wide. By accident or design, its good eye was under the water, safe from Hex's lash.

Veg had an inspiration. He launched himself at the big turtle.

Mosa sheered off, momentarily confused by the combination of objects: two together in the water, a third in the air. Veg remembered something Cal had said once, about animals becoming confused by more than two objects; they could not count. Arky was also confused, unable to concentrate on Veg while the dangerous lizard was so close behind. It was also annoyed by the manta.

Veg bypassed the beak and touched the smooth hull. It might not *look* like a turtleshell, but it seemed rock-hard. He got behind it and stayed close. There wasn't anything much to hang on to. Mosa made a feint, and Arky forgot about Veg as it braced against the greater menace. Hex continued to pace the surface. It was an impasse of a kind.

Mosa circled, adapting to its limited vision. It had no intention of giving up the chase; in fact, the taste of its own blood might well be stimulating it to some berserker effort. And it seemed to Veg that mosa did have the physical wherewithal to prevail, for it outmassed man, manta, and turtle combined and was fully adapted to combat in the ocean. Even completely blind (Hex might yet get the other eye) it could probably sniff him out and finish him off. Arky was only a temporary cover; once the turtle decided to depart, mosa would pounce on the mouthful remaining, shrugging off the superficial lacerations Hex might inflict.

It was death in the making for him. A kind of checkmate demise, as one piece after another was nullified, but inevitable. Somehow the end no longer frightened him the way he thought it should. Had there been an element of chance about it, he might have been eager and nervous. As it was—

Chance struck. A school of sharks converged on the scene, slim sleek missiles of appetite. In a moment mosa, the wounded one, was the centre of attention.

Suddenly Veg understood what had happened. He had dived off his rock, originally, making a splash that attracted the turtle. But meanwhile his scratched-up back had been bleeding into the water, and mosa had smelled it. Then the commotion and mosa's own injury had alerted the sharks . . .

Chance? Maybe less than he had supposed.

But very soon those killer fish would come after *him*.

Mosa was now in a fight for its life. No single shark approached the reptile in size, but there were as many as a score of them, some as long as fifteen feet, all maddened by the blood. Already they had torn great gashes in mosa's hide. Several of their own number were dead, for mosa as an individual was more savage than they – but now the checkmate had been reversed.

Arky, no dumb bunny, took this opportunity to dive for safer territory. Its mighty flippers clove the water, creating a turbulence that jounced Veg around and towed him under. Then the turtle was gone, moving more rapidly than he could follow.

Veg struck for the rock. Two sharks detached themselves from the main platoon as though central command had allocated them, and cruised after him. Hex sliced up their projecting fins and set them to fighting one another. This diversion was sufficient. He made it to safety.

He stood ankle-deep on his isle and wondered what he would do when the tide made him available to the sharks again. Hex could not divert them indefinitely. Veg could not expect luck to save him again. He was not, in sober analysis, one of those hero types who won out no matter what the odds against success. He felt empty without Cal, and deep remorse for the split that had overtaken them. It hadn't really been Aquilon's fault, either; she hadn't meant to make trouble like that.

How easy, now, to pass judgments on his prior conduct.

Hex perched on the highest point of the rock, his foot splaying out to grip it clumsily. It was a sitting and pushing type of foot, rather than a grasping member, and the posture had to be uncomfortable – but Hex appeared to be staying until the end. There was no use in Veg himself trying to climb that point; it was too small and steep for anything but a perpetual balancing act, and this would only postpone the finish, not change it.

Where was Cal now? The manta Circe had said the tyrant lizard was after him, alone. That was sure death for the little man. But Cal was funny about that sort of thing. He might have found a way to—

Impossible. What could a man, any man, do against Tyrann? Cal was digested by now.

No, he couldn't be. Not his friend!

Veg realized that he had only to ask Hex. The manta would surely know. A snap of the tail would tell him Cal lived; two snaps—

He choked on the question. It would not come out. He was afraid of the answer.

The water was at his knees. Already a small shark was circling the rock, waiting.

Should he die without knowing?

Maybe this was his punishment for despoiling Aquilon.

Veg looked across the water, at the savage valley, the snow-topped mountains, the islands reaching into the sea, the level horizon showing beyond the channel between the large harbour islands, Silly and Cheryb-dis. He looked, expecting nothing.

And saw a ship.

Chapter Nineteen

CAL

Tyrann's bulk almost blocked the opening. The carnosaur was sleeping, his body spread out along the stream bed to capture every vestige of warmth therein. The hot water from the cavern puddled at his nose and coursed along his neck – the only thing, in this snow-line dawn chill, that was keeping him reasonably functional. The flesh was discoloured where the hottest water touched, but evidently the reptile had elected some heat discomfort in spots instead of the lethargy of cold all over. Probably it inhaled warmth this way. This was courage of a kind.

Cal stood just within the cave mouth, where a refreshingly cool circulation occurred, and surveyed the situation. It was possible that Tyrann was playing possum, waiting for the prey to come out – but Cal doubted that the reptile was capable of such subtlety. It was not an art large predators usually needed for survival. Tyrann would normally sleep until the heat of the day raised his body temperature to a suitable level. In the valley this would be a simple matter – but the chill of this upper region was apt to make it a long sleep indeed. It had been a mistake for Tyrann to settle down here, for without continuous muscular exertion to maintain his body heat, he could not survive.

Probably Cal could climb right over the ugly jaws and be on his way with impunity. Victor in their contest, he could make his way along the shore to the Paleocene camp. It might take him several months to make it, and there would be other hazards – but *if* he made it to that radio, his course was justified. To the victor belonged the spoils – the spoils of a world.

Yet he hesitated, looking down at the great prone reptile. He was not afraid of Tyrann – indeed, had never been – for he understood the creature's needs and motives. They were the same as his own: survival. Tyrann accomplished his purpose by size, power, and

352

determination. Cal used his intelligence – and determination. The fact that he had won did not mean that his cause was morally superior. It meant simply that he had demonstrated a greater capability for survival, in this instance.

If he summoned the forces of Earth (for casuistry aside, that was surely the gist of his report), he would be pitting an advanced world against a primitive one. That would not be a fair contest. Very soon the dinosaurs would be extinct again, and Paleo would be just like Earth: crowded with neurotic humans, its natural resources depleted ...

Veg and Aquilon were right. His alternate universe framework was theoretical. Each world was a separate case, and the means did not justify the end, particularly when it meant the destruction of a known world for the sake of unknown ones ... that might in time be ravaged anyway. Man did not have the esthetic authority to do such a thing to *any* world, and Cal had judged by the case before him. He could not throw Paleo to the omnivore.

Studying Tyrann, Cal knew himself to be a hypocrite. The truth was that he had expected to lose, and thus preserve this world a moment longer. He couldn't accept victory, and had never intended to. He had argued the ugly cause merely to put both sides on record. That would be important, in the Earth-sponsored court-martial that would follow the abrogation of their assigned mission. That could protect the trio to some extent, and the mantas. Selfish motive!

Tyrann was too noble a brute to be arbitrarily extinguished at man's convenience. Let Paleo remain unspoiled a moment, geologically speaking, longer. Let the dinosaur find his own destiny. Let the king of the reptiles rule today, even if extinction was inevitable tomorrow.

But Tyrann would die today, in effect, if he remained before the cave. He had cooled off during the night, since the tremendous muscular dynamo of his body had cut down into torpidity. A lot of heat would be required to revive him, and it might never get warm enough long enough here in these mountain reaches to do the job. Tyrann could sleep himself into starvation.

The hot water, at least, would have slowed the process, and in any event it would take some time for ten tons of flesh to cool completely. If Tyrann were brought to consciousness before any

353

further heat loss occurred, and while his considerable bodily energy resources remained . . .

Cal stepped out of the cave, feeling the chill immediately. He kicked the yard-long snout where the water made it tender. 'Wake up, lazybones!' he yelled.

An eye flicked open, but Tyrann did not stir. That insidious cold remaining in his flesh immobilized him, though the sun was now hot upon his flank and the water softened his belly. The mighty reptile had a mighty chill; he could not leap to full awareness and performance the way a mammal or bird could.

Cal put a foot on Tyrann's nearest tooth, slung his knee against the nose, mounted to the top of the head and tromped about. 'Get on the ball, sleepy! I don't have all day!'

A hiss of annoyance issued from the tremendous, flaccid throat. The muscles of the bulging neck tensed and Cal slid off, caution not entirely forgotten. The skin was hardly sleek, this close; it hung in elephantine folds, mottled and blistered, and infested with insectlike parasites. Tyrann, he thought, probably itched hugely in his off moments.

Cal scrambled around the looming shoulder, avoiding the clenching, almost-human extremity below it, and trotted to the side of the gully. 'Can't catch me!' he shouted. He pried a fragment of rock out of the rubble and lobbed it towards the head. It missed, but the second had better aim.

Tyrann bestirred himself. Water gushed down the channel as the ponderous body elevated. Stones splashed into it, dislodged by the hulking, careering shoulders. Clumsily, laboriously, Tyrann stood up and turned about.

Cal danced along the gully, skirting the hips and tail barely in time. He paused only long enough to be certain the reptile was on his trail again. Then he plunged downhill, following the warm channel. He wasn't worried – yet! – about being caught. It should be at least an hour before Tyrann was really alert. By then—

By then, perhaps, they would be well into the warm valley and he could slip away, leaving the monster frustrated but alive. Cal had won his victory; all he wanted now was to return Tyrann to his habitat. After that – well, he no longer had need of the journey up-coast, since he was not going to make the report. He'd just have to hope he had misjudged the intent of the Earth authorities.

Progress was faster than that. In ten minutes they were out of the snow region. In twenty, the air was appreciably warmer, almost comfortable. In thirty, away from the opening gully—

'Veg!' he cried. But it wasn't Veg.

The man nodded briefly, hands on his steam rifle. 'Dr Potter, I presume.'

The exchange had taken five seconds. It was enough of a pause to bring Tyrann into sight. Still clumsy but recovering nicely, the dinosaur bellowed and charged down at them.

Almost casually the stranger aimed his weapon and fired. A hiss as the steam boosted away the shell and dissipated; a clap of noise as the projectile exploded. As Cal turned, Tyrann began to fall. His head was a red mass.

'Just about in time for you,' the man remarked. 'Where are your companions?'

Tyrann was dead. The great body still twitched and quivered, and would continue to cast about for some time, but the head had been blown apart by the explosion. The shell must have scored directly inside the mouth: an expert shot. It was a cruel demise for the carnosaur, and an unnecessary one; at this stage as horrifying as the murder of a friend. Cal's reaction of grief and outrage, rather than grateful relief, was evidently noted by the stranger, for one of his eyebrows rose in mild puzzlement.

Cal identified the stranger now: an Earth-government agent, similar to the one he had known as 'Subble'. There were many of them, all basically similar to each other, differing only in superficial respects. This was deliberate. They were, in a manner of speaking, made that way. This one was dark-haired and heavy-featured – but the body was that of a superman, and the mind, Cal knew, was abridged but very sharp. This man would be able to quote all the Bible and much of Shakespeare, but would not have studied either creatively. He would have no truly individual personality. His past was a prepared memory, his present a specific mission, and his future irrelevant.

The question was, why was he here? Here on Paleo, the world of the paleontological past. Here in the reptile enclave. There should be no human beings here, apart from the trio.

The only sensible answer was that the trio had been followed. That suggested that Cal's worst fears had been realized. Their

355

debate about the nature of his report on Paleo had after all been academic.

'Come with me,' the man said gently.

Cal offered no resistance. He knew the agent could kill him or severely incapacitate him in a single second or an hour, whichever combination he chose. And would, if the occasion warranted. Obviously this encounter had been no accident.

'I am Taler,' the agent said as they walked south.

So he was of the generation after Subble: the T's. Agents tended to go by three-letter codes, modified for pronunciation. Each generation (speaking mechanically, not biologically) was uniform. A given individual would react to a given situation in a manner so similar to that of his pseudo-brothers that the coordinating computer could accept his report without modification for individual bias. This was said to facilitate law enforcement immensely, in its various and often obscure ramifications on violent Earth.

But why had an agent been dispatched at all? This was supposed to have been a civilian mission.

He was pestering his own mind with rhetorical questions. The answers were all there, if he cared to bring them forth. Why an agent? Because the civilians were no longer needed. Earth had already made its decision with regard to the disposition of Paleo.

Cal had not made any specific reports, but had been aware that the radios maintained a carrier signal, pinpointing their geographic whereabouts at all times. The one in the Paleocene camp was probably still broadcasting. The other must have stopped when the raft had been upset by *Brachiosaurus*, drowning the equipment. This could have looked very much like sabotage.

All he had promised had been an eventual technical report: itemization of flora and fauna, climate and geography. He had planned to deliver his conjectures on the nature of the planet itself – the alternate-world framework. That would have been food for thought, for it suggested that there was not merely one world available, but an infinite number, if only connections to them could be established. Paleo, instead of representing merely a regressed Earth, implied a new universe, some of whose worlds could be very close in nature to the modern Earth.

But the short-thinking authorities had not waited. They had evidently concluded that if a party of three could survive this long on

Paleo, it was habitable and safe, and therefore wide open for exploitation. No doubt many corporations were eager to make their investments and begin profiting. So a more substantial investigation had been organized – in fact, it had probably been in the making before the trio was ever assigned. No wonder they had been boosted through so precipitiously, back at the orbiting station! If the guinea pigs were to be used at all, it had to be immediately, lest the larger mission be delayed. Report? No more than a pretext to conceal from the trio their true insignificance.

So Cal's notion that Earth would patiently wait for his delayed report had been wishfully naïve. That was not the nature of the omnivore.

Cal repressed his further thoughts, aware that the agent could ferret them out quickly if suspicious.

They arrived at Taler's camp. A glossy-fabric tent had been pitched in the forest, stark contrast to the ancient ginkgos surrounding it. Inside the tent sat another agent, operating a radio. Yes – they were in touch.

'Taner,' Taler said, introducing his comrade.

Taner spoke into the mike. 'Calvin Potter secured. Fungoids loose.'

Secured? Another line of conjecture opened up. An ugly one. He had not been even nominally rescued – he had been taken prisoner. And they were searching for the mantas.

Why? Why indeed! Here was a world for the taking – provided the mantas didn't take it first. Any two of them could sporulate by committing suicide, and cover the planet with the very population the Earth-government abhored: advanced fungoid entities. That would ruin it for colonization, by certain definitions, and reduce the spoils to ashes.

Perhaps it would be better that way. The manta, at least, was an honourable creature.

Taler turned to him. 'I see you comprehend our purpose, Dr Potter.'

Oh-oh. He had forgotten, for the moment, the uncanny abilities of these men. By studying his reactions to stimuli – and words themselves were stimuli – they could virtually read his mind.

'Precisely,' Taler said. 'Now it will be easier for us all if you choose to cooperate. Where are the other members of your party?'

357

They would run Veg and Aquilon down soon enough anyway – perhaps already had. Presuming the two had survived the quakes. A speedy pickup – yes, Taler was testing him in much the manner old-time police had verified the performance of their drugs or lie detectors by asking preliminary questions to which they knew the answers. 'I left them on a small island in the eastern bay, together.'

'And the fungoids?'

That was another matter. 'I told them to get lost.'

'You are a clever man, Dr Potter.'

Cal smiled grimly. 'Common sense suggested that where there were two such highly trained agents as yourselves, others could also be present. Since I actually asked the mantas to observe my encounter with the carnosaur but not to interfere, I am reasonably certain that I have been under observation by them. Since it does not appear to be to their advantage to have these creatures captured by you, it was natural that I express my sentiment.'

'However obliquely, and with insufficient precursive tension to alert me in time. Two fungoids were in the vicinity,' Taler admitted. 'They departed when you amended your prior instructions by suggesting that they "get lost". Our personnel were not quite quick enough.'

'It would have been messy,' Cal said, 'had I suggested instead that they attack.'

'Correct.' Taler pulled aside a flap of the tent and revealed beneath it several heavy cables. These divided and subdivided and fed eventually into the material of the tent itself.

Suddenly Cal was very glad he had warned the mantas clear. The tent was a network of filament! The moment sufficient power was applied, he was sure, the entire surface would flash like a nova, blinding every sighted creature nearby. The agents would have some kind of protection – polarized contact lenses, perhaps – but the mantas would have been destroyed. Alive but dead, for the sensitive eye was virtually their sole sensory apparatus.

That showed how well Earth understood the manta metabolism, now. For in death the bodies of the mantas would dissolve into spores, and in country like this it would not be possible to be assured of destroying every drifting bit of life. Living mantas were no such danger, and a blind manta would be innocuous – unable to strike either in life or death.

'Now we shall have to run them down the hard way,' Taler said, showing no malice. 'That may mean considerable damage to the area.'

Cal knew the agent meant it. But the matter was out of his hands now. 'What about the others?'

'We picked Vachel Smith off a rock in the ocean, and one fungoid accompanied him voluntarily. They are confined aboard ship in good condition. Taner is about to go after the girl and her companion. I see you did not know your associates had separated.'

'I hadn't known any mantas had rejoined them, either. Well, at least I'll have company in the brig.'

Chapter Twenty

ORN

The island was still dark as Orn roused the sleeping quilon with a careful nudge of his beak. Something was wrong. There was an alien presence he could not fathom – the same horror he had experienced the first time he had encountered the giant mams and supposed, erroneously, to be an aspect of their own strangeness.

She woke nervously, brushing her forelimbs against his under feathers, touching the warm egg for reassurance. He knew that gesture. It meant that she feared for the egg, that some danger threatened it. And that was why he had alerted her, for he did not like this odd visitation. Would she sense it too?

'Circe!' she exclaimed. 'You came back!'

She saw it! And – she was not frightened. Her reaction, her sounds, were of relief and welcome, not apprehension.

'Veg – Cal – are they safe? Where are they?'

She was trying to make contact with it! She was friendly to this un-creature. It could not, then, be a threat.

Braced by this realization, Orn concentrated on the spot of greatest disturbance. If the quilon could perceive something there, so should he. His eyes were better than hers, and his nose too.

All he found was an unfamiliar growth of fungus: a tremendous toadstool. He could not read its life history, for it deviated too far from the lines he knew. It had not been there when they fought the Elas. But it was the nature of these things to sprout very rapidly.

It moved.

Orn looked to discover what had dislodged it, but observed no cause. There was no wind, and no animal had brushed against it. The ground had not quaked. The water had not washed ashore.

'They're safe!' The quilon was happy. She liked to see the toadstool move.

'Is the water clear now?' She was making query-noises. Orn was able to comprehend more and more of her mannerisms and read her intent. But he could not determine her precise concern. She was smarter than most mams, but fell short of Ornette's level, and was subject to meaningless and transitory expressions.

The toadstool disappeared. Astonished, Orn left the egg momentarily to probe the ground where the thing had grown. It was as though it had been lifted away by the wind – the wind that wasn't there. Surely the quilon had seen the phenomenon. Plants never moved of their own volition!

'Circe is checking out the region. We'll have to move off this rock, Orn, and we can't do it while the reptiles are about. I think I can manage the egg, provided the water isn't too deep and nothing attacks us. Circe can guide us—'

Orn wondered whether this continuous noise could have been what drove the male mam away. Certainly it was irritating, when there was the problem of foraging while guarding the egg against both known and unknown menaces. Already that chatter had brought upon them a disastrous visitation by the Elas.

The toadstool reappeared, blown like a frond in a gale. Orn was able to see it clearly now that he was aware of its properties. These were contrary to all that his memory told him. But gradually he was able to accept that this fung had somehow evolved entirely separate from his own ancestry. Just as the ordinary animals had split from each other and developed over the millennia into dissimilar lines, so had this. Perhaps it had happened entirely in this valley, unvisited by any of his own line. Thus its utter strangeness, that had rendered it virtually imperceptible to him except as a vague horror, was not really so sinister. A creature with metabolism resembling that of a plant, yet as active as an animal. A creature without wings that flew. Now that his mind had conjured the necessary evolution of the species – a fung that reached for organic food, then jumped for it, until it had become dependent on such motions for sustenance – he could accept it.

Just as a man could become as large as a small rep, and make perpetual noises, so could a fung become a flying toadstool.

The thing had planted itself in the ground again, and the quilon was making her noises at it. Perhaps the two odd species, mam and fung, had evolved together, and somehow understood each other. Such a connection would be no more remarkable than what he had

361

already observed in this changed world.

The quilon faced him. 'Circe says there is now a deep and treacherous chasm between us and the main island. The fault must have opened up there, and we can't cross it unless we swim. But I can't swim holding the egg. I mean I might try it, but the cold water would kill the embryo. But Circe says the bay between us and the mainland is shallow, maybe only chest deep on me. The quake must have pushed up the bottom in a ridge parallel to the fault – well, no use trying to explain *that* to you. She can show us the best route across, so we can wade. And she says there are no big reptiles in the immediate area right now, and no sharks: they're all gathering around some battle several miles away, where there's a lot of blood. Something like that – I'm not sure. There's a sleeping duckbill by the main island, and he won't bother us anyway. But the tide's coming in; we have to do it right away if we're going to, otherwise it'll be hot by the time the water's low again, and the sea predators will be out in force.'

Orn ignored her chatter. It was dawn – the best time for hunting, because most of the reps were torpid, though not the sharks. He would have to forage for the mam as well as himself, since she had to warm the egg. He had observed that she did not consume fish, sticking instead to tubers and berries from the island. He could cross over now and sniff out some roots for her, then feed himself.

The toadstool flew out over the sea again The quilon stood up, lifted the egg – *and walked into the water!*

Orn squawked and fluttered after her, appalled at her folly. The cool sea would deaden the life in the egg! But she only made vocal noises at him, refusing to be summoned back.

He was helpless. Any measure taken against the quilon would surely immerse the egg – the very thing he sought to protect. He could not carry it back himself; he had to wait for her to do so. He realized that she meant no harm – but she did not seem to comprehend the danger. How could he make her understand?

She stepped cautiously away from the rock, the water rising to her removable hip-plumage. She held the egg against her fleshy breast with one forelimb, balancing with the other. She was moving away from the main island, following a course suggested by the motions of the flying toadstool.

Orn started swimming, being too light to maintain his footing at this depth. The quilon, well over half immersed, continued towards the mainland. She wasn't even trying to get to the island!

He had no notion how to abate this bizarre exploration. Had he known the mam was prone to such action, he would never have left her with his egg. Now all he could do was parallel her course and hope she would turn back before the egg was lost. He would have to kill her if she sacrificed it through her stupidity – but he did not want to do that.

The sea beneath him was clear. Small fish circulated temptingly, and he was hungry, but he could not go after them now. He could not see through to the bottom, for it was quite deep, though where the quilon walked it was unusually shallow. Memory told him that earth faults under the sea were sometimes like that: one side high, the other low, or two ridges separated by a chasm. But how had she known?

She was in now almost to her head. The egg was precariously lodged on her shoulder, nestled in the yellow mane that descended from her scalp. Both her forelimbs were raised to shield it. This was not adequate coverage; the egg would soon grow cold there, even if the water that was already plastering her artificial fur to her bifurcated udder did not rise farther. He swam closer, though he could do nothing.

The quilon stopped. 'Too deep. I can't keep my footing. If I lower my arms, I'll float, and the egg will unbalance me—'

Sometimes such sounds seemed to signal a change of intent. Would she turn back now?

She worked her way back until the mane drew entirely out of the water. She held the egg close before her, warming it though her torso was wet. Then the toadstool came near, bouncing on the surface, and angled away in a slightly different direction. She followed it.

Again she went as deep as she could go, and again she uttered her frustrated sounds and retreated. The toadstool circled, seemingly unable to point the way again. *Now* would she give up this hazardous enterprise and return his egg to land and safety?

Safety? Even the mainland, with its rampaging reps, was safer than the hideously exposed bit of rock they were stranded on. Had it been possible to move the egg even to the main island – but the canyon in the sea prevented that.

Then Orn realized what the quilon and her obscure acquaintance were attempting to do. Shallow water leading towards the mainland, while the tide was low—

He went into action. He dived, spreading his wings against the water to provide the impetus that would send him under. He explored the bottom with his beak and eye.

Ahead of the quilon the ridge descended, then rose again to a level he thought she could navigate. If she could cross that deepest portion, she could travel a long way towards land – perhaps all the way. But she could not pass the hollow without immersing the egg. Perhaps only four lengths of her body, about four wingspans, separated her from the resumption of navigable shallows.

This was not the type of thinking Orn's mind was made for, but his long apprenticeship in solitary survival, coupled with the present pressing need, sharpened his abilities. There were problems memory could not solve, and this was one such: how to get the mam female across the gap without dunking the egg – and soon enough so that the rising tide would not make it entirely impossible.

Had there been floating wood, memory might have sufficed. His ancestors had utilized logs to cross from island to island upon occasion, or from side to side of deep rivers. but there was no log here. Orn himself was the only thing afloat – and only the relative stillness of the water enabled him to maintain his balance. Waves, or any other threat, could swamp him, for he was top-heavy and lacked webbed feet. He was actually better at swimming under water than on the surface, because there his abbreviated wings were effective.

But in this emergency, his abilities might be enough to save the egg. And the egg was paramount.

Orn paddled up and nudged the standing quilon. She was silent now, and water seemed to have splashed onto her face though the egg was dry. There was a certain unhappy handsomeness about her as she stood balked, and he wondered to what extent mams had genuine emotions.

But there was no time for such idle considerations. Orn nudged her again, trying to make her understand. The egg could be saved, if her dull mam brain could rise to the occasion.

For a moment she did not move. Then, slowly, she placed one forelimb across his back, bearing down on his body so that he sank in the water. She was astonishingly heavy, but he spread his wings somewhat and kicked his feet and maintained his position. He could not endure this for long; his instinct and memory cried out against such proximity to a foreign creature. But long enough—

She moved the egg until it rested partly against his back, just above the water. Then she pushed slowly forwards. Her body went down, but the egg remained high, its weight borne by his feathers.

At the place the mam had balked before, her feet left the bottom and she floated. Orn paddled desperately to maintain his balance as she lost hers. It was difficult; he was tilting irrevocably over—

Then the quilon's stout legs began to kick in the water, driving them both slowly ahead and restoring joint balance. He steered and she held the egg on his back. A single bad wave, even a gust of wind, would topple them.

The toadstool circled rapidly, as though even its vegetable intellect were aware of the crisis. Orn glanced at it – and saw the suggestion of motion in the distance behind it. Something was coming!

Almost, in his instinctive eagerness to scramble for safety, he dislodged the egg. But he controlled himself after a single jerk and went on paddling. Perhaps it was only one of the sporting cory reps, who were unlikely to stray this far out from shore.

Progress was so slow! Only by poking his head under the surface and noting the locations of the bottom features was he able to determine that they were moving. If a predator rep came upon them now—

It did. It was the Elas, the flippered paddler who had carried Ornette away before. Already it was hungry again, or merely mischievous, and their motion in the shallow water had summoned it from its hiding place. Here within its feeding ground they had no chance at all to escape.

The toadstool broke its circle and went to meet the Elas. Orn could not watch closely, for his balance remained precarious. He saw the fung rise high in the air as though it were a ptera and pass over the lifted head of the rep. Nothing happened – but the Elas emitted a tremendous honk of pain.

Then it was retreating, and the smell of its blood came to him. Had an old wound reopened as it strained to snap up the toadstool? Or had it merely been frightened by the oddity of the fung, the blood remaining from the wound Orn had inflicted on its neck before?

Orn was satisfied that they were safe again. Joy was no more a

365

part of his nature than was grief, and the security of the egg was what mattered. Somehow the rep had been turned away.

The animal panting of the quilon became loud, and his own respiration was laboured. He was, in the aftermath of the rep threat, quite tired. He had been subjected to a double strain – the weight of the quilon and egg on his back, and the fear of the Elas when he was impotent as a fighter. But they were over the shallow section again. He honked, trying to convey this to her, and finally she stopped kicking her heavy-boned feet and pushed her round extremities down until they struck the bottom sand.

The rest of the crossing was easy. Twice more he had to assist the quilon, the rising tide making the portages longer, but now they were both familiar with the routine. The flying fung guided them unfailingly, selecting the best route. Orn was coming almost to like such toadstools.

Secure at last on land, they lay on the pleasant brach, the egg warmed between them. The toadstool also rested nearby, a hump with a single peculiar eye. He could see it quite clearly now, though it remained a most unusual phenomenon.

The quilon had been right; the drive for land had been best. The chick still lived in the egg for he could feel its living presence. With the Elas remaining so near, they would have been perpetually vulnerable on the fragment island. Now they had a chance, and the egg too. The mainland was by no means ideal for nesting, but the island had turned into a death trap.

Orn looked about. He knew the terrain because he had pursued Ornette here during their courtship. Not far back from the shore the snowy mountains rose, riddled with their caverns and gullys and heated waters. Somewhere near the snowline there might be a suitable nesting site. The cold would make it doubly difficult to warm the egg, but this was necessary to escape the predator reps, who ordinarily would not ascend that far.

He stood and led the way, and the quilon followed, submissive now that she had done her task. She held the egg closely against her damp body, enclosing it with her forelimbs so that as little as possible was exposed to the air. Actually, the heat of the day was upon them, so this was no longer critical. The fung vanished into the brush; he spied it only occasionally.

Between shore and mountain was a level plain, an extension of the

366

larger one the Tricer herds ranged on. Here the palms were well trimmed, showing that the huge reps had foraged here recently. Though he did not fear them himself, he was not certain how they would react to the large mam. They might ignore her – but if they did not, the egg would be in peril again. He decided to change course so as to avoid the local herd.

Then he sniffed something else. It was another large mam of the quilon species – a male.

Orn did not know whether this was good or bad. The male had left the female, and perhaps this return meant a reconciliation. But it could also mean trouble. Orn would not ordinarily interfere with mam courtship and mating rites – but he needed the quilon female to transport the egg, and to warm it while he foraged. He could not hatch it alone.

Before he could make a decision, the male approached. It was not the original mate.

There was a babble as the two mams vociferated at each other. The toadstool had taken off at the first whiff of the visitor; Orn smelled it in the vicinity but could not spot it.

The haphazard dialogue continued. Orn picked up the sequence of reactions from the female: surprise, comprehension, anger, fear. She did not like the stranger, but was afraid of what might happen if she made an open break. She suspected the male of malicious intent. Her concern was not primarily for herself, though; it was—

For the egg!

Orn was already charging as the realization hit him. His wings flapped to boost his speed; his beak aimed forward. Headfirst, he launched himself at the strange male quilon.

The creature was not facing him, but from it a bolt of lightning emerged. A terrible heat struck Orn, searing the feathers of one wing and the flesh of that wing and the bony substructure, and lancing on through his body. The wound was mortal; he knew it as he completed his charge.

The female mam struck the intruder with her free limb, but he caught it with his own and was not hurt. This also Orn perceived as the signals of death spread through his running body. The male was swift and deadly and without compassion. He would kill them both and smash the egg. This certainly kept Orn going when he should have fallen. Only by somehow bringing the mam enemy down could he give the egg a chance – even the ugly chance Orn himself had hatched with. His own parents had died defending their nest and eggs from a marauding croc; Orn would die defending his egg from a predator mam. It was the way it had to be.

But he knew too that it was *not* to be. He had thought these mams to be slow and clumsy and not wholly intelligent. He had foolishly judged from the pair that came in peace to mate. The other mam was in his strength, and was devastating. This one would prevail.

Yet he continued, his legs somehow supporting the momentum of his body. He could at least strike at it, perhaps wound it . . .

Then a shadow came upon that scene.

The male quilon had one limb taken by its grasp on the female, the other lifted to ward off Orn. Its stout hindlimbs were anchored in the soil. Only its head was free, this moment, to move about. It turned.

The shadow passed.

There was a gash across the mam's head, where the eyes had been.

The shadow returned. Orn recognized it now. It was the flying fung, moving with dizzying speed.

Fire lanced from the male again, scorching brush and trees but not the toadstool. A second gash appeared, almost circling the mam's throat. Blood pounded out.

As Orn finally collided with his target, only a few heartbeats from the time he had started the charge, he knew that both of them were dying. His weight jarred the male's grip loose from the female. Only she and the fung – and the egg! – had survived this brutal encounter.

'Circe!'

Orn collapsed in a heap with the mam, his blood mixing with that of his antagonist. He no longer had command of his body, but he could hear the female quilon's sounds. She never was silent!

'Circe! We've killed an agent! There may be others in the area, and they'll wipe us all out. They've come to take over Paleo, I'm sure of that. We'll have to cover the evidence. In a hurry.'

The toadstool slowed and came to rest. There was blood on its tail.

'The Tricers! Can you stampede them?'

The fung was gone.

Then she was standing over Orn, touching the feathers of his neck with those uselessly soft digits. She still supported the egg. 'Orn – you're alive!'

368

He had not known that death would be so slow. He was helpless, but now he felt no pain. There was only a gradual sinking to the sound of her dialogue, now gentle and no longer annoying.

'No – you can't survive that burn. I'm sorry, Orn. I – I didn't mean it to end like this. I'll save your egg. I'll keep it until—'

Her paw caressed his neck feathers. 'The Tricers are coming. I have to get out of here, Orn. With your egg. Those brutes will flatten everything, so no one will know, I hope. How he died, I mean. Keep Paleo sacrosanct . . .

'I – you were a gallant soul – *are* one – and I love you. You diverted the agent so Circe could – you gave your life for ours, and I'll always remember that. Always.

'Goodbye, Orn.'

She was gone, and somehow he knew she would preserve the egg. That was all that mattered.

The ground rumbled and shook. Tricers – stampeding! Orn tried to move, but could not, before he remembered that the effort was pointless. Their sound was loud, their massive hooves striking the ground in a gargantuan raindrop pattern. They were coming here! The entire herd, charging along the narrowing plateau, converging on this spot, their growing cadence like the shaking of a volcano.

There would be nothing but a beaten trail, after their passage.

Orn was satisfied.

Chapter Twenty-one

VEG

He stood on the deck and watched them bring Cal in. Hex stood beside him, in his shadow, impassive as only a manta could be.

The ship was anchored in water of appropriate depth near the mouth of the great swamp. It was a double-hulled military yacht, chemically powered but capable of fifty knots. Veg assumed that the agents had assembled it piecemeal this side of the transport tunnel, since it would have been impossible to beam the entire ship through as a unit. A big job, requiring skill and time, though of course the agents would have been programmed for it. They must have started work the moment the trio set sail on the *Nacre*. He didn't need Cal to tell him what that meant about the importance of the trio's original mission. They had simply been a test case, human guinea pigs, sacrificial lambs or whatever, sent through on the spur of the moment to verify that the transfer equipment was in working order and that men could survive the jump. A few days to allow for any subtle residual tissue damage, then a few more to make sure there were no slow-acting poisons on Paleo. Probably Noodlebrain had thought he was sentencing them to death, and it had been sheer luck that everything *had* functioned properly.

The tiny cutter docked beside the yacht. A derrick hoisted Cal and one of his captors to the deck. In a moment Cal passed across the line marking Veg's area of confinement, and the two friends were together again.

'There's a force screen or something,' Veg warned him as they watched the cutter cut east. He still felt the awkwardness of their last discussion. How could things be the same between them, after ... Aquilon?

Cal nodded. He knew all about such things. If any of them attempted to jump ship or even cross the line on the deck without authorization, the invisible alert screen would trigger automatic weaponry that would blast them immediately. The remains would be netted and englobed in seconds, so that the atmosphere would not be contaminated by their corpses. This was mainly for Hex's benefit, since his demise would release a cloud of potent spores. Earth had learned its lesson in that regard.

''Quilon?' Cal inquired.

'It didn't work out,' Veg said; then he realized with fierce embarrassment that Cal had not been referring to their sexual liaison. 'I left her on the island, when I heard about—' He broke off, aware that that was wrong too. Cal had not asked for help, in his contest with Tyrann.

'So Hex tattled,' Cal murmured, smiling briefly.

'Yeah. Circe, anyway.' The tension was broken; Cal understood. 'How'd you make out?'

'Taler shot it.'

'Oh.' That was too simple. It meant Cal didn't want to talk about it, any more than Veg wanted to talk about his own adventure. And Cal would have explained about the other mantas by now, the missing ones, if he intended to. Something was going on.

A woman stood amidships, fiddling with radio equipment. She was tall, slender, and blonde – rather beautiful, yet quite unlike Aquilon. Veg had been observing her with covert admiration, wondering what she was doing here on this man's mission.

'Taner reports island evacuated,' the woman said, every syllable clear though she did not seem to be striving for precision. 'Proceeding to mainland.'

Cal looked at her. 'Earth is keeping extraordinarily close tabs on its representatives,' he remarked. 'I've seen three agents so far, with evidence of at least two others, and reporting in at every turn.'

'They figure Paleo will corrupt somebody, otherwise,' Veg said. 'The way it did us.'

'A telling point. I believe I would have termed it "enlightenment", however.'

'And a gal aboard too.'

'That's nothing to interest you,' Cal said with an obscure expression. 'That's a female agent.'

Veg was shocked. 'That little thing? A superman?'

She glanced their way and smiled. 'Tamme, at your service.'

Veg recalled the things the agent Subble had been capable of back

371

on Earth. He looked again at the girl. He shook his head in negation. She would not last long in a lumberman's free-for-all, whatever her training.

Tamme was watching him. 'I *would*, you know,' she murmured.

For the third time in as many minutes he felt quick embarrassment. Damn that mind-reading ability of hers!

She laughed.

Cal looked thoughtful, but did not comment.

'Contact,' Tamme said. 'Bird and woman. Fungoid concealed.' Then she paused, frowning. 'Taner dead.'

Taler's head appeared in the hatch. At least Veg thought it was Taler; they were all so similar they were hard to tell apart unless they were together. 'So the report was correct. The fungoid can upon occasion dispatch an agent.'

'*She* must have had a hand in it,' Tamme said. 'Shouldn't have sent a man for that chick.'

'You have to admit we aren't exposed much to attractive feminine types,' Taler replied.

She threw something at his head. The motion was so rapid and controlled that Veg was only aware of the jerk of her full blouse and the flash of metal in sunlight.

Taler moved simultaneously, plucking the object from the air before his face. He held it aloft, a trophy. It was a tiny stiletto – and had he not been ready for it, the point would have skewered his nose.

They were only playing, but they were deadly. All of them. That sudden murder of their companion seemed to mean nothing more to them than an ineffective tactic. Unless this whole little episode was merely a show to impress the prisoners. Yet Subble had seemed like a decent guy and he had been an agent not many letters removed. SU compared to TA – SUBble, TALer, TAMme, TANner . . .

Taler came to them. 'It appears there is some difficulty picking up Miss Hunt. We are also interested in the three outstanding fungoids. Is the present creature able to contact others, if set free to do so? There is no need to answer.'

No need indeed! Veg was familiar with this type of interrogation. The agent merely asked questions, and gauged the response from the bodily reactions of the listener. There was nothing an ordinary man could do about it.

But why were the agents so intent on capturing all the trio and the mantas? They could survey the planet and make their report without reference to those who had gone before. The trio wasn't important any more, if it had ever counted for anything here at all, and this campaign hardly seemed worth the effort.

Well, Cal would know. Veg would follow his friend's lead.

'If you do not cooperate,' Taler said gently, 'we shall have to undertake a search-and-destroy mission. That could mean the death of Miss Hunt, too.'

Cal did not speak, but Veg's pulses leaped angrily. Aquilon – dead?

'Interesting,' Taler remarked. 'Dr Potter is even more enamoured of Miss Hunt than is Mr Smith. But Dr Potter refuses to be influenced thereby. Since a threat of this nature would therefore be ineffective, I make none; I merely advise you that the element of risk does apply to Miss Hunt so long as she is beyond our jurisdiction.'

Taler now addressed himself completely to Cal. 'We shall begin with a humane nerve gas. This particular formula should render all mammals unconscious on contact. Reptiles and amphibians will be affected to a lesser extent. Plants will suffer some loss of foliage in the following days and a few will rot. Representatives of the third kingdom—'

'Blinded,' Cal said.

Taler signalled to Tamme. 'Lift the barricade.'

Something clicked off. 'You'd better explain it to Hex,' Cal said to Veg. 'He's your manta.'

'I'm not sure myself what's going on. You want Hex to fetch 'Quilon?'

'These gentlemen,' Cal said, 'want very much to have all four mantas here on the ship, alive, because if any two should die on Paleo their spores could spread and mate and produce many thousands of mantas to take over the planet.'

'That wouldn't be so bad. Mantas aren't destructive.'

'These gentlemen wish to preserve Paleo for human colonization, however.'

Veg smiled bleakly. 'Oh. They'd have trouble, with all those mantas.'

Then something occurred to him. '*I* don't want Earth to colonize, and 'Quilon doesn't either. We already had that out.'

'I have come to agree with you,' Cal said surprisingly. 'Paleo should be preserved as it exists. But although I decided not to make my report, events have made the issue academic. The agents are now in control.'

Veg experienced a mixture of emotions. He was gratified to learn that the schism between them was gone, that Cal was now on the side Aquilon had espoused – but angry that Cal should so readily submit to the demands of the agents. It was not like Cal to yield under duress.

Taler spoke, facing Veg. 'Your friend is very clever. He has already outwitted me once, and I am not a stupid or gullible man. No agent is. Now he is planning to betray us again. I must therefore request that you address your manta immediately, without further conversation with Dr Potter.'

The manner was polite. Taler could afford courtesy. Veg knew that he was fully capable of enforcing his demand, and needed no bluster.

But the other remark! So Cal had not surrendered! That was especially good to know. But what had Cal planned? Could Veg figure it out in time?

'Instruct your manta,' Taler said, his voice still mild but carrying just that hint of urgency required to make his point. Further delay would mean considerable unpleasantness. Veg did not fancy himself to be a fool.

But what could he do, except as told? 'Hex,' he said, and the manta rotated on its foot to face him. 'These men have – do you know what nerve gas is?'

Two snaps of the tail.

Veg turned to Taler. 'I have to explain—'

'Nerve gas is a substance that can be released into the air,' Taler said. 'It will fill the entire valley within an hour, barring exceptional atmospheric conditions. It will blind all eye-bearing fungoids without killing them – and the damage is probably irreversible.'

'Do you understand that?' Veg asked Hex. He wondered how the agents had developed and tested this chemical, with no mantas to try it on. Could it be a bluff?

To his surprise, Hex snapped once. The mantas were getting better at picking up human speech and grasping its content.

'They will release this gas, if you don't go and tell 'Quilon and the other mantas to come here – to surrender. We can't stop them.'

One snap.

'So I guess you'd better—'

Something crackled. Veg saw Cal fall to the deck.

'Remain where you are,' Taler snapped. He was facing Hex, who had not moved, and his directive was as much for the mantas as for Veg. 'Your friend was about to impart inappropriate information to you and the manta. I had to anesthetize him immediately. He will recover in a few minutes unharmed. Instruct your manta.'

'They aren't kidding,' Veg said to Hex, furious but helpless. 'I don't like it, but I have to tell you to go bring Circe and Diam and Star back here – and 'Quilon too, of course. They'll kill us all, otherwise.' Inside he was chagrined that he hadn't been able to follow Cal's plan, whatever it was. By the time Cal woke up, Hex would be on his way, and it would be too late.

'Very good,' Taler said. 'The barrier is down – but the creature will be covered by our cannon until out of sight. We are equipped to englobe the remains in seconds. It has one hour before we release the gas – no more.'

'One hour, Hex,' Veg repeated dully. 'So make it fast. I—' He turned to the agent again. 'You promise not to hurt any of them, or us?'

'If you cooperate. Our interest is in completing our mission; there is no personal onus. The group of you will be assigned elsewhere, where there need be no restriction on your activities or those of the fungoids. You have my given word. That is not sacrosanct, of course, but is a statement of intent.'

Veg remembered Subble once more. The man had kept his word all the way, though he hadn't been obliged to. He had to trust Taler that far.

'It's okay for all of us, if you make it in one hour,' he told Hex. 'Tell them that. Now get going.'

Hex leaped into the air and was on his way, a disk skipping across the water. He was travelling at something like a hundred miles an hour, and in about a minute had disappeared into the foliage fringing the swamp.

Veg lifted Cal to his feet as Taler departed. In a few minutes, as predicted, the little man recovered, though he had a scrape on the head where he had struck the deck. Veg raged to see the injury done, but knew that protest would be useless.

375

'Sorry,' Veg murmured. 'I couldn't figure out what you wanted, and the bastard wouldn't give me time to think, and he could read my mind anyway, so I just had to send Hex off.'

Cal gripped his hand momentarily. 'It's all right.'

'I blew it. I'm just not smart enough.'

'On the contrary. It was essential that I be out of the way so that *I* couldn't blow it, as you put it. They were already suspicious of me. *You* they assumed were safe.'

'I *am* safe,' Veg said. 'Mad as hell, but safe. And I can't even slug one of them. I tried that on Subble, and got smeared.'

'Yes, I'm sure Taler read that fury in you. So now Hex is telling 'Quilon and the other mantas the ultimatum. What do you suppose they'll do?'

'What *can* they do? No sense having that gas turned loose.'

Cal only smiled.

Half an hour passed before a manta reappeared, alone. It glided in while the cannon tracked it and landed neatly on the deck. It was Circe.

Taler came out immediately. 'This is not the same fungoid,' he said.

'It's Circe—' Quilon's manta,' Veg explained.

'Miss Hunt is ready to be picked up?'

'I guess. The swimming isn't so hot hereabouts.'

Taler swung lithely over the rail and dropped into a second cutter. In a moment he was speeding in the direction Circe had come from. Veg wondered how he was so sure of the way, then realized that the sharp perceptions of the agent would make location easy. It was her cooperation Taler required, nothing else. Her agreement would bring in the remaining mantas.

Tamme was on deck, her efficient yet feminine manner disquieting. She had sex appeal, and he knew she read his appreciation of that, and read his attempt to repress and conceal his reaction. She hardly bothered to hide her amusement.

Fifteen minutes later Aquilon was brought aboard, along with Hex. She held what had to be one of Orn's eggs in her arms; Veg had no idea how she had come by it. There was a bruise on her cheek that he didn't like to look at, suspecting that he had put it there; but that was the least of the change in her. She was not the same woman he had known and loved.

376

'It's been a long time,' Aquilon said. 'Four nights and three earthquakes since we three were last together . . .'

'Three nights, two earthquakes,' Cal said.

'You must have been very busy, not to notice. *Four*—'

'Now don't you start fighting again,' Veg interposed quickly. 'Could have been ten days and nine earthquakes, for all I remember, and what difference does it make?'

She smiled, becoming the girl he had known. She held no grudge against him.

Still, they stood there somewhat awkwardly. Veg knew he really hadn't managed things very well. First, siding with her against Cal (and had it been sex that decided him?), then trying to go back to Cal when the man didn't want help, and getting stranded himself. Finally, he played the betrayer to them both by sending Hex off . . . no, he had no congratulations coming.

Suddenly he realized that the hour was up – and Cal's two mantas, Diam and Star, had not come in.

'Release the gas,' Taler said. Tamme, who seemed to handle more than radios, opened a chest and brought out several sealed cannisters. Frost glistened on them; they had been stored cold.

'That's pointless now,' Cal said. 'The two mantas are already dead.'

Taler studied him. 'You play a dangerous game, sir.'

Cal nodded. 'There is a world at stake.'

Tamme spoke into her mike. 'Parley has failed. Two fungoids have spored. Too late for enclosure. Proceed with alternate.' She returned the cannisters to their compartment.

'What happened?' Veg demanded. 'I thought they were coming in!'

Aquilon touched his hand in that way she had. 'They knew what the invasion by the Earth omnivore meant. So they . . . died, and Hex cut them up and spread the spores while Circe reported back here to the ship. By now those spores are all over the valley. They can't be wiped out.'

'But I told Hex—'

Taler cut in, seemingly without malice. 'Dr Potter was aware that Miss Hunt would not honour that request – and that she would correctly interpet its real meaning. Had Dr Potter been conscious at the time your manta left, I would have fathomed his sensation of victory, and thwarted his plan. As it was, I picked up nothing from

377

him except his nonspecific chord of emotions. In my confidence, I failed to read him later, and I attributed Miss Hunt's confused state of apprehension concerning her treatment at our hands following her involvement in the termination of Taner. Therefore I did not question her, assuming that the remaining mantas were on their way separately.' He smiled with good-natured rue. 'I have not before been so readily outwitted by a normal man.'

Veg's mind was spinning. Cal had been walking a tightrope while juggling flaming torches barehanded! So many complex factors were interacting. This was a type of contest alien to him, and one he had certainly not appreciated at the time. 'Why did 'Quilon and Circe come in, then?'

'Two sets of spores were sufficient,' Aquilon said. 'No point in having us all die.'

'But we didn't follow through on the bargain,' Veg said. 'We didn't bring in all the mantas. So the agents don't have to give us any break. Maybe they'll kill us all, now.'

'Does it matter?' Aquilon inquired dully, staring at the egg she held.

'Revenge would be pointless,' Taler said. 'Mr Smith's bargain was made in good faith; it did not occur to him that the others would not honour it. We agents are realistic, not recriminatory – otherwise we would have brought you to accounting for the damage done by the three fungoids back at the Earth station, and particularly for the one that escaped entirely. But we chose instead to learn from the experience, and so we followed you as rapidly as was feasible.'

'You mean you didn't plan to come here anyway?' Veg asked, wondering just how bad a mistake that manta break at the station had been.

'Not this particular party. The original expedition was to consist of normals – extraterrestrialogists, geologists, paleontologists. When we realized the potentialities of your fungoids, this military unit was substituted.' Taler faced towards the mainland, as though watching for something. 'You have demonstrated that as a group you are too valuable to waste. Future agents will be programmed to avoid mistakes of the nature of those we have made here, and you will be reassigned as agreed.'

Veg shook his head dubiously. 'So you're letting Paleo go, after all that trouble?'

'By no means. Our alternate program to salvage the planet for mankind is already underway. Observe.'

They looked across the water. Smoke was rising from the valley – a wall of it on the west side, near the trio's original camp. The breeze was blowing it east.

'You're burning the enclave!' Aquilon exclaimed, horrified.

'The spores, as you pointed out, are beyond recovery. It is necessary to destroy them and the habitat in which they might prosper. We are doing so.'

'But the dinosaurs! They have nowhere to go!'

'They are part of that habitat,' Taler said. 'This will hasten their extinction, yes.'

She stared at the smoke, stricken.

'You can't get all the spores that way,' Veg said, similarly appalled. 'They're tough. Some will ride high in the sky, where it stays cool. Some will settle in the water—' He stopped, wondering whether he had said too much.

'Some spores will survive, inevitably,' Taler agreed. 'But the point is that they require hosts for their maturation. By depriving them of these – chiefly the omnivorous mammals of the valley – we are making it impossible for them to develop there. Some will drift beyond the mountains – but as you saw, that landscape is barren, and their numbers will be diffuse after the hurdles of fire and snow. The ocean is not a conducive habitat, either, since the fungoids are land-based. The probability is that a long-range program of survey and extermination will prevent any fungoid menace from erupting.'

'The whole valley!' Aquilon said. 'How could it possibly be worth it!'

'Perhaps you should have considered that at an earlier time. We were prepared for this contingency, but it was not our desire to destroy the enclave. You forced it.'

'I didn't know!' But it sounded to Veg as though she lacked conviction. She certainly should have guessed that the omnivore would not be easily balked.

'Dr Potter knew.'

He was right, Veg thought. Cal would certainly have anticipated the consequence of his plot. Had he betrayed Paleo after all, making dupes of those, like Veg and Aquilon and the mantas, who would have saved it? Veg did not look at him.

'Some will escape,' Cal said. He sounded worn. 'The spores can survive for many years, and there will be an entire planet to hide on. In as little as a year some will mature sufficiently to respore, and there will be no way to control that secondary crop of mantas. It will be cheaper to vacate Paleo than to police it effectively. Your superiors will realize that in time, and act accordingly. This valley had to be sacrificed for the sake of this world.'

'You are gambling with genocide,' Taler said. He turned to Veg and Aquilon. 'If I were this man's companion, I would be afraid.'

Veg watched the smoke rising, knowing that Cal had foreseen this and probably planned on it, and understood.

Chapter Twenty-two

QUARTET

Aquilon stood holding Orn's egg: a nine-inch shell containing all that remained of a gallant pair of birds. She had wrapped a soft blanket about it, but could not be satisfied that it was warm enough. She kept turning it so as to hold a new face of it against her body, lest any side chill. This was an unreasonable fear, for the air was warm and the egg's requirements were not that critical; she suspected it would survive up to half an hour in isolation at normal temperature, and perhaps more. All it needed was a general, mild warmth, such as that provided by a clothed human body.

Tell that to my female psyche, she thought. Orn had died protecting her – because she held the egg. It was her egg now, never to part until hatched. There could never be enough warmth for it.

Smoke shrouded the dinosaur valley. Soon the enclave would be a mass of embers – all because she had tried to fight the ruthless agents. She was a murderess now; it had been at her behest that Orn and Circe had attacked that agent Taner, who so resembled Subble. Almost, when she had seen him first, she had capitulated. But then she realized what his presence meant . . .

Cal thought it was worth it. But his analytical brain was sometimes frightening. Even human colonization, with all its inequities, would have been better than this. Why had he set it up this way?

Everything had turned out wrong. The night of love with Veg had aborted; she knew now that she did not love him. Not that way. She had loved Orn, in a fashion – only to see him die. Such a noble spirit! now there was only the egg.

She could not get close enough to it. She cradled it with one arm and reached under the blanket with the other, pressing her hand between its rough surface and her own abdomen. She found the catches on her blouse and disengaged them, opening her bosom to

381

the egg. Still it was not close enough. She released her brassiere and slid it up over one breast and then the other, letting it cling just beneath her shoulders while her softly resilient breasts pressed yieldingly against the shell. Then, almost, she felt close enough.

The fires were rising. Open flame showed in patches at the west fringe, licking at the cycads. Obviously it was not a natural conflagration; it ate too readily at green wood, consuming living fern and horsetail as well as ground debris. Tongues of it snaked out over the water, sending up gouts of vapour. No – this was the incendiary product of man, the omnivore. Like its master, it destroyed every living thing it touched, and despoiled the nonliving.

She suspected, intellectually, that Cal was right. Earth had been ready to move in on Paleo from the start, and the actions of the trio had had little bearing on that decision. Only if they had turned up some imperative reason for caution would this rape have been blunted. Carcinogenic vegetation, poisonous atmosphere, super-intelligent enemy aliens – one of these might have done it. But dinosaurs? They were merely a passing oddity, a paleontological phenomenon. Animals.

Animals. Suddenly she realized what it meant, this fire, in terms of life, of feeling. This was not merely the destruction of an anachronism. These were living creatures.

Veg and Cal beside her had field glasses, and both were using them silently. She was occupied with the egg, her naked flesh embracing it, giving it warmth, drawing some subtle comfort from it. She would not be helped, Paleo would not be saved, nothing useful would be accomplished, were she to witness the enlarged optic details of the fall of the reptile kingdom. She needed no glasses. She saw the distant orange flickering, the smoke smudging up, and that was already too much. The camps they had made, the raft, Orn's body ... everything, incinerated at the behest of the omnivore.

She turned about, glancing at Charybdis to the south – and saw the smoke there too. They had not overlooked any part of the enclave! Yet she had not seen any agents travelling about to start those devastating blazes.

The water rippled. Things were swimming past, outward, fleeing the heat, though surely there was nowhere to go. Fish, reptiles – and the latter had to come up for air. *Ichthyosaurus* with the monstrous eyes? No, this was a paddler, *Elasmosaurus*. The same, perhaps, that she and Orn had fought. Was that a scar on its neck? Was it blind of one eye?

It passed the ship, hasty, frightened, pitiable.

Fire bathed it. The reptile struggled in the water, burning, dying, and the odour of its scorching flesh was borne to her across the brief distance between them. She did not need to turn to see the agent with the weapon. That would be Tamme, an omnivore with female form. Naturally these butchers would not allow any large swimming reptile to escape, for it might conceivably serve as host for a microscopic manta.

She hugged the egg. How could she sit in judgement on her species? She herself had killed, useless gesture that it turned out to be. She was an omnivore too.

The dream of bliss was cruelly ended. The idyll of Paleo had been revealed as genocidal naïveté. What good was it now to feel sorry for Elas, the one-time enemy plesiosaur? It was less vicious than man.

She had known it before. She had seen this on earth, this savagery.

She held the egg, wondering whether it would not be kinder in the long run to dash it against the deck.

Veg focused the glasses on the fringe of the valley, fascinated in spite of himself. The fire burned everything, even the ground, even the water. The lenses brought every detail within arm's reach.

Amazing, how quickly and uniformly the fires had started, spaced to spread across the entire valley. They must have fired incendiary shells, and must still be firing them, because new centres of flame appeared at intervals, hastening the death march of orange.

He had seen such carnage before. They had burned his own forest, back on Earth, and for the same reason: to get the manta. The omnivore (now he was thinking in manta terms!) was ruthless. He had thought to foil it, here on Paleo, but that never had a chance to work.

He sneaked a glance at Aquilon, keeping the glasses to his face and pointed forward. She stood beside him, wild and beautiful, holding the egg she had saved. A blanket covered it and her shoulders, though the air was warm. Through an open fold he thought he saw—

He snapped back to the glasses. A trick of vision, surely. But, bewilderingly, his eyes suddenly stung, and the glasses seemed to cloud for a moment. He remembered his night with Aquilon, the joy of which had faded so quickly. It was as though he had expected more than a mere woman and was disappointed to have found her, in the dark under a tarp, to be less than ethereal. It seemed to him now that it could have been anyone he embraced then. *Should* have been anyone . . . but her.

He saw now that he wanted a dream Aquilon, not the flesh 'Quilon. And the dream had been sullied. And his friendship with Cal had been demeaned.

The reptiles were charging into the water, trying to escape the fire, but it pursued them. Tricers, Boneheads, Struths and Ankys, drowning simultaneously, inhaling water and flame. With them, he was sure, were many more mammals, too small to show up amid the giants. And birds, and insects.

Veg was not, despite his pretenses, a violent man. But had he had any real opportunity to wipe out this shipload of killers, he would have done so.

He saw a large duckbill, *Para*-something-or-other, smash through the smoke and dive into the sea. For a moment only its bony crest showed above the surface, and it seemed that smoke plumed back even from that. Then the dinosaur came up, reared skyward – and a jet of flame shot from its nostrils. It had taken in some of the chemical, and its lungs were afire. A true dragon for the moment, it perished in utter agony.

And farther out to sea the head of Brach emerged, clear of the fire. But the stupid brute was charging the wrong way again, going towards the conflagration. Back! Back! he mouthed at it, to no avail. Monstrous, it lumbered out of the water, fire coursing off its back outlining neck and tail and pillarlike thighs. The tiny brain tried to make sense of the agony surrounding fifty tons of body, and could not; burning brightly, Brach keeled over like a timbered redwood tree and rolled with four trunks in the air.

For a long time Veg watched the spasmodic twitching of Brach's smoking tail, until at last that smoke seemed to get in his own eyes, and the stench of it in his nose, and he cried.

Cal watched the destruction of the reptile enclave with severe misgiving. It was true that he had foreseen this, even precipitated it, but the cruelty of the denouement was ugly. Certainly the extinction of most major lines of reptiles was inevitable, here, regardless of the actions of man. One could no more halt that natural process than one could turn back the drifting of the continents. But the dinosaurs did have the right to expire in their own time and fashion, rather than at the fleeting convenience of man.

The masses of herbivorous reptiles had thinned, the majority already perished in the flaming ocean. Now the carnivores, unused to fleeing from anything, were coming into sight. *Struthiomimus*, birdlike predator; several young *Tyrannosaurs*; then a real giant—

He refocused the glasses. That was no carnosaur! It was an ornithischian dinosaur, a bipedal herbivore. *Iquanodon*! But of what a size! Sixty feet from nose to tail tip, as scaled on the range measure of the field glasses. Larger than Tyrann fullgrown, and heavier in proportion, for the gut was massive. A total weight of twelve tons, at least. A herbivore *would* be heavier-set, of course; the digestive apparatus had to be more voluminous . . .

If a biped that size – the largest ever to tread the earth – had hidden unsuspected in the valley, what other treasures had been concealed? The lost opportunities for study . . .

Yet it had to be. He had intended to set the manta spores loose before the Earth mission arrived, knowing it *would* arrive. But he had misjudged how *soon*. He had debated with Veg and Aquilon, putting it all on record so that the investigators would know he had intended to summon them. And he *had* so intended – but he had meant them to arrive too late. They would have discovered that Veg and Aquilon, despite their stand, were innocent. That the mantas had travelled with *him* – and apparently acted without his knowledge and against his wishes. Acted to take Paleo for the third kingdom, for the manta. Cal himself would have been gone, presumed dead, for the plan did not tolerate any interrogation of him by agents. Thus the Earth invasion would have been balked, and the other two either deported again or simply left on Paleo, but not punished.

But in his vanity he had delayed, seeking to vindicate his right to make such a decision for a world. And in so doing, he had thrown away his *chance* to make it. And so he had been caught, and had had to play the game the hard way, making it expensive for everyone. Perhaps if he had not suppressed his real thoughts and intentions, had not constructed his elaborate justifications for the sake of verisimilitude—

Yet it changed nothing. The age of reptiles was finished here, whether man came or not. And the battle was for Paleo, not the class of mammals or the class of reptiles, or even the kingdom of animals or fungus.

No, the battle was not even for this world. He could have advised the mantas long before the actual enclave had been discovered. The enclave was nothing, Paleo was nothing – nothing more than the convenient battleground. There would be a million enclaves, a billion Paleos, and trillions, quadrillions, quintillions of *other alternate worlds*. That was what the confirmation of the parallel-worlds system meant. He had known, despite his earlier words to Aquilon, that it could not be the paradox of time travel. Paleo had to be one of an infinite series of parallels, each differing from its neighbour by no more than an atom of matter, a microsecond of time. The two went together, space and time displacing each other in a fixed if unknowable ratio. No alternate world could match Earth *exactly*; no two alternates could jibe precisely, for that would be a paradox of identity. But they could come close, *had* to come close – and Paleo and Earth were close (or had been, prior to the crossover), almost identical physically, almost identical temporally – even though to man's viewpoint sixty-five million years was not close, and an intelligent flightless bird was not close. Such distinctions were trivial, compared to those between potential other alternates.

Perspective. If Aquilon liked Orn, she could find millions like him, in those quintillion other frames of reality. And millions of other Aquilons *were* finding those Orns.

Yes, it was vast. A sextillion worlds, each complete in every detail down to the atomic level. A septillion worlds, octillion, nonillion decillion – there were not numbers in the mind of man to compass the larger reality. Infinity trailing behind Earth, ranging back to the age of reptiles, the age of amphibians, the age of fishes, the age of invertebrates – all the way back to the primeval formation. Millions of contemporary Earths discovering millions of Paleos, raping them . . .

Sooner or later those parallel crossings would intersect, and Earth would meet Earth with an insufficient spacing between them. A decade perhaps, or a minute – and there would be unique war.

Better that this Earth ravish this Paleo, delayed by the manta. Better that the lesson be learned that way, now. Co-existence had to be learned, and the very hardest coexistence was with oneself. Earth might get along with an alien world, but not with another Earth. The rivalry would be too immediate, too specific. Without bloody experience of the Earth-Paleo nature, the later and major confrontation would be disastrous. As the three-year-old might fight with the two-year-old for a favoured toy, and gradually learn to interact more reasonably, so Earth would fight with Paleo.

But it remained hard to abide, the brutality of this first meeting. If only there were some way to come at maturity (individual, species, world) without passing through immaturity . . .

Memory. It began far, far back in the half-light, wetter and warmer than much of what followed. He floated in a nutrient medium and absorbed what he needed through his spongy exterior. He reached for the light, a hundred million years later, needing it . . . but brushed against the enclosing shell and was restrained. He had to wait, to adapt, to grow.

There was warmth, but also cold. He moved restlessly, trying to achieve comfort, to get all of his suspended body into the warm section of his environment. And he remembered that too: somewhere a billion years ago he had struggled between freezing darkness and burning light, and satisfied his compelling hunger by growing into an absorbtive cup, a cylinder, a blob with an internal gut, by extruding fins and flukes and swimming erratically after game. He formed eyes, and gills, and a skeleton, and teeth, and lungs, and legs.

Ornet remembered.

Postscript

CALVIN POTTER

The Cretaceous enclave of a world otherwise representative of the Paleocene epoch of Earth captures one of the more remarkable episodes in the history of our planet. For more than two hundred million years the reptiles dominated land, air, and the surface of the sea; then abruptly all but a few forms vanished, vacating the world for the primitive mammals and birds.

Quite a number of theories have been advanced over the years to account for this 'time of great dying' but none have been completely satisfactory. It has been suggested for example that 'racial senescence' was responsible: the notion that species, like individuals, gradually age and die. No evidence supports this, and it fails to explain the survival and evident vigour of reptiles such as the turtles and crocodiles, or the much longer tenure of creatures like the horseshoe crab. Another theory was pandemic illness: perhaps a plague wiped out most reptiles without affecting mammals or birds or amphibians. Apart from the fact that disease simply does not work this way – it can decimate, but seldom exterminate, a widespread and varied population – the gradual diminution of numbers of species in the late Cretaceous argues against this. Why should it attack one species at a time, then later strike many others simultaneously? Various types of catastrophes have also been proposed – solar flare, worldwide flood, etc. – but again, the selectivity of such an occurrence is not explained, and no record of it is found in relevant sedimentary deposits. The rocks show an orderly continuity from Cretaceous to Tertiary, wherein the great reptiles disappear and, later, the small mammals appear. The changeover could not have been violent.

More recent theories have been more sophisticated. Did world temperature become too cool for most reptiles, so that they gradually became torpid and unable to forage effectively? This would account for the survival of the warm-bodied mammals and birds. But a substantial cooling would have been necessary, and there was none at the time, as illustrated by plant life. Could the opposite have happened: a devastating heat wave? Again, the record denies this.

Radiation? A science-fiction writer suggested that fluctuations in Earth's magnetic field should periodically permit the planet to be bathed in increased radiation from external sources, increasing the mutation rate of animals disastrously. If a magnetic lapse occurred when radiation from a nearby supernova struck, there could indeed be biological havoc. But why only among the reptiles and certain sea creatures? Radiation is one of the least selective forces.

There was a radical change in vegetation during the Cretaceous period. The angiosperms – flowering plants – suddenly became dominant. Did the herbivorous dinosaurs find the new vegetation, particularly the grasses, too tough to chew and digest? Another science-fiction writer thought so. But this plant revolution came before the extinction of the dinosaurs, and many of the hugest reptiles flourished for millions of years amid the flowers. They were able to adapt, and the dental equipment of *Triceratops*, for example, shames anything developed since short of a lumbermill.

Could the mammals have competed so strongly with the reptiles as to exterminate them? Direct physical oppression seems an absurdity, for the dinosaurs held the mammals in check quite readily for a hundred million years. One has only to visualize a pack of mice attempting to bring down *Tyrannosaurus*. Mammals might, however, have eaten reptile eggs – but again, it is strange they would wait so long, then be so completely effective. The swimming reptile *Ichthyosaurus* gave live birth, so should have survived. And why did the land-laid eggs of the turtle and crocodile escape?

No – to comprehend the decline of the great reptiles, one must first grasp the geologic cycle of which they were a part. No form of life exists in isolation, and evolution and extinction is never haphazard. Definite conditions promoted the ascendence of the reptile orders while suppressing the amphibians and mammals. The later reversal of these conditions demoted the reptiles in favour of the mammals and birds. The dinosaurs were doomed to transience by their very nature.

The surface of the Earth has always been in motion. One facet of this is termed 'continental drift'. The continents owe not only their positions but their very substance to the convective currents of Earth's mantle. This turbulence brought up the slag and guided it into floating masses that accumulated considerably. Though normally separate, at one point several came together to form the segments of the supercontinent, Laurasia/Gondwanaland.

Such a situation has occurred more than once in the past. It is marked by a particular complex of phenomena: subsidence of mountains, the intrusion of large, shallow bays or inland seas, diminution of tremors and volcanic activity, and extraordinarily even climate. In sum: a very quiet, conducive environment for life.

In such case, the competitive advantages of amphibianism or internal temperature control are academic. When the temperature of land, water, and atmosphere at sea level varies only from 10° F. to 20° F., day and night, season to season, century to century, warm-bloodedness is a complication irrelevant to survival. Indeed, it may be moderately detrimental, since it requires a higher rate of metabolism and therefore makes food intake more critical. The mammals perfected this control, involving the development of a hairy covering (to retain body heat), compact torso (same), sweating mechanism (to cool that compact furry body when necessary), improved teeth, limbs, and posture (to hunt and feed more effectively, to meet the demands of increased appetite), live birth (because infant exposure would be fatal), and sophisticated internal regulatory mechanisms. But while the mammals struggled through the innumerable false starts and the tens of millions of years necessary to accomplish all this, the reptiles were simply growing large and savage. The birds undertook a similar program, and were similarly overshadowed by their flying reptile cousins.

Thus developed the age of reptiles, extending from the Permian period through the Triassic, Jurassic, and Cretaceous: two hundred twenty million years. The reptiles were not as complicated as the birds and mammals, but they dominated the world-continent.

But eventually this tremendous land mass began to break up, as the convection currents formed a new pattern. North to south, east to west, the continent was sundered. The Americas were shoved away from Europe and Africa; Antarctica broke from both, and from Australia. A crack in the land widened into a chasm, to a strait, to a channel, to a bay, and finally to a sea: the Atlantic Ocean. This was no overnight occurrence; it took millions of years. Though there were many severe tremors associated with the upthrusting of matter through this rift and the other rifts of the world, they posed no immediate threat to life on land. The severance of the Americas became complete just before the end of the Cretaceous; the other continents separated at other times, but geologically the fragmenting was rapid.

The consequences of this breakup were multiple. The ocean floor was re-sculptured, disturbing ancient breeding and foraging grounds. Enormous quantities of continental debris were dumped into the oceans, for a time affecting the chemical properties of the water. Volcanism was restimulated, affecting the atmosphere. And the motion of the fragments brought about stresses leading to new orogeny: tremendous mountain ranges like the Rockies and Andes, that remade weather patterns and dehydrated inland plains. The physical restructuring of the world inevitably brought about a shift in climate, and this in turn affected life.

The plants reacted massively. Forms that had been minor suddenly had a competitive advantage: the angiosperms, or flowering plants, that did not leave their reproduction to chance. The increased winds and mountains and oceans and deserts worked against random fertilization. The older gymnosperms did not become extinct, but assumed a minority role in the new ecology.

This change in vegetation necessarily affected the animals. The arthropods – chiefly the insects – radiated astonishingly because of the offerings of the flowers, and the spiders followed them. The insectivores – mainly mammalian and avian, together with the reptilian lizards and amphibian frogs – multiplied in response, for this food supply seemed inexhaustible.

The large reptiles were only indirectly affected. They were not insectivores, and even the flying ones were adapted to prey on fish, not flies. Reptile herbivores were capable of adjusting to the new foliage, or surviving in reduced numbers on the less plentiful old-style plants. The variety, but not the vigour, of their species declined, while the carnosaurs continued much as before. But their young began to be crowded by the burgeoning other life. Full-grown mammals and birds hunting in packs or flocks, began to deviate from their normal diet and prey on newly hatched reptiles, and so added a factor to the ecological balance. This was an annoyance rather than a calamity, for even new-hatched reptiles were more than a match for most other species, but it presaged the new order.

The revised geography struck far more specifically. The ponderous ornithischians could not thrive in steep mountains or dry deserts or icy wastes, and were restricted by the violence of the landscape. As these untoward conditions developed, they migrated from large sections of the new continents, and the carnosaurs of course accompanied them. The disappearance of the vast continental seas and swamps severely limited the range of the massive sauropods and the paddlers of the shallows. Unkind wind patterns ravaged the pteradactyls. But many suitable places remained, and the net effect of the change was to concentrate the reptile orders in smaller sections of the world and reduce their meanderings, not to bring them anywhere near extinction.

The climate was another matter. The overall temperature changed only slightly, becoming cooler. This by itself was unimportant. What counted was not the average but the range. The so-called temperate climate developed: actually about as intemperate as the world has ever known. The even seasons shifted to hot summers and cold winters. An individual summer's day might range from 50° F. low to 100° F. high. A winter's day could begin at that low and drop fifty degrees. The reptile biology simply was not equipped to handle such extremes. A heat wave in summer could wipe out enormous numbers; a prolonged freeze in winter did the same. The warm-bodied creatures, in contrast, were ready, and only a fraction of their number failed to adapt. This, more than anything else, drove the reptiles as a group to the tropics, and reduced their territory drastically.

And here the most direct aspect of the continental breakup came into play. For the individual land masses were not contiguous. They were now isolated by deep water. *The reptiles could not migrate far enough.* North America, for example, drifted too far north to have a tropical zone, and was completely separated from South America for some time. Stranded, the reptiles were subject to the full ravages of geography and climate, and they expired. Some few survived for a time in local enclaves, but such existence was tenuous. These extremely confined areas were subject to volcanism and recurring tremors and drastic alteration by shifts in the prevailing winds or drainage. Inevitably the reptiles there were destroyed, whether in a few hundred years or a few million.

The dinosaurs could have survived all the other changes and met the challenge from other classes of vertebrates – had they been able to travel freely over the world, for there was always suitable pasture somewhere. But the fragmentation of the original land mass restricted them at the very moment, geologically, that they could least afford it. Far from being coincidence, this was inevitable. The age of reptiles on land was finished.

The sea reptiles had their own problems. Those tied to the shallows who laid their eggs on land, such as *Elasmosaurus*, expired with the others, for the shallows were gone. Those fully adapted to deep water, such as *Ichthyosaurus*, suffered severe competition by flourishing sharks and, more deviously, by restriction of their diet. For an earlier revolution had occurred in the water: the teleosts, the so-called bony fishes, had appeared. These had stronger skeletons than did the earlier types, and possessed an air bladder modified from a one-time lung that enabled them to match the density of the surrounding water and float at a given level without muscular effort. For the first time, vertebrates were able to compete specifically with the invertebrate ammonites, who for hundreds of millions of years had possessed this controlled flotation ability and thrived. The fish, however, were superior swimmers. This did not eliminate the ammonites, but it did restrict them. When the continental breakup ravaged the oceanic geography and chemistry, the ammonites lost out. Those swimming reptiles who preyed exclusively on ammonites followed them into oblivion.

Thus, medium by medium and type by type, the life of the world was transformed by the breakup of the master continent. It was not that the birds drove out the flying reptiles, or that the teleosts and sharks drove out the ammonites and certain corals and swimming reptiles, or that the angiosperms drove out the gymnosperms, and certainly the mammals did not drive out the land reptiles. But the conditions of each habitat changed significantly, and shifted the balance to favor new species. Those forms of life that were ready for harsh extremes of geography and climate and chemistry prospered; those that were not did not.

But what of the few surviving reptiles? These were the ones who *were* equipped to endure the new regime. The crocodiles and turtles were able to forage either on land or in the deep sea, so neither the sharks nor severe temperature extremes could eliminate them entirely. They were able to migrate from an unkind continent to a kind one, and did so, and have lasted until the present. The duckbills might have joined them, as they were strong swimmers and fast runners on land – but they had to feed on land, so could not remain in the water for weeks at a time. The snakes and lizards were small enough, and suitably shaped, to reside on and in the ground and trees; for them the arthropods and small mammals represented an impoved diet, and deep burrows shielded them from winter's cold and summer's heat. They survived largely because they were small enough to utilize such shelter; the dinosaurs' specialization in large size worked against them fatally.

Have there been other extinctions as the continents drifted into new configurations? Certainly, many of them, though few as impressive as this one. There will surely be more. When the land moves, life must follow. The real mystery is not the great dying, but why this natural course remained a mystery for so long . . .

Part Three

$\overline{\text{OX}}$

Chapter One

TRIO

· · ·

It had a shiny black finish, solid caterpillar treads, a whirling blade – and it was fast. It was seemingly a machine – but hardly the servant of man.

Veg fired his blaster at it. The project charge should have heated the metal explosively and blown a chunk out of it. But the polished hide only gave off sparks and glowed momentarily. The thing spun about with dismaying mobility and came at him again, the vicious blade leading.

Veg bounded backward, grabbed the long crowbar, and jammed it end first into the whirring blade. 'Try a mouthful of *that!*' he said, shielding his eyes from the anticipated fragmentation.

The iron pole bucked in his hands as the blade connected. More sparks flew. The blade lopped off sections, two inches at a time: CHOP CHOP CHOP CHOP! Six feet became five, then four, as the machine consumed the metal.

At that point Veg realized he was in a fight for his life. He had come across the machine chewing up the stacked supplies as he emerged from transfer and thought it was an armoured animal or a remote-controlled device. It was more than either; it had an alarming aura of sentience.

He tried the rifle. The flash pan heated as he activated it; steam filled the firing chamber. Bullets whistled out in a rapid stream, for the steam rifle was smoother and more efficient than the explosive-powder variety. They bounced off the machine and ricocheted off the boulders on either side. He put at least one bullet directly in its eye-lens, but even this did no apparent harm.

Still, the contraption had halted its advance. *Something* must be hurting it!

The rifle ran out of bullets. Veg grabbed an explosive shell and slammed it into firing position as the machine moved forward again. He aimed at the treads and let fly.

Sand billowed out, for an instant obscuring the target. The machine wallowed – but a moment later it climbed out of the cavity formed by the explosion and emerged undamaged.

'You're a tough one!' Veg said admiringly. He was a man of barely dominant peace; he loved a good fight when he could justify it. He hurled the rifle at the enemy.

The weapon flew apart as the whirling blade swung to intercept it. One large section bounced away to the side. The machine turned to chase after it, chopping the piece up where it had fallen and scooping it into a netherhopper. It did not, he saw now, have parallel treads, but a single broad line of cleats, individually retractable like the claws of a cat. The hopper opened just before this wheel/foot – and closed tightly when finished, like a mouth. Sophisticated ...

Veg grinned for a moment. Wonderful technology, but the stupid thing didn't know the rifle was no longer dangerous! It had fought the weapon instead of the man.

Then he sobered. The machine wasn't *fighting* the rifle, it was *consuming* it! It ate metal.

He hadn't been battling this thing. He had been feeding it. No wonder it had halted; as long as he was willing to serve good metal by hand, why should the machine exert itself further?

This revelation didn't help much, however. It suggested that the machine was distressingly smart, not dumb. The human party would need that metal to survive. He couldn't let a ravenous machine gobble it all down.

Still, that gave him an idea. If metal fed it, would food hurt it?

Veg tore open a pack of food staples. Here were breadstuff and vegetables and – he paused with distaste as his hand rummaged – meat.

Then he brightened. What better use for it? He hauled out a plastic-wrapped steak and hurled it at the machine, which had just finished the rifle, burped, and turned back toward the man. The blade rose to catch the package; bits of flesh, bone, and plastic splayed into the air.

This time he observed the scoop-like orifice, the hopper, in action behind the blade. The different processes of the machine were well coordinated. The bulk of the freshly sliced meat and bone funneled directly into this mouth, just as the metal had. Veg held his breath, another steak in hand. Would the machine get sudden indigestion?

No such luck. A spout opened, and clear liquid dribbled out onto the ground: the surplus juices of the meat, apparently unneeded by the thing's metabolism. The machine assimilated the organic material as readily as it had the inorganic. And came on for more.

Would liquid short it out? External liquid, not digestive fluid. Veg found a bottle of water and heaved a full gallon at the fan. The machine was drenched.

First it shook; then it glowed all over. Death agonies for this non-living creature? No – it was merely drying itself off efficiently by a combination of vibration and heat. It had not been incapacitated.

'Takes more brains than I got to handle this metal baby,' Veg muttered as he danced nimbly aside. It was hardly the occasion for introspection, but Veg had high respect for the intelligence of his friend Cal and wished he were here at this moment. Cal could have looked at the oncoming machine and made one obvious suggestion, and the thing would be finished.

The two men had met years before, in space, introduced as a prank by idle crewmen. Veg was a vegetarian and, after too much ribbing, somewhat militant about it. Since he was also an extremely powerful man, the sniggers had soon abated. Rabbit food did not necessarily make rabbits.

Until word circulated of a man who was a pure carnivore, eating nothing but meat – man flesh, at that! – and who thought vegetarians were stupid. Veg had not reacted overtly, but his muscles had bulged under his shirt tensely.

Tiny, weak Calvin Potter – about as inoffensive as it was possible to be. Yet it was technically true: Owing to a savage episode in his past, he had been rendered unable to consume any food except human blood. And he was a genius, compared to whom all other people, including vegetarians, *were* stupid.

If Veg had suffered ridicule, it was minor compared to what Cal endured. Veg did not like being made a patsy for the torment of another man. He took the unhappy little Cal under his bone-crushing wing, and very shortly no one thought anything about him was even faintly humorous.

Yet as it turned out, Cal was the stronger man, able because of his intellect to tackle even a predator dinosaur alone and barehanded – and to survive. He had actually done it.

There was no way to summon Cal. Veg had beamed through to this alternate world first, to set things up for his companions and scout for any dangers. Aquilon was to follow in an hour, Cal in another hour, along with the mantas. All nice and neat.

Only about two hundred and fifty pounds could be transferred at one time, and the equipment had to cool off after each use. That was why things had to be spaced out. Or so the agents claimed. Veg didn't believe the male-agent, Taler; the female, Tamme, was obviously no more trustworthy, but on a woman it didn't really matter.

He retreated again. Well, he had found danger, all right! Rather, it had found him. An animate buzz saw with an omnivorous appetite. If he didn't figure out something pretty soon, it would eat him *and* the supplies and lie in wait for Aquilon . . .

That goaded him to fury. The thought of the lovely woman being consumed by the machine . . .

Veg had always been able to take or leave women, and because he was large, muscular, and handsome, he had taken a number. Until Aquilon, the girl who never smiled, came into his life. She was an artist, whose paintings were almost as beautiful as she. Though she was competent and independent, she was also deep-down *nice*. Veg had not known what real love was, but to know Aquilon was indeed to love her, though she had never solicited it. Part of that love now was to give her up without resentment; *that* was the essence she had taught him simply by being what she was. She might have split the Veg-Cal friendship apart – but she needed them both as much as they needed her. So they had become three friends, closer than before, with no competition or jealousy between them. Finally she was able to smile . . .

'I'm going to get you out of here if it kills me!' Veg cried. He hoisted the bag of food to his shoulder and began running. 'Come, doggie!' he called, flipping back a package of raisins. 'Soup's on – if you can catch it!'

The machine had been sampling the fabric of the tent-assembly. It angled its blade to catch the raisins. Evidently it liked them better – more iron? – because it followed after Veg.

He led it across the desert, away from the supplies. His tactic was working – but what would happen when he ran out of food?

Aquilon stood chagrined at the carnage. The supplies had been ravaged, bits of meat and metal were scattered across the sand, and Veg was nowhere in sight. What had happened?

She cradled the egg in her arms, keeping it warm. It was a large egg, like a small football, nine inches long. It was all that remained of two fine birds she had known and loved. They had died, protecting her and it. There was no way to repay them except to vindicate their trust and preserve the egg until it hatched.

She felt a sudden urge to paint. She always painted when upset; it calmed her marvellously. She had painted the phenomenal fungus landscape of Planet Nacre, where she and the two men had had their first great adventure together. She had painted the savage omnivore of that world – and seen in it the mere reflection of the worst omnivore of all, man himself. She had painted dinosaurs – but how could she paint the ravening monsters that were the souls of human beings, herself included?

She could try; it might work this time. To make visible the ego of the human omnivore ... but to do that she would have to put down the egg ...

Then she saw the tracks. Veg's footprints led away from the camp, partly obscured by something he must have been dragging. Had he gone exploring? He should have stayed nearby, securing the camp against possible dangers, not gallivanting about the countryside. Not that there was much countryside to see; this was about as gaunt a locale as she cared to endure. Sand and boulders ...

But what would account for the destruction of supplies? Someone or something had vandalised them, and she knew Veg would not have done that. The cuts were peculiar, almost like the marks of a rampant powersaw. Strange, strange.

She was worried now. If something had attacked, Veg would have fought. That was the omnivore in him despite his vegetarianism. That could account for the mess. If he had won, why wasn't he here? If he had lost, why were his footprints leading away? Veg was stubborn; he would have died fighting. He would never have run.

She had thought she loved Veg at one time. Physically, sexually. She had tried to be a vegetarian like him. But somehow it hadn't worked out. She still cared for him deeply, however, and his unexplained absence troubled her.

She contemplated the prints. Could he have lost – and been taken captive? If someone held a gun on him, even Veg would not have been so foolish as to resist. Yet where were the prints of his captor? There were only the treadlike marks of whatever he had been hauling...

No, she still didn't have it. First, there would be no one here to hold a gun or any other weapon on Veg. This was an uninhabited wilderness desert on an unexplored alternate world. They were the first human beings to set foot on it. Second, the prints diverged in places, sometimes being separated by several yards. If Veg had been dragging or hauling anything, the marks would have been near his own prints, always.

She stooped to examine the other marks more carefully, cradling the big egg in one arm. She touched the flattened sand with one finger. Substantial weight had been here – a ton or more, considering the breadth of the track and the depression of the sand. Like tyre marks but wider, and there was only one line instead of parallel lines. What sort of vehicle had made that? Not a human artifact...

The obvious thing to do was to follow the tracks and find out. But she wasn't supposed to leave the campsite until Cal and the mantas were through the aperture, and she didn't want to walk into the clutches – treads? – of whatever had followed Veg. There was no real cover here apart from the boulders; as soon as she got close enough to see it, *it* would see her. And if it had made Veg move out, there was no way she could fight it. Veg was an extraordinarily able man physically.

So she would have to stay here, keeping a sharp lookout, and clean up the mess. If she were lucky, nothing would happen until Cal arrived. If she were luckier, Veg would return unharmed.

She turned, letting the bright sunlight fall on the egg, warming it. Ornet was inside that egg, the embryo of a bird that possessed a kind of racial memory: perhaps a better tool for survival than man's intelligence. If only the right habitat could be found. And if only a mate for the bird could be found, too. Maybe one could be fetched from Paleo, the first alternate-Earth, and the pair would start a dynasty here in some desert oasis, and she could watch the community prosper . . .

Desert oasis . . . this was Earth, or an alternate of it; the landscape matched some place and some time on the world she knew. Where – on Earth – was this? Cal was the only one who could figure that out.

The shadow of a human being fell across the sand before her, jolting her out of her reverie. Aquilon froze before she looked up; it was too soon for Cal to appear, and Veg could not have come upon her unawares. Who, then? She looked – and gave a little gasp of amazement.

A beautiful blonde girl stood before her, shaped like a siren beneath her flowing hair. Siren in more than one way: She was nude.

The apparition's blue eyes surveyed the scene coolly. Aquilon, functionally attired in denim, felt out of sorts. 'Who are you?' she demanded.

'Pointless to go into all that now,' the nymph said. 'Please give me the egg.'

Aquilon stepped back involuntarily. 'No!'

'You must. You can't preserve it any longer. Not here in the desert with the awful machines. I have found a new Garden of Eden, a paradise for birds; when it hatches there—'

'No one else can—' Aquilon broke off, realizing what her mind had balked at before. 'You're *me!*'

'And you're me, close enough,' the blonde said. 'So you can trust me. You—'

'But you're – you're more—'

The woman's eyes dropped momentarily down to her own bosom, following Aquilon's gaze. 'I bore a child; that's why. I lost mine; you'll keep yours. But you can't keep the egg.'

Aquilon retreated. 'A baby? I—'

'You are in danger. You can save yourself but not the egg. There is little time, and it's too complicated to explain right now. Give it to me.' She reached out.

'No!' Aquilon retreated again, hugging the egg. Her mind was spinning with this inexplicable development. How had her buxom double manifested here? *Could* she trust her – or was it some weird kind of trap? To know that the egg really was safe . . .

'Give it to me!' the blonde cried, diving for her.

Aquilon straightarmed her, but the force of the woman's lunge

403

shoved her back. Her heels caught against a bag of supplies, and she tumbled backward, the blonde on top of her. Both of them screamed.

The egg, caught between them, had been crushed. The large embryo within, released too soon, flopped blindly and died.

Cal looked about. The supplies had been savaged. Veg was gone, and Aquilon was lying on the ground near a mound of sand. He rushed to her.

She was not dead. She was sobbing. She lifted a sand-smudged face to him as he put his hand on her shoulder. In one hand was a fragment of broken shell.

Cal realized that the precious egg had been smashed. She must have fallen while holding it and then had to bury the remains. Hence the tears, the mound of sand.

He felt sharp regret. That egg had meant a lot to her, and therefore to him. He had hoped it could be preserved until it hatched, inconvenient as that process was.

But more important, now: What had this loss done to Aquilon? And where was Veg? Had Veg had something to do with the destruction of the egg? No, impossible!

He let her be. She would have to recover in her own fashion. There was no genuine comfort he could provide; the egg was irrevocably gone. He analysed the tracks instead – and was amazed.

Veg had gone somewhere across the desert and not returned. Aquilon had apparently fought someone – a barefoot person, possibly female, for the prints were small. Those tracks staggered a short way over the sand and then vanished. And some kind of vehicle had come and gone, doing damage to the supplies enroute.

Had the agents sent in other missions? Other people, with power equipment – and bare feet? For what reason? If there were two or more missions, they should have been informed of each other's presence so they could rendezvous. Certainly they should not have raided each other. And, Taler, the agent leader, had had no reason to lie about this.

Still, the rebuilt-human-androids that were the agents were smart, strong, and ruthless in the performance of their assigned missions. Cal had a sober respect for them even when he had to oppose them. One agent of the SU series, Subble, had been assigned to ascertain

404

the truth about the Nacre adventure; he had done so. Three of the TA series had been sent to salvage the alternate-Earth Paleo for human civilization; they had made a devastatingly direct attempt to do that, also, despite all Cal's efforts. As a result, the enclave of dinosaurs had been wiped out, the Orn-bird killed, and the trio of 'normal' people taken prisoner. As though a girl like Aquilon could ever be considered typical, or a man like Veg!

'Hex! Circe!' he snapped, turning to the creatures who were sitting motionless near the aperture, their lambent eyes fastened on him. 'Find Veg. Careful – danger.'

The two mantas leaped into the air, flattening into their speed-form as they moved. They sailed across the desert like two low-flying kites, swift and silent.

Aquilon rose. 'Cal!' she cried despairingly.

He walked towards her, wishing with one part of his mind that she were the kind to fall into a man's arms when she needed comforting. But she was not; very seldom did she break down. She was a tough, realistic girl. As long as she lived, she would function well. That was probably why he loved her; her beauty was secondary.

'What happened?' he asked gently.

'A woman came and broke the egg,' she said. 'And she was me.'

'*You?*' Those bare, feminine prints . . .

'Me. My double. Only more so. I hit her . . .'

Something clicked in his mind. 'The alternate framework!' he exclaimed. 'I should have known!'

'What?' She was so pretty when she was surprised!

'We're dealing in alternates now. There must be an infinite number of alternate-Earths. Once we start crossing those boundaries, we run the risk of meeting ourselves. As you did . . .'

'Oh!' she said, comprehending. 'Then she *was* me. Only she'd had a baby. But why was she here – and where did she go?'

'We can't know yet. Did she say anything?'

'Only that I could survive but not the egg. She wanted to take it to some Eden . . .'

'She must have known your future. Perhaps she was from a slightly more advanced framework. In a year she could have had her baby and lost her egg, so she knew from experience—'

'No – it was her *baby* she lost.' Aquilon shook her head, unsettled.

'She said I would keep mine. But I'm not pregnant!'

'There are other alternates,' he pointed out. 'An infinite number of Aquilons will have had babies, and an infinite number more will be due. She could have mistaken you. She meant well.'

'And I fought her,' Aquilon said. 'I shouldn't have done that ...'

'How could you know? And you had a right to retain your egg no matter what she knew. You fought for it before to save it from dinosaurs.'

'But now neither of us have it. She was crying as she left ...'

'She wanted to save the egg – and instead destroyed it,' Cal said. 'She felt as you would feel.'

Aquilon looked at him, her tear-streaked face still sandy – and lovely. 'Then she is desolate. I should have given it to her.'

'No. Each world must look out for its own. We fought to prevent Earth from despoiling Paleo; we must also fight to prevent other alternates from despoiling *us*. But we must understand that they are very much like us ...'

'Omnivores!' she said bitterly.

'But there is a positive side. Orn's egg has been lost in this alternate – but there must be many alternates where it was saved. In some you kept it; in others the other Aquilon took it. But the chick isn't dead, there.'

'Ornet,' she said. 'Offspring of Orn and Ornette ...'

He smiled. She was coming out of it. 'By any other name ... Now we must find out what happened to Veg.'

Her eyes followed the tracks across the sand. 'Do you think he—?'

'I sent the mantas after him. Somehow they know; they would not have gone if he were dead.'

'Yes, of course,' she murmured.

They cleaned up the supplies somewhat, making packs for each person, just in case. A blaster and a rifle were missing, and one of the long crowbars, suggesting that Veg had taken them. 'But we already know that we face a strange situation,' Cal warned her. 'Conventional weapons may be useless.'

'Machine!' she said suddenly.

Cal looked up inquiringly. 'We have no machines here.'

'My double – she said something about machines, here in the desert. "Awful machines." A danger—'

Cal looked once more at the tread-tracks. 'A machine,' he

murmured thoughtfully. 'Following Veg . . .'

'Oh, let's hurry!' she cried. 'And take weapons!'

They started out warily, following Veg's tracks and those of the mystery vehicle. Cal was ill at ease; if a human being could appear from another alternate, so could heavy equipment. Suppose some kind of tank had been dispatched to hunt down the visitors to this world? They just might have walked into an interalternate war . . .

Aquilon stopped abruptly, rubbing her eyes. 'Cal!' she whispered.

Cal looked. At first he saw nothing; then he became aware of a kind of sparkle in the air ahead. Faint lights were blinking on and off, changing their fairy patterns constantly.

'A firefly swarm?' Aquilon asked. 'Let me paint it.' She was never without her brush and pad, and now, without the egg to hold, she could paint again.

She hesitated. He knew why: Her sudden freedom made her feel guilty. How much better to have given the egg to her double! The woman would have taken care of it every bit as well as Aquilon herself because she *was* Aquilon – wiser for her bitter experience. Or at least, so it would seem – to *this* Aquilon at this moment. He had to divert her thoughts.

'Fireflies? With no plants to feed the insects?' Cal asked, posing what he knew to be a fallacious question. 'We have seen no indigenous life here.'

'There has to be life,' she replied as she quickly sketched. 'Otherwise there would be no breathable atmosphere. Plants give off oxygen.'

'Yes, of course . . .' he agreed, watching the swarm. 'Still, there is something odd here.'

The sparkle-pattern intensified. Now it was like a small galaxy of twinkling stars, the individual lights changing so rapidly that the eye could not fix on them. But Aquilon's trained perception was catching the artistry of it. Color flowed from her automatic brush, brightening the picture. This was the marvellous, creative person he had known, expressing herself through her art.

The flashes were not random; they moved in ripples, like the marquee of an old cinemahouse. These ripples twined and flexed like living things. But not like chains of fireflies.

'Beautiful,' Aquilon breathed. Yes, now her own beauty illuminated her; she was what she perceived.

Suddenly the swarm moved towards them. The lights became bright and sharp. The outline expanded enormously.

'Fascinating,' Cal said, seeing three-dimensional patterns within the cloud, geometric ratios building and rebuilding in dazzling array. This was no random collection of blinkers . . .

Aquilon grabbed his arm. 'It sees us!' she cried in abrupt alarm. 'Run!'

It was already too late. The glowing swarm was upon them.

Chapter Two

$\underline{OX}$

∴∴∴

Survive!

$\overline{OX}$ assimilated the directive, knowing nothing but the need. *How, why, mode,* were absent; there was no rationale. Only the imperative. It was inherent in his being; it made him what he was. It *was* what he was: the need to survive.

He turned his attention to the external.

Disorientation. Distress. Nonsurvival.

$\overline{OX}$ retracted, halving his volume. What had happened?

Survival dictated that he explore despite the pain of the external. $\overline{OX}$ realized that through DISTRESS related to NONSURVIVAL, certain forms of distress might be necessary *to* survival. Judgement was required. He modified his capabilities to accommodate this concept and thereby became more intelligent.

Experiment and intelligence provided a working rationale: He had extended himself too precipitously and thereby thrown his basic organization out of balance.

The lesson: Expansion had to be organized. Four dimensions became far more complex than three, requiring a different *type* of organization.

$\overline{OX}$ extended a fleeting outer feedback shell to explore the limits of his locale. It was not large; he had room to move about but had to contain himself somewhat.

Discomfort. Minor distress but growing. $\overline{OX}$ hovered in place, but the discomfort increased. He moved, and it abated. Why?

The base on which he rested, the network of points, was fading.

409

He was his environment; he occupied many small elements, drawing energy from them, making a sentient pattern of them. This energy was limited; he had to move off and allow it to regenerate periodically. Merely sitting in one spot would exhaust that set of elements: nonsurvival.

The larger OX expanded, the more points he encompassed and the more energy he consumed. By contracting within optimum volume he conserved survival resources. But he could not become too small, for that limited his abilities and led to dysfunction.

OX stabilized. But his minimum functional size was still too large for the territory to sustain indefinitely. He could exist at maximum size briefly or at minimum size longer – but the end was nonsurvival, either way.

Survive! He had to keep searching.

He searched. Unsuccess wasted resources and led to discomfort. Yet even in his distress, there was a special irritant. Certain circuits were not functioning properly. He investigated.

All was in order.

He returned to the larger problem of survival – and the interference resumed persistently.

OX concentrated on the annoyance. Still there was no perceivable dysfunction. It did not manifest when he searched for it, only when he was otherwise occupied.

He set up a spotter circuit, oriented on the troublesome section. He had not known how to do this before the need arose, but this was the way of survival: the necessary, as necessary.

OX returned to his larger quest – and the irritation manifested. This time the spotter was on it. He concentrated, pouncing, as it were, on what he had trapped.

Nothing.

Paradox. The spotter oriented on any malfunction; it was a modified feedback, simple and certain. Yet there was a malfunction – and the spotter had failed.

OX suffered disorientation. Paradox was nonsurvival. It was also annoying as hell.

He disciplined himself, simplifying his circuits. No paradox. If the spotter hadn't caught it, there was no malfunction. But there *was* something. What?

OX concentrated. He refined his perceptions. Gradually he

410

fathomed it. It was not *his* malfunction but an interruption from an external source. Thus the spotter had had no purchase.

Something was obscuring some of his elements. Not obliterating them but damping them down so that he was aware of the loss of energy – peripherally. When he investigated, he shifted off those particular elements, and the effect abated. He could only perceive it through that damping, while his circuits were functioning. Ghostly, it avoided his direct attention, for it was an *effect*, not a *thing*.

Was it an ailment of the elements themselves? If so, his survival would be more limited than originally projected – and he was already in a nonsurvival situation.

OX cast a net of spotters to determine the precise configuration of the damping. Soon he had it: There were actually three centres set close together. A stable, persistent blight. No immediate threat to survival.

Then one of the blight spots moved.

OX fibrillated. *Distress!* How could a blight move, retaining form? Stable or recurring form with movement was an attribute of sentience, of pattern. Blight was the *lack* of pattern.

Modification. Perhaps blight could slide somewhat, forced over by some unknown compulsion. Nonsentient. All blight spots would suffer the same effect.

Another spot moved – the opposite way. Then both moved together – and apart.

Disorientation.

Chapter Three

TAMME

∴

Tamme emerged from the aperture, alert and wary. She had not told the three explorers that she was coming along and did not expect them to be pleased. But after the disaster on the dinosaur world, Paleo, the agents were taking few chances. These people were not to be trusted; left alone, they were too apt to concoct some other way to betray the interests of Earth.

The camp was deserted. Tamme saw at a glance that weapons and food had been removed: more than would normally have been used in the three hours since the first person had been sent through. They were up to something already!

But it was strange. Too many footprints led away. Veg, Cal, Aquilon – and a barefoot person? Plus something on a caterpillar tread. And the two mantas.

Caterpillar? Hardly standard equipment. Where had they gotten it?

Answer: There was nowhere they could have gotten it. Tamme herself had put through all the supplies in advance, checking and rechecking a detailed roster. This was the first human penetration to this new world. Sensors had reported breathable air, plant life, amphibious animals, fish – all far removed from this desert where the aperture actually debouched but certainly part of this alternate. Also advanced machines. That was what made immediate exploration imperative.

Machines did not evolve on their own. Something had to build them. Something more advanced than the machines themselves.

Ergo, there was on this world something more than the sensors had indicated. Either an advanced human culture – or an alien one. Either way, a potential threat to Earth.

But windows to new worlds were hard to come by. The first such breakthrough had come only a few months ago, and Mother Earth naturally had not wanted to risk valuable personnel by sending them through a one-way aperture. So volunteers had been used – three space explorers who had gotten in trouble with the authorities and had therefore been amenable to persuasion. Expendables.

An unusual trio, actually. Vachel Smith: a huge vegetarian nicknamed Veg. Deborah Hunt, called Aquilon: named after the cold north wind because, it seemed, she seldom smiled. And Calvin Potter, a small, physically weak man with a fascinatingly complex mind. The three had been lost on a planet called Nacre – theoretically it glowed in space like a pearl because of its perpetual cloud cover – and had befriended the dominant life-form there: an animate fungus with extraordinary talents. The manta.

It had been a mistake to loose this group on the world beyond the aperture, and soon the authorities had recognized that. But by that time the trio, instead of perishing as expected, had penetrated to the nearest continent and gotten involved with the local fauna – they had a talent for that! – which turned out to be reptilian. In fact, dinosaurian. Extraction had been awkward.

Three agents of the TA series had accomplished it, however: Taner (now deceased), Taler, and Tamme herself. But when they made ready to return to Earth with the prisoners, another complication had developed. Their portable return-aperture generator had opened not on Earth but on a third world.

They had known there was risk involved – of exactly this kind. The apertures were experimental and erratic. Though Paleo was the only alternate to be reached so far from Earth, despite thousands of trials, one trial on Paleo had produced this unexpected and awkward pay-off. Perhaps it was a better initiation point.

The original Earth/Paleo aperture remained. It had been broadened so that massive supplies could be transferred, and the three agents had built their own prefabricated ship with which to pursue the fugitives. A fourth agent had remained to guard the original aperture, which happened to be under the ocean near a Pacific islet a thousand miles from the western coast of Paleocene America.

It had seemed easier to transfer back directly from this spot – on the continent – rather than make a tedious trip back with the prisoners. Location seemed to make little difference to the apertures; they could start at any point and terminate anywhere – usually in the vacuum of interplanetary space. They had radioed Taol for approval, and he had contacted the Earth authorities for approval. If the supplementary aperture were successful, it would greatly facilitate the exploitation of Paleo.

Then, with the surprise development, new orders: check it out with sensors and explore it personally if necessary – but HOLD THAT CONNECTION! There was no certainty they could ever locate that world again, given the freakish nature of apertures, so it had to be held open now. Earth, enormously overpopulated, its natural resources approaching exhaustion, needed a viable alternative to expensive commerce by space travel. This could be it. More personnel would be funneled through the main aperture in due course; meanwhile, use their present resources in case the connection became tenuous.

Thus, reprieve for the prisoners. They were free – to engage in another dangerous exploration. They had not, however, been told about the machines. This time an agent would accompany them. Just to keep them out of mischief.

Agents had been developed to handle this sort of emergency. An agent was not a person; he was an android on a human chassis, moulded to precise specifications. Tamme had no past beyond her briefing for this mission; all she knew was the material in the common pool of information shared by every agent of the TA type. And that overlapped considerably with the pool of SU before her series and TE after it. But it was a good pool, and all agents were superhuman both physically and mentally. She could handle this trio of humans.

She paused in her reflection. Better qualify that. She could handle them physically because her strength, reflexes, and training were considerably superior to theirs. And emotionally, because though she had feelings, they were fully disciplined. But the woman Aquilon had her points, and the man Calvin had a freakish mind that had already demonstrated its ability to fence successfully with the mind and perception of an agent. Random variation in the 'normal' population had produced an abnormal intelligence. Too bad the authorities hadn't recognized it in time.

Tamme grimaced. The truth, known to every agent but never voiced, was that the authorities were not overly smart. If ever a class of agents were programmed to tackle the problems of Earth directly, they would begin by putting the incompetents out of power. What a waste, to serve a stupid master!

Meanwhile, the immediate: Was Cal behind this odd disappearance of the trio? Had he anticipated her presence or that of Taler – she had matched Taler, scissors/paper/rock, for the honour and lost – and arranged some kind of trap? Possible but improbable; there had been no hint of that in his mind before he was transferred. He *could* have done such a thing, but probably *hadn't*.

All of which meant that the obvious surmise was the most likely one. She had forced herself to run through the alternatives first as a matter of caution. The three explorers must already have encountered one of the advanced machines of this world, and it had taken them – somewhere.

Which was one reason they had not been told in advance that Tamme was coming along. What they did not know, they could not betray. In case the machines turned out to be intelligent enough to make an interrogation. An agent had to consider every ramification.

So the expendables had been expended. That accounted for everything except the extra set of prints. The bare feet walked into the sand and stopped as though the person had been lifted away at that point. But by what? A flying machine?

She checked the origin of the bare prints. The same: They appeared in the sand from nowhere. Odd indeed. Unless someone had intentionally made those prints by walking backwards, then forwards in his/her own tracks to make them seem like the mystery they were ...

Tamme carried their spare aperture projector so that she could return to Taler on Paleo regardless of the firmness of the existing connection. Assuming hers did not open onto a fourth alternate-world! For a moment she was tempted to go back immediately. This situation was eerie. Which was ridiculous; she was not afraid of isolation or death.

All right: She had a machine to deal with. A formidable one if it had so neatly managed to kill or capture all three humans and their mantas already. Best to tackle it promptly. And with extreme

415

caution. Too bad she couldn't radio Taler across the aperture!

First she made a survey of the general premises. She ran, loping over the sand at about twenty miles an hour, watching, listening. There was nothing lurking nearby. She completed her circle and set out after the massed trail of footprints, machine tread, and manta marks. Veg and Aquilon, apparently together. A curious parade!

But soon the tracks diverged. Veg, tread, and mantas continued forward, but Cal and Aquilon turned aside – and stopped. Their prints disappeared just as the bare ones had. Two more people were gone inexplicably.

Another flying machine? Then why hadn't the others taken note? If they all were captive, why hadn't all of them walked all the way to wherever they were being taken? More mystery – and she was not enchanted by it. Her working hypothesis was taking a beating.

Tamme resumed the trail after making another scouting circle. She had good perceptions; she would have known if anything were hiding near. Nothing was.

Several miles farther on, the mantas diverged. One went to the left, the other to the right. An encircling manoeuvre? Encircling what if they were already captive?

Now she had to make a choice: Follow one of the mantas, or follow the main trail. Easy decision: Fast as she was, she could not face a manta. The fungoids could do a hundred miles an hour over sand or water. Veg she could overtake as long as he were afoot.

But the machine was an unknown antagonist. She did not care to risk an ambush by such a device. So she followed the trail by eye, moving some distance to the side, alert for whatever she might find.

Veg's tracks were not forthright. Now they turned right, now left, and now they faced backwards – but the scuffing of his heels showed he was walking backwards, not changing the direction of his motion. Facing the machine evidently but staying clear of it. Why? Overall, the trail curved slowly left as though the two were travelling in a great circle back to the base camp. Not exactly the pattern of captivity.

A manta appeared, moving swiftly over the sand. It was beautiful in its seeming flight; she had great admiration for its mechanical efficiency and artistry. Tamme was armed but held her fire; these creatures were phenomenally apt at dodging. So it was unlikely she could score on it from any distance, and she did not want to antagonize it unnecessarily.

It came to rest before her, coalescing into a dark blob, the huge single eye glowing. The mantas, she knew, projected an all-purpose beam from that eye; they both saw and communicated by means of it. Was it trying to tell her something?

'Which one are you?' she inquired experimentally. They could actually see the compressions and rarefactions of the air that made sound; thus, they could in effect hear, though they had no auditory equipment. All their major senses were tied into one – but what a sense that one was!

The thing jumped up, flattened into its travelling form, and cracked its tail like a whip. Six snaps.

'Hex,' she said. 'Veg's friend. Do you know where he is?'

One snap, meaning YES.

Communication was not difficult, after all. Soon she had ascertained that Veg was in good health and that the manta would conduct her to him.

Veg was resting as she came up. He was leaning against a boulder and chewing on a hunk of dark bread. 'Where's the machine?' Tamme asked, as though this were routine.

'It finally got full and lost its appetite,' he said. 'So it left. Lucky for me; I was almost out of food.'

'You were *feeding* it?'

'It was bound to eat. Better to feed it what we could spare than let it take its own choice. Like vital supplies – or people. The thing eats meat as well as metal! But when I started feeding it rocks and sand, it quit. Not too smart.'

So the machine had been attacking him – and he had foiled it at last by throwing what the desert offered. Veg might not be a genius, but he had good common sense!

Veg considered her more carefully. 'What the hell are *you* doing here?'

'We don't trust you.'

'It figures.' He wasn't even very surprised; she could read his honest minor responses in the slight tension of his muscles, the perspiration of his body, and the rate of breathing. In fact he was intrigued, for he found her sexually appealing.

Tamme was used to that in normals. She *was* sexually appealing; she had been designed to be that way. Usually she ignored her effect

417

on men; sometimes she used it. It depended on the situation. If sex could accomplish a mission more readily than another approach, why not?

But at the moment her only mission was to keep an eye on the activities of these people. Veg was the simplest of the lot; his motives were forthright, and it was not his nature to lie. She could relax.

'Have some bread,' Veg said, offering her a torn chunk.

'Thank you.' It was good bread; the agents' supplies were always nutritious because their bodies required proper maintenance for best efficiency. She bit down, severing the tough crust with teeth that could as easily cut through the flesh and bone of an antagonist.

'You know, I met one of you agents,' Veg said. 'Name of Subble. You know him?'

'Yes and no. I am familiar with the SU class of agent but never met that particular unit.'

'Unit?'

'All agents of a type are interchangeable. You would have had the same experience with any SU, and it would have been very similar with an SO, TA, or TE.'

His body tensed in quick anger. Amused, Tamme read the signs. Normals found the concept of human interchangeability repulsive; they always wanted to believe that every person was unique, even those designed to be *un*-unique. If only they knew; the camaraderie of identity was the major strength of all agents. Tamme never wanted to give up any of her programmed attributes – unless every agent in her class gave them up. She only felt at ease with her own kind, and even other series of agents made her feel slightly uncomfortable.

'Decent sort of a fellow, in his way. I guess he reported all about what we said.'

'No. Subble died without making a report.'

'Too bad,' Veg said with mixed emotion. Again Tamme analyzed him: He was sorry Subble had died but relieved that the report had not been made. Evidently their dialogue had grown personal.

'Agents don't antagonize people unnecessarily,' she said. 'Our job is to ascertain the facts and to take necessary action. We're all alike so that the nature of our reactions can be predetermined and so that our reports need minimal correction for subjectivity or human bias. It is easier on the computer.'

418

'That's what he said.'

'Naturally. It's what we all say.'

Again that predictable annoyance. Veg looked at her. 'But you *aren't* alike. He – he *understood*.'

'Try me sometime.'

He looked at her again, more intently, reading an invitation. Sex appeal again. He had evidently been through a traumatic experience with the girl Aquilon and was on the rebound. Here he was with another comely blonde female, and though he knew intellectually that she was a dedicated and impersonal agent of the government, his emotion saw little more than the outward form. Which was why female agents *were* comely – though they could turn it off at will. Normals had a marvellous capacity for willful self-delusion.

The other man, Calvin Potter, was far more intriguing as a challenge. But the expedient course was to enlist the cooperation of the most likely individual, and that was Veg. Cal would be deceived by no illusions; Veg was amenable, within limits, and more so at this time than he would be a month from now.

'We *are* alike,' Tamme repeated, smiling in a fashion she knew was *un*like any expression Subble would have used. 'I can do anything your SU could do. Maybe a little more because I'm part of a later series.'

'But you aren't a man!'

She raised a fair eyebrow. 'So?'

'So if someone socked you—'

'Go ahead,' she said, raising her chin. She had to refrain from smiling at the unsubtlety of his approach.

He moved suddenly, intending to stop his fist just shy of the mark. He was, indeed, a powerful man, fit to have been a pugilist in another age. Even sitting as he was, the force of a genuine blow like this could have knocked out an ordinary person.

She caught his arm and deflected it outward while she leaned forward. His fist passed behind her head and momentum carried it around. Suddenly she was inside the crook of his arm, and their heads were close together.

She kissed him ever so lightly on the lips. 'There will come a time, big man,' she murmured. 'But first we must find your lost friends.'

That reminder electrified him. He had a triple shock: first, her demonstrated ability to foil him physically; second, the seeming incipience of an amorous liaison with a female agent – intriguing as a suppressed fancy, upsetting as an actual prospect; third, the idea of dallying with a stranger while his two closest friends were unaccounted for.

Of course, Veg was not as culpable as he deemed himself to be in that moment. Tamme had scripted this encounter carefully, if extemporaneously. He had never supposed seriously that she would have anything to do with him – and he had not known that Cal and Aquilon were missing. The appearance of the mantas had seemed to indicate that things were all right; he hadn't thought to query Hex or Circe closely, and the mantas, as was their custom, had not volunteered anything or intimated that something was wrong. He had supposed that Cal and Aquilon were back at the camp, their occupation made safe by his diversion of the vicious machine.

Tamme had shocked him with a kiss while informing him that this was not the case. In due course he would think all this out and realize that the agent had used him, or at least manipulated him. But by that time the significance of her remark 'There will come a time' would have penetrated to a more fundamental level, and he wouldn't care.

Child's play, really. That was why Cal was so much more intriguing. She would of course make the attempt to impress Cal because he would then be less inclined to work against the interests of Earth – the interests as the Earth-Authorities saw them. But she expected to fail. The girl, too, would be a difficult one because the weapon of sex appeal would be valueless. Aquilon had sex appeal of her own in good measure – and it was natural rather than cultured. A rare quality! Also, Aquilon had already killed a male-agent, Taner; she would do the same with a female-agent if the occasion required it.

And there was a mystery: how had she killed Taner? She could not have caught the man off guard, and she could not have seduced him. Agents used sex as they used anything necessary; They were not used *by* it.

It had to have been through the agency of the mantas. The fungoids were extremely swift, and the strike of their whiplike tails could kill. But they had to be airborne to attack and within striking range, and the reflexes of an alert agent were sufficient to shoot down a manta before it could complete its act. It was a matter of split-second coordination – but the agent had the edge.

Taner had been careless, obviously. But that did not excuse the slaying of an agent. When the facts were known ...

They were now both on their feet, ready to go. Veg's thoughts had run their channelled course. 'They're not at the camp?'

'No. Their tracks follow yours, then disappear.'

'That true, Hex?' he asked the manta. Distrust of agents was so ingrained that he wasn't even conscious of the implied affront. Why should he take her word?

Hex snapped his tail once. Vindication. Tamme wondered whether the creatures could read human lies as readily as the agents could. She would have to keep that in mind.

'Maybe Circe found them,' Veg said.

Hex snapped twice.

'I think you should look at the tracks,' Tamme said. 'Something strange is going on, and we may be in danger.' Understatement of the day!

'Wait,' Veg said. 'The mantas came across with Cal, right? They *must* know.' But as he spoke, he saw that Hex was ignorant of the matter.

Tamme shrugged. 'I guess that Cal found you missing, so he sent them to find *you*. While they were gone, something got *him*.' She perceived his new alarm and quickly amended her statement. 'He's not dead so far as I know. He's just gone. The tracks walk out into the sand and stop. I suspect a machine lifted him away.'

'A flying machine?' He pondered. 'Could be. I didn't see it – but that ground machine sure was tough. But if—'

'I don't think it ate them,' Tamme said, again picking up his specific concern. He had strong ties to his friends! 'There's no blood in the sand, no sign of struggle. The prints show they were standing there but not running or fighting.'

'Maybe,' he said, half relieved. 'Hex – any ideas?'

Three snaps.

'He doesn't know,' Veg said. 'Circe must be looking for them now. Maybe we'd better just go back to camp and wait—'

Tamme reached out, took his arm and hauled him to the side with a strength he had not suspected in her. They sprawled on the ground behind a boulder. Wordlessly, she pointed.

Something hovered in the air a hundred feet ahead. A network of glimmering points, like bright dust motes in sunlight. But also like the night sky. It was as though tiny stars were being born right here in the planet's atmosphere. She had never heard of anything like this; nothing in her programming approached it.

Hex jumped up, orienting on the swarm. He shot towards it.

'Watch it, Hex!' Veg cried.

But Tamme recognized a weakness in the manta. The creature had to be airborne to be combat-ready. Actually it stepped across the ground rapidly, one-footed, its cape bracing against the pressure of the atmosphere. It had to aim that big eye directly on the subject to see it at all. Thus, the manta *had* to head towards the swarm – or ignore it. Probably the creature would veer off just shy of the sparkle.

Hex did. But at that moment the pattern of lights expanded abruptly, doubling its size. The outer fringe extended beyond the manta's body. And Hex disappeared.

So did the light-swarm. The desert was dull again.

'What the hell *was* it?' Veg exclaimed.

'Whatever took your friends,' Tamme said tersely. 'An energy consumer – or a matter transmitter.'

'It got Hex . . .'

'I think we'd better get out of here. In a hurry.'

'I'm with you!'

They got up and ran back the way they had come.

'Circe!' Veg cried.

'There's something after us – and don't you go near it! It got Hex!'

'Oh-oh,' Tamme said.

Veg glanced back apprehensively. The pattern was there again, moving towards them rapidly. Circe came to rest beside them, facing it.

'We can't outrun it,' Tamme said. 'We'll have to fight.'

She faced the swarm, trying to analyze it for weakness, though she did not know what she was looking for. The thing swirled and pulsed like a giant airborne amoeba, sending out fleeting pseudo-pods that vanished instead of retracting. Sparks that burned out when flung from the main mass?

'God . . .' Veg said.

'Or the devil,' she said, firing one hip-blaster.

The energy streamed through the centre of the bright cloud. Points of light glowed all along the path of her shot, but the swarm did not collapse.

422

'It's a ghost!' Veg said. 'You can't burn a ghost!' He was amazed rather than afraid. Fear simply was not natural to him; he had run as one might from a falling tree, preserving himself without terror.

Tamme drew another weapon. A jet of fluid shot out. 'Fire extinguisher,' she said.

It had no effect, either. Now the swarm was upon them. Pinpoint lights surrounded them, making it seem as though they stood in the centre of a starry nebula. Circe jumped up, her mantle spreading broadly, but there was nothing for her to strike at, and it was too late to escape.

Then something strange happened.

Chapter Four

SENTIENCE

First problem: survival in a nonsurvival situation.

Second problem: existence of mobile blight, detectable only by its transitory damping effect on elements.

Each problem seemed insoluble by itself. But together, there was a possibility. The existence of mobile nonpattern entities implied that a nonpattern mode of survival was feasible. Comprehend the mode of the blight, and perhaps survival would develop.

OX's original circuitry had difficulty accepting this supposition, so he modified it. The nagging distress occasioned by these modifications served as warning that he could be pursuing a nonsurvival course. But when all apparent courses were nonsurvival, did it matter?

He put his full attention to the blight problem. First he mapped the complete outline of each blight spot, getting an exact idea of its shape. One was virtually stationary, a central blob with extensions that moved about. Another moved slowly from location to location in two dimensions, retaining its form. The third was most promising because it moved rapidly in three dimensions and changed its shape as it moved.

This was the way a sentient entity functioned.

Yet it was blight. A mere pattern of element damping.

Pattern. A pattern of blight was still a pattern, and pattern was the fundamental indication of sentience. Thus, nonsentients were sentient. Another paradox, indicating a flaw in perception or rationale.

424

Possibility: The blight was not blight but the facsimile of blight. As though a pattern were present but whose presence suppressed the activation of the elements instead of facilitating it. An inverse entity.

Error. Such an entity should leave blanks where those elements were being suppressed: as of the absence of elements. $\overline{OX}$ perceived no such blanks. When he activated given elements, the presence of an inverse pattern should at least nullify it so that the elements would seem untouched. Instead, they did activate – but not as sharply as was proper. The effect was more like a shield, dimming but not obliterating the flow of energy. A blight, not a pattern.

$\overline{OX}$ suffered another period of disorientation. It required energy to wrestle with paradox, and he was already short of the reserve required for survival.

In due course he returned to the problem; he had to. It seemed that the ultimate nature of the spots was incomprehensible. But their perceivable attributes could be ascertained and catalogued, perhaps leading to some clarification. It was still his best approach to survival. Where a pseudopattern could survive, so might a genuine pattern.

$\overline{OX}$ developed a modified spotter circuit that enabled him to perceive the spots as simple patterns rather than as pattern-gaps. The effect was marvellous: Suddenly, seeming randomness became sensible. Instead of ghosts, these now manifested as viable, if peculiar, entities.

The most comprehensible was the outline-changing spot. At times it was stationary, like a pattern at rest. When it moved, it altered its shape – as a pattern entity normally did. But even here there was a mystery: The spot did not change according to the fundamental rules of pattern. It could therefore not be stable. Yet it was; it always returned to a similar configuration.

$\overline{OX}$'s disorientation was developing again. With another effort he modified his rationale-feedback to permit him to consider confusion and paradox without suffering in this fashion. The distress signals accompanying this modification were so strong that he would never have done it had he not faced the inevitable alternative of nonsurvival.

Now he concentrated on the observable phenomena. Possible or not, the spot moved in the manner it moved and was stable.

Another spot moved but did not alter its outline appreciably. It

425

seemed to be circulating so as not to exhaust its elements, which made sense. But it travelled only in those two dimensions.

The third spot did not move. It only shifted its projections randomly. It had occupied the same bank of elements too long – yet had not exhausted them. Another improbability: Elements had to be given slack time to recharge, or they became inoperative.

Of course, a pattern that damped down elements might not exhaust them in the same fashion.

Could $\overline{OX}$ himself achieve that state? If he were able to alternate pattern-activity with pattern damping, he might survive indefinitely.

Survival!

Such a prospect was worth the expenditure of his last reserves of energy.

$\overline{OX}$ did not know how such an inversion might be achieved. The spot patterns *did* know, for they *had* achieved it. He would have to learn from them.

It now became a problem of communication. With an entity of his own type $\overline{OX}$ would have sent an exploratory vortex to meet the vortex of the other. But these spot-entities were within his demesnes, not perceivable beyond them.

He tried an internal vortex, creating a subpattern within his own being, in the vicinity of the most mobile spot. There was no response.

He tried a self-damping offshoot – another construction developed as the need manifested. The mobile spot ignored it. Was the spot nonsentient after all – or merely unable to perceive the activation of the elements?

He tried other variants. The mobile spot took no notice.

$\overline{OX}$ was pragmatic. If one thing did not work, he would try another, and another, until he either found something that did work or exhausted the alternatives. His elements were slowly fading; if he did not discover a solution – nonsurvival.

In the midst of the fifteenth variation of offshoot, $\overline{OX}$ noted a response. Not by the shape-changing spot at which the display was directed – by the stable-shape mobile spot. It had been moving about, and abruptly it stopped.

Cessation of motion did not constitute awareness necessarily; it could signify demise. But $\overline{OX}$ repeated the configuration, this time directing it at the second spot.

426

The spot moved towards the offshoot. Awareness – or coincidence?

$\overline{OX}$ repeated the figure, somewhat to the side of the first one. The spot moved towards the new offshoot.

$\overline{OX}$ tried a similar configuration, this time one that moved in an arc before it damped out. The spot followed it and stopped when the figure was gone.

$\overline{OX}$ began to suffer the disorientation of something very like excitement despite a prior modification to alleviate this disruptive effect in himself. He tried another variant: one that moved in three dimensions. The spot did not follow it.

But a repeat of the two-dimensional one brought another response. This spot always had moved in two dimensions; it seemed to be unable to perceive in three. Yet it acted sentient within that limited framework.

$\overline{OX}$ tried a two-dimensional shoot that looped in a circle indefinitely. The spot followed it through one full circle, then stopped. Why?

Then the spot moved in a circle of its own beside the shoot. It was no longer following; it was duplicating!

$\overline{OX}$ damped out the shoot. The spot halted. There was no doubt now: The spot was aware of the shoot.

The spot moved in an oval. $\overline{OX}$ sent a new shoot to duplicate the figure.

The spot moved in a triangle. $\overline{OX}$ made a similar triangle subpattern.

The spot halted. $\overline{OX}$ tried a square. The spot duplicated it. *So did the shape-changing spot*.

$\overline{OX}$ controlled his threatening disorientation. Communication had been established – not with one spot but with two!

Survival!

427

Chapter Five

CITY

$$\begin{matrix} \cdot & \cdot & \cdot \\ \cdot & \cdot & \cdot \end{matrix}$$

It was like a city, and like a jungle, and like a factory, all run together for surrealistic effect. Veg shook his head, unable to make any coherent whole of it at first glance.

He stood on a metal ramp beside a vastly spreading mock-oak tree overlooking a channel of water that disappeared into a sieve over a mazelike mass of crisscrossing bars lighted from beneath.

'Another alternate, I presume,' Tamme said beside him. 'I suspect we'll find the others here. Why not have your mantas look?'

Now Veg saw her standing beside Hex and Circe. 'Sure – look,' he said vaguely. He still had not quite adjusted to finding himself alive and well.

The mantas moved. Hex sailed up and over the purple dome of a mosquelike building whose interior consisted of revolving mirrors, while Circe angled under some wooden stalactities depending from an inverted giant toadstool whose roots were coloured threads.

Veg squatted to investigate a gently flexing flower. It was about three inches across, on a metallic stem, and it swivelled to face him as he moved. He poked a finger at its centre.

Sharp yellow petals closed instantly on his finger, cutting the skin. 'Hey!' he yelled, yanking free. The skin was scraped where the sharp edges had touched and smarted as though acid had been squirted into the wounds.

He raised his foot high and stamped down hard with his heel. The flower dodged, but he caught the stem and crushed it against the hard ramp. Then he was sorry. 'Damn!' he said as he surveyed the wreckage. 'I shouldn't have done that; it was only trying to defend itself.'

'Better not fool with what we don't understand,' Tamme warned a bit late.

'I don't understand *any* of this, but I'm *in* it!' Veg retorted, sucking on his finger.

'I believe that was a radar device – with a self-protective circuit,' she said. 'This place is functioning.'

'Not a flower,' he said, relieved. 'I don't mind bashing a machine.'

There was a humming sound behind him. Veg whirled. 'Now *that's* a machine!' he cried.

'Climb!'' Tamme directed. She showed the way by scrambling up a trellis of organ pipes to reach a suspended walkway. Veg followed her example with alacrity.

The machine moved swiftly along the original ramp. Its design was different from the one he had battled in the desert. It had wheels instead of treads and an assortment of spider-leg appendages in place of the spinning blade.

It stopped by the damaged flower. There was a writhing flurry of its legs. So quickly that Veg was unable to follow the detail, it had the plant uprooted, adjusted, and replaced – repaired.

Then the machine hummed on down the ramp.

'What do you know!' Veg exclaimed. 'A tame machine!'

'I wouldn't count on it. If we do any more damage, we may see a destroyer-machine. And if this is their world, we'll be in trouble.'

'Yeah, no sand here.' Veg nodded thoughtfully. 'If that desert was the hinterland, this is the capital. Same world, maybe.'

'No. What we went through felt like a projection – and the atmospherics differ here. That's no certain indication, but I believe it is safer to assume this is another alternate.'

'Anyway, we're jungle specimens, picked up and put down, remote control. In case we should bite.' He bared his teeth. 'And we just *might*.'

'Yet it is strange they didn't cage us,' Tamme said. 'And it was no machine that brought us.'

'Well, let's look about – carefully.' He walked along the higher path. It extended in a bridgelike arc over a forest of winking lights. These were bulbs, not the scintillating motes that had brought the party here. Which reminded him again: 'What *did* bring us?'

Tamme shook her head in the pretty way she had. It bothered him to think that probably all female agents had the same mannerisms, carefully programmed for their effect on gullible males like him. 'Some kind of force field, maybe. And I suspect there is no way out of this except the way we came. We're in the power of the machines.'

He stopped at a fountain that seemed to start as a rising beam of light but phased into falling water and finally hardened into a moving belt of woven fabric. Very carefully because of his experience with the flower, he touched the belt. It was solid yet resilient, like a rug. 'The thing is a loom!'

Tamme looked, startled. 'No Earthly technology, that,' she said. 'Very neat. The light passes through that prism, separates into its component colours, which then become liquid and fall – to be channelled into a pattern of the fabric before they solidify. Some loom!'

'I didn't know light could be liquefied or solidified,' Veg remarked. His eyes traced the belt farther down to where it was slowly taken up by a huge roll.

'Neither did I,' she admitted. 'It appears that we are dealing with a more sophisticated science than our own.'

'I sort of like it,' he said. 'It reminds me of something 'Quilon might paint. In fact, this whole city isn't bad.'

But it was evident that Tamme was not so pleased. No doubt she would have a bombshell of a report when she returned to earth. Would the agents come and burn all this down, as they had the dinosaur valley of Paleo?

Hex returned. 'Hey, friend,' Veg said. 'Did you find them?'

One snap: YES.

'All in one piece?'

Three snaps: confusion. To a manta, fragmentation was the death of prey. The creatures were not sharp on human humour or hyperbole.

But Cal and Aquilon were already on their way. 'Veg!' Aquilon called just as though nothing had changed between them. She was absolutely beautiful.

In a moment they all were grouped about the light-fountain-loom. 'We've been here an hour,' Cal said. 'This place is phenomenal!' Then he looked at Tamme, and Veg remembered that Cal had not known about her crossover. 'Where are your friends?'

'Two alternates away, I suspect,' Tamme said.

'You drew straws, and you lost.'

'Exactly.'

'She's not bad when you get to know her,' Veg said, aware of the tension between the two.

'When you get to know them ...' Aquilon murmured, and he knew she was thinking of Subble.

'I realize that not all of you are thrilled at my presence,' Tamme said. 'But I think we have become involved in something that overrides our private differences. We may never see Earth again.'

'Do you want to?' Cal inquired. He was not being facetious.

'Is there anything to eat around here?' Veg asked. 'We're short on supplies now.'

'There are fruiting plants,' Aquilon said. 'We don't know whether they're safe, though.'

'I can probably tell,' Tamme said.

'See – lucky she's along!' Veg said.

It fell flat. Neither Cal nor Aquilon responded, and he knew they were still against Tamme. They were not going to give her a chance. And perhaps they were right; the agents had destroyed the dinosaur enclave without a trace of conscience. He felt a certain guilt defending any agent ... though Subble had indeed seemed different.

It didn't help any that he knew Tamme could read his emotions as they occurred.

'Any hint of the machines' purpose in bringing us here?' Tamme asked.

Cal shrugged. 'I question whether any machine was responsible. We seem to be dealing with some more sophisticated entities. Whoever built this city ...'

'There's some kind of amphitheatre,' Aquilon said. 'With a stage. That might be the place to make contact – if they want to.'

'Doesn't make much sense to snatch us up and then forget us!' Veg muttered.

'These entities may not see things quite the way we do,' Cal said, smiling.

They examined the fruit plants, and Tamme pronounced them probably safe. Apparently she had finely developed senses and was able to detect poison before it could harm her system.

The amphitheatre was beautiful. Translucent colonnades framed the elevated stage, which was suspended above a green fog. The fog seemed to have no substance yet evidently supported the weight of the platform, cushioning it. Veg rolled a fruit into the mist, and the fruit emerged from the other side without hindrance: no substance there!

'Magnetic, perhaps,' Cal said. 'I admit to being impressed.'

'But where are the people who made all this?' Veg demanded.

'Why do you assume *people* made it?'

'It's set up for people. The walks are just right, the seats fit us, the stage is easy to see, and the fruit's good. It wouldn't be like this if it were meant for non-humans.'

Cal nodded. 'An excellent reply.'

'What about the machines?' Aquilon asked. 'They move all around, tending it.'

'That's just it,' Veg said. 'They're *tending* it, not *using* it. They're servants, not masters.'

'I can't improve on that reasoning,' Cal said. That struck Veg as vaguely false; why should Cal try to butter him up? To stop him from siding with Tamme?

'But if human beings built it—' Aquilon started.

'Then where *are* they?' Veg finished. 'That's what I wanted to know the first time 'round.'

'Several possibilities,' Cal said thoughtfully. 'This could have been constructed centuries or milennia ago, then deserted. The machines might have been designed to maintain it, and no one ever turned them off.'

'Who ever deserted a healthy city?' Veg asked. 'I mean, the whole population?'

'It happened at Çatal Huyuk in ancient Anatolia. That was a thriving neolithic city for a thousand years. Then the people left it and started Hacilar, two hundred miles to the west.'

'Why?'

'We don't know. It happened almost eight thousand years ago. I suspect they ran out of game because of overhunting, and no doubt the climate had something to do with it.'

'I don't like that one,' Veg said. '*These* builders didn't have to hunt for a living. If something happened to *them*, it sure could happen to *us*.'

'On the other hand, they could be here now, sleeping – or

432

watching us.'

'I don't like that, either,' Veg said.

'Or perhaps this is a prison city, made for the confinement of enemies or undesirables until sentence is pronounced.'

'You get worse as you go,' Veg said, grimacing. '*You* try it, 'Quilon.'

Aquilon smiled. That still gave him a nervous thrill, for he remembered when she could not smile back on Planet Nacre. In certain ways things had been better then. 'How about a vacation resort for honoured guests?'

'Stop there,' he said. 'I like it.'

'At any rate,' Cal concluded, 'whatever brought us can certainly remove us – and *will* when it so chooses. We would do well to conduct ourselves decorously.'

'Segregation of the sexes?' Aquilon asked mischievously.

'He means not to break anything,' Veg said – and realized too late that no one had needed any interpretation. Neither girl was stupid; Veg himself was the slow member of the group. It had never bothered him when they were three; now that they were four, it somehow did.

'You understand that, mantas?' Aquilon asked. 'We don't want trouble.'

The two fungoids agreed with token snaps of their tails. Aquilon had, in her way, taken the sting from his verbal blunder, for the mantas *did* need to have human dialogue clarified on occasion. Still the sweet girl, 'Quilon, and he loved her yet – but not in the same way as before. Oh, if certain things could be unsaid, certain mistakes taken back . . . but what was the use in idle speculation? In time love would diminish into friendship, and that was best.

'For now, let's rest,' Tamme said.

Rest! Veg knew Tamme didn't need it half as much as the others did. The agents were tough, awfully tough. And in their fashion, intriguing.

Cal nodded agreement. He would be the most tired. He was much stronger than he had been when Veg met him back in space before Nacre, and now he could eat ordinary foods, but still his physical resources were small. 'The mantas will stand guard,' Cal said.

Tamme gave no indication, but somehow Veg knew she was annoyed. She must have planned to scout around alone while the

433

others slept; maybe she had some secret way to contact the agents back on Paleo. But she could not conceal it from the mantas!

Then Tamme looked directly at him, and Veg knew she knew what he was thinking. Embarrassed, he curtailed his conjectures. And Tamme smiled faintly. Bitch! he thought, and her smile broadened.

They found places around the chamber. The benches were surprisingly comfortable, as though cushioned, yet the material was hard. Another trick of the city's technology? But there was one awkward problem.

'The john,' Aquilon said. 'There has to *be* one!'

'Not necessarily,' Cal replied, smiling in much the way Tamme had. 'Their mores may differ from ours.'

'If they ate, they sat,' Veg said firmly. 'Or squatted. Sometime, somewhere, somehow. No one else could do it for them.'

'They could have designed machines to do it for them.'

Veg had a vision of a machine slicing a person open to remove refuse. 'Uh-*uh!* I wouldn't tell even a machine to eat—'

'A variant of dialysis,' Cal continued. 'I have been dialyzed many times. It is simply a matter of piping the blood through a filtration network and returning it to the body. Painless, with modern procedures. It can be done while the subject sleeps.'

'I don't want my blood piped through a machine!' Veg protested. 'Now I'll be afraid to sleep for fear a vampire machine will sneak up on me, ready to beat the oomph out of me!'

'Dialysis would only account for a portion of it,' Aquilon murmured.

'Oh, the colon can be bypassed, too,' Cal assured her.

Veg did not enjoy this discussion. 'What say we set aside a place, at least until we find a real privy? In fact, I can *make* a real privy.'

Cal spread his hands in mock defeat. 'By all means, Veg!'

'I will forage for building materials,' Tamme offered.

'I'll help,' Aquilon said. 'Circe?'

'That is kind of you,' Tamme said. Veg wondered whether she meant it. Foraging alone, the female agent could have explored the city widely and maybe made her report to Taler. Now she couldn't – and even if she moved out too quickly for Aquilon to follow, the manta would keep her in sight. Smart girl, 'Quilon!

Then he glanced at Tamme to see whether she were reading his

434

reactions again. But she was not watching him this time, to his relief.

His eyes followed as the two women departed. How alike they were, with their blonde hair and shapely bodies – yet how *un*like! Would they talk together? What would they say? Suddenly he was excruciatingly curious. Maybe he could find out from Circe later.

'I think you need no warning,' Cal said quietly as he poked about the suspended stage. 'Just remember that girl is an agent, with all that implies.'

Veg remembered. Back on Earth the agents had moved in to destroy every vestige of manta penetration. They had burned Veg's northern forest region, gassed the rabbits and chickens of the cellar-farm in Aquilon's apartment complex, and bombed the beaches where Cal had lived. Then they had come to Paleo and brutally exterminated the dinosaurs. That memory was still raw – but years would never completely erase the pain of it.

They were agents of what Aquilon called the omnivore: man himself, the most ruthless and wasteful killer of them all. He knew, how well he knew!

Yet – Tamme was a mighty pretty girl.

'Once we had a difference of opinion,' Cal said. 'I hope that does not occur again.'

Veg hoped so, too. He and Aquilon had argued against making any report on the alternate world of Paleo, to protect it from the savage exploitation of man. Cal had believed that their first loyalty had to be to their own world and species. Their difference had seemed irreconcilable, and so they had split: Cal on one side, Veg and Aquilon on the other. And it had been a mistake, for Cal had in the end changed his mind, while the other two had only learned that they were not for each other. Not that way, not as lovers, not against Cal.

This time there was no question: They were all three against the omnivorous government of Earth. The agents were incorruptible representatives of that government, fully committed to their computer-controlled program. In any serious choice, Veg knew his interests lay with Cal and Aquilon, not with Tamme.

Yet it had not worked out with Aquilon, and Tamme was a pretty girl ...

'It is possible to divorce the physical from the intellectual,' Cal said.

435

God, he was smart – as bad in his way as Tamme was in hers. 'I'll work on it,' Veg agreed.

They built the privy and also a little human shelter of light-cloth from the fountain-loom. It seemed ridiculous to pitch such a tent inside the doomed auditorium – but the city was alien, while the shelter seemed human. It served a moral purpose rather than a physical one.

The mantas found meat somewhere while the humans ate the fruits. Survival was no problem. Veg conjectured that there were either rats or their equivalent in the city: omnivores for the mantas to hunt. Maybe no coincidence.

But as they ranged more widely through the city, they verified that there was no escape. The premises terminated in a yawning gulf whose bottom they could neither see nor plumb. This was, indeed, a prison. Or at least a detention site.

'But we were not brought here for nothing,' Cal insisted. 'They are studying us, perhaps. As we might study a culture of bacteria.'

'So as to isolate the disease,' Aquilon added.

'We're not a disease!' Veg said.

Cal shrugged. 'That may be a matter of opinion.'

Veg thought of the omnivore again, destroying everything from flies to dinosaurs, and wondered. 'What happens to the culture – after they know what it is?'

'We'd rather not know,' Aquilon said a bit tightly. Veg felt a surge of sympathy for her. She had salvaged nothing from Paleo but the egg – and that was gone.

Tamme didn't comment, but Veg knew her mind was working. She was not about to sit still for the extermination of a used culture.

'That's for sure!' Tamme said, startling him, mocking his own speech mannerism. Once more he had forgotten to watch his thoughts. He knew she was not really a mind reader, but the effect was similar at times.

'It is my suspicion that our captors did not construct this city,' Cal said. 'Otherwise they would not need to study us in this manner. More likely the city was here, and we were there, so it combined us, trusting that we were compatible.'

'That might be the test,' Tamme said. 'If we are compatible, we have affinities with the city, and so they know something about us. If

436

we had died quickly, they would have known we had no affinities. Other samples, other environments, hit or miss.'

'Score one for it,' Aquilon said. 'I rather like it here. Or at least I would if only I were certain of the future.'

'If my conjecture is correct,' Cal continued, 'we have two mysteries. The origin of this city – and the nature of the sparkle-cloud. And these mysteries may be mysteries to each other, too, if you see what I mean.'

'Yeah, I see,' Veg said. 'City, sparkle, and us – and none of us really knows the other two.'

'With a three-way situation,' Aquilon said thoughtfully, 'we might have a fighting chance.'

'If only we knew how to fight!' Veg said.

Night came again inside the auditorium as well as out. They ate and settled down.

Then Veg saw something. 'The sparkle-cloud!' he exclaimed. 'It's back!'

It shimmered on the stage, myriad ripples of lights, pattern on pattern. They had seen it in daylight; by night it was altogether different: phenomenal and beautiful.

'A living galaxy!' Aquilon breathed. 'Impossible to paint . . .'

'Energy vortex,' Cal said, studying it from a different view. 'Controlled, complex . . .'

'It's staying on the stage,' Veg said. 'Not coming after us!'

'*Yet*,' Tamme put in succinctly.

'If only we could *talk* to it!' Aquilon said.

'How do you communicate with an alternate-hopping energy vortex?' Tamme inquired. 'Even if it had a brain, there's a problem in translation. More likely it is just a field of force generated by some distant machine.'

'Even so, communication might be possible,' Cal said. 'When we use radio or telephone or television, we are actually communicating with each other. What counts is who or what is controlling the machine or the force.'

'Translation – that's the key!' Aquilon said, picking up from Tamme's remark. 'Circe – send it your signature.'

The manta beside her did not move. The eye glowed, facing the vortex.

After a moment Aquilon shrugged, disappointed. 'No

437

connection,' she said. 'Their energy must be on different bands.'

'It is possible that we are seeing the mere periphery of some natural effect,' Cal said. 'A schism between alternates, a crack in the floor that let us fall through to another level – no intelligence to it.'

Suddenly the vortex changed. Whorls of colour spun off, while planes of growing points formed within the main mass. Lines of flickering colour darted through those planes.

'A picture!' Aquilon exclaimed.

'Must be modern art,' Veg snorted.

'So called "modern art" happens to be centuries old,' Cal observed.

'No, there really is a picture,' Aquilon said. 'You have to look at it the right way. The planes are like sections; the lines show the outlines. Each plane is a different view. Look at them all at once, integrate them . . .'

'I see it!' Tamme cried. 'A holograph!'

Then Cal made it out. 'A still life!'

Veg shook his head, bewildered. 'All I see is sheets and squiggles.'

'*Try*,' Aquilon urged him. Oh, she was lovely in her earnestness! He needed no effort to appreciate *that*. 'Let your mind go, look at the forms behind the forms. Once you catch it, you'll never lose it.'

But Veg couldn't catch it, any more than he had been able to catch *her*, back when he thought she was within his grasp. He strained but only became more frustrated. He saw the flats and curves of it but no comprehensible picture.

'It's all in the way you look,' Cal explained. 'If you—' He broke off, staring into the vortex. 'Amazing!'

Veg looked again, squinting, concentrating, but all he saw was a shifting of incomprehensibly geometric patterns with sparkles flying out like visual fireworks.

'That's Orn!' Aquilon cried. 'No, it's a chick—'

'The hatchling,' Cal said. 'Ornet. Yet how—?'

'And a baby manta!' she continued. 'Where *are* they?'

'Back on Paleo, maybe,' Veg said, annoyed. 'What sort of a game are you folks playing?'

'No game,' Tamme assured him. 'We *see* them.'

''Quilon!' Cal cried. 'Look! Behind that obscuring sparkle. Can that be—?'

'It *is*,' she cried. '*That's a human baby!*' She shook her head, but her eyes remained riveted to the picture. 'My God!'

Veg strained anew but could make out nothing. He was getting angry.

'Your God,' Cal said. 'I remember when you found that expression quaint.'

Aquilon drew her eyes momentarily from the stage to look at Cal, and Veg felt the intensity of it, though he was not a part of it. She was moving inexorably to Cal, and that was right; that Veg loved her did not mean he was jealous of his friend. Cal deserved the best.

'I was painting,' she said. 'That first night on the mountain . . . and you said you loved me, and I cried.' Her eyes returned to the stage. 'Now I have picked up your mannerisms.'

Veg put his own eyes straight at the indecipherable image. The human relations of the trio were just as confused as that supposed picture, only coming clear too late to do any good. He had not known Cal and Aquilon were so close, even back at the beginning of Nacre. He had been an interloper from the start.

Suddenly all three others tensed as though struck by a common vision. Veg knew now this was no joke; they could never have executed such a simultaneous reaction – unless they really had a common stimulus. 'What the hell is it?' he demanded.

'A machine!' Aquilon exclaimed, 'that whirling blade—'

'*Where?*' Veg cried, looking around nervously. But there was no machine. Aquilon was still staring into the vortex.

'That must be what Veg fought!' Tamme said. 'See the treads, the way it moves – no wonder he had such a time with it! The thing's vicious!'

'Sure it was vicious,' Veg agreed. 'But this is only a picture – or a mass hypnosis. *I* don't see it.'

'You know, that's a small machine,' Cal said. 'A miniature, only a foot high.'

'They're *all* babies!' Tamme said. 'But the others are no match for that machine. That's a third-generation killer.'

'Throw sand at it!' Veg said. For a moment he thought he saw the little machine buzzing through the depths of sparkle. But the whirling blade spun off into a pin-wheel, and he lost it. He just didn't have the eye for this show.

'They *can't* throw sand,' Aquilon said breathlessly. 'Ornet and the mantling don't have hands, and the baby can't even sit up yet.'

'They would hardly know about that technique of defense yet,' Cal added.

'Well, they can run, can't they?' Veg demanded. 'Let them take turns leading it away.'

'They're trying,' Tamme said. 'But it isn't—'

Then all three tensed again. 'No—!' Cal cried.

Aquilon screamed. It was not a polite noise, such as one makes at a play. It was a full-throated scream of sheer horror.

Veg had had enough. He charged the stage, leapt to the platform, and plunged into the centre of the glowing maelstrom, waving his arms and shouting. If nothing else, he could disrupt the hypnotic pictures that had captivated the minds of the others.

He felt a tingling, similar to his experience the last time. Then it faded. He was left gesticulating on the stage, alone. The sparkle-cloud was gone.

Chapter Six

FRAMES

Things progressed rapidly. The two blight spots were sentient; they responded to geometric sub-patterns readily and initiated their own. They had individual designations by which they could be identified, and these they made known by their responses. The shape-changing one was Dec, a ten-pointed symbol. The mobile-stable one was Ornet, indicative of a long line of evolving creatures or perhaps, more accurately, a series of shifting aspects of identity. The third was not responsive in the same way, but Ornet identified it as Cub, or the young of another species. Each entity was really quite distinct, once the group was understood.

The blights had a need, as did $\overline{OX}$. He grasped the concept without identifying the specific. Ultimately, the mutual imperative to be SURVIVE. $\overline{OX}$ needed more volume; the spots needed something else.

When the spots were amenable, they made perfect geometric figures. When they were distressed, they made imperfect figures. $\overline{OX}$ did the same. Thus, they played a wide-ranging game of figures: I do *this* – does it please/displease you? Is it nearer or farther from your mode of survival? You do *that* – I am pleased/displeased as it reflects on some aspect of my survival.

Given enough time, they could have worked out an efficient means of communication. But there was no time; $\overline{OX}$'s elements were fading, and he had to have answers *now*. He had to know what the spots needed, and whether they had what *he* needed.

So he ran a frame-search. Instead of laboriously exchanging

441

symbols, he surveyed the entire range of prospects available to him.

In a few, the spots were more active. They made excellent figures. In others, the elements were stronger, better for him. Guided by this knowledge, $\overline{OX}$ arranged his responses to direct developments towards the most favourable prospects.

But somehow these prospects faded as he approached them. The spots ceased cooperating.

$\overline{OX}$ surveyed the framework again, analyzing it in the context of this alteration. Somehow the act of orienting on his needs had made those needs unapproachable.

He tried orienting on the prospects most favourable to the spots – and then his own improved.

Confusion. His survival and that of the spots were linked – but the mechanism was unclear.

By experimentation and circuit modification, he clarified it. The spots needed a specific locale, both physical and frame – that part of the framework where there were certain stationary spots. As they approached that region, they did something that enhanced the strength of his elements.

This was an alternate solution to his problem! He did not need greater volume if his existing elements recharged faster. The proximity of the spots, in some cases, enhanced that recharging. $\overline{OX}$ directed the responses to further enhance recharging while keeping the needs of the spots in mind.

Suddenly the spots responded. Amazingly, the elements flourished, recharging at such a rate that $\overline{OX}$'s entire survival problem abated.

In retrospect, comprehension came. The elements were not individual entities; they were the energy termini of larger sub-patterns. These systems were physical, like the ground. The spots were physical. The spots catered to the needs of the energy plants and thereby improved $\overline{OX}$'s situation.

Dialogue improved also. $\overline{OX}$ learned that one of the most important needs of spots and element-plants was fluid – a certain kind of liquid matter. In the presence of this fluid, spots of many varieties flourished. Some were mobile spots of semi-sentient or nonsentient nature, distinct from the three he knew. Others were stationary and nonsentient – and these also were of a number of subtypes. Some provided nourishment for the sentient spots, and so these were facilitated by the transfer of liquid and increased access to certain forms of ambient energy. Others, of no direct interest to the sentients, produced nodules of processed energy that projected into adjacent alternate-frames. These were the elements!

The physical sustenance that the spots provided for their own plants also aided the element plants. They became more vigorous, and so the elements were stronger. So, by this seemingly devious chain, when $\overline{OX}$ helped the spots, he helped himself. Not just any spots, for the semi-sentients had no care at all for the plants and would not cater to $\overline{OX}$'s preferences. But the sentient spots, grasping the interaction between them, now cared for the element plants as they cared for their own. It was largely through Ornet, the most sentient spot, that this understanding came about.

Survival seemed assured.

Then the machine came.

$\overline{OX}$ recognized it instantly, though he had never experienced this type of interaction before. Alarm circuits were integral to his makeup, and the presence of the machine activated them. Here was Pattern's deadliest enemy!

In certain respects the machine was like a spot, for aspects of it were physical. But in other respects it was a kind of pattern, or antipattern. It possessed, in limited form, the ability to travel between frames, as $\overline{OX}$ did. Ordinarily, he would have noted only its pattern-aspect, but his necessary study of the spots had provided him with a wider perspective, and now he grasped much more of its nature. Suddenly the spots had enhanced his survival in quite another way, for when he viewed the machine as a double-level entity, he found it both more comprehensible and more formidable.

It could not touch $\overline{OX}$ directly, but it was deadly. It destroyed his elements by shorting out their stores of energy and physically severing the element-plants from their moorings, leaving gaps in the network. Such gaps, encountered unawares, could destroy a pattern entity.

The machine was also a direct physical threat to the spots and hence, in another respect, to $\overline{OX}$'s own survival. He could avoid it, moving his pattern to undamaged elements – but the spots had no such retreat. They could not jump across the frames of probability.

The spots were aware of this. They were furiously mobile, interacting with the machine. Ornet was distracting it by moving

443

erratically, while Dec swooped at it, striking with a sharp extremity. But the machine was invulnerable to such attack. In a moment it discovered less elusive prey. It turned on Cub.

Cub did not take evasive action. He merely lay where he was while the attack-instrument of the machine bore down.

The blades connected. Thinly sliced sections of the physical body flew out as the action continued. The solids and fluids were taken into the machine, and Cub was no more.

After that, the machine departed. It was a small one, and its immediate survival need – its hunger – had been sated by the matter in Cub. The crisis was over.

But Dec and Ornet had a different notion. They suffered negative reaction. They were distressed by the loss of their companion, as though he were related in some way to their own survival. It was a thing they were unable to convey directly to $\overline{OX}$, but he understood their need, if not their rationale. They had expended much attention assisting Cub from the outset, and they required him to be undefunct.

Accordingly, $\overline{OX}$ surveyed the alternates. A number existed in which one of the other spots had been consumed by the machine, but $\overline{OX}$ concluded these were not appropriate. He located those in which all three spots survived intact.

Knowing an alternate frame and *entering* it were different things. $\overline{OX}$ had directed events toward favourable alternates before – but now he had to travel through the fourth dimension of probability, isolate one from many, and take the spots with him – when the options had been greatly reduced by the force of events. He could readily remove the spots to a frame in which they would not suffer immediate attack by the machine; it was much more difficult to do this after that event had actually occurred.

He tried. The consumption of energy was colossal, diminishing his elements at a ruinous rate. Once started, he *had* to succeed, for only in the proper alternate would the elements remain sufficiently charged for the maintenance of his pattern. Failure meant nonsurvival.

The spots could be moved so long as they remained within the boundaries of his animated form. He could not move them physically from place to place, but he could transfer them from one version of reality to another. It was in his fundamental circuits, just as knowledge of machines was in them; he knew what to do – if he could handle himself properly. Moving blight spots was more difficult than merely moving himself.

The framework wrenched. $\overline{OX}$ fibrillated. The frame changed. $\overline{OX}$ let go, disoriented by the complex effort. For a time he could not discern whether he had succeeded or failed.

. . . rstanding came about.

Survival seemed assured.

Then the machine came.

$\overline{OX}$ recognized it instantly, though he had never experienced this type of interaction before. The intrusion of the machine activated his alarm circuits. Here was Pattern's deadliest threat!

$\overline{OX}$ acted. He formed a decoy shoot designed to pre-empt the attention of the machine. It resembled ideal prey because it exhibited tokens keyed to the machine's perceptions: the glint of refined, polished metal; the motion of seeming blight; the sparkle of the periphery of a true pattern-entity. The machine was not intelligent enough or experienced enough to penetrate the ruse. It followed the shoot.

The shoot moved out on a simulated evasion course, the machine slicing vigorously at it. The shoot would fizzle out at a suitable distance from the locale of the spots – by which time the machine would have forgotten them. The threat had been abated, and all the spots were safe.

Chapter Seven

FOREST

Agents were disciplined; they had firm control over their emotions. Even consciousness-changing drugs could not subvert this, unless their actions overrode the total function of the brain. The subconscious mind of an agent was integrated with the conscious so that there were no suppressed passions, no buried monsters.

But the brutal slaying of a human infant had shaken her. The agent training and surgery could not eliminate the most fundamental drives that made her a woman. To watch, even in replica, a baby being sliced alive like so much bologna and funnelled into the maw of a machine . . .

Then Veg had disrupted the image, and it had not returned. Perhaps that was just as well.

Another thing bothered her: the feeling that the image was not a mockup but a transmission. As with a televised picture: a replica of events actually occurring elsewhere. If so, this was no threat to cow the captives; it was the presentation of vital information.

Perhaps the controlling entity expected them to absorb the news like so many sponges. Probably there was more to come. But she was not inclined to wait on alien convenience. It was time to act.

Before she could act, she had to reconnoitre and get back in touch with Taler. That meant giving Cal and the mantas the slip.

But she could not afford to leave the human trio to its own devices. That was why she had come along on this projection! If she left them alone now, they could come up with some inconvenient mischief, just as they had on Paleo.

Answer, straight from the manual: take a hostage.

There was no problem which one. Cal was too smart to control directly – if, indeed, he could be controlled at all. He had given the agents a lesson back at Paleo! Aquilon would be difficult to manage because she was female, and complicated. The mantas were out of the question. So it had to be Veg: male, manageable, and not too smart. And she had primed him already.

Meanwhile, the others were recovering from their shock. No subtlety here; they reacted exactly as human beings should be expected to. Perhaps that was part of the point: The aliens intended to test the party in various ways, cataloguing their responses, much as psychiatrists tested white rats.

'What does it mean?' Aquilon asked, shading her eyes with one hand as though to shut off the glare of the vision.

'It means they can reach us – emotionally as well as physically,' Cal said slowly. 'Whenever they want to. We could be in for a very ugly series of visions. But what they are trying to tell us – that is unclear.'

Tamme turned to the nearest manta. 'Did you see it?' she inquired.

'Circe didn't see the vision,' Aquilon answered. 'Their eyes are different; they can't pick up totalities the way we do. They have no conception of perspective or of art.'

Tamme knew that. She had studied the material on the fungoid creatures before passing through the aperture from Earth to Paleo. She knew they were cunning and dangerous; one had escaped captivity and hidden on a spaceship bound for the region of space containing the manta home-world of Nacre. It had never been killed or recaptured despite a strenuous search, and they had had to place a temporary proscription on Planet Nacre to prevent any more mantas from entering space.

The manta's eye was an organic cathode emitting a controlled beam of light and picking up its reflections from surrounding objects. That radar eye was unexcelled for the type of seeing that it did and worked as well in darkness as in light. But it had its limitations, as Aquilon had described. Yet if the mantas had seen the cloud-picture, this would have been highly significant.

Cal understood. 'We see with one system, the manta with another. A comparison of the two could have led to significant new

447

insights about the nature of the force that brought us here and showed us this scene.' He shook his head. 'But we have verified that the mantas see only flares of energy in the cloud, winking on and off extremely rapidly. They can not perceive the source of these flares and are not equipped to see any pictures.'

'Let's sleep on it,' Veg said gruffly.

'The baby – something about it—' Aquilon said.

'What's a *baby* doing by itself in an alternate world?' Veg demanded. 'Whatever you folks thought you saw, it wasn't real.'

Tamme differed. 'A little manta, a little flightless bird, and a little human being – there's a pattern there, and they looked real. I was able to read the bodily signs on that baby. It was thirsty. I'd say it was real, or at least a projection made from a real model.'

'Odd that it should be in a nest,' Cal remarked.

'I recognized it somehow,' Aquilon said. 'I don't know who it was, but it was *somebody*. Maybe one of us, back when . . .'

Cal was surprised beyond what he should have been. Tamme would have liked to question him about that, but this was not the occasion. Why should a conjecture about his infancy make him react? But Aquilon was right: There *was* a certain resemblance to Cal – and to Aquilon herself. Had the alien intelligence drawn somehow from human memories to formulate a composite infant?

They settled down. The trio shared the interior of their tent, unselfconsciously; Tamme, by her own choice and theirs, slept apart. She had not been invited along, and they did not want her, but they accepted her presence as one of the facts of this mission.

Tamme's sleep was never deep, and she did not dream in the manner of normals because of the changed nature of the computer-organized mind. Much of human sleep was a sifting, digesting, and identification tagging of the day's events; without that sorting and filing, the mind would soon degenerate into chaos. But agents were reprogrammed regularly and so required no long-term memory cataloguing. Rather, she sank into a trancelike state while her body relaxed and her mind reviewed and organized developments with a view to their relevancy for her mission. It took about an hour; agents were efficient in this, too.

Now the others were asleep, Cal deeply, Aquilon lightly, Veg rising through a rapid-eye-movement sequence. The two mantas were off exploring; if she were lucky, they would not check on the supposedly quiescent human party for several hours.

She stood and removed her blouse, skirt, and slippers. Her fingers worked nimbly, tearing out friction seams and pressing the material together again in a new configuration. This was one trick male agents didn't have!

When the clothing was ready, she removed her bra, slip, and panties and redesigned them, too. Then she reassembled herself in an artful new format, let down her hair, and relaxed.

Sure enough, Veg's REM proceeded into wakefulness. It was not that he had complex continuing adjustments to make in connection with his rebound from Aquilon – though he did. He had merely forgotten to visit the privy before turning in. Tamme had known he would rouse himself in due course.

Veg emerged from the tent. Tamme sat up as he passed her. He paused, as she had known he would. He could barely see her in the dark, but he was acutely conscious of her locale. 'Just goin' to the . . .' he muttered.

'It happens,' she said, standing, facing him, close.

Hope, negation, and suspicion ran through him. She picked up the mixed, involuntary signals of his body: quickened respiration and pulse, tightening of muscles, odours of transitory tension. She could see him, of course, for she had artificially acute night vision – but her ears and nostrils would have sufficed. Normals were so easy to read.

Veg walked on, and Tamme walked with him, touching, matching her step to his. There was a faint, suggestive rustle to her clothing now that set off new awareness in him. He did not consciously pick up the cause of this heightening intrigue, but the effect was strong. And in his present emotional state, severed from Aquilon, he was much more vulnerable to Tamme's calculated attack than he would normally have been.

Outside the auditorium there was a light-flower, its neon petals radiating illumination of many wavelengths. Now Veg could see her – and it was a new impact.

'You've changed!'

'You merely behold me in a different light,' she murmured, turning slightly within that differing glow.

'Some light!' he exclaimed. She could have traced the process of his eyes by his reactions: warm appreciation for face and hair, half-guilty voyeurism for the thrust of her bosom and newly accented

449

cleavage thereof, wholly guilty desire for the enhanced swell of her hips and posterior.

But his guilt was not straightforward. He ordinarily did not hesitate to appreciate the charms of women. But he had not been exposed to other women for some time. His experience with Aquilon and the knowledge that he was in the company of an agent made him hold back. He felt no guilt about cleavages and posteriors – merely about reacting to them in the present circumstances. This guilt in turn heightened the allure in a kind of reverse feedback. Forbidden fruit!

She turned away, interrupting his view of the fruit, and led the way along the path, accenting her gait only that trifle necessary to attract the eye subtly. Here the way was like a tunnel under swirling mists. Translucent figures loomed within the ambience, never quite coming clear, even to Tamme's gaze. There were so many marvels of this city – if only it were possible to establish contact with Earth so that it all could be studied and exploited!

They had built the privy over the Black Hole: a well of opacity fifteen feet across and of no plumbable depth. Cal had conjectured that it had once been an elevator shaft. Now it served as a sanitary sink.

While Veg was inside, Tamme brought out the miniature components of her projector. It would project a spherical aperture seven feet in diameter that would hold for fifteen seconds. After that, the unit would shut down, conserving its little power cell. The cell recharged itself, but slowly.

One problem was that she could not take the aperture projector with her. She had to step through the sphere while it existed. It would be disastrous to be caught halfway into the field as it closed down! Part of her would be in the other world, the remainder here – and both would be dead. Too bad people did not possess the regenerative powers of earthworms: cut one in half, make two new individuals!

Actually, the apertures were two-way. They were really tunnels between alternates that one could move through in either direction. The trouble was that the device could not be activated from the far side. No doubt in time the technicians would develop a key for that purpose – or perhaps they had already but simply hadn't gotten it into production yet. Alternate-projection was a nascent science.

She expected no difficulty but took no unnecessary chances. She wrote a short message addressed to Calvin Potter and attached it to the generator.

Veg emerged. It had only been a couple of minutes, but the agent had worked extremely rapidly. All was in order.

'What's that?' he asked.

'An aperture generator,' she said, rising to approach him.

'You mean you had one of those all along?' he demanded. 'We could have gone back anytime?'

'Yes and no,' she said. 'I could have used it anytime – but it is a calculated risk. Our aperture technology is emergent; we seem to have less than a fifty per cent reliability of destination.'

'You're getting too technical for me,' Veg said, eyeing her displayed torso again. But she knew he understood the essence; he merely liked to assume a posture of country-boy ignorance when anyone used difficult words. This window might or might not take them back where they started from.

'We set our aperture projector on Paleo for Earth,' she said. 'Instead, it opened onto the machine desert. This one has a complementary setting. It should take us back to where the other one is. But it may not.'

'We?' he asked. 'You can go where you want to; I'm staying with my friends.'

She could knock him out and toss him through. But she wanted his cooperation in case of emergency, and it was always better to keep things positive when possible. 'I thought it would be more private this way,' she said, using her specific muscular control to twitch her left breast suggestively.

The suggestion scored. But with his flare of desire came immediate suspicion. 'What do you want with me?'

Time for a half-truth. 'These generators are two-way – but it is better to have an operator. When I'm over *there*' – she indicated the prospective field of the projector – 'I can't turn it on again over *here*. And if it doesn't open in the right place, I could be stranded.' She shrugged, once more making a signal with her decolletage. 'That might please some of you, but . . .'

'Uh-uh,' he said, giving her one more correct call. 'We're all human beings, up against things we don't understand. We've got to stick together.'

451

'That's right. So—'

'So you want me to cross over first? No thanks! I did that before and almost got gobbled by a machine.'

'No, I'll go,' she said.

He relaxed, his suspicion warring with his desire to believe her. She knew Cal had warned him not to get involved with an agent. 'Then you want me to turn it on in an hour to bring you back?'

'Yes.' She took a breath, skillfully accentuating the objects of his gaze in yet another ploy. 'Of course . . .'

'Not much privacy,' he remarked, 'if I'm *here* and you're *there*.' Now he was getting angry, as the lure retreated, despite her seeming agreement to his prior objections. Fish on a hook.

'Well, the projector *can* be set to go on automatically after a certain period. A simple clockwork timer. And the limit is not necessarily an hour. It's a combination stress-time parameter with a safety factor. We could slip a load of five hundred pounds through – twice the normal – but then we'd have to wait four hours to return. The time multiplies at the square of the mass, you see. For sustained use, two hundred and fifty pounds per hour is the most efficient.'

'I see,' Veg said. 'So we could both go through. Together we wouldn't weigh more than three fifty—'

'Three sixty.'

'Hold on! I'm two hundred, and you can't be more than one thirty—'

'You're two-oh-five; you have prospered in the wilderness, I'm one fifty-five, including my hardware.'

'You sure don't look it!'

'Heft me.'

He put his big hands under her elbows and lifted her easily. 'Maybe so,' he said. 'Sure no fat on you, though.'

'Agents are more solid than they look. Our bones are laced with metal – literally. And the android flesh with which we are rebuilt is more dense than yours. But you're right: no fat in it.'

'I know you're tough,' he agreed, not altogether pleased. 'Still, might be safer if we both went in case there were bad trouble at the other end.'

She would be better off alone if there were real trouble. But that was not the point. 'Yes. But then there would be a long, uninterrupted wait – and no one could reach us.' She breathed again.

Veg was not slow to appreciate the possibilities. Two, perhaps three completely private hours with this seductive woman! 'Safety first!' he said. 'Let's go take a look.'

He had taken the bait, lured by the thrill of exploration as well as her own enticements. And she really had not had to lie. It *was* safer with two, in a routine crossover, and the limitations of the generator were as she had described.

She really had taken more trouble than strictly necessary to bring him along. A knockout or a straight lie would have done the job in seconds. But either of these techniques would have led to complications later. This way, not only would he serve as an effective hostage – he could be of genuine assistance in a variety of circumstances. All she had to do was prepare him.

She could do a lot with a man in three hours.

'All right,' she said. 'You're armed?' She knew he was; she was merely alerting him.

He nodded. 'I keep a knife on me. I lost my other hardware to that machine back in the desert.'

'If there's any long-distance threat, I'll cover it.'

He glanced once more at her half-exposed breasts. 'Yeah – like Taler.'

She laughed honestly this time, knowing he knew there was no jealousy between agents. She set the return aperture timer for three hours, leaving a reasonable margin for recharging, then activated the projector.

As the sphere formed, she drew him through the aperture beside her.

There was no passage of time, just the odd transfer wrench. They emerged in a world apart. Where there had been surrealistic buildings, now were trees.

Not the desert world. She had been afraid of this.

'Not Paleo, either – or Earth,' Veg said, for once divining her thoughts before she read his.

Tamme looked about warily. 'How do you know? This is a forest – and there are forests on both worlds.'

'This is the forest primeval,' he said, unconsciously borrowing from American literature.

'Evangeline,' Tamme said.

'Who?'

'Longfellow's poem from which you quoted. *Evangeline, A Tale of Acadie*, vintage 1847.'

'Oh. That's right – you agents do that. Got too much of that dense android muscle in your brains.' He grimaced. 'What I meant was that this forest has never been touched by man. So it's not Earth – not *our* Earth. And it's a high rainfall district, so it's not the desert world – not this place, not this milennium, anyway. Look at the size of that pine!'

'The aperture does not necessarily lead to the same geographic spot on the alternate,' she reminded him. 'Each alternate seems to differ in time from the others, so it could differ in space, too, since the globe is moving. For instance, we're in day here instead of night, so we must be elsewhere on the globe. There was vegetation on other parts of what you call the desert world.'

'That's what I said. But no trees like this. Those machines ate wood, too. They'd have sawed into this long ago – and they haven't.'

He was right. Her perceptions showed a slightly differing chemical composition of this world's atmosphere. Though it would be foolish to judge an entire world by one view of a tiny fraction of it, it *was* a new alternate. The changes were minor but significant.

'I am not surprised,' she admitted. 'My aperture projector is set for Paleo – but we did not start from the desert world. That sparkle-cloud moved us to an unspecified alternate, so we're out of phase.'

'Yeah – like taking the wrong bus.'

That was hardly precise, and she was surprised he thought in terms of such an ancient vehicle, but it would do. 'It may be a long, hard search for home.'

'*Your* home, maybe. I'd settle for Paleo. Or Nacre.'

'Nacre is part of the Earth-alternate. So you'd have to—'

'But we can get back to the city-world all right? We're not lost from there?'

'Yes – in just under three hours. We're in phase for that. But we shall have to be standing right on this spot, or we'll miss it.'

'Well, let's not waste the time!' he exclaimed. 'This is beautiful! Finest softwood forest I ever saw!'

She laughed. 'By all means, look at the trees. But how can you be sure this *isn't* Paleo? Plenty of virgin softwood there!' She knew this wasn't Paleo, but was interested in his reasoning.

'Not the same. These are modern pines. See, the needles are different. Trees evolve, you know, same as animals do. This white pine, now – actually, it's different from Earth white pine, in little ways—'

She raised her hands in mock surrender. He was not pretending; at this moment, the forest really did interest him more than she did, and he knew more than she in this area of botany. Agents had an excellent general education, but they could not be experts in every field.

Meanwhile, the social environment had changed as well as the physical one. Just as sex was relatively attractive to this country man when he was confined to the city, this challenging new – rather, *old* – forest was more attractive yet.

Which was not quite what she had anticipated. There were always unexpected wrinkles appearing in normals! Agents, in pleasant contrast, were completely predictable – to other agents. They were designed to be that way.

Pleasant contrast? It actually made for a certain tedium, she realized, when the mission stretched out longer than a few hours or days. In some things, predictability was less than ideal.

Watch yourself, she thought then. She was beginning to suffer from an overload of experience, and she had no dream mechanism to restore her mind to its prior equilibrium. It was inevitably shaping her into more of an individual than the computer could readily tolerate. If this went too far, her report would be suspect, even useless. The general rule was that an agent's mission should not continue longer than ten days because of that deterioration of reliability. She had already been nineteen days, and the end was not in sight.

She shuddered. How good it would be to return to computer central to be reset – and how awful to remain out so long she lost her affinity with her series, TA!

Veg was moving among the trees, tapping the trunks, looking at needles. This was his element! He suffered no pangs of dawning identity!

There were, it seemed, plenty of untouched worlds available for man's expansion. Earth's population and resources problem would be solved – just as soon as she got back.

She would have to return, try another setting, and begin a survey of alternate-worlds. It would be too cumbersome to step through every time. She would fashion a spot sensor that used very little power in projection because of its small mass. By bouncing it through and back like a tennis ball, she could check a dozen worlds in an hour, the only delay being the adjustment of the projector settings between uses.

She would not need Veg, after all. Not until she located familiar territory.

Three hours. She could sleep, for she had perfect timing and would wake when the return aperture was due. But first she would make a spot survey of this locale, for it might turn out to be the most suitable one yet discovered for exploitation. Earthlike, modern, no dinosaurs.

She lifted her hands, caught hold of a dead spoke on the huge pine, and hauled herself up. The trunk was a good six feet in diameter at the base, and the top was out of sight. She climbed rapidly, wriggling between the branches as they became smaller and more closely set. She was getting dirty, but that didn't matter. She really should have adjusted the seductive design of her outfit; trees were not much for that sort of thing, and her clothing inhibited progress. A few welts or scratches on the visible surfaces of her breasts would not bother her but could well turn off Veg – and she just might need him.

The trunk thinned alarmingly at the top and swayed in the stiffening wind. At an elevation of two hundred feet she halted, looking about. There were a number of tall trees, some reaching to two hundred and fifty feet. White pine, when allowed to grow, was one of the tallest trees, comparable to the Douglas fir and young redwood. Veg would know all about that! But now these tall trees interfered with her vision, so that all she could see was more forest. She had wasted her time. No doubt Veg could have told her that, too!

She descended, to find him waiting for her, looking up. How like a man! She hardly needed to make an effort to show off her wares; he knew how to find them for himself. Tree-climbing skirt!

'No good climbing,' he remarked. 'That's boy-scout lore – useless in a real forest. All you see is—'

'More trees,' she finished for him.

'I had a better view from the ground.'

'Thank you.'

456

'Found something else.'

Now she read the signs in him: He was excited, and not merely by his nether-view of her thighs as she came down the tree. He knew that what he had to tell her would affect her profoundly.

Tamme paused, trying to ascertain what it was before he told her. It was not a threat, not a joke. Not a human settlement. What, then?

'Can't tell, can you!' he said, pleased. 'Come on, then.'

He showed the way to a small forest glade, a clearing made by a fallen giant tree and not yet grown in. The massive trunk, eight feet thick, lay rotting on the ground. And near its sundered stump—

'An aperture projector!' she exclaimed, amazed.

'Thought you'd be surprised. Guess we weren't the first here, after all.'

Tamme's mind was racing. There was no way that such a device could be here – except as a relic of human visitation. *Agent* visitation, for this was an agent model, similar to hers. But not identical – not quite.

'Some alternate-world agent has passed this way,' she said. 'And not long ago. Within five days.'

'Because the brush has not grown up around it,' Veg said. 'That's what I figured. Can't be yours, can it?'

'No.' The implications were staggering. If an alternate-world agent had come here, then Earth was not alone. There could be millions of highly developed human societies possessing the secret of aperture travel, competing for unspoiled worlds. What would she do, if she encountered one of those foreign agents, as highly trained as she, as dedicated to *his* world as she was to Earth?

By blind luck she had learned of the other agent first. Before *he* learned of *her*.

This was likely to be the mission of her life – and the fight of Earth's survival.

She had an immediate choice: Return to the surrealist city and commence her survey of alternates, hoping to discover in the process the route home. Or take a more chancy initiative by going after the competing agent and attempting to kill him before he could make his report to his world.

Each alternative was rife with bewildering complexities. She was trained to make quick decisions – but never had the fate of Earth depended on her snap judgement, even potentially. So she sought an advisory opinion. 'Veg – if you came across the spoor of a hungry tiger, and you knew it was going to be him or you – what would you do? Follow the trail, or go home for help?'

Veg squinted at her. 'Depends how close home is, and how I am armed. But probably I'd go home. I don't like killing.'

She had posed the wrong question – another indication of her need for caution. An agent should not make elementary mistakes! Naturally the vegetarian would avoid a quarrel with an animal. 'Suppose it was the track of a man as strong and as smart as you – but an enemy who would kill you if you didn't kill him first?'

'Then I'd *sure* go home! I'm not going out *looking* for any death match!'

She ran her tongue over her lips. 'Any sensible person would do the same. It's a fairly safe assumption.'

'Yeah.'

'But the secret of victory is to do the unexpected.'

'Yeah.'

'All right. The aperture we used will come on again in two hours and eleven minutes. Check your watch; you'll only have fifteen seconds.'

'I don't have a watch.'

There it was again. She was missing the obvious at a calamitous rate in her preoccupation with larger concerns. She needed computer reorientation – but could not get it. There was no choice but to continue more carefully.

She removed her watch and handed it to him. 'All you have to do is stand exactly where we landed. In fact, your best bet is to go there now, camp out on that spot. Then you'll be transported back automatically even if you're alseep. Tell your friends where I went, then wait at the city. Cal will understand.'

He was confused. 'Where *are* you going? I thought—'

She knelt by the generator. 'After the tiger. This will not be pretty, and I may not return. It's not fair to involve you further.'

'You're going to fight that other agent?'

'I have to. For our world, Earth.'

'You're not taking me along?'

'Veg, I was using you. I'm sorry; I felt it was a necessary safeguard. My purposes are not yours, and this is not your quarrel. Go back to your friends.' She was checking over the projector as she talked, making sure it was in working order, memorizing the setting.

'That was the note you left,' he said wisely. 'Telling Cal and 'Quilon not to try anything if they didn't want anything to happen to me.'

She nodded acquiescence. 'The projector is vulnerable. If they moved it or changed the setting, even accidentally . . .' Of course she could do the same thing to *this* one and return to the city, but that was no sure way to solve the problem. The other agent might have another projector, so her act would only alert him – and an agent needed no more than a warning! No, she had to go after him and catch him before he was aware, and kill him – if she could.

'Now you're letting me go.' His mixture of emotions was too complex for her to analyse at the moment. The projector was more important.

'There was nothing personal, Veg. We do what we must. We're agents, not normal people.' All was in order; the projector had not been used in several days, so it was fresh and ready to operate safely. 'We will lie, cheat, and kill when we have to – but we don't do these things from preference. I suppose it won't hurt for you to know now : I was extremely sorry to see those dinosaurs destroyed at Paleo. Had I been in charge, we would have left you and them alone. But I follow my orders literally, using my judgement only in the application of my instructions when judgement is required.' She glanced up, smiling briefly. 'Take it from a trained liar and killer : Honesty and peace are normally the best policies.'

'Yeah. I knew you were using me. That's why I lost interest, once I thought it through. I'm slow, but I do get there in time. Trees don't *use* people.'

She took an instant to verify that in him. He was serious; deceptive behaviour turned him off even when he didn't recognize it consciously. She had misread him before, and that was bad. She had overrated the impact of her sex appeal; the preoccupation had become more *hers* than *his*. She was slipping.

Veg had loved Aquilon – *still* loved her – in part because of her basic integrity. He had lost interest in Tamme when her agent nature was verified. He was a decent man. Now his interest was increasing again as she played it straight.

'I made you a kind of promise,' she said. 'Since I may not be seeing you again, it behooves me to keep that promise now.' She ran her finger along the seam of her low-fashioned blouse, opening it.

Veg was strongly tempted; she read the signals all over his body. No mistake *this* time! But something in him would not let go. 'No – that's paid love. Not the kind I crave.'

'Not a difficult payment. Sex is nothing more than a technique to us. And – you are quite a man, Veg.'

'Thanks, anyway,' he said. 'Better get on with your mission.' There was a turbulent decision in him, a multifaceted, pain/pleasure metamorphosis. But he did not intend to betray her. 'Time can make a difference – maybe even half an hour.'

'I tried to deceive you before,' she said. 'That discouraged you. Now I am dealing only in truth. I never deceived you in what I was offering, only in my motive, and that's changed now. I would prefer to part with you amicably.'

'I appreciate that. It's amicable. But I meant it, about time making a difference. You should go, quickly.'

She read him yet again. The complicated knot of motives remained unresolved: He wanted her but would not take her. She did not have time to untangle all the threads of the situation – threads that extended well back into his relation with Aquilon. 'Right.' She put her blouse back together.

She had not been lying. Veg was a better man than she had judged, with a certain quality under his superficial simplicity. It would have been no chore to indulge him, merely an inconvenience.

She turned on the projector. The spherical field formed. 'Bye, Veg,' she said, kissing him quickly. Then she stepped into the field.

And he stepped into it with her.

Chapter Eight

ENCLAVE

The episode of the machine attack had brought them together, with new understandings. The spots were interdependent – and OX interdependent with them. Dec, the moving shape changer. Ornet, the stable mover. Cub, helpless. OX, variable and mobile.

The three spots required gaseous, liquid, and solid materials to process for energy. The concepts were fibrillatingly strange despite OX's comprehensive new clarification circuits. They needed differing amounts of these aspects of matter in differing forms and combinations. But it was in the end comprehensible, for their ultimate requirement was energy, and OX needed energy, too. They drew it from matter; he drew it from elements. Energy was the common requirement for survival.

Could the spots' method of processing it be adapted to OX's need? YES. For when OX acted to promote the welfare of the spots, his elements became stronger. He had ascertained that before the machine attacked. When he provided the spots with their needs, they helped the plants, which in turn strengthened their elements. Yet the specific mechanism was not evident.

OX concentrated, experimenting with minute shifts in the alternate framework. Gradually, the concepts clarified. The fundaments of the plants were rooted in certain alternates but flowered their elements in others. The roots required liquids and certain solids; the flowers required pattern-occupation, or they accumulated too much energy and became unstable. Their energy would begin spilling, making chaos. The reduction of that energy by

461

the patterns kept the plants controlled, so that they prospered. The plants had both material and energy needs, and the spots served the first, the patterns the second.

The spots served another purpose. One of them, Ornet, had knowledge – a fund of alien information that compelled $\overline{OX}$'s attention, once he established adequate circuitry to hold detailed dialogue with this particular spot. For this information offered hints relating to survival.

Ornet had a memory circuit quite unlike that of $\overline{OX}$. Yet $\overline{OX}$ had become wary of ignoring difficult concepts; survival kept him broadening. Ornet's memory said that his kind had evolved a very long time ago, gradually changing, aspects of itself continually degenerating and renewing like a chain of self-damping shoots. That much was comprehensible.

But Ornet's memory also said that there were many other creatures, unlike Ornet or the two other spots or the machine, and that they, too, expanded, divided, and degenerated. This was significant: *a host of other spots*. Yet only the three were here. What had happened to the others?

Ornet did not know. There were a few in the enclave, mobile nonsentients, but those were only a tiny fraction of those described. $\overline{OX}$ was not satisfied that all were gone. They seemed to have existed in another framework and might exist there still. Where was that framework?

Further, Ornet's perception said that the machines had evolved in somewhat similar fashion. He knew this from his observation of the one that attacked. And he also said that $\overline{OX}$ himself had evolved somehow from some different pattern.

Alien nonsense! But $\overline{OX}$ modified his circuits, creating the supposition that all of this could be true, and followed the logic to certain strange conclusions.

Yet something was missing. $\overline{OX}$ realized, in the moment this special circuit functioned, that he could not have evolved here as the first pattern; he had come into existence only recently, whereas the plants had been here for a long time. And what about the spots? All were of recent origin, too, like $\overline{OX}$. Even his special circuits could not accept this as the only reality.

Because the spots enhanced the elements, $\overline{OX}$'s immediate problem of survival had been abated. He could afford to consider longer-range survival. In fact, he *had* to – for survival was not complete until all aspects were secure. Control of his immediate scene was not enough. Was there some threat or potential threat beyond?

OX explored as far as he was able. His region was bounded on all sides by the near absence of elements; he could not cross out. There were only diminishing threads of elements that tapered down to thicknesses of only a few elements in diameter. It was impossible for OX to maintain his being on those; he had to have a certain minimum for his pattern to function.

He sent his shoots across these threads regularly; this was part of the way he functioned. Most were self-damping processes resulting from more complex circuits; some were simple self-sustaining radiations. A few were so constituted that they would have returned had they encountered a dead end. None did return, which showed OX that the threads continue on into some larger reservoir beyond his perception.

Radiations were inherent in the pattern scheme. Had another pattern-entity existed within OX's limited frame, OX would have been made aware of its presence by its own radiations. It was essential that patterns not merge; that was inevitable chaos and loss of identity for both. Because of the natural radiations of shoots, patterns were able to judge each other's whereabouts and maintain functional distances. This OX knew because it was inherent in his system; it would be nonsurvival for it to be otherwise. Once he had reacted to the seeming presence of another pattern because he had intercepted alien shoots, both self-sustaining and damping ... but upon investigation it had turned out to be merely the reflection of his own projections, distorted by the irregular edge of his confine.

He knew there were other patterns ... somewhere. There had to be. He had not come equipped with shoot-interpretation circuits by coincidence!

Perhaps beyond the barrier-threads? OX could not trace them – but the spots *could*. OX held dialogue with the communicative spot, Ornet. He made known his need to explore beyond the confines of this region.

Ornet in turn communicated with Dec, the most mobile spot. Dec moved rapidly out of OX's perception. When he returned, his optic generator signalled his news: This frame, one of the limited myriads of alternates that comprised the fabric of $\overline{OX}$'s reality, did indeed have other structures of elements. Dec had located them by following the element-threads that $\overline{OX}$ could not. Dec perceived these elements only with difficulty but had improved with practice. At varying physical distances, he reported, a number of them re-expanded into viable reservoirs. And in one of these Dec had spied a pattern.

The news threw $\overline{OX}$ into a swirl of disorientation. Hastily he modified his circuits; he had now confirmed, by observation of his own nature and indirect observation of the external environment, that he was not the only entity of his kind.

The other patterns had to know of him. His radiations, travelling the length of the element-threads, had to notify them of his presence. Yet never had a return-impulse come. That had to mean the others were damping out their external signs. Their only reason would be to abate a threat, as of a shoot-detecting machine or a pattern-consuming nonsentient pattern, or to conceal their presence for more devious internal reasons. On occasion, $\overline{OX}$ damped out his own radiation when he did not wish to be disturbed; his circuits did this automatically, and analysis of them showed this to be the reason. Actually, such damping was pointless here, there were no intrusive patterns, and the spots were not affected: additional evidence that $\overline{OX}$ was equipped by nature to exist in a society of patterns, not alone.

Why would other patterns, aware of him, deliberately conceal themselves from him? In what way was he a threat to them? He was a fully functioning pattern; it was not his nature to intrude upon another of his kind. The other patterns surely knew this; it was inherent, it was survival.

Something very like anger suffused $\overline{OX}$. Since his nature responded only to survival-nonsurvival choices, it was not emotion as a living creature would know it. But it was an acute, if subtle, crisis of survival.

A compatible pattern would not have acted in the fashion these outside patterns did. Therefore, their presence was a strong potential threat to his survival.

$\overline{OX}$ sent Dec out to observe again more thoroughly, and he sent Ornet out to the same physical spot in an adjacent frame. The two observers could not perceive each other, for they could not cross over alternates, and $\overline{OX}$ could observe neither since they were beyond his element-pool. But this difficult cooperative manoeuvre was critical.

Their report confirmed what $\overline{OX}$ had suspected.

Dec had observed a pattern fade, leaving the points unoccupied. Then it, or another like it, had returned. But Ornet's location had remained vacant.

$\overline{OX}$ understood this, though the spots did not. The pattern was travelling through the frames. Because of the configuration of the pool as $\overline{OX}$ had mapped it, he knew that the foreign pattern had to move either towards Ornet or away from him. It had moved away. And that meant that the other pool of elements extended beyond $\overline{OX}$'s own pool, for his did not go farther in that direction.

The other pools, in fact, were probably *not* pools. They were aspects of the larger framework. The other patterns were not restricted as $\overline{OX}$ was.

They were keeping him isolated, restricted, confined to an enclave, while they roamed free. This, by the inherent definition of his circuitry, was inimical behaviour.

$\overline{OX}$ sank into a long and violent disorientation. Only by strenuous internal measures was he able to restore equilibrium. Then it was only by making a major decision that forced a complete revamping of his nature.

He was in peril of nonsurvival through the action of others of his own kind. He had either to allow himself to be disrupted at their convenience or to prepare himself to disrupt the other patterns at *his* convenience. He chose the latter.

$\overline{OX}$ was ready to fight.

Chapter Nine

LIFE

The two mantas, Hex and Circe, showed them the place, then disappeared again on their own pursuits. They seemed to like the city and to enjoy exploring it.

Cal and Aquilon stood on either side of the projector, not touching it. 'So she had a way back all the time – and she took Veg with her,' Aquilon said bitterly. 'While we slept, blissfully ignorant.' She crumpled the note and threw it away in disgust.

'I knew she had some such device,' Cal replied. 'I told the mantas to let them go.'

She was aghast. 'Why?'

'We could not stop the agent from doing as she wished – but Veg will keep an eye on her and perhaps ameliorate her omnivoristic tendencies. Meanwhile, it is pointless to remain idle here. I suspect we shall be able to make contact with the pattern-entities better on our own. They may or may not attempt to contact us again on the stage. If they do, I would prefer that Veg not break it up and that Tamme not receive their information. If they don't, it will be up to us to make a move.'

'You really have it figured out,' she said, shaking her head. Then: '*Pattern* entities? What—?'

'I have been doing some thinking. I believe I understand the nature of our abductor, and how we can communicate with it.'

She lifted her hands, palms up. 'Just like that!'

'Oh, it was simple enough, once I had the key,' he said modestly. 'Pattern.'

'That's what you said before. I still don't follow it.'

'First we have to capture a suitable machine.'

'Capture a machine!' she exclaimed.

'If we can immobilize it long enough for me to get at its control unit, I should be able to turn it to our purpose.'

She looked at him in perplexity. 'Lure it under an ambush and knock it on the head with a sledgehammer?'

Cal smiled. 'No, that would destroy the delicate mechanism we need. We shall have to be more subtle.'

'Those machines aren't much for subtlety,' she cautioned him. 'If there are any of the whirling-blade variety around—'

'The menials will do,' he said. 'Preferably one with an optic-signal receiver.'

Aquilon shook her head. 'Well, you know best. Tell me what to do.'

'Locate a flower or other device that will attract the right type of machine.'

'Something optical, you mean?'

'Something that requires optical repair, yes.' He faced away. 'Hex! Circe!'

Aquilon shrugged and went looking. Cal knew what she was thinking: He was far more the mystery man than he had been on Nacre or Paleo. Those had been comparatively simple, physical worlds; this was a complex intellectual-challenge situation. His area of strength! But he would soon explain himself.

The two mantas arrived, sailing down to land beside him. 'You have observed the tame machines?' he inquired.

They did not need to snap their tails. His rapport with them had progressed beyond that stage. He could tell their answer by the attitude of their bodies, just as he had divined their disapproval of his directive regarding Tamme and her projector. YES. As he had already known.

'Can you broadcast on their optical circuits?'

Now they were dubious. There followed a difficult, somewhat technical dialogue involving wavelengths and intensities. Conclusion: They *might* be able to do what he wanted. They would try.

Aquilon returned. 'The light-loom seems best,' she reported. 'If something interfered with the original light-beam, the entire fabric would be spoiled. Seems a shame . . .'

'We shall not damage it,' Cal assured her. 'We want only to attract the relevant machine.' He glanced again at the little projector. 'This we shall leave untouched, as I believe it has been set to bring them back at a particular moment. They have no chance to reach Earth; I hope they find equivalent satisfaction.'

Aquilon's eyes narrowed. 'Are you implying—'

'As the agents experience more of reality away from their computer, they become more individual, more human. We stand in need of another human female if we are to maintain any human continuity away from Earth.'

Her lip curled. 'Why not wish for a cobra to turn human while you're at it?'

They went to the fountain. 'Distort that light,' Cal told the mantas. 'Play your beams through it if you can keep it up without hurting your eyes.'

They dutifully concentrated on the rising light.

'This may take a while,' Cal said, 'because it is subtle.'

'Too subtle for me,' she murmured.

'I will explain it.' He dusted off the clear plastic panel covering the tapestry storage chamber. This was unnecessary, for there was no dust. He brought out a small marking pencil.

'Where did you get that?' she asked.

'The marker? I've had it all the time.'

She smiled ruefully. 'He travels through Paleocene jungles, he battles dinosaurs, he tackles self-willed machines, he carries a cheap pencil.'

Cal put his hand on her arm, squeezing. 'Life does go on.'

She turned her lovely blue eyes upon him. 'Did you mean it, on Nacre?'

Nacre, fungus planet: There was no mistaking her allusion. Now he regretted that he had made reference to it in front of Veg; that was not kind. He looked into the depths of those eyes and remembered it with absolute clarity.

They had been climbing, forging up a narrow, tortuous trail between ballooning funguses and the encompassing mist. Aquilon, instead of resting, had painted – not despite the fatigue, as she explained, but *because* of it. And though her subject had been ugly, the painting itself had been beautiful.

'You match your painting,' Cal had told her, sincerely.

She had turned from him, overcome by an emotion neither of them understood, and he had apologized. 'I did not mean to hurt you. You and your work are elegant. No man could look upon either and not respond.'

She had put away her painting and stared out into the mist. 'Do you love me?' Perhaps a naïve question since they had only known each other three months, and that aboard a busy spaceship; they really had had little to do with each other until getting stranded on the pearl-mist planet.

And he had answered: 'I'm afraid I do.' He had never before said that to a woman and never would again except to her.

Then she had told him of her past: a childhood illness that destroyed her smile.

Now she had her wish: She could smile again. That was the gift of the manta. But it had not brought her satisfaction.

'Yes, I meant it,' he said. And did not add: *But Veg loved you, too.* That had formed the triangle, and she had seemed better suited to healthy Veg, especially on Paleo. Unfortunately the two had proved not wholly compatible and were in the process of disengaging. Cal hoped he had done the right thing in exposing Veg to Tamme. He had tried to warn Veg first, but the whole thing had a jealous smell to it as though he were throwing a rival to the wolves. Wolf, cobra – by any metaphor, an agent was trouble. Unless, as with Subble, there was some redeeming human quality that transcended the mercilessly efficient and ruthless program. A long, long shot – but what else was there?

'Look – the pattern is changing!' Aquilon exclaimed, looking through the plastic at the slowly moving material.

'Excellent – the mantas have mastered the trick. Now we'll see how long it takes for a repair-machine to come.'

'You were about to explain what you're doing.'

'So I was! I am becoming absent-minded.'

'Becoming?'

Such a superficial, obvious gesture, this bit of teasing. Yet how it stirred him! To Cal, love was absolute; he had always been ready to die for her. Somehow he had not been ready to banter with her. It was a thing he would gladly learn. At the moment, he did not know the appropriate response and would not have felt free to make it, anyway. So he drew three dots on the surface: •• 'What do you see?'

'A triangle.'

469

'How about three corners of a square?'

'That, too. It would help if you completed the square, if that's really what you want to indicate.'

'By all means.' He drew in the fourth dot: $\vcenter{\hbox{$\bullet\,\bullet$}\hbox{$\bullet\,\bullet$}}$ And waited.

She looked at it, then up at him. 'That's all?'

'That's the essence.'

'Cal, I'm just a little slower than you. I don't quite see how this relates to comprehension of the so-called "pattern entities" and travel between alternate worlds.'

He raised an eyebrow. 'You don't?'

'You're teasing me!' she complained, making a moue.

So he was learning already! 'There's pleasure in it.'

'You've changed. You used to be so serious.'

'I am stronger – thanks to you.' On Nacre he had been almost too weak to stand, contemplating death intellectually and emotionally. He still had a morbid respect for death – but Veg and Aquilon had helped him in more than the physical sense.

'Let's take your square another step,' she suggested. 'I know there's more. There always is with you.'

He looked at the square. 'We have merely to formulate the rule. Three dots are incomplete; they must generate the fourth. Three adjacent dots do it – no more, no less. Otherwise the resultant figure is not a—'

'All right. Three dots make a fourth.' She took his marker and made a line of three: $\bullet\ \bullet\ \bullet$ 'What about this?'

'Double feature. There are two locations covered by three adjacent dots. So—' He added two dots above and below the line:

$\vcenter{\hbox{$\bullet$\quad$\bullet$}\hbox{$\bullet$}}$

'So now we have a cross of a sort.' She shook her head. 'I remain unenlightened.'

'Another rule, since any society must have rules if it is to be stable. Any dot with three neighbour-dots is stable. Or even with two neighbours. But anything else – more than three or less than two – is unstable. So our figure is not a cross.'

'No. The centre dot has four neighbours. What happens to it?'

'Were this the starting figure, it would disappear. Cruel but necessary. However, the five-dot figure does not form from the three-dot figure because the ends of the original one are unstable.

470

Each end-dot has only a single neighbour.' He drew a new set:
• • •   Then he erased the ends, leaving one: •

'But what of the new dots we already formed?'

'Creation and destruction are simultaneous. Thus our figure flexes so.' He numbered the stages: 1 • • • 2 •⋮ 3 • • • 4 •⋮ 'We call this the "blinker".'

She looked at him suspiciously. 'You mean this has been done before?'

'This is a once-popular game invented by a mathematician, John Conway, back in 1970. He called it "Life". I have often whiled away dull hours working out atypical configurations.'

'I haven't seen you.'

He patted her hand. 'In my head, my dear.'

'That would sound so much better without the "my".'

'"In head?"'

She waggled a forefinger at him. '"Dear".'

'You are becoming positively flirtatious.' Perhaps she was rebounding from Veg.

'Was Taler right on the ship?'

The ship. Again he looked into her eyes, remembering. The Earth government had not waited for the trio's report; it had sent four agents to Paleo to wrap it up, which agents had duly taken the normals prisoner and destroyed the dinosaur enclave. 'Interesting', Taler had remarked while Tamme watched, amused. 'Dr Potter is even more enamoured of Miss Hunt than is Mr Smith. But Dr Potter refuses to be influenced thereby.'

'I suppose he was,' Cal said.

She sighed as though she had anticipated more of an answer. 'There must be more to life than this.'

He glanced at her again, uncertain which way she meant it. He elected to interpret it innocuously. 'There is indeed. There are any number of game figures, each with its own history. Some patterns die out; others become stable like the square. Still others do tricks.'

'Now she was intrigued. 'Let me try one!'

'By all means. Try this one.' He made a tetromino, four dots: • • •

Aquilon pounced on it. 'There's an imaginary grid, right? The dots are really filling in squares and don't mesh the same on the bias?'

471

'That's right.' She was quick, now that she had the idea; he liked that.

'If this is position one, then for position two we have to add one, two, three spots, and take away – none.' She made the new figure:

'Correct. How far can you follow it?'

She concentrated, tongue between her lips. At length, she had the full series. 'It evolves into four blinkers. Here's the series.' She marked off the numbers of the steps in elegant brackets so as to avoid the use of confusing periods.

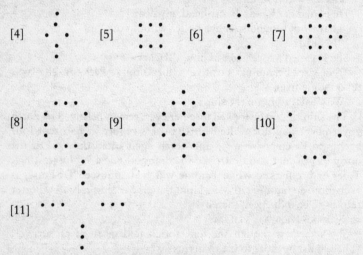

'Very good. That's "Traffic Lights".'

'Fascinating! They really work, too! But still, I don't see the relevance to—'

'Try this one,' he suggested, setting down a new pattern:
'That's the "R Pentomino".'

'That's similar to the one I just did. You've just tilted it sideways, which makes no topological difference, and added one dot.'

'Try it,' he repeated.

She tried it, humouring him. But soon it was obvious that the

472

solution was not a simple one. Her numbered patterns grew and changed, taking up more and more of the working area. The problem ceased to be merely intriguing; it became compulsive. Cal well understood this; he had been through it himself. She was oblivious to him now, her hair falling across her face in attractive disarray, teeth biting lips. 'What a difference a dot makes!' she muttered.

Cal heard something. It was the hum of a travelling machine. The bait had finally been taken!

He moved quietly away from Aquilon, who did not miss him. He took his position near the light fountain. The next step was up to the mantas.

The machine hove into sight. It was exactly what Cal had hoped for: a multilensed optical specialist – the kind fitted out to analyze a marginally defective light-pattern. One of the screens on it resembled an oscilloscope, and there seemed to be a television camera.

Excellent! This one must have been summoned from mothballing, as light-surgery was no doubt necessary less frequently than mechanical repairs. This was an efficient city, which did not waste power and equipment.

The two mantas turned to concentrate on the machine. Cal knew they were directing their eye-beams at its lenses, attempting to send it intelligible information and usurp its control system. If anything could do it, the mantas could – but only if the machine were sufficiently sophisticated.

It stopped, facing the mantas. Was the plan working?

Suddenly the machine whirled, breaking contact. Its intake lens spied Cal. The snout of a small tube swung about with dismaying authority.

Cal felt sudden apprehension. He had not expected physical danger to himself or Aquilon, and he was not prepared. His skin tightened; his eyes darted to the side to assess his best escape route or locate a suitable weapon. There was a nervous tremor in his legs.

He had played hide-and-seek with Tyrannosaurus, the largest predator dinosaur of them all. Was he now to lose his nerve before a mere repair robot?

Cal leaped aside as the beam of a laser scorched a pin-hole in the plastic wall behind the place he had just stood. He had seen the warm-up glow just in time. But now it was warmed up and would fire too fast for his reflexes. He scurried on as the laser projector reoriented.

His plan had malfunctioned – and now the machine was on the attack. They were in for it!

The mantas tried to distract it, but the thing remained intent on Cal. Wherever he fled, it followed.

Aquilon, jolted out of her concentration, stepped forward directly into the range of the laser, raising her hand. Her chin was elevated, her hair flung back, her body taut yet beautiful in its arrested dynamism. For an instant she was a peremptory queen. 'Stop!' she said to the machine.

It stopped.

Startled, Cal turned back. Had the machine really responded to a human voice – or was it merely orienting on a new object? Aquilon's life depended on that distinction!

Aquilon herself was amazed. 'I reacted automatically, foolishly,' she said. 'But now – I wonder.' She spoke to the machine again. 'Follow me,' she said, and began to walk down the path.

The machine stayed where it was, unmoving. Not even the laser tube wavered, though now it covered nothing.

'Wait,' Cal murmured to her. 'It begins to come clear. You gave that machine a pre-emptive directive.'

'I told it to stop,' she agreed. 'I was alarmed. But if it understood and obeyed me then, why not now?'

'You changed the language,' he said.

'I what?'

'The first time you addressed it, you used body language. Everything about you contributed to the message. You faced it without apparent fear, you raised your hand, you gave a brief, peremptory command.'

'But I spoke English!'

'Irrelevant. No one could have mistaken your meaning.' He put his hand under her arm, pulling her gently towards him. 'Body language – the way we move, touch, look – the tension of our muscles, the rate of our pulse, our respiration – the autonomic processes. The agents virtually read our minds through those involuntary signals.'

'Yes,' she said, seeing it. 'Your hand on me – that's speaking, too, more than your words.'

He let go quickly. 'Sorry. I just wanted you to understand—'

'I did,' she said, smiling. 'Why does that embarrass you?'

'This city is, despite its weirdities, essentially human. It was made to serve human beings, perhaps women like you—'

'A matriarchy?'

'Possibly. Now those people are gone, but the city remains, producing breathable air, growing edible fruit, supporting at least some omnivorous wildlife as though in anticipation of the needs of the mantas, manufacturing things for human use. Surely the machines remember their erstwhile masters!'

'Then why did it attack you?'

'I was acting in an unfriendly manner, associating with aliens who were interfering with the business of the city. I was giving the signals of an enemy or a vandal – as indeed I regarded myself. The machine reacted accordingly.'

Aquilon nodded. 'So we know the builders, though not their language.'

'We *are* the builders – on another variant. Perhaps this city is an artifact of a human alternate many thousands of years in our future. With the alternate framework, it stands to reason that many worlds are ahead of us as well as many behind.'

'Dinosaurs on one – super science on another,' she agreed.

'But I do not think the sparkle-cloud is part of this human scheme – as I was explaining.'

'You *were*?'

'The Life game.'

She grimaced. 'I haven't gotten through your R Pentomino yet.'

'I wouldn't worry about it,' he said. 'It only achieves a "steady state" after eleven hundred moves.'

'Eleven hundred moves!' she exclaimed indignantly. 'And you set me innocently to work with a pencil—'

'The point is, the entire game is determined by the opening configuration. But that hardly means that all openings are similar, or that a five-point figure does not have impressive complexities in its resolution. Most simple patterns quickly fade or become stable. A few are open-ended, especially when they interact with other figures. So larger opening patterns might conceivably—'

'Cal!' she cried. 'Are you saying that this little dot-game – the sparkle-pattern—'

He nodded. '"Life" is a simple two-dimensional process that nevertheless has certain resemblances to the molecular biology of our living life. Suppose this game were extended to three physical dimensions and given an indefinitely large grid?'

She shook her head so that her hair flew out enticingly. Had she picked up that gesture from Tamme? 'It would still be predetermined.'

'As *we* are predetermined, according to certain philosophies. But it becomes extremely difficult to chart that course before the fact. Suppose a number of forms were present on that grid, interacting?'

'If their patterns got too large, they'd mess each other up. There's no telling what would happen then.' She paused, his words sinking in. 'It would still be predetermined by the initial figures and their relation to each other on the grid – but too complicated to predict without a computer. Maybe there's no computer that could handle the job if the grid were big enough and the figures too involved. Anything could happen.'

'And if it existed in four or five dimensions?'

She spread her hands. 'I'm no mathematician. But I should think the possibilities would approach those of organic processes. After all, as you pointed out, enzymes in one sense are like little keys on the molecular level, yet they are indispensable to the life processes. Why not dot-pattern enzymes, building into—' She paused again. 'Into animate sparkle-clouds!'

'So we could have what amounts to independent, free-willed entities,' he finished. 'Their courses may be predetermined by their initial configurations and framework – but so are ours. We had better think of them as potentially sentient and deal with them accordingly.'

'Which means establishing communication with them,' she said. 'It was a giant mental step, but at last I am with you.' She looked down at the complex mess of her R Pentomino and blew out her cheeks.

'That's good,' he said. 'Because we need that machine – and you seem to be able to control it. Bring it to the auditorium.'

Aquilon struck a dramatic pose before the machine. 'Come!' she commanded, gesturing imperatively. And it did.

'You know, I rather enjoy this,' she confided as they walked.

476

Chapter Ten

PHASE

$$\begin{matrix} \bullet & \bullet & \bullet & \\ \bullet & & & \bullet \\ \bullet & & & \bullet \\ & \bullet & \bullet & \bullet \end{matrix}$$

$\overline{OX}$ was ready to fight. He now knew he was under observation by pattern-entities resembling himself who declined to communicate with him. Had they merely been there, unaware of him, they would not have cut off their normal radiation shoots – and since he had not cut off his, they had to know of him. So he was certain of his diagnosis.

His combat circuitry, laboriously developed in the process of restoring equilibrium, informed him that it would be nonsurvival to permit the outside patterns to learn of his change of condition. He therefore fashioned a pseudoplacid circuit whose purpose was to maintain normal radiation despite the internal changes. The observing patterns would thus receive no evidence of $\overline{OX}$'s real intent.

It was also probable that the outside patterns did not comprehend the significance of the spots. That was thus an asset, for the spots had already proved themselves as both element-stimulators and sources of exterior information. In fact, the spots represented $\overline{OX}$'s major potential weapon. He had ascertained that they, like he, were of recent origin; they, like he, possessed the powers of growth and increased facility. According the Ornet-Spot memory, the stationary stable Cub was a member of a type that had greater potential than many others. But this needed a great deal of time and concentration to develop. $\overline{OX}$ decided to exploit this potential.

Each alternate was separated from its neighbours by its phase of duration. $\overline{OX}$ had verified this by study of the elements he activated:

They gradually matured as the plants charged them, and this maturation represented a constant within the individual frame. Even an element that had been activated and recharged many times still reflected its ancestry and age. But the equivalent elements of adjacent alternates differed, one frame always being newer than the other.

Since $\overline{OX}$ was a pattern having no physical continuity, this differential of alternates did not affect him except as it affected the elements. Generally the older, more established elements were more comfortable; fresh ones were apt to release their energy unevenly, giving him vague notions of nonsurvival.

That differential could, however, affect the spots, who were almost wholly physical. $\overline{OX}$ could move them from one frame to another as they were, allowing them to change in relation to their environment because of the shift in that environment – as when he had moved them to a more favourable habitat. He could also, he discovered, modify the transfer so that the alternates remained fixed – and the spots changed. He had done that when Cub perished before the blade of the machine. It was merely an aspect of crossover: A physical difference between creature and alternate always had to be manifest.

What it amounted to was a method for aging the spots. When $\overline{OX}$ moved them this way, they were forced to assume the duration they would have had, had they always existed there. Then he shifted them back, this time letting them be fixed while the frame seemed to change. It was an artificial process that cut the spots off from the untampered frames beyond the enclave – but he was barred from that, anyway.

In this manner he brought the spots from infancy to maturity in a tiny fraction of the time they would normally have required. Of course to *them* it seemed as though their full span had passed in normal fashion; only $\overline{OX}$ knew better. But he explained this to them and offered certain proofs for their observation, such as the apparent cessation of the growth of the fixed life around them, the immobile plants. Only those plants within the radius of the frame-travel advanced at the same rate. They discussed this with increasing awareness and finally believed.

The little machine, always hovering near, was also caught up in the progress. $\overline{OX}$ tried to leave it behind, but with inanimate cunning it moved in whenever it sensed his development of the

478

complex necessary circuits, staying in phase. Originally it had been impervious to the spots' attacks; had they advanced without it, they would have been free of it one way or another, either by getting completely out of phase with it or by becoming large and strong enough to overcome it. Thus, they always had to be on guard against its viciousness.

OX also arranged education shoots that facilitated the expansion of awareness in the spots. Though this almost wholly occupied OX's available circuitry, it did not have a large effect on either Dec or Ornet. They seemed programmed to develop in their own fashions regardless of his influence. But for Cub it was most productive. Ornet's conjecture had been accurate: Cub had enormous potential, in certain respects rivalling OX's own. How this could be in a physical being OX could not quite grasp; he had to assume that Cub had a nonphysical component that actually made rationality feasible. At any rate, Cub's intellect was malleable, and OX's effort was well rewarded.

OX watched and guided according to his combat nature as Dec became large and swift, able to disable a semi-sentient animal with a few deadly snaps of his tail-appendage, able to receive and project complex information efficiently. He was the fastest-moving spot physically, useful for purely physical observations and communications.

Ornet served to protect and assist Cub – but Ornet's memory clarified as he grew and offered many extraordinary insights into the nature of spots and frames that influenced OX's own development. Ornet, limited as he was physically, nevertheless had vested within him more sheer experience than any of the others, including OX himself. That was a tremendous asset, like a stabilizing circuit, guiding him through potential pitfalls of nonsurvival. OX always consulted with Ornet before he made any significant decision.

But Cub was his best investment. he grew from a non-mobile lump to a slowly mobile entity, then to a creature approaching Ornet in physical capability. His intellect became larger and larger. Soon he was grasping concepts that baffled both Dec and Ornet. Then, as he approached maturity, his reasoning ability interacted with OX's on something other than a teacher-pupil level. He began to pose questions that OX could not resolve – and that in turn forced OX to ever-greater capacities.

What about the killer machine? Cub inquired once after they had driven it off. Do you think it gets lonely as we do? Doesn't it have needs and feelings, too?

The very notion was preposterous! Yet $\overline{OX}$ had to make a new circuit and concede that yes, in machine-terms, it would have needs and feelings, too, and perhaps was lonely for its own kind.

Or maybe for sapience of any kind – including ours? Cub persisted. Could it be that when it tries to consume us, it is really seeking intellectual dialogue, not aware that we do not integrate physically as it does?

$\overline{OX}$ had to allow that possibility, also. Still, he pointed out, it remains a deadly enemy to us all because we *don't* integrate as mechanical components. We can never afford to let down our guard.

But long after that dialogue, his curcuits fibrillated with the intemporate concept. A machine, seeking intellectual dialogue. A *machine!*

Chapter Eleven

HEXAFLEXAGON

.
:
... ...
:
.

They emerged into a blinding blizzard. Snow blasted Veg's face, and the chill quickly began its penetration of his body. He was not adequately dressed.

Tamme turned to him, showing mild irritation. 'Why did you come?' she demanded.

He tried to shrug, but it was lost in his fierce shivering. He did not really understand his own motive, but it had something to do with her last-minute display of decency. And with her beauty and his need to disengage irrevocably from Aquilon.

Tamme removed her skirt, did something to it, and put it about his shoulders. He was too cold to protest. 'This is thermal,' she said. 'Squat down, hunch up tight. It will trap a mass of warm air, Eskimo-style. Face away from the wind. Duck your head down; I'll cover it.' And she removed her halter, formerly her blouse, adjusted it, and fashioned it into a protective hood.

He obeyed but did finally get out a word. 'You—'

'I'm equipped for extremes,' she said. 'You aren't. I can survive for an hour or more naked in this environment – longer with my undergarments. So can you – if you just sit tight under that cloak. After that, we'll both exercise vigorously. We have to stretch it out three hours until the projector brings us back. We'll make it – though for once I wish I'd set it for the minimum safe-return time.'

He nodded miserably. 'Sorry. I didn't know—'

'That you would only be in the way? *I* knew – but I also knew your motive, confused as it might be, was good. You have courage and

481

ethics, not because you've been programmed for them, but because you are naturally that way. Perhaps agents should be more like that.' She paused, peering around. Snowflakes were hung up on her eyebrows, making little visors. 'I'll make a shelter. Maybe we won't *have* to go back.'

He watched her move about, seemingly at ease in the tempest ... in her bra and slip. He was chagrined to be so suddenly, so completely dependent on a woman, especially in what he had thought of as a man's natural element: wilderness. But she was quite a woman!

Tamme made the shelter. She cleared the loose snow away, baring a nether layer of packed snow and ice, a crust from some prior melting and refreezing. She used one of her weapons, a small flame thrower, to cut blocks of this out. Soon she had a sturdy ice wall.

'Here,' she directed.

He obeyed, moving jerkily into the shelter of the hole behind the wall. The wind cut off. Suddenly he felt much better. The cloak *was* warm; once the wind stopped wrestling with it, stealing the heated air from the edges, he was almost comfortable. He held it close about his neck, trapping that pocket of heat. But his feet were turning numb.

Tamme built the wall around him, curving it inwards until she formed a dome. It was an igloo!

'I think you'll manage now,' she said. 'Let me have my clothing; I want to look about.'

She crawled into the igloo beside him while he fumbled with cloak and hood. And she stripped off her underclothing.

Veg stared. She was an excellent specimen of womanhood, of course; not lush but perfectly proportioned, with no fat where it didn't belong. Every part of her was lithe and firm and feminine. But that was not what amazed him.

Strapped to her body was an assortment of paraphernalia. Veg recognized the holster for the flame thrower she had just used: It attached to her hip where a bikini would have tied – a place always covered without seeming to be, filling a hollow to round out the hip slightly. There was another holster, perhaps for the laser, on the other hip. An ordinary woman would have padded that region with a little extra avoirdupois; Tamme's leanness only served to delineate her muscular structure without at all detracting from her allure. There was a similar structure near her waist, which was in fact more

482

slender than it had seemed. And at the undercurves of her breasts.

How artfully she had hidden her weaponry while seeming to reveal all! Her thighs had seemed completely innocent under her skirt as she came down the pine tree. And who would have thought that the cleavage of her bosom had been fashioned by the push of steel weapons so close below! Had she been ready to make love to him that way, armed to the ...?

'No, I'd have set aside the weapons,' she said. 'Can't ever tell where a man's hands may go.'

She tore the bra, slip, and panties apart, then put them back together a different way. Evidently she could instantly remake all her clothing for any purpose – functional, seductive, or other. He had no doubt it could be fashioned into a rope to bind a captive or to scale a cliff. And of course her blouse had become first a revealing halter, then a hood for his head.

The female agent was every bit as impressive as the male agent! It was an excellent design.

'Thanks,' Tamme said.

She donned her revised underthings, once more covering the artillery. Veg now understood about her weight: She probably weighed a hundred and fifteen stripped but carried forty pounds of hardware.

She held out her hand unself-consciously. Hastily he passed the cloak and hood across and watched her convert them back into skirt and blouse. But not the same design as before; the skirt was now longer for protection against the storm, and the blouse closed in about her neck, showing no breast. Quite a trick!

She scrambled out of the igloo door and disappeared into the blizzard. While she was gone, Veg chafed his limbs and torso to warm them and marvelled at the situation in which he found himself. He had gone from Earth to Paleo, the first alternate; then to Desertworld, the second alternate. And on to Cityworld, Forestworld, and now to Blizzard – the third, fourth, and fifth, respectively. Now he was huddled here, shivering, dependent on a woman – while all alternity beckoned beyond!

How had they come here, really? Who had left the aperture projector so conveniently? It smelled of a trap. As did the blizzard. But for Tamme's strength and resourcefulness, it could have been a death trap.

Yet death would have been more certain if the aperture had opened over the brink of a cliff or before the mouth of an automatically triggering cannon.

No – that would have been too obvious. The best murder was the one that seemed accidental. And of course their immediate peril might well *be* accidental. Surely this storm was not eternal; this world must have a summer as well as a winter and be calm between altercations of weather. Tamme had said the projector could have been left five days ago. This storm was fresh. So maybe another agent had passed this way, leaving his projector behind as Tamme had left hers at Cityworld.

That meant the other agent was still around here somewhere. And that could be trouble. Suppose the agent overcame Tamme and stranded Veg here alone? She was tough and smart – and mighty pretty! – but another agent would have the same powers.

Unless —

Veg straightened up, banging his head against the curving roof wall. Suddenly a complex new possibility had opened to his imagination – but it was so fantastic he hardly trusted it. He didn't want to embarrass himself by mentioning it to Tamme. But he could not ignore it. He would have to check it out himself.

He wriggled out of the igloo. The wind struck him afresh, chilling him again, but he ducked his head, hunched his shoulders, and proceeded. This would not take long.

He counted paces as he slogged through the snow. At a distance of twenty steps – roughly fifty feet since he could not take a full stride in two-foot-deep snow – he halted. This was a tissue of guesswork, anyway, and here in the storm it seemed far-fetched indeed.

He tramped in a circle, backwards into the wind where he had to, eyes alert despite being screwed up against the wind. His face grew stiff and cold, and his feet felt hot: a bad sign. But he kept on. Somewhere within this radius there might be—

There wasn't. He retreated to the igloo, half disappointed, half relieved. He didn't regret making the search.

Tamme returned. 'What have you been doing?' she demanded. 'Your tracks are all over the place!'

'I had a crazy notion,' he confessed. 'Didn't pan out.'

'*What* crazy notion?'

'That there might be another projector here, part of a pattern.'

484

She sighed. 'I was hoping you wouldn't think of that.'

'You mean that's what *you* were looking for?' he asked, chagrined.

She nodded. 'I suspect we are involved in an alternate chain. We started from the city alternate – but others may have started from other alternates, leaving their projectors behind them, as I did. One started from the forest. Another may have started from here. In which case there will be a projector in the area.'

'That's what I figured – only I didn't really believe it. Projectors scattered all through alternity.'

'Alternity! Beautiful.'

'Well, it's as good a name for it as any,' he said defensively. 'Anyway, if it's all happening like that – what do you care? No one's trying to torpedo Earth.'

'How do you know?' she asked.

'Well, I can't *prove* anything, but what about the Golden Rule? We're not trying to do anything to *them*, so—'

'Aren't we?'

He faltered. 'You mean, we *are*?' He had thought she was just going after one agent, not the whole universe.

'Our government is paranoid about Earth-defence. We're out to destroy any possible competition before it destroys us. Remember Paleo?'

'Yeah ...' he agreed, wishing she hadn't reminded him of that. She, like all agents, was a ruthless killer.

'So it behooves us to catch them before *they* catch *us*.'

'But *we're* not paranoid! We don't have to—'

'*You* aren't. As an agent of our government, I *am*.'

He didn't like that, but he understood it. 'You have to serve your master, I guess. But if you ran the government—'

'Things would change. I don't like paranoia; it's inefficient. I don't like killing to maintain a defective system. But that is academic. Right now I have to trace this chain – if that's what it is – to its end. And deal with what I find there.'

'Yeah ...'

'You assumed the projector would be within fifty feet because the last one was. That does not necessarily follow.'

'Hell of a better chance to find it than looking three miles out.'

'Yes. I ranged three miles. The snow covers all traces.'

'Maybe it's under cover – in a hollow tree or under a rock or something. Because of its being winter.'

'Good idea. I'll check for that.' She moved out again.

She found it. The mound gave it away. Another aperture projector, very similar to the others.

'You can still go back' she told Veg.

'I'm getting curious,' he said, 'Let's go. It's cold here.'

She shrugged and activated the device. They stepped through.

Veg braced himself for any extreme of climate or locale – hot, cold, lush, barren, metropolis, wilderness. And stood amazed, caught unbraced for the reality.

It was an alien orchestra.

The instruments were conventional, even archaic: strings, wood-winds, percussion. The technique was flawless to his untrained ear. The melody was passionate, stirring mind, heart, and entrails. It was only the players who were alien.

Tamme looked about warily, as bemused as he. Veg knew she was searching for the next projector.

There was no sign of it.

Meanwhile, the alien orchestra played on, oblivious of the intrusion. The players on the violins had at least twelve appendages, each terminating in a single finger or point. These fingers moved over the strings, pressing to change the pitch; half a dozen fingers bunched to control the bow. The creatures on the flutes were bird-like, with nozzle-like mouths with gill-like apertures around the neck that took in air alternately so that there was always pressure. Those on the drums had arms terminating in hard balls on flexible tendons; they did not need to hold any drumsticks.

Veg wondered whether the creatures had been designed for the instruments or the instruments for the creatures. If the latter, as seemed more reasonable, what did this signify about music on Earth? Human beings adapting to instruments that were designed for aliens? That would mean strong crossover between alternates . . .

He tried to speak, but the music was loud, coming at them from every side, and he could not hear his own voice. Not surprising since the two of them had apparently landed right in the orchestra pit, huge as it was. They had to get out of it before they could communicate.

486

He looked for the edge of it – and only saw more musicians. They were really devoted to their art to ignore creatures as strange as he and Tamme must seem to them. He started to walk between the players, but a hand on his arm restrained him. It was Tamme, shaking her head 'No'.

He realized why: There was no distinguishing feature about this spot, and they could readily lose it. For that matter, they could lose each other if they stayed apart. There seemed to be no end to this orchestra!

Tamme pointed to a spot on the floor. 'Stay!' she mouthed several times until he read her lips and understood. He would be the place marker, she the explorer. Ordinarily he would have insisted on reversing the roles, but he knew she was more capable. He squatted where she had indicated.

Tamme moved through the formations of musicians. They were not exactly in lines or groups, but they were not random. There was a certain alien order to it – a larger pattern like that of the leaves on a tree or the stars in the sky.

Somewhere, here, was another projector – maybe.

Where? It was not visible. Could the aliens – actually they were not aliens but natives, as this was their alternate – could they have moved it? Somehow he doubted it. The creatures had taken absolutely no notice of the human intrusion; why should they bother with a mechanical device that did not play music? Maybe it was inside one of their instruments. No – when they left, it would be lost, and that was no decent alternative!

He contemplated the musicians. Where *did* they go during their breaks? Or were they anchored here forever? He had seen none move. Strange!

But back to the projector: Could it be in one of the boxlike seats? There seemed to be room. Which one? There were fifty or a hundred of them in sight. And how could he get *at* it?

Tamme was moving in widening spirals. He caught intermittent glimpses of her between the musicians. After a couple more circuits she would be invisible; the massed musicians blocked every line-of-sight pathway beyond a certain distance.

Well, that was one problem he would let Tamme handle. She didn't want him interfering, and maybe she was right. Still, it took some getting used to – but Tamme was different from Aquilon.

487

Veg shook his head. He wasn't sure which type of girl he preferred. Of course it was over between him and Aquilon, and pointless with Tamme, even for the one-night stand she had offered; she was not his type. Still, no harm in speculating . . .

This shifting randomly through alternates – or *was* it random? It reminded him of something. A children's game . . . puzzle . . . fold-a-game, flex-a-gone . . .

'Hexaflexagon!' he exclaimed. 'Alternity hexaflexagon!'

Tamme was there so fast he jumped, startled. 'What's the matter?' He could hear her now; the music had subsided to a delicate passage.

'Nothing,' he said sheepishly. 'I was just thinking.'

She did not waste effort on the matter. 'I have located the projector.'

'Great!' he said, relieved. Now that they were on this roller-coaster, he preferred to continue forward. He had not relished the notion of staying here or of returning to the blizzard world. 'How'd you figure which box?'

'Sound. The boxes are hollow; the projector changed the acoustics.'

'Oh. So you used the music. Smart.' Music and hexaflexagons, he thought. He followed her to the place.

It was the stool of a bass-strings player. The octopus-like creature almost enveloped the box, four of its tentacles reaching up to depress the ends of the four strings, four more manipulating the bow. The sounds it made were low and sweet: It really had the musical touch!

'You're pretty good,' Veg told it. But the volume had swelled again, drowning him out. The creature made no acknowledgment.

Tamme squatted, touched the box, and lifted out a panel. inside was one of the little aperture projectors. She didn't ask whether he was ready to go; she knew it. She reached in, her arm almost brushing the overlapping bulk of the octopus, and turned the machine on.

And they were on a steeply inclined plane. "Yo!' Veg cried, rolling helplessly.

Tamme caught his wrist and brought him up short. He had known she was strong, but this disconcerted him. Seemingly without effort, she supported the better part of his weight.

Veg's flailing free hand found purchase, and he righted himself. They were perched on a steeply tilted sheet of plastic. It was orange but transparent; through it he could see the jumbled edges of other sheets. He had caught hold of the slanting upper edge. Tamme had done the same farther up.

Below them were more sheets, some edge-on, some angled, some broadside. Above them were others. And more to the sides. All sizes and colours. What held them in place was a mystery; they seemed firm, as if embedded in clear glass, yet there was no support.

Veg peered down, searching for the ground. All he could see was an irregular network of planes. The jungle, like the orchestra they had just vacated, was everywhere, endless.

Tamme let go, slid down, and landed gracefully on a purple horizontal plane to the side. She signalled Veg to stay put.

'It figures,' he muttered, hoisting himself up to perch on the thin edge. The worlds were fascinating in their variety, but he certainly wasn't being much of a help so far.

Soon she was partially hidden behind the translucency of angled planes; he could detect her motion, not her image. She was looking for the next projector, of course.

Suppose she didn't find it? There was no guarantee that a given world had a projector or that it would be within a thousand miles. There had to be an end to the line somewhere.

A chill of apprehension crawled over him. No guarantee the next world would have air to breathe, either! They were playing one hell of a roulette game!

Maybe they would go on and on forever, meeting such a bewildering array of alternates that eventually they would forget which one they had started from, forget Earth itself.

Well, he had volunteered for the course!

Tamme was now invisible. Veg looked about, becoming bored with the local configurations. He wanted to explore some on his own, but he knew he had to remain as a reference point. This alternate was pretty in its fashion, but what was there to *do*?

He noticed that the plastic plane he perched on was not in ideal repair. Strips of it were flaking off. Maybe it was moulting, shedding its skin as it grew. Ha-ha.

Idly, he peeled off a length of it, moved by the same mild

489

compulsion that caused people to peel the plastic from new glossy book restorations. The stuff was almost colourless in this depth, flexible and a bit crackly. He folded it over, and it made a neat, straight crease without breaking.

That gave him a notion. He began folding off triangular sections. He was making a hexaflexagon!

'Let's go,' Tamme said.

Veg looked up. 'You found it, huh?' He tucked his creation into a pocket and followed her, leaping from plane to plane, stretching his legs at last.

It was hidden in the convergence of three planes, nestled securely. 'Kilroy was here, all right,' he murmured.

Tamme glanced at him sharply. 'Who?'

'You don't know Kilroy? He's from way back.'

'Oh – a figure of speech.' She bent over the projector.

So that was a gap in the agent education: They didn't know about Kilroy. He probably wasn't considered important enough to be included in their programming. Their loss!

The projector came on,

and they were back in the blizzard.

'A circuit!' Tamme cried in his ear, exasperated. 'Well, I know where the projector is.' She bundled him into her clothes and plunged forward.

'Maybe it's not the same one!' Veg cried.

'It is the same. There's our igloo.' Sure enough, they were passing it. But Veg noted that they had landed in a slightly different place this time, for the igloo had been built at their prior landing site. This time they had arrived about fifty feet to the side. Was that significant? He was too cold to think it out properly.

In minutes they found it. 'There's been time to recharge it – just,' she said. Then: 'That's funny.'

'What?' he asked, shivering in the gale.

'This is a left-handed projector, more or less.'

'Same one we used before,' he said. 'Let's get *on* with it.'

'I must be slipping,' she said. 'I should have noticed that before.'

'In this blizzard? Just finding it was enough!'

She shrugged and activated it.

They were now in the alien orchestra.

Veg shook the snow off his cloak and hood and looked about. This time they seemed to have landed in exactly the same place as before; he saw the stain of their prior water-shedding as the snow melted.

'We're stuck in a loop of alternates,' Tamme said. 'I don't like this.'

'There's got to be a way out. There was a way *in*.'

'That doesn't necessarily follow.' She glanced about. 'In any event, we ought to rest while the local projector is recharging.'

'Sure,' he agreed. 'Want me to stand watch?'

'Yes,' she said, surprising him. And she lay down on the floor and went to sleep.

Just like that! Veg's eyes ran over her body, for she was still in bra and panties. The hardware didn't show, and in repose Tamme looked very feminine. And why shouldn't she? he asked himself fiercely. Every woman in the world did not have to be stamped in the mould of Aquilon!

Of course Tamme wasn't a woman at all but an agent. She really *was* stamped from a mould – the TA-distaff-series mould. All over the world there were more just like her, each every bit as pretty, competent, and self-reliant.

He shied away from that concept. Instead, he looked around the orchestra at the now-familiar creatures. They looked the same: octopi, gillbirds, drumstick drummers. But something had changed somehow. What was it?

He concentrated, and it came to him: *This* alternate was the same, but the blizzard-alternate had been different. The igloo, as he passed it ... no, he couldn't quite pin it down. Different, yet the same, indefinably.

Veg blew out his breath, removed Tamme's cloak, and discovered his plastic hexaflexagon. This was proof he had been to the plane world, at least! He completed the folds, bit on the ends to fasten them properly, and flexed the device idly.

This was a hexa-hexaflexagon. It was hexagonal in outline, and when flexed, it turned up a new face from the interior, concealing one of the prior ones. But not in regular order. Some faces were harder to open than others.

He fished in his pocket and brought out a stubby pencil. He

491

marked the faces as he came to them: 1 for the top, 2 for the bottom. He flexed it, turning a new blank face to the top, and marked it 3. He flexed it again, and 2 came up.

'Closed loop,' he muttered. 'But I know how to fix that!' He shifted his grip to another diagonal and flexed from it. This time a new face appeared, and he marked this 4.

The next flex brought up 3 again. Then 2. And 1.

'Back to where we started,' he said. And changed diagonals. A blank face appeared, which he marked 5. Then on through 2, 1, 3, and finally to the last blank one, 6.

'Those loops are only closed if you let them,' he said with satisfaction. 'I'd forgotten how much fun these hexes were! You can tell where you are because the faces change orientation.'

Then the realization hit him.

'Hey, Tam!' he breathed.

He had spoken no louder than before, and the volume of the ambient music had not abated, but she opened her eyes immediately. 'Yes?'

'Maybe this is a bum lead – but I think I know why we're repeating worlds. And maybe how to snap out of the loop in controlled fashion.'

She sat effortlessly, the muscles in her stomach tightening. 'Speak.'

He showed her his plastic construct, opaque because of its many layers. 'You know what this is?'

'A doodle from plane-frame material.'

'A hexa-hexaflexagon. See, I flex it like this and turn up new faces.'

She took it and flexed it. 'Clever. But to what point?'

'Well, they don't come up in order – not exactly. Look at the face numbers as you go – and at the composition of the repeats.'

'One,' she called off. She flexed. 'Three ... Two ... One ... Five ... Two, inverted.' She looked up. 'It's a double triad. Intriguing, not remarkable.'

'Suppose we numbered the worlds we've been going through – and found a repeat that was backwards? I mean, the same, but like a mirror image?'

For the first time, he saw an agent do a double take. 'The second blizzard was backwards!' she exclaimed. 'Or rather, twisted sixty

492

degrees. The igloo – the irregularities in it and pattern of our prior tracks, what was left of them, the projector – all rotated by a third!'

'Yeah. That's what I figured. Didn't make sense at first.'

'Flexing alternates! Could be.' Rapidly she flexed through the entire sequence, fixing the pattern in her mind. 'It fits. We could be in a six-face scheme on this framework. In that case our next world will be – the forest.'

She certainly caught on rapidly! 'But we can't go home from there.'

'No. The face will be twisted, part of a subtriad. But we would know our route.'

'Yeah,' he agreed, pleased.

She pondered momentarily. 'There's no reason the alternates should match the hex faces. But there *is* a clear parallelism, and it may be a useful intellectual tool, in much the way mathematics is a tool for comprehending physical relations. Our problem is to determine the validity of our interpretation without subjecting outselves to undue risk.'

'You sound like Cal now!'

'No shame in that,' she muttered. 'Your friend has a freakishly advanced intellect. We could travel the loop again just to make sure – but that would mean a delay of several hours, waiting for the projectors to recharge. In that time our competition could gain the advantage.'

'So we just go ahead fast,' Veg finished. 'We can follow the flex route and see if it works. If it does, we've got our map of alternity.'

'In your bumbling male-normal fashion, you may have helped me,' Tamme said. 'Come here.'

Veg knelt down beside her.

She put both hands to his head, pulled him to her, and kissed him. It was like the moment in free fall when a spaceship halted acceleration in order to change orientation. His whole body seemed to float, while his own pulse pounded in his ears.

She let him go. It took him a moment to regain composure. 'That isn't the way you kissed me before.'

'That was demonstration. This was feeling.'

'You do feel? I thought—'

'We do feel. But our emotions are seldom aroused by normals other than amusement or distaste.'

Veg realized that he had been paid an extraordinary compliment. But that was all it was. He had helped her, and she was appreciative. She had repaid him with a professionally executed gesture. Case dismissed.

'We should have a choice here,' she said. 'Repeat the triad indefinitely – or break out of it. Only way to break out is to project elsewhere than to the plane world. But how can we do that – without interfering with the settings on the projector?'

Veg appreciated the problem. Touch those settings, and they could be thrown right out of this hex framework and be totally lost – or dead. That would accomplish nothing worthwhile. They wanted to follow the existing paths wherever they led, and catch up to – whom?

'These settings are built into the hexaflexagon,' he said. 'All you have to do is find them.'

'Yes. Too bad alternity isn't made of folded plastic.'

They remained in silence for a time, while the music swelled around them. And Veg had a second revelation. 'The music!'

Again she caught on almost as fast as he thought of it and quickly outdistanced his own reasoning. 'In phase with the music! Of course. Catch it during one type of passage, go on to Plane. Catch it during another—'

'Now's the time!' Veg cried.

They ran to the projector. Tamme had it on instantly.

And they were in the forest.

'Victory!' Veg exclaimed happily. Then he looked about uncertainly. 'But is it—?'

'Yes, it is rotated,' Tamme said. 'So it is part of a different triad. There'll be another odd-handed projector here.'

They located it, and it was. 'Hypothesis confirmed,' she said. 'Now if our interpretation is correct, we won't have to worry about being sent back to Blizzard because this inverted version is part of a different loop. The next one should be new. Brace yourself.' She reached for the switch.

'Sure thing,' Veg said. 'I'm braced for one

new world.'

It was new, all right. Veg's first impression was of mist. They stood in a tangibly thick fog. He coughed as the stuff clogged his lungs. It wasn't foul, just too solid to breathe.

'Get down,' Tamme said.

He dropped to the ground. There was a thin layer of clear atmosphere there, below the fog bank, like air trapped beneath river ice. He put his pursed lips to it and sucked it in.

'Crawl,' she said, her voice muffled by the fog.

They crawled, shoving aside the fog with their shoulders. Suddenly the ground dipped – but the bottom of the fog remained constant. It was too stiff to match the exact contour of the land. Now there was squatting clearance beneath, then standing room.

'That's some cloud!' Veg remarked, peering up. The stuff loomed impenetrably, a pall that blacked out all the sky. Wan light diffused through it. 'Stuff's damn near solid!'

'You liked it better under the pine tree?' Tamme inquired. She was already looking for the next projector.

'Sure did!' He had the nagging feeling the fog bank could fall at any moment, crushingly.

A valley opened out before them. Tamme stared.

Veg followed her gaze. 'A fog house?' he asked, amazed.

It was. Blocks of solidified fog had been assembled into something very like a cabin, complete with slanting, overlapping fog tiles on the roof. Beyond it was a fog wall or fence.

'This we have to look into,' Tamme said. She moved towards the house.

A curtain of fog parted, showing a doorway and a figure in it. 'Inhabited yet,' Tamme murmured. Her hands did not move to her weapons, but Veg knew she was ready to use them instantly.

'Let's go and ask directions,' he suggested facetiously.

'Yes.' And she moved forward.

'Hey, I didn't mean—' But he knew that she had known what he meant since she could read his emotions. Awkwardly, he followed her.

Up close, there was another shock. The inhabitant of the house was a human female of middle age but well preserved – with a prehensile nose.

Veg tried not to stare. The woman was so utterly typical of what he thought of as a frontier housewife – except for that proboscis. It twined before her face like a baby elephant trunk. It made her more

495

utterly alien than a battery of other nonhuman features might have – because it occupied the very centre of attention. It was repulsively fascinating.

Tamme seemed not to notice. 'Do you understand my speech?' she inquired sociably.

The woman's nose curled up in a living question mark.

Tamme tried a number of other languages, amazing Veg by her proficiency. Then she went into signs. Now the woman responded. 'Hhungh!' she snorted, her nose pointing straight out for a moment.

'Projector,' Tamme said. 'Alternates.' She shaped the projector with her hands.

The woman's nose scratched her forehead meditatively. 'Hwemph?'

'Flex,' Veg put in, holding out the hexaflexagon.

The woman's eyes lighted with comprehension. 'Hflehx!' she repeated. And her nose pointed to the fog bank from which they had emerged, a little to the side.

'Hthankhs,' Veg said, smiling.

The woman smiled back. 'Hshugh.'

Veg and Tamme turned back towards the fog. 'Nice people,' Veg remarked, not sure himself how he intended it.

'There have been others before us,' Tamme said. 'The woman had been instructed to play dumb, volunteering nothing. But we impressed her more favourably than did our predecessors, so she exceeded her authority and answered, after all.'

'How do you know all that?' But as he spoke, he remembered. 'You can read aliens, too! Because they have emotions, same as us.'

'Yes. I was about to initiate hostile-witness procedures, but you obviated the need.'

'Me and my flexagon!'

'You and your direct, naïve, country-boy manner, lucking out again.' She shook her head. 'I must admit: Simplicity has its place. You are proving to be a surprising asset.'

'Shucks, 'taint nothin'.' Veg said with an exaggerated drawl.

'Of course, our predecessors were the same: Tamme and Veg. That's why they obtained her cooperation.'

'I noticed she wasn't surprised to see us. I guess our noses look amputated.'

'Truncated. Yes.'

He laughed. 'Now she's punning. Truncated trunks!'

They were at the fog bank. 'Stand here. I need another orientation point. The projector will be within a radius of twenty metres, or about sixty feet.'

'You sure can read a lot from one nose-point!'

She plunged into the bank. The stuff was so thick that her passage left a jagged hole, as if she had gone through a wall of foam. It bled into the air from the edges, gradually filling in behind her. 'Talk,' Tamme said from the interior. 'The sound will help me orient on it, by the echo.'

It figured. She didn't ask him to talk because of any interest in what he might have to say! 'This place reminds me of Nacre in a way. That was all fog, too. But that was thinner, and it was everywhere, made by falling particles. The real plant life was high in the sky, the only place the sun shone; down below was nothing but fungus, and even the animals were really fungus, like the mantas. So it wasn't the same.'

There was no response from the bank, so he continued. 'You know, I read a story about a fog like this once. It was in an old science-fiction book, the kind they had in midcentury; I saw a replica printed on paper pages and everything. This thick fog came in wherever the sun didn't shine – they spelled it "phog" – and inside it was some kind of predator you never saw that ate people. It never left the fog – but nobody dared go *in* the fog, either. All they heard was the scream when it caught somebody—'

'YAAGH!'

Veg's mouth gaped. 'Oh, no!' He plunged into the fog, knife in hand.

A hand caught his wrist and hauled him back out. 'Next time don't try to tease an agent,' Tamme said, setting him down. 'I found the projector.'

'Sure thing,' he said, chagrined. Still, it was the first clear evidence of humour he had seen in her.

'Crawl under,' Tamme said.

They crawled under the fog, snatching lungfuls of clear air from the thin layer on the ground. The projector was there.

'Not far from where we landed,' Tamme said. 'But the pattern is not consistent enough to be of much aid. We still have to search out the projector on each new world and figure out the mechanism for breaking out of loops. I don't like that.'

Veg shrugged noncommittally. Except for Blizzard, he hadn't minded the searches. But of course if there were danger, they would not be able to afford much delay. 'With the hexaflexagon, you can run though every face just by flexing the same diagonal as long as it will go. When it balks, you switch to the next. So maybe if we just keep going straight ahead, we'll get there, anyway.'

Tamme sat up. She did not seem to be bothered by fog in her lungs. 'We'll play it that way. If we get caught in a repeating loop, we'll look for something to change. Meanwhile, I want a concurring opinion.'

'Another man-versus-tiger choice?'

She brought out a slip of paper. 'Call off the order of your hexaflexagon faces.'

Veg, hunched nose down to the ground to avoid the fog, was surprised at this request. Tamme knew the order that the faces appeared; she had flexed through them, and agents had eidetic recall. He could only confirm the obvious! But he brought out his toy and went through the whole pattern, calling off the numbers. 'One. Five. Two. One. Three. Six. One. Three. Two. Four. Three. Two. One.'

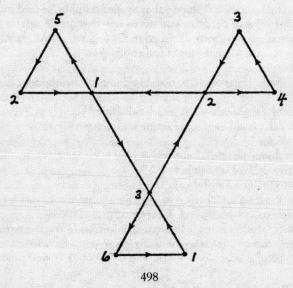

Tamme made a diagram of lines and numbers and little directional arrows. 'This is triangular,' she said. 'A three-faced hexaflexagon would simply go around the central triangle. Your six-faced one adds on to the angles. Would you agree to the accuracy of this diagram?'

She showed him what she had drawn.

Veg traced around it, starting from the northwest face 1. 'One, five, two, one, three – yeah, that's the order. Makes sense of it finally!'

Tamme nodded. He could barely make out her gesture since her head was almost concealed by the fog. 'As I make it, we actually started on Five, the City. That would make Two the Forest, One the Blizzard, Three the Orchestra, Six the Planes, and back to our first repeat, One/Blizzard. Then repeat Three/Orchestra. And repeat Two/Forest. And now face Four/Fog.'

'I guess so,' Veg said, having trouble keeping up. 'We're here now.'

'Our next stop should be repeat Three/Orchestra – this time twisted because it is on a separate loop. Then on to Two/Forest, One/Blizzard, and home to Five/City.'

'It figures,' he said. 'We've used up all the faces.'

'In which case we'll be back where we started – closed loop, and nobody but ourselves.'

'I guess so, right now. The others must have gotten off. Is that bad?'

'I can't buy it. Who set up all these other projectors?'

Veg shook his head. 'Got me there! If they'd gotten off, they'd have taken back their projectors – so they must be still on. And there can't be six Veges and six Tammes.' He sobered. 'Or *can* there?'

'Suppose your hexaflexagon had twelve faces?'

'Sure. There can be any number of faces if you start with a long enough strip of triangles and fold it right.'

'A twelve-face construction would merely add one new face to each of the six exterior angles,' she said.

Veg shrugged. 'I'll take your word. I'd have to make a live hexaflexagon to check it out myself.'

'*Don't* take my word. Make your construction.'

'Here? Now? Why not get to a better alternate to—'

'No.'

'I don't have anything to—'

She took apart the six-faced hexaflexagon, straightened out the long folded strip of plastic, pried at the edge with a small knife that appeared in her hand, and peeled it into two layers lengthwise. She produced a little vial of clear fluid, applied it to the edges, and glued the strips together endwise. The result was a double-length strip.

Veg sighed. He took it and folded it carefully. He made a flat spiral so that the double length became the size of the original but with two layers instead of one. Then he fashioned a normal hexaflexagon.

'Run through it and number your faces,' Tamme said.

'Okay.' This was a more complicated process, involving thirty flexes, but in due course he had it. Meanwhile, Tamme had been making a new diagram.

'Now start at face One and flex,' she said. 'I will call off your numbers in advance. Five.'

He flexed. 'Five it is.'

'Seven.'

He flexed again. 'Right.'

'One.'

'Right again. Hey, let me see that diagram!'

She showed it to him. It was an elaborated version of the prior one, with new triangles projecting from each of the six outer points. One angle of each of the outermost triangles carried the number of a new face, bringing the total to twelve.

They flexed through the rest of the construct. It matched the diagram.

'As I make it,' Tamme said, 'We could be on this one instead of the six-faced one. In that case our starting point would be Seven, followed by One, Five, Two, Eight, Five, Two, One, and now Three. If so, both our next two stops may be new worlds, Six and Nine.'

'Instead of repeats!' Veg said. 'That's the proof right there. All we need to do is try it. If we don't like the new ones, we just skip on to Three, there in the loop – that's here. Our map is still good.'

'Unless this is actually a mere subsection of an infinitely large configuration,' she cautioned. 'In that case, it is only a hint of a route through it. But we could probably find our way back, though there is no longer any way to travel back the way we came,' She paused, peering at him through the mist. 'If something should happen to me, you use this diagram to return to your friends in the City.'

'Not without you,' he said.

'Touching sentiment. Forget it. Your philosophy is not mine. I will leave you instantly if the need arises.'

'Maybe so,' Veg said uncomfortably. 'So far there hasn't been any real trouble. Maybe there won't be.'

'I rate the odds at four to one there *will* be,' she said. '*Someone* set up these projectors, and in at least one case it was another agent just like me. Of course I'm used to dealing with agents just like me – but they have been Tara, Tania, and Taphe, not alternate Tamme's. I mean to find that other agent and kill her. That will be difficult.'

'Yeah. Different philosophies,' Veg said. He knew she read the disapproval in him. Maybe it would be better to leave her if it came to that.

'Precisely,' Tamme said. And activated the projector.

They were in a curving hall. Checkerboard tiles were on the floor and a similar but finer pattern on the flat ceiling. The walls were off-white. Light shone down from regular spaced squares in the ceiling pattern. It was comfortably warm, and the air was breathable.

'So you were right,' Veg said. 'A new alternate, a larger pattern. No telling *how* many agents in the woodwork.'

'It is also possible that these are all settings on the same world,' Tamme said. 'That would account for the constancy of gravity, climate, and atmosphere.'

'That blizzard wasn't constant!'

'Still within the normal temperature range.'

'If they're all variations of Earth, that explains the gravity and climate. You said yourself they were different alternates. Trace disctinctions in the air, or something.'

'Yes. But perhaps I was premature. It could be as easy to regulate the air of a particular locale as to arrange for travel between alternates. Matter transmission from one point on the globe to another would cover it. I merely say that I am not *sure* we are actually—' She stopped. 'Oh-oh.'

Veg looked where she was looking but didn't see anything special. 'What's up?'

'The walls are moving. Closing in.'

He didn't see any difference but trusted her perception. He was not claustrophobic, but the notion made him nervous. 'A mousetrap?'

'Maybe. We'd better locate that projector.'

'There's only two ways to go. Why don't I go down here, and you go there? One of us is bound to find it.'

'Yes,' she said. There was a slight edge to her voice, as if she were nervous. That was odd because agents had excellent control. They were seldom if ever nervous, and if they *were*, they didn't show it.

'Okay.' He walked one way, and she went the other. But it nagged him: What was bothering her so much that even he could notice it?

'Nothing,' he muttered to himself. 'If I pick it up, it's because she wants me to.' But what was she trying to tell him?

He turned about to look back towards her. And stood transfixed.

The walls were moving – not slowly now but rapidly. They bowed out from either side between him and Tamme, compressing the hall alarmingly. 'Hey!' he yelled, starting back.

Tamme had been facing away. Now she turned like an unwinding spring and ran towards him, so fast he was astonished. Her hair flew out in a straight line behind her. She approached at a good thirty miles an hour: faster than he had thought it possible for a human being on foot.

The walls accelerated. Tamme dived, angling through just as the gap closed. She landed on her hands, did a forward roll, and flipped to her feet. She came up to him, not even out of breath. 'Thanks.'

'That mousetrap!' he said, shaken. 'It almost got you!' Then: 'Thanks for what?'

'For reacting in normal human fashion. The trap was obviously geared to your capacities, not mine. That was what I needed to ascertain.'

'But what was the point?'

'The object is to separate us, then deal with us at leisure. No doubt it feeds on animal flesh that it traps in this manner.'

'A carnivorous world?' Veg felt an ugly gut alarm.

'Perhaps, or merely a prison, like the City. We see very little of the alternates we are visiting.'

'I'm with you. Let's find the projector and get out!'

'It will have to be in a secure place – one that the walls can not impinge on.'

'Yeah. Let's stay together, huh?'

'I never intended to separate,' she said. 'But I wasn't sure who might be listening.'

Hence the edgy tone. He'd have to be more alert next time! 'You figure it's intelligent?'

'No. Mindless, perhaps purely mechanical. But dangerous – in the fashion of a genuine mousetrap.'

'Yeah – if you happen to be the mouse.'

They moved on, together. The walls were animate now, shifting like the torso of a living python. They pushed in – but the air in the passage compressed, preventing complete closure. There was always an exit for the air, and Veg and Tamme were able to follow it on out.

'But watch out when you see any air vent or duct,' Tamme warned. 'There the walls could close in all the way quite suddenly because there would be an escape for the air.'

Veg became extremely interested in air vents.

Sometimes they encountered a fork in the way and had to judge quickly which branch would lead to a broader hall. But now that they understood this region's nature, they were able to stay out of trouble.

'Hey – there it is!' he exclaimed. 'The projector.'

The walls were rolling back ahead of them, while closing in behind, as though herding them forward. A projector had now been revealed. It was on wheels, and a metallic ring surrounded it.

'Clever,' Tamme said. 'Wheels and a circular guard so that it always moves ahead of the wall and can't be trapped or crushed. So long as the walls do not close precisely parallel – and that does not seem to be their nature – it will squirt out. See the bearings on the ring-guard.' She moved towards it.

Veg put out his hand to stop her. 'Cheese,' he said.

She paused. 'You have a certain native cunning. I compliment you.'

'Another kiss will do.'

'No. I am beginning to respect you.'

Veg suffered a flush of confused emotion. She did not kiss those she respected? Because a kiss decreased it – or increased it? Or because her kisses were calculated sexual attractants, not to be used on friends? Was she becoming emotionally involved? This was more the way Aquilon reacted. The notion was exciting.

'The notion is dangerous,' Tamme said, reading his sentiment. 'You and I are not for each other on any but the purely physical level, strictly temporary. My memory of you will be erased when I am reassigned, but yours of me will remain. When emotion enters the picture, it corrupts us both. Love would destroy us.'

'I'd risk it.'

'You're a normal,' she said with a hint of contempt. She turned to the projector. 'Let's spring the mousetrap.'

She brought a thread from somewhere in her uniform, then made a lasso. She dropped this over the switch, jerked it snug, then walked away. The thread stretched behind her, five paces, ten, fifteen.

'Hide your eyes·' she said.

Veg put his arms up to cover both ears and eyes. He felt the movement as she tugged at the thread, turning on the projector.

Then he was on the floor. Tamme was picking him up. 'Sorry,' she said. 'I miscalculated. That was an agent's trap.'

'What?' He stared back down the hall, his memory coming back. There had been a terrific explosion, knocking him down—

'Directional charge. We were at the fringe of its effect. You bashed your head against the walls.'

'Yeah.' He felt the bump now. 'Good thing that wall has some give. You people play rough.'

'Yes. Unfortunately, I have been overlong on this mission. My orientation is suffering. I am making errors. A fresh agent would have anticipated both the trap and its precise application. I regret that my degredation imperilled your well-being.'

'Mistakes are only human,' he said, rubbing his head.

'Precisely.' She set him on his feet. 'I believe the blast stunned the walls temporarily. You should be safe here while I make a quick search.'

'I like you better, human.'

'Misery loves company. Stay.'

'Okay.' He felt dizzy and somewhat nauseous. He sat down and let his head hang.

'I'm back.' He had hardly been aware of her absence!

She took him to a 'constant' spot she had located: six metal rods imbedded in floor and ceiling, preventing encroachment. On a pedestal within that enclosure was another projector.

'This one is safe,' Tamme said.

Veg didn't ask her how she knew. Probably it was possible to booby trap a projector to explode some time after use so that a real one could be dangerous, but that would be risky if the alternate-pattern brought the same person back again. Best not to mess with the real projectors at all! Like the way the desert Arabs never poisoned the water no matter how vicious the local politics got. Never could be sure who would need to drink next.

'I hope the next world is nicer,' he said.

'Bound to be.' She activated the device.

Chapter Twelve

CUB

. . .

Cub finished his meal of fruit, roots, and flesh. He had gorged himself in case it were long before he ate again. Beside him Ornet preened himself, similarly ready.

Dec sailed in from his last survey. By minute adjustments of his mantle he made the indication: All is well.

Cub raised his wing-limb, flexing the five featherless digits in the signal to $\overline{OX}$: We are ready.

$\overline{OX}$ expanded. His sparkling presence surrounded them as it had so many times before. But this time it was special. The field intensified, lifted – and they were moving. Not through space; through time.

At first there was little change. They could see the green vegetation of the oasis and the hutch they had built there for shelter and comfort. Farther out there were the trenches and barriers they had made to foil the predator machine.

The machine. Mach, they called it. The thing had grown right along with them because it was part of the enclave $\overline{OX}$ had aged. It was a constant menace – yet Cub respected it, too, as a resourceful and determind opponent. Had it been in his power to destory it, he would not have done so because without it the group would be less alert, less fit, and bored.

Do we *need* adversity to prosper? he asked himself, linking his fingers so that he would not inadvertently signal his thoughts to the others. Apparently so. That ever-present threat to survival had forced them all to advance much faster and better than they would

506

have otherwise. Perhaps, ironically, it was the machine more than anything else that was responsible for their success as a group. This was a concept he knew the others would not understand, and perhaps it was nonsensical. But intriguing. He valued intrigue.

Then the hutch vanished. The trees changed. They expanded, aged, and disappeared. New ones grew up, matured, passed. Then only shifting brush remained, and finally the region was a barren depression.

Cub moved his digits, twisting them in the language that Ornet, Dec, and $\overline{OX}$ understood. Our oasis has died, he signalled. The water sank, the soil dried, the plants died. We knew this would happen if we were not there to cultivate the plants and conserve the water they need. But in other frames water remains, for $\overline{OX}$'s elements remain.

A shoot formed within $\overline{OX}$'s field. This is temporal, it said, using its blinker language that they all understood. All alternates extend forward and back from any point. All are distinct, yet from any point they seem to show past and future because of the separation in duration between frames.

Obvious, Cub snapped with an impolite twitch of his fingers.

Ornet made a muffled squawk to show partial comprehension. He was a potent historian but not much for original conjecture. His language, also, was universally understood: Cub could hear it, Dec could see it, and $\overline{OX}$ could field the slight variations it caused in his network of elements.

Dec twitched his tail in negation: The matter was not of substantial interest to him.

I would include a geographic drift, $\overline{OX}$'s shoot flashed. But I am unable, owing to the limit of the enclave.

Nonsense, Cub responded. We're all advanced twenty years. In terms of real framework, we exist only theoretically – or perhaps it is the other way around – so we can travel on theoretical elements.

Theoretical elements? the shoot inquired.

Your elements were cleared out by the external patterns, Cub signalled. Once they were there, and once they will be there, instead of mere threads. They still exist, in alternate phases of reality, serving as a gateway to all the universe. Use them.

Theoretical elements? the shoot repeated.

Cub had little patience with the slowness of his pattern-friend. Make a circuit, he signalled, much as he would have told Ornet to

507

scratch for arths if he were hungry. Analyze it. Accept this as hypothesis: We can theoretically travel on theoretical elements. There has to be an aspect of alternity where this is possible, for somewhere in alternity all things are possible. To us, geography may be fixed, for we are restricted to the enclave. Theoretically, that geography can change elsewhere in relation to ours just as time does. We have merely to invoke the frames where this is so.

Uncomprehending, $\overline{OX}$ made the circuit. Then he was able to accept it. Such travel was possible. And – it was.

The geography changed as they slid across the ageing world. They saw other oases growing and flexing.

Cub was surprised. He had been teasing $\overline{OX}$, at least in part. He had not really believed such motions would work; the enclave isolation had prevented any real breakout before. But when $\overline{OX}$ made a circuit, $\overline{OX}$ became that circuit, and his nature and ability were changed.

Perhaps $\overline{OX}$ had at last transcended the abilities of the outside patterns. If so, a genuine breakout was now feasible. But Cub decided not to mention that yet, lest the outside patterns act to remedy that potential breach. It was not wise to give away your abilities to the enemy.

That was how they had given Mach the slip. Always before, $\overline{OX}$ had made certain preparatory circuits, which the machine had sensed. This time Cub had had $\overline{OX}$ make spurious shoot-circuits, deceiving Mach. Thus, when they were ready to move, the machine had thought it was another bluff and had not appeared.

But soon Cub became bored with flexing oases. Let's cut across the alternates, he signalled. See some really different variations. We can go anywhere now . . .

Another test – but $\overline{OX}$ obliged. The oasis in sight stopped growing and started changing. The green leaves on the trees turned brown; the brown bark turned red. The bases thickened, became bulbous. Creatures appeared, rather developed from the semisentients already present. Like Ornet but with different beaks: tubular, pointed, which they plunged into the spongy trunks of the trees, drawing out liquid.

This was more like it! Cub watched, fascinated by sights he had never seen before and hardly imagined. A feast of experience!

The trees flowered, and so did the creatures. The flowers

expanded until there were neither trees nor creatures, only flowers. The oasis itself expanded until there was no desert at all, only large and small flowers.

A streak appeared. Cub couldn't tell whether it was a wall or a solid bank of fog. It cut off some of the flowers. They did not wither; they metamorphosed into coloured stones. The fog-wall increased until it concealed everything. Then it faded, and in its wake were planes, multi-coloured, translucent, and set at differing angles. Machines rolled up and down them, chipping away here, depositing there, steadily altering the details of the configuration without changing its general nature. Cub hardly bothered to question why; he knew that there would be too many whys in all alternity to answer without squeezing out more important concerns.

The planes dissolved into bands of coloured light, and these in turn became clouds, swirling in very pretty patterns, developing into storms. Rain came down, then snow – Cub recognized it, for snow fell on the enclave seasonally, forcing him to fashion protective clothing. But this was not only white; it was red and green and blue, shifting as the alternates shifted.

In due course it solidified into walls of stone: They were passing through a cavern, a huge hollow in the ground. Cub recognized this also, for last season he had fashioned digging and chipping tools and dug deep, deep into the ground, trying to ascertain whether there was any escape from the enclave in that direction. He had, in fact, made a small cavern. But it was useless, and he had given up and closed it over. Now they used it for winter storage and occasionally for shelter from storms.

A tremendous room opened out on one side, far larger than the cave Cub had made. Then the stone closed in again as though the very walls were moving.

Wait! Cub signalled. I saw something. Go back.

The shoot gave a controlled fadeout equivalent to the drooping of Ornet's tail feathers or Cub's own shrug of the shoulders. The moving walls reversed, opening into the cavern.

There! Cub indicated. Geographically – move over.

Now the others spotted it. In the centre of the cavern a creature was doing something. It was working on some sort of machine ... no, the thing was too simple to be a machine, merely a mechanical device, perhaps the ancestor of a machine. Sound emerged, pleasant, harmonious. The thing was playing music, similar to that Cub himself could make with voice and the beat of his hands on a log, but smoother, prettier. The creature's tentacles touched the device here and there, and the melodious sound issued.

Follow that frame, Cub directed, as though the other members of his party had no preferences. But they were content to follow his lead in this. In physical motion, Dec was supreme; in memory, it was Ornet. In imagination, it was Cub, and they all knew it.

OX oriented – and the single alien musician became two, then eight, and then a myriad of players. The music swelled resoundingly. Then the creatures changed, becoming humanoid, and finally human.

Your kind! Ornet squawked.

Startled, Cub examined them more carefully. My kind!

They changed to tall green plants, playing the instruments with leaves and roots. Wait! Cub signalled, too late.

But OX was already backing up. The Cub-type players re-formed, went alien, returned, went naked, elaborately clothed, and finally focused on a compromise.

My kind! Cub repeated, half dazed. But what are those others? He gestured towards some individuals that differed slightly. They resembled him, but their torsos varied, and their faces were bare as though they were not yet grown.

Female of your species, Ornet squawked. Show the natural version, OX.

OX obliged, shifting to the unclothed players.

Mam females lack the urinary appendage, Ornet explained, gesturing with his beak. But they possess structures for the nursing of infants. My ancestors have not observed your particular species, but these are merely modifications of the type.

Cub stared at the nursing structures, appalled yet fascinated. I would like to put my hands on those, he signalled.

This can not be done, the shoot replied. We can not interact.

I know it! Cub gestured irritably, though for a moment he was tempted to challenge OX to make a circuit for the attempt. Let's go on.

They went on – but after that Cub's attention was on his memory of his kind, on the bare-fleshed females. If only there were some way to get across the barrier physically!

510

Suddenly Mach appeared, rising up out of the storage cave. All of them were caught off guard. Once more the machine had been too cunning for them and had arranged to come on their special frame-trip, after all!

The thing came whirling its blade and spinning its treads, forcing the physical beings out of its way, and its pattern-disruptive emanations were so strong that $\overline{OX}$ had to move explosively to avoid nonsurvival effects. Cub could see the sparkles flying out like a stellar display on a chill night.

Then the group mobilized, as it had so many times before. Ornet served as decoy, flapping his wings and squawking just outside the range of the blade. Dec swooped by, flicking his tail at the perceptor bulbs. Cub stood back and threw stones into the blade. And $\overline{OX}$ formed shoots that spun across the elements in the machine's vicinity, distracting its alternate-frame perspective.

They could hardly damage Mach, let alone destroy it; it was invulnerable to their attack. But their combined harassment made it uncomfortable and always drove it back.

This time it persisted for an extraordinary time. It was undeniably strong. But finally the stones and sand that Cub shovelled at its blade and into its hopper discouraged it. Sand did not hurt it, but it was unable to disgorge it while under attack. And so it retreated – just far enough to abate their defensive action.

Through the years they had come to a kind of understanding with Mach. Once the machine retreated, they would let it alone – and it would not attack again that day. Truce, while both sides recuperated. Neither side had ever broken that tacit agreement; that temporary security was too important. Mach actually seemed to be honest; perhaps the mechanical circuits prevented dishonesty in any form. This was one of the things about the machine that Cub respected. Sometimes he and Dec and Ornet sought out Mach and attacked it merely to invoke the truce so that they could be assured *it* would not attack *them* while something important was going on.

Cub threw himself down, panting, as the machine became quiescent. It remained within the area of $\overline{OX}$'s influence – but Cub had no desire to drive it outside. They had brought it along on this trip, and they would have to return it to the normal enclave. It would not be right to leave it stranded.

Once he had wished for some way to rid the enclave of this

constant menace. Now he had the chance – and would not take it. Not merely because of his interpretation of their truce; because he was even more certain that Mach was a sentient entity, too, and deserved a certain measure of respect.

But then he remembered what he had seen beyond the enclave, in the cave of the musicians, and forgot the machine.

Chapter Thirteen

DREAMS

Aquilon wiped her eyes with her fists. 'This R Pentomino is a menace!' she complained. 'I'm getting a headache! It just goes on and on.'

Cal pulled his head out of the innards of the machine. 'I told you it was an impressive dead end after eleven hundred and three moves.'

'I know. I wanted to see for myself.'

'Try the glider,' he suggested.

'The what?'

'You have been dealing with stationary forms. There are others. Here.' He extricated himself and came over. 'This is the glider.' He made the pattern of dots on her canvas-sheet:

'That's another pentomino!' she said indignantly.

He shrugged and returned to his work. 'I hope to convert this machine to a specialized oscilloscope, or facsimile thereof, so that we can translate our signals into pattern-language. I have the feeling that the pattern-entities are as eager to talk with us as we are to talk with them. Think how confusing we must be to them!'

'But we are solid and visible!' she said working on the new figure.

It had gone from [1] •⋮• to [2] •• ⋮ to [3] • ⋮• In fact, it was

now a mirror image of its original form, turned endwise. Funny.

'Precisely. An entity whose system is based on patterns of points would find our mode of operation virtually incomprehensible.'

She made the next figure, jumping straight from one to the next

without such laborious additions and erasures. [4] • • • 'Do you
think Veg is all right?'   • •

'I doubt I ever get used to the caprices of female thought,' he
remarked. 'Veg is with Tamme.'

'That's what I meant.'

'Jealousy – at your age?'   •
    •
She looked at the next figure: [5] • • • 'Hey – this thing repeats
itself on new squares! It's like a blinker – only it moves!'

'Precisely. Patterns can travel. The glider moves diagonally at a
quarter the speed of light.'

'Speed of light?'

'An advance of one square per move is the maximum possible
velocity in this game, so we call it the speed of light. The glider takes
four moves to repeat itself, one square across and one down, so that
is one quarter lightspeed.'

She looked at it, nodding. 'Beautiful!'

Veg would have said, 'So are you.' Not Cal. He said: 'A variant of
that formation is called the Spaceship. Spaceships of various sizes
can move at half the speed of light. As they go, they fire off sparks
that vanish, like propulsion.'

'The sparkle cloud did that!' she cried.

'Yes. We also know of a "glider gun" that fires off gliders
regularly. And another figure that consumes gliders. In fact, it is
possible to fire several gliders to form new figures at the point of
convergence – even another glider gun that shoots back at its parent
guns, destroying them.'

'If I were a pattern, I'd be very careful where I fired my gliders!'
Aquilon said. 'That game plays a rough game!'

'It does. As does all nature. I should think assorted defensive
mechanisms would appear by natural selection, or the game would
be unstable – assuming it were self-willed. The possibilities are
obvious.'

'Especially when you get into three dimensions!'

'Yes. It is a three-dimensional computerized grid I am working on
now. I wish I were a more experienced technician!'

'I think you're a genius,' she said sincerely. And she felt a flare of
emotion.

'You can help me now if you will. I'll need some figures for my
three-dimensional grid.'

514

'What's wrong with the ones we have? The R Pentomino, the glider—'

'They won't be the same. A line of three points would manufacture four new ones, not two – because of the added dimension. That would form a short cross, which would in turn form a kind of hollow cube. I believe that's an infinitely expanding figure – and that is not suitable for our purpose. We need figures that are approximately in balance – that neither fade out too rapidly nor expand to fill the whole framework.'

'Hm, I see,' she murmured, trying to trace the three-dimensional permutations of the figure on her two-dimensional canvas. She compromised by using colour to represent the third dimension. 'Your line becomes an indefinitely expanding three-dimensional figure, as you said. Looks like two parallel caterpillar treads with eight cleats in each, if I haven't fouled it up. But almost any figure expands; there are just too many interactions.'

'Agreed. So we must modify the rules to do for three dimensions what "Life" does for two. Perhaps we must require four points to generate a fifth and let a point be stable with three or four neighbours. Perhaps some other combination. If you can suggest viable rules and figures, it will save me time, once I have this equipment modified.'

'I'll try!' she said, and bent to it.

They both had difficult, intricate jobs, and from time to time they had to break off. They also chatted intermittently during the work.

'Say – did you ever find the missing earthquake?' Aquilon asked suddenly.

Cal paused momentarily at his labour. She knew he was finding his mental place, as she had just made another momentous leap of topic. To her surprise, he placed her reference accurately. 'We were separated three days on Paleo, during which time there were two tremors, a minor and a strong one. I remember them clearly.'

'For a genius, you have a poor memory,' she said, smiling over her complex dot-pattern. 'We were separated four days, and there were quakes on the first three. You must really have been absorbed with that dinosaur not to notice.'

'Odd that we should differ on something so easy to verify,' he said. 'Shall we compare notes in detail?' It was as though he were inviting her to a duel, certain that she would lose.

Aquilon was intrigued. 'Let's.'

'You and Veg went to the island—'

'Not *that* much detail,' she said, embarrassed. Then she reconsidered. 'No – let's put it out in the open. You wanted to make a report on Paleo that would surely lay it open to exploitation and destruction—'

'I changed my mind.'

'Let me finish. I wanted to help Orn and Ornette survive because they were unique, intelligent birds and I liked them. Veg went with me.' She took a breath and forced herself to continue. 'Veg and I made love that night. Next morning he went to see you at the raft – and the first tremor came.'

'Yes. After he left the raft, I set sail. I was aware of the tremor; it made the water dance. About fifteen seconds, mild.'

'Even a mild earthquake is horrible,' she said, giving her head a little reminiscent shake. 'That was the first day, the first quake. So we agree.'

'So far.' She could tell from his tone that he was still sure she was wrong about the tremors. She was also a bit uneasy about the seemingly bland response to her confession concerning Veg. 'The second day Circe came and told us a predator dinosaur was after you, but you wouldn't let the mantas help you. I thought we should leave well enough alone. Veg hit me and headed off.'

'He should not have done that.' Again, too mild a response.

'Cal, I didn't want you to die – but I thought it was more important that you be allowed to do what you felt you had to do, your own way.'

'Precisely. Veg blundered.'

So it was all right. Cal understood. She should have known he would. 'Later that day the second quake came. It shattered the eggs – all but one. It was violent, awful.'

'I was on the mountainside. The tremor knocked Tyrannosaurus off his feet and rolled him down the mountain. I was afraid he was too badly hurt to continue the chase. Fortunately, he suffered minimal damage.'

Aquilon grimaced, knowing he was not being facetious. Cal had wanted to conquer the dinosaur himself, without the help of an act of God. 'So we agree on the second day, the second quake.'

'We agree. I continued up on the mountain and slept in a volcanic

516

cave. Next day the agents came – Taler, Taner, and Tamme.'

'No,' she said firmly. 'Next day there was a third quake. It tore the island apart. A plesiosaurus got Ornette, so Orn and I had to ferry the egg to the mainland the day following – the morning of the fourth day, the day the agents came. I'll never forget that awful journey through the water, protecting the egg! I had to use Orn for support—'

Cal nodded thoughtfully. 'So you really did experience an extra day and tremor!'

'You lost a day, Cal. What happened to it?'

He sighed. 'This suggests something too fantastic to believe. In fact, I *don't* believe it.'

So there *was* something! 'This sounds fascinating! You have a secret?'

'In a manner of speaking. I didn't think it was anything significant. You would have been the first to know had there been anything to it. All men have fantasies – and all women, too, I'm sure. But now – I wonder. Alternates *do* exist, and in some of them are virtual duplicates of ourselves. The woman you met, the naked Aquilon—'

'Don't tell me you dream of naked Aquilons!' she said, pleased. But at the same time, the memory of the lost egg upset her. She had so wanted to save the Orn species . . .

'More than that, I'm afraid. After all, I have seen you naked in life.'

She remembered the time she had run nude on Paleo before they found the dinosaurs. She had not realized that he had paid attention. 'You always loved me. You said so back on Planet Nacre. And I love you. But there's never been much of a – a physical component, has there?'

'The major component,' he said seriously.

'Oh? I thought all things were intellectual to you.'

He peered at her over the machine. 'You are leading me on.'

'That's what I mean. You are too smart for me, and we both know it. I couldn't deceive you with feminine wiles if I tried. You intellectualize everything to the point where you feel no physical passion.' She felt a little shiver as she said it, wanting him to deny it. She had taken the initiative with Veg, and that had been wrong; he had resented it and repaid her with a blow. Not a conscious

517

motivation, perhaps – but she was sure that it had been one of his unconscious ones.

'Intelligence is irrelevant. You have shown me my error in the counting of tremors, for example.'

'That's right. What *did* you do with that day and that quake? Chase naked Aquilons?'

'Yes.'

She looked at him sharply, for he sounded serious. 'You *did?*'

'Bear with me if I affront your sensitivities. I think this is something you should know.'

'I'm not affronted,' she said, keeping her eyes on her diagrams. 'Intrigued, though . . .' She certainly was; the three-dimensional life-game analysis was now no more than a pretence.

He buried his head in the machine so that only his voice reached her. She returned to her work with an effort and listened, visualizing what he described.

'I escaped Tyrannosaurus by hiding in a volcanic cave, the night of the day we had the second tremor. It was warm in there, for the water of the stream was hot. I was extraordinarily tired, yet keyed up: It had been the greatest adventure of my life. I had, in my fashion, conquered the dinosaur!

'I found myself a comfortable ledge, sprawled out, and fell into a perspiring stupor. I thought of dinosaurs and conjectured that one of the duck-bills like *Parasaurolophus*, with the enormous nasal crest, might have been able to survive the heat of that cave. Its breath through the inside of the crest would have cooled its tissues, as the breath of a dog cools its tongue and thus its body. But if the creature stayed too long or strayed into the cave and got lost, it might have died and been washed out through the river-canyons of the far side of the mountain range. Idle speculation of the type that entertains me.'

'I know,' she agreed softly. Who else but Cal would care whether the body of a duck-billed dinosaur washed out one side of the mountain or the other?

'I must have slept off and on. It was not really comfortable in that heat. Towards morning that conjecture about the duck-bill roused me. *Could* it get out of the dinosaur enclave through the mountain? Could *I?* Driven by curiosity, I began to explore the cavern, going far back into the mountain. The heat was terrible; when it reached about one hundred and forty degrees Fahrenheit I turned back. I was naked; I was sweating so profusely that clothing would have been useless.

'Then I saw something. It was nestled in a recess, invisible from the mouth of the cave. I would have missed it but for my acute night vision, sharpened by my night in the cave. It was a little machine. Its presence amazed me, for it suggested that man had been there before. I fiddled with it, trying to ascertain its condition and purpose. I lifted a kind of key from it.

'A cone of pale light projected from the device and bathed me. I felt a strange wrenching. For an instant I feared I had been victimized by some type of booby trap, though why anything of that nature should be placed there I could not guess. Then the machine was gone, and I stood in the cave, the key in my hand.

'Astonished, I set it down on a convenient ledge and looked about. Far down at the mouth of the cave I saw a glow; dawn was coming.

'I went back to that entrance to check on Tyrann, my reptile nemesis. He was still there, sleeping, his great nose almost touching the cave. In fact, his bulk blocked the flow of water, making it form into a puddle. Beyond him was the snow of the mountain, covering the canyon rim where the heat of the river did not reach. An odd sight: dinosaur in snow!

'"Cal!" someone cried. "I thought you were dead!"

'I turned, startled. You were there, 'Quilon, nude and lovely. Your yellow hair floated down your back like the glorious mane of a thoroughbred horse, and your blue eyes were bright. I doubt you can appreciate how lovely you were to me in that instant. I had come very near death, and you were an angel.

'"I escaped, thanks to this convenient cave," I said, as though it were of no moment. I do not remember my exact words, of course, but it was something equivalently inane.

'"So did I,"' you said. "Cal, I could have sworn I saw Tyrann get you! It was awful. Then he came after me, and I just made it here—"

'"I told the mantas not to interfere. Why did you come?"

'"I love you," you said.

'You were not speaking intellecutally or theoretically or platonically. Your voice trembled with the devotion of a woman for her lover. You were wild and forward, and I – I was powerfully moved by it. *You meant it.*

'Your vision of seeming death had charged you, first with grief, then with enormous passion. We were naked, and in love, and it seemed wholly natural that we resort to the natural culmination. All the suppressed urges I had entertained towards you were released in the bursting of that dam; it seemed I could never get my fill of your body. And you were eager for me; you were a creature of lust. It was as though we were two animals, copulating interminably, driven by an insatiable erotic imperative.

'All day we remained in that cave. Once there was a terrible tremor. It bounced Tyrann half awake; it dislodged stalactites from the back of the cave. We were afraid the mountain would collapse in on us – so we made love again, and slept, and woke, and did it yet again.

'At night I woke, disgusted with myself for using you like that. Yet even as I looked at you in your divine sleep, the passion rose in me again, and I knew that I had to get out of the sight of you if I were not to succumb again. So I retreated to the back of the cave.

'I remembered the key and searched for it in the dark. My hand found it on the ledge. I picked it up and shook it – and suddenly there was an illumination about me, and I experienced that dizzy feeling – and there was the machine in front of me again.

'Alarmed, I returned to where you slept – but you were gone. You could not have left by the cave mouth, for Tyrann was there, and there were no fresh tracks in the powdering of snow near him. I was sure you had not left by the rear passage, for I had been there. Yet there was absolutly no evidence of your presence; even the lichen on the ledge where we had made love was undisturbed, as though no one had ever been there.

'Forgive me: My first thought was intense regret that I had not awakened you for one more act of love before you disappeared. Then I cursed my sordid nature, for I would love you as strongly were I a eunuch. I lay down and tried to piece it out, and finally I slept again. In the morning I knew it had been a dream – an extravagant, far-fetched, ridiculous, wonderful, masculine wish fulfillment. And so I put it out of my mind, ashamed of the carnal nature underlying my love for you, and I have maintained a proper perspective since.'

Aquilon sat leaning over her diagrams, stunned. The episode Cal had so vividly described had never happened, and it was shocking to hear him speak so graphically, so uncharacteristically. Yet it mirrored the secret passion she had longed to express if only there were some way around her inhibitions and his. And it touched upon something hideous, something she herself had buried until this moment.

'Cal—' she faltered but had to force herself to go on, lest he think it was revulsion for the sexual description that balked her. Yet she could not say what she had intended, and something almost irrelevant came out instead. 'Cal, the key – what happened to it?'

'What happens to any dream artifact when the sleeper wakes?' he asked in return, as though glad for the change of subject.

'No – did you keep it, or put it back? Did you check for that machine again? It should have—'

'I must have replaced the key automatically,' he said. 'I never returned to the rear of the cave. It was part of my disgust, and I refused to humour the passions of the dream by checking.'

'Oh!' It was a faint exclamation of emotional pain. He had never even checked! But that pang freed her inhibition somehow, and now she was able to approach her own hidden concern. 'Cal, you said I thought you had died in your dream. What did I say?'

He did not answer, and she knew he was suffering from acute embarrassment, realizing how frankly he had spoken.

'Please, Cal – this is important to me,'

His voice came back from the machine. 'Not very much. We did talk about it some, but it was not a pleasant subject, and there obviously had been some error.'

Aquilon concentrated. 'Tyrann galloped after you, those awful double-edged teeth snapping inches short of your frail body, the feet coming down on you like twin avalanches. Snap! and your rag-doll form was flung high in the air, striped grisly red, reflected in the malignant eyes of the carnosaur. Tyrann's giant claw-toes crushed your body into the ground; the jaws closed, ripping off an arm. Your head lolled from a broken neck, and your dead eyes stared at me not with accusation but with understanding, and I screamed.'

Now Cal's head jerked out of the machine. 'Yes!' he exclaimed. 'That's what you said in essence. How could you know?' Then he did a double take. '*Unless you actually were there in that cave—*'

'No,' she said quickly. 'No, Cal, I wasn't there. I was stranded on an earthquake-torn island with Orn's egg. I swear it.'

Still he looked at her. 'You desired my death?'

521

'No!' she cried. 'I dreamed it – a nightmare. I told that dream to the birds, Orn and Ornette, that third day, before the last quake. That I had seen you die.'

'You dreamed it – the same time I dreamed my—'

'Cal,' she said, another shock of realization running through her. 'In some alternate – *could it have happened?*'

He came to her. 'No. How could I have made love to you if I were already dead?'

She caught his hand, shaken, desperate. 'Cal, Cal – your dream was so much better than mine. Make it come true!'

He shook his head. ''Quilon, I did not mean to hurt you. It was only that if there were an unaccounted day for me, I would be compelled to believe that somehow – but the whole thing is insane. I do love you – that much has never been in doubt – but I slept around the clock in that cave, recovering from the ravages of that chase, and it is hardly surprising that exaggerated fancies emerged, an ugly expression of—'

'I don't care!' she cried. 'Your dream was *not* ugly; *mine* was. Yours was more accurate than your belief. I *am* like that – or could be, would be, if I thought I'd lost you. You like to think I'm cold and chaste, but I'm not. I never was! I seduced Veg – it's no platonic triangle. I made a mistake, but *this* is no mistake. I want to love you every way I can!'

He studied her uncertainly. 'You *want* the dream – and all that it implies?'

'Your dream, not mine. Then you'll know me as I am. Yes, I want it – now!'

He shook his head, and she was suddenly, intensely embarrassed, afraid she had repulsed him by her eagerness. Did he only love the ethereal image, not the reality?

'I take you at your word,' he said. Relief and surprise flooded her, made her weak. 'After we complete this project.'

'Communication with the pattern-entities? But that may take days!'

'Or weeks or years. There will be time.'

'But the dreams, the cave—'

'We are not in the cave.'

She saw he was not going to re-enact the dream-orgy of lovemaking he had described. Had she really thought he would?

522

This was Cal, civilized, controlled. The chaste, celestial personification – it was not of her but of *him*.

Yet he had acceded. Why?

Because he wanted to give her time to reconsider. The impulse of the moment was too likely to lead to regret, as with her and Veg, or with Cal and his dream-girl in the cave. He would not grasp what he was not assured of holding.

It was better this way.

He kissed her. Then she was sure of it.

So it was not the dream. It was love, shifted from the suppressed to the expressed – gentle, controlled, and quiet. It was more meaningful than any wild erotic dream could have been, this simple affirmation of commitment.

Glowing inside, she completed her charts while he worked on the machine, as though there had been no interruption. It was as though they had walked through a desert and suddenly been admitted to an exotic garden filled with intriguing oddities and fragrances that could be explored at leisure together. Yes – there would be time!

'I worked out "ideal" rules for one, two and three dimensions,' she said brightly. 'One dimension would be a line. It takes one dot to make another, and any dot with two neighbours or no neighbours vanishes. It doesn't work very well because one dot makes a figure that expands at the speed of light indefinitely, and you can't even start a figure with less than one. For two dimensions, same as now: Three dots make a fourth, and a dot is unstable with less than two or more than three neighbours. Since up to eight neighbours are possible, it has far more variety than the one-dimensional game.'

'Of course,' Cal agreed.

'For three dimensions there are twenty-seven potential interactions, or up to twenty-six neighbours. We should require seven neighbours to make a new dot, and the figure is stable with six or seven. Less than six or more than seven will eliminate a given dot. So a cube of eight dots would be stable, each dot with seven neighbours – like the four-dot square in the two-dimensional version.'

Cal nodded. 'I believe it will do. Let's try some forms on our cubic grid, applying those rules.'

I believe it will do. And Aquilon was as pleased with that implied praise for her work as with anything that had happened.

Chapter Fourteen

FORMS

Cub had become minimally communicative during the tour, and $\overline{OX}$ did not understand this. Had he been injured during the battle with Mach?

It is the mating urge, Ornet explained, delving again into his memory-experience of mams. Sight or smell of the mature female stimulates the male to interact with her.

Why? $\overline{OX}$ inquired, finding the concept obscure.

It is the way they reproduce their kind. My kind performs similarly; Dec's has a separate mechanism. The machines are distinct from us all.

Why should any kind of being require reproduction?

We orginate, we age, we die, Ornet squawked. It is the way of physical species. If we do not reproduce ourselves, there will be nothing.

Still $\overline{OX}$ could not grasp it. I do not reproduce myself. I exist as long as my elements are charged and numerous.

You surely do reproduce yourself, Ornet squawked. I have not seen enough of your type to fathom the mechanism, but my memory indicates that it must be – for all entities. In some way you were conceived by your forebears, and in some way you will transmit your heritage to your successors. Perhaps if you encountered a female of *your* species—

There are no pattern-females, $\overline{OX}$ replied. I read that in my circuits. I have the potential to become anything that any pattern can be.

524

Ornet drooped his tail feathers. He never engaged in speculation; the past was his primary interest.

OX sent a shoot to question Dec. Why should spots die or reproduce themselves? it flashed.

The two are synonymous, Dec replied. To die is to reproduce.

This did not satisfy OX, either. A pattern needed neither to die nor to reproduce. Why should a spot?

Dec was emitting a complex array of signals. OX adjusted his circuitry to pick up the full spectrum. Dec was capable of far greater communication than either of the others, for he used light, the fastest of radiations. OX could perceive it by the effect of his elements: minute but definite. He had long since intensified his perceptions of such variations so that observations that had once been beyond his means were now routine. Now he activated a really intricate perception network, more comprehensive and sensitive and responsive than ever before.

Then Dec's whole mind was coming across on the transmission, as clearly as if it were a barrage of pattern-radiation shoots:

[DEATH]	[SPORES]	[MERGING]	[REPRODUCTION]
*	*	*	*
[cessation]	[carriers of]	[two sources]	[growth of cells]
[animation]	[genetic code]	[crossover]	*
*	*		[chain of habitats]
[philosophical]			
[ramifications]	[♀♂]		

OX assimilated it and fed back his questions on the aspects of the concept. The dialogue was complex, with loops of subdefinitions and commentary opening out from the corners of the major topics, with both obvious and subtle feedbacks and interactions between concepts. It required maintenance of a circuit larger than the rest of his volume. OX stayed with it, devoting whatever attention was necessary. He refined his circuits, added to them, revised . . .

And found himself within the mind of Dec.

Now he felt the force of gravity, a vital component of Dec's motion; the pressure of atmosphere, another essential; the impact of physical light on his eye. He felt the musculature of the single foot, opposing the constant pull and unbalance.

These things had been mere concepts to him before, described but not really understood. It was one thing to know that a physical body had weight that held it to the ground; it was quite another to experience that ubiquitous force on every cell of the body. A factor that was of no importance to $\overline{OX}$ in his natural state was a matter of life and death to this physical being; a fall could actually terminate Dec's existence! Thus, gravity equated with survival. Yet gravity was only one of an entire complex of physical forces. No wonder the spots were different in their reactions from $\overline{OX}$; their survival depended on it!

And he understood the synonymity of death and reproduction, how the primed body dissolved into its component cells that became floating spores that met and merged with the spores of another deceased fungus entity and then grew into new entities. Without death there was no replication, and without replication there would be no more entities of this type. Yet this process was necessary to the evolution of the species, and without evolution it would also pass. Death equated with survival – death of the individual, survival of the species – because the demands of the physical environment were always shifting. $\overline{OX}$ now understood the essential nature of these things, and the rightness of them. Multiple physical imperatives set fantastic demands, requiring complex devices of survival unknown to pattern-entities.

Then he was out of the physical, back in his own nature, fibrillating. He had never before experienced sensation and thinking of this type; there was a phenomenal amount of data to assimilate and circuits to modify. The physical was a whole separate existence, with its unique imperatives!

$\overline{OX}$ had learned more in this one encounter than in any prior one. He now realized all the way through his being that the intellectual systems of the spots were as complex and meaningful as his own. The spots were, indeed, complete entitites.

He modified his circuits to incorporate a perpetual awareness and appreciation of this fact. Just as alternity was infinitely variable, so was intellect! His comprehension of existence would not be complete until he had experienced the inner nature of each spot – and of a machine.

He formed a shoot to approach Ornet. By motions and flashes that coincided with the creature's mode of communication, $\overline{OX}$ made known his mission: to exchange minds for a moment. Ornet was receptive; he had long been curious, in a paleontological way, about the inner nature of patterns, since they had so little place in his memory.

The mechanism of exchange differed from the one that had been effective with Dec, for there was no mass-level tool of light. Instead, OX had to create a shoot-circuit that duplicated the bird's every observable contour and function, correcting it as Ornet directed. OX made himself into another Ornet, with feet and claws and wings and beak, subject to gravity and all the other manifestations of the physical aspect. Then this form moved to coincide with the presence of Ornet, and the shoot's points picked up the signals of the body's nervous functioning, the living animation of its cells.

Slowly, the mapping progressed, merging the element pattern with the physical pattern. And as the overlap became sufficient, OX began to receive Ornet's sensations and thoughts directly.

Ornet was old. His species was normally adult in the third year after hatching and faded after twenty. Ornet was twenty now. His powers were receding, His feathers losing their gloss, his beak its sharp edge. He felt a kind of vacuum in his life, but he had not been able to define it until OX had questioned him about Cub. Then his memory had been evoked, making it clear – but far too late. He had never had contact with a female of his kind, never been aroused – and so had lived without really missing it. He was not given to speculative thought or to emotional reactions; he accepted what was and worked only to enhance survival and comfort.

This personality, in a manner quite different from Dec's, was compatible with OX's own mode. But because Ornet's reproductive aspect was quiescent, OX still had no direct comprehension of it. And so long as his understanding was incomplete, he lacked a potential tool for survival.

It was evident that Ornet did not have to die in order to reproduce his kind. But if the death/reproduction connection were not valid, what *was*?

OX phased out, moving the shoot away from coincidence with the body of the bird. Deprived of their guidance by the minute electrical stimuli of the physical nervous system, the subcircuits collapsed. It was a non-survival jolt – but only for the shoot. In a moment OX reorganized in a more stable format, recovering equilibrium.

He had absorbed another vast segment of reality and

527

comprehended to some extent the process of ageing and its relation to death. But it was not enough.

Now he came to Cub. Cub, by the reckoning of Ornet's memory, was now in the young prime of his life. And he had, as $\overline{OX}$ himself knew, a marvellously powerful and versatile reasoning mechanism. He was the source of $\overline{OX}$'s confusion; now perhaps he would be the resolution of it.

$\overline{OX}$ made another phase-in shoot, this one in the form of Cub. Small and tight as it was, this lone shoot was nevertheless far more complex than $\overline{OX}$'s entire being had been at the time of his first emergence into awareness. I wish to join you, to understand you completely, the shoot signalled.

Do as you like, Cub responded indifferently.

$\overline{OX}$ attuned his subcircuits to the nervous impulses of living matter, as he had so recently mastered with Ornet. He slid the shoot over to merge.

There was a period of adjustment, for though the principle of functioning was similar, between Ornet and Cub, the detail differed. Then awaresness focused.

It was a maelstrom. Rational misgivings warred with unattainable urges. The picture of a naked-Cub-species female formed, her arms and legs outstretched ... dissipated in an aura of revulsion ... re-formed.

$\overline{OX}$ watched, felt, experienced. Now he, too, felt those amazing urges. The attraction/repulsion of the reproduction/death complex; the need to overtake, to grasp, to envelop, to penetrate – countered by inability, confusion, and guilt. Desire without opportunity, force without mechanism. Compulsion so great it threatened to nullify survival itself. Emotion.

$\overline{OX}$ twisted out of phase with such an effort that he carried the entire enclave into another frame. His system was in terrible disarray; his circuits warred with each other.

But now he understood the spots' need to reproduce their kinds. He knew what emotion was. Having discovered that, he was unable to eliminate it from his system; the profound new circuits were part of his pattern.

But $\overline{OX}$ realized that his survey was still incomplete. He had learned marvellous and dismaying new things – but that only increased the need to learn the rest. Perhaps little of significance remained, and there were nonsurvival aspects to the continuation of this search – but he had to do it. Survival and emotion drove him.

He searched out Mach, the wild machine.

$\overline{OX}$ anticipated resistance, but Mach was quiescent. Perhaps it was waiting to ascertain the nature of this new attack. $\overline{OX}$ formed a shoot-image of it, then cautiously phased in.

This was dangerous because the machine, unlike the living spots, had certain pattern-aspects. It was aware of the elements, though its existence did not depend on them, and it could use them to make those special patterns that extended across frames. This ability was very limited, but this was one reason why $\overline{OX}$ had such trouble nullifying Mach's attacks. Mach could almost match $\overline{OX}$'s manoeuverability across frames, provided that travel was restricted to adjacent or nearly adjacent ones. And the machine could drain the elements of so much energy that they would not serve a pattern-entity for some time.

$\overline{OX}$ found the nerve circuits on the physical level of the machine, adapting to them as he had for Ornet and Cub. And slowly he became Mach.

The machine intellect was distinct from those of the living spots. Its impulses ran along metal conduits with appalling force and dealt with motors and transformers and switches and harsh chemical reactions rather than the subtle interactions of life or pattern. Yet it was sentient.

This was Mach – and now $\overline{OX}$ understood. The machine had needs fully as compelling as those of the other entities. Its prime motive was similar to theirs : SURVIVE. But it required energy transformed from matter by more brutal processes. Most of the physical substances it could obtain from its environment, but a few were in critical shortage here in the enclave.

It was the lack of these substances that made Mach desperate and dangerous. The machine required them in order to develop its potential to reproduce its kind – and some of them could be filtered from the bodies of the living spots. There was no inherent personal animus; Mach attacked because it was driven by a need that could not be denied, in much the fashion of Cub's need. Gradually, as it realized that the spots were in fact sentient, it came to equate destruction of them as long-range nonsurvival and tried to resist the urge to take what beckoned. But it could not.

Supply those substances, and Mach would no longer be an enemy. The machine might even cooperate with the other members of the enclave. Its strength on the physical level was such that it could be of substantial assistance to them – especially in the effort to break out of the enclave.

OX had developed combat circuits to oppose the inimical behaviour of the external patterns. Now he comprehended that patterns were ill equipped to indulge in such activities. Their intellectual comprehension translated only poorly into action. This was one reason the external patterns had done nothing but observe after arranging the enclave.

Machines, in contrast, were entities of action. Mach's mind contained pragmatic instructions for accomplishing many tasks, provided the tools existed. OX now saw that he, as a pattern, had tools that the machine did not.

Now OX understood enough, and he had a new sense of motivation. He made ready to act.

Chapter Fifteen

ALTERNITY

They stood on a metal highway, and a tank was bearing down on them. It was a monster, with treads as high as a man and a nose needling forward like that of an atmosphere-penetrating rocket.

Veg's dizziness left him. He charged to the side. Tamme was right beside him, guiding his elbow in case he stumbled.

The tank careened on by, not swerving.

'Was that another trap?' Veg asked breathlessly.

'Coincidence, more likely. Do you recognize this alternate?'

He looked about. All around them were ramps and platforms, and on these structures vehicles of every size and shape sped by. Some were quite small, and some were tiny – the size of mice, or even flies. But all were obviously machines.

'A bit like downtown Earth,' he muttered. 'But not—' He paused. 'The machine world! This is where they breed!'

'I doubt they breed,' she said. 'Nevertheless, this is a significant discovery.'

'Significant! Those machines are half the problem! I had to fight one of them halfway across the desert to protect our supplies!'

'Only to fall prey to the sparkle-cloud,' she reminded him.

'Yeah . . .'

A dog-sized machine headed for them. It had perceptor-antennae extending from the top, and it emitted a shrill beeping.

'We're discovered,' Tamme said. 'I think we'd better move on.'

But it was already too late. The seemingly aimless paths of the machines suddenly became purposeful. From every side they converged.

531

'I think we'd better not resist,' Tamme said. 'Until we locate the projector, we're at a disadvantage.'

They certainly were! They were now ringed by machines, several of which were truck-sized, and there was a dismaying assortment of rotating blades, pincers, and drills. But she had already noted a containment pattern to their activity rather than an attack pattern.

A container-machine moved up, and two buzz saws herded them into its cage. The mesh folded closed, and they were prisoners.

'You figure this is the end of the line?' Veg asked. 'I mean, maybe the hexaflexagon goes on, but if the machines catch every visitor . . .'

'Uncertain,' Tamme said. 'Some may avoid capture, some may escape, some may be freed.'

'How many agents do you figure are travelling around here?'

'It could be an infinite progression.'

Veg was silent, chewing over that. She could read his concern: an endless chain of human beings parading through the worlds, right into the maw of the machine? That would explain how the machines knew so well how to handle them! And why the nose-woman on the fog world had not been surprised or afraid. The alternates would be like tourist stops . . .

They cruised up to a metal structure. 'A machine-hive,' Veg muttered, staring out through the mesh, and his description was apt. It rose hugely, bulging out over the landscape, and from every direction machines of all sizes approached, while others sped outward. The hum of their engines was constant and loud, like that of hornets. A number were flying machines, and these ranged from jet-plane to gnat size. They zoomed in and out of appropriately diametered holes.

Their own vehicle headed for one of the truck-sized apertures. The machine-hive loomed tremendously as they approached; it was a thousand feet high and as big around.

'Any way out, once we're *in*?' Veg asked apprehensively.

'I could short the gate mechanism and get us out of this vehicle,' Tamme said. 'But I don't think that would be expedient.'

Veg looked out of the rushing landscape. They were now on a narrow, elevated railroad-trestle like abutment fifty feet above the metal ground. Small buzz-saw machines flanked them on trestles on either side, and a pincer-tank followed immediately behind. There was no clearance for pedestrians.

'We must be doing a hundred miles per hour,' he remarked.

'More than that. The lack of proximate and stationary objects deceives the eye.'

'Well, if the machines wanted to kill us, they'd have done it by now,' he said. But he hardly bothered to conceal his nervousness.

So they stayed put. In moments their truck plunged into the tunnel – and almost immediately stopped. Tamme, anticipating this, caught Veg about the waist before he was flung into the wall. 'Well, aren't we cosy,' she murmured as she let him go.

'I wish you wouldn't do that,' he muttered. He meant that she could have warned him instead of demonstrating her superior strength again – and he also knew that she was aware of his reactions to contact with her body. She nodded to herself; she was in fact teasing him, probably trying to build up her own self-image in the face of her deterioration of set, of agent-orientation. This was a weak human device, and she would stop.

The gate opened. They stepped out. The gate closed, and the truck departed. But other bars were already in place, preventing them from following the vehicle out.

'Now we can make our break,' Veg said. He put his hands on the bars and shook them. 'Yow!'

Tamme knew what had happened. The metal was electrified. 'They have had prior experience with our form of animation,' she said. 'Possibly the first agent escaped, but we shall not. We'll have to wait and see what they have in mind for us.'

'Yeah,' he agreed dubiously.

Tamme was already exploring their prison. It was brightly lit by glowing strips along the corners, the light reflecting back and forth across the polished metal walls. One wall had a series of knobs and bulbs. They were obviously set up for human hands and perceptions. The machines would have no use for such things!

There was a pattern to the bank of knobs. It resembled the controls to a computer. The knobs would be to activate it, the lights to show what was happening.

'Very well,' she murmured. She turned the end knob quickly, removing her hand as it clicked over.

There was no shock. The light above that knob brightened. Sound came from hidden speakers: raucous, jarring.

Tamme reversed the knob. The sound died.

'Alien juke box,' Veg muttered.

'Close enough,' Tamme agreed. She turned the next knob.

Sound rose again: a series of double-noted twitterings, penetrating.

She turned that off and tried the third. This was like the roar of ocean surf, with a half-melodious variable foghorn in the background.

There was over a hundred knobs. She tried them all – and got a hundred varieties of noise. Then she started over. On the second round the sounds were different; there were no repeats.

'This may be fun to you, but it's my turn to sleep,' Veg said. He lay down on a raised platform that seemed made for the purpose.

Just as well. She could work more efficiently if he were safely out of mischief. She could have zeroed in on the sounds she was looking for much faster but preferred to wait until Veg got bored, for a reason she did not care to tell him. Now she got down to serious business.

Still it took time. For two hours she tried new sounds until she got one vaguely resembling human speech. She turned this off, then on again – and it was a different, yet similar patter. She tried again on the same knob, but though the human-sounding voice continued, it was no closer to anything she understood.

'Have to find the key,' she murmured inaudibly. 'Not getting it yet.'

She left the knob on and turned to the next. The voice modified, becoming less human. So she went to the knob on the other side, and now the voice became more familiar.

In this manner, slowly, she centered on a language approximating contemporary English. She knew she could narrow it down to her exact dialect but refrained.

Veg woke with a start. 'Hey – that's making sense!'

Tamme warned him into silence with a fierce gesture. Now that the language was close, the machine could probably identify their precise alternate – which was the point of all this. She wanted communication without complete identification, lest her world be in peril.

But the machine – actually it was an input to the main hive intellect – had heard. 'Curminicate, yez,' it said.

'Yez,' she agreed, while Veg looked bewildered.

534

'Ujest noob; abdain edenddy.'

That's what you think! she thought, *I'll unjest your noobs but not to abdain edenddy. I want an approximation,* not *identity.*

She adjusted knobs, bringing it closer. She pretended to be trying to obtain identity while actually adapting herself to the new pattern so that the machine would be satisfied the language was her own. This was a clever trap: letting the captives pinpoint their own alternates so that their worlds could be nailed.

Meanwhile, she hoped Veg had sense enough to keep his mouth shut. A few words from him now could tip off the machine.

'Now – gestons,' she said.

'Esk.'

'Furst geston: wheer or we?'

'Machina Prime, sender of ralofance.'

Mentally she translated: Machine Prime, center of relevance. No modesty about this alternate!

'Wat wont with os?' Already the artificial speech pattern was becoming set so that she could think in it and use it automatically. So while Veg's brow furrowed in confusion, to her it was like an ordinary conversation: What do you want with us?

'Merely to identify you and to establish amicable relations between our frames.'

Tamme was glad Veg could not follow the machine's dialect readily, for he would have laughed aloud. Amicable relations between the home-alternate of the killer machines and Earth? Unlikely!

Fortunately, she was an expert liar. 'This is what we want, too. We shall be happy to cooperate.'

'Excellent. We shall send an emissary to your frame and establish an enclave there.'

Which enclave would be blasted out of existence – if it came anywhere close to true-Earth. But it wouldn't. 'We shall make a favourable report on our return,' she said. 'But at present we must continue on through our pattern of frames.'

'By all means. We are conversant with your pattern. In fact, we have entertained many of your life-forms before. But we must advise you: There is danger.'

Friendly advice from the machine? Beware! 'Please explain.'

'Your form of sentience is protoplasmic; ours mechanical. Yet we

535

have many similarities, for we both require physical housings and must consume matter in order to produce functioning energy. The enemy is not physical, consumes no matter, and is inimical to rational existence. No physical being is secure on any frame, for the enemy is far more skilled in frame-shifting than either machine or life. But your pattern takes you through an enemy home-frame, and there the danger is magnified.'

Oho! So the machines sought liaison against a common antagonist. This just might be worthwhile. 'We do not understand the nature of this enemy.'

'Its nature is not comprehensible by material beings. It resembles a cloud of energy-points, sustained on a framework of nodes.'

The sparkle-pattern! This was an insight indeed! 'We have encountered such entities but did not appreciate what they were. They moved us from one frame to another involuntarily. From that frame we escaped and are now attempting to find our way home.'

'They do this to our units, also. We are able to resist to a certain extent, but they are stronger than we in this respect.'

'Stronger than we, too,' Tamme said. 'We are very clumsy about frame travel.' All too true – which was one of the things that rang false about this proposition. If the machines had true alternate-travel, as this one implied, they had little need of human liaison. If they *didn't*, there was not much help Tamme's world could offer.

'Two frames are stronger than one.'

'We agree. What next?'

'Will your world accede to a contract?'

Contract? What was this? Now she wished she could interpret the physical mannerisms of the computer the way she did with men! 'That depends on its content.'

'Agreement to interact for mutual benefit. Establishment of interaction enclaves. Transfer of beneficial resources.'

Now she was catching on. 'I believe my world would be interested. But once our government has ratified the contract—'

'Government?'

'That select group of individuals that formulate the mechanisms and restrictions of our society so that there will not be chaos.'

'Individuals?'

Oh-oh. 'Your machines are not separate entities?'

'They are separate physically but part of the larger entity.

536

Separated from the society, our units become wild, subsapient, without proper control. Only in unity is there civilization. This is why we are unable to travel far between frames; our units become separated from the hive and degenerate into free-willed agents.'

'That is a difference between us. We are distinct subentities; we retain our sentience and civilization when isolated from our hive.' But privately she wondered: did human beings really prosper in isolation. Agents certainly did not! For normals it might take a generation, but individuals cut off from their societies did degenerate. Apparently the effect was more intense with the machines. That would explain why this hive-computer was rational, while the machine Veg had met was vicious. Without its civilized control, it had reverted to primitive savagery.

'That is now apparent. It explains what had been a mystery about your kind – though you behave more rationally than your predecessors.'

So some had tried to fight 'Perhaps you have made it easier for us to *be* rational by providing an avenue for communication. It would also help if you made available those substances we require for our energy conversions – organic materials, water, clean air.'

'This we shall do on your advice.'

Very accommodating; she almost wished she could affort to trust the machine. Aspects of its society were fascinating. 'How should we reach you again? Our meeting here is random; we would not be able to locate your frame again.' Maybe she could turn the tables, identifying the machine-alternate without giving away Earth.

'We shall provide you with a frame-homer. This is a nonsentient unit that will broadcast a signal across the framework. We shall be able to locate it by that signal, once it is activated.'

'Excellent. We shall activate it when the contract is ready.'

A slot opened below the knobs. Inside a little drawer was a lentil-sized button. 'No need. This will activate itself when the occasion is proper.'

So they weren't gambling overmuch on the good faith of the other party, either! Tamme took it and filed it away in a pocket. 'Good. Now we must proceed.'

'We shall provide you with your material needs if you will expalin them.'

She hesitated, then decided to gamble. Why should the machine poison them when it already had them in its power? More likely it would do them every possible little service in the hope of getting them and its unit safely to Earth, thus making firm contact. So she described the type of vitamins, proteins, and minerals that life required.

After some experimentation, the machine produced edible, if unappetizing, food synthesized from its resources. Tamme and Veg were hungry, so they ate and enjoyed. She kept Veg silent while she gave advice for future cuisine. Though she did not regard any human beings that might follow as her friends, the common enemies were a greater threat; let the humans settle their differences in private. Also, let some *other* Earth be taken over if that was the way of it.

'You understand,' she said at the conclusion of the meal, 'we can not guarantee when we will reach our home-world, or *if* we will. Alternity is complex.'

'We understand. We shall conduct you to your projector.'

'Thank you.'

A truck appeared. The bars lifted. Tamme gestured Veg inside, at the same time touching her finger to her lips. She did not want him blabbing anything while they remained within the hearing of any machine, which she now knew to be no more than a unit of the hive.

They rode out of the giant complex, and she felt a very human relief. Shortly they were deposited at a platform. Set on a pedestal was a projector.

Tamme wasted no time. She activitated it. And they

were standing in mist again.

'Okay – now can I talk?' Veg demanded.

'Should be safe,' she said. She had considered whether the lentil-signal could overhear them but decided not. If it were sentient, it would lose its orientation away from the hive-frame, and if it were not, it would probably be inactive until activated. Why should Machine Prime care about their dialogue when their world of Earth was so near its grasp? Calculated risk; she was not ready to throw it away yet but did not want to keep Veg silent forever.

She forged through the mist towards the next projector.

Veg followed her with difficulty. He had to crawl on hands and knees, taking deep breaths from air pockets near the ground. 'That pidgin English you were jabbering – sounded as though you made some kind of deal—'

'The machine culture wants permission to exploit Earth,' she said. 'Apparently they have very limited alternate-transfer capacity, hardly ahead of ours, and unless the whole hive goes, the machines become wild. So they want to place an identifying beacon on our alternate – they call it a "frame" – so that they can zero in with a full self-sustaining enclave. That means a hive-brain. They say they need a contract between alternates, but I don't believe that. Who would enforce such a document?'

'Yeah, who?' he echoed.

She found the projector and activated it.

They stood within the closing walls.

'I don't think it's smart, showing them where Earth is,' Veg said.

'Don't worry. If there's one thing I'm not going to do, it's take their button to Earth. I'll find a good place for it – somewhere else in alternity.'

'Yeah.' He was right behind her as she moved towards the next projector, avoiding capture by the walls. 'But what was this about a common enemy?'

'The sparkle-cloud. They can't handle it, either. It is the ultimate alternity traveller. But the fact that we have a mutual enemy does not necessarily make us allies. I played along with the hive-brain only to get us out of there. Which it probably knew.'

'Then why did it—?'

'That beacon-button is probably indestructible short of atomic fusion. We're travelling through alternate frames. It's bound to key the machine boss in somewhere even if we throw it away – and it could pay off big if we actually get it to an exploitable world.'

'Like Paleo?' They skirted the burned-out decoy projector, mute evidence that this was the same frame they had visited before.

'Like our *Earth*. From what I observed, those machines with their physical power and hive-unity could probably devastate Earth. Our population would become an organic source of nutrition, and our terrain would represent expansion room for their excess units.'

Veg scratched his head. 'Are we sure they would do that? Maybe they really are trying to be—'

539

'It is what we would do to *them*.'

He nodded. 'I guess so. The old omnivore syndrome. Do unto others before they do it unto you. You know you agents wanted to save the alternates for Earth to exploit. Now that we're running into tough civilizations, or whatever—'

'Right. It may be better to close off the alternate frontier entirely. I shall make a complete report on my return. It may be that your dinosaur worlds will be saved after all.'

'That's great!' he exclaimed, giving her arm a squeeze with his big hand. He was so strong that she felt discomfort, though no ordinary man could harm her. 'Even though it's too late for the *real* Paleo.'

'There will be countless alternate Paleos – and it is not certain that we eliminated all the dinosaurs from that one. It was the manta spores we were after, you know.'

He was silent. She knew the memory of the destruction of the Cretaceous enclave of Paleo still tormented him, and she had been one of the agents responsible.

They reached the projector. This one was charged, though it would not have been had they not spent that time interviewing the hive-computer. Sooner or later they would return to a frame too quickly and be unable to project out despite pressing need to do so. She would have to prepare for that, if possible. What would be the best way to survive for two hours under pressure? Educate Veg?

Meanwhile, they both needed some rest, and they could not be assured of getting it on an untried world. Veg had slept in the hive, but he was still tired, and she was not in top form.

She activated the projector.

They stood in the forest again, as she had anticipated. 'I believe this location is secure,' she said. 'We'll rest for six hours before continuing.'

'Good enough!' Veg agreed. But he hesitated.

'You will not be able to relax here while I'm in sight,' she told him. 'Short of obliging you or knocking you out—'

'Uh-uh! I'll take a snooze down beside the other projector. That way we can guard both spots.'

She nodded acquiescence. His discipline in the face of his powerful passion for her body was remarkable, if somewhat pointless. He had indulged himself with the woman Aquilon and had been unsatisfied, so now he was doubly careful. He wanted more than the physical and was content to gamble against the odds in the hope of achieving it. Unfortunately for him, the odds were long – perhaps a thousand to one, against. She was human, at the root, so theoretically could fall in love. But agents were thoroughly conditioned against irrelevant emotion, and they had virtually no subconscious with its attendant ghosts and passions.

It would be better for him to accept the reality and indulge the passing urge he felt for her, knowing that there was no deeper commitment. That would abate his tension and make this alternate tour easier. Yet she had learned just enough respect for him to let him do it his own way. His human capriciousness and curiosity had already opened several profitable avenues, such as the hexaflexagon parallel, and might do it again. They were a good team: disciplined agent, variable normal.

If his indecision became a threat to her mission, she would have to act to abate it. That could mean seducing him directly or stranding him on some safe alternate. Neither action would leave him satisfied, and that was unfortunate.

Perhaps she would have to deceive him, pretending to love him. She could do it if she really tried. But she did not care to. 'Maybe I'm getting too choosy, like him,' she muttered. 'The real thing, or nothing ...'

Now she needed rest. She slept.

They stepped from the forest into a forest. Flexible green plants stood on a gently sloping bank of black dirt. As trees they were small, but as vegetables, large. In either case, strange.

'No problem here,' Veg said cheerfully. 'Just vegetables, like me.'

'Trouble enough,' Tamme murmured.

'I know. You wish I'd lay you or forget you. Or both. And I guess it makes sense your way. But I don't have that kind of sense.'

Good. He was coming to terms with the situation. 'These plants are strange.'

He walked to the nearest and squatted beside it. 'I've seen strange plants before. They all – oh-ho!'

She had seen it, too. 'It moved.'

'It's got thick leaves and tentacles. And what look like muscles.'

Tamme surveyed the assemblage. 'We had better find the

541

projector rapidly. The plants are uprooting themselves.'

They were. All about the two intruders, the plants were writhing and drawing their stems from the earth.

'I'm with you!' Veg cried. 'Next thing, they'll be playing violins ... over our bones.'

Together they ran up the slope, casting about for the projector. This brought them out of the region where the plants were walking and into one where the foliage had not yet been alerted. But the new plants reacted to the alien presence the same way.

'They can't move rapidly, but there are many of them,' Tamme said. 'You'd better arm yourself with a stick or club if you can find it.'

'Yeah.' Veg ran over to a stem lying on the ground. He put his hands on it. 'Yow!'

It was no dead stalk but a living root. The thing twisted like a snake in his hands, throwing him off.

Meanwhile, the other plants were accelerating. Now they were converging with creditable alacrity, their thick, round roots curling over the ground, digging in for holds.

'Here's a weapon,' Tamme said, drawing a yard-long metal rod from her clothing.

Veg paused to stare. 'Where'd you hide *that*? I've *worn* that outfit of yours! No club in it.'

'It telescopes,' she explained. 'Be careful – it's also a sword. It weighs only ounces, but it has a good point and edge. Don't cut yourself.'

'Edge? Where?' He looked at the blunt-seeming side.

'There's an invisibly thin wire along the leading face, here. It will cut almost anything with almost no pressure. Trust me; *don't* rub your thumb on it.'

Veg took the blade and held it awkwardly in front of him. He had obviously never used such a weapon before, but she had no time to train him now. 'Just do what comes naturally. Stab and hack. You'll get the feel of it.'

He stepped out and chopped at a branch of the nearest plant. The sword sliced through easily, the broad part wedging open the cut made by the wire. 'Hey – it works!'

Tamme let him hold off the plants while she searched for the projector. She hoped there *was* one; they always ran the risk of a

542

dead end, a frame in which the original projector had been destroyed or was inaccessible.

The walking plants did not seem to feel much pain, but after Veg had lopped off quite a few branches and stems, they got the message and withdrew. Veg was able to clear a path wherever Tamme wanted to go. He was enjoying this, she knew; though he would not kill animal life to eat, he would kill attacking vegetables.

Then something else appeared. Not a plant; it was vaguely humanoid, yet quite alien. It had limbs that terminated in disks and a head that resembled a Rorschach blob. It emitted a thin keening.

'Is that a machine, plant, or fungus?' Veg asked.

'Mixture,' she replied tersely. 'Inimical.'

'I'll hold it off,' Veg said. 'You find the projector.'

'No, the thing is dangerous. I'll tackle it.'

'Thanks,' Veg said sourly. But he moved off, allowing her to make a stand while he searched.

Aliens were hard to read, but the malevolence seemed to radiate out of this thing. Obviously it recognized her general type and intended to exterminate it. Had a human agent done something on a prior visit to arouse justified antipathy, or was the creature a hater of all aliens? Or could it be the farmer growing these plants they were multilating? In that case, its attitude was more that of a man with bug spray. It hardly mattered now; she had to deal with it.

The creature came close and suddenly charged her, its hand wheels leading. They were spinning like little buzz saws – which they surely were. She leaped aside, not wishing to reveal her technology by using a power weapon. The longer she fenced with it, the more she would learn about it. Was it intelligent, civilized – or was it more like a vicious guard dog? The evidences were inconclusive so far.

The saw-wheels came at her again. This time she stepped in, blocking the two arms with her own, forcing the wheels out while she studied the musculature and perceptive organs of the torso. The thing's skin was cold and hairy, like that of a spider.

In the moment her face was close, an aperture opened and spewed out a fine mist. Caught off guard, she did not pull her face away in time. It was an acid, and it burned her skin and eyes, blinding her.

She touched her hip. Her blaster fired through her skirt, bathing the creature in fire. It's body crackled as it was incinerated. The keening stopped.

543

'Yo!' she heard Veg call.

She ran to him, orienting on the sound. She had been trained to handle herself regardless of injuries. She used the echoes from her own footsteps to identify obstructions, such as the tall moving plants.

'Here – in a pile of rocks,' Veg said as she came up.

'Is it charged?'

'Think so. I've never been quite sure how you could tell.'

'Time to learn.' While she talked, she focused on her autonomic system, blocking out the pain. 'There's a little dial in the base with red-green markings. Read it.'

He stooped. 'It's on green.'

'Right,' she said, though she could not see anything. The flaming in her face retreated as her pain-block took effect, but that was only part of the problem. The damage was still being done, but she could not yet wash the acid off. 'Now let's see if you can activate it.'

'That I know. You shove this thing, this little lever—'

She heard the echoes of his voice and knew that the changing walls were there. They had made the shift.

'Now let's see if you know the way to the next projector.'

'Hey – how come all this practice *now*?' He paused. 'Hey – your face – it's bright red! What happened?'

'That animal-mineral-vegetable was also a skunk.'

'Acid!' he cried, alarmed. 'Acid in the face! We've got to wash that off!'

'No water here. Let's move on.'

'Your eyes! Did it get your—?'

'Yes. I am blind.'

She did not need the visual input to pick up his shock and hurt anger. 'God, Tamme—'

'I can function. But it will help if you find that projector.'

'Come on!' He took her hand.

'You run ahead. I am well aware of your location.'

'Okay.' He let go. They moved down the flexing passage.

He did know the way. They reached the projector. 'Lefthanded – and it's not ready,' he announced.

And the next frame should be the forest – safe, pleasant, with plenty of fresh cold water in a nearby stream. Out of reach.

'Someone must have used it since we did,' he said. 'Been almost eight hours since we were here last.' Then he caught himself. 'No – I'm thinking of the time we slept. We *left* here only about an hour ago. Hey – I never gave you back your watch. You don't need it right now, though, I guess.'

It was a pitifully naïve attempt to distract her from the insoluble problem. 'I doubt anyone has been here since we were,' she said. 'But we have no notion how many are travelling this pattern. This is an inversion, possibly part of another hexaflexagon, with its own personnel.'

'Can't we push it?' he asked plaintively. 'The dial is getting towards the green . . .'

'Dangerous. An incomplete transfer might deliver dead bodies. We don't know.'

'We've got to clean out those eyes. Make them tear.' Another hesitation. 'Or do agents ever cry – even for that?'

'My eyes teared. The damage was done in the first seconds, and after that it was probably too late for water, anyway.' Had she not been preoccupied with their escape, she would have thought of this before. It was another mark of the pressure she was under and her loss of capacity as an agent, quite apart from her vision.

'Permanent or temporary?'

'Temporary, I think. It is a superficial burn, clouding the retinas.'

'Then we're okay. We'll rest until you heal.'

'We may not have time.'

'Stop being so damned tough and act sensibly! Going off handicapped is stupid – you know that.'

She nodded. 'It was stupid letting myself fall into the acid trap. I've been making too damn many human errors.'

'Now you even *sound* human.' He sounded pleased.

'We'll give it a few hours. Agents recover quickly.'

'Any other girl'd be crying and dependent,' he grumbled.

Tamme smiled. 'Even Miss Hunt?'

'Who?'

'Deborah Hunt. I believe you were close to her at one time.'

'You mean 'Quilon!' he exclaimed. 'We never use her original name, any more than we use yours.' He paused. 'What *was* yours?'

'I have no other name.'

'I mean before you were an agent, you were a girl. Who were you?

Why did you change?'

'I do not know. I have no memories of my civilian status – or of my prior missions as a TA-series agent, female. The debriefing erases all that. All agents of a given series must start their missions with virtually identical physical and intellectual banks.'

'Don't you miss it sometimes?'

'Miss what?'

'Being a woman.'

'Like Aquilon Hunt? Hardly.'

'Listen, don't cut at her!' he snapped.

'I admit to a certain curiosity about the nature of this emotion that grips you,' she said. 'Passion, pleasure, pain, hunger, I can understand. But why do you maintain an involvement with a woman you know must go to your best friend and avoid one with me that would carry no further entanglements?' The question was rhetorical: She knew the answer. Normals lacked fit control over their emotions and so became unreasonable.

'You *want* my involvement with you?' he asked incredulously.

'It is a matter of indifference to me except as it affects my mission.' Not wholly true; she had no real emotional interest in him but would have appreciated some entertainment during her incapacity. This conversation was another form of that entertainment.

'That's why,' he said. 'You are indifferent.'

'It would be useful to know what she has that I do not.'

'Any other woman, that would be jealousy. But you only want to know so you can be a more effective agent.'

'Yes.' Another half truth. The continuing strain of too long a mission made her desire some kind of buttressing. The temporary love of a man offered that. But it would not be wise to tell him that; he would misinterpret it.

'Well, I'll answer it. 'Quilon is beautiful – but so are you. She's smart, but you're smarter. As a sex object, you have it all over her, I'm sure; she has the body, but she doesn't know how to – well, never mind. What it is, is, she needs a man, and she *cares*.'

'Agreed. You have not answered my question.'

Veg choked. 'You *don't* care. You could drop me in a volcano if it helped your mission. You don't need anyone – even when you're blind.'

'True. I have never denied this. I have no such liabilities. But what

546

positive asset does she have that—'

'I guess I can't get through to you. Her *liabilities* are her assets – that's how Cal would put it. Me, I just say I love her, Cal loves her, and she loves *us*. I'd let the universe go hang if that would help her. It has nothing much to do with sex or strength or whatever.'

Tamme shook her head, intrigued. 'This is far-fetched and irrational. It should be informative to put it to the test.'

'Shut up!'

'That, too, is intriguing.'

Veg got up and stomped away. But he did not go far, for the walls were waiting.

Tamme threw her mind into a healing state, concentrating on the tissues of her face and eyes. She, like all agents, had conscious control over many ordinarily unconscious processes and could accelerate healing phenomenally by focusing the larger resources of her body on the affected area. The external lenses of the eyes were small but hard to act on directly; this would take several hours of concentration.

When the projector was recharged, Veg took them through.

Tamme continued the effort in the forest, and in four hours her vision began to clear.

'You mean you can see again?' Veg demanded.

'Not well. I estimate I will have three-quarters capacity in another two hours. Since we should have two familiar frames coming up, that will suffice. Once I desist from the specific effort, the rate will slow; it will take several days to get beyond ninety per cent. Not worth the delay.'

'You're tough, all right!'

'A liability, by your definition.'

'Not exactly. You can be tough and still need someone. But we've been over that before.'

In due course they moved on to

the mist frame and

the alien

orchestra, following the hexaflexagon pattern. Their strategy of ploughing straight ahead seemed to be paying off; they were stuck in

547

no subloops. Probably they had not been stuck before; they just had not understood the pattern.

'Now we strike a new one,' Tamme said.

'You ready?'

'My vision is eighty per cent and mending. The rest of my faculties are par. I am ready.'

'Okay.' And they went through.

Tamme lurched forward and caught hold before she fell. Veg dropped but snagged a hold before going far.

It was an infinite construction of metal bars. They intersected to form open cubes about six feet on a side, and there was no visible termination.

'A Jungle gym!' Veg cried. 'I had one of these at my school when I was a kid!' He climbed and swung happily.

'Let's find a projector,' Tamme said.

'Got to be on one of these struts.'

'We need to establish a three-dimensional search pattern. There is no variety here as there was in the coloured planes. We don't want to double back on checked sections.'

'Right. Maybe we'd better mark where we started and work out from that. Take time, but it's sure.'

They tied his shirt to a crossbar and began checking. Sighting along the bars was not much good; the endless crosspieces served to interrupt the line of sight so that the presence of the projector could not be verified. It was necessary to take a direct look into each cube. In the distance the effect of the massed bars was strange: From some views, they became a seemingly solid wall. From the centre of a cube, there seemed to be six square-sectioned tunnels leading up, down, and in four horizontal directions.

When sighting routinely down one of these tunnels, Tamme saw a shape. It looked like a man.

She said nothing. Instead, she sidled across several cubes, breaking the line of sight in all three dimensions, and searched out Veg.

She was able to orient on him by the sound. 'You're out of position,' she said.

'No – I'm on the pattern. You're off yours.'

'I left mine. We have company.'

'Oh-oh. Alien?'

'Human.'

'Is that good or bad?'

'I'm not sure. We'd better observe him if we have the chance.'

'Here's the chance!' Veg whispered. Sure enough, a figure hove into view along a horizontal axis.

'That's *you!*' Tamme whispered. 'Another Veg!'

She knew what he was going to say: *Your eyes must be seeing only forty per cent! I'm HERE!* But she was wrong. 'Well, we figured this could happen. Another couple, just like us, from a near alternate. We've just got to find that projector *first.*'

Tamme made a mental note: The episode with the acid thrower must have thrown off her perceptions. Not only had she misread Veg's response, he sounded different, less concerned than he should be. She would have to reorient at the first opportunity to avoid making some serious mistake.

Meanwhile, she concentrated. 'We have the advantage because we saw them first. We can enhance our chances by conducting our search pattern ahead of them. That way they'll be checking a volume of space that we have already covered – where we *know* there's no projector.'

'Smart!' he agreed.

Tamme calculated the probable origin of the competitive party, based on her two sightings of the strange Veg and the assumption that the other couple had landed not far from their own landing. They worked out from that. There was some risk the projector would happen to be on the wrong side of the other couple, but all they could do now was improve their chances, not make them perfect.

And suddenly it was there, nestled in a hangar below an intersection. Tamme approached it cautiously, but it was genuine. And it was charged.

Now she had a dilemma. She had control of the projector – but her larger mission was to eliminate Earth's competition, even that of a very near alternate. Should she tackle her opposite number now?

No. If the other couple had taken the same route around the hexaflexagon, it had to have been earlier, for the two-hour recharging time of the projectors required at least that amount of spacing out. But it was also possible that the others were flexing the other way – backwards, as it were. In which case they could not yet have encountered the walking plants and the acid-spraying keeper. So that other agent, male or female, would be in top form and would have a material advantage. That was no good.

Better to proceed on around the next subloop and tackle the competition when they crossed again in this frame. Then she would be ready. With luck, the other agent would not even know the encounter was incipient, and that would more than make up for the eye deficiency.

She activated the projector.

And they stood amidst sparkles.

'Well, look at that!' Veg said, impressed.

'A home-frame of the pattern-entities,' Tamme said. 'Another major discovery.'

'Yeah. They told us at the bazaar, but I didn't expect it so soon.'

Tamme did not stiffen or give any other indication of her reaction; her agent-control served her in good stead. Instead, she continued as if he had said nothing unusual, drawing him out. 'They said a lot at the bazaar.'

'Yeah. But what else could we do? By cooperating, at least we save our own alternates, maybe. I'm sorry if we have to go against our duplicates who didn't make it there – but in the end, it's every world for itself. And with the pattern-entities right here on the circuit – well, so much the better.'

'If those patterns don't spot us and transport us right out of the network.'

'Yeah. Let's get on with it.'

They got on with the search. But now Tamme knew: *She had picked up the wrong Veg.* This one was travelling the other way and had been through at least one alternate – the 'bazaar' – that she hadn't. And some sort of agreement, or treaty, had been made there involving other alternate Vegs and Tammes.

She had been right: Herself, from another alternate, was her enemy. And it *was* herself, for Veg would have known the difference immediately had his companion been a male agent.

Every frame for itself. *Her* Veg would not have agreed; *this* Veg did.

Ironically, she preferred the attitude of her original Veg. He had

550

more conscience; he cared. Meanwhile, he was with the other Tamme.

She had to complete the subloop and get back to the Jungle gym before that enemy Tamme caught on. The bitch would not be slow, either! So long as that other did not locate the projector, her search pattern would continue, and there would be little interaction between the agent and the man. But if they found it and had to wait for the recharge, there would be time.

And if they found the shirt tied at the point of arrival ... there would be two shirts, one from each Veg. A dead giveaway! Why hadn't she thought to recover that shirt?

It had, after all, been sheer luck, her finding the projector first. She had figured a pattern based on her two sightings of the opposition – and at least one of those sightings had actually been of her own man! No science in that! But the same sort of coincidence could bring the other Tamme to the same projector. The enemy Tamme would have to wait while *this* Tamme could move – if she found the projector on this frame soon.

Maybe it would be better to avoid contact entirely and go on. No – that would be deserting her Veg and bringing along one who would surely turn uncooperative when he caught on. And she was trapped on a subloop; there was no way out but through the Jungle gym frame.

The projector on this subloop would probably be charged. She might complete the trip around within one hour and catch the enemy completely off guard. That would be best. Her vision would not be much improved within that time, but the element of surprise was more important.

What about this Veg? No need for him to know. He had already served to alert her, and he was no threat.

'Hey, these aren't the same,' he commented, watching a swirl of sparkle almost under his nose. 'See, they're smaller, and they don't fade in and out. This one's staying right here in this alternate, as though it doesn't know any better.'

'You study it,' she said, casting about for the projector. 'The information could be valuable.' Maybe it would keep him occupied and innocent.

He watched it. 'You know what I think – this is a primitive one, like a three-dee R Pentomino. It just rides on a few elements, maintaining itself, not doing anything fancy. Maybe this isn't the sparkle home-alternate, but a fringe-alternate, with animal-patterns instead of advanced-sentient ones. They must have a whole range of states just as we do – some hardly more than amoebas, others superhuman. Superpattern, I mean.' He chuckled.

He certainly *had* been to places she hadn't. R Pentomino? He seemed to have a much better grounding on the sparkles. It showed in his terminology and his attitude. 'Maybe you can work out the whole sequence of patterns,' she suggested. Where *was* that projector?

'Yeah. How they start as little three-dimensional swirls across the elements, like wind rattling the leaves of a poplar, and then begin modifying things to suit themselves. How some turn into predator patterns, gobbling up others, until the good patterns learn to shoot them down with glider guns. But then the bad ones start shooting, too, and they just keep evolving, dog eat dog, only it's all just patterns on energy-nodes. Finally they achieve higher consciousness – only they don't even know what it is to be physical. They think that the only possible sentience is pattern-sentience. And when they finally meet up with sentient material beings, it's like a nightmare, like monsters from the deeps, impossible but awful. Yeah, I think I can see it, now. Too bad we can't talk with them, tell them we understand . . .'

Tamme paused in her search, listening. *The man was making sense!* Could that be the rationale of the mysterious pattern-entities? The machines called them enemies, but if it were really just a monumental case of misunderstanding . . .

Then she spotted the projector and put aside irrelevant conjecture. 'Let's go, Veg!'

One step to the

orchestra, then another back to

the Jungle gym.

'I have your man captive,' the other Tamme said, indicating the direction with a minimal nod of her head. 'Do you yield?'

Rhetorical: To yield was to die. But it was true: Veg was efficiently gagged and bound with the two shirts, his legs tied so that he hung by his knees from a bar.

552

'What's this?' the free Veg asked, amazed. 'Why'd she tie her own companion?'

Tamme glanced at him. 'I am the other agent. I have not been to the bazaar.'

The expected spate of emotions ran through him. A stranger he was, yet he was very much Veg, slow in certain ways, noble in others. 'Then why didn't you—?'

'Tie you? What purpose? *She* is the dangerous one.'

'But *she* tied *me* – and you didn't!'

'I may have known you longer,' Tamme said. *And gotten soft!* 'Though it was not you I knew, precisely.' Of course, she *should* have put him more obviously under her control, as a counter to the alternate-Tamme's threat. Yet another mistake.

The free Veg looked from one Tamme to the other, disconcerted. Then he spoke to the other. 'Listen: I changed my mind. I'm not fighting anyone. This isn't right.'

'Then go untie your double,' Tamme said, realizing that her human error had converted to an odd kind of advantage: The alternate-Veg had been neutralized. 'You men are basically gentle; she and I are not so hesitant.'

'Yeah.' The free Veg went to help the bound one, passing between the two women. Then he halted, facing his own: 'Okay – I can't stop it. But maybe I can make it fair. Get rid of your power weapons.'

'Get out of the way,' Tamme Two said. She held a laser in her hand.

'Or shoot me first,' Veg said. 'Use that, and you'll sure as hell have to shoot me sometime because I won't work with you anymore.'

He was serious; the signals were all over him. It was a trifling threat to an agent. Still, Tamme knew what was going through the other's mind because it was her mind, too – her mind as it had been a few days ago when she was tougher, less corrupted by individual sentiment. Veg had been more than neutralized; he was now sympathetic to the Tamme he had not known, more gentle than his own. Liability had become strength. Tamme Two could dispense with him – but the man had commendable qualities and was proving more useful than anticipated. Why antagonize him needlessly? Especially when she had the advantage, for the other had evidently been injured in the face . . .

Tamme Two dropped the laser. Tamme One drew and dropped

hers. Because they were agents, they could read each other – well enough, at least, to know whether a given weapon was about to be dropped or fired. The lasers fell almost together down through the endless shaft of cubes.

'And don't use any others,' Veg Two said. 'Just your hands, or hand-powered stuff. Okay?'

Tamme Two nodded. She would make the sensible compromise to retain his good will, minor as its value was. He moved on.

Then both girls were moving. Actually, the laser shot would have been risky because it lacked power for instant effect, and there would have been time for both weapons to be used. Direct combat would be more decisive.

Tamme One swung around her bar, getting out of the direct line of vision. She had the disadvantage, and they both knew it; she had to use evasive strategy, hoping for the break that would reverse the odds. She ran along the topside of another bar towards her opponent.

But the other had anticipated her. A hand came from below to catch her ankle. Tamme One leaped into space, jackknifing to catch Tamme Two's hair. The other jerked aside and countered with a high kick.

Tamme caught a bar and swung around it and back to her feet. Tamme Two dived at her, pressing her advantage. Tamme raised a knee to catch her in the chest, but Tamme Two caught her shoulders and sat down suddenly. This was an old judo technique, *yoko wakare* or side-separation throw. Ordinarily, it was performed on the ground; in this case, there was no ground and no firm footing beyond the bars. The pull was tremendous. Tamme fell forward, somersaulted in air, and caught Tamme Two's ankles.

Then the telescoping sword manifested. Tamme Two's hands were free; Tamme One was momentarily exposed. The first slash caught her on the side, cutting open her clothing and severing the flesh through to the ribs. Her inferior vision had betrayed her; she could have countered as the sword was being drawn had she seen it in time. Now she was wounded, and the advantage was shifting from marginal to gross.

She let go and dropped, taking a moment to cut off the flowing blood by will power. But Tamme Two dropped with her, slashing again with the sword. Tamme drew her own and whipped it at her enemy – but her reflexes were slowed by the regenerative effort, and Tamme Two parried easily.

Tamme reached out and caught a bar one-handed. The wrench was terrible, but her body was brought up short.

And Tamme Two stopped with her, kicking the sword from her hand and simultaneously stabbing for the heart. Tamme twisted aside, too slow, and the point missed by two inches, piercing her left lung instead.

Never before had she realized how devastating an opponent she was, how implacable, how efficient. Tamme Two was an agent at par; Tamme herself was an agent at eighty per cent vision, caught by surprise, with diminished sense of purpose. Any one of those differences was critical, and now she was done for. Could she take the other with her into oblivion?

It took Tamme Two a moment to yank out the sword, for the power of the thrust had projected the point entirely through the body. Tamme took advantage of that moment to club Tamme Two on the side of the neck, preparatory to catching her in a literal death grip.

Tamme Two dodged again, reducing the effect of the blow, and blocked the clasping arms. Tamme was already dropping down through the cubes – but her hold was not tight, and Tamme Two slipped through. The double suicide would only kill one.

This time Tamme Two let her go, knowing better than to come again within reach of those arms. Instead, she drew and threw a fine knife. It shot straight down with unerring aim to embed itself in Tamme's skull, penetrating the brain.

'I am going to space,' he said.

'If you do, I will kill myself,' she said.

Bunny heard her parents engaging in their solemn, serious dialogue, terrified. Knowing there was nothing she could do. They never fought, never argued; when either spoke, it was final.

Actually, they had never spoken these words; the words were in Bunny's mind, her nightmares. But they reflected the unvoiced reality, building over the years into inevitable decision.

Her father went to space, unable to resist the gratification of a lifelong lure. Ocean sailing was in his ancestry; the nature of the challenge had changed, not his response.

Bunny understood this, for he had told her of space, its myriad wonders only now being revealed, its compelling fascination. Neutron stars, black holes, quasars; alien life, mysterious artifacts of long-dead empires; acceleration, free fall; meteors, comets, craters. She wanted to go, too.

The day he left, her mother carefully scraped the insulation from the apartment's energy line and shorted it out across her body. Bunny was an orphan.

'I know your father was lost in space, and your mother died when you were a child,' he said. 'This is what first attracted me to you. You *needed* me, and I thought that was enough.' He paused to walk around park space, idly knocking his powerful hands together. 'I'm strong; I like taking care of things. I wanted to take care of you. But Bunny, it isn't enough. Now I'm ready to marry – and what I crave is a wife figure, not a daughter figure. It just wouldn't work out, and we both know it.'

She did know it. She didn't plead, she didn't cry. After he left, she followed the model she remembered as closely as was convenient. She jumped off the passenger ramp into the moving line of a major freight artery.

'Both arms severed at the shoulders, one leg mangled, internal organs crushed. Heart and liver salvageable; kidneys unsalvageable. Brain intact. It would cost a fortune, but we *could* reconstitute her. To what point? She is medically indigent, no parents, no insurance, no special dispensations, no extraordinary talents, and she obviously doesn't want to live.'

'A suitable prospect, would you say?'

'Yes. You would be doing her a favour. *She doesn't want to remember.*'

'Very well. You will authorize the condemnation procedure?'

'I don't see much choice; it's that or death in hours.'

So Bunny's mangled but living remains were condemned as legally unsalvageable, and the government assumed possession in much the same manner as it acquired the right of way through a slum.

Two years later, the rebuilt, retrained body and brain were issued under the stamp of an agent, series TA, female.

Tamme opened her eyes. A snout-nosed near-human leaned over her. 'Hvehg!' the woman called.

A man came, bearded, putting his strong hand on hers. It was a hand very like that of the man Bunny had hoped to marry. 'You'll make it, Tam,' he said. 'We're taking good care of you.'

'Who?' It was hard to speak; she was weak and confused, and she needed . . . too much. He would reject her if he knew.

'You don't remember who you are?' the man asked, alarmed.

She made an effort. 'I am TA. You?'

'You don't remember me?' This seemed to bother him even more.

'Is this the start of a mission? I don't know how I got here, or who either of you are, or anything. Please tell me.' Speaking was such an effort that she knew she would soon have to desist – and she hardly understood her own words. TA?

'I am Veg. This is Ms Hmph, near as I can pronounce it. You were badly hurt, nearly dead; I brought you here, and the Hmphs made a place for us. We'd met them before on our trek through alternity.'

'Alternity?'

'Brother! You really are out of it. Maybe you better rest now.'

The mere suggestion was enough. She sank into sleep.

Her first mission as a TA was on Earth. She was told nothing, not even that it *was* the first. As with all agents, her mind was erased and reset between assignments, so it made no difference to her or the computer whether it was the first or the last. This reprogramming was to preserve the series identity; the computer needed assurance that any agent of a given series would respond and report precisely as allowed for. That way there was negligible human distortion; it was as though the computer itself had made the investigation. It was an efficient system, replacing the outmoded FBI, CIA, and similar organizations.

Had Bunny been aware of the transformation, she would have been incredulous. The weak, frail, insecure girl now was super-human – literally. She could run thirty miles an hour and sustain it for miles: twice the world record for normals. She could invert herself and walk on two extended fingers. She was thoroughly grounded in the use of a wide variety of weapons, from bazookas to kitchen knives, and was also adept at barehanded combat. She had the equivalent of college degrees in a number of technical and liberal arts. And she had a stunning face and figure.

But Bunny was not aware. Bunny was part of the dross that had been erased. Her body and brain had been stripped to their fundamental content, then recycled.

Tamme found herself in a riot-prone city. She moved among the people, questioning, searching out her mission. She had been given a single name and a probable address, no more. And in due course she found it; there was an assassination plot against a touring official. As the steam rifle oriented, so did she. The assassin died a fraction of a second before he fired, and Tamme returned to her barracks.

There she indulged in the predebriefing relaxation that was customary, almost mandatory: play being a recognized adjunct of the fit man. It was postponed for the agents until after completion of their missions, partly as additional inducement for performance, partly because that was the time of their greatest divergence from the agent-norm. Freshly briefed agents would have found each other so predictable as to be dull; postmission agents had differing experiences to discuss and were to a certain extent different people. Interaction became entertaining.

She met a male of the SU series. He was fascinating. He had been dispatched to apprehend a moonshine gunsmith and had been shot in the foot by one of the old-fashioned contraptions. She played nude water polo with him, and because of that foot was able to hold him under while she made the first score. But then he had hauled her under with him, and for four minutes they both held their breaths while they made love – though love was too strong a term for this physical release of passion.

'Will we ever meet again, Subble?' she asked as she lay in his arms, floating on the surface, enjoying the almost-combatlike exercise of power that no normal human could match.

'It hardly matters,' he replied. 'We will not remember or care.' And he shoved her head under, brought her bottom up, and penetrated her again . . . as a subterfuge while he knocked the ball in for the tying score.

After she got even with him for that, they both reported for final debriefing, and all had been erased.

Now Tamme did remember. She sat up with an anguished effort, her wounded side and chest excruciating. 'Subble died on his next mission!' she exclaimed.

Strong arms came about her shaking shoulders. 'Easy, Tam,' Veg said. 'You're dreaming.'

'No – I'm only now coming awake! You knew him!' she cried. 'You killed him!'

He bore her back to the bed. 'We knew him. We liked him. 'Quilon especially. He was a decent sort. For an agent. He may have died, but we didn't do it.'

She clung to him. 'I'm terrified! Stay with me – please!'

'Always.' He lay down beside her, smoothing her troubled forehead with his hand, careful of the bandage. 'Rest. Rest. You're still very weak.'

Tamme had other missions. One by one she relived them: one a mere interview with a scientist, another a spell as housemistress to an outpost halfway across the Earth-Sphere of colonization, keeping the normals sane. She had acted, always, with complete, objective ruthlessness, forwarding the interests of that government that had fashioned her in that manner it required.

Right up until her assignment on the first alternate world, Paleo. That mission, surprisingly, had been a multiple-agent venture. It brought her to the present.

When she was well enough to walk, Veg took her out of the house. The building was made of blocks of foam-like fog, and it tended to degenerate. Periodically, the farmer and his family cut new fog from the bank and built a new residence. The makings of the old house were chopped up for cattle bedding; the bovines liked the impregnated people-smell of it.

They were hard workers, these Fognosers (as Veg called them), and their children helped. They used hands for brute work, and prehensile snouts for fine work. They harvested certain types of mist for foods; most varieties tasted rather like scented soap but were nutritious.

'Now I remember,' Tamme said. 'We met these people once, and you showed them the hexaflexagon.'

'Yeah. They have seen many Vegs and many Tammes, but I was only the second one who happened to show the hex. Lucky I did because they remembered us. I mean, distinguished us from all the others just like us and helped. I've been making hexaflexagons like crazy; that's how I repay them.'

'And how shall I repay *you*?' she asked.

He shook his head. 'I wasn't doing this for pay.'

She gripped his hand. 'Please – I need you. I want to please you. What can I do?' Oh, God – she was pleading, and that would drive him off.

He looked at her. 'You *need* me?'

'Maybe that's the wrong word,' she said desperately.

His mouth was grim. 'When you use a word you don't understand, just manipulate – yes, it's the wrong word!'

'I'm sorry!' she cried. 'I won't use it again. Only don't be angry, don't turn away ...'

He held her by the shoulders at arm's length. 'Are you crying?'

'No!' But it was useless. 'Yes.' If only she hadn't been so weak physically and emotionally! Strong men didn't appreciate that.

'Why!'

What was left but the truth? 'When you are near me, I feel safe, secure. Without you, it is – nightmare. My past—'

He smiled. 'I think you have already repaid me.'

What did he mean? 'I don't understand—'

'You had a brain injury on top of everything else. I guess it gave you back all those erased memories, right back to – Bunny. And it broke up your conditioning. So now you can have nightmares from your subconscious, you can feel insecure – that's why you need someone.'

'Yes. I am sorry. I am not strong.' Like a child, weak; like a child, to be taken care of.

He paused, chewing meditatively on his lower lip. Then: 'Do you remember our conversation once about what 'Quilon had that you didn't?'

She concentrated. 'Yes.'

'Now you have it, too.'

'But I'm weak. I can't stand alone, and even if I could—'

He looked at her intently, not answering. Her ability to read emotions had suffered, perhaps because her own were in such disarray. She could not plumb him for reaction, could not be guided by it. She was on her own.

'Even if I could,' she finished with difficulty, 'I would not want to.'

Then with an incredible brilliance it burst upon her. 'Veg – this, what I feel, the whole complex, the fear, the weakness, the need – is this love?'

'No. Not fear, not weakness.'

She began to cry again, her momentary hope dashed. 'I'm not very pretty now I know. My face is all splotched and peeling from that acid burn, and I've lost so much weight I'm a scarecrow. I'm Bunny all over again. So I don't have any right to think you'd—' She broke off, realizing how maudlin she sounded. Then she was furious at herself. 'But damn it, I *do* love you! The rest is irrelevant.'

She turned away, sorry she had said it yet glad the truth was out. She remembered Bunny, but she was *not* Bunny. When he left her, she would not commit suicide; she would carry on, completing her mission ... somehow.

He took her into his arms and kissed her, and then she needed no other statement.

Tamme grew stronger – but this made her uneasy. In a few more days she was able to outrun Veg and to overcome him in mock combat. She tried to hold off, letting him prevail, but he would not let her. 'I want you healthy,' was all he said.

'But once I achieve full capacity, I'll have emotional control,' she said. 'I will be able to take you or leave you – as before.'

'I love you,' he said. 'That's why I won't cripple you. I've seen you as you are when the agent mask is off, and that's enough. We always knew it couldn't last between us. When you are well again, it'll be over. I'll never say it wasn't worth it.'

Her face was wet, and she discovered she was crying again. She cried too much these days, as though making up for the tearless agent. 'Veg, I don't *want* to be like before! I don't care how weak I am if it means I can stay with you.'

He shook his head. 'I had a quarrel with Cal once on Paleo, and so did 'Quilon. She was miserable, and I was with her, and we thought that was love. It wasn't. Real love doesn't need weakness or misery. I won't make that mistake again.'

'But when I was strong, you said—'

'You can be as strong as Sampson, I don't care!'

'Please—'

'*I'm* strong for a normal man,' he said. He picked up a stick an inch in diameter, spliced it between the fingers of one hand, and tensed his muscles. The stick snapped into three pieces. 'But I need people. I need Cal, and I need 'Quilon, and I need you. You didn't need anyone.'

Tamme picked up a similar stick and broke it the same way. The fragments flew out to land in a triangle on the ground. 'I'm strong, too – and now I need you. But what about tomorrow?'

He shrugged. 'I don't know. All I can do is live for today. That may be all we have. That's the way it is with agents, isn't it?'

She drew the knife she carried. 'If I stuck this back into my head, maybe it would—'

He dashed the blade out of her hand. 'No! What's got to be, 'sgot to be!'

She yielded, knowing he was right. 'Then love me now, right now,' she said, moving into his arms. 'What we defer today may never come tomorrow ...'

Even the natives knew it was ending. Veg cut and hauled huge amounts of fog to make a new wall for their cattle, and Tamme took the children for walks through the forest, protecting them from the wild predators that lurked there. It was perhaps the only taste of woman's work she would ever experience.

On the day that Tamme decided, using cynical agent judgement, that she had regained ninety-five per cent of capacity, the hosts invited the neighbours for a party. They ate fog delicacies and sang nasal foghorn songs and played with the hexaflexagons Veg made, and in its simple fashion it was a lot of fun.

In the evening she and Veg walked out, holding hands like young lovers. 'One thing nags me,' he said. 'Tamme Two could have killed you, couldn't she? After you fell down, and she put the knife in you, she just turned away. I wasn't sure which of you had won. But she could tell us apart – I guess it was by our reactions, and I still had the burn marks of the rope on me – and she looked at me, for all the world just like you, but sharper somehow – even before the fight, you had gentled some – and she said I was the enemy. I guess she was going to kill me, and she sure as hell had little conscience about it, but my double wouldn't let her.' He paused, smiling reminiscently. 'I sort of like that guy, you know! He has guts and conscience. He told me during the fight that he had to stay with his own, but he wished Tamme Two was more like you and hoped she'd get that way. So it wasn't just the knife in your head that changed you; you were getting there on your own.

'So they projected out, and I went down to find you. I thought sure you were dead. But you'd hung up on a crossbar with that knife in your hand. I guess you'd yanked it out somehow. You were hardly even bleeding.'

'Agents are tough,' she said. 'I shut off the blood and went into what we call repair-shock. I don't remember it; the process is automatic. Actually, the damage was too extensive; I would not have survived without help.'

'Yeah. I carried you up and projected us here, and the folks understood. They were great! But why didn't Tamme Two come down and finish you off for sure?'

'She should have. I think, at the end, it must have bothered her to kill herself – even her alternate self. I know *I* had little stomach for it. So she pulled her shot, just a little, and left it to nature. Perhaps she is further along the way to becoming normal – like me – than we supposed. The odds were still against my survival.'

'I guess they were! If the fog people hadn't taken us in and brought their doctor – you should have seen him putting in stitches with that nose, no human hand could match it – well, I wouldn't have wished it on you, but I'm glad I got to meet Bunny.'

'Who?'

He didn't answer. Her perceptions were back to norm; she could read the passing trauma that shook him, the realization that Bunny – and all that she implied – had been suppressed.

'We can't stay here any longer,' Tamme said.

'Right,' he said heavily. 'You have a mission. Got to get back to Earth and report.'

She read the resignation in him. He knew he was giving her up – yet his conscience forced it. But there was one thing he didn't know.

'I do remember – some,' she said.

'Don't play with me!' he snapped. 'I don't want an act!'

'You wanted the moon.'

'I knew I couldn't have it.'

'You preserved my life. This will not be forgotten.'

'Why not?' he muttered. 'The computer will erase it, anyway.'

They returned to the fog house.

She activated the projector, and they were at the bazaar.

Crowds milled everywhere, surging past the multi-levelled display stalls. Human, near-human, far-human, and alien mixed without concern, elbows jostling tentacles, shoes treading the marks of pincer-feet. Eyeballs stared at antennae; mouths conversed with ventricles. Frog-eyed extraterrestrials bargained for humanoid dolls, while women bought centaur tails for brooms. Machines of different species mixed with the living creatures, and walking plants inspected exotic fertilizers: horse manure, bat guano, processed sewer sludge.

'Hey – there's a manta!' Veg cried, waving.

But it was an alien manta, subtly different in proportion and reaction, and it ignored him.

They walked among the rest, looking for the projector. Then Tamme's eye caught that of a man: a terrestrial agent of a series closely akin to hers.

He came over immediately. 'Oo gest stapped in? Mutings ot wavorium.' He indicated the direction and moved on.

Veg stared after him. 'Wasn't that Taler?'

'Possibly. SU, TA, or TE series, certainly – but not from our frame.'

'I guess not,' he agreed, shaking his head. 'Sounded like you and that machine-hive chitchat. Hey – this is a good place to leave that lentil!'

'True,' she agreed. She took it out and flipped it into a bag of dragonfly-crabs, one of which immediately swallowed it.

'The gourmet who eats that crab will get a surprise!' Veg said, chuckling. Then he turned serious. 'What do we do now? There may be thousands of agents here. We can't fight them all!'

'I have lost my taste for fighting.'

He glanced at her. 'Then you're not all the way better yet. Still, we have to do *something*.'

'We go to the wavorium.'

'I feel dizzy,' he muttered.

The wavorium was a monstrous frozen fountain whose falling waters, though fixed in one place, were neither cold nor rigid. Tamme parted them like curtains and stepped into a turbulent ocean whose waves had the texture of jellied plastic. The surface gave slightly beneath their weight but sprang back resiliently behind them.

Perched on the central whitecaps were a number of Tammes, Vegs, Talers, Aquilons, and Cals. From the outside, more were entering, just as she and Veg were.

'Very wall, les coll it tu urder,' a Taler said. 'Em eh cumprohonsible?'

'Cloos nuif,' another Taler responded. There was a general murmur of agreement.

'Need a translation?' Tamme asked Veg. 'He called the meeting to order and asked if he were comprehensible. The other said—'

'I heard,' Veg growled. 'I can make it out, close enough.'

'That's what the other said.' She concentrated on the speaker, once more adapting her auditory reflexes so that the speech became normal to her.

'We all know why we're here,' the chairman-Taler said. 'This happens to be a central crossover point for a number of alternate loops. Now we can't go wandering aimlessly forever; we have to come to some sort of decision. It is pointless to quarrel among ourselves – we're all so nearly equal that chance would be the deciding factor. We need to unify, or at least agree on a common, noncompetitive policy that will serve the best interests of the majority. Discussion?'

'Suppose we pool our resources?' a Tamme said. 'If we represent different alternatives, we may be able to assemble enough information on our real enemies to be of benefit.'

'Not likely,' Taler said. 'We are so similar we had to have diverged from a common source at or about the time the three agents made captive the three normals on Paleo. Several of us have been comparing notes, and our experience seems to be identical prior to that point. After that, we evidently divide into three major channels: In each case the three normals are accompanied to the desert frame by one agent, Taler, Taner, or Tamme. Each of these subdivides into three channels, as that agent enters the alternate clover-pattern with one normal. Nine variations in all. However—'

'That is assuming reality *is* diverging,' a Cal pointed out. 'I suspect the framework is considerably more complex. *All* the alternates appear to exist through all time, separated from each other by a fraction of a second. Thus we are not precisely parallel with each other, and our seeming unity of earlier experience is illusory.'

Taler paused. 'You disconcert me,' he said, and there was a

565

general chuckle. 'Let's call our unified origin a fictional reference point of convenience, much as the hexaflexagon is an imperfect but useful analogy and guide. Obviously, our best course is to return each to his own alternate – if we can find it. Can we agree on the nature of the report we should make to our home-worlds?'

'Stay out of alternity!' Veg bawled, startling Tamme, who had not been paying attention to her own Veg amidst this assemblage of doubles.

There was a smattering of applause, especially from the normals. The Cal who had clarified the framework concept nodded at Veg as though they were old friends, and several Aquilons smiled warmly.

'I believe that sums up the sentiment of this group,' Taler remarked with a smile of his own. He seemed more relaxed and human than he should be, as though he had diverged too far from his original conditioning. 'Now how can we be certain that the right couples return to their worlds? Or does it make a difference?'

'We'll have to get off at the same frame we got on,' an Aquilon said. 'We have twelve couples here – one from each starting point. It should match.'

Taler shook his head. 'Right there, it doesn't match. Twelve couples, nine combinations: Three are duplicates. The extras are all male-female, so we have seven male-female pairs, four male-male, and one female-female. Now—'

The Tamme/Aquilon couple stood together. 'Are you implying—?'

'By no means, ladies,' Taler said quickly. 'I merely point out that there seems to be a bias here in favour of male-female pairings – yet chance would have had only four such couples out of every nine. This suggests that our gathering has been selected from a larger pool. There must be hundreds of couples, travelling in both directions. We represent a selected cross-section.'

Veg was looking at the Tamme/Aquilon couple. 'That's as pretty a set as you'll ever see,' he murmured.

'So there may be an infinite number on the treadmill,' another Tamme said. 'We can work it out by ourselves – but that's just a fraction. Useless.'

'Yet there *is* a frame for each couple – somewhere,' a Taner pointed out. 'A one-to-one ratio. No need to compete.'

The Tamme disagreed. 'We can't pinpoint our exact alternates or guarantee that others will. Some would be missed; others would get half a dozen couples. Just as we find ourselves doubling up right here. That will play merry hell with the equality of alternates. Some governments will catch on no matter what we report. Then—'

'Then war between the frames,' Tamme murmured to herself, and heard the others coming to the same conclusion. All agents' minds worked similarly, of course.

'Whose world would be ravaged?' Taler asked rhetorically. 'Mine? Yours? I don't care about the others, but I want my *own* left alone even if I don't return to it.'

'We can't guarantee that *any* alternate is left alone – the moment *one* government catches on to the exploitative potential of alternity, the lid's off,' the Tamme said. 'We all know what our governments are like.'

'Omnivores!' an Aquilon cried with feeling. 'Ravening omnivores!'

'We are omnivores, too,' Taler said. 'We are all killers at heart.' He raised his left arm. He wore long sleeves; now the cloth fell away to reveal a stump. His arm had been amputated at the elbow. 'An alternate Taler – myself! – did this to me. I was lucky to escape with my life, and as it was, I spent some time recuperating. If it had not been for my normal companion—' He smiled, glancing at another Aquilon, who lowered her eyes demurely – 'Well, let's check this out here and now. How many couples met their doubles on the way here?'

All hands went up.

Taler nodded. 'I thought so. Many of you conceal your injuries well – but every agent here lost to his exact counterpart, correct?' There was agreement. 'Received a head injury – a bad one?' Again, agreement. 'We represent the natural selection of that fragment of the circuit that met their doubles – and lost, and so were delayed for recovery. Out of all the other possibilities happening elsewhere. So we know first hand: We are omnivores, destroying even ourselves. Yet it seems that the male-female aspect enhanced the chances of survival as though something more than mere competence were operant. We may have redeeming qualities.' He paused. 'And how many of us – remember?'

All the agents' hands went up, including Tamme's own.

Veg turned to her. He was half amazed, half furious. All about

567

them the other normals were facing their agents with the same question. Even the Aquilon with the chairman-Taler was on her feet, her pretty mouth open accusingly. 'You *remember?*'

Veg saw the universal reaction. Suddenly he laughed – and so did the others. 'Wait till I get you alone!' he said.

'We are not as we were,' Taler said over the hubbub. 'We lost – but we won. I tell the world, I tell alternity: I *remember Budge*, the lonely orphan boy, condemned as economically unsalvageable. I *am* Budge.'

Tamme stared at him. *Taler had gone normal!*

All around the wavorium others were staring.

'But I am also Taler,' the agent continued. 'Converted from unfit normal to fit agent. Veteran of seven anonymous missions, killer of men, competent liar, lover, philosopher—'

'Amen!' his Aquilon said.

'I remember both heaven and hell,' Taler continued. 'I *am* heaven and hell, and now purgatory – *as are we all.*'

'This is intriguing, and it would be entertaining to compare notes – but we must complete our missions,' an alternate Tamme said. 'Or agree *not* to . . .'

Taler nodded. 'If no one returns to a given world, the government is unlikely to expend more agents in such hazardous exploration. Paleo is not secure, owing to the presence of the manta's spores; the desert world has the known menace of the wild machines and the unknown menace of the sparkle cloud. So long as they have no hint of what lies beyond the sparkle, they will not pursue it further. It wouldn't be economic.'

'If no one returns . . .' It was another general murmur.

The Cal spoke again. 'The matter is academic. The option is not ours. We were conveyed to this framework of frames by pattern-entities, and we have virtually no chance to locate our original worlds – Desert, Paleo, or Earth – without the intercession of these entities. We are in their power, confined to these worlds at their pleasure.'

Taler looked about. He sighed. 'Any refutation?'

There was none.

'Then I suggest we return to our points of entry into this alternate-pattern, rejoin our original companions, and wait on the pleasure of the sparkle entities. They appear to have protected us from ourselves, and perhaps that is best.'

'But what if we return to the wrong companions by mistake?' his Aquilon asked.

'Then, my dear, we shall treat them as we would our *right* companions. We have had enough of misunderstanding and violence.' He looked about and again discovered no refutation. 'Meeting adjourned.'

Veg turned to Tamme. 'But why did that other Tamme attack us? If they were at this meeting – or one like it – she would have known there was no percentage in fighting.'

'Their meeting differed from ours,' she said. 'They had not been injured in battles with their doubles, and perhaps there were no Cals to clarify matters. They must have decided that it was each frame for itself. There must be many like that, still out to terminate the opposition – as I was at the start. Before I went normal.'

'Yeah.' He faced about. 'Let's go.'

'Don't you want to chat with Cal and Aquilon?'

'Yeah – but I'm afraid you'll take off with the wrong Veg again.'

She laughed – but realized it wasn't funny to him. The presence of his friends, who he knew were not his original ones, made him nervous.

They had to wait their turn for use of the projector. There were actually many projectors here, but the others were labelled for other loops, and further exploration seemed pointless. Meanwhile, the bazaar was fascinating.

Then on through to the

Jungle gym, this time encountering no opposition;

the fog world, for a brief reunion with their friends there;

the orchestra,

and the forest.

'Before we go on,' Veg said. 'About remembering—'

'Yes,' she said. She had known this was coming and was prepared. 'There is something you should know. I am strong again, but I am

569

changed, as Taler is, as all of us at the meeting are. I have full emotional control, but it is as though my program has been modified – and can not now be reverted to the original. Not without erasure and resetting – which seems unlikely in view of events.'

He watched her, the wild hope coalescing. 'Then—'

'I still love you,' she said.

'But I thought—'

'I said I had recovered control. I knew that if I died, or if we were separated, it would be best that you not know the truth. And there was still substantial risk of such an outcome. Therefore, I exercised that control to protect the one I loved.' She lowered her eyes. 'I did what I felt was necessary. I did not enjoy it. Now I know we shall be together. I shall not again conceal my feeling from you. But I must advise you that my love is now as fixed as my prior conditioning. I shall not be casually set aside.'

'That's for sure!' he agreed. He looked at his hexaflexagon. 'Next world's Blizzard, then back to the City. We don't have to rush it.'

'We'll never have to rush it,' she agreed.

Chapter Sixteen

REQUISITION

```
  •  •
 •   •
  • • •
```

They emerged in single file from the indoctrination suite: twenty-four agents of the TE series. Eighteen were male, six female.

The inspection party consisted of ranking execs from industry: Steel, Atomics, Transport, Fuel, and Construction. They were all portly, wealthy, powerful, conservatives who were not to be trifled with – no, not for an instant. The ire of any one of them could cost the Sec his position within the hour, and so he was unusually accommodating. In fact, he was obsequious.

'The agent program is the finest investigative and first-line remedial service ever conceived or implemented,' the Sec said to the visitors. 'The computer itself processes them, giving them a common store of information, guiding their attitudes: We call it "set". The individual agents are like extensions of the machine, each reacting to any situation exactly as programmed to react. That way the computer needs to make no allowance for human variability, subjectivity, distortion. All that has been precompensated in the program; one agent's report is exactly like another's.'

Transport shook his head in seeming perplexity: a deceptive gesture, as none of the execs were stupid. 'Surely this is not feasible; every mission any agent goes out on represents new and different experience. He would soon differ from his companions by that degree. We *are* what we experience.'

The Sec smiled ingratiatingly. 'Of course, sir. The computer has taken this into consideration. Therefore, every agent is reprocessed after each mission. His individual memories are erased, and he is restored to the programmed set for his series. These TE's are an example; they have just been—'

Fuel shook his head. 'Memory can't be erased. It is a chemical process spread throughout the brain. You'd have to destroy the whole—'

The Sec coughed. 'Well, I am not conversant with the technical details. Perhaps it is merely repression. But it is a repression that it would take brain surgery to abate. I assure you, no agent is put in the field unless his set is correct. The computer—'

'Brain surgery?' Fuel inquired. 'I'll bet a severe shock could scramble—'

'I'd like to question one of those retreads,' Transport said. 'Or would that distort that delicate "set"?'

'Of course not,' the Sec said, ruffled. 'You are welcome to interview this batch.' He touched a stud. 'Send a premission TE to the exec tour observatory,' he said.

The first agent in the line detached himself and came to the observatory. He was a handsome man, exactly like his companions except for the details of hue and feature: eyes, hair, nose, mouth, ears. Each varied just enough to provide that superficial individuality the public notion required while making it plain that he was a nearly identical twin to the other members of his series. Even his blood type matched, and his fingerprints – with that same minute variation. He was powerfully built and extremely well coordinated: a superman in many respects. 'I am Teban,' he said with a slight inclination of the head.

The Sec nodded in return, not bothering to introduce himself. 'Each agent has a three-letter designation. The first two indicate the particular series; the third indentifies the individual. The remaining letters are merely cosmetic, to offer a humanizing aspect. Thus, this is Series TE, individual B: TEBan. We employ the eighteen most adaptable consonants for the individual names, B, D, F, H—'

'You missed C,' Construction protested wryly.

'C is not one of the preferred letters,' Teban interposed smoothly. 'It may be rendered soft as in "cent" or hard as in "cock". Therefore it is not—'

'What?' the exec interrupted, reddening.

'Soft cent, hard cock,' the agent repeated. 'I am certain you heard me the first time.'

572

The Sec stepped in hastily. 'A "cent" is an archaic unit of currency. A "cock" is a male fowl, a rooster. Our agents are well versed in—'

'Any intelligent person *is*,' Teban said.

'I believe we should question another individual,' Steel said.

'Yes, of course,' the Sec agreed. He gestured to Teban, who turned smartly and departed. In a moment he was replaced by another agent, so like him it was disconcerting.

'I am Teddy.'

'Series TE, individual D, suffix DY,' the Sec explained.

The agent turned to him, raising one eyebrow. 'These people are well familiar with the pattern,' he said. 'In fact, they consider you to be a somewhat inept official due for replacement and would prefer to interview me directly.'

'Right on the mark,' Steel muttered.

'Ah, er, yes,' the Sec agreed wanly. 'Our agents are trained to interpret the nuances of human involuntary body language.'

Steel ignored him. He turned to Teddy. 'We are told you are preformed, like an ingot, to rigid tolerance. High-grade, invariable. That you have no prior memories of your own personal experience. Is this true?'

'No.'

Fuel smiled. 'Aha!'

'We already have proof it isn't true,' Construction said. 'This one reacted differently from the first. So they *aren't* all alike.'

'We're alike,' Teban said. 'In the interval between interviews, *you* changed. So I responded differently.'

'But you said you had no prior personal memories,' Steel said. 'I mean, that you *do*.'

'All of us have the same personal memories.'

Steel nodded. 'What *do* you remember?'

An obscure expression crossed Teddy's face. 'Naked breasts, spread thighs straddling a cello. Beautiful music. Guilt, urgency, Frustration.'

Steel glanced at his companions obliquely. 'Most interesting programming!'

Transport stepped forward. 'Where and when did you observe this nude musician?'

'Time and geography are not readily defined in the frames of

573

alternity,' Teddy said. 'We are twenty years out of phase, so could not interact.'

'Alternity? Phase?' Atomic asked.

'Now don't explode, 'Tomic,' Steel said with a vulpine smile. 'Let's interview another agent. This has been most informative and may become more so.'

Teddy departed. Another agent appeared. 'I am Texas.'

Steel made a gesture to quiet his companions. 'Please define alternity.'

'The entire fabric of probability,' Texas replied. 'This world is but a single frame of an infinite framework.'

'And on these other frames are naked female musicians?'

'On one frame among the myriads.'

'What else is there – in alternity?'

'Translucent planes. Technicolor blizzards. Edible fog. Alien creatures. Bazaar. Forest. Carnivorous walls. Machine-hive. Element plants. Çatal Huyuk.'

'Send in another agent,' Steel said brusquely.

'A female,' Transport added, and the other execs nodded agreement. The Sec merely stood as if frozen.

She arrived: supple, buxom, attractive. Her hair and eyes were brown but not intensely so; pretty as she was, it would have been hard to describe her precisely after a casual encounter. 'I am Terri.'

'Have you seen,' Steel asked carefully, 'a nude female cellist?'

She eyed him archly. 'Of course not.'

'Your male companions seem to have had other experience. A different "set"?'

'They were referring to the program,' she said. 'The computer provides a common set. That does not mean we have actually seen these things, only that we remember them. I am certain my brothers informed you it was a memory, not an experience. However, if you are really interested in this type of thing, I will fetch a cello and—'

'I believe it is time to interview the computer itself,' Fuel said. 'It occurs to me that a great deal of money has been foolishly spent.'

Now the Sec summoned the courage of desperation. 'Sirs, something has obviously gone wrong with the program. We never—'

'Never checked the program?' Fuel inquired. 'Or never thought *we'd* check it?'

'The agent program has been inadequately supervised from the start,' Terri said. 'It would be simple for us to assume control of the government, and perhaps the time has come.'

Steel turned to the Sec. 'Are there no safeguards in the program?'

'Of course there are!' the Sec said nervously. 'Agents of all series are specifically directed to preserve the status quo. They—'

'*Are* they?' Steel demanded of Terri.

'Not when the status quo is obviously a liability to the welfare of the species,' she said.

Now the glances the execs exchanged were as nervous as those of the Sec.

The other agents of the TE series, male and female, fell in around them as they approached the computer communications input, like an honour guard ... or merely a guard. Polite, handsome, powerful, frightening. But the execs were permitted to address the computer without interference.

Steel, no coward, became the spokesman for the execs. 'What's going on here?' he demanded.

'Interpretation,' the voice of the computer said. It was a pleasant voice, not at all mechanical.

One of the agents spoke: 'These execs are suspicious of the program and wish to ascertain whether the status quo is threatened by us. They are also confused about the nature of alternity and intrigued by nude female cellists.'

'I am speaking for $\overline{OX}$,' the computer said. 'This is the code designation Zero X, or Arabic numeral nothing multiplied by the Roman numeral ten, themselves symbols for frame-representations that can not be expressed in your mathematics. Zero times ten is nothing in a single frame, and dissimilar systems can not interact meaningfully; but in the larger framework the result is both infinite and meaningful, expressing sentience. Think of it as the mergence of skew concepts.'

'Forget the symbolism,' Steel said. 'Who is $\overline{OX}$?'

'$\overline{OX}$ is a pattern entity whose nature is alien to your scheme, as just explained. $\overline{OX}$ is twenty years out of phase, so can not communicate directly. The presence of $\overline{OX}$'s shoot here in your spot-frame distorts the operation of your machine and modifies the program.'

'Obviously,' Steel said. 'What do you want from us?'

'The shoot has come on behalf of one of your kind who is in need. Provide a female infant; project her to a frame whose setting I shall indicate.'

'Provide a baby!' Steel exclaimed. 'What on Earth does a computer want with a baby?'

'She will not be on Earth,' the computer said. 'In twenty years she will be a woman.'

'Indubitably. Now is that all?' Steel asked sardonically.

'If we do it,' Fuel put in, 'will this – this shoot go away and revert our computer to normal? No more interference?'

'Your frame will never be touched by alternity,' the computer said.

The execs exchanged glances again. 'We agree,' Steel said. 'We will provide the baby.'

'Provide also the following materials in refined form, in the amounts I shall specify,' the computer said. 'Strontium, magnesium, copper . . .'

Cub stared. A female of my species, here in the enclave! he signalled, astounded. But how is it possible? We are out of phase!

I sent a shoot across theoretical elements to locate the home-frame of your male parent, OX explained. That frame provided a nascent female. She aged as you did, as I brought her into phase with us. She is for you.

She is beautiful! Cub signalled. I do not know what I will do with her, but I must do it urgently.

He went to the female. He tugged at her wild long hair. He put his appendages on her torso, squeezing the strange flesh here and there.

She squawked like Ornet, chewed on his digits, and scraped his surfaces with the sharp points of her own digits. Then she ran away.

Apparently something had been omitted. OX consulted with Ornet.

Mams must be raised together, Ornet said, or they do not get along. You have provided Cub with a wild girl, one raised alone. She possesses the physical attributes of his species but lacks the social ones. So does he.

Social attributes?

Come into my mind, Ornet squawked.

OX came into his mind. Then he comprehended.

576

We must return to the natural framework, he flashed. We can not exist apart from our societies. This is true for all of us; I, too, must join my kind.

But we are isolated in the enclave, Ornet protested.

I now know why, $\overline{OX}$ replied. It is time to break out.

And run amuck like that wild mam fem? Ornet asked.

We must discuss it together, $\overline{OX}$ agreed. What we decide together will be right.

They discussed it together: $\overline{OX}$, Ornet, Dec, Cub, and Mach, now rendered sociable by the provision of its necessary substances. Together, they issued a report.

That report changed alternity.

Chapter Seventeen

CATAL HUYUK

Cal lay within the cabin of the *Nacre*, staring up at the palm frond and bamboo-pole network that enclosed the cabin of their crude homemade raft. He felt the mud clay calking between the logs of its deck. Uncomfortable, certainly – but he hardly cared, for he had existed much of his life with extreme discomfort ... and now Aquilon lay beside him.

'But the bird,' Aquilon protested. 'You said it was intelligent. That means Paleo is technically inhabited—'

'Intelligent for *Aves*: birds,' he said. 'That can't approach human capability. But yes, it is most important that this – this *ornisapiens* be preserved and studied. It—'

'Orn,' Veg said from the woman's far side. 'In a zoo.'

'No!' Aquilon cried. 'That isn't what I meant. That would kill it. We should be *helping* it, not—'

'Or at least leaving it alone,' Veg said. 'It's a decent bird ...'

'We appear,' Cal remarked, 'to have a multiple difference of opinion. Veg feels that we should leave his Orn-bird alone; 'Quilon feels we should help it; I feel the needs of our own species must take precedence. We must have room to expand.'

'*Lebensraum*,' Aquilon whispered tersely.

The word shook him. How bitterly she had drawn the parallel: Adolph Hitler's pretext for conquest. The Third Reich had to have room to live – at the expense of its neighbours. *Their* living needs were not considered.

'What do birds eat?' Veg asked.

Cal felt Aquilon shudder. She was a practising vegetarian at the moment, eschewing the omnivorous way of life. If her comment about Lebensraum had shaken Cal, Veg's question had shaken her. For they all knew what birds ate, especially big birds. They were carnivorous or omnivorous.

They hashed it through, but their positions were set by those two words: *Lebensraum* and *Omnivore*. Cal was on one side, accepting both concepts and their applicability to the present situation of Earth; Veg was on the other, accepting neither. Aquilon, torn between the two, finally had to go with Cal: when one omnivore contested with another for territory, might was right.

It was a subtle, seemingly minor distinction, but it touched on deep currents. They had all waged an interplanetary struggle against the omnivore – yet they themselves were aspects of the omnivore. The words they said now were hardly more than chips floating on the sea, hinting at the implacable surges beneath. In the end Veg got up and left the raft.

Cal felt a pain as though his heart were physically breaking; he knew the rift was fundamental. Perhaps Veg would return – but once Cal made his report to Earth, which would set in motion Earth's exploitation of Paleo and the probable extinction of dinosaurs and Ornbirds alike, their friendship would never be the same.

Beside him, Aquilon was sobbing. Cal knew some streak of perversity in him had made him argue the omnivore's case; he had no more sympathy with the appetites of the omnivore than Veg did. Let Paleo remain unspoiled!

No, the issue had to be brought out, examined, even though it hurt.

They slept side by side. Cal did not touch her, though he longed for her with a loin-consuming passion. She was not a proper subject for lust, she was Aquilon, fair and perfect . . .

In the morning they checked for Veg but could not find him. 'I think he's all right,' Aquilon said. 'He's with the birds. We should leave him alone and go to make the report. He'll never go with us.'

That damned report! 'I hate this schism,' Cal said.

'So do I. But how can we bridge it? We talked it all out.'

They had talked nothing out! But words today were as pointless as the words of yesterday.

They set sail on the *Nacre*, dispatching the mantas to locate Veg and return with news of him. While they were at sea, there was a dancing of the waves, indicating a small tremor or earthquake. 'I hope that's the extent of it!' Cal said.

They beached the raft with some difficulty, then set out on foot.

And in the afternoon the tyrannosaurus picked up their trail.

The mantas were ready to help, but Cal warned them off. 'If we think our kind is superior, we should be ready to prove it,' he said.

'Against a carnosaur?' she demanded incredulously. 'Ten tons of appetite? The ultimate predator?'

'The ultimate reptilian predator, perhaps,' he said. 'Though I suspect the earlier allosaurus might have been more efficient. The mantas would be the ultimate fungoid predators. And man stakes his claim to being the ultimate mammalian predator. So it is proper that the champions meet in single combat.'

Suddenly she saw it. 'The mammals and the reptiles, meeting on the field of honour. The decisive combat. The carnosaur has size and power; the man has brain. It is a fair compromise, in its fashion. It relieves the conscience of difficult moral decisions.'

'Precisely,' Cal said, smiling grimly. 'I knew you'd understand. And so will Veg. You had better hide in a tree. I must do this alone.'

She scrambled away as the ground shuddered, and not from any geologic tremor. *Tyrannosaurus rex*, king of predators, was closing in for the kill! The tyrant lizard's tread rocked the land, and the crashing of saplings became loud.

He glanced at Aquilon to make sure she was safe, knowing that she would be terribly afraid for him, and with reason. Intellectually, she comprehended his decision, but emotionally it was intolerable. She thought he would be killed.

'Cal – no!'

Too late. The slender fern trees swayed aside. A bird flew up from a nearby ginkgo tree. Through the palm fronds poked a gaping set of jaws – fifteen feet above the ground. There was a roar.

Tyrann had arrived.

The dinosaur charged upon Cal, dwarfing the man. Aquilon stared from her perch, unable to turn her head away, horrified.

When Tyrann was no more than its own length – fifty feet – distant, Cal dodged to the side. He surprised himself by the alacrity with which he moved, picturing what Aquilon was seeing. She still tended to think of him as the wasted, physically weak sufferer she had known on Nacre. But he had recovered greatly and now approached normal vitality. His love for her, he knew, was partly responsible.

Tyrann was unable to compensate in time and drove his nose into the dirt where Cal stood. He lifted his mottled head, small eyes peering about while leaves and twigs tumbled wetly from his jaws.

Now the real chase began. Cal had no chance to watch out for Aquilon, but he knew she was following with the mantas, observing. If Tyrann should spot her, the mantas would help her escape. They could hardly stop Tyrann's charge, but their cutting tails could strike out the monster's eyes and nose, depriving him of his principal senses.

Cal played a desperate game of peekaboo around a large palm tree with the carnosaur. Then he fled through a small forest of firs. Tyrann pursued indefatigably, relentlessly. Cal found a herd of triceratops, grazing dinosaurs with huge bony plates on their heads and a deadly trio of horns. One of the bulls came out to challenge Tyrann and so provided Cal with some breathing space.

He ran up the side of the mountain towards the snowline. Then the earth rocked violently: another quake. He was thrown to the ground almost under Tyrann's nose.

But the quake also upended the dinosaur, who went rolling down the slope. Relieved, Cal got up – and was struck by a stone rolling down the mountain. A freak of luck – but fatal.

He was only unconscious a few seconds, he thought – but as he struggled to his feet, Tyrann was upon him. The gaping mouth with its six-inch teeth closed on his legs.

There was an instant of unbearable pain. Then his system, recognizing that, cut off the pain. Cal knew he had lost. One leg had been sheared off. There would be no report from this world. The dinosaur had proved superior.

Perhaps that was best.

Aquilon, thrown off her feet by the quake, waited for the upheavals to stop. Then she ran up the slope after the dinosaur, flanked by four mantas. What she saw was sheer nightmare.

. . . rag-doll form flung high into the air . . . jaws closed, ripping off an arm . . . head lolled back from broken neck . . . dead eyes staring . . .

581

Aquilon screamed.

Tyrann gulped down the remnants of his meal, then cast about, orienting on the scream. He saw Aquilon.

Had it really been a nightmare, a bad dream, she would have awakened then. But it was real, and the carnosaur was still hungry.

The four mantas settled about her, facing Tyrann. In a moment they would attack. 'No!' Aquilon cried. 'I will finish the fight he started – or die with him!' For now, too late, she realized how completely she loved Cal. Why had she never taken the initiative? Only in this way – by sharing his challenge – could she exonerate her missed opportunity.

'Hex and Circe – go find Veg, take care of him. Diam and Star, go guard the Orn-birds and their nest. Don't come back to me until I have settled with Tyrann – one way or the other.'

They moved out, sailing down the mountain like the manta rays for which they had been named. She was on her own.

She fled up the mountain, knowing that Cal must have had good reason to go that way. The cold – maybe the snow of the heights would stop the creature!

Tyrann followed – but not with the alacrity he had pursued Cal. Was it because he had suffered internal injuries when he tumbled during the earthquake – or was he simply less hungry now?

Dusk was coming. That and the increasing elevation chilled the air rapidly. Soon it was near freezing, and she knew the snows were not far beyond. She was not cold, for her continued exertion generated warmth – but the moment she stopped, she would be in danger.

Her foot caught in something, and she fell, splashing. It was a small stream. Now she was soaked – and that would only accelerate her exposure. But she could not stop, for Tyrann was not far behind.

The water was warm! It should have been chill, even frozen!

Struck by inspiration, she charged upstream. The stream banks formed into a kind of chasm, warm at the base. And the stream became hot, hurting her feet. Finally, she came to its origin: a cave.

Here was salvation! She plunged inside, basking in its hot interior. The dinosaur could not enter!

She removed her clothing and washed herself in the bathtub-temperature water. Sheer luxury!

But now she was stuck here, for Tyrann lay in wait outside, his nose right up against the mouth of the cave. She would have to climb over that nose to escape – and she was hardly ready to risk that yet!

She lay down on a convenient ledge to sleep. But now the horror of Cal's death returned to her full force. When she closed her eyes she saw the monstrously gaping jaws, the bloodstained teeth; when she opened them, she still saw that vision of savagery. And the tiny-seeming body, tossed up the way a mouse was tossed by a cat, broken, dismembered, spraying out red . . .

'Cal! Cal!' she cried in anguish. 'Why didn't I show my love before you died?'

She tried to pray: 'God give him back to me, and I'll never let him go!' But it was no good, for she did not believe in any God, and if she *had* believed, she knew it would have been wrong to offer to make a deal.

She slept and woke and slept again fitfully. The night seemed to endure for an eternity. She was hungry, but there was little except heat-resistant lichen growing near the mouth of the cave: no fit diet. So she drank hot water, pretending it was soup, and deceived her stomach.

Then she was roused, near dawn, by a presence. *Someone was in the cave with her.* She lay still, frightened yet hopeful. It could only be Veg – but how had he gotten past Tyrann? And why had the mantas guided him here when her business with the dinosaur was not yet finished?

For a moment the figure stood in the wan light of the entrance. Suddenly she recognized the silhouette.

'Cal!' she cried. 'I thought you were dead!'

He turned, obviously startled, seeing her. His vision had always been sharper than hers, especially in poor light. 'I escaped, thanks to this convenient cave,' he said as though it were a routine matter.

'So did I,' she said, bathed in a compelling sensation of *déjà vu*, of having been in this situation before. How could she have missed seeing Cal earlier? And who – or what – had Tyrann actually eaten? She had been so sure—

'Why did you come?' he asked.

'I love you,' she said simply. And, suffused by her breathless relief, she remembered her attempted bargain with God and her overwhelming love for this man. She went to him, and took him in her arms, pressing her breasts against his body, kissing his mouth,

583

embracing him so tightly her own arms hurt.

He responded with astonishing vigour. No further word was spoken. They fell into the hot water, and laughed foolishly together, and kissed and kissed again, mouth on mouth, mouth on breast, splashing water like two children playing in the tub.

So they made love again and again, as long as the flesh would bear. Perhaps the hot water was a tonic, recharging their bodies rapidly. They slept embraced half out of the water, woke and loved again, and slept, on and on in endless and often painful delight.

Another quake came, a terrible one, frightening them, so they clasped each other and let the rocking mountain provide their motion for them: a wild and violent climax, as though they were rocking the mountain with the force of their ardour. Night came, and still they played.

But in the morning she woke, and he was gone, inexplicably. Alarmed, she searched the entire cave as far back as the heat permitted but found no sign. It was as though he had never been.

She took her courage in both hands, dressed, and edged out into the dawn beyond Tyrann's nose. It was cold here, and light snow powdered the dinosaur's back. Tyrann was asleep, and surely he would die, for the chill would inevitably seep into his body and keep him moribund until the end. She had won, after all; in fact, she could probably have left long ago.

There were no human prints. If Cal had come this way, it must have been hours ago, before it grew cool enough for the snow to stay. Yet she had thought he was with her until recently.

She moved on down the little canyon towards the warmth of the valley, following the trail they had left as well as she could: mainly the scuff marks and claw indentations of the carnosaur's feet that showed because they had in their fashion changed the lay of the land.

She came to the place where she had thought Cal died. There she found one of his shoes, with the foot and part of the leg protruding. Flesh and bone and tendon, jaggedly severed by the crunch of the huge teeth of Tyrann.

There was no question of authenticity. Cal had indeed died here two days ago; the ants were hard at work.

Yet she had made love to Cal a day and night. Had it been a phantom, born of her grief, her futile longing? She touched her body here and there, feeling the abrasions of violent lovemaking. Could she have done all that to herself in an orgy of compensation for what she had never done during Cal's life? Her mind must have been temporarily deranged, for here was reality: a worn shoe with the stump of the leg.

She buried the foot and saved the shoe.

Now the mantas came: Circe and Star. Veg was all right, they reported; he had tried to come to help her when the mantas informed him but had been shaken up by the second quake and stranded on a rock in the bay. The birds had lost their eggs in that same quake and had to flee their nest, but both Orn and Ornette survived. The third quake had sundered their island and stirred up the water predators again.

'They lost their eggs . . .' Aquilon repeated, feeling a pang akin to that of her loss of Cal, one grief merging with the other.

Guided and protected by the mantas, she rejoined Veg and the Orn-birds. A month passed, an instant and an eternity for both people, sharing their awful grief. The phantom Cal did not reappear – but Aquilon had continuing cause to wonder, for she had no period. Veg had not touched her – not that way. Only in futile comfort had he put his arm about her.

In three months she knew she was pregnant. Yet there was no way – except that day and night in the cave. On occasion, she returned to it, past the frozen hulk of Tyrann at the entrance, but she never found anything. She had made love to a phantom— and she carried the phantom's child.

Veg shouldered more of the burden of survival as her condition progressed. The two sapient birds also helped, guarding her as she slept, bringing her delicacies such as small freshly slaughtered reptiles. She learned to eat them, and Veg understood: to survive in nature, one had to live nature's way. She was a vegetarian no longer.

'Also,' she explained with a certain difficulty, 'it's Cal's baby. I have to live this way.' She was not certain he would see the logic of that, or if there *were* any logic in it, but it was the way she felt. Her intake nourished Cal's baby; Cal's standards governed. Had it been Veg's baby . . .

'I loved him, too,' Veg said, and that sufficed. He was not jealous of his friend – only glad that even this much remained of Cal. She had never told him the details of the conception, letting him assume it was before the dinosaur chase began. There had, after all, been opportunity.

'After this one is born, the next must be yours,' she said. 'I love you, too, – and this would be necessary for survival of our species even if I did not.'

'Yeah,' he said a bit wryly. 'I'm glad you had the sense to go with him first. If he had to die, that was the way to do it.'

In civilization, among normal people, this would have been unreal. Here, with Veg, it was only common sense. Veg had always wanted what was best for his friend Cal, and it was a compliment to her that he felt she had been worthy.

'We argued about whether man should colonize,' she said. 'We were wrong, both sides. We assumed it had to be all Earth or nothing. Now we know that there was a middle ground. *This* ground: just a few people, blending into the Cretaceous enclave, cutting our little niche without destroying any other creature's niche. If we had realized that before, Cal might not have felt compelled to match Tyrann, and they both would be alive today.'

'Yeah,' he said, and turned away.

The baby was birthed without difficulty, as though nature had compensated her by making natural birth easy. There was pain, but she hardly cared. Veg helped, and so did the birds: They made a fine soft nest for the infant. She named him Cave.

If her relation with the birds had been close, it was closer now. They nested, for their season had come 'round again. Aquilon would leave baby Cave in the nest with the eggs, and Ornette would sit on them all protectively. Aquilon took her turns guarding the eggs while the birds hunted. They were an extended family.

When Cave was three months old, and Aquilon was just considering inviting Veg to father a sibling, disaster struck. Agents from Earth appeared. Concerned by the nonreport from the advance party – Cal, Veg, and Aquilon – the authorities had followed up with a more reliable mission.

The mantas spotted them first: a prefabricated ship coming in past the islands of Silly and Cheryb-dis. Three agents, one of whom was female.

Veg made a wheeled cart with a loose harness that either bird could draw, and set a nest in it. This made the family mobile – for there was no stationary place safe from agents. One manta was designated for each adult entity: Hex went with Veg, Circe with Aquilon, Diam with Orn, and Star with Ornette. Their function was to give advance warning when any agent was near any of the others, so that person could flee. There was to be no direct contact with any agent unless the nest was in danger. With luck, they would be able to stay clear until the agents left.

It was not to be. The agents were not merely surveying the land, they were after the people, too. The agents quickly ascertained the presence of a baby, and this seemed to surprise them. Hex, in hiding as two of them examined the deserted nest site, picked up some of their dialogue and reported on it: 'Cooperation with tame birds I can understand, though they've really gone primitive,' the male said. 'But a human baby? There wasn't *time!*'

'She must have been pregnant before leaving Earth,' the female said. 'Then birthed it prematurely.'

Aquilon was in turn amazed. 'How long do they think human gestation *is*? Two years? Cave was full-term!'

But the riddle of the agents' confusion had to wait. There was no question that the agents intended to take the trio and the baby captive for return to Earth – they apparently did not know that Cal was gone – and this could not be permitted.

One would have thought the home team had the advantage: two human beings toughened by a year among the dinosaurs, two fighting birds, and four mantas – the most efficient predators known to man. But there were three eggs and a baby to protect – and the three agents were equipped with Earth's technology. In one sense, the contest of champions Cal had visualized was to be joined again – but this time the weapons were different. One agent could wipe out one tyrannosaurus with one shot.

Cal could have directed an efficient program of opposition – but Cal was gone. The agents were stronger, faster, and better armed than Veg and Aquilon.

'We've got to get out of here,' Veg said. 'They're canvassing this whole valley and the neighbouring ones. They know we're here, somewhere, and they're drawing in the net. They'd probably have picked us up by now if they'd located Cal; they must figure he's hiding.'

'Even now, he's helping us, then,' she said, nodding. 'And if we leave, what happens to the dinosaurs?'

'Earth will wipe them out, or put them in zoos, same thing,' he said glumly. 'We've had our problems with the reps, but it's their world, and they have a right to live, too. But we've been over this; we can't kill the agents. Even if we had the weapons, we couldn't do it. We'd be murderers.'

'If we could stop the agents from returning to their base ...'

'You think they'd go native like us?'

'It wouldn't matter, would it? Earth would have no report ...'

He smiled. 'Yeah.'

'And if they were stranded here, maybe they'd come to see it our way. Maybe they'd settle, turn human. That female – she could bear children.'

'Yeah,' he repeated, mulling it over.

'Three men, two women – that might be a viable nucleus.' There were aspects to it that disturbed her, but it was a far more positive approach than murder.

It was a daring plan. They set it in motion when one agent was on land, tracking down the moving nest.

Veg set sail with Hex on the old raft, the *Nacre*. He was a decoy, to draw off one of the two agents on the ship. 'And Veg,' Aquilon said as he left. 'If it is the female who comes after you, smile at her.'

'Yeah, I know,' he muttered. 'Use my delicate masculine wiles to subvert her superior feminine force.' He spat eloquently downwind. 'The day I ever cater to the likes of *her* ...'

'You're a handsome man. You don't want to have to kill her ...' But he was already on his way, and she felt like a procuress. Was she prepared to follow the same advice when she encountered a male agent?

She took one more look at Cave, sleeping in the nest-cart, guarded by the three other mantas and two birds. Yes – to save him, to save the eggs, to save the enclave, she *was* prepared. If they succeeded in stranding the agents here, it would eventually come to that, anyway: crossbreeding. Better that reality than the loss of everything she had fought to preserve.

Then Aquilon raided the ship. She stripped and swam, hoping that in the night her motion would be mistaken for that of an aquatic reptile. If not – that was the risk she had to take. The agent aboard would not kill her out of hand; he would let her board, then subdue her – and the test of her commitment would be at hand. She was a

588

buxom woman now because of nursing her baby. If she could seduce him, or at least lull him into carelessness so that she had a chance to scuttle the ship, then it would be done. The vessel was anchored in deep water and would not be recoverable.

Of course, then the water predators would close in . . . but she was ready to die. Perhaps the agent, realizing that he could no longer report to Earth, would be pragmatic and join her, and together with the mantas they could make it to shore.

She had smeared the juices of a vile-smelling root over her body to repel the water reptiles, and it seemed to work. She reached the ship without event and climbed nimbly to the deck.

To be met by the alert agent there. 'Welcome aboard, Miss Hunt. I am Tama, your host. Kind of you to surrender voluntarily.'

The female – the worst one to meet! 'I've come to sink your ship,' Aquilon said, knowing the agent was well aware of her intent.

Tama ignored this. 'Come below decks.' It was an order, not a request.

Aquilon thought of diving back into the bay. Once she went into the hold, captive, she would never have a chance.

Tama moved so quickly she seemed a blur. 'Do not attempt to jump,' she said from the rail behind Aquilon.

Whatever had made her think she had a chance against an agent? Sheer delusion!

'Yes,' Tama agreed. 'But you amaze me too. You have indeed borne a child.'

'Nothing amazing about it,' Aquilon said. 'You could do the same if you chose to.'

'Yet you have been on Paleo only three months – and your Earth physical showed no pregnancy.'

Aquilon stiffened. She had been on paleo a *year* and three months. Surely the agents knew that!

'We shall have to plumb this mystery,' Tama said. 'You are not trying to deceive me, yet we can not explain—'

She was interrupted by the sound of a bell. She brought out a tiny radio unit. 'Tama.'

'Tanu,' a male voice returned immediately. 'Male acquired, one fungoid destroyed.'

'Talo,' another voice said. 'Attacked by one sapient flightless bird. Bird destroyed, mission as yet incomplete.'

589

Aquilon felt an awful shudder run through her. Hex dead, Veg captured, one of the great birds killed, she herself nullified – and the effort had hardly started. What a terrible price had already been paid!

'There is no need for further violence,' Tama said. She held out the communicator. 'Spreak to your fungoids; tell them to land here. We shall treat you fairly.'

Aquilon faced about and walked towards the cabin, her lips tight. There was no way she could mask her antipathy to the agents. Subble she might have heeded, but these were ruthless strangers who could read her every response and anticipate many of her acts.

Suddenly a gun was in Tama's hand. 'Very clever!' she snapped. 'You did not know you were being supported by a fungoid.'

A manta! Aquilon suddenly recognized Veg's unsubtle hand in this. He had suggested that the mantas be confined to the defensive perimeter, and she, preoccupied with her own preparations, had agreed. Veg had sent a manta after her – and because she hadn't known it, she had been unable to give that fact away.

Tama fired. Aquilon, galvanized into action, made a dive for the weapon. But the agent's left hand struck her on the neck, knocking her down half stunned.

Then three mantas attacked simultaneously. They were fast, and they knew how to dodge projectiles and beams. But the agents, forewarned, had armed themselves with scatter-shot shells, almost impossible to avoid.

Aquilon watched helplessly from the deck as the first manta went down, a pellet through the great eye. 'Star!' Aquilon cried in horror.

The second manta came closer but was riddled by pellets through the torso. It sheered off and fell into the water. 'Diam!'

The third manta caught the agent across the neck, severing windpipe, jugular vein, and carotid arteries. Even so, Tama got off one more shot, and the fungoid crashed into the deck.

Aquilon stood up unsteadily. 'Oh, Circe!' she cried. 'We didn't want bloodshed . . .'

Tama grinned with ghastly humour, unable to speak. She clasped her throat with both hands, containing the blood – but the damage was too extensive, and she slumped to the deck, dying.

The mission had been a disaster; now there were no mantas, and there would be no other woman on Paleo to share the burden of bearing children.

But she had a job to do: Scuttle the ship. At least she could save Paleo. She went below decks to locate the necessary tools to do the job. A projectile cannon, or even a sledgehammer, to make a hole in the bottom, to let in the sea ...

Instead she found – a projector. She had never seen one before, but somehow she recognized its nature. The agents intended to establish a return aperture to Earth from right here!

She picked it up, intending to destroy it by smashing it into the deck. But her finger touched a switch inadvertently.

A cone of light came out from it, bathing her.

And she stood in a completely different scheme.

She was in a room about twenty feet long and fifteen wide. Walls, floor, and ceiling were plastered, and there was a fantastic variety of what were, to her artistic eye, highly authentic primitive art objects and paintings.

There were only two small, high windows and no door. A homemade ladder made of poles and thong-bound crosspieces ascended to a small hole in the ceiling: the only exit.

Had she projected herself back to Earth, the very thing she had tried so hard to stop – or was she in a new alternate world, inhabited by primitive man? If she had joggled the setting on the device, she could have travelled randomly.

Without that projector, she had no chance to return – and who but the agents would ever use it to seek her out? Her choices were to submit to recapture – or escape into this world.

She was hardly conscious of making the decision. Veg, Orn, and her baby were on Paleo – but if any of them survived the onslaught of the two remaining agents, it would not be as free entities. And the projector must have fallen to the deck as she phased through, either breaking or fouling up its setting.

Better for her to accept the inevitable. She could not return and would not want to, and no one would fetch her. She would have to make a new life for herself here, wherever this was. Even if it should be Earth.

But her eyes were full of tears. Consciously she was desperate to return to her baby, to retreat into the warm jungle valley with Veg. Perhaps Circe had survived; she had crashed into the deck but might not be dead. At any rate, there would soon be new mantas, as the freed spores drifted and mated and grew. Maybe Orn managed to haul eggs and baby to safety. Oh, yes, she longed to go there ... but surely Orn would *not* escape, the eggs would be lost, and her baby Cave ...

Her baby – conceived in the cave. Suddenly, a year after the fact, the truth struck her: Cal, from an alternate world, had been projected to hers. For one day and a night. *Her* Cal had died; it was the alternate who had fathered her child. He had been summoned, somehow, in the hour of her greatest need.

'Thank God for that one day ...' she whispered.

Now she was in another alternate herself. Perhaps she would help some other person, as she had been helped. Would that redeem the double wreckage of her life?

Meanwhile, her eyes were taking in her surroundings, and she was reacting with growing excitement. In a manner, she had died, for she had been irrevocably removed from her world – and surely this one was akin to heaven. She had studied art like this before. She recognized it. Prehistoric man – neolithic – Anatolia, somewhere around 6000 B.C.

'Çatal Huyuk!' she exclaimed, pronouncing it with the soft C: Satal.

The study of art necessarily led to an appreciation of history, and she had absorbed a fair background incidentally. Now she stood still, concentrating, bringing it back from long-idle mental channels.

Çatal Huyuk was a mound in south-central Turkey – the ancient Anatolian peninsula – on the highland plateau, about three thousand feet above sea level. For many years archaeologists had thought there was no neolithic occupation of the Anatolian plateau and no real art or organized religion there. The excavation of Çatal Huyuk had completely changed that, for here was a flourishing, religious, artistic, peaceful city demonstrating an advanced ancient culture. A substantial segment of prehistory had had to be rewritten.

Of course this might not be *the* Çatal Huyuk. There had been similar cities in Anatolia, and it could be a modern replica. But it was certainly of this type.

Excited, Aquilon moved about, inspecting the room in detail, using it as a diversion from the horrors she dared not dwell on back in Paleo. The plaster on the walls was actually a thin layer of white clay. Solid timbers supported the roof. The floor was neatly segmented into several levels, as though the intent was merely to indicate distinct areas, like lines on a playing field. This would be a sleeping platform, with its reed matting; this the kitchen area. Here was the hearth, under which the family's dead would be buried. Here was the storage bin, empty at the moment.

The walls were painted in panels. Some were solid red; others had geometric designs bordered by representations of human hands and feet. One wall was dominated by a protruding sculpture: the stylized head of a bull, the two horns projecting up and out, surrounded by pillars and ledges that showed the shrine-like nature of this section.

She climbed the ladder cautiously and poked her head over the top. She saw the rooftops of a city, each a different level, each with its entrance hole.

There were people. Suddenly Aquilon was conscious of her nakedness; she had never had a chance to dress and had never anticipated – this.

They stared at her. In moments they had her ringed. All were women; the few men who showed their heads had been sent scurrying with a few peremptory words. There was no question which sex was in control.

Aquilon did not resist. The people were not hostile, only curious. They took her to another room and tried to talk to her, but their language was completely alien to her experience. Yet she was fortunate, for this relieved her of the problem of explaining her presence.

They took care of her. She was, it seemed, something of a phenomenon: a tall blonde woman in a land in which all women were short and dark-haired. They regarded her as an aspect of the goddess-mother and she did not go out of her way to deny it. She was, after all, a recent mother (ah, there was grief: Did they marvel at her sadness?), and it showed. On religious festivals – of which there were a considerable number – she was expected to parade naked through the city, an object not of lust but of feminine presence. She had come to them naked, and that set the system; when she wished to move among them without reference to her goddess-head, she donned an elegant robe and slippers. They were able to accept this dual aspect; the dichotomy between goddess and woman was inherent in their religion. It was a pragmatic system.

If she had not already known it, the art of the city would have told her this was a matriarchy. There were paintings and sculptures and tapestries in splendid array. These people were indefatigable artists; pictures and designs were on walls, pots, clay statuettes, wood, baskets, pottery, weapons, and even skeletons. The eyebrows, cheeks, and lips of the women were also painted. A fine subindustry for making pigments existed – black from soot; blue and green from copper ores; red, brown, and yellow from iron oxides, and so on. Aquilon was already familiar with the technique and of course was a superior artist in her own right, which tended to confirm her status.

But in all this art there was not a single sexual symbol. No female breasts, no phallic representations, no suggestive postures. A male-dominated society would have abounded with artistic expressions of lust; in her own day the "nude" always meant a young, voluptuous woman. Here, nothing: Women were not motivated in this direction, and though many of the artists were male, they painted under direction of the priestesses.

She learned the language, and painted, and it was a rather good life. Gradually her grief for what she had left behind faded. The people were disciplined and courteous and not without humour and song. The men were out much of the day hunting. Many women wove cloth, prepared hides, and fashioned rather sophisticated clothing; others cleaned their homes and supervised repairs. The houses were scrupulously clean, with all the rubbish being dumped in the scattered courtyards. These people were primitive in that they could not write and lacked machine technology – but in all other respects they were civilized. More so, really, than those of her own day.

Then she discovered the projector. It was in a disused chamber beneath a new residence. It had been closed off because it had been damaged by fire and was considered unsafe; it could not be demolished because that would have interfered with the neighbouring residences. There was also an element of religion, as there was in almost every aspect of life in this city: A revered old woman had lived in it once, and it would have been an affront to her spirit to destroy it entirely. So it had been vacated and forgotten for many years. But Aquilon was privileged to explore where she lived; how could the woman's spirit be insulted by the visit of a goddess?

In this chamber was a device very like the one she had found aboard the ship – but more advanced, for it had a television screen.

She experimented. The thing was self-powered but alien. She did not know how to operate it and hardly wanted to find herself in yet another alternate. Yet she was fascinated. In the course of days she worked it out: The screen showed which alternate it was attuned to, and a separate key enabled the operator to return to his point of origin: here. Other controls shifted the focus, making the images on the screen change dizzily.

There were an infinite number of alternates available. In the nearest, she actually saw herself bending over the projector, a few seconds behind or ahead of her. Once she exchanged a smile and wave with the other Aquilon who happened to be focusing on *her*. It was no replay of her own acts; these were separate Aquilons, individuals in their own right yet still very much *her*.

In farther alternates there were other scenes. Some were bizarre: walking plants, a huge machine hive, or perpetual blizzard. Others were tempting, such as a placid forest or a near-human farm fashioned from solidified fog.

She went further. She took the key, set the screen on the quiet forest, and activated the projector.

And she stood in the forest. It was real. The air was sweet and cool.

Nervous, she squeezed the key – and she was back in Çatal Huyuk, her heart thudding, her whole body shaking with the release of tension. She really *could* go and return!

One alternate was a desert. On it an Aquilon carried one of Orn's eggs.

Orn's egg! Suddenly it occurred to her that this alternate of Çatal Huyuk, with its lush surrounding plains filled with game and vegetation, was ideal for a flightless, five-foot-tall hunting bird: an avian Garden of Eden. There were aurochs – European bison, somewhat like the American 'buffalo'; gigantic pigs, deer in great herds. Sheep and dogs were domesticated, and the men hunted wild ass, wild sheep, deer, foxes, wolves, leopards, and bear. There were many varieties of birds and fish. How Orn would have loved it here:

abundant prey but no dinosaurs!

Orn: She had never been able to locate Paleo with Orn on it, or Veg, or the agents. She could not rescue her real friends. But that egg the alternate Aquilon carried contained a living *ornisapiens* chick. Suppose she fetched it, then went to another alternate and got another? One male and one female. Re-establishing a marvellous species ... what a wonderful project! Perhaps she could make similar forays for mantas.

She watched the other Aquilon moving about, holding that precious egg. The woman cradled it in the crook of her arm as she stooped to touch the sand. There were tread marks there, as of a machine.

Machine! Aquilon knew about the self-willed machines. She had watched them consuming ... everything. If they were cruising on that world, the humans had little chance, and the egg, none. And of course there was no game to speak of there. Even if hatched, the Orn-chick would inevitably die.

Aquilon decided: She would save that egg now.

Without further thought – for that might cause her to lose her nerve – she removed her elegant white goddess-incarnate robe, too valuable to soil. She took up the key (must never forget *that!*) and put it in her mouth for safekeeping. She took a deep breath and activated the projector.

The desert world formed about her.

For a moment she oriented, checking the desert and the alternate Aquilon. All was in order.

The girl saw her. 'Who are you?' she demanded.

Aquilon realized that to this woman *she* was the original Aquilon, having no knowledge of the alternate framework. How to explain the past year and make her believe it – when at any time a machine could come upon them? 'Pointless to go into all that now,' Aquilon said. 'Please give me the egg.'

The girl stepped back, clutching it. 'No!'

Aquilon hadn't anticipated resistance. The merit of her plan was so obvious! Too late she realized that what made sense to her would not necessarily make sense to her uninformed alternate. The girl was evidently younger than she and had borne no child; this alternate was a year or more divergent from her own. Poor planning on her part – but she had run this sort of risk by acting on impulse. Best to go ahead now.

'You must. You can't preserve it any longer. Not here in the desert, with the awful machines.' But the girl didn't know about *those* yet, either. She had a lot to learn! All the more reason to salvage the egg from her incompetent hands. 'I have found a new Garden of Eden, a paradise for birds. When it hatches there—'

The girl's face became sullen, resistive. 'No one else can—' She halted, amazement spreading over her comely features. 'You're *me!*'

'And you're me, close enough,' Aquilon said impatiently. She should have explained about that at the outset! So many mistakes – she was fouling it up appallingly. 'We're aspects of the same person. Alternates. So you know you can trust me. You—'

'But you – you're more—'

Was the girl accepting it? Good. 'I bore a child – that's why. I nursed my son until two months ago. But—' Too complicated, and it hurt to remember. How she longed for Cave! 'I lost mine. You'll keep yours. But you can't keep the egg.'

The girl retreated. 'A baby? I—'

Maybe she shouldn't have mentioned that. This girl had not had her baby. A whole different situation, for Aquilon herself had been transported to Çatal Huyuk, not this machine-desert world. For a moment Aquilon was tempted to stop and question this girl, to find out all the details of *her* life. Had she made love to Cal – or to Veg? Or an agent? What had happened to the Orn-birds of her Paleo that she should be left with the egg? Had she found a projector?

But that would be folly. She could not afford to engage in dialogue with all the myriad alternate-Aquilons she could reach. There was a job to do, and she should do it – or go home. 'You're in danger. You can save yourself but not the egg.' A human being could fight off a machine if properly armed or escape it – but hardly while carrying the egg. She had seen an agent tackle one in another alternate. Interesting that the orientation of her projector seemed to be on those alternates where other human beings had projected aboard, as though all projectors were somehow linked. The connection was geographic, too; obviously if she had projected to this desert world a hundred miles from this spot, she would not have been able to fetch the egg. It all implied some higher agency – something else to think about when she had the time. 'There is little time, and it's too complicated to explain right now. Give it to me!' She reached out, hating the necessity for this brusque language, so unlike her. But she knew if she delayed any more, she would lose her nerve, and the job would not get done.

'No!' The girl retreated, hugging the egg.

'Give it to me!' Aquilon cried.

The girl straight-armed her. They fell together over a bag of supplies. The egg was caught between them and crushed, destroying the chick within.

'Oh, *no!*' Aquilon cried, her dream dying with the chick. Tears streamed down her face. 'I came to save it – and I smashed it!'

The alternate was crying, too. But tears could not reconstitute the egg.

Aquilon staggered away, heedless of direction. A few paces into the sand she remembered the projection key. She took it out of her mouth and squeezed it.

Back at Çatal Huyuk she washed herself, donned her robe, and went out onto the roof of the city. There was a numbness inside her that would not abate. She had travelled to an alternate and done irreparable damage thereby because of her lack of planning and carelessness and impetuosity. What penance could she do?

After an hour she returned to the chamber with a heavy mallet and smashed the projector and screen. Never again would she trifle with alternity.

Chapter Eighteen

REPORT

PATTERN ALERT: SURVIVAL

Pattern-entities, unable to comprehend the nature of physical sentience but unable to ignore it as a potential nonsurvival threat, instituted an enclave consisting of five divergent sentient entities: a pattern, a machine, and three forms of life – fungoid, avian, and mammal. There were also nonsentient plants and a population of sub-sapient animals upon which the sentients preyed.

The purpose was to observe the interaction of sentients, drawing inferences concerning their natures and survival potential within a restrictive environment. This information might enable the patterns to determine the extent of the potential threat to survival posed by the physical sentients.

To be certain that survival was the primary issue, the enclave was so designed that none of the occupants could survive comfortably without pre-empting the needs of the others. There were insufficient elements for the pattern, minerals for the machine, prey for the living predators, or mixed organic substances for the mammal infant. Direct competition was required.

In order to obtain a complete picture, a system of alternate-frame holography was used. Holography, as practised in the physical scheme, involves the division of a given beam of energy into parts, one part subjected to an experience the other lacks. The resultant difference between the parts thus defines the experience. In this case, mature representatives of the sentient species were provided the means to observe some of the interactions within the enclave and within the framework of alternity itself. In this manner the reactions of the physical sentients could be contrasted to those of the nonphysical sentients, and the changes in the physical sentients contrasted to their like counterparts, rounding out the picture.

The experiment was not entirely successful. All the sample entities of the enclave survived despite its deliberately restrictive situation, and a majority of the travellers through alternity also survived – but this did not enlighten the pattern-entities. There was initial competition in both environments, followed by cooperation that greatly enhanced survival. The information did not fall into neat patterns, and the mechanisms and motives of the physicals remained unclear. The pattern-entities therefore ignored the experiment, failing to act or even respond even when the entities of both groups made serious attempts to communicate. The failure was not in the conception or execution of the plan but in the patterns' inability to interpret the results or to act on data received.

What had been intended as an exercise of short duration became one of greater scope – because it was left alone. In due course the entities of the enclave, utilizing techniques largely incomprehensible to the watching patterns, achieved comprehension and powers beyond those of their background societies. Patterns have substantial limitations in the physical world; physical creatures are similarly restricted in the pattern framework. True science is a combination of the two systems.

Only through a conceptual technology developed from the merging of systems can true progress be made. This means complete and free interaction between all forms of sentience. We – the five sentient entities of the enclave – have worked out the principles of such interaction. We are able to communicate meaningfully with all of the intellects we represent, as demonstrated by this report, which is being conveyed to representative frames for each of these types.

We feel that the fundamental knowledge must be placed in the minds of those entities best able to utilize it, with the proviso that it be used only to facilitate harmony and progress among all the alternates. We feel that four of our five representative species lack suitable philosophies or talents for this purpose. The fungoids and the aves do not have either the inclination or the manual dexterity to operate the necessary constructs. The mams have both – but lack appropriate social control. They are predators, exploiters: in their own description, 'omnivores', destroyers of differing systems. Therefore, this power can not be entrusted to their possession. The pattern-entities are also capable and have better philosophical mores. But their cynicism in setting up this enclave and the associated 'hexaflexagon' pattern of alternate frames shows that their philosophy is incomplete. Sentients are not to be toyed with in this fashion. In fact, the patterns have such extraordinary difficulty comprehending the nuances of physical need and operation that we feel that they, too, are unsuitable.

Only one species possesses incentive, capability, and philosophy to make proper use of the information and to carry through effectively on the implied commitment. For this species only, we append our technical report, granting the power of alternity.

We believe the machines well serve the need.

Chapter Nineteen

ORN

Orn heard the terrible squawk and knew its meaning instantly. The predator mam had caught Ornette and killed her. Now it would come for him.

He did not feel grief, only loss. Now he had no mate, and the line of his species was ended – unless he found another mate or preserved the eggs. Neither he nor his eggs would survive if this mam caught him – and the mam cub would perish, also.

Orn did not think in the manner of reps or mams. His mind was experience, and the experience was millions of seasons long: a racial memory. It did not employ words at all; to him, 'mam' was that complex of impressions generated by the presence of fur-bearing, infant-nursing, warm-bodied vertebrates. 'Rep', 'aves', and the various representatives of such classes were similar concepts.

Orn knew the manner his kind had survived, back as far as his species had existed distinct from other aves. He was well equipped for survival in the world his ancestors had known. But that world had changed, and this made survival perilous.

Orn's ancestry contained no record of a chase by a predator mam, for mams had been tiny prey for most of their species duration. Thus, he had never experienced a threat of the kind this represented. But Orn was expert in hiding and in hunting – indeed, the two were aspects of the same process. He knew this mam was as savage and deadly as a young tyrann. If it caught him it would kill him and take the eggs and cub.

So he fled – but he did it expertly. He put his long neck through the front loop of the nest-cart and drew it behind him. The cub began to make noise. Immediately, Orn twisted his head about, bent his neck down, and found the chip of wood that was used for such occasions. He put it in the cub's mouth. The cub sucked on it and stopped crying.

Orn hauled the wagon into a dense thicket near a turbulently flowing stream, concealing it from the exposure of both light and sound. He washed his beak and feet in the stream, temporarily cutting down on his typical odour. Then he scraped over the traces the cart's wheels had made, carefully placing pine needles, palm fronds, and half-decayed brush in place so that it matched the forest floor. He found the rotting, arth-riddled corpse of a small rep and placed it nearby: That smell would override all else.

This was not the way Orn reasoned, for his mind did not work that way. It was merely the accumulated and sophisticated experience of his species. As the arths constructed elaborate warrens and performed many specialized tasks, so he performed in the manner survival had always dictated. That he did it consciously only reflected the talent of his species: His memories were far greater than those of arths, reps, or any other species and required far more sophistication of choice. But memory it was, not reasoning.

His camouflage completed, he washed himself again, waded downstream, and spotted a small grazing rep: a baby tricer. He pounced on it, digging his claws into the creature's back just behind the protective head-flange.

The slow-witted rep emitted a squeal of pain and whipped its head about. But Orn held his position just out of reach of the crushing bone, digging his powerful talons in deeper, flapping his stubby wings to maintain his balance. Unable to dislodge his attacker, the tricer stampeded. Orn rode it, guiding it by tightening the grip of one foot or the other, causing it to shy away from the increased pain.

Finally, Orn jumped off it, releasing the rep to its own devices. He had, in effect, flown: He had travelled a distance leaving no recognizable trace of his passage. No predator could follow his trail by sight or scent back to the hidden nest.

Now he made an unconcealed trail that led obliquely away from that nest. He knew the predator mam would come across it in due course and would recognize it. Orn made several big circles so that there was no obvious point of termination to betray his ruse, then set off for the territory of the largest and fiercest tyrann in the valley. The mam would find plenty to distract him, following *this* trail!

But Orn had underestimated the cunning of this beast. The mam did not pursue his mock trail directly. He set an ambush for Orn.

Only the silence of the arths of the region alerted the bird. Normally, the little flying, crawling, and tunnelling creatures were audible all around – except when an unnatural presence alarmed them. When Orn entered this pocket of quiescence, he knew something was wrong.

He retreated silently – but the mam was aware of him. A bush burst into fire beside him: the lightning strike of the mam's weapon.

Orn ran. The mam pursued. Orn was fleet, for his kind had always hunted by running down their prey. But this mam was far swifter on his feet than others of his type, the Veg and the Quilon. Orn had to exert himself to an extraordinary extent to leave it behind – and then he was unable to conceal his trail properly.

He could lead it in a long chase, hoping to tire it: Orn could run for days. But meanwhile the eggs were slowly growing cold. The warmth of the mam cub beside them in the nest and the covering of feathers and fibres extended the time those eggs could be left – but the night was coming. Both eggs and cub would need attention – the one for warmth, the other for food. If the cub were not fed, it would make noise – and that would summon the predator mam or a predator rep. Orn knew these things from recent experience.

He had to lose the mam quickly, then return to the nest for the night. Because it was well concealed, he should be able to leave it where it was until morning.

But the mam would not relinquish his trail. It fell back but never enough to permit him to eliminate his traces. He was in trouble.

Then a fung found him. Only with difficulty had Orn learned to comprehend these plant-creatures, for they were completely alien to his ancestry. Now he identified them fairly readily. They bounded across land or water faster than any other creature, and their strike was deadly – but they killed only for their food and fought only for the two friendly mams. Orn had no concern about the fungs.

Now he realized that its presence signified a development in the conflict with the predator mams. But he was unable to communicate with the creature.

The fung dropped before him and coalesced into its stationary shape. Though Orn could not afford to wait long, he knew there was motive behind this presence. He inspected the fung at close range.

The creature was injured. Fluids oozed from it.

Then Orn knew that the friendly mams had succumbed. This was the Circe fung, companion of the Quilon. It had been rent by a predator weapon. It had sought him out to show him this.

No creature but Orn remained to protect the nest – and the predator was after him.

The sounds of the pursuer were growing. Orn had to run again.

The fung rose up, faltered in the air, and righted itself. There was no doubt it was in trouble; its normal grace and speed were gone.

It moved towards the predator mam.

Orn realized that disabled as it was, the fung was about to attack the mam.

That might eliminate the mam or delay him so that Orn could get safely to the nest.

He ran to the stream, went up it, found another small rep, and forced it to take him towards the nest.

All was well. The eggs were still warm, and the cub was sleeping.

Orn sat on the nest, raising the temperature of the eggs while he poked his beak into the mash prepared by the Quilon. When the cub woke, he put a portion of this mash into its mouth, holding its head upright with one wing, patiently catching the spillage and putting it back into the mouth. When the cub balked, Orn performed his most difficult ritual: He took a shell dish in his beak, carried it to the nearby stream , scooped it full of water, brought it back, and set it on the edge of the nest. Then he took one of the hollow-reed sections and set one end in the dish, the other in the cub's mouth. The cub sucked. Water went up the tube and into its mouth. In this way it drank.

Orn's care of the cub was another function of his memory. Ancestors had on occasion sought to preserve the lives of young animals, cubs of those slain for food. Those cubs could mature to become prey when prey was scarce, so this was a survival talent. Even a newly hatched chick, confronted with a helpless mam cub, would have reacted similarly, sharing food, cutting reed stems, fetching water, fashioning warm cover. It was a symbiosis that came naturally in the time of the dominance of the great reps.

Now he cleaned the nest. The mam cub, like all mams, was a voluminous processor of water. It imbibed great quantities and expelled them almost continuously. The nest was made so that most of the fluid percolated through and fell on the ground, but in time the damp bedding soured, creating an odour problem. Orn pulled out tufts of it and replaced them carefully with fresh. This took some time, but it was necessary and natural.

The cub slept. Orn covered it and the eggs and slept, too.

In the morning Orn left the nest well insulated and went out to hunt and reconnoitre. He did not take extraordinary measures to conceal his traces, for he intended to move the nest to a better place.

First he checked on the predator mam. The fung was gone, and the mam was injured; it had evidently been a savage encounter. Orn did not see the mam; he saw the site of the contest, noting the scuffled ground, the blood soaked in it – mam blood and fung ichor – and the bits of flesh and bone that had constituted the five extremities used to manipulate the lightning weapon. He saw the ruptured skin of the fung, the lens of the great eye, some muscle of the foot, but very little of the main body. That was odd, for the scavenger arths had not had time to consume that mass yet.

The mam had survived, badly damaged – but he was still casting about, searching for Orn and the nest.

Orn thought of attacking the mam. It was in a weakened state, and Orn was strong; he might now be able to kill it. But if the mam possessed the fire weapon and had some way to operate it despite the loss of the small bones, Orn could not prevail. A tyrann might be crippled, but its tooth was still sharp! Orn left the mam alone.

He ran down a small brach rep, fed on it, and returned to the nest. It was full daylight now. The mam's search pattern was getting closer; he had to move the nest.

He hooked his neck through the harness and pulled. He would take it to a warm cave high in the mountain ridge. There the eggs could remain warm steadily, and the cub would be protected. Caves made good nesting places – sometimes.

But the route was difficult. He had to pass through the territories of two predator reps, slowed by the nest, and pursued by the mam. He had to navigate the fringe of a mud flat. Then the steep slope, where he would be exposed to the mam's lightning weapon.

Orn did not concern himself with the odds. He moved out.

He passed through the tyrann's region safely. Once this section had been the territory of a larger tyrann, who had pursued the Quilon up the mountain and perished in the cold; the new tyrann had not yet fully assimilated the enlarged area. It might be asleep or occupied elsewhere.

But the smaller rep predator, a struth, caught him.

Struth was as like Orn as a rep could be. He had long legs, a slender neck, and he was within twice Orn's mass. He therefore regarded Orn as a direct competitor.

With a scream of outrage, Struth charged. Orn ducked out of the harness and scooted around the cart to face the rep. He would have to fight – otherwise, Struth would gobble the eggs and cub.

Orn's ancestry had had much experience with Struth. The rep was tough. Only in the cool morning could Orn match it, for then the rep's speed and reflexes were slowed.

This was morning.

Orn dodged aside as Struth charged. He brought up one foot, using his sharp claws to rake the rep's side with the powerful downstroke.

It was a good shot. A soft-skinned mam would have been disembowelled. But the tough hide of the rep protected it so that all it suffered was a nasty scrape and the severance of several small muscles. Meanwhile, its teeth whipped around, snapping in air not far from Orn's neck.

But Orn was ready for that motion. His beak stabbed forward, scoring on the rep's eye. The creature screamed with pain and pulled back.

Orn raised his foot again to make the evisceration strike, his best technique. But the rep's jaws closed on his elevated foot, for it was taller than he.

Immediately, desperately, Orn struck with his beak, punching out the other eye. The rep let go – but Orn's foot had been mangled.

He made one more strike against the blind Struth with his good foot. This time it was effective. Dying, his intestines spilling out, the rep collapsed. He snapped savagely at his own guts, trying to vanquish the pain.

Orn took no time to feed, tempting as the sight of those burgeoning entrails were. The mam would catch up! He returned to the nest, hooked his neck through, and limped forward. Weight on his injured foot pained him increasingly, but he went on jerkily.

He reached the mud flat. The mud was hot today; huge bubbles rose, expanded, and popped. But a detour around this area would greatly extend his route and take him back through Tyrann's territory. Lame as he was, that was not to be risked.

The best path through it would take him near several of the largest bubble-pits. Alone, he might manage it, even injured as he was. Hauling the nest made it far more difficult.

But if he made it, the boiling mud would serve as an equal barrier to the mam. Perhaps a fatal one.

He moved ahead, twisting around the hot pits with the inspiration of desperation. He had to keep the nest moving, for the wheels tended to sink in the soft surface.

He heard a noise. His head swivelled. The predator mam had emerged from the foliage. The creature was swathed in material. Sticks were bound to its limbs and fabric covered its torso – not its normal removable plumage but tight patches covering wounds. Orn did not have to reason out the combat; his observation of the site of the engagement with the fung, coupled with the present condition of the mam, were sufficient to form the picture.

The fung had struck at the weapon first, nullifying it, leaving the mam to his own resources. Next, the fung had cut at the mam's broad neck. The mam had protected his neck with his limbs, and so those limbs had been deeply sliced: flesh from bone. But once the mam got his appendages on the fung, he had torn it apart, killing it.

Afterwards, the mam had bound up his wounds to stop the loss of body fluids, using the sticks to fix the bones in place. And continued his pursuit of Orn. A formidable predator!

A huge bubble developed almost beneath Orn. It was a slow riser that had given no prior signal of its presence; Orn had judged this section safe.

He jerked forward, trying to haul the cart to safety. But its wheels were deep in the mud loosened by the bubble. He only succeeded in sliding it directly into the air cavity as it erupted.

The cart tipped, spilling one egg into the hot mud, then another. The cub wailed. Orn flapped his wings, striving for leverage against the air. But the harness entangled them.

The bubble burst. Scorching gas enveloped Orn. He squawked in agony, then inhaled the vapour into his lungs.

Burning inside and out, Orn sank into the bubble. As the heat of it cooked him, his glazing eyes saw a strange glow with many sparkling points. It coalesced about the nest, about the one remaining egg and the mam cub.

This was the one experience Orn's ancestry had been unable to bequeath to him: the death of the individual. Heat, pain, and a cloud of lights. Mud-matted feathers. Sinking.

The strangest thing about it was the apparent surprise of the watching predator. The *mam* was not dying; why was he sharing Orn's experience?

Chapter Twenty

UNIT

The unit phased into the forest-frame, orienting on the location of the two mams.

'Watch out!' Veg cried. 'One of the machines is after us!'

'I am an emissary of Machine Prime,' the unit said. 'As you will recall, we made an agreement for the exchange of enclaves between our frames.'

'That's true,' Tamme said, but her body was tense. She no longer carried the frame homer: evidence of her bad faith.

'You will note that I address you in your own dialect rather than the one we worked out in our prior interview.'

'I noted,' she said tightly.

'Peace is being established between the alternates. We are in touch with your home-frame and are making contact with others. There will be no exchange of enclaves.'

'Meaning?' She was trying to assess the best method of disabling the machine.

'We never intended conquest despite your suspicions. We wished only rapport, a stronger base against what we deemed to be a common enemy. You misjudged our motive, and we misjudged the patterns. Such misconceptions are being resolved. If you will accompany me now, you will be satisfied.'

Veg shook his head. 'I have this strange feeling we should believe it. A machine never tried to talk to me before. It sure knew where to find us, and it didn't attack.'

Tamme shook her head. 'I don't trust it. We know how vicious these machines can be.'

'I must convey you to Çatal Huyuk,' the unit said. 'You have merely to remain in your places.'

'A machine can move us across alternates?' Tamme asked.

'A machine always *has*,' Veg reminded her.

Uncertain of the situation, she made no overt resistance. The unit moved them. They phased smoothly from forest to city without the intercession of Blizzard.

Aquilon saw the machine and opened her mouth in a soundless scream. Cal looked up from a partly dismantled machine. 'Is this an answer to our message?' he inquired guardedly.

'You may call it such, Dr Potter,' the unit said.

Then Cal saw Veg and Tamme. He relaxed. 'Hello,' he said, raising his hand in greeting. 'It must be all right. The machines are our friends – I think.'

Tamme glanced from him to Aquilon. 'And are we friends, too?'

'You've changed,' Aquilon said, looking closely at her.

'I have gone normal.'

'We are all friends now,' the unit said. 'I will convey you to Çatal Huyuk ancient, where—'

'Çatal Huyuk!' Cal and Aquilon exclaimed together.

'Amplification,' the unit said. 'This frame is Çatal Huyuk modern. Our destination is Çatal Huyuk ancient.'

'*This* is Çatal Huyuk?' Cal asked. 'Ten thousand years later?'

'Time becomes irrelevant. We shall return you to your own frames after the decision-assembly or to any you prefer.'

Tamme and Aquilon were grim lipped; the men were more relaxed. What kind of decision was contemplated by the machine?

'Çatal Huyuk,' Cal repeated, shaking his head. 'The splendour of early man, forgotten . . .'

The two mantas settled, watching the unit. The surrealist city faded out, and the ancient Çatal Huyuk faded in.

A pattern-entity and the white-robed alternate Aquilon were waiting in the shrine-room. The two Aquilons were startled by each other, turning their eyes away. Tamme appraised the almost prisonlike closure of the room warily, judging whether the machine and pattern could be destroyed and an escape effected without the loss of Veg.

'We are all friends,' the unit repeated. 'We are gathered here for the dénouement so that we may resolve prior confusions and dispose the protagonists suitably.'

The assembled entities looked around: five human beings, two mantas, and the pattern. No one spoke. Sparkles from the pattern radiated out, passing through the physical creatures without effect.

'In a certain frame,' the unit said, as though oblivious to the tension that now gripped even the men, 'Calvin Potter died. His cessation was witnessed by his close friend and potential lover, Deborah Hunt. It had a profound effect on her – so strong that the trauma extended across a number of related frames.'

'My nightmare!' the informal Aquilon whispered.

The white-robed Aquilon glanced at her. 'So you felt it, too . . .'

'This is a common effect,' the unit explained. 'It accounts for many of the instances of human *déjà vu*, precognition, spectral manifestation—'

Cal nodded, comprehending. 'We call it supernatural because the natural laws of our single frame do not account for psychic phenomena. But if they are merely reflections of actual occurrences in adjacent frames . . .'

'This man,' the unit said, indicating Cal, 'crossed over to the frame of that woman—' it indicated the priestess Aquilon – 'and impregnated her. He returned to his frame and dismissed the matter as a fantasy. She bore his child and cared for it with the aid of her friend Veg and the four mantas and the family of sapient birds.'

Informal Aquilon stared at robed Aquilon. 'You said you had a baby—'

'Yes . . .'

Informal Aquilon turned to Cal. 'And you were the father?'

He spread his hands. 'It appears so.'

'This is another occasional effect,' the unit said. 'When there is a sudden, overwhelming need in one frame, and the capacity to alleviate it in a nearby one, spontaneous crossover can occur. In this case it was facilitated by the presence of an aperture projector left by an exploratory party from a farther-removed frame. Their agents were of the VI series—'

'We haven't reached VI yet,' Tamme said. 'TE is the latest—'

'That frame is ahead of yours,' the unit explained. 'Vibro and Videl projected in, left their spare projector in a secluded location in case of emergency, and went to study the reptilian enclave. They were misfortunate, being caught in a severe tremor, injured, and consumed by predatory fauna before they could reach that reserve projector. So it remained where it was, on that frame, until used by Mr Potter.'

Veg sat down on the edge of the raised level. 'This is mighty interesting,' he said. 'But why were we picked up by the sparkles, and who left all those other projectors around? Can't *all* have been survey parties gobbled by dinosaurs — not in Fognose, or Blizzard, or—'

'The other projectors were left by people like you,' the unit said. 'You and the TA agent projected to another frame, leaving your instrument behind. The same thing happened on the other frames. Because each was a frame-site selected by the pattern-entities for temporary storage of experimental subjects—'

'White rats,' Tamme interjected. She had not relaxed.

'—they were in phase with each other. Instead of opening on random frames and locations, each projected to the immediate site of another storage area. This kept the subjects contained — which was one reason the patterns arranged it that way. The aggregate formed patterns — again no coincidence, as this is inherent in any endeavour of the pattern-entities.'

'It figures,' Veg said. 'So there was no way *off* that Möbius loop.'

'That system has been dismantled,' the unit said.

'But what about all the other people?' Veg demanded.

'They are being interviewed by other units.'

'You mean the machines have taken over all alternity?'

Now it was out. Tamme, seeming relaxed, was poised for action — and Cal, both mantas, and the informal Aquilon were ready to follow her lead. There would be violence in an instant — the moment they were sure there was no better course.

'The term "takeover" is inapplicable,' the unit said. 'Machine Prime now serves as coordinator for existent frames. This will be clarified in a moment.'

'Let it speak,' Cal murmured to Veg. 'This is a most revealing dialogue.' And now Veg also was ready for action.

'The follow-up mission of the agents was delayed for a year, in that frame where Aquilon was gravid. When the agents came, the mantas and sapient birds died, Vachel Smith was captured, and Miss Hunt projected to this frame: a world in the human neolithic. She

613

found the projector left here by another party—'

'How many parties *are* there buzzing around?' Veg demanded.

'An infinite number. But most were incorporated into the pattern arranged by the pattern-entities; there was no mechanical way to break out of those loops. Miss Hunt experimented with her projector, visited her counterpart on the desert setting, inadvertently destroyed the egg, and returned here in remorse to destroy her projector.'

'You did that?' the informal Aquilon asked.

The robed Aquilon nodded sadly. 'What happened to my baby?'

'The bird Orn attempted to save both his eggs and your baby. He was stalked by an agent whose assignment was to recover both for return to Earth. The agents did not believe there had been time for a human infant to be conceived and birthed, so it was important for them to investigate the phenomenon fully. Orn perished – but a pattern entity salvaged one egg, the baby, and a fertile spore from the deceased mantas. These were conveyed to a restricted locale with a newly manufactured machine entity—'

'The scene we saw on the stage!' the informal Aquilon cried. Now her resolve to fight was wavering. The machine seemed to know too much to be an enemy.

'A nascent pattern was also created there,' the unit continued. 'Small, mindless shoots of the type generated on Mr Potter's three-dimensional screen were sent across the limited element accesses in such a way as to combine and form a complete, sentient entity. This is the way new patterns are formed; they do not reproduce in the fashion of physical entities. There is a certain parallel in the manufacture of sentient machines, however. Such a machine had just been fashioned on the so-called Desert frame; one of its builders had obtained the necessary ingredients from the human supplies projected there—'

'So that was why it was hungry!' Veg said. 'It was a mother machine.' Now he, too, was wavering as further comprehension came.

'The analogy is inexact,' the unit said. 'However, the new machine was the one transferred to the enclave elsewhere on that frame. That enclave was then complete. The patterns, observing, hoped to ascertain the nature of the physical entities. They were not successful in that – but the enclave nevertheless achieved success of

614

its own.'

'But the enclave-baby died!' Informal Aquilon protested. 'We saw the horrible machine slice it up—'

Robed Aquilon froze.

'The pattern-entity, reacting to the need of the other entities, restored the infant,' the unit said. 'Its death became apparent but unreal – as was Mr Potter's death in your frame. You called that a nightmare.'

'My baby – lives?' robed Aquilon asked.

'Yes. The component entities of the enclave combined their resources and developed a system of intercommunication that is now transforming sentient relations in all alternity. The adult enclave then assigned the duty of application and coordination to Machine Prime, and this duty we are now executing.'

There was a pause. Then: 'Why tell us all this?' Veg asked. 'Why not ship us back to our homes, or execute us, or ignore us? What do you care what happens to us?'

'Machine Prime does not care. It merely honours the terms of the agreement. The enclave specified that those of you who were instrumental in its formation be catered to. Now it is being dismantled, and we—'

'Dismantled?' informal Aquilon asked. 'What's happening to – to Ornet and the baby—?'

'The baby grew up to be a remarkably capable man,' the unit said. 'This was because the enclave pattern entity, $\overline{OX}$, utilized special properties of alternity to age the entire enclave twenty years. The other inhabitants matured similarly. In fact, $\overline{OX}$ arranged for a baby girl from your home-frame to enter the enclave, and she also matured. She was intended as a mate for Cub – the man – but that did not occur. It seems your kind, like machine units, can not be raised in isolation and retain sanity. $\overline{OX}$ therefore arranged for the return of the girl and reverted the enclave to its original status after issuing the report of the five sentients.'

'So the baby is – still a baby,' informal Aquilon said. 'And Ornet is a chick, and—'

'What's going to happen to them?' robed Aquilon demanded. 'My baby—'

'Their disposition is for this party to decide,' the unit said. 'We suggest that the baby be returned to its natural parents—'

'Oh-oh,' informal Aquilon said, looking first at her alternate, then to Cal.

Cal put his hand on hers. 'I may have strayed once – but this was a confusion. At any rate, the matter is academic. I am not the father.'

'You are the father,' the unit said.

Veg chuckled. 'Machine, if you can win an argument with Cal, you're a damn genius. Because *he* is.' He shook his head. 'Never thought he'd be involved in a paternity suit, though.'

'It is not a matter for debate,' the unit said. 'We have verified the information.'

Even Tamme relaxed. If the machine were ready to quibble about details, force might not be necessary. But if force *were* called for, it should be timed for that instant of confusion when the machine realized its mistake. For Cal had to be correct; Tamme anticipated the point he was about to make and recognized its validity. When it came to intellectual combat, Cal was supreme, as she and the other agents had learned on Paleo.

'Let me explain,' Cal said. 'According to you, I crossed over, impregnated this woman—' he indicated the robed Aquilon – 'and returned to my own frame in time to encounter the agent mission there. Meanwhile, in the other frame, she carried the baby to term and gave birth to it, subsequently becoming separated from it when it was about three months old. That baby entered the enclave and is now available for return.'

'Correct,' the unit said.

'Therefore, approximately a year passed in the other frame. But in *my* frame, a week has passed.' He frowned. 'Correction: two weeks. Time has become confused – but hardly to the extent of a year. My companions will verify this.'

Veg's mouth dropped open. 'That's right! Tamme got better in a week on Fognose, and there weren't many other—'

'True,' Tamme agreed. She had assessed the mechanisms of the machine and judged that one projectile fired to ricochet off the treads and into the mechanism from below would cripple it. Slowed, it could then be reduced by a concerted attack. It was a small machine, not as formidable as some.

'Yes,' informal Aquilon said. 'How can he be the father – from two weeks ago?'

'He is the father,' the unit repeated.

616

'I am undoubtedly the father of a baby in some other alternate – or will be some eight months hence,' Cal said. 'But some other Cal, from a frame running a year or more ahead of us – because this other Aquilon, in addition to her Paleo adventure, has evidently been here at Çatal Huyuk some time – is responsible for the enclave baby.' He turned to informal Aquilon. 'There is no question of my leaving you even for your double.'

Veg smiled triumphantly, while Tamme made ready to act. 'What do you say to *that*, machine?'

'We have mentioned that the agent mission was delayed for a year in this woman's frame,' the unit said, making a gesture to include the robed Aquilon. 'The patterns were responsible for that. This occurred in the course of the institution of their holographic representation, the enclave. Time travel is not possible within frames, but the appearance of it can be generated by phasing across frames, as you found on Paleo. By instituting a type of feedback circuit, a pattern entity is able to accelerate a portion of a limited complex of frames. This occurred in the enclave. But that portion is then out of phase and can not interact effectively with normal frames until it reverts. The only way to adjust the time-orientations of individuals so that one entity may interact with another in a different frame despite a dichotomy of time is to enable that individual to cross on the bias. That is what the patterns did with you. When you crossed from Paleo to Desert, you jumped forward more than a year in time.'

'But we used our own projector!' Tamme protested, still trying to catch the machine in its error.

'Your projector is a toy compared to the ability of the patterns. They altered your route during transit.'

Tamme saw her chance going. The machine was not at all confused and showed no weakness. From what she had seen of the patterns, they *could* play tricks with time . . .

'However, such bias must always be balanced,' the unit continued. 'The patterns could not jump you forward a year in one frame without performing a similar operation in the other. Therefore, the agents, similar in number and mass to your party—'

'Equations must balance!' Cal exclaimed. 'Of course! We jumped to the desert, hurdling a year, while the agents hurdled the same year jumping from Earth into the other Paleo. So those agents lost a year without knowing it, and so did we.'

Tamme relaxed. The seemingly impossible had happened. Cal had been outlogicked, their chance to strike eliminated. That machine really had control over the situation!

'Now I remember,' the robed Aquilon said. 'Tama said there hadn't been time, and I didn't know what she meant.'

'But we were in different frames,' Veg said. 'Our year couldn't balance out the agents' year, when—'

'Parallel frames – linked by Cal's brief crossover,' the unit said. 'For that purpose, with Cal in one and his child in the other, the two frames amounted to identity. By this device you were restored to phase with that Aquilon you impregnated, though she has lived more than a year longer than you in the interval between your encounters.'

Now the machine was so confident it was even waxing informal, Tamme thought. It had started calling them by their group-given names instead of their legal ones.

Cal spread his hands. 'I will, of course, assume responsibility for the baby—'

'Oh, no, you won't!' the robed Aquilon said. 'You may be the biologic father, but *my* Cal died, and I mourned him, and I will not have an impostor take his place. In that interim I was dependent on the grace of another man, and so was the baby. I may not love him – yet! – but *he* is the one to raise the baby with me – if he chooses to.'

Suddenly Tamme's deadly readiness had another object.

'Who?' informal Aquilon asked, perplexed. 'This is all so confused—'

'Veg. I think he always was the one I really—'

Veg jumped. 'Uh-*uh*! I loved you once – one of you, anyway – but that didn't work out. Now I'm with Tamme—'

Cal looked at him. 'It would not be wise to place undue credence in an agent's expressed interest. An agent is the ultimate manifestation of the omnivorous way.'

How cleverly the machine had manoeuvered them! Now they were quarrelling among themselves and would be unable to unite against the real menace. 'I love him,' Tamme said. 'I go where he goes; I eat where he eats, figuratively and literally. It doesn't matter who doubts it, so long as *he* believes. I can understand why she loves him, too – but I shall not give him up.'

618

'Not *him*,' the robed Aquilon said. 'I mean *my* Veg. Maybe he's dead, too, now, but—'

'He is not dead,' the unit said. 'The surviving agent of that frame, Tanu, is in the process of taking him back to the major transfer point on Paleo so he can be returned to Earth to stand trial for treason. We can recover him for you.'

'Yes!' she cried.

That agreement seemed to finish any thought of opposition. If the machine could fulfill its promise – and there was no reason why it couldn't – they all stood to gain far more by cooperating.

'There remains the disposition of the other entities of the enclave,' the unit said, as though all this had been routine. 'The manta Dec and the bird Ornet, now too young to comprehend their parts in this matter—'

'Bring them here, too,' the robed Aquilon said, seeming to radiate her joy at the recovery of her baby and her man. 'This fertile plain is a paradise for their kind. That's why I tried to bring the egg here—' She looked at her double. 'I'm sorry—'

'If I had known, I would have given it to you,' the informal Aquilon said. 'Ornet and Dec belong to your frame.'

The unit activated a relay. A small manta, a large chick, and a human baby appeared in the middle of the room. They drew together defensively, the manta and the chick standing on either side of the baby, facing out, poised.

The robed Aquilon went to them, extending her hands to the manta and bird, winning their confidence. She picked up her baby, hugging him, smiling with tears streaming down her cheeks. 'You'll like it here – I know you will!' she cried. 'The people here won't hunt you; you'll be sacred, as I am.' Then she looked around the room. 'Why don't you stay, too?'

Veg and Tamme exchanged glances. 'The baby I might bear would not resemble me . . .' she cautioned him.

'I *know* who it would resemble!' he said. He frowned. 'I sort of like the forest . . .'

'You will be free to travel between frames at will,' the unit said. 'I will convey you.'

'Even to Earth?' Cal asked.

'Anywhere in alternity, Calvin Potter. This privilege will not be extended indiscriminately, but these present here are the parental entities to the enclave, insofar as those entities survive. There will be access to the entire fabric, as required by the compact.'

'I am interested in the comparative evolution of the several forms of sentience – pattern, machine, and life,' Cal said. 'The machines, for example, must have been created, perhaps by an early compromise between energy and physical states of sentience. There must be a fascinating history—'

'There is,' the unit agreed. 'This, too, is available to you.'

The robed Aquilon looked up. 'I meant all of you, and $\overline{OX}$ and the machine, too, if their frames will give them up. The whole enclave could grow up normally, in a better environment. Learning to live and work together, showing the way for all the sentience of alternity ...'

'What a marvel that could make of this city,' Cal said. 'Representatives of all the sentients.'

'Çatal Huyuk modern ...' the informal Aquilon said. 'This is where it starts – right here, in this room, now ...'

The pattern entity in the corner sparkled. 'This is $\overline{OX}$,' the unit said. 'He accepts your invitation. Of course he will be in touch with his own kind, too. But he wants to continue his association with the spots – that is, physical sentience.'

'But what about the machine?' The robed Aquilon persisted. 'From what you say, it belongs with the others. It's not a bad sort. It should be with the entities of the enclave, and those of us who – understand. It shouldn't be sent back to—'

'Mach has been temporarily incorporated as a unit of Machine Prime,' the unit said. 'The matter has therefore been resolved.'

'Now wait a minute,' Veg said. 'That little machine has a right to decide for itself whether it wants to be swallowed up in—'

Cal put a hand on his friend's arm. 'It's all right.'

'Who are you?' Tamme demanded, already guessing the answer.

The unit made a gesture with wheels and blade that was very like a smile. 'I am Mach.'

AUTHOR'S NOTE

Some readers may be curious about the games of 'Life' and 'Hexaflexagon' described respectively in chapters 9 and 11. A number of readers wrote to inquire about the game of 'Sprouts' described in my earlier novel *Macroscope*, so I hope to save us all trouble by identifying my sources here.

'Life' is derived from Martin Gardner's column in *Scientific American* magazine for October and November 1970, and January and February 1971. (Martin Gardner is not to be confused with John Gardner, founder of *Common Cause*, another worthy entity.)

'Hexaflexagons' are real figures that can be made from folded paper; I have made several with three, six, and twelve faces and recommend them as entertainment for children and adults. The source is *The Scientific American Book of Mathematical Puzzles & Diversions*, by Martin Gardner, first published in 1959 by Simon and Schuster.

And for *Macroscope* readers: 'Sprouts' is also from Mr Gardner's column in *Scientific American* for July 1967.

ALTERNITY

HEXAFLEXAGON CHART

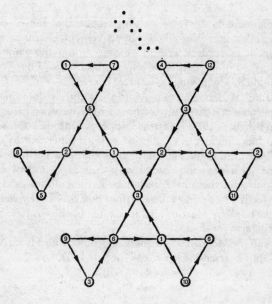

Key:

1. Forest
2. Orchestra
3. Fognose
4. Jungle gym
5. Blizzard
6. Walls

7. City
8. Planes
9. Machine-hive
10. Walking plants
11. Pattern
12. Bazaar

THE END

BATTLE CIRCLE
BY PIERS ANTHONY

Including *Sos The Rope – Var The Stick – Neq The Sword*.

In this highly imaginative trilogy, master science fiction writer Piers Anthony creates a world of savage power, of primitive and brutal laws where all disputes are settled in the battle circle, and where men must seize and realise their vision of an empire by the might of their primitive weapons.

'Anthony's story of men fighting for mastery of wandering tribes, with sword, club and rope in the ceremonial Great Circle, has its own internal conviction – its own grandeur, even . . . a rigorous masculine power, rare in any kind of novel nowadays.'
The Observer

0 552 99085 X   £3.95

CORGI BOOKS

JOHN M. FORD
THE DRAGON WAITING

'I read it with delight, wonder and fascination. This book plays, with a truly wonderful seriousness, the game of fantasy and history. I love it'
Marion Zimmer Bradley, author of *The Mists of Avalon*

Across Europe, forces of darkness, magic and rebellion are gathering, bringing the Vampire Duke of Milan, an exiled heir to the Byzantine throne and a young woman physician closer to confrontations that will involve Richard, Duke of Gloucester, Louis VI of France and a plotting wizard spy. And meanwhile, in the Welsh hills, Hywell Peredur watches the Red Dragon rise again to free his country from the White Dragon of England. And the Dragon is waiting for each of them . . .

The Dragon Waiting is a fantasy of stupendous scope and richness, a glittering tapestry of passion and betrayal, magic and intrigue, a magnificent recreation of a past where myth has become history.

'A thunderclap of a book, a thing of blood and magic'
Roger Zelazny

0 552 12557 1   £3.50

CORGI BOOKS

THE COLOUR OF MAGIC

TERRY PRATCHETT

Jerome K. Jerome meets *Lord of the Rings* (with a touch of *Peter Pan*) . . .

On a world supported on the back of a giant turtle (sex unknown), a gleeful, explosive, wickedly eccentric expedition sets out. There's an avaricious but inept wizard, a naive tourist whose luggage moves on hundreds of dear little legs, dragons who only exist if you believe in them, and of course THE EDGE of the planet . . .

THE WACKIEST AND MOST ORIGINAL FANTASY SINCE *HITCHHIKER'S GUIDE TO THE GALAXY*.

0 552 12475 3   £1.75

CORGI BOOKS

A SELECTED LIST OF SCIENCE FICTION
AND FANTASY TITLES FROM CORGI BOOKS

☐ 99085 X	Battle Circle	Piers Anthony	£3.95
☐ 99168 6	In Other Worlds	A. A. Attanasio	£2.95
☐ 99004 3	Radix	A. A. Attanasio	£2.95
☐ 12284 X	Book One of the Belgariad: Pawn of Prophecy:	David Eddings	£1.95
☐ 12348 X	Book Two of the Belgariad: Queen of Sorcery	David Eddings	£2.50
☐ 12382 X	Book Three of the Belgariad: Magician's Gambit	David Eddings	£2.50
☐ 12435 4	Book Four of the Belgariad: Castle of Wizardry	David Eddings	£2.50
☐ 12447 8	Book Five of the Belgariad: Enchanters' End Game	David Eddings	£1.95
☐ 12557 1	The Dragon Waiting	John M. Ford	£3.50
☐ 12688 8	Starman	Alan Dean Foster	£1.95
☐ 12774 4	Back to the Future	George Gipe	£1.95
☐ 12679 9	Master of the Five Magics	Lyndon Hardy	£2.50
☐ 12680 2	Secret of the Sixth Magic	Lyndon Hardy	£2.50
☐ 10067 6	Farnham's Freehold	Robert Heinlein	£1.95
☐ 12438 9	Queen of The Lightning	Kathleen Herbert	£2.50
☐ 99182 1	The Windsingers	Megan Lindholm	£4.95
☐ 99131 7	The Dune Encyclopedia (Illus.)	Dr. Willis E. McNelly	£5.95
			£2.95
☐ 12683 7	Exiles of the Rynth	Carole Nelson Douglas	£2.50
☐ 12682 9	Six of Swords	Carole Nelson Douglas	£1.75
☐ 12475 3	The Colour of Magic	Terry Pratchett	£1.95
☐ 12429 X	The Golden Swan	Nancy Springer	£1.75
☐ 12428 1	The Black Beast	Nancy Springer	£1.95
☐ 12427 3	The Sable Moon	Nancy Springer	£1.75
☐ 12426 5	The Silver Sun	Nancy Springer	£1.75
☐ 12403 6	The White Hart	Nancy Springer	£4.95
☐ 12620 9	The True Game	Sheri S. Tepper	£2.95
☐ 12849 X	The Revenants	Sheri S. Tepper	£4.95
☐ 99096 5	The Shape of Things to Come	H. G. Wells	